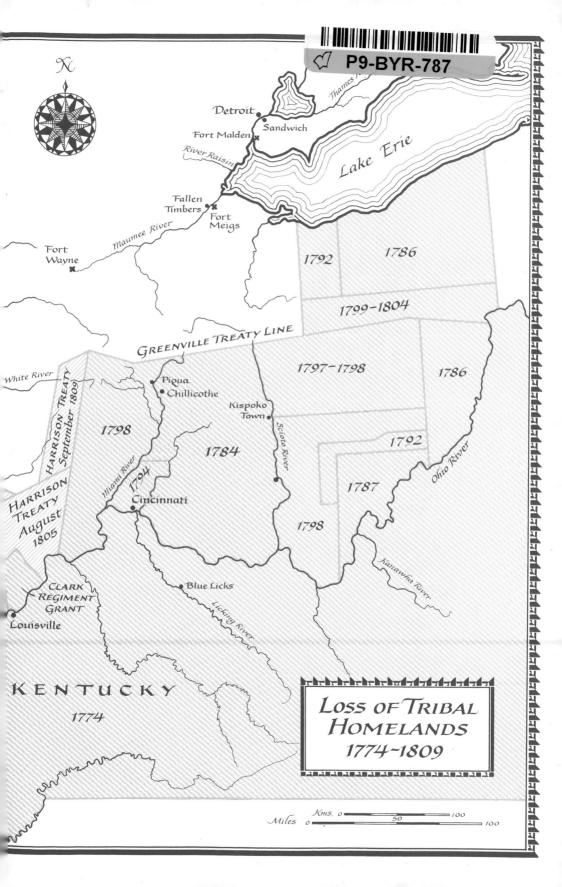

N

Detroit
Sandwich
Fort Malden
River Raisin
Thames River
Lake Erie

Fallen Timbers
Fort Meigs
Maumee River

Fort Wayne

1792      1786

1799–1804

GREENVILLE TREATY LINE

White River

HARRISON TREATY September 1809

1798

1797–1798      1786

Piqua
Chillicothe

Kispoko Town

Scioto River

1792

Miami River

1794

1784

Ohio River

HARRISON TREATY August 1805

Cincinnati

1787

1798

Kanawha River

CLARK REGIMENT GRANT

Louisville

Blue Licks

Licking River

KENTUCKY

1774

LOSS OF TRIBAL HOMELANDS 1774–1809

Kms. 0      50      100
Miles 0      50      100

Also by James Alexander Thom
Published by Ballantine Books


*Long Knife*

*Follow the River*

*From Sea to Shining Sea*

# PANTHER
# IN THE SKY

*The Open Door, Known as the Prophet, Brother of Tecumseh*

# PANTHER IN THE SKY

## James Alexander Thom

BALLANTINE BOOKS · NEW YORK

Frontispiece: George Catlin, *The Open Door, Known as the Prophet, Brother of Tecumseh,* 1830. National Museum of American Art, Smithsonian Institution. Gift of Mrs. Joseph Harrison, Jr.

Endpaper and frontmatter maps based on original research by the author. Inquiries should be addressed to the author, care of Ballantine Books.

**Library of Congress Cataloging-in-Publication Data**

Thom, James Alexander.
        Panther in the sky.

1. Tecumseh, Shawnee Chief, 1768–1813—Fiction.
2. Shawnee Indians—Fiction. I. Title.
PS3570.H47P36     1989      813'.54     88-48012
ISBN 0-345-30596-5

Design by Holly Johnson
Manufactured in the United States of America

First Edition: April 1989

10 9 8 7 6 5 4 3 2 1

*For Mari and Rhu,*
*who keep me from fossilizing*

# *Acknowledgments*

Without the kindness and wisdom of several present-day Shawnees, I could not have understood the oneness, the comforting inclusion, of tribal life I have portrayed in this book. In the embrace of the Shawnee Nation United Remnant Band of Ohio—descendants of Shawnees who followed Tecumseh to the end in the War of 1812—my heart has melted and my mind has expanded. Members of other bands have given me insights into the patient and forgiving nature of their race, and all have delighted me with the keen sense of humor of a people too long stereotyped as stern and humorless. I cannot put into words the gratitude I owe to Tukemas/Hawk Pope and his wife, Meenjip Tatsii, to Walking Song, Kiji Wapiti, Crow Woman, to Don Rapp (Gay-Nwaw-Piah-Si-Ki) of the Eastern Band, and to many others with whom I have had shorter councils. They have done their best to help me see and understand, and any failure to convey the spirit of their people is my fault, not theirs. I can hardly hope that this book will live up to all their expectations, but they know how I tried. They trusted me because I made it plain to them that my question was "What did it all mean?"

I am grateful also for the guidance, friendship, and technical information given by many non-Shawnee experts and aficionados, such as Don Ekola, J. Martin West, Harve Hildebrand, Art Two Crows, Pete Rollet, Dr. Mike Pratt, and Richard Day, who have familiarized me with everything from folklore and period weapons to details of dress and battle plans.

Whenever I begin work on a new book I am reborn into a new world. This time it was more so than ever. Entering the round world of this splendid people, sharing their bittersweet heritage, learning and retelling the story of their beloved leader, has enriched my life.

James Alexander Thom
*Bloomington, Indiana*

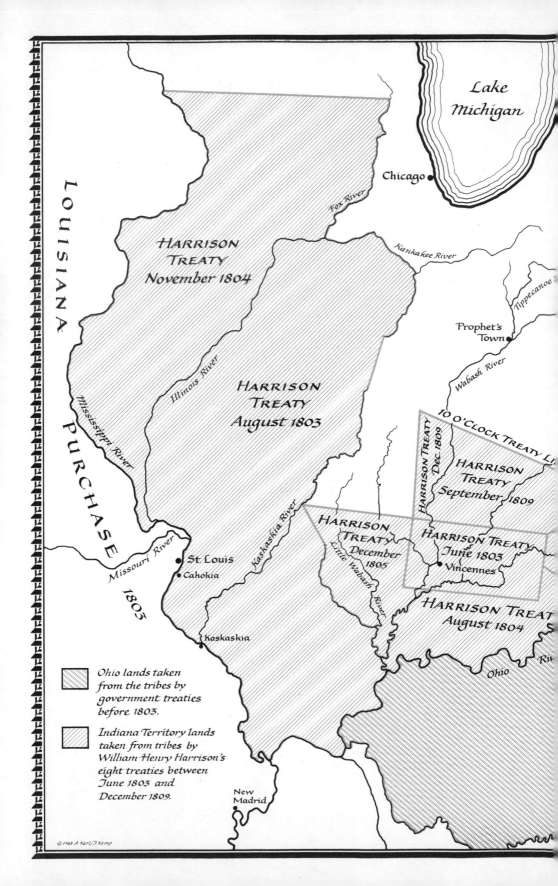

Lake Michigan

LOUISIANA PURCHASE

1803

Mississippi River

Missouri River

Fox River

Chicago

Kankakee River

HARRISON TREATY November 1804

Illinois River

HARRISON TREATY August 1803

Tippecanoe

Prophet's Town

Wabash River

10 O'CLOCK TREATY LI

HARRISON TREATY Dec. 1809

HARRISON TREATY September 1809

HARRISON TREATY December 1805

Kaskaskia River

Little Wabash River

St. Louis

Cahokia

HARRISON TREATY June 1803

Vincennes

HARRISON TREATY August 1804

S

HARRISON TREAT August 1804

Ohio

Riv

Kaskaskia

Ohio lands taken from the tribes by government treaties before 1803.

Indiana Territory lands taken from tribes by William Henry Harrison's eight treaties between June 1803 and December 1809.

New Madrid

© 1988 A. Karl / J. Kemp

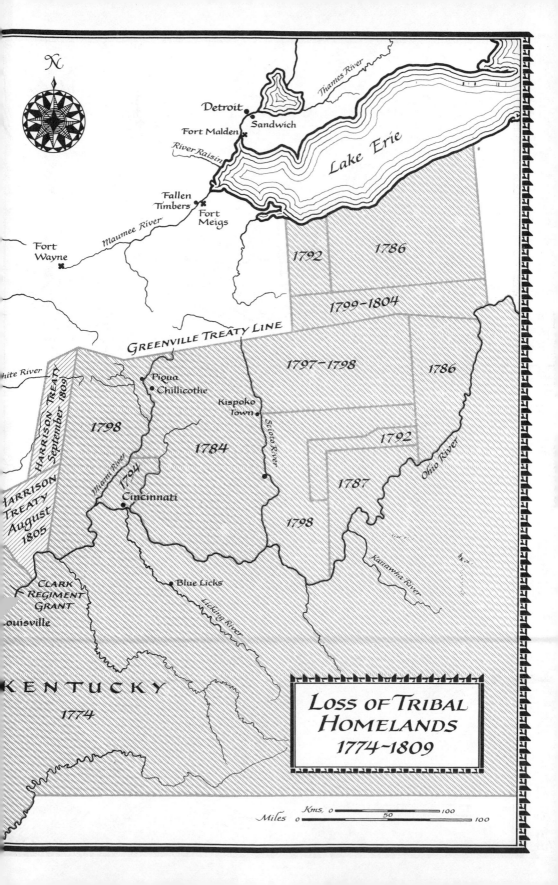

N

Thames River

Detroit
Sandwich
Fort Malden

Lake Erie

River Raisin

Fallen
Timbers
Fort
Meigs

Maumee River

Fort
Wayne

1792    1786

1799–1804

GREENVILLE TREATY LINE

White River

HARRISON TREATY September 1809

Piqua
Chillicothe

1797–1798    1786

Kispoko
Town

1798    1784    Scioto River    1792

HARRISON
TREATY
August
1805

Miami River

1794

Cincinnati

1787

1798

Ohio River

Kanawha River

CLARK
REGIMENT
GRANT

Blue Licks

Louisville

Licking River

KENTUCKY

1774

LOSS OF TRIBAL
HOMELANDS
1774–1809

Kms, 0    100
Miles 0    50    100

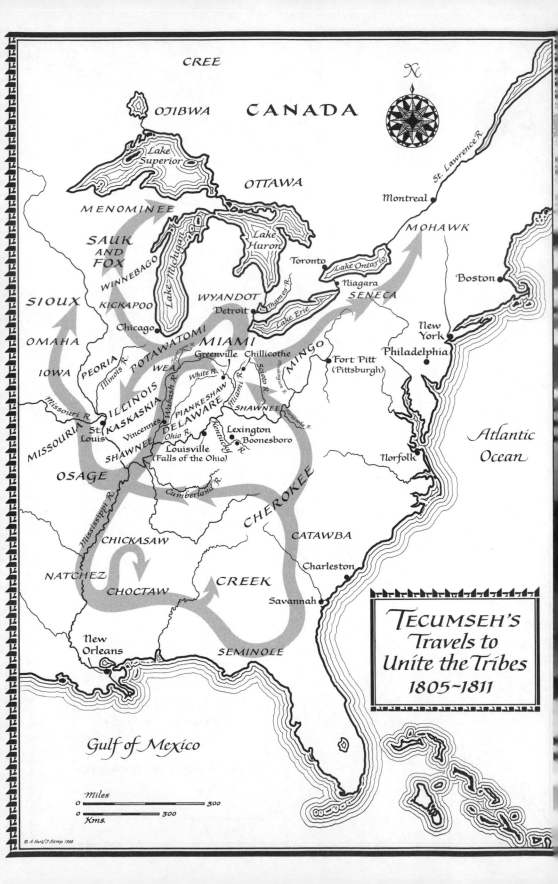

CREE

OJIBWA

CANADA

Lake Superior

OTTAWA

St. Lawrence R.

Montreal

MENOMINEE

MOHAWK

SAUK AND FOX

Lake Huron

WINNEBAGO

Lake Michigan

Boston

SIOUX

KICKAPOO

WYANDOT

Toronto

Lake Ontario

Niagara

SENECA

New York

OMAHA

PEORIA

Chicago

POTAWATOMI

MIAMI

Detroit

Lake Erie

Thames R.

MINGO

Fort Pitt (Pittsburgh)

Philadelphia

IOWA

Illinois R.

WEA

Greenville

Chillicothe

Muskingum R.

Scioto R.

Missouri R.

MISSOURIA

ILLINOIS

KASKASKIA

Wabash R.

White R.

Miami R.

DELAWARE

SHAWNEE

Kanawha R.

St. Louis

KASKASKIA

Vincennes

PIANKESHAW

Ohio R.

Kentucky R.

Lexington

Boonesboro

SHAWNEE

Louisville (Falls of the Ohio)

Norfolk

OSAGE

Mississippi R.

Cumberland R.

CHEROKEE

Atlantic Ocean

CHICKASAW

CATAWBA

Charleston

NATCHEZ

CHOCTAW

CREEK

Savannah

New Orleans

SEMINOLE

Gulf of Mexico

TECUMSEH'S Travels to Unite the Tribes 1805~1811

Miles
0                    300
0
Kms.            300

© A. Karl / J. Kemp 1988

TECUMSEH'S
Activities in
the War of 1812

CANADA

Thames River

Moraviantown •
• Battle of the Thames
Arnold's Mill
WALPOLE ISLAND
• Chatham

Lake St. Clair

MICHIGAN
TERRITORY

Fort Detroit
• Sandwich
Detroit River
Monguagon •
Fort Malden
• Amherstburg

Pelee Point

Lake Erie

PELEE ISLAND

BASS ISLANDS

KELLEY'S ISLAND

River Raisin

Sandusky Bay

Fort Miami
Fallen Timbers ✗
Fort Meigs
Fort Stephenson

OHIO

Maumee River

Sandusky River

- - - - -   British Retreat
September–October 1813
Naval Battle
✗   Battle

Kms.
0       40
0       40
Miles

# PROLOGUE

*On This Side of the Circle of Time*

*Thames River, Ontario*
*October 5, 1813*

Once again the People were fleeing on a road of hunger.

Through the foggy autumn woods a brown river flowed westward, and along its south bank the gaunt families slogged eastward. Their voices murmured in a dozen Algonquian tongues, though mostly they were silent, turned inward upon their misery and fear. They numbered more than twenty hundred, women and coughing children and ancients, most afoot, a few on horseback and travois, strung out more than two miles along the mud-clogged road. Their feet slithered and sucked in the cold muck.

So many times Tecumapese, whose name meant Watcher of the Shooting Star, had fled like this with her people ahead of the armies of the Long Knives. The first time she had been a young woman, not yet a mother. Now she was fifty-five summers of age, and in her own memory this was the seventh flight. It always happened in the autumn. The American armies always drove them out at harvesttime, making them face winter without food or shelter.

Cold rain had fallen for six days while the Redcoat army of their allies the British retreated along the lakeshore and then up this river road. The wheels of their cannons and baggage wagons and the hooves of their horses and beef cattle had churned the dirt road into ruts of mud. And now the Indian refugees came following, carrying sodden bundles, their blankets and clothes ragged, drenched, and soiled, their leggings soaked through and clotted with mud. Half were barefoot; the mire had swallowed their moccasins.

Through the murmur and hush of their slow passage purled the crying of hungry babies, and that was the sound that most tormented Star Watcher.

The leaves of the big oaks, elms, and beeches all around were gold, the

3

maples and sumacs were vermilion to livid. When a gust of cold wind stirred the fog, showers of rainwater and yellow leaves would come down. It was the time of year when a woman's heart was meant to be absorbed in the harvest and the yield of the hunt, in corn parching and bean shelling, in acorn gathering and walnut breaking, in drying venison and buffalo meat over smoky fires, in rendering bear oil and tanning hides.

But the autumn colors were not in the heart now, only in the eyes. The leaves that had fallen had been mashed and trampled into the mud with the blackened old leaves of other years. Once again because of the Long Knives there would be no harvest.

Star Watcher sat on her mare in the chilly morning air looking back for stragglers as her people stumbled by. Her brother Tecumseh had put upon her the burden of keeping the people together and hurrying them on. Upon the shoulders of their younger brother, the Prophet, he had put the task of leading them to the town of the Jesus Indians, where they might find food and shelter. And upon himself Tecumseh had taken the warrior's task of defending the rear, of harassing and delaying the Long Knife army like wolf pack around bison herd, to give the helpless ones and the ponderous Redcoat army time to move ahead up the river to a defensible place. With less than a thousand warriors he had slowed the advance of General Harrison's four thousand Long Knives. But still the Americans came on and were perhaps not more than five miles behind now, and the people could not be allowed to fall behind or sit and rest. But some had strayed aside or fallen down and gotten lost, and one of the lost ones was her own grandnephew.

Star Watcher was a strong, erect woman whose graying hair hung down her back to her waist in one thick braid. On each russet cheekbone was the thumbprint of red paint with which the Shawnee women of all ages marked their faces. She wore a beaded deerskin dress and leggings, with a damp red woolen English blanket drawn around her shoulders. She was handsome, queenly looking, mother of many: of the children of her own loins, of her little brothers whom her mother had left with her, and of many more whose mothers and fathers had died by the guns and diseases and whiskey of the American white men. And now she was also the mother, as Tecumseh had joked grimly to her yesterday, of all these exhausted and homeless ones, the families of his warriors.

"Go on, old Grandmother," she coaxed. "Go on, sister. Hurry on. The town of the Jesus Delawares is near ahead. Hurry on. Be strong!" Her searching gaze fell upon a Peckuwe Shawnee woman she knew. "Sister," she called. "Have you seen today the little boy of Nehaaeemo?"

The Peckuwe woman, who was leading a small child with each hand, shook her head, scowling, and called back: "I have my own to take care of on this hard way we go! Am I to look out also for half-bloods whose mother lets them stray?"

Star Watcher's dark eyes flashed, and her lips set firm. She kneed her mare and rode as skillfully as a warrior in among the people and halted the horse in the woman's way, stopping her. She leaned down close to the woman's startled face. Her breath came in white puffs in the dank air as she spoke, voice quick and low: "Listen to me with all the power of your attention. We speak of a good little boy whose mother goes mad in her head with worry, a woman who has too many children to hold one by each hand like you. Nehaaeemo is of my own blood. Do not speak with a knife tongue of her or of a lost boy. When the road is hard we must say soft words to each other. Did not Our Grandmother Kokomthena, the Creator, give us this as one of the Rules of Living?"

The woman, now looking at the ground, nodded. "I swallow my bad words."

"*Weh-sah,* good," said Star Watcher. "Now, go along. I know you are tired and your little ones have short legs, but you must hurry on."

"Yes," said the woman, who now looked up with tears in her eyes. "And I pray the little boy will be found. I shall watch for him with my own eyes."

Star Watcher smiled at her and nodded, then turned her mare and rode back among the stragglers, shepherding them. How many had strayed off to lie down and rest? What would happen to them when the Long Knives found them? From nearly thirty years ago she could remember seeing a Kentucky horse soldier with a sword chase and hack seven women who had fallen behind in their flight from Maykujay Town. She gazed back down the river and shuddered with fear and hatred. It was quiet back there now, the frightening quiet the prey listens to when it knows it is being hunted. This quiet was in a way more fearsome than the battle thunder of yesterday, when Tecumseh and his warriors had fought the Americans all morning at the Chatham bridges on the Forks of the river Thames.

For thirty years her brother had been fighting to save his people's world, and though this now seemed a hopeless time, so had the many other times when he had turned like a trapped panther and torn his pursuers apart. He had come to be the chief of chiefs, loved and trusted by many peoples, the last free chief, the one who would not sign treaties with the Americans, the one who saw far ahead.

It was now just as it had been most of her life, the People fleeing, the war chiefs protecting them—except that now they were not in their home-land anymore. Now this river alongside the retreat was not the Scioto-se-pe or the Miami-se-pe, or the Wabash-se-pe or the Maumee-se-pe, those clear green rivers of the Shawnee homelands, but a muddy river with a British name, in a northern land, home of Wyandots, Ottawas, Ojibways, Potawatomies, not of Shawnees.

Suddenly, above the drone of voices, shouting arose and cries of "Tenskwatawa! Father!" Star Watcher turned and looked upstream and saw her younger brother, the Prophet, riding back toward her from the front of the column. She reined her mare around and stood waiting for him, dreading that he was bringing word of some new trouble ahead.

Tenskwatawa, whose name meant He-Opens-the-Door, rode close to her, a long cloak draped behind him, his many-colored turban pulled down as usual on the right side to hide his blind eye. The cold, wet weather was making his nostrils leak mucus onto the silver ring in his nose and into his mustache. Open Door was not a good rider, and Star Watcher sighed with fond pity as the great shaman of the Shawnee nation hauled at the reins and conducted a grunting struggle to guide his horse, while people scurried to get out of his way. Everything he did had always been like this. He was a legend of awkwardness. Considering what a blundering fool he was, it was a miracle how much he had done for the People.

"Sister," he panted, "we in front saw the smoke from the Jesus town! We are almost there!"

"*Weh-sah!* That will give the People strength of heart. But you, brother, you should have ridden ahead into the town, to prepare for us, and sent a rider back to tell me."

"Ah . . . yes." He squinted his good eye, realizing that he had made a typical error of judgment. Then he said, as if to justify himself, "I came to tell you, Nehaaeemo is in the worst of grief for her little son George. She wails and dirties her face with mourning, and will listen to no word of hope—"

"Listen!" Star Watcher interrupted him, turning to look toward the rear. People down the road were shouting. Her face brightened when she heard the name they were calling.

Around a bend far down the road Tecumseh came riding into view surrounded by people on foot and followed by a horde of mounted warriors. She first discerned him at this distance by the great curved white plume in his headdress. Some of the people on the road in front of him were women and gray-hairs. Some children and feeble elders were being helped along, even carried, by warriors. Star Watcher knew what this meant. Tecumseh and his fighting men had been gathering up the stragglers and lost ones as they came along. Star Watcher remembered one of the teachings she had given him over and over when he was a boy growing to warrior's age: "Always protect the People. That is all a warrior is for." And he had lived by that.

Now Tecumseh had seen her, and he raised a hand and called out in his mighty voice that could be heard over multitudes and distances. He rode out from the others and came ahead at a canter on his muddy white horse.

It was then as he drew closer that Star Watcher saw two things at once, one of which gave her joy, the other terror.

He held a child on the saddle in front of him: the little lost boy, son of Nehaaeemo.

But Tecumseh's face was painted as she had never seen it before, red on one side, black on the other. War and death. She felt a chill pass down from her scalp through her neck and bosom, and her heartbeat quickened, aching. She kicked the mare's flanks and hurried down the road to meet him. Open Door followed. Many people were shouting, some wailing. When she was close to him she saw the whiteness of his beloved smile, shining through the terrible red and black. How all the People loved this brother of hers and depended upon his strength and vision! But she was bound to him as no one else was. She had been as much mother as sister to him; her very name had been changed at his birth to show that she was a watcher over his life.

He reined in and reached and squeezed her hand, then Open Door's hand. Then he dismounted and lifted the dirty, frightened little half-breed boy down from the saddle, grimacing with pain. She saw that there was a bloody bandage on her brother's left arm. "Here is this little one," he said. "He was beside the road, crying and hungry. Take him to Nehaaeemo and tell her to guard her children better than she has done."

Star Watcher slid down from her saddle, drew the sniffling child close to her hip, and sheltered him in her blanket. She looked at Tecumseh's slit, bloodstained left sleeve and the seeping poultice rag bound around his upper arm, then at his face, half red, half black, her eyes asking questions. But he said nothing about that. He was tense with haste, like a drawn bow. "We will meet the Long Knives today in the way I have yearned to meet them," he said. "The British general can run no farther and has promised to stand with us this time and fight them with all his power. We will have his cannons and his Redcoats to help us, and this time we will draw back no more. Here today we will defeat the army of my great enemy Harrison, or here we will leave our bones. I told General Procter that if he puts his tail between his legs and runs away again, my warriors will walk away from him and leave him to the bayonets of the Blue-Coats.

"My brother, my sister, here is what you must do about the Sacred Bundle, and about our grain seeds. . . ."

As he instructed them about those irreplaceable belongings of the tribe, his chieftains and warriors began riding up. Star Watcher looked first for her husband, Wasegoboah, Stands Firm. He was a gray-hair, but still brawny and quick and always near Tecumseh, one of the thirty longtime followers who had designated themselves the protectors of his life.

Her husband dismounted and came to stand near her, looking at her intently. She smiled at him, but he did not smile. In the intensity of his eyes there was something so terrible, so full of pain, that she wondered if he had a wound somewhere. He stood beside her, his arm touching hers, but did not tell her anything, even when she probed his face with her eyes. His look and silence filled her with such dread as her brother's red and black war paint had done. As a gust of cold wind blew more yellow leaves down all around, there seemed to be a mournful death-moan inside her head.

Tecumseh was saying now, his eyes gleaming with passion:

"Today every breath I draw will give me strength to kill Harrison. Weshemoneto, the Master of Life, will put into my hands the fate of this evil man who has done more than anyone to ruin our People!" He turned to mount his white horse, but then paused and returned to Star Watcher. He gripped her wrist in his hand, which, for the first time in her memory, felt cold. He looked straight and deep into her eyes, and his hard face went soft. The lines of the angry frown vanished from between his brows for a moment, and she could see his eyes again as she had seen them long ago before they had ever been angry: large eyes, eyes that had seemed to try to draw forth the meaning of everything they saw, eyes of a hazel color flecked with green and brown, unlike any others ever seen in this dark-eyed family. Old Change-of-Feathers, who had been the principal Shawnee shaman when Tecumseh was born, had explained that the child's eyes contained the light of the Eye of the Panther, the shooting star that had gone over when he was born, and how well she could remember that, the greatest omen she had ever seen. Now Tecumseh murmured, so softly that only the familiar movements of his lips told her what he was saying, one of the rules of Kokomthena, Our Grandmother, that Star Watcher herself had taught him over and over when he was a boy: *"Weshecat-welo k'weshe laweh-pah."*

"May we be strong by doing what is right," she repeated.

Then he mounted, without even seeming to favor his wounded arm, and rode off up the road toward the fording place, not looking back.

Stands Firm was turning away to his horse, to follow Tecumseh. Star Watcher grabbed his arm fiercely and made him look at her. She said, "I do not see Thick Water with him. Is he killed?" Thick Water was Tecumseh's most tenacious bodyguard, always so close by him that Tecumseh now seemed like a man without his shadow; Thick Water's absence seemed an omen, as if Weshemoneto had withdrawn his cloak of protection from around her brother.

Stands Firm replied: "No. Tecumseh sent him away."

She shuddered. Somehow this sounded even more ominous than if the bodyguard had been killed in the battle yesterday. "Why did he send him away? *Wahsiu, my husband! What do you think?"

"He told him to go bring back some Wyandots who had deserted us. He tried also to send me away from him, to send me to stay by you and help you with these people."

She hung tight to his sleeve. *"Wahsiu,"* she hissed at him, her eyes wild with doubt, "what is the bad thing that you are not saying out loud?"

He drew his arm out of her grasp. "My wife, I must go. . . ."

She remembered her brother's war paint, the red and the black, and she guessed. Her eyes drilling into her husband's, she demanded:

"He had a sign?" She was thinking of the foreknowledge of death that her father and her older brother had taken into battle with them on their last days. *"He had a sign?"* She almost squealed the question at him, leaning forward and starting to tremble. The little boy beside her whimpered.

"By our fire last night a red leaf fell upon him from a tree. All of us with him heard the noise of a bullet, though no gun was shot anywhere. Then he told us that he will fall today. Yes, *neewa,"* Stands Firm groaned, his lips drawn in a grimace, his eyes wet and squinting, "he had a sign, yes!"

She recoiled as if she had been shot. Then she lashed out with her work-hardened hand and clouted the side of his head, screaming at him, "Say no!" Passing warriors turned to look.

He tasted blood, and his ear rang from the impact. She had never struck him before, nor anyone, not even children. He grabbed her wrist before she could slap him again and forced her trembling arm down to her side. His heart was quaking, as was her whole body.

"Forgive me, *wahsiu,"* she groaned. "I want you to say he had no sign."

"That I know you want. But he did. Now you must let me go on. When we fight the Long Knives today he wants me beside him in Thick Water's place."

"Now you lie! You said before that he tried to send you away!"

"He did try to. But then he had the sign and saw in it that I might save him if he falls."

She tried to find hope in this, but hope was faint. She struggled to make herself calm. "Then go, my husband. Be strong. Do what you can if it happens. I pray for your safety as I always have done. Your heart and mine are one heart." She could hardly speak but had to tell him these things before he went into battle. He was as good a husband as any woman had ever married, though he had spent most of the years of their marriage in the farthest corners of the land, helping Tecumseh try to unite the tribes.

Star Watcher and Stands Firm gripped their right hands together almost until they hurt, and he pressed his forehead against her temple. She shut her eyes, and the eyelids stung with salt.

Then he was gone from her side, and when she opened her eyes he was swinging onto his horse's back as nimbly as a young warrior, and the horse was already kicking up mud, surging into a gallop up the road, her old husband going off with a hope of protecting her brother, while she, fearing that there was not a hope, put her hands under the little boy's arms and lifted him onto the pommel of her saddle. She swung on behind him, saying, "Come, now. Your mother wants you so much." She saw Open Door riding far ahead already, going toward the missionary town, knowing nothing of Tecumseh's sign. The little boy at last spoke:

"Ai, I am cold!"

"Yes, you are cold. But do you know there is a secret way to make yourself never feel cold again? You can learn it when you get a little older. The warriors and grandfathers know the secret, but you have to be old enough to learn." She talked to the child to keep from flying out of her head. She remembered when the boy Tecumseh had learned the secret on the coldest day in anyone's memory, and how his body and hands had always given off warmth after he learned it. How will such good secrets be taught, she wondered, if the Long Knives win? When you have no home, you forget everything, even who you are.

Then she remembered that Tecumseh's hand had been cold today, and her hope grew smaller still.

She rode through the column of hundreds of warriors of many tribes who were following her doomed brother up the road to ford the river to the battleground, the Shawnees, Miamis, Wyandots, Potawatomies, Ottawas, Ojibways, Menominees, Delawares, Sauks, Foxes, Kickapoos, Winnebagoes, Senecas, even Sioux and Creeks from places far west and south, the broadest brotherhood of nations any chief had ever united for any cause, those who had been with him for many seasons and those who had come to join him after he had proven he could shake the world. They rode and trotted along toward a battle in which they all could expect to die, their weapons rattling, their bone and quill and silver ornaments chattering and jingling, their faces painted with stripes and dots and circles, robes and leathers flapping, following her brother to go and fight still again the American army of Harrison the land stealer.

Star Watcher talked to the little boy as she rode past the warriors to catch up with the refugees, the mothers and wives and sisters and children of all these warriors who might die today. "We must be with our families," she told the boy. "We must live on, and not forget the good things we know.

Weshemoneto the Great Good Spirit favors our People. Though the white man's God is strong, the Master of Life knows we are right, and gives us Tecumseh to save us."

"I am *cold,*" groaned the little boy.

She held the blanket tight around him and hugged him closer to her belly. "Did you know, I was holding my mother when Tecumseh was born? Did you know, I first saw the shooting star that went over when he was born? Oh, yes," she groaned, "he was like my own little boy, and Our Grandmother the Creator told me what to teach him to make him good and kind. . . . For when the Panther's Eye shot through the sky, it was foretold that he would be good and full of vision, and the strongest of all our leaders." She bit her upper lip and breathed deep breaths. And then she said, in a voice that sounded softer in her own head:

"That was in the ending of the Time Before. Yes, when the Long Knives were still on the other side of the Beautiful River. Yes! Yes, what a happy people we were in the Time Before! Sometime we will be happy again, for everything comes back around. . . . Oh, let me try to tell you how beautiful and terrible was the Panther Star on that night. . . ."

She was remembering the first time she had seen the life that was Tecumseh, remembering it because now she believed that she had seen him alive for the last time. And through the blur of her tears as she rode and talked, everything was muddy brown and gray, and the falling leaves were little drifting smears of gold and red.

In her mind she saw Tecumseh's red-and-black face. And his white smile, like light through clouds.

*Everything comes back around.* He is still alive and believes that he can win this day, she thought. He believes that he can kill our greatest enemy on this day. He means to do this even though he expects to die!

"The shooting star," she said to the little boy, "was the color of his eyes. The color of a panther's eyes, when a panther crosses your path and turns to look at you. . . ."

# PART ONE

PART ONE

# CHAPTER 1

*On the Other Side of the Circle of Time
Old Piqua Town     March 9, 1768*

Turtle Mother squatted, naked and sweaty, in the center of the birth hut. Her daughter knelt at her right and an old midwife at her left.

The pain returned with its rushing sound. The light of the little campfire outside the hut blurred in Turtle Mother's sight and became two campfires, moving apart from each other and then together again. She gripped the center post of the hut and groaned, and pushed down with all the strength of her torso. Her breathing was fast and hard. She pressed as if she must turn herself inside out. She felt as if she would die of this. But with her first two she had felt as if she would die, too, and had not, so she was not afraid. Still, even knowing she would not die of this, she felt as if she would.

Then the pain drew back a little way, and Turtle Mother squatted there with her hands still on the post and drew slow breaths. Sweat was coursing down her cheeks, growing cool in the night air, and the coolness felt good. She was aware of her daughter's hands as they pressed and stroked her flanks and eased the pain. The girl's hands were gentle and cool, but strong.

As the rushing sound of the pain lessened, the sounds of the night came to her ears again. She heard the piping of the little tree frogs. She heard Wind Spirit whispering high in the treetops outside the shelter, the spring trickling through its rocks nearby, and in the distance the quickening beats of a drumming grouse. She heard the voice of her husband, Pucsinwah, Hard Striker, who was talking with their son Chiksika beside the campfire outside the hut.

Her daughter's hand now stroked her brow and wiped sweat out of her eyes. The girl had moved closer around in front of her. The girl's eye reflected firelight for a moment as she moved, then her thick hair shadowed

15

it. She was only ten years old, but already she was like a woman in the wisdom of her heart, and she understood, the way an animal understands, without word teaching, the coming of life. Thus she knew how to help and soothe her mother in the labor of birth instead of being afraid and helpless. For a moment, Turtle Mother was able to smile at her daughter. Then the mighty coming-down began again, and her smile turned to a grimace, and she turned her head aside, and again the firelight shimmered and divided. This time the pain was greater and longer, and it forced noises from her throat, awful noises.

Hard Striker by the fire outside heard his wife's pain and feared for her. Though he was the principal war chief of all the Shawnees, he was a man who felt the pain in others. Turtle Mother was a perfect wife for a man, but birth was always uncommonly hard for her, and each time she gave him a child he was afraid he would lose her. Looking toward the shelter, he said to his son Chiksika, "A man cannot know how that feels."

It was not the kind of thing that a father would have tried to express to an ordinary boy of twelve. But Chiksika, like his sister, was wise and good beyond his age. His name meant "the Chickasaw," for he had been born while his parents traveled through the lands of that nation, down in the southern lands beyond the hunting grounds of Kain-tuck-ee. Chiksika was as near manhood and ready to become a warrior as most boys were at sixteen or seventeen. He listened well to everything his father said and tried to understand it all.

Now Hard Striker said to him, "I have felt the hurt of a musket ball in my body, and of the tomahawk several times. But surely a woman's pain is worse than those." He squinted and looked toward the shelter. When he spoke again his voice was thick with feeling. "Sometimes you will hear men and boys make mockery of women, saying they are weak and silly. My son, never let your lips speak such things."

"No, Father. I promise."

Hard Striker drew a small leather bag from under his robe, a bag decorated with quillwork. He shut his eyes and moved his lips, making a silent incantation. The firelight gleamed on the planes and ridges of his craggy face. Raising his hand high, he shook the medicine bag to make its contents rattle. Two of the items in the bag were dried snippets from the birth cords of his first two children. Every man chose for himself what was good medicine to carry, and to Hard Striker the bond of his family was the best of all things. He sensed that life was a form of fire, that the bodies of people were a way of containing the sacred fire of the sun and carrying it about on the earth, and that the fire was kept by woman and passed on to the next generation somehow through this cord. So the cord was powerful and good medicine. Now he passed the bag back and forth through the smoke of the campfire, praying. After a while he put the bag away. He glanced toward the shelter and thought with tenderness of what his wife and daughter were sharing in that dim place. The girl herself would someday have to suffer this same pain, before many years, he knew, because she would be beautiful like her mother, and her man would want to be upon her often. Hard Striker wondered who that man would be. He felt time moving, going around. He remembered when his daughter had been born. Now she was old enough to help at another child's birth. And before many years she would be bearing. She was called Sky Watcher, because she had seemed to be staring hard at the sky when she first opened her eyes. The chief, remembering that, looked up at the starry sky through the still-leafless trees. It was good to have a clear look at the stars and to be in the quiet of the woods instead of in a town at the time of a birth, because the *unsoma* were clearer and more true when the world was quiet. For this reason Hard Striker liked to build a birth shelter away from the smoke and noise of towns for his wife when she bore children. The *unsoma* were the name-signs that came at the time of a child's birth or in the ten days following it. The *unsoma* were brought by the Messenger Spirits, and one had to be alert to detect them and not catch a wrong sign. It was necessary to be open to the signs no matter what else was on one's mind, and there was a great deal now on Hard Striker's mind.

When Turtle Mother had begun having the pains of birth, the family had been on the trace to the main Shawnee town of Chillicothe, on the Miami-se-pe. Cornstalk, the nation's principal chief, had called for a council of all the Shawnee septs to be held there, to talk about the problem of white men.

As chief of the Kispoko, or warrior, sept, Hard Striker would be a most important member of the council. Though he was known throughout the nation as a fair and far-seeing man, and his opinions weighed heavily even on matters that had nothing to do with war, this council was sure to have much discussion of war, because the white people were becoming very troublesome. For years they had crowded the Shawnees off their lands farther east, until the nation had congregated here in the O-hi-o lands above the great Speh-leh-weh-se-pe, the Beautiful River—the O-hi-o-se-pe, as it was called by most peoples. On the other side of the Beautiful River lay the Sacred Hunting Ground of Kain-tuck-ee, where all tribes could hunt but none could live, because it was a land occupied by the ghosts of a giant race, whom the tribes had massacred there hundreds of years before. The Algonquian nations all hunted there, but primarily the Shawnees, Miamis, and Delawares. This had been the way of Kain-tuck-ee through many ages.

Kain-tuck-ee was a sacred and bountiful and lonely land; because it was empty of people, it was full of game.

But now an evil thing was being done about Kain-tuck-ee. White men were counciling with the Iroquois, ancient enemies of the Shawnees, trying to buy Kain-tuck-ee from them. The Iroquois neither lived nor hunted in Kain-tuck-ee and thus had nothing to lose by selling that land to the white men, as the white men in their cunning well knew. The whites were also trying to buy parts of Kain-tuck-ee from the Cherokees, who lived southeast of it. If the white men tried to settle in the Sacred Hunting Ground, surely there soon would be war with them. Already white hunters and settlers were intruding on Shawnee lands near the head of the Beautiful River, despite treaties that were supposed to keep them on the other side of the mountains.

And so the matter of the council was very much on Hard Striker's mind. But for this moment, he was trying to concentrate upon the important thing that was happening here in the circle of his family in a clean and quiet place under the stars; he kept the power of his thoughts directed to his wife, Methotasa.

Her name meant A-Turtle-Laying-Her-Eggs-in-the-Sand. That had been the *unsoma* seen at the time of her own birth, the sign seen in a sandy creekbed far to the south, in the Muskogee land. Turtle Mother was a Creek woman, warm and fertile like her homeland beside the Tallapoosa. And as the turtle lays her many eggs, so would Turtle Mother bear many children, as the world and seasons rolled round and round and the stars turned slowly above.

The world was good, so very good. And to be born a Shawnee was the best fortune in this good world. The Shawandasse, called the South Wind People because of their origins in those warm lands, were the happiest, bravest, and most honorable of all people, and the Kispoko, his sept, were the bravest of all the Shawandasse. Of course other tribes and septs believed that about themselves, but Hard Striker knew it was true in the case of his people. In his mind there was nothing wrong in the entire circle of the world—except the one great trouble.

The coming of the white men.

For as long as Hard Striker could remember, the whites had been like some distant, rumbling thunder from the east. They were a strange, greedy people, takers of everything, bringers of noise, drunkenness, and disease. Since before the time of Hard Striker's grandfather the Shawnee people had migrated, trying to keep a distance between themselves and the whitefaces. Sometimes it had not been possible to keep a distance. The Shawnees had been caught between the French white men and the English white men in one of their wars a few years ago, and that was when Hard Striker had been hit by an English musket ball. Again in a few more years there had been more trouble with the whites, and Hard Striker had gone with Pontiac, the Ottawa, to fight the Englishmen.

That had been five years ago. Now the white people were still coming, until by now they had disturbed even the oneness of the Shawnee nation.

For now some of the chiefs—including Cornstalk, the principal chief—had come to believe that the whites could never be held back and that the Shawnees should make peace with them and stop trying to hold them back. The white men, because of their superior numbers and weapons and tools, presumed themselves to be a superior race, and some chiefs were beginning to believe this themselves and were ready to let them have their inevitable way. But Hard Striker had seen enough of the whites to believe that his own race was superior to them, both in body and spirit, and he meant to plead in the council at Chillicothe that a superior race, particularly one that stood right in the eyes of the Master of Life, should never have to bow down and lick the feet of an inferior race, no matter how rich and numerous they were. The saddest sight Hard Striker could remember was that of the great Pontiac giving up his struggle two years ago and signing a peace treaty with the white men. Hard Striker was never going to put his mark on a treaty. He was going to remind all the chiefs in the council that Weshemoneto, the Great Good Spirit, had put this beautiful land here for the red men and would not like for them to yield it to intruders who had not stayed on their own land beyond the Eastern Water. Hard Striker did not mean for his son Chiksika or his daughter Sky Watcher, or this child now being born, or any child yet to be born, in his family or in his tribe, to grow up like scavenger dogs in a world ruled and ruined by greedy, smelly, diseased whitefaces. And he would use the greatest force of his mind and tongue to keep the nation from being wedged apart by them.

In the shadows within the shelter, Turtle Mother clutched the post and strained once again and felt the great slow mass stretching her. But it was coming now. At last it was coming down, and her body was giving it away to the world. Sky Watcher was saying nice things to her, and the midwife's hands were under her, ready to help the baby come out. Turtle Mother yielded everything at last and felt the immense relief, the pricklings and twinges inside. The grimace of pain melted from her face, and with a serene smile she looked down for the first sight of this new life she had made. There were flashing aftershocks of pain still, and sliding, oozy sensations in her loins, and warm smells of blood and slime and excrement coming up, and the midwife lifting and pulling away the gleaming creature, and then the birth sac, and talking in a soft, urgent voice, while Sky Watcher crooned happily and readied a bed of clean hides spread over a cushion of boughs. As Turtle Mother reclined with a long sigh, Sky Watcher helped the mid- wife clean the slime off the infant. Then they laid the little hot blob of life upon Turtle Mother's bosom between her swollen breasts. She moved gentle hands over the infant, feeling it in the darkness for any faults. The baby was still on its cord. She explored the little damp groin and said in a breathy whisper, "There is his little *passah-tih*. Go tell your father it is a son."

Sky Watcher stooped to go out, then paused and gasped.

The sky above the stark treetops was suddenly filling with a greenish light; it was like the night lightning on a horizon, except that it was not a flash, but a growing light. "Ai!" she cried, pointing up. Her father and brother were just looking up. And as they gaped at the sky, seeing the stars fade in the strengthening light, something shot over, something like a fire-arrow but much more intense, and yellow-green like the eye of a panther, streaking southward. Though it was silent, it seemed to hiss on the brain, to sizzle over the uplifted eyes.

Hard Striker and Chiksika had risen by the fire-ring with their mouths open, watching the thing pass beyond the silhouetted branches of the leafless treetops. Turtle Mother where she lay inside the shelter did not see the thing, only the brief, strange glow outside the door.

For a moment then as the darkness and the stars returned and the warm yellow light of the campfire replaced the cold green light of the sky, nothing was said. The apparition with its tail of stardust stayed in their minds, making them dumb, until Hard Striker at last closed his mouth and drew a slow breath and turned to his son, eyes glittering, and exclaimed:

"It is the *unsoma!*" His gaze fell upon Sky Watcher poised in the entry of the shelter. "Daughter! You saw it!"

"Yes! And Father, a son is here!"

"A son! Ah-i-ee! Oh, what a man this will be, with such a sign as that! Ah!" He raised both hands toward the place where the light had gone, hands trembling with the unspeakable wonder of it.

Inside the shelter, Turtle Mother placed the baby on the robe beside her and raised herself on an elbow. Now the midwife gave her a strand of boiled sinew, and Turtle Mother looped it around the umbilical cord and tied it tight. Then a hand's width from the knot she took the tough cord between her front teeth and severed it with a sawing bite, the taste of the fluid in her mouth. The child's limbs twitched, and a high, pure, quavering wail came forth.

"Now, sister," Turtle Mother murmured to the midwife, "when the sun comes up go and bury the sac beyond three creek valleys or more."

The midwife gave a sly smile. It was a secret among women, kept from husbands, that there would be a year free from pregnancy for every stream that flowed between the birthplace and the discarded sac. Turtle Mother loved children, but she did not want pain like that again for a long time.

Sky Watcher came back in and moved to sit in a way so she could hold her mother's head in her lap. "Mother," she said, her voice breathy with awe, "it was a green star! A sign!"

Her mother nodded, her eyes glittering. The infant, lulled by Turtle Mother's familiar heartbeat, stopped crying. "Now, *wahsiu,*" Turtle Mother called softly. "Husband, come now and see your son, born under a sky sign. He is ready."

Hard Striker pulled his knife from the sheath that hung from his neck and bent over to run the blade through the flame. It was a fine, long knife with a narrow blade made even more narrow by years of sharpening. A French officer had given it to him years ago during the war with the British. In those years Hard Striker had taken many scalps with this knife, three of them the scalps of English soldiers he had killed, two the scalps of white intruders since that war. Whenever he held the knife, his hand would cause his soul to remember. All the sharp warrior memories lived in the knife: the eruptions of gunfire and smoke in ambushes, howls and hard blows in sun-dappled green woods, pounding heartbeats, hot blood spurting on moss, the feel of this knife cutting scalp to the hard skullbone . . .

But this same knife he now passed through the flames with tenderness in his heart, for this was also the knife with which he skinned and cut meat to feed his family and with which he did the sacred family thing he was about to do now.

With the blade purified he went into the dark shelter and knelt beside his wife. He pressed his cheek against hers, and with a swollen heart he murmured to her of his great esteem and gratitude. She breathed on his eyelids, smiling. Then he sat back on his heels, and she lifted the baby to him. He cradled it on his left forearm. Sky Watcher held up a clay-bowl oil lamp, and in its tremulous light he looked down at the wriggling baby and inspected it, his eyes soft in his hawklike face. He studied it from its damp black hair and its tiny nostrils to its sprig of a penis and the miniature fingernails and toenails. The little mouth, shapely as a flower bud, was already alive with sucking motions. Sky Watcher uttered a little musical laugh of sheer delight. Hard Striker chuckled. "*Weh-sah,* good!" he breathed. He murmured to it: "*Neequithah,* my son." Then he placed the infant on its back on his wife's arm and leaned over with his French knife. He took the end of the umbilical cord between his left thumb and forefinger, feeling the wonderful strangeness of it, which was unlike any of the

animal tissues a man ever touched. He put the sharp edge of the blade to
the cord, just outside the threadknot, and gently sliced off the loose end.
He leaned back and looked at it. One end had been severed by her teeth,
the other by his knife. When it was dry, he would put it in his medicine bag,
where ten years ago he had put in that of his daughter and twelve years ago
that of his first son. He looked at his wife's tired, beautiful face for a long
while. Chiksika had come in and was looking over his father's shoulder.
Now all the little family of Hard Striker was in this tiny, warm space under
a bark roof beneath the white stars, and it was the center of the world.

"When we go to Chillicothe," he said, "we will speak at once to Change-
of-Feathers." Change-of-Feathers, Old Penegashega, was the chief medicine man of the Shawnee nation, an ancient who had lived through many
years of the past and seen still more years into the future. "I yearn to hear
what he will tell us about the *unsoma* that crossed the sky."

Turtle Mother nodded, her eyes intense. Then she looked down at the
infant by her breast. She knew that a great sign always foretold a remarkable
life, and that a remarkable life was most often a hard life. "Yes. Yes," she
said. "I tremble to think of what it must mean!"


Hundreds of people came running out of the town to meet Hard Striker.
People had seen the sign and learned of the war chief's new son. And so
now they came running, women and children in their deerskin dresses and
tunics, their faces full of happiness and curiosity, from among the bark
houses and the hide-covered lean-tos, through the garden plots, around the
ends of pole fences, coming down the road, calling greetings, to meet their
warrior chief and his family. Behind them came warriors and chieftains,
walking instead of running, as men should for the sake of their dignity, but
they were walking fast and sometimes breaking into a trot in their own
eagerness to know. The town lay under a haze of dust and woodsmoke, on
a broad plateau above the marshy bottomlands of the Little Miami-se-pe. On
the far side of the curving river rose grand, rocky bluffs crested with forest.
It was a beautiful town, of several hundred silver-gray, bark-covered, loaf-
shaped *wigewas* and peak-roofed council houses, a town built among the
giant elms, maples, and oaks that grew on the plain. The packed-earth
streets between the houses were wide and striped by shadows of the leafless
trees in the sunlight, and there were hundreds of Shawnees moving in the
streets. The air was full of the aromas of cooking, of baking meal-cakes, corn
chowders, and roasting meats, and the drone of thousands of voices. The
whole town was vibrant with the excitement of this great gathering of the
septs. From within the heart of the town came drumbeats, the chattering

of rattles, the songs of wooden flutes, the yips and laughter of many children.

Hard Striker rode at the head of his family, grinning, his hand held high. His wife with her new baby on her arm rode wrapped in a blanket, lying on a travois that trailed behind the horse her son Chiksika was leading, and her daughter walked beside the travois. The girl was dutiful and stayed beside her mother, though in her eagerness to be among the young people from the many towns, she seemed to be almost dancing as she walked. Her face was smooth, russet, and her small, even teeth gleamed white. Her eyes were as brown and big as buckeye nuts. The long, shiny, blue-black braid of her thick hair swayed behind her as she walked, reaching her waist, and around her head was a strand of mottled-glass trade beads. Sky Watcher was already aware that she was beautiful, and she was forever happy and grateful for it. There was seldom a morning when this girl awoke without a smile already on her face, because everything in her life was as good as it could be.

Now the people were surrounding the family, running back to the travois to see Turtle Mother and her new child, patting their hands together and dancing around, crying out like birds in their delight. "A-hi-ee! A boy, then!" "And you saw the light go over?" "Will he be named 'Flying Star'?" Turtle Mother smiled her lovely, wise smile at the horde of faces above her and answered "Yes" or "Maybe" to their queries, sometimes reaching up to touch the hands of friends.

Hard Striker rode in a glory of pride, saluting the approaching chiefs while with his sinewy left arm he controlled his stallion, which was excited by the milling crowd and tried to prance and caper. Hard Striker was proud of his new son's portentous birth and of his handsome family. He rejoiced in the warmth of the greetings. To a Shawnee, the love and respect of one's tribesmen were all the wealth one could need. The bond of kinship among the People was a world in itself, and within a sept this bond was so strong and all-embracing that the whole sept was, in effect, a family, *the* family. No Shawnee child whose parents were killed by war or disease ever had to become an orphan, because all adults were fathers and mothers and uncles and aunts to all children. The only unbearable punishment for any crime was banishment from the tribe. It seldom happened. Death was preferable. It was considered better to be a dead person than a living nonperson, which one became if he was put out of the tribe. Thus in the round wholeness of the living tribe there was a warmth that made even the hardness and hunger of winter bearable. Life was never easy or certain for the red men, especially now that the white men were unsettling their world, but there was always the great comfort of not having to be alone against the hardships of the world. So whenever Hard Striker returned like this into the presence of the People, his heart would glow in his breast. And now it was especially so because of what had happened under the shooting star.

Now he saw Black Snake, his main chieftain, coming down the road toward him, cloaked in a red blanket, his roach headdress bristling, one brawny, braceleted arm raised in greeting. With Black Snake walked the great Black Fish, village chief of Chillicothe, a compact, graceful man whose bearing made him seem much taller than he was. Also coming was a large, broad-faced elder with a feather-tipped staff in his hand, his wrinkled visage very intense. Ah! It was Penegashega himself, Change-of-Feathers, the Chalagawtha shaman whom Hard Striker had intended to seek right away, and Change-of-Feathers in his own eagerness had come out to meet him. Surely it is a great matter, this of my son's name-sign, the chief thought, if Change-of-Feathers comes forth at once from the council fires to speak to me of it. Look at the thought in his eyes! There is much there! Surely, then, this is a most important thing that has come upon us!

Hard Striker reined in and dismounted when he reached the shaman and the chiefs. His family's entourage stopped behind him. Black Fish took his hand, and his thin, hard lips seemed to melt suddenly with the warmth of his smile. "Welcome, my brother, to Chillicothe. My people are honored."

"Black Fish, my brother. May we do great good in this council. May Weshemoneto smile on this town."

Now Change-of-Feathers took Hard Striker's hand, and his eyes searched Hard Striker's face.

"First Warrior! Always I rejoice to see my son the Kispoko, and now on this day, more than ever before."

"Father, I thank you. When I come through the trees and see this great town, my soul sings as if I were coming home. And now on this day more than ever I am happy to see my wise father and take his hand. You do me honor to come forth and welcome my family."

"When the flying star went over, I saw in the eyes of a dream that a child was born in its very light. Was my vision true?"

"Exactly. Within the same breath, both came, the star and my son. All my family remarked on it with wonder."

Change-of-Feathers, plainly much moved, took a deep breath and let it out with a shudder, and tears brimmed in his eyes. He held Hard Striker's hand fervently in his own. Change-of-Feathers' hands were soft and loose-fleshed, like his large body, but vibrantly strong, and one felt a living power flowing from their touch. Never a warrior, Change-of-Feathers had an air of gentleness about him, and his face, though manly, was tender and wise and expressive, rather like a grandmother's. A row of puncture tattoos ran from ear to ear across his cheekbones and the bridge of his nose. Change-of-Feathers went back now to greet Turtle Mother and to look at the infant. He studied it, murmuring something to himself. He put his soft hand on Turtle Mother's head, then stroked the baby's brow, opened its eyelids, and turned again to Hard Striker. "My son," he said, "the coming of the flying star was a good sign for these councils, but it was yet more, because a son was born to our war chief. No other child was born in our nation on that night, from what we have heard." The people were quiet now, Black Fish and Black Snake standing with them listening, the women and children listening from nearby. A cool breeze sighed in the grasses and the weed stalks in the meadow and shook the feathers of Change-of-Feathers' staff. "Listen," the medicine man went on. "It means more than I can yet explain. Eagle Speaker and I have talked of this. Eagle Speaker too had a dream." Eagle Speaker was a seer, a younger man than Change-of-Feathers and a Bear Walker, one of the Shape Shifters through whom messages were often given to the People. "In the dream of Eagle Speaker, there was a long-tailed star in the sky for a year and then the earth shook, throwing things down. I must go out to fast and listen before I can know all it means. Cornstalk himself wants to know what they mean. He waits to see you in his lodge, and to learn of the child. For the naming of your son, you should know this:

"That passing light was the color of the panther's eye. Several times our fathers have seen such stars. It is believed that it is the Eye of the Panther that forever moves in the night sky. This child's eyes have that color.

"You are the chief of the Kispoko, called the Panther sept. You were traveling, passing from one place to another, when it came. That, too, has meaning. We see a panther only when he crosses our path. The panther says, *'Nila ni tha'mthka:* I cross someone's path.' And so we call the passing panther Tha'mthka. Think of this. I will tell you more when I can.

"But come. Cornstalk waits to welcome you, and the councils can begin. Hard Striker, my son, I have great joy in the birth of your boy. Great leaders are given to the People in times of the greatest need. By our law, only a Chalagawtha or a Thawegila can be the chief of all this nation, and your son is Kispoko. But in a time of war, the war chief is powerful. The whites will force us to wage war or surrender. A time of greatest need is coming. We shall see. Our lives are in the hands of Weshemoneto. Perhaps he will send this war chief across the path of the whitefaces. Come now."

Hard Striker, as if in a trance of thought, swung onto the back of his horse, and all the people began moving back toward Chillicothe, following their chiefs and the shaman, the young ones running and skipping, barely aware of all these portents. And as they paraded into the crowded town, Hard Striker was deciding something. He looked over the heads of the people and saw the hazy blue bluffs looming above the town, beyond the river. He saw this with his eyes, but in his soul he was seeing the panther. He had already decided the name he would give his son. Tha'mthka. Tecumseh. The Panther Crossing the Sky. The Shooting Star.

And his daughter. One could change one's name if another name became more right. Sky Watcher had been a good name for her until now. But she had first seen the shooting star, and she had helped this marked child into the world. She herself was already blessed with uncommon goodness and wisdom, the guardian virtues. She was most important to this child's life. A truer name for her would be Star Watcher, Tecumapese.

# CHAPTER 2

*Kispoko Town, on the Scioto River*
*Spring 1768*

Sometimes in spring Turtle Mother would hang the cradleboard from a limber bough near the garden clearing. Breezes would move the bough and cause the cradleboard to turn slowly and bob gently in the sun-dappled shade, and the baby would see the green of leaves, the golden flashes of sunshine, blue sky, red birds darting, women's brown bodies bending and moving in the bean fields and vegetable gardens, all this revolving, everything in motion, the colors and the songs and laughter of the women and the twittering of birds sometimes making him squeal and chortle, sometimes lulling him to sleep. Days passed and seasons turned.

Or sometimes she carried the cradleboard on her back while she worked, and here too was motion, motion as she hoed amid the hot, summer-green smell of bean and corn leaves, motion as she pounded grain to meal or scraped hides to make leather beside the door of her husband's lodge and talked with her daughter or told her stories of the People or sang with her, and the baby knew their two voices among the hundreds of voices in the town, and he was content when their two voices were calm and happy and near. He seldom cried, for the motions and the sounds and the colors of the peaceful days delighted all his growing perceptions. In his soft skullcase moved the surd, formless billows of baby thought, the gradual coalescence of patterns and recognitions, of needs and satisfactions, always with the motions, the nearnesses, the sounds. His mother's round, brown, dark-nippled breasts hung over him, her hand released him from the straits of the cradleboard, fondled him, cleansed him, and anointed him with oil, delighting his naked skin, and then the oozy nipple would meet his sucking lips, and he would nourish himself blindly like a root in the earth, lulled by the oldest of all the sounds, her pumping heart. If he opened his eyes, he would see her glinting eyes above him, her large hand moving slowly

27

to discourage some buzzing, tickling fly, and beyond, the leaves moving, the clouds moving. Or he would watch his own fat little hand clench and open or experimentally extend a finger at a time, perhaps knowing or perhaps not knowing that it was a part of him instead of one of the familiar moving things of the sensual world around him.

And sometimes the face of his sister, Star Watcher, would move into the round of his little world and loom before him with its white smile and its songs and its cooing and clucking sounds. Her face was as welcome as his mother's, her caresses as kind, her skin as warm, her voice as musical; the only difference was that her little nipples did not give food.

And he came to know other faces, too: his father's, usually high above him smiling down, the eagle feather in his hair translucent with sunlight, the silver bobs of his earrings glittering just out of reach, the deep roll of his voice filling the world. And his brother's face, a different smile, dark hair without a feather or other ornaments, and the funny popping sounds he would make with his lips to start the baby giggling. Still the days passed and the seasons turned.

Then came days when he was kept close to his mother's skin inside a musky-smelling animal hide, dark with interesting and tickly short hairs on it, and when the robe was opened the air on his skin was cold, a sensation new and needing to be understood. In those days there was always the sharp odor of smoke, and sometimes he would stay enchanted for long times by the light and movement of flames, contemplating fire and the moving shadows it made above him, hearing its soft or sharp little sounds. The fire was another familiar to him, always there, moving and making sounds, like another member of this family. Sometimes at night he would wake up, and though he could hear his mother's heartbeat and her breathing, and feel the warmth of her skin, he could not see her or anyone else in the darkness of their *wigewa,* no one except the fire. It was always there, though sometimes it would be burned down to silent, shimmering embers, and though it looked different then from the flames, it still had motion and he would recognize it, and make sounds to it, wordless talk in the cold darkness between two warm and living things, baby and fire.

Still the days and nights passed and the seasons turned.

His bones were growing straight in the straight cradleboard. Constrained in it much of every day, his limbs and backbone and the back of his head aligned by its straight wooden back, he was unconsciously being molded into that erect posture that characterized the Shawnees and made them seem an unusually proud and handsome people. Chiksika, now in his thirteenth year, was nearly as tall and straight as his father the chief, whom he emulated in every way. Chiksika and Hard Striker were often gone for many days at a time in the winter, gone together with their horses and guns and bows, just the two of them or with other men of the town, to hunt up or down the river and in meadowlands to the west and south for meat and hides, leaving Turtle Mother and Star Watcher and the baby in Kispoko Town. Sometimes during their absences there would be howling, shrieking blizzards, and the snow and cold winds would force their way into the bark house. It would be hard to keep the fire alive, and the smoke would blow back down through the smokehole, filling the house, stinging their eyes, and making their throats hurt. During such times there might be much discomfort and distress, the mother and daughter huddling together in robes, trying to keep the baby warm, and they would murmur anxiously to each other about the safety of Hard Striker and Chiksika, who were living out in it somewhere without even a *wigewa*. The baby could feel their distress as well as he could feel the cold and the smoke, and he would cry a great deal then, his little voice muffled by the robes and the shriek and moan of the snowy gale outside. In this first winter of his life there were several weeks of such white and screaming weather, and then weeks when the wind would stop blowing and the stars would come out, but the still air would be so cold that trees would crack and the snow on the ground would crunch loudly when people walked by outside. The hunters found little during these times or could not travel back to Kispoko Town because of the cold, and some days there was no food anywhere in the whole town, and then dogs and old horses would be killed and divided. Several old people and some children died from the cold and hunger and from sickness brought on by the cold. It was not uncommon in the lives of the Shawnee to suffer like this in midwinter. Some of the people lacked fingers and toes they had lost by freezing in winters past, and there was danger in going outside one's lodge even to gather wood for the fires.

Sometimes this winter there was nothing for Turtle Mother and Star Watcher to eat for days. This they could bear because they understood and knew it would end eventually, but when a mother has had no nourishment for a long time, she cannot explain to her baby why her milk is not nourishing and why his stomach hurts and he never has the good sleepiness. And he cries.

But sooner or later a hunting party would return over the snowy meadow trail, wrapped to their ears in blankets and hides, their horses snorting frost, and these hunters would raise their cold-stiffened arms and cry a halloo to the village. Venison and bear and fowl, frozen rock hard, would be unloaded from the shivering horses and would be given not just to those hunters' own families but to whoever was most weakened by hunger in the tribe. If there were five hundred hungry people in the town and one carcass, somehow it would be managed so that every person would receive either a sip of meat broth or a shred of flesh.

But sometimes a hunting party would come in with nothing, nearly dead from exposure, and if they came when the famine was most dire, there might be at most a hunter's lame, scrawny horse to butcher, and the people would relish a taste of meat, even though it was bad meat, and then with it stuttering and gurgling in their bellies they could smile and hope for another day, for another and luckier hunting party to ride in, for their own husbands and fathers and brothers to arrive, for a warm wind to melt the snow and ice, or for some miracle from Weshemoneto: an elk getting trapped in broken ice in nearby Scippo Creek or the discovery of a part of a beaver carcass unfinished by wolves.

Then at last Hard Striker, Chiksika, and their hunters rode in across the twilit snow, yelling happily for help to unload and distribute the huge, hide-wrapped bundles of buffalo and elk and venison under which their horses were staggering in the deep snow. Soon, then, Hard Striker's lodge was cozy with the heat from the cookfire and full of the delicious aroma and the flare and sizzle of roasting fat meat and the laughter and the familiar voices, happy, singing, tale telling. The baby was fed broth from a horn spoon and some warm marrow, strange tastes that caused him to look astonished and make serious faces, but then his stomach at last was content, and he went to sleep warmed by his parents' bodies in their bed. And through the bark walls came the laughter and pleasant voices of the other people of the village who also had been fed.

And so the days and nights passed, and the spring came again. And the baby born under the shooting star, whom Change-of-Feathers had decided was destined to be a war chief of unusual courage and vision, passed from his first year into his second, and then similarly into his third, for it was a brief time of peace, and in times of peace the world rolls smoothly through its rounds, allowing its children to learn and play and become what they may.

# CHAPTER 3

*Kispoko Town, on the Scioto-se-pe*
*January 1771*

This time there was no flying star over her childbed, but once again Turtle Mother's labors were to produce a birth that the Shawnees would never forget. She was becoming a legend among mothers.

This time, her daughter was not present to soothe her and help her. Star Watcher had just come to the age to be a woman, and the moon had caused her blood to flow down for the first time, frightening her. Turtle Mother, already starting to labor, had explained it all to her and told her to put certain of her belongings into a bundle and go to the lodge at the end of town where each woman had to go when this was happening to her, whether it was her first time or she had been doing it for years. When the blood was coming down, they were not supposed to be touched or smelled, or even seen, her mother told her, except by other women who were bleeding, too. Hearing this, Star Watcher had looked afraid and ashamed. She already knew of the women's lodge, of course; other girls and women had told her about it, and even her own mother had gone away there regularly during the times when she was not pregnant. But now that it was her own time, Star Watcher suddenly had felt herself to be loathsome. There was a boy in the town, a fine Chalagawtha boy named Wasegoboah, or Stands Firm, who played eyes with her. "Will Stands Firm know," she had asked her mother, "that I am in the moon lodge? What will he think of me?"

And so Turtle Mother had had to pause in her labor and reassure her daughter. Most girls were taught about the blood moon by their grandmothers, not by their own mothers. But Star Watcher's grandmothers were dead in the south lands, so now Turtle Mother had to tell her: "There is really no evil in the bleeding time. It only means that your body is old enough to make itself ready to bear children. Men want us to go apart at

31

these times because men cannot understand some things. They are troubled because they smell something. A man fears and hates what he does not understand. He believes game will smell the blood on him, and flee. He believes that if a woman in her moon steps over him, he will become weak. If a man is going to war and his wife has her moon, his war party may be called back.'' She chuckled, then groaned and grew tense, then relaxed, and smiled again.

"Sometimes, women have pretended to have their moon, in order to save their husbands from going to war. That is clever, but it is bad because it deceives the People. There is great medicine in the moons, my daughter, but it is not all medicine. There are many ways a woman can fool a man, by knowing things he does not know. But some such fooling is not right.''

Star Watcher, even in her anxiety, had listened hard to understand all this, and she had tried to understand it in terms of Stands Firm. As if knowing this, her mother had said then:

"If Stands Firm learns that you are away to the women's lodge, then he will like you even more. He will like you in more ways. He will not be able to help himself. . . .''

She had paused again and held herself tense for a while as a pain passed through. Then, after a while, regaining her breath, she had smiled a sly smile at her daughter and said to her almost in a whisper:

"Men only *think* they are in control of things. Woman guides man's path more than he would ever believe. But a woman who is wise will always let him believe he guides his own path. A woman who brags that she directs him, she makes him very mad. And he will send her apart from him just as if she were in her blood moon.'' Turtle Mother's eyes had glittered with the fun of sharing this great secret, even in her time of strain.

The girl, as mystified by all these strange new confidences as she was by the aches and the moist heat and the tickling sensations in her loins, had looked intently into her mother's eyes and asked: "How does one come to know these secrets?''

"Where does knowing come from?'' Turtle Mother had said. "The secrets are being spoken in your belly now. Is not the closest of the spirits Our Grandmother, Kokomthena, our Creator? And is it not said in Our Grandmother's very first law that we must be apart from others when we are in our blood moon? Why then do you think this is? Our Grandmother understands men's minds, for did she not create them?

"Daughter, listen: Do not dread to go to the women's lodge. You will be surprised. It is a very *good* place. Many such truths as I have just told you about men and women can be learned there. Listen to the women there as they talk. You will have a good time there, though of course this is a secret that men do not know. So we let them think as they like. Listen. Here is a good thing they do not even think of. For those five days a woman enjoys rest from the work of her home! Ha! Now you smile!"

"When I come back," the girl had said, rubbing her cheek against her mother's, "there will be another little brother or sister that I can hold."

"Yes, my daughter. Another one. But maybe not so little." She had become aware that she was carrying much baby this time.

And then after the girl had walked away in the snow to the women's lodge with her little bundle of belongings, and the sun had become red in the treetops in the west, Turtle Mother's pains had quickened and grown stronger, and the midwives had come in to prepare her. There were only women in the house now. Her husband, Hard Striker, and son Chiksika were away hunting. Their hunting trips were anxious times now, for the white men were more and more at large in Kain-tuck-ee, and there had been fights with them. This time her husband and his hunters had been gone for more than a week.

Now that Star Watcher could not be here to take care of little Tecumseh during the childbirth, the boy had been put in the care of relatives.

After it started, it began to seem to Turtle Mother that this birth would not be as hard as the others, even though her belly was very heavy. The child emerged soon. It was a boy, not unusually large. But strangely, the pain was still coming down.

And suddenly one of the midwives exclaimed, "Hai! Another one comes!"

Immediately there was an unusual excitement in the *wigewa,* for twins were very rare among the Shawnee.

This boy was almost exactly like the first. Turtle Mother squatted, looking at the two slick little black-haired squirmers before her and thinking for the first time in her life how good it was that a woman had two breasts.

But the pain had not stopped, and she feared that somehow she had been hurt inside by her double burden. She was suddenly very much afraid, afraid that she would die from a hurt inside, while her husband and sons and her daughter were gone from the *wigewa,* that she would die and leave these twins newborn.

And then as the midwives were preparing to take the afterbirths, one cried out that there was another head. This was beyond belief. Turtle Mother swayed, wild-eyed and frightened, her body pushing as if she must get rid of this unheard-of thing. One of the midwives nearly fainted. They were almost too disconcerted to finish their work but fumbled with the tangle of slippery cords, and in the wet mess, and finally pulled down a cramped, wrinkled, dark runt of a baby, who began squalling at once in a

voice big enough for all three. His harsh, terrible wail could be heard for
a great distance around the *wigewa,* and people came out into the snow with
bemused expressions and looked toward Hard Striker's lodge. They were
still standing there when one of the midwives rushed out to fetch the
Kispoko medicine man.

For never in the memory of any living person had a woman delivered
three babies at once in a Shawnee town.

When Hard Striker rode in with his hunters two days later, the runt of the
newborn litter was still howling. He had scarcely stopped since the moment
of his birth. He would scream until his contorted little face was engorged.
"Only when the nipple is in his mouth," Turtle Mother groaned, "does he
cease."

"What did you say?" Hard Striker asked. He was stunned by the news
of the three babies at once, and he could not hear her words over the
screaming of the runt.

She put her nipple in the runt's mouth and then repeated in the wonderful silence, "Only when he eats does he quit shrieking. And even now,
listen to him complain." The baby growled and mumbled angrily as he
sucked. Turtle Mother looked haggard from loss of sleep, and so did the
neighbors who had come to greet their chief and to see what he would do
about this poor unhappy little monster.

Hard Striker turned toward the doorway and asked the neighbors hovering there if they would like to go home to their own *wigewas* for a while
so he could examine his new sons. And he exclaimed: "Think of it! Three
of them! Ha! Think of it! I could start a new tribe!"

"Yes," replied Corn Dog, a bleary-eyed neighbor. "That would be a
good idea, a new tribe. On the other side of the river."

Hard Striker was worried and upset, and this joke made him angry, but
he did not show it. He told the people: "We got much meat. My own son
Chiksika killed two bucks and a doe. In a while we will share meat. Now
let me look at my sons. Three of them! Think of it! Ah! Tecumseh, my son!
Come up in my arms!" The little boy, home from his aunt's, was hugging
his father's leg and trying to climb. Hard Striker lifted him and tossed him
twice and caught him to make him laugh. Then, still holding him, he knelt
to watch the runt baby sucking furiously, making his fierce noises. The other
two newborns were asleep, wrapped in a doeskin on the mat beside her.

"I need another teat," Turtle Mother said wistfully.

"Ha, ha! That would be something! Three of them! Think of it! Where
is daughter?"

"She is in the women's lodge."

"Ah." A momentary sadness crossed his face. "She is a woman now. Was she scared?"

"She went happily."

"Good. She is always happy. May she always be happy." While he talked and held Tecumseh, Hard Striker with his free hand was pulling down the robe and examining the two sleeping babies. "They look good," he said. Then to her, with tenderness thickening his voice, he said, "My wife. You become a legend. I have the greatest woman of our nation. Even greater I think than Tall Soldier Woman." Nonhelema, Tall Soldier Woman, Cornstalk's sister, was a great female Shawnee village chief. Her town was across the river, on the Peckuwe Plains. "Now let me see this one," Hard Striker said. He knelt closer to his wife and began to study the suckling infant. His face went grim. Tecumseh sat on his father's thigh and regarded the baby with equal gravity.

"He does not look promising," Hard Striker said.

"He is weak," she admitted. "All his strength is in his mouth." The fire crackled, and the feeding baby muttered and gulped.

Then Hard Striker asked the awful question, because something was becoming apparent to him even though the baby was cradled in her arm.

"Is he crooked?"

She sighed, bit her lower lip, and blinked. "He is crooked." And then she rushed on. "No doubt he was crowded in the womb. But his bones are still soft; surely the cradleboard will straighten his body as he grows!" She had been giving this much thought during the long, sleepless two days since the babies' birth. She had fingered every inch of the little warped body with pity and agony and fear in her heart, and had come to believe that there was a slight chance he could grow straight and not be forever lame or deformed. He did not have any fused joints, any strange holes in his bones, or any terrible growths or markings on him. He was simply a cramped, spindly thing with a narrow and lopsided head, like a bean. He would not necessarily become a cripple, she believed. But he *was* dubious.

"I should talk with the shaman," Hard Striker said. He frowned. The Kispoko village medicine man was lacking in wisdom and spiritual power, compared with Change-of-Feathers. He had ideas that were alien to traditional teachings, and many of the women in the sept were afraid of him because of such ideas. One of the ideas he had put forward was that if a baby looked as if it would be crippled, a sufferer and a burden to the tribe, it should be left out to die. The Shawnees never did this, but Turtle Mother knew this shaman sometimes recommended it, and she was afraid.

Hard Striker turned his eyes away from the runt, as if it hurt him to look at it anymore. She saw that look in his eyes and feared what he might be thinking. Her husband had talked often with the shaman and knew that sometimes it would make sense not to allow a certain child to grow up. Animal herds keep themselves strong and healthy, he knew, by weeding out the weak and sick, and the Kispoko, being the warrior sept, should keep itself as strong and vigorous as it could. Still, though Hard Striker understood the sense of it, he was troubled by the idea.

The Kispoko medicine man came, and after looking thoughtfully at the screaming runt for a long time and then sitting with his eyes shut and a feathered medicine stick in his hands, he rose and went out into the snow. Hard Striker followed him out, and they stood in the cold under the stars. The medicine man began walking among the *wigewas,* and after a while the two men were far enough toward the edge of the town that they could hardly hear the baby crying. It seemed that it would be easier to talk about its fate without its voice in their ears. Behind them, the soft light from fires leaked out of cracks and passageways of the bark huts, making little yellow rays of warmth on the trampled snow. Beyond the edge of the village there lay only frigid darkness, and Hard Striker could not keep himself from thinking of an infant left to die in such cold and darkness.

He said, his breath condensing in the terrible cold, "I wonder if the cradleboard would straighten him."

"I fear," said the shaman, "that he would cry himself to death long before then. And your family would grow sick from lack of sleep. Maybe," he added after a pause, "your neighbors would try to persuade you to silence him anyway. It is bad for the chief of the sept to have such a troublesome thing in the midst of his own family."

Hard Striker's heart was heavy with dread and sadness. It did not seem that the shaman was going to counsel him to let the poor creature live. Hard Striker had been hoping that some hopeful word might come from him.

Now the shaman said:

"I think, though, that it could be dangerous not to nurture an infant born as one of three. That is a sign of much power. It is a great *unsoma,* like the shooting star. Maybe the Great Good Spirit means to test your faith and wisdom by giving you this loud and ugly one."

The medicine man did not say it to the chief, but he was wondering whether the loud one might even be the work of Matchemoneto, the Evil Spirit, and he feared that great trouble could come to a village where a creature of the Evil Spirit was being raised. On the other hand, to abandon such a creature might bring even more evil upon the town. The shaman had never faced a problem like this, and he was bewildered by it, and it was made worse by being in the family of the chief.

Hard Striker felt that the medicine man might be thinking about Match-emoneto. He had thought of this, too. He had wondered which would be worse, to risk offending the Evil Spirit or to live with a creature of the Evil Spirit in one's family. Any person in the tribe had his own medicine bag and could, if alarmed by this loud one, make witchcraft against it or against the whole family.

And so now the two most powerful men of the Shawnee warrior sept stood in the dark with the intense cold upon their heads, while pity and fear worked in their hearts.

Turtle Mother sat looking in wonderment at the ugly little creature in her arm. It was not nursing now, and yet it was not crying. Its strange little face was for once in repose. It seemed to be asleep. The firelight limned the side of its head. She could hear footsteps crunching on the snow, coming toward the *wigewa,* just one person's footsteps. She knew it must be her husband. Her heart pounded with fright as the door flap opened and his hand, then face, then body, slipped into the firelight.

He sat down with his legs folded and held his hands over the fire, his face full of serious thought. But he said nothing for so long that finally she said:

"Do you notice that he has stopped crying?"

"Yes."

After a while she asked, "What says the shaman?"

"He says that the little one is his own *unsoma.* He says that he should be named Lalawethika."

"He-Makes-a-Loud-Noise."

"Yes."

"And . . ."

"And the naming day will be in seven days, so we must think of names for the other two as well, and watch for their signs."

He looked across the fire at his wife's face now, and he saw that a rill of tears had started down each side of her nose. Her chin was crumpled with crying, but she was smiling, too. Her body began to quake with voiceless sobs.

"I know you were afraid," he said. "But have the Shawnee ever abandoned their children to the wolves?"

"My husband," she said when at last she could speak. Her eyes were swimming in tears. "I am so happy."

# CHAPTER 4

*Kispoko Town
Summer 1772*

Tecumseh, now in his fourth summer, was squatting in the sunlight with other little naked children watching Chiksika win the arrow-and-hoop game in the meadow when word came about the white-face.

The hoop rolled fast, because it was thrown by a very good hoop roller named Thick Water, about nine years of age, tall and long-armed. The hoop was made of limber green hickory with a mesh of willow strips inside. It would be rolled along a smoothed path, and boys alongside the path would try to shoot their arrows through it as it passed. A boy who could put an arrow through the hoop would then get to throw the hoop over arrows sticking in the ground, and he could keep any arrows he encircled with his throw. Chiksika, quick and unerring, had already won arrows from all the players his own age and now was winning them from young warriors, some of them years older. Whenever he won another arrow, he would bring it over and lay it on the ground in front of Tecumseh, who had the honor of guarding them for his big brother. Tecumseh would laugh and clap his hands together, then hunker more protectively over the growing pile of arrows while Chiksika swaggered back out, smiling and sweating, to win more. Such a hoard of arrows was a treasure. It took hours to make an arrow: to find and split and shave down a straight-enough shaft, to trim and attach the right-size feathers, and especially to get or make a good arrow-head. Not many boys, not even many men, knew how to flake flint into arrowheads anymore. For years the tribes had been dependent upon guns bought from white traders or captured in war, and even for the making of arrows, pieces of iron or brass were often used instead of flint, as they would not shatter when they struck a tree trunk or rock. But the metal-tipped

38

arrows were not used in the arrow-and-hoop game, because any boy who had one would not risk losing it so easily.

And so Chiksika was just nocking another arrow to his bowstring, yelling cheerfully, and Thick Water, skinny, brown, and shining with sweat in the hot sunlight, was just getting poised to roll the hoop down the line again, when excited shouting was heard:

"Long Knife! Whiteface!"

At once everyone in the meadow tensed with alarm. Children looked confused and ready to run. Many people came running from the direction of the Scioto-se-pe, pouring out of the willow shade into the sunlight, some carrying clubs and staffs, some swishing willow switches through the air and yelling that a captured whiteface was being brought in to run the gauntlet.

The game players howled with delight and went sprinting off to join the running, shouting people. Chiksika ran to Tecumseh. He snatched up his arrows, crying, "Come! Hurry, little brother!" Tecumseh did not need to be called. He always followed Chiksika whenever and wherever he could. They sped through the sunny grass toward the running mob, their hearts racing with excitement, yipping and howling. Tecumseh had hardly a notion what this was all about; he was yelping and running only because Chiksika was. His little legs pumped furiously as he tried to keep up, and his heart felt as if it would fly out of his mouth. Another little boy, running in front of him, bits of chaff stuck to his oiled buttocks, tripped and fell, and Tecumseh tumbled over him into the tall grass but scrambled to his feet and kept going at full tilt, his little feet padding on the ground. The air was full of dust and voices. Soon Chiksika had reached the edge of the stampeding crowd, and Tecumseh was still right behind him, charging alongside the welter of skirts, leggings, and bare legs.

Chiksika dodged in through the doorway of his father's lodge, and Tecumseh tumbled into the gloom after him. A kettle of meat and hominy was simmering aromatically over the cookfire, but no one was tending it. Everyone had left in a hurry. Chiksika dumped his arrows beside a wall and snatched up a long hickory staff. He grabbed Tecumseh's hand and pulled him out the door, back into the stream of running people, who were heading toward the center of the town.

Beside a brush fence in front of a *wigewa* sat an ancient woman too frail and bent to join the throng, but not too old to shriek encouragement and cackle with the joy of it all. Chiksika skidded to a stop before her, and Tecumseh ran into him from behind. "Old Grandmother," Chiksika yelled into her ear, "I borrow this!" and he plucked a thin branch out of her fence and thrust it into Tecumseh's hand, telling the woman, "We will bring it

back with whiteface blood on it!'' Then he was off again, Tecumseh on his
heels.

Now they were going up the wide, packed-earth avenue that led to the
grand council lodge, and on both sides of it the people were lining up,
laughing, shouting, holding their sticks and clubs and switches, slashing
them through the air to hear their vicious sound, hundreds of people of all
ages. Most of the men were nearly naked in the summer heat, wearing only
loincloths, their bodies agleam with sweat and the oil they put on to protect
their skin from insects, the women wearing light frocks of doeskin or bright
trade cloth or only small lap aprons. The children cavorting among them
wore nothing but oil and dust.

As Chiksika and his little brother ran along the lines of excited people,
they saw their mother, holding two of the triplets in her arms, and Star
Watcher holding the little Loud Noise, who was crying lustily.

Nearer to the lodge they came upon Stands Firm, the young warrior who
was Star Watcher's suitor. Chiksika and Stands Firm admired each other and
often hunted together, so Chiksika sprang into line next to him. They
smiled at each other with a happy ferocity in their eyes and whipped their
sticks noisily through the air. The shiny metal ornaments in Stands Firm's
decorated ears shook and glinted with his motions. Tecumseh stood between the two youths, hip high to them, full of admiration and excitement
but still scarcely understanding what was happening. Stands Firm said:

"I hope the Long Knife gets this far. I will be the one who knocks him
to his knees if he does! Ha!''

"Ha, ha! Or I will!''

"He surely won't get past the two of us!''

Soon the parallel lines of people grew more subdued, looking down the
line, waiting for the white man to appear. The lines were very long; there
were people here not only from Kispoko Town but also many from the
other Shawnee towns across the river. The captive might well not make it
this far.

"They say this whiteface wants to become one of our people," Stands
Firm said.

"He does?" said Chiksika, surprised.

"I talked to the one who caught the whiteface and brought him here.
They say he was very good on the trail, that he does not like being a white
boy.''

"Eh, so,'' Chiksika replied, looking bemused. "I can understand that.''
But his eagerness to whip the whiteface was diminished a little, somehow.
It would be harder to hate somebody who *wanted* to be a Shawnee.

Now a drum sounded up by the lodge, a slow, two-beat rhythm, like a heartbeat, growing faster and faster. Then it stopped. Hard Striker appeared in front of the lodge, wearing red leggings and a chest-plate made of rows of colored quills. He held in his left hand a long pole decorated with scalplocks. He struck the ground twice with the butt of his pole, and then the drum beat twice. Everyone looked down the other way then. The voices rose to an excited murmur.

And then at that far end, two hundred paces away, a single figure was thrust out between the two rows of townspeople. His blue coat made him easy to see. Then two warriors stepped close to the captive and cut and tore away all his clothing. Now he was even more conspicuous. Little Tecumseh's mouth gaped. Here was something he had never seen before: a person whose whole body was white like a fish's belly. This image was so strange, and so curiously beautiful, that it was as if he were not really standing here but hearing one of the old ones tell a legend. There were legends of people with white bodies, and Tecumseh had seen them in his mind while listening.

But he was here, with the dust and the crowd, their howling laughter. This was real, and the moment was frightful. He cringed back and wrapped his arms around Chiksika's leg, dropping his switch, his face contorting as if he were going to cry.

"No, no," Chiksika exclaimed, leaning down over him, frowning, pulling his arms away. He picked up the stick and put it in Tecumseh's right hand. Then he pointed toward the white slip of a figure down the way and said loudly in his ear: "That is a whiteface! He is bad. When he runs past us here, you must try to hit him. That's what this stick is for: to hit him as hard as you can. Don't be afraid, little brother. Do you hear me?"

The child nodded. His eyes were still wild with fright, but he always did what Chiksika said. He would do anything to please his brother. In his mind he remembered the hoop rolling between the two lines of boys, and he thought now that this striking of the white person must be some sort of a game, like arrow-and-hoop.

Tecumseh had heard of whitefaces often, and he had sensed the tone in which they were mentioned, as when bad spirits were spoken of, but he had never imagined that the thing called a whiteface could be actually a person who was white all over, that the white-bodied whiteface would come by like a hoop in a game, that he was supposed to hit it with a stick, that it would come close enough to be hit with a stick. He was afraid now of what was about to happen. But he was also eager to do anything that would make his brother smile on him.

Then there was a drumbeat at the lodge. The voices rose to a scream.

At the other end of the line, a warrior hit the white person from behind with a long staff, nearly knocking him off his feet, and as he staggered and hesitated, all the people near him began lashing at him with their switches.

Then he suddenly sprinted away in a crouch, and he was coming up the line very fast, white legs pumping, white arms held up to fend off blows to his head. As he came, the sticks slashed out at him, hundreds of them, blurred and whistling. The people near Tecumseh were practically dancing with eagerness as he came on; their hands strained with their grip on their sticks and switches. Tecumseh was trembling with the awful excitement.

The runner was coming so fast that many of the whips were missing him. He stumbled once, over a staff someone had thrust at his legs. His hands touched the ground, but he righted himself and came on, crouching and staggering, sometimes jerking his head aside in pain, but still coming fast.

At ten paces the bloody welts on his white skin were plain, and he seemed to be weakening. There was black hair on his groin. His face was a bloody grimace. Now his sprinting step had been beaten out of him, and he was merely weaving and plodding and trying to stay upright. He was coming so slowly now that everyone was hitting him, some more than once. His eyes were rolling wildly. Suddenly he sagged to his knees under the blow of a stout pole.

For an instant Tecumseh could see the blood-spattered white body falling to the dust right before him; then a mass of bare legs and skirts blocked his sight as the people moved in to surround the fallen figure. Then it was all dust and howling, the whistling and slashing of limber whips. It went on for a long while before Chiksika came back to Tecumseh from the center of it, and his sweaty face bent down to the child, happy and crazy-eyed. His hand grasped Tecumseh's arm and pulled him. "Come! Use your stick! You must count a coup on the Long Knife!" He wedged a way in among the milling people and pushed Tecumseh forward. "Now hit him!"

The white body was curled up, on elbows and knees, still moving, struggling to rise. The strange white skin was crisscrossed with welts and bleeding cuts, smeared with blood and smudged with dust and dirt from the street. Switches were still slashing and smacking, making blood spray, and the body twitched with the blows. The white person's head, its dark hair lank with sweat and blood and spotted with bits of chaff, turned slightly, and now Tecumseh saw the side of the face, very close. It was all red with blood, and only the teeth showed white now.

"Hit him, little brother!" Chiksika shouted in the child's ear.

And now Tecumseh, all sick and frightened and confused inside, feeling as he had never felt before, did what his big brother told him to do. He raised his stick and whipped at the living thing before him. The Shawnees did not whip their children, so he did not know what whipping felt like; only in accidents at play had he ever felt pain. The turmoil rose and rose inside him, and he slashed again and again with his stick, the stick from the cackling old grandmother's fence. He got closer over the cringing, bloody body and whipped with all his might. He was not whipping a person now, he was lashing out against his own unbearable feelings. He was fighting against a terror. He loved and hated this poor struggling thing before him, and it was blurred by his tears.

Other people were still whipping at it, and Tecumseh was now so close over it that some of their sticks hit his own arms and back. One blow stung his ear so sharply that his nose began to run. But he kept whipping, even though now he knew that whips hurt terribly. Everything was red and yellow. Tecumseh sobbed and screeched and whipped and could not stop.

Finally it was Chiksika himself who took hold of Tecumseh's arms and pulled him off. The battered body was flat on the ground now and no longer moving. The people were backing off, re-forming their two lines.

"Eh! You are a fury!" Chiksika told the child. "The whitefaces had better be wary of Tecumseh! Ha, ha!"

But the child was too sick and dizzy to hear the words. And for once, Chiksika's pleasure did not make Tecumseh laugh.

The young white man was taken away to a lodge where women would feed him and heal his wounds with herbs and ointments. He had proven himself strong and brave by not crying out once, and thus it was assured that he would be adopted into the tribe.

And so Chiksika would tell people: "Yes, he must be strong, to be alive after the beating our Tecumseh gave him! Ha, ha!"

Tecumseh was sick and troubled by dreams for several days after that, but soon the easy flow of the summer days soothed his soul, and everything was as it had been.

One day as the light of the late afternoon sun glowed golden in the village and over the woods and meadows all around, Hard Striker sat by his lodge with his wife and waited for Tecumseh to come in from play. The child came running, tired, hungry, and happy, and he saw his father summoning him with a wave of his hand. He came and stood before him, and Hard Striker said:

"My son, I have something to tell you about yourself. It is the most important thing you will ever know. It is time to tell you because I think you are old enough now." His father's face was like stone, but his voice was soft and warm.

"You were born under a great sign, the sign of the Panther leaping across the sky. To be born under a great sign means that you will have a great thing to do, and your life will not be easy."

It was as if his father's voice itself had weight, and he felt the weight settle on him.

His life, which had always been play and love and happiness, with everything easy to understand, was changing.

That night he dreamed of whitefaces, of a white bird, of yellow dust and great thunder noises, and he woke up crying.

His mother had to hold him until he was quiet.

She put her cheek against his and whispered to him: "For once it is not your little brother Loud Noise who cries in the night. Now go back to sleep. You are in your family, and all is good."

# CHAPTER 5

## *Kispoko Town*
## *June 1774*

S ee this," Chiksika told Tecumseh, kneeling beside him in a sunny
glade in the deep green woods. The forest there was of enormous
hardwoods. The ground under the trees was pleasantly open and
free of deadwood and underbrush, because it was close to the village, and firewood gatherers kept it clean. Chiksika pointed at a plant. Many
other plants like it were growing in the glade. "This is the poison vine that
made your skin itch last spring. Know it by the three notched leaves. You
must know the shape of the leaves and stay out of it. But if you do get it
on your skin . . . Come here now." He rose and walked a few steps and
knelt again. "Now see this plant." It had a light green, oval-shaped leaf.

"I know that one," Tecumseh said. He knelt beside Chiksika, his small
bow in his left hand. "In the summer it has the little orange flowers, and
the little hummingbirds go to it."

"Yes. Good," said Chiksika. "And now see this, how much juice comes
out when I break the stem. Now, brother, if you get the poison plant on
your skin, then you should come and get this plant, and mash the stems and
leaves and rub their juice on your skin, and the itch will stop, and the sores
will go away. This is what Mother put on you to cure you when you got
into the poison plant."

"Ah!"

"Is it not good how Our Grandmother Kokomthena who lives beside
the moon has made the world?" Chiksika said, smiling and squeezing
Tecumseh's shoulder. "She has created something for everything. If she
makes a poison, she also makes something to cure the poison."

"Yes. But why did she make the poison?"

Chiksika paused. That was the kind of question Tecumseh would always
ask in the middle of a lesson. Now Chiksika replied: "So that there will be

more to know, and to show us how much she thinks of us. Do you remember the root I showed you which cures the bite of the rattlesnake?''

"Yes. Pocono."

"Good. Now I know you are going to ask me why Our Grandmother made the rattlesnake with poison, so I will answer before you ask. This she did so that we will be careful not to step on him. He has a privilege not to be stepped upon. But she also put a warning noise on him so that a careless person will not be bitten by mistake.''

Tecumseh thought for a moment. "Then why," he asked, "did not Our Grandmother put a warning noise on the poison ivy?''

Chiksika shook his head, then laughed. "You!" he exclaimed, and popped him on the head with his fingertips.

"Or on the copperhead snake?" Tecumseh kept on.

"So you will have to stay alert and watch for things! And so there will be more for you to learn. Now." He reached out and touched the jewel-weed plant again, and he said in the voice he used when he was reaching the main point in a lesson, "You will see that wherever the poison leaves grow, nearby grow these that cure the poison. Everything in the world Our Grandmother created just so. For every evil spirit there is a good spirit. But one must learn everything, or these creations will do you no good. Do you see?''

Tecumseh nodded. He rubbed a jewelweed leaf between his finger and thumb and felt its healing juice, and he thought how wise the Creator had been. He smiled at Chiksika, white teeth flashing in his coppery face. "Now what else?" he said.

Chiksika laughed aloud. "More! More! My little brother wants to know everything before he is seven summers old!''

"Yes! What about the mockingbird? When his funny noises made me laugh this morning, you said you would tell me about why he makes such funny talk.''

"Ah. For this reason," Chiksika said. "It is to guard the place where he lives. He learns the songs of many other birds. Then he sits near his home and makes himself sound like a forest full of birds. And so, when other birds come near his territory, they will think it is already crowded with too many birds and will go away.''

"Ah! How smart he is!''

"Oh, yes. Kokomthena made all the birds and animals smart in their ways, so they can get along. The birds are a people, just as we are, and the wolves are a people, and deer and bears. And all are smart in their ways. A great hunter is one who knows how the different races of animals are smart. If he knows this, then he can think like them and know where they will be at a time of the day. The Great Good Spirit made Kokomthena very wise, so that she could create smart and happy creatures on the world."

"Tell me about her little dog and the Skemotah."

Chiksika put his hand on Tecumseh's shoulder and smiled. "It is like this. Kokomthena is always busy making something. She does not make people and animals anymore, because she finished them. But what she makes now is the Skemotah. She weaves on it every day, in her home near the moon. You tell me what the Skemotah is."

"It is a big basket, or like a seine."

"And is for what?"

"When the world ends, she will fish for all the People. The good ones she will lift to heaven in the seine, and the bad ones will fall through and be lost."

Chiksika said, "I think you know this story very well already, little brother."

"Yes. But what about her little dog?"

"Here it is about her little dog. All day every day she weaves the Skemotah. When she is finished with it, there will be nothing else for her to do, and so the world will end, and that is when she will fish for the good ones to take to heaven. But every night, when Our Grandmother Kokomthena is tired from her weaving and goes to sleep, her little dog wakes up . . ."

Tecumseh laughed and clapped his hands. "Because he has been sleeping all day at her feet!"

"Yes. And when she goes to sleep, the little dog is ready to play. So he takes the Skemotah in his teeth and unravels all she has woven that day. And so because of her little dog, the world has not ended yet."

Tecumseh smiled, then looked thoughtful. "The little dog is bad. But what he does is good for us. I would not want the world to end."

"Would you not? Would you not want to go to heaven?"

"Someday. But not yet."

"Ah. Why not now?" Chiksika was smiling at his little brother's solemn concentration.

"Because I cannot, yet."

"Why?"

"Because our father says I have a great thing to do. I do not yet even know what it is. But the world cannot end until I have done it."

Chiksika was delighted by this. "Ha, ha!" He hugged Tecumseh to his side, and his laughter was rich and loud in the quiet woods. Tecumseh was infected by it, and his own child's laugh rang out. It was a joy to learn to understand the world he lived in, and his brother Chiksika was his primary teacher, even more than was his father, who had less time because all the people in the tribe were in his care. It was as if his father had hundreds of children, many of them much older than himself. Tecumseh understood this about the chief and was very proud of his father. But it was Chiksika who was Tecumseh's first teacher, protector, hero, and friend. And just as Chiksika in childhood had always trailed after his father, and emulated him, and absorbed everything he said, just so Tecumseh did Chiksika. He had long ago decided he would be just like his brother.

Chiksika did not try to shake off his younger brother. It was not just that he liked being the object of such adulation. He enjoyed the child's voracious curiosity and his untiring vitality. The boy was remarkable. His mind caught and held everything that entered it. He could recite tribal lore word for word after hearing it once, but he liked to hear it over and over so that he could examine it in his mind. And already, at six years, he was the champion among his peers in every sort of hunting or fighting or game-playing skill. With his little hickory bow he could put arrows almost unerringly into any mark. He could outrun many of the ten-year-olds, was a quick, strong, and tricky wrestler, and rode a pony as if he were a part of it. Chiksika, himself acknowledged as one of the most promising young bucks in the sept, saw Tecumseh as even more promising; he was aware always of his little brother's destiny signs, and he felt a sacred duty to help guide him along the path to a worthy manhood.

Suddenly now Chiksika raised his head. Someone was running through the woods, coming close. Chiksika tensed and crouched, though no danger was likely this close to the town.

Now they saw the figure coming, flitting through the sunbeams in the deep green woods, naked except for breechcloth and moccasins, muscular and graceful. Chiksika raised his arm and shouted:

"Stands Firm! *Pe-eh-wah,* this way!" The youth veered toward them and trotted up, his silver ear ornamentation jouncing heavily. His usual smile of greeting was not on his face.

"Here you are! Quick! Come to the council lodge. Your father calls for everyone. Great trouble with the Long Knives! They have burned the Wapatomica towns of our people!"

"Burned the towns?"

"Yes! With an army they went up the Muskingum, and burned the towns at the Forks! Hurry!" He turned and sprinted back toward the town, summoning them to follow. Chiksika and Tecumseh plunged into the woods and caught up with him. Chiksika's blood felt as if it were boiling through his veins; his soul was full of the silent scream of outrage. Could this really be true, that the whitefaces had dared do such a thing?

Tecumseh listened from the edge of the crowd and felt the anger and
excitement of the warriors growing as they were told of the events. As he
heard the chiefs of the Wapatomica towns tell of it, he tried to see it in his
mind.

It had started when some of the worst sort of Long Knives had tricked
some of the followers of Tah-ga-ju-te, a great Mingo chief, and murdered
them. The Mingo was a peaceful chief, a friend of both white men and red
men. His wife had been a Shawnee woman.

Among the murdered Mingos had been all the members of the chief's
family. The white men had butchered them into pieces. The chief had sworn
revenge. He had sworn to take ten scalps for each murdered member of
his own family. He had told the white leaders at Fort Pitt that he was not
going to wage a general war, and that he would put down the hatchet when
he had had retribution. A few of his Shawnee relatives had helped him carry
out his vow, and then they had put down their weapons. But the white
leaders, in their fear and anger, had then raised an army and attacked six
Shawnee towns, burning them and their crops. Their governor chief in
Virginia was now raising a bigger army to come farther into the Shawnee
country and burn more Shawnee towns. The army was gathering at Fort
Pitt, and there were so many soldiers that the smoke of their cookfires hid
the hills and the stink of their dung on the ground could be smelled for a
mile. They would probably come next to these towns here on the Peckuwe
Plains, including Cornstalk's Town and Kispoko Town.

And now with this invasion threatening, Cornstalk, main chief of all the
Shawnees, was calling for his people to remain at peace with the white men,
to appease them, to avoid war against so large an army.

But many of the Shawnees were in a rage about the murders and about
the burned towns. They felt that the Long Knives must be stopped now and
punished, or they would grow more bold and aggressive.

After the council had gone on for hours, and all had had their say, Hard
Striker rose to speak. Tecumseh, proud and excited by the sight of his father
standing before the hushed crowd, breathed fast and listened. He was
determined to remember his father's words as he always remembered stories and lessons.

"My brothers, my people," the chief said, his deep voice rolling over the
council ground. "Do you remember that only a few moons ago I went to
the Mingo chief and spoke to him about the dangers the white men bring?
This I did. But he said he had always been a friend to the white men as well
as the red, and that he would not guard himself against them.

"I warned him, but he would not listen, and now he has paid the price. All his family was butchered, and now he sits in bitterness. And the trouble that started in his camp now sweeps toward our own homes.

"Listen! Do you think we will stop this trouble by sitting still and smiling at the whitefaces, as he did? Do the whitefaces build their army of thirty hundred just to come and sit and smile at us and talk friendly talk? Listen! The Mingo was not crushed because he was weak or afraid. He is a strong and brave man. No! He was crushed because he believed in the friendship and the word of the Long Knives.

"You know me. I am a war chief. Long have I warned you that we must stand firm against the whitefaces, and never let them reach onto our land even with the toes of their boots. Many of you have echoed my belief.

"It is bad what the Long Knives have done to the Mingos, and to the Wapatomica towns. But if these evil acts have blown the mist of foolish trust from our eyes, then this was good. Now with clear sight we see that the whitefaces want to come here and burn our towns and our crops, so our children will be cold and hungry in the coming winter. The Mingo's trouble was their excuse to come to our side of the river and try to walk on us. Now surely our eyes are clear!

"Listen! The Master of Life would not look upon us as worthy men if we bent to beg at the white man's feet, for the white man is wrong and we are right. Now the Master of Life calls upon us to do with strength and courage what is our duty to do: to put these white intruders back out of our country! This country was given to our People.

"I ask you, warriors of the Kispoko Shawnees, and all men of other septs who sit among us today, to be brave and righteous! I press for war to resist the Long Knives. When we sit in council with our great chief Cornstalk, I will tell him this, and I hope that I may tell him that all my warriors are with me! *Neweh-canateh-pah Weshemoneto!*"

The hundreds of voices of the Kispoko men responded in a roar: "Ho! The Great Good Spirit favors our People!"

Tecumseh had quailed, listening to his father's words. Now a fearful excitement crowded up in his breast, for though he knew little of war, he was old enough to understand that there would soon be a great disruption of all things he knew.


Hard Striker was sure that he had swayed most of his warriors to back him for war in the great council with Cornstalk. But that night his wife was looking at him with narrowed and cunning eyes, and he suddenly realized that his hardest battle of persuasion might still be ahead of him. As his wife,

Turtle Mother was the Kispoko women's chief, and the women's chief was the peace chief. If the women of the sept decided against war, they had many ways of influencing the men, both in open council and by private persuasion. If Turtle Mother wanted no war against the white men, she could set the women in motion to change the men's minds. So Hard Striker decided to watch her closely and see which way she was leaning.

When she put the pot of succotash before him and knelt across from him, he shut his eyes and thanked Weshemoneto for the good world he had given them to live in, then prayed to Kokomthena with thanks for the corn and beans she had created. Then he smiled at his wife across the fire and reached with his horn spoon into the pot. She smiled sweetly back at him and filled her spoon also.

He nibbled some of the corn from the edge of his spoon, saying, "Mmmmm. *Mmmm!*" Chiksika and Star Watcher and Tecumseh filled their spoons and began eating, watching their parents, aware of some wordless tension between them. The triplets were already asleep under a blanket on the bed at the end of the room. Loud Noise had been a good, quiet child for a change that evening, and the household of the chief was calm and pleasant.

"How good this food is," he said to his wife.

"How good it is to be all together here and in good health, all our family safe," said Turtle Mother. "May nothing ever harm this family or take any of us from the others."

Hard Striker stopped chewing for a moment, then resumed. He knew what she meant by that. He swallowed and said:

"May no bad people ever drive us from this bountiful and sacred land."

Turtle Mother stopped chewing for a moment, then resumed. She knew what he meant by that. She swallowed and said:

"May we have peace. For, as our great chief Cornstalk has told us, if we anger bad men, they will bring armies into this bountiful and sacred land, and make us suffer."

Hard Striker's eyes flashed. But then he smiled at her again and blew on his succotash to cool it. He said, "If a child kicked this pot of food into the fire, and then did excrement in your bed, and you petted him and asked him to be nicer, do you think he would be nicer, and do that no more?"

"*Mat-tah,* no," she said.

"The Long Knives," he said, "have done that to the Wapatomica towns. If we go to them at a treaty and pet them and ask them to be nicer, they will smile behind their hands to each other and then come into this valley to throw our food in the fire and do excrement on the graves of our ancestors. My wife, they must be punished for what they did, and stopped from coming here. The whitefaces must bleed now in the east, or we will bleed and weep all the way to the sunset.''

Tecumseh shivered at what these quiet words made him see in his mind. He could remember, as in a dream memory, red blood on white skin. He did not realize that his father and mother were arguing. He presumed that they were always of one mind. Chiksika and Star Watcher knew they were arguing and refrained from saying anything.

Turtle Mother's face was now like a mask. But through her glittering eyes Star Watcher could see anger and fear and doubt and resolve all marching back and forth in her soul.

Turtle Mother finished the meal in this tense silence and said nothing while cleaning up afterward. Without a word she scoured the cookpot with sand. And then in the feeble light of the fire she worked for a long time with awl and sinew to repair a moccasin. She was thinking hard. Most of the times when Hard Striker glanced through his pipe smoke at her, her face looked so defiant that he was sure she was preparing her peace speech for the women. He worried and grew irritated by turns but did not try to talk with her again about it, because he thought it would work out better if she thought than if she stiffened in argument.

It was not until the next morning that he knew. Before full daylight he opened his eyes and saw that she was up on her elbow looking at his face in the gloom. Her naked body was warm against his side, and her musk was strong in his nostrils.

She said softly, "You tell me that you will punish the Long Knives. You do not say that *they* might win. If they were to win, killing many of our young men, then they would surely come on here to punish our People. And that would be even worse than asking them for peace.''

He thought. Then he said, "Yes, but they will not win. Because we are better, and we are right. I have told you how we slaughtered the British soldiers in the woods at the head of the Beautiful River in the Long War. They do not know how to fight in the forest." He talked low, not wanting the children to awaken to this kind of talk.

She said, "I do not want my son Chiksika harmed or killed. Nor do I want that for you. . . .''

"Then do not speak the words of it. That is bad medicine to speak of it.''

"But you must know how much I do not want that.''

"So this is what you will tell the women to say? That we should cringe before the Long Knives and let them infest our sacred lands?''

She stared at him. Her breast was on his arm, and he did not want to die. But he wanted to do right.

Finally she said:

"Because I honor you, *wabsiu*, I will not speak out against what you want to do. But listen. If my son dies, if the Long Knives win and then come here to harm my children or molest my daughter, perhaps I will be bitter with you forever."

A pulsating scream pierced the stillness of the night. It was taken up by hundreds of other voices, which swelled to such a shriek that Tecumseh felt the hair rise on the back of his neck. A hide-covered drum beat like a huge, fast heart, and the flames of a bonfire soared higher than the roof of the council lodge. All the people of Kispoko Town were gathered around the council ground. In the center were the bonfire and a war post.

The post was a peeled log as thick and tall as a man. It had been painted red, and it stood there, as yet untouched but nonetheless the focus of everyone's attention.

The drumbeats went on like a pulse after the scream had died down. Then the line of warriors shuffled out into the center. The chatter of deer-hoof rattles tied to their feet and ankles joined the rhythm of the drum; then the ululating war cry rose again, pouring from their throats.

The line of dancers was long. There were several hundred of them, their faces and naked bodies painted in colors, shining in the firelight with oil and sweat. They stepped high, touched their toes to the earth, and then thumped their heels down, their sinewy bodies arching, then crouching, their knives and tomahawks glinting in the light of the blaze. Their eyes were bulging, crazed. At first the dance was a pantomime of stealth, as they stalked their enemy. Then it built in passion and noise. They leaped, swung, and twisted their bodies in the motions of combat, chopping and stabbing the air with their weapons, repeating and repeating the war cry.

Chiksika had told Tecumseh that when one reached this stage of the dance, one could see his enemies before his eyes, and thus one was striking and slicing not the empty air, but the vision of the enemy. One can sometimes feel the blade hit flesh, he had said. And if one feels the blow like that, it is a sign that when the real battle is fought, the blow will actually cleave enemy flesh. Therefore one must dance with the utmost exertion, even to the point of exhaustion, with the heart full of fire, in order to make the enemy's vision appear. To do the war dance with half a heart, Chiksika had said, was to go half-prepared into battle.

Chiksika now was second in the line of dancers. Before him was Blue Jacket, formerly the white youth who had been whipped in the gauntlet. He was a promising warrior now, as much a Shawnee at heart as Chiksika. They were transported. The war post had become a whiteface soldier in a scarlet coat. Blue Jacket and Chiksika circled close around the war post, war cries tearing their throats; they dodged and spun as they closed upon it. Blue Jacket leaped high, and with a lashing blow as quick as the strike of a snake he struck the blade of his tomahawk into the very crown of the red post. Then Chiksika's blade stuck beside it.

Outside the circle of firelight, Tecumseh yelped. He had seen blood spurt from the post.

# CHAPTER 6

## On the Ohio River
## October 10, 1774

There was no moon, but in the starlight Hard Striker could see the other war canoes and the rafts moving alongside through the mist on the surface of the great river, every vessel loaded with as many warriors as it could carry without sinking.

They were now in the middle of the river. Hard Striker was in the prow of a large canoe. The whole sky was brilliant with stars. The water of the Beautiful River gurgled under the bark hull of the canoe.

As he always did the night before going into battle, Hard Striker looked up to try to see his warrior's star. Long ago when he was a young man courting Turtle Mother in her Creek village, he had learned from the Creeks their belief that the soul of every warrior was guarded by a particular star. She had pointed out to him which star was his own, and since then, as war chief of the Shawnees, he had lived and fought under one of the two stars that lined up with the Guide Star of the North. Now he had to turn in the canoe and look back over his shoulder to see the star. He looked at it for a moment and then returned his gaze to the river. His hand on the prow of the canoe felt the rub and flow of the water against the hull, as if the canoe were a living thing swimming on the living water. He could feel too the living strength of the eight paddlers whose strokes drove the vessel toward the east shore, closer and closer to the enemy's camp. Hard Striker now was thinking of the plan of the battle.

It was to be a battle plan unlike any he had ever followed. It was Cornstalk's plan, for Cornstalk at last had agreed to lead the tribes against the Long Knife army. So many of his people wanted to fight the white men that Cornstalk had agreed, but with reluctance. Since it was Cornstalk's war plan and Cornstalk was a brave and intelligent chief, it probably was a good plan, though it was not the red man's usual way of fighting.

Usually a war party would make a surprise raid upon a force or a town
it could surround and then, if resistance became too great, would withdraw
and await a more favorable chance. This time, though, there would be no
better chance. The whiteface army camped at the mouth of the Kanawha-se-
pe was now about the same size as Cornstalk's force, ten hundred men. But
in a few days it would be three times larger, because the white chief
Governor Dunmore was coming down the great river from Fort Pitt with
a much bigger army. And so Cornstalk had decided to engage this smaller
part of the army before the two parts of the white force could unite. If the
attack succeeded, there would be many captured guns and powder horns
with which to arm more warriors for war against the other part of the army,
which was still far up the river.

The enemy camp was on a wedge of land where the Kanawha-se-pe
flowed into the O-hi-o, a mile downstream. From here in the middle of the
great river Hard Striker could sometimes see the glimmer of a far-off
bonfire, a tiny light like a spark that would then vanish in the blackness of
the shoreline forest. Above the wedge of land there was a faint glow of
firelit smoke from the campfires.

Cornstalk's plan was to place a line of warriors across that wedge of land,
from the O-hi-o to the Kanawha-se-pe, before daylight. This would trap the
soldiers on the point of land so they could not retreat. Cornstalk had learned
in the Seven Years' War between the British and French that if white
soldiers were crowded into tight places, they could be annihilated by warriors shooting from cover around them. If Cornstalk's ten hundred warriors
could advance down the wedge undetected before daybreak, they could
crowd the white soldiers into just such a tight place.

It did seem like a good battle plan. With Cornstalk's Shawnees were
some Mingos, Delawares, and Wyandots. If these allies could do to this
army what the red men had done to the British army of Braddock nearly
twenty years before, then there was a chance to stop the other part of the
army and save the Indian towns. If this battle failed, the Shawnee nation
would be left with two unbearable choices: surrender to the Virginia governor, on the white man's terms, or destruction of the villages and crops in
the face of winter.

And so this day would be a great and important day. This would be as
important as any battle the Shawnee men had ever fought in all their history
since the Beginning. Hard Striker prayed as the vessel moved through the
starlit mist of the river. He prayed that the Long Knives would be caught
by surprise, that in their confusion they would get in the way of each other's
guns, that they might even be overrun while still in their blankets. They had

no suspicion that Cornstalk was crossing the river. The rafts and pirogues and canoes were silent. Some of the chiefs were so sure it would happen this way that they were already exulting.

As the war chief, Hard Striker should have been exulting with them. But, strangely, his confidence was overshadowed by a dread and a sadness. Perhaps it was because of the unfamiliar tactics Cornstalk was using. Perhaps it was because so many of Hard Striker's own kin and beloved would be exposed to danger in this uncommon battle. His son Chiksika. His closest friend and subchief, Black Snake. The fine warrior Stands Firm, who, it was understood, would one day be the husband of his daughter, Star Watcher. Too much confidence would put them all in terrible danger.

Of course it was good to be confident and to hope for an easy victory, as this strengthened the spirit. But even in victorious combats, one must be prepared to see one's own friends and relatives die around him and to bear the grief after that. He had borne such grief often enough in his years. And if one were the war chief, the weight of all deaths had to be borne upon one's own soul.

This was what Hard Striker was thinking in his canoe upon the misty river under a sky full of cold stars, when suddenly, despite the river of hot blood in his veins, he shivered. He turned quickly to look again at his warrior star in the north.

He could not see it!

As if it had suddenly burned out, it was not there. The Guide Star twinkled, and the other star on the line with it. But he could not see his own warrior's star, and his heart suddenly was cold.

He shut his eyes. When he opened them and looked again, the star was there. But he had failed to see it before, and that was a sign he fully understood. It changed everything.

Nothing had changed in the world around him—the soft, gurgling, trickling music of the water, the breathing of the paddlers, the dark shapes of the war canoes and rafts, the dark line of the eastern riverbank growing larger and clearer ahead, the glow of the enemy's campfires downstream— but ice was in his heart, and he understood the sad and glorious meaning of it: that he was to die before this day was through. He had not been able to see his warrior's star, and that meant he would be gone.

He would have to tell his son, of course. It was bad luck and unfair not to tell blood kin that such a thing had been foreseen. But it could be a bad thing to tell it, because it might well diminish Chiksika's spirit before the battle, his first battle.

So it would be necessary to tell him in a way that would strengthen, not weaken, his heart.


When there was barely enough predawn light to see by, the thousand warriors left their vessels on the riverbank and stole through the gloom of the woods toward the army's camp and began to form a battle line across the wedge of land between the two rivers. Their deployment was slow and tense, for the morning was still, with no wind to cover the whisper and rustle of their movement through the autumn-dry woods. The ground was rough, studded with mossy boulders and outcroppings, and the trunks of great dead trees lay everywhere. It would provide good cover when the battle began, but now it slowed the formation of Cornstalk's battle line, and it would not be long before the white soldiers would be rolling out of their blankets and the chance to catch them sleeping would be past. The Indians' battle line was less than a mile from left to right, so every warrior was hardly an arm's reach from his nearest comrade, and they could be in sight of each other, even within whispering distance of each other, and this was good. Also good was that the sun would be coming up behind the warriors' backs and thus would be in the eyes of the soldiers.

Cornstalk came along the line to the place where Hard Striker had stationed his Kispoko warriors. With him were his sister Tall Soldier Woman, a handsome, rawboned, middle-aged woman a hand taller than most men, and Black Hoof, a mature Chalagawtha warrior chieftain with glittering black eyes. Tall Soldier Woman was the only living woman warrior of the Shawnee nation. It had been a long time since she had been to war, but this was to be an uncommonly important battle, and so she was there, in charge of the warriors of her village. She was armed with a pistol and a knife. Now these chiefs knelt under a huge beech tree with Hard Striker and Black Snake and looked through the graying woods toward the army camp and made their final decisions.

"They do not stir yet," said Hard Striker. "If we move forward now, perhaps we can still catch them in their blankets."

"Yes," Cornstalk said. "But listen, we must also consider: maybe they are so quiet because they know we are here, and lie in wait for us. The spies say that their commander is General Lewis. He was in the battle with Braddock, and surely has learned from that to be wily. Therefore I say that we must not rush recklessly into their camp. We must get close in among them with the stealth of the hunter."

"I agree," said Hard Striker. "So our people must be told to stay on line as they move down, with a brother on either hand. And to keep this line even if we are pushed back."

Cornstalk nodded. "Above all, we must not allow them to push us back beyond this place. If they did, our line would extend and grow too thin."

"And so we must give our men heart to be very strong," Tall Soldier Woman murmured in her beautiful, low voice, "to be strong even though the battle may be the whole day long. Too many of them believe it will be a quick victory. They might be deceived."

"My sister is wise," Cornstalk said to her. "Now. There is little time. We must tell them this that we have said, and be moving before the sunlight touches the treetops."

"Weshemoneto is with us," Hard Striker said, and all the chiefs touched hands before parting.

*Weshemoneto is with us,* Hard Striker had said, even though he knew that before this day was done he would instead be with Weshemoneto.

On a thong around his neck Hard Striker wore a bone from the spine of a fox. He closed his hand around it. This was his *pa-waw-ka,* the personal token through which Weshemoneto's power came to him. It felt now as if it were burning and quivering in his palm. With his eyes closed the chief held it for the duration of four breaths. The smell of dew-damp wood ashes from the soldier camp clung in his nostrils.

Now he went to his son Chiksika, who was strutting and flexing his muscles behind a big fallen ash tree a few yards away, working his nervousness into a fighting passion. "Come down with me," Hard Striker said softly in his ear. "I have something you must hear."

They squatted beside each other, and Hard Striker put his hand on the oiled braid of Chiksika's scalplock. First he told him what had been decided about the attack. Then he said:

"My son, we have a chance to do a great thing here today for our People. Weshemoneto is beside me today, and for as long as I can, I am going to fight much stronger than I ever have before. You must make your name today by being as strong as you can be . . . because after this day you will have to take my place in our family."

Chiksika stiffened and turned his painted face to his father's in the gray half-light, his mouth open. "Hear me," Hard Striker hurried on. "Sometime today I will fall and not rise again. I have seen it. Hsh! I will have no protest from you! *Wehshe-cat-too-weh,* be strong! Live long. Protect your mother and your sister. Raise your little brothers to be great men, so they will always bring honor to our family. Help them to earn their *pa-waw-kas* as I helped you with yours. Mark no treaties. Promise me!"

Chiksika nodded. Hard Striker's eyes were blurred for a moment by tears; feeling his son nod had moved him to an almost unbearable tenderness. He pressed his forehead against Chiksika's temple for an instant, then pushed him to arm's length. His hand, still tingling with the power from the *pa-waw-ka*, gripped Chiksika's scalplock, and he shook him with affectionate roughness. "This is to be your first day as a Shawnee warrior," he told him. "Stay beside me. You and I will be deadly. I believe that Weshemoneto means to give me time to do great things today before he takes me off. So please help me, my son. In this great day and for as long as you live. Never disgrace yourself or our family. I charge you never to let the white men rest in our country. Always teach Tecumseh that this is his sacred burden, too. Promise me that!"

"I promise you that, my father." Chiksika's voice sounded almost strangled, but Hard Striker could feel through his hand that his son was steady, not trembling.

"Good! Now we must go along and tell our people how to fight today. Soon the sun will touch the trees. *Wehshe-kesheke,* a fine day!"

# CHAPTER 7

## Kispoko Town
## October 12, 1774

Turtle Mother tore loose her braid and shook her hair out so that it hid her face. She ripped open the front of her dress and dirtied herself with ashes and mud and began rocking on her haunches and howling. Tecumseh was terrified. This was beyond his ability to comprehend.

When the warriors returned from the Kanawha-se-pe, Chiksika had come home covered with bandages, limping, and had gone straight to his mother and put his hands on her shoulders and said something to her. She had shrieked and started this, and it was terrible to be near her. The triplets became so agitated that Star Watcher had to take them from the lodge to the house of relatives in another part of the village. She made Tecumseh follow and help her bring the little ones.

The whole Kispoko Town had become a terrible place. In many of the houses other women were wailing and keening. It had been raining, and the ground was covered with wet, cold, muddy dead leaves. The air was chilly and misty so the woodsmoke stung the eyes. Bandaged warriors were walking or riding through the streets. Some were displaying the fresh scalps that hung on their rifles and lances, but their faces were grim. Tecumseh led his little brother Loud Noise and trudged through this forlorn scene, scarcely seeing it, his soul still overpowered by the sight and sound of his mother's grief. He could not understand why his father did not come home and make her smile.

Later during that strange and terrible day, Tecumseh slipped away from his sister and went toward his home and stood a little way off and looked at the house and listened to his mother's wailing voice, his whole body shaking with the agonies he felt. Over the doorway of the house now hung a white mourning cloth. He looked at the white cloth and remembered how

61

she had looked: her face hidden in her black hair, her hands tearing open her garment and spreading ashes and dirt on her bosom.

Chiksika had much to explain to the family. He sat with them in their aunt's lodge, and while Star Watcher took care of the three little brothers and listened in the shadows beyond the fire, her eyes glinting with tears, Chiksika said:

"A great war chief is honored by being buried close to the battlefield where he dies. So our father was buried down there, by the Beautiful River.

"We painted his face black. We put him in a grave in the ground, with bark around him. We sprinkled in the sacred tobacco from the four sides of the grave. He lies with his head toward the setting sun. In the grave there is no stone or metal, as those can strike a fire in the grave. There is a hole in the bark in the end of the grave so his spirit can pass through. That is how our father is buried, and now you can see it in your mind, and know where he is.

"We came back across the river on the rafts and in the canoes, in the dark after a whole day of battle. We did not win. More whiteface soldiers were coming down, and we did not have enough gunpowder left, and so Cornstalk saw that we could not win in that place. Oh, we had many scalps. Twenty of our people died, but four or five times that many of the soldiers we killed, and surely two hundred of them we wounded. They lay everywhere in the woods crying in their pain. Yes, we did them much more harm. But we did not win. No. We came back across the river with our dead ones and all who were hurt. And then our allies, the Wyandots, the Delawares, and the Mingos who were with us, they chose to go back to their villages rather than fight another battle against the Long Knives.

"When those allies rode away, there came a darkness over the face of Cornstalk. He did not call them cowards, for they had fought well the whole day. But when they turned to ride the trails to their own homes, they could not look at his eyes.

"And we buried our dead then, and followed Cornstalk home. All the way there was a thundercloud upon his face, for he had advised us not to go to war, and he had led us only because we had wanted to go. He will call a council of all the nation soon, and from that we will learn whether to go to war again or go ask the white chief for peace and mercy. Do you hear all this, Tecumseh?"

The boy nodded. He was listening and understanding as well as he could, but the spirits were whirling his head around and making him see things. He was seeing his father in the ground encased in the bark of trees, with his face blackened and his head toward the sunset. He was seeing the warriors who had come to the village with terrible wounds. Some of them had been brought home on litters because they could not walk. Some, like Chiksika and Stands Firm, had come limping. One had walked in without one of his eyes and another without one of his hands.

And Tecumseh kept seeing his mother and hearing her shrieks. Always she had been calm and happy and clean. Now she had become something else, something as unsettling as the wounded men, because her husband had not come home. Tecumseh said:

"Will our mother die? Is she dying now?"

Chiksika leaned over and put his hand on Tecumseh's neck. "She will not die. The part of her that was our father's has died and gone to be with him. But the part of her that is our mother stays with us. Now for a year she is not to bathe or change her clothes, nor dress her hair. She will not laugh, and she will stay in the *wigewa* when the dances are held. Tomorrow all our people will go and give her a Condolence Day, for she was the chief's woman, and then she will cease to cry aloud. For the rest of the year she will weep only in silence but will remain unkempt. When that year is past, you will then see her as she was before."

Star Watcher leaned toward the fire, listening intently to all this. She knew that she would have to do very much for her mother and for the children during that year, and she needed to understand how everything would be. And she kept wondering also about the hurt that made Stands Firm limp.

"Who will become chief of the Kispoko now? Will it be you?" Tecumseh asked Chiksika.

He shook his head. "She-me-ne-to, Black Snake. He will now be the war chief of the Shawnees. I am not old enough for that. As for our own family, soon we will move to Chillicothe Town."

Star Watcher gasped. "Leave our father's town?"

"After this it will be Black Snake's Town. Chillicothe is the town of Black Fish, the principal peace chief. By the old laws it is the peace chief's duty to take us as his, and care for us. Everything will be different now, because of the whitefaces. Maybe there will not even be any towns." He wished he had not said that. It was too ominous. His gaze passed over the little group, his sister and his four little brothers. Chiksika was now the oldest male in the family, and it would be his responsibility to protect them and to hunt meat for them all, and above all to keep his promise to his father. He must raise all his little brothers to be strong men who would bring honor to the family. Chiksika looked at the helpless brood, thinking of this, and even though he hurt in every part and was shaken with exhaustion, he felt his father's life-power spread in him, and he felt what it was to be his father and to love them as his father had.

There would be so much to do. This family would require so much
of him that he would scarcely have time to be a young man. Though he
had fully become a man in these last two days, he was scarcely over being a
boy.

But Chiksika did not resent this burden that fate had put upon his back.
His father, Hard Striker, had taught him that the purpose of a Shawnee
man's life is to be worthy of Weshemoneto's approval, and that worthiness
lay in serving the family and the People. Now events had placed him early
in that position to serve them, so there was no question in his mind that their
needs were above his own desires.

But if the council chose to continue the war against the Long Knives, he
himself might be killed soon, too soon to keep his promises. He would have
to talk to Tecumseh soon about those promises.


Chiksika and Tecumseh sat late by the fire. Chiksika had laced a brown-
haired scalp onto a hickory hoop and was flensing the skin side with the
edge of his knife blade. "This," he said, pointing to the scalp, "is what a
white man looks like after he has been made into a good white man. The
only good white men look like this."

He said that he had killed three white men but had only this one scalp
because it had not been possible to get to two of the bodies in the fighting.
"Surely there never was such a war before," Chiksika said. "For the day
afterward my ears could not hear anything."

"Why do you want the hair of this man?" Tecumseh asked. It seemed
strange to him that part of a man was being dressed as one dresses the hide
of a beaver or muskrat from a trap. His father had owned many old scalplocks, but Tecumseh had never thought about them very much because they
were old and dry. Chiksika said:

"It is the way to count, and to help remember. There are untruthful men,
who would boast that they had killed more enemies than they had. But if
they do not have the scalps, they do not have to be believed."

"You told me you killed three, but here is the hair of only one."

"Those who were near me in the battle know I killed three. I can expect
anyone else to believe me only about this one."

The brothers were talking softly. Though Chiksika had made a name in
his first battle and should have felt triumphant, the emptiness where his
father's life had been was too dark and heavy.

After a while Chiksika said, "Now listen well, little brother, for I have
very important words to say to you, about our father in battle, and about
us."

Tecumseh embraced his knees and looked from the fire to Chiksika's profile.

"Our father told me before the battle that he would die. But then he fought as only the greatest warriors could ever fight. I myself saw him kill four officers. He said to kill the Redcoat officers first because the other soldiers would not know what to do if the officers did not tell them and make them do it. One of those I killed was an officer, though not this good one here. Perhaps I killed even more. Sometimes you do not know if one dies, and I had many in my sights. Even those without red coats are easy to see and shoot in the woods. Without war paint their light faces are as clear to see as the egg of a quail in the grass." Tecumseh envisioned this. Chiksika went on. "We fought the whole day. Our father fought even after he got a broken bone in his face and a broken bone in his knee. He was red all over with blood from his wounds, but he never grew slow or hid himself. I stayed close to him all the time. I thought I could protect him from the bullet or blade that was meant for him. I saved him once from a soldier. He saved me three times. I saved him again, from an officer with a sword. But finally I could not save him from one of the hundreds of bullets that forever came forth from their smoke. I held him in my arms, and his blood from his chest and mouth ran on me. He said he could see his warrior's star at last, that it was growing near him, that it was big and bright like the sun. He smiled even with the blood in his mouth and told me that he would not be lost beyond, because he could go by the star."

Tecumseh's body was trembling like that of a frightened rabbit, but his heart was growing huge inside him as he heard all this about his father in battle. Chiksika said now:

"He gave me promises to keep and to give to you. You must never forget these promises, even if I die in a battle. He said we must always protect our family and bring honor to it. That we must try to teach our little brothers the same. Are you remembering?"

Tecumseh nodded, his throat swollen. He always remembered what Chiksika taught him. Now Chiksika said:

"He told me to help you earn your *pa-waw-ka* when you are ready. He told me not to let you forget the burden you are marked to carry, and that we are never to sign treaties with the white men."

They were silent for a moment. They could hear the gurgling river nearby.

"Those are many promises," Tecumseh then said in a little voice. "They will be hard to keep."

"Very hard to keep. The worst times for our People are coming. For the Long Knives are braver enemies than we thought." Chiksika breathed deeply, wincing with the pain of a hurt rib. He said, "But our father once taught me, a brave enemy is a great gift. He said I will understand that someday. Maybe I am beginning to understand that already."

"I," said Tecumseh, shivering, "do not understand that yet. Maybe I am not old enough."

"They are a strong enemy, but we are stronger because we are right. As for me, I am going to kill white men until our father's death no longer hurts my heart."

Black Fish walked out to the edge of town to meet Hard Striker's family when they arrived at Chillicothe, and Chiksika, seeing him come forth, remembered a day almost seven years ago when the family had come here, and Black Fish had honored them then, too, by coming out to greet them like this. Then it had been a day of sunshine, and there had been a new life in the family, the baby Tecumseh; now the sun was hidden by gray clouds, and the family came mourning for a life lost. Turtle Mother's tangled hair hid her face.

Black Fish was known as a demanding teacher of youth, but he was also the principal peace chief of the Shawnee nation and was famous for his warm and generous heart. Though his broad, bony face did not soften with a smile as he came forward with outstretched hand, his eyes glittered and he seemed to radiate a pulling power. When Chiksika stood with him and held his hand, he felt warmed and strengthened, as he had used to feel in the presence of his father. Black Fish's lips were thin like a gash in leather, but from this hard-looking mouth came a soft greeting.

"My heart and my village are open to embrace the family of our great and brave war chief, whose last day brought honor to the warrior sept of our nation. You will share everything we have. Your mother and sister we surround with love and protection, and everything I know I shall teach to your little brothers. Come, let me welcome your mother, and let me see again the sons she bore under the great signs."

Very soon after the family arrived in Chillicothe, scouts began bringing bad news to the town.

The two armies of the Long Knives, one having crossed the Beautiful River from the battleground and the other having come down from Fort Pitt in boats, were closing together near the Shawnee towns down on the Scioto-se-pe. The thousands of soldiers were close enough now to threaten Cornstalk's Town and Tall Soldier Woman's Town and Black Snake's

Town. They had penetrated into the heart of the Shawnee country, and now they could easily march up and destroy all those towns and their crops, as they had done to the Wapatomica towns of the Shawnees during the summer. Such destruction would leave virtually all of the Shawnee nation to face winter without food or shelter. The only choices were a plea for peace and mercy or the most enormous and terrible sort of battle on the plains, close enough to the towns that the women and children and old people would be in danger. Cornstalk called a full council.

Chiksika sat as a warrior in council for his first time. Cornstalk faced the chiefs and warriors and asked them whether they wished to fight again. Chiksika and Black Snake and Black Fish and a few others stood up. But most said it would be better to sue for peace. With a terrible darkness in his face, Cornstalk threw his hatchet down so hard that its blade was buried. "Why did you not choose for peace when I advised it, before the battle?" he cried. "Now we have lost our war chief and many of our sons for nothing. The white men's god was very strong and did not let us stop them. And so now we must go on our bellies like snakes and ask this white governor to have pity on us and spare our women and children, and now he will feel even stronger. But, yes," he finished in a sad voice, "now we will crawl to him and ask for mercy. And what will this mercy cost us? I know not what his terms will be, but I expect that there will be more whitefaces than ever feeling bold enough to come into our country!"

Cornstalk was right. The white men's treaty demanded the right to go down and build houses and towns in the sacred hunting ground, Kain-tuck-ee, on the other side of the Beautiful River. Cornstalk had to give his word that he would never raise the hatchet again against the whites. The chiefs who signed had to promise that they would not allow their young warriors to molest the white people who came down to Kain-tuck-ee to settle. "Hear my prophecy," Black Fish said after the treaty, which he had refused to sign. "They say the river will be the boundary. The white men will demand that we stay on our side, but they will not stay on theirs. They will come across the river into our country and steal our horses and shoot our game, and they will shoot us when we go there to hunt. It will be bad."

Star Watcher had many friends in Chillicothe and was glad to see them. But some of these girls were growing up to be not so pretty as she, and they seemed to resent it that this young woman of marriageable age had come to live in their town, bringing such beauty that she turned the heads of many young warriors from them toward her. Some of those girls began to treat her as if they did not like her, and she did not understand it.

But her mother, who at that age had been the most beautiful girl of her own town, could see what was happening, even though she was still in her mourning time.

"They will worry about you until they get married, my daughter," she said. "Or until *you* get married."

Star Watcher looked down at her hands and sighed. The only person she had ever thought of marrying, Stands Firm, now lived miles away, in their old home. Then she looked up with a wistful smile.

"But I already have a family to take care of," she said.

"Listen to Loud Noise," Turtle Mother said.

The runt of the triplets was jabbering in his bed. He who had cried so much in his first days did not cry much more than an ordinary child now, but he talked all the time he was awake, even though he knew hardly any words yet. But sometimes Star Watcher and her little brothers thought they could almost understand what he was trying to say. They thought that they had heard the words before.

Finally one evening Turtle Mother tried to explain it to them. She was still in the same torn and dirty clothes of mourning, and her hair was still loose around her face as she worked, and she still never smiled, but she cut and carried firewood, kept a cookfire going, ground corn, repaired the house, made clothing and moccasins for her children, and took care of them when they were sick or hurt, just as she always had, with the help of Star Watcher. And though she did not laugh or sing as she had used to, she still taught them.

"The tongue your little brother is speaking," she explained, "is the secret language of Kokomthena, Our Grandmother who created us. Our Grandmother speaks Shawnee tongue, and all other tongues, but also she has her own language, which children can understand until they are four summers of age. Then when they learn to speak Shawnee tongue, they forget Our Grandmother's tongue. But sometimes when we hear a child talking, we think we remember some of the words. When Loud Noise becomes four, very soon now, this winter, then he will forget how he talked this way."

"Ah," exclaimed Tecumseh, squeezing his hands together and looking at his mother with widened eyes, "Tell us stories of Our Grandmother. How she made Kispoko warriors. Tell about Rounded-Sides, and about Our Grandmother's Silly Boys!" Tecumseh yearned to hear the old stories that told where the People had come from. He had been hearing Black Fish talk so many times lately about the frightful coming of the Long Knives, and of their lies and broken treaties, and of the way they made trouble and brought disease and death, that everything seemed to be under a dark cloud, and he longed to hear again the old sure stories that made his head fill up with bright sky and limitless waters, and giants and round men, and clay people, and great serpents with horns, and the Great Turtle with the world on his back, those stories that made him think that the People had once enjoyed happier and more magical times and perhaps might again someday.

Tecumseh knew the magic was still alive, though perhaps asleep or gone away to hide in these times. The shamans, in fact, had sacred bundles in which were kept, among other great medicines, feathers of the Thunderbirds and a bit of the flesh of the King of the Great Horned Snakes. Women in the time of their moon were not allowed to pass within sight of where the bundles were kept.

The bundle owned by the Chalagawtha Shawnees was stored in a small house next to the shaman's lodge, and sometimes it hung from a tall pole near Black Fish's lodge, and the ground around the pole was always kept swept. Tecumseh had stood looking at the bundle often, and in looking at it he had felt a power coming from it, a power that had seemed to hum like a bee tree and had made him see white light and green water even though he was looking at the shapeless brown bundle with feathers attached to it. Yes, there was still magic being kept by the People, by the old men who knew things. But in these times when everything was darkened by the coming of the white men, all the old beautiful and terrible magic that had used to visit the People seemed to be in hiding, and a boy could see it only in his dreams or when an adult told the old stories.

"To begin," Turtle Mother said, talking from behind the shaggy hair that hung from her head, "Weshemoneto, the Great Good Spirit, the Master of Life, who is like a mighty wind in the shape of a man, made Our Grandmother Kokomthena, and told her that she would be the Creator of people, that she should create people so that the world would not stand empty, and so someone could see its beauty. And so Our Grandmother got busy at once. Our Grandmother first created the Delawares. When she had finished them, she thought, Now I am skillful enough to make some Shawnees. So she filled her hands with clay and made an old man and an old woman, and blew in their noses to bring them to life. They were the first sept of the Shawnee. Her grandson, Rounded-Side, watched her do this and smiled. Then she created a young man and a young woman, and then she told them she was tired and was going home, and she told them to play with each other and make some children, who would be the rest of the Shawnee septs.

"But Our Grandmother had grown tired of making people, and she forgot to give the young woman her *massih*, and she forgot to give the young man his *passah-tih,* and so they did not know how to make children. She went home, calling Rounded-Side to come with her. She told him, 'Do not stay and tease them, they have to play with each other and make children.'

"But Rounded-Side was one of those who, when they are told not to do something, think it must be fun to do that."

The children looked at each other and giggled when she told them that. Rounded-Side was the kind of child they pretended not to be. Turtle Mother went on:

"So he told Our Grandmother, 'I am going to hunt deer. I will come home later.' Our Grandmother was suspicious, but she was too tired to make him obey, and she went home. She needed to rest, and to think up ways for her creations to make a living. For she was concerned about how they would be, even though she had lost interest in creating them. To this day, she cares how we are, and when the Lightning or the Wind or the Animal Masters visit her in her home by the moon, sometimes she has them bring messages and instructions down to us.

"Of course Rounded-Side sneaked back to watch the young man and young woman play with each other. And he teased them because they did not know how to make children. How could they, without their genitals? So he teased them. They had tried making little children out of black mud, but had thrown them away across the water when they would not breathe or move.

"For two years the young couple were unable to connect themselves to make children. And to tease them, Rounded-Side created the Peckuwe Sept and the Kispoko Sept, and laughed, and said, 'It is this easy! Yet you two cannot do it!' "

Turtle Mother's voice, as she spoke the words of Rounded-Side, was lilting and saucy, as it had always been when she told such stories, but if she was allowing herself to smile, the smile could not be seen. Her children were smiling at the tone of Rounded-Side's mocking voice. He was mischievous, but not in a wholly evil way, and children liked to hear about him because he was like them.

"Then in two years Our Grandmother was rested, and she came down. She had thought of many things to give her creations so that they could live and be healthy and good. She was not displeased that Rounded-Side had made the Peckuwes and the Kispokos. It was all right with her if someone else was making people, for she had grown tired of it, as I said before.

"Then Rounded-Side introduced Corn Woman and Pumpkin Woman to the People. Weshemoneto had made Corn Woman and Pumpkin Woman so they could help them grow food to eat. And so that the Kispoko would never be lonesome, Rounded-Side created other tribes, and gave them to the Kispokos as enemies to fight, for their joy is in fighting."

Tecumseh smiled at this. His father had often told him that the Kispokos were the best of all warriors, and this was the reason why. Rounded-Side had made them that way.

"Our Grandmother then gave a Sacred Bundle to each sept," Turtle Mother said. "In each bundle there is some of the flesh of the Great Horned Serpent. And though that flesh has been there for hundreds of hundreds of years, it is still fresh, and seeps blood. Anyone who has been present on occasions when the bundles are opened will tell you that is so, that they saw it themselves. There will come times when you will see for yourselves. Now, in the Sacred Bundle of the Kispoko, she put something special. Do you know what that was?"

"Feathers from the Thunderbirds," said Tecumseh. He knew that the Thunderbirds were the terrifying but good forces that guarded the door of the house of Heaven. Their beating wings made thunder, their flashing eyes made lightning. But the Shawnees knew that the Thunderbirds were good powers, and that was why they had no fear of storms, as some people did.

"Yes," Turtle Mother said. "Feathers from the Thunderbirds. And also an ancient tomahawk, with a head shaped like three leaves. Our Grandmother then told us what she had been thinking about while she rested. She taught us how to take care of ourselves, how to hunt, how to build houses, how to find Spirit Helpers, who would teach us how to make sick people well. She taught us how to have ceremonies and dances to entertain her and honor her, and how to be good and worthy. She gave each sept its song to sing, and she gave us the *Kweh-tele-ti-weh-nah,* which are the Shawnee laws we live by.

"And," Turtle Mother said now, with a strange catch in her voice which, had she not been in mourning, someone might have supposed to be a hidden chuckle, "*this* time Our Grandmother remembered to give them their genitals, which they found to be very interesting."

# CHAPTER 8

*Chillicothe Town*
*October 1775*

Tecumseh ran between the lodges, his moccasined feet rustling the fallen leaves, carrying his hickory bow in his left hand and a bloody rabbit in his right. His face, a face almost beautiful in the symmetry of its features and the smoothness of its coppery-brown skin, was alight with a dimpled, white-toothed smile and a glitter of triumphant excitement in the hazel eyes.

Never had the boy seen anyone, even Chiksika or any grown hunter, shoot an arrow more swiftly and surely than he had just done.

Now he ran dodging among the bark houses and cookfires, springing over stick fences and startled dogs, toward his family's *wigewa,* his spirit nearly bubbling over with the desire to tell about it. He felt the rabbit's swiftness in his own legs now; as he sprinted through the town he *was* the rabbit. The men had always said that when a worthy hunter kills an animal, that animal's own kind of power goes into the hunter, whether it is the strength of a bear, the fleetness of a buck, or the noble courage of an elk. Not all men agreed that a rabbit was enough of an animal to give its spirit to a hunter; some said the Keepers of the Game did not deal in the little spirits of rabbits and squirrels. Some said rabbits and squirrels did not even have spirits, but not many people believed that. Most people believed every animal, no matter how small and weak, had a spirit. The squirrels, in fact, sometimes showed that they were controlled by very powerful spirits and even carried omens. Tecumseh was not old enough to remember it, but when he was a baby there had been a great migration of squirrels. Hundreds of hundreds of them had rushed southward through the forests as if in flight from doom, and many of them had drowned in the Beautiful River when they tried to cross it. Sometimes small animals would do such unusual things, said the shamans, and bad events usually followed.

Whatever the truth was about the spirits of small animals, Tecumseh now felt the rabbit's swiftness and power in his own legs, and he sprang with a happy whoop over a pole fence near his home, and in his memory he saw again what had happened: the rabbit springing and dodging through the dry weed stalks and over a fallen log, a blur of brown and flashing white. And Tecumseh himself running in the same direction over the field, swinging his bow around, aiming it ahead of the rabbit and letting the arrow go with a sinewy *twung!* Oh, if only Chiksika could have been there to see that miraculous shot! The story of it was desperately wanting to be told, and already Tecumseh could see the astonishment and approval in Chiksika's face. And so now Tecumseh sprinted toward the door of his family's house like a rabbit about to dive into its burrow.

When he burst in through the low doorway the dim interior was dense with woodsmoke and steam and body smell. Beyond the flames of the fire in the center of the room his mother knelt naked, her brown shoulders agleam with oil in the beam of daylight from the smokehole above, and Star Watcher bared to the waist in the steamy room, stood over her, picking and pulling at her mother's wet, tangled, black hair with a horn comb. Tecumseh had lifted the rabbit high to announce his feat but was stopped in confusion by this scene.

His mother, wincing from the pull on her hair, squinted at him through lanky wet strands, her teeth showing either in a grimace or a smile. He could hardly remember how she had ever looked with a smile.

"Little brother," Star Watcher said, "go out."

"I shot this," he blurted. "I shot it running! Where is Chiksika? What are you doing?"

"Go out," she repeated in a high voice. "Come home when the sun is down." And then Tecumseh heard a sound he had not heard for a year: his mother's laughter.

"Good, my son, my hunter!" she said, and her laughter was music. "We are proud of you! But go out for a while. It is time for me to become clean and be as I was before."

Tecumseh stood with his mouth open for only a moment; then he understood, and his heart leaped from one joy to another. He started as if to go to her and fling his arms around her, bloody rabbit and all, but Star Watcher hurried to him and put her hand firmly on his shoulder and told him again, "Go out. Be happy about this day, and come back when we are done."

"Where is Chiksika?" he asked. He was glowing warm all through, and he wanted to be near his big brother and share all this with him. Much of the dark cloud seemed to be off of the world today, and the boy felt the way he sometimes did when he heard the stories of the old bright days of the Beginning.

"Your brother," she said, "is at the council lodge with Black Fish and the men. Some English soldiers are in the town."

"English?" He felt a chill in his scalp. He knew English were white men. But his sister was smiling and for some reason did not seem alarmed that white soldiers were here.

"Chiksika will tell you. He knows more. These English want to be allies, they say. Go now."

Now almost dazed by the whirl of good events of the day and the fearsome thought of white soldiers in Chillicothe Town, Tecumseh turned to go out, to go and find Chiksika. He heard his sister laugh behind him.

"Little brother," she said, "you can leave the rabbit here for me to cook. You don't have to carry it everywhere!"

When he ran off in the direction of the council lodge, he had his bow and quiver, though not his rabbit. The rabbit did not matter so much now. His head was too full of other things. It did seem that he should have the bow, because of the white soldiers. Just in case.

The packed ground of the street was hard and dry. There were no clouds in the sky, and in the sunlight the yellow-and-red leaves, those that had not yet fallen, were waving, trembling and hanging on against a cold breeze. Most of the adults walking or standing outside their lodges had blankets drawn around them. The cold air was fragrant with hardwood smoke and the aromas of roasting meat and baking Shawnee cake. From the end of the street where the council lodge stood came the drone and jabber of many excited voices, and he could see that a large part of the town's population was there near the lodge. When he had gone out early this morning in the cold half-light to hunt, there had been no one outside the lodges, except here and there a woman squatting or a man facing a tree, making steamy water. He had hunted a long time this morning among the corn and bean fields and in the meadows along the river, and he had gone south among the trees and fields of the bottomlands below the town, among the hundreds of dead, gray trees whose bark had been stripped off to cover the *wigewas* of the town; then he had moved up the slope toward the woodland hills and had stalked around a large, trickling spring where he had hoped to find some animals drinking.

Springs of water were among the greatest blessings, and towns were always built where good springs were. Tecumseh knew he had been born right beside a spring, near Piqua Town. He had heard that story often enough, the story that a star had gone over the moment he was born. He remembered his father telling him that the star meant he was to be very important to the People someday, somehow. Other people told the story often, too. Sometimes when people would tell that story they would say it with the same tone in their voices that they had when they told the creation stories, and it would seem strange to realize that they were talking about him. Those were magic stories, about great powers and vast skies and bright waters, and most of the time Tecumseh did not feel there was much magic in the world. There were the usual people saying and doing the usual things, always the sad and angry talk about the coming of the Long Knives; always the women were hard at work in the fields or the houses; always the men went out on the long hunts, or to the councils, or sometimes to war. To live was hard and often uncomfortable. Sometimes one's eyes were red and sore from smoke, or one's skin itched from insect bites or the poison plants, or one's hands and feet were so cold they stung, and often in the winter one's belly would be empty for so long that it would hurt, and one's arms would feel so weak from hunger that they were hard to lift. And often there would be the long funerals for people who had died, those long funerals in which one would have to behave in just such a manner and do just such a thing and walk in just such a line, every moment for days, though one would rather run or hunt or play or listen to storytellers. Life was a hard and stark thing, and often if there was magic at the funerals, it was the cautious magic required to satisfy the departing spirit and to keep out of its way until it had entirely left the village and gone on by one of the Roads back to the Creator. There were many rituals the living had to do when a corpse was going to the grave.

But sometimes, when one least expected it, there would be some *good* magic: something Cyclone Person would whisper in the treetops; or something a raccoon or fox, standing nearby and unafraid in the woods, would say with its eyes; or something little Loud Noise would say in Our Grandmother's tongue but was understandable anyway—at least understandable in the heart.

And there was the magic in the dreams. Once, when Tecumseh had carelessly, sleepily, lain down with his head toward the west, lying as the dead lie in their graves, he had had a death dream, a dream in which huge-headed men had come riding swiftly, screaming, through yellow smoke, to kill him. From that dream he had leaped into wakefulness, sitting up in his bedding with a slamming heart, and had seen first the shimmering coals of a night fire with the dim shapes of beloved friends sitting around it looking at him. Though he had not been able to see their faces, he had known they were beloved friends. And then they had faded, and he had seen shimmering coals still, but this time in the familiar firepit of his own mother's lodge, with the usual shapes of his mother and sister and little brothers all asleep. He had known then that he was truly awake, that he had been in two dreams, one deeper than the other. The next day he had told his mother about that dream, and she had told him that he had dreamed of his death because he had slept with his head toward the west, as the dead do, and that probably he had nearly gone away in his sleep. She had seemed very frightened, telling him this. She had warned him many times since not to go to sleep that way again.

And then one day not long ago, while traveling with Chiksika to Piqua Town, Tecumseh had been standing in the woods near that spring where he had been born, and through his feet suddenly he had felt the earth trembling. Though he had seen nothing change on the earth in his real eyes, though he had seen no trees move or even a leaf stir, he had felt through the soles of his feet that the deep earth was unsteady, and it had made him lurch and almost fall down. With his real eyes he had seen only one sign of what was happening: the water from the spring had appeared to be running backward for a moment, running uphill toward its source. Then it had stopped and run as before, and he had become steady again.

It was said that sometimes the Great Turtle that holds up the Earth gets restless, and when it does the world trembles and waters act strangely. It was, in fact, the Great Turtle who had made it possible for the People to come to this land; the Turtle had moved, and a sea of water between this land and the Old Land had run off so that the People could cross over. Then the Turtle had settled back, and the sea had filled up again. That had happened long before the memory of anyone now alive, but the story of it had been brought along through the ages by the tribal Singers.

When Tecumseh had told Chiksika about the trembling earth and the spring water running uphill, Chiksika had told him that no one else in Piqua Town had felt the earth tremble. No one in the town had lurched or staggered, except the usual men who bought rum from traders. Chiksika then had looked at him with strange eyes and said, "It is good. Sometimes you will feel and see something no one else does. Remember that is your gift. When it is time for you to understand what they mean, the meaning will come. But if you are ever to understand them, you must always try to be worthy of your gift. If you ever fail to be worthy, the Great Good Spirit will never reveal what these signs mean, and they will only trouble you, and you might go crazy from them."

It was when he was near springs of water that Tecumseh most often felt the magic that was in the world.

Now, trotting up the street toward the council lodge where the crowd was gathered, Tecumseh was thinking about signs and could feel upon himself the weight of the gift. As his father had told him, his life would not be easy; like a chief or a shaman, he would have more duties to do than an ordinary warrior, and the People would rely upon him, because the Panther Star in the sky at his birth had pointed him out.

"Oh," a woman cried to another woman, "here they come!"

"Look at them," the other squealed. "Such beautiful soldiers!"

Tecumseh could not see them yet, but he could feel a thrill of excitement running through the crowd of people. Though he was tall for his age, he could see only the backs and shoulders of the grown-up people in the pressing crowd. He was being jostled backward now by people who were surging back, making way. So he slithered forward among them, and suddenly he was on the front edge of the crowd, and there in the open, not five paces away and coming toward him, were the two biggest and most elegant men Tecumseh had ever seen. Chief Black Fish was walking between them, and he looked little. These two were glittering and blazing in the sunlight, their hair silver, their faces pale pink and grim with importance. Tecumseh looked at them with his mouth open, too stunned to move back.

Their coats were scarlet wool and covered with gold-colored metal buttons and braids of golden thread. Gleaming silver gorgets the shape of new moons flashed at their throats. Brilliant silk sashes crossed their chests, and from these hung knives as long as a man's arm, ensheathed in black leather trimmed with silver; these, Chiksika had told him, were the weapons for whom the Long Knives had been named. The soldiers wore black leggings that reached to their thighs. And on their heads, atop the silver curls that covered their ears, they wore huge black headdresses of bear fur with plates of silver and gold in front. These men looked like sun gods.

If these were what whiteface soldiers were like, Tecumseh thought, how brave his father and brother must have been to go and fight ten hundred of them! The only white men Tecumseh had seen before were French traders, who were small, dirty men, and the naked man in the gauntlet.

Now he drew back as the giant white men came closer. He saw that Black Fish had a proud, pleased look in his eyes as he strode forward with one of these mighty men on either side.

They passed directly in front of Tecumseh, and their tread was very heavy. He was devouring with his eyes every detail of them, and through their shining glory now he was beginning to see and sense other things. The one closest to him had a sheen of sweat on his face, and there was a sore-looking red boil on his neck above his tight collar. The white of his trousers was smudged with dirt. There were spots on the scarlet coat, like those of meat grease on a dirty blanket. His leather shoes creaked and his long knife rattled as he walked by, and he sounded as if he had trouble breathing.

Then Tecumseh's keen nostrils were assailed by the man's smells. Eddying in the air around him were the dense, sour odors of old sweat and smoke in wool, of mouth rot and tobacco, even traces of the odors of urine and excrement. Tecumseh's nose wrinkled, and he recoiled. Even his mother, who had not bathed herself or changed her garment in the year of her mourning, had never smelled like this. Chiksika had told Tecumseh that white men had a bad smell about them. But Tecumseh had not guessed it could be like this. He wondered how they could bear to be near each other.

And even under that repulsive stench, Tecumseh detected something else, or so he thought.

This giant, stern-faced man, who looked like a sun god, who was as thick as a large tree and taller than any warrior, walking through the town under the protective hospitality of Black Fish, smelled afraid.

"I smelled fear on him," Tecumseh said to Chiksika later that day. "Can this be so?"

Chiksika paused. He had one finger in a little jar of ocher, with which he was painting lines and dots from the corners of his eyes to his ears. He was preparing for the war dance that was to be held for the white soldier chiefs.

"Yes," Chiksika replied. "It is plain that they have some fear among us. Here is why, I think: Only last year these men were our enemies. They were with the white chief Dunmore when he came with his army. They were numerous then. Now there are just these two chiefs amid our people. These two and some men who brought horses loaded with gifts. And new guns, and much powder and lead for the guns. They are a little afraid because last year we were their enemies and we killed many of them." Chiksika held up his mother's old French trade mirror with his left hand and ran a line of paint along his right temple.

"Guns? Our enemies bring us guns?"

"Here is the way of it, little brother. These men come to say they now wish us to be their allies. These men tell us they belong to the British king across the Great Water over there." He pointed with his paint-stained finger toward the east. "You have heard of the king of England. They are his. Now they want us to call that king our father. They say he is the chief of the mightiest nation in the world. Here is what has happened since last year among the white men. This they told in council today:

"They say that their king beyond the Water is angry with the white men who live on this side. The ones we call the Long Knives. They say the Long Knives are not obedient to their king anymore, and grow saucy. They say there have already been some battles between the king's soldiers and the Long Knives. That there will surely be a war.

"They say the English king does not want the Long Knives to come into our country and take our land from us. They say we are under the protection of their king. They say that king wants us to be strong and to drive the Long Knives out of Kain-tuck-ee. And so he sends us guns and powder. And new blankets and good knives made in his country over there. And he will let his Redcoat soldier chiefs help us drive the Long Knives out of Kain-tuck-ee. Black Fish likes this. He says he wants to help the king's soldiers do this. And so we will have a war dance for the English king's soldier chiefs tonight." He dipped his finger in his paint jar again, leaned toward the mirror, and made another line on his face.

"But," Tecumseh said, remembering something, "there was a treaty made last year after the battle. Do you remember? That we would not raise our hand against the white men anymore? Was that not a kind of promise to them? I thought only the white men broke promises."

"That treaty," Chiksika replied, "was made by the white chief Dunmore of Virginia. He belongs to the English king. So that treaty is not broken. It is only the Long Knives who come into our country and bother us now, not the king's white men. And the king wants us to stand against those Long Knives."

Tecumseh thought of this and nodded. But he remembered something else. "Did not Cornstalk promise he would never raise his hand against *any* white men?"

"You remember things well. Cornstalk did so. And he has already told these English chiefs that he cannot help them, because of that promise. Cornstalk made himself helpless. But Black Fish did not mark a treaty. And the Shawnee law is that a man who does not make a promise is free to do what his heart tells him, even if the chief above him is bound by the promise. Black Fish is free to help the British soldiers fight the Long Knives." Chiksika stopped painting his face and looked at his little brother. "Therefore Black Fish is very glad he did not mark the treaty. He believes that this purpose of the king of England will be a good thing for saving the People from the intrusion of the Long Knives."

Tecumseh had no more questions. There was so much to think about from this day. He remembered now:

"Brother! Have you ever shot a running rabbit, while you were running? And did you know our mother is out of her year of mourning?"


It was the twentieth day of the Hunter's Moon, cold and gray, and most of the leaves had fallen to the ground, when Black Fish summoned Tecumseh to his lodge and told him that it was time for him to start earning his *pa-waw-ka*. A chill of dread seized Tecumseh, for he had seen other eight-year-old boys in past winters earning their *pa-waw-kas,* and he knew it was going to be worse than anything he had ever had to do.

"When you have your *pa-waw-ka,*" Black Fish told him, looking at him with sharp eyes, "you will be able to get power from the Great Spirit when you most need it. You will wear your *pa-waw-ka* all the time, and when you have great trouble or terrible suffering, you will hold the *pa-waw-ka,* and the power and comfort will come like sacred fire into you through your hand. Your *pa-waw-ka* will be your most treasured thing. Sometime it might keep you alive, or help you defeat your strongest enemy. You even more than most warriors will need such a power to turn to because of the duties you will have someday. Because it is so important, you cannot get it easily. There is no short or easy way to get anything of great importance. Do you understand?"

Tecumseh nodded. "Yes, Father."

"You must obey me. Every morning for the next four moons you will have to do this, at the beginning of every day. After the first morning you will probably say, 'I cannot do this again.' But you will have to do it the next morning, too. Even when the snow is on the ground and ice is on the river, you will have to do it. If, even one morning of that time, your spirit is not strong enough to make you do it, you will fail to earn the favor of Weshemoneto. Do you promise me now that you will do it each morning?"

Tecumseh shuddered. But he replied, "I promise, Father."

Black Fish nodded, his craggy face unsmiling. "Good. Tomorrow morning at the first daylight you will begin. Your brother Chiksika long ago earned his *pa-waw-ka.* He will tell you how to strengthen your heart for it. Go to his lodge in the morning as soon as you are awake."

The next morning when Turtle Mother squeezed Tecumseh's foot to wake him up, the first thing he heard was sleet hissing and pattering on the bark roof of the *wigewa.* He had hoped it would be one of those sunny, mild days that sometimes occur during the Hunter's Moon.

"Come," said his mother. "It is time for you to go to Chiksika's lodge." Star Watcher smiled to encourage him.

He left the warm envelopment of his sleeping robe and dressed, standing as close as he could get to the fire, shivering and almost sick with dread. Outside the *wigewa* the air was raw and icy. Sleet pelted his face and hands like tiny arrows of ice. He shivered and set off at a hunch-shouldered run down the lane. The bare trees and hulking huts were black against the hissing gray sky. It had rained most of the night before the sleet started. The path was covered with mashed, sodden, dark leaves, speckled white with sleet, dotted with puddles of cold rainwater. His moccasins were soaked at once and squished and splatted as he ran through the hissing gloom. He hoped that Chiksika would have a blazing fire in his hut but was afraid that he would not.

Chiksika was not married yet and lived alone. His little *wigewa* was about two hundred paces from the river, and Tecumseh could hear the river water running even at that distance. The river was high and fast from the night's rain, and Tecumseh was frightened. The ordeal ahead would be dangerous as well as miserable.

When he turned back the door flap and ducked in, the little space was very warm with a smokeless fire of white oak. Chiksika was sitting on the opposite side of the fire, dressed and waiting. His weapons and medicine bag hung on a post behind him, and on his spear hung the scalp he had taken from the soldier at the battle of the Kanawha-se-pe. The brass trim of his gun gleamed with the firelight. The gun was a rifle he had taken from a dead enemy in that battle, a much better gun than the musket he had used before. The room was cozy and interesting, one of Tecumseh's favorite places to visit, and it would have been a good place to sit on such a wet, dismal day, drinking hot sassafras or mint tea and hearing Chiksika tell stories. But for the next four moons, clear into the depth of winter, his visits to Chiksika's hut were not to be such pleasures.

"Take off your clothes, little brother," Chiksika told him even before he could sit to warm himself by the fire. "You will want to get this done as quickly as you can."

When Tecumseh stood naked, his clothes on the ground, his tough, slender little body agleam like copper, Chiksika began the instruction.

"You remember what our father told us about the sacred fire. Tell me."

"Yes. The People have the fire that was lit long ago. There are men whose duty it is to tend the fire and never let it go out."

"Just so," Chiksika said, "there is a fire inside the spirit of every Shawnee warrior. What does Shawnee mean?"

"It means People of the South."

"Yes. And when we came up into this place of cold winters, the Sun gave each of us some of himself to keep us warm when we hunt in the winter and are away from the sacred fire of our home. Now listen to what I say:

"When you begin to earn your *pa-waw-ka*, you will be naked like this, and you will leap into the river every morning, in the deep place there so that even your head will be under the water."

"Yes."

"When you do this, only the fire of the Sun inside you will keep you from turning to ice. So listen: When you go into the river you must think very hard of the fire inside you. You must pray Weshemoneto will blow on it and make it flame up. The fire inside you must be greater than the cold on your skin. It is like when you are hunting in winter and you tell yourself that cold does not matter, that it is just a feeling, just as warmth or pain or pleasure are just feelings, and if you make yourself warm inside, you are able to bear it.''

"Yes. I have done that. You taught me.''

"On the day when you earn your *pa-waw-ka,* you will have to go under ice in the river, and not one time but four times. It is cold today, but it is warm compared with the way it will be on that day. That is why we start now. Day by day you must get used to calling for the fire inside you. When the snow comes it will get harder to do, but as you do this each day you will learn to talk to Weshemoneto and ask, so that he will hear, for his breath to fan the fire inside you. And so, by the time of the coldest day, when you have to go under the ice four times, he will know your voice well, and he will know you have prayed every morning and are worthy to find your *pa-waw-ka,* and he will keep you from turning into ice as you go down to the river bottom for it. Do you understand this quite well?''

"Yes.''

"Then you are ready?''

"Yes.''

"Then come. We shall walk down to the river.''

*"Walk?"*

"I said walk.''

"I saw other boys last winter, and they ran. They ran down, and they ran back.''

"Yes, but you are Tecumseh, son of Hard Striker. In this family we do not show anyone we are concerned with pain or fear. In this family we walk down to the river. We leap into the water so that we go all the way under. And then we walk slowly and with dignity out of the river and back to the hut. I have seen boys from other families who go into the river and out so fast that they are like a skipping stone, and only get wet on one side. And people laugh at them.'' Chiksika was smiling as he said this, and it was funny enough to make Tecumseh smile, even in his dread.

"Did you walk when you did this?'' he asked Chiksika.

"Yes. Our father walked beside me. Slowly and with dignity.''

"Then I will walk slowly and with dignity.''

"Then let us go down. I advise you to start praying now, because the sleet will try to freeze you even before you get to the river. Come.'' He stood up.

Tecumseh took a deep breath, swallowed hard, began trying to pray, turned, and stepped out from the warm house into the wet, chilly gray of the morning.

Even more shocking than the icy sting of the sleet was the sight of the people standing there in their blankets. He had not seen a single person on his way to Chiksika's hut, but now dozens of people were standing along the path to the river, some with their blankets and hide robes pulled up over their heads, all looking at him. Tecumseh was outraged. He felt colder than cold and more naked than naked because they had come out to watch him. And he could see by their faces that they were in a jolly, mocking mood. People had not come out in numbers like this to watch other boys. This must be, he thought, a part of the burden of being favored.

"Don't forget to pray," Chiksika reminded him. "And *they* are the reason why you must go slowly and with dignity."

Tecumseh turned outside the door and began walking toward the distant river. The sodden ground under his feet had a thin crust of sleet on it, which he stepped through with each pace. His feet and ankles and even his calves began to ache with cold. The cold rain and melting sleet were running down his skin everywhere. It felt coldest between his shoulder blades and in the cleft between his buttocks.

"Look at his skin! Like a plucked duck!"

"You had better run, Tecumseh!"

"Look at his little *passah-tih!*" shrieked a coarse widow-woman of the tribe. "Like a little twig! And where is his little bag of balls? Has it frozen and fallen off? Ha! Heeee! Heheee!" Her remarks made the others cackle and inspired them to make similar remarks and jokes.

"Remember to pray," Chiksika reminded him again. "They're only trying to make you forget."

And so Tecumseh prayed with all his might and walked in spite of his desire to run. The wet ground squished, and the taunts kept coming, and the grinning faces kept leaning in front of him, and the terrible distance to the terrible gray river looked like a mile. His breath was coming in gasps, and he was shuddering uncontrollably, and the people along the way were remarking on it. It was as if he were in a gauntlet where the people used taunts instead of whips.

"Stand straight," Chiksika murmured in his ear. Tecumseh straightened his back and shoulders, which had become hunched. Straightening up made him feel colder and more vulnerable.

"Pray for the fire!" Chiksika hissed when at long last they were almost to the river's edge. The water was fast, loud, gray as flint, dimpled with raindrops and sleet. Tecumseh prayed with all his might. He clenched his teeth to keep them from chattering. The wind was icy, blowing from the river onto the front of him. His naked skin was taut as a drumhead all over him. And now they were standing on the mud-slick bank of the river, and his feet and hands were numb, and the river looked too terrible. The surface was choppy and shivering in the wind gusts, steaming with rain spatters. He felt as if he were stiff as ice already and feared that he could not move to go in. All his insides were shaking and shuddering.

"Pray," Chiksika hissed again. "Make him hear you! Remember the Shawnee fire, the Sun!"

Tecumseh with his last bit of will clenched his fists and tensed every muscle to stop quaking. Weshemoneto, he cried inside, help me do this! Blow on the Sun and make me warm!

"Now," Chiksika commanded in a merciless whisper, "go in."

"I . . . can't."

"Little brother," Chiksika whispered, "you have done well. Believe me. I have a secret: it is warmer in the river than in the wind. Go in!"

With a desperate gasp, believing everything Chiksika told him, Tecumseh forced his stiffening leg muscles to spring, and with the name of the Great Good Spirit echoing in him, he leaped off the shore, sure that he would die in the river and now ready to. For an instant he saw the dark shape of his body against the gray sky reflected on the water.

And then with a great, slamming heartbeat he splashed into the water, and what Chiksika had said was true: it *was* warmer than the wind! It was not at all warm, but it was not as cold as the wind, and that surprise was enough to make the prayer work. Suddenly the cold was no longer inside his body, but only on the skin. His flesh was not frozen after all, and he could move!

When his head broke the surface he gasped a chest full of air. Chiksika and the people on the bank, and the village and trees beyond and the gray sky were blurred by the flow of water over his open eyes, cold gray, but inside him the warm power was blossoming. He was swept by joy. Weshemoneto had heard him and answered! And the noises coming out of Tecumseh's throat now were gasps of laughter. Even as he thrashed in the river and paddled toward the shore he saw a grin on Chiksika's face and heard the people laughing, but now laughing not at him but for him, sharing his joy.

"Now come out," Chiksika called. He knew the truth of cold, that even if one had mastered it and learned to bear it, it could still quickly kill a person who was not hardened to it. "Come out," he called again.

So Tecumseh waded out of the cold water into the colder wind, wisps of steam coming off his body, his skin tortured by the cold but his spirit feeling strong and worthy, steady and hot, and with the people cheering him he walked with Chiksika his brother and teacher, slowly and with dignity, back up through the sleety grass and wet leaves and puddles, toward Chiksika's hut. He was not even thinking of the warmth in the hut now, nor of his clothing nor of food nor of hot drink, but of the strength that he had found burning inside himself and of his faith in the Great Good Spirit, who had kindled it in him when he had needed it. He understood that it was a sacred fire inside him and that it would never go out as long as he lived, as long as he could will it to keep burning, and that it would be an even greater fire when he finally earned his *pa-waw-ka.* Never had he wanted anything as he wanted that! As he and his wonderful brother walked side by side, Chiksika said, "Look up. There is blue sky through the clouds."

"Yes," he replied, surprised to hear how his voice quavered. He thought of sunshine. He thought of the part of the sun burning inside him.

"If the sky clears," Chiksika said, "that means it will be much colder tomorrow morning."

Each morning after that, Tecumseh was surprised to discover, the air felt just as cold and the river looked just as terrible. He had expected the fire to be burning in him every morning when he awoke; he had expected to feel strong and sure when he went to Chiksika's house; he had expected the ritual to become easier.

But it did not. Every morning the dread would be in him. It seemed that his skin and flesh could remember the awful cold better than his heart could remember the warm power and the joy. Thus every morning the test of his will had to be repeated, and every morning he would fear that Weshemoneto was not going to hear his prayer. He would find himself praying at night that the next day would be mild, and then he would be ashamed of himself, and would doubt his worthiness, and would think that perhaps Weshemoneto was withholding his help because Tecumseh had been timid and prayed for mild weather. Every morning he went through these doubts all over again. He wanted to ask Chiksika why it never became easier, but he did not want him to know that he was weak.

And as the winter deepened, another discouraging thing happened. The river water grew colder and colder, and it was no longer a refuge from the biting cold air and wind.

After just a few days the people had stopped coming out to watch him go to the river. At first he had resented their presence. But when they no longer came and did not even seem to care about his ordeal anymore, he began to realize that they had in a way been a help to him, since he could never have let them see him fail.

Chiksika did not have to be told that his little brother was having trouble with his ordeal. Every boy had trouble with it. Chiksika himself had quailed before each morning's plunge. And even though more than ten winters had passed since he had earned his *pa-waw-ka,* he still relived the shock of it every morning as he watched Tecumseh's lithe little body splash into the cold gray water. And every morning as they walked back to the *wigewa* his own heart would soar and flame up with joy because Tecumseh had again triumphed over the cold.

One morning after a month of the ordeal had gone by, Chiksika leaned over the fire in his hut and told Tecumseh:

"Tomorrow you will have to go to the river without me. I must leave the town with a hunting party. We are going a long way west, to the ground between the Big Miami-se-pe and the Whitewater. It is harder to find game toward the Beautiful River because of the whitefaces. We expect more luck west of the Miami-se-pe. That country is several sleeps from here, and we might be gone for six or seven days. You must promise me that you will come down and go into the river every morning, just as if I were here. It will be harder."

"Yes," Tecumseh admitted, knowing how true this was. "It will be harder."

"But you will do it."

"I promise I will do it."

"Think of the honor of our father."

"I will not make anyone think his son is weak."

"Good. I have arranged for Eagle Speaker to go to the river with you every day while I am gone. He will live here in my house while I am gone, and you will come here as usual." Chiksika noticed the firm, angry set of Tecumseh's mouth, the insulted look in his eyes, and he explained quickly: "It is the rule that a man must always be on the shore when a boy goes into the river in winter. It is not to spy on you and make sure you do it, little brother, but to pull you out if you get cramped."

The insulted look passed from Tecumseh's face. Chiksika went on: "Eagle Speaker may have some important things to say to you. He is one of the Bear Walkers. He, like Change-of-Feathers, had a dream the night you were born. To have Eagle Speaker near you when you are in this ritual will be good. You can talk to him about dreams you have. And if he has signs about what will happen with the people, perhaps they will help you understand your own." He looked up. He listened to the wind. The bark slabs of the roof were creaking and rubbing, and once in a while a gust would make smoke from the fire puff back down from the smokehole. "We have come far into this winter without a snowfall, or ice on the river," he said. "The signs were for a hard winter, but it comes late. I think that it will snow before I come back. I hope so. Snow can help hunters, if it is not too bad a snow. But I expect that one morning, perhaps as soon as tomorrow, you will have to go to the river in the snow, and I will not be here to help you." He smiled ruefully. "Are you ready for a day like that?"

"I will pray very hard, my brother."

"Good. And pray for our hunters, too. We need the prayers when we go far from home in the winter."

Chiksika did not say it, but he was thinking not just of the dangers of the severe winter far from home, but also of the many white men who now ranged through the country on this side of the Beautiful River. They were of the most dangerous and lawless kind, who stayed ahead of the advance of their people and paid no heed to treaties. They had murdered several lone Shawnee hunters in the last few months.

Eagle Speaker was an odd man who talked little and had a far look in his eyes. But unlike some far-gazing men, he also noticed details and subtle things close by. He seemed to understand exactly how Tecumseh was feeling about something at any moment and even what he was thinking.

His presence at the morning ritual was as comforting as Chiksika's had been. On the first few days when there was snow on the ground, Eagle Speaker seemed to give off a warmth that kept the whiteness of the snow from being too chilling. Before long, to walk naked through the snow was no worse than walking naked through sleet or cold rain.

For several days Tecumseh had thought about the shaking earth. It had been on his mind. And he was thinking about talking to Eagle Speaker about it one morning after the river plunge, when Eagle Speaker surprised him by saying:

"For a long time I have had dreams about the ground trembling. Now since I have been with you I have had those dreams every night. I believe the dream has something to do with you."

Those words made Tecumseh's heart leap. He and Eagle Speaker were sitting close to the fire ring in Chiksika's hut. Tecumseh was wrapped in a robe to get the chill out of his limbs. He said: "Sometimes I have felt the earth shudder under my feet when no one else did. Sometimes it has almost thrown me to the ground."

Eagle Speaker sat very still for a long time, and something was passing in the air between them, something invisible, something like the hum of power Tecumseh had felt from the Chalagawtha medicine bundle. Finally Eagle Speaker asked, "Did you see anything when you felt this?"

"I saw water run backward, uphill. Nothing else."

Eagle Speaker gasped. His eyes were shut. He said: "When I dream of the trembling ground, I see the water in a river stopping and swirling around and then going back where it came from, like the big waves that flow up on the sand at the edge of the big lakes with a roar and then run back. Have you seen this?"

"My brother says we will travel to Mis-e-ken someday to see the big lake. But I have not seen that yet."

"There is something I do not know yet about this," Eagle Speaker said. "It is the time when it will happen. It is not soon; maybe it is a lifetime away. It is to be in a year of deep troubles. The year will begin with a light in the sky. The animals will be upset. There will be war that year. I have seen a bundle of sticks tied together with thongs, then the thongs broken and the sticks scattered. These things I see in the dream. But then when all these things are bad, I see the earth shake and the water in the river go backward, and then the bundle of sticks is again tied together. Perhaps these things that I have seen, you should keep them in your mind, too. Change-of-Feathers has told me you were born when the star shot over the sky. That was when I dreamed of these signs. And I can remember a few days later your family riding into Chillicothe, and the people saying there had been a birth in Hard Striker's family while the green star was passing over."


By the fourth cold moon, Tecumseh had become very much hardened. He had mastered his body enough to walk slowly down to the river even in snow. He could make the Sun flare inside him and keep himself from shaking, even on days when he had to pause at the river's edge and throw big rocks to break the ice. Chiksika had gone out with several hunting parties during that time, sometimes coming home with much meat, sometimes with none. He had seen no whitefaces on this side of the Beautiful River, but on one hunt his party had found the frozen body of a Peckuwe man who had been shot several times through the body and his fingers and scalp removed, then left for the carrion eaters. Around him were the prints made by white men's hard-heeled footwear. Every one of the victim's belongings had been stripped off and taken away. Only a beaded pouch had been overlooked, and by the beadwork Chiksika had been able to identify the Peckuwe man. Chiksika had recounted this through clenched teeth and hardened lips. His hatred for the Long Knives was growing to be the most important thing in his soul. He said he could hardly wait for the winter to be over, so that he could join the soldiers of the English king and go down into Kain-tuck-ee and kill the Long Knives who were settling there. He said he wanted to bathe himself in their blood.

Tecumseh could hardly wait for the end of winter also, but it was because he wanted the ordeal of the cold river to be over. Like Chiksika, he was shocked and angry about the Long Knives, but the ordeal of the river was closer to him just now. It was his main preoccupation, and most other matters seemed far away.

Then came a morning early in the Hunger Moon when the sky had cleared after a week of snows, and it had suddenly become so cold that trees had cracked like gunshots in the night. When the sun came up that morning it shone through a glittering haze. The air itself was freezing. When his mother woke him up her breath was clouding even though she had already put wood on the fire. Only the center of the *wigewa,* a few feet right around the fire itself, was even slightly warm. She looked worried and told Tecumseh:

"You will need to pray very hard this morning, because this is that kind of cold that makes fingers and toes come off. One's heart must be of fire on such a day or it will become ice. Pray hard and be careful." She did not say it, but she wished very fervently that he would not have to go into the river on a day like this. She was afraid.

"I have grown very strong," he told her to keep her from worrying. But he was scared. It was on just such a day, which could be judged the coldest day of the winter, that Black Fish might declare that the time had come for him to do the four dives and find his *pa-waw-ka.*

And it proved to be so. When he arrived at Chiksika's lodge, his ears and nostrils stinging with cold, Black Fish himself was waiting for him in the hut with Chiksika. People in nearby *wigewas* were peeking out their doors. "Tecumseh, my son," the chief said, "take off your clothes and we will go down to the river. This will be the final day. I will pray with you as you go into the river. All will be well. I have been told that you are a very strong boy."

It was so cold that Black Fish instructed him to hold his hands over his genitals as they walked down. "So they won't freeze off before you ever enjoy them," he said.

The surface of the snow was frozen in a crust that broke with sharp edges as he walked, but his feet were so numb at once that he felt no pain in walking. Many people had come out to watch. They stood wrapped to their ears in blankets and robes, shifting from foot to foot, and the steam from their mouths froze into glittering clouds. Many of these were people who had taunted him in the beginning, but they were silent now, and he could see sympathy in their eyes. Chiksika had told him that although it was not common for boys to die or be seriously harmed by this, some did get frostbitten fingers or toes, and some became very sick. And of course in past years a few had died from the shock.

As they walked down now, their faces grave with prayer, Tecumseh could hear blows being struck and saw that some men were already breaking the ice for him with axes and heavy poles. He was thankful that he would not have to break the ice himself, for the ice looked thick and strong, and he imagined that he had just enough heat and strength in him for the four dives and no more.

He was using all the strength of his will to keep from shuddering or groaning. His teeth were chattering, and the cold air was searing his nostrils as he breathed. He was praying with such concentration that behind his eyes he could see the flames of the inner fire being fanned by Weshemoneto's breath.

Now they came to the river and walked out on the ice, to the edge of the hole the men had made. The water in the hole was full of crushed and broken ice, which moved and gnashed as the current flowed under.

"Three times you must go under the water, and three times you must climb out," Black Fish said. "The fourth time you must go to the bottom and grasp whatever your hand finds, and bring it up. Waste no time now, my son. Go!"

Tecumseh gasped a deep breath and jumped feet first through the floating fragments of ice, which had already in the intense cold begun freezing together again. The shock was less than he had expected; the air had been so cold that even this icy water was a little less so. The fire burned in him, and so far he was all right.

Blowing and gasping, he surfaced and quickly scrambled out onto the ice. This was the worst shock of all. The cold air on his wet skin pierced him so deeply, he felt that the fire would go out entirely. He felt as if his whole body lay on the edge of a great knife. The people on the shore were praising and encouraging him, but their voices sounded as thin and piping as birdcalls through the ringing in his head. He heard Black Fish say, "Again!" He turned and plunged in again. Again he scrambled out. As he turned to plunge in the third time, he was aware of a strange rattling at his ears and realized that his wet hair had frozen. "Again," said Black Fish's voice, and he leaped once more.

Now as he tried to climb out, gasping desperately for breath, he knew that his body was growing weak and clumsy. His hands and feet, even his elbows and knees, could feel nothing, not even the hard ice. His heartbeat fluttered inside his heaving chest like the wings of a trapped bird. Chiksika's face appeared above him, and it was tense and full of worry. Then Tecumseh was at last standing on the ice again, somehow standing up even though every part of him was quaking as if to shake him apart.

"Now," Black Fish said. "Find your *pa-waw-ka*." For a moment Tecumseh's aching brain could not quite remember what this meant. Then he remembered what he had yet to do. Chiksika's voice came into his head: "Pray!"

Now Tecumseh prayed, not with words but with a desperate outreaching of his soul to Weshemoneto, and this time, crouching over, his body bending as stiffly as old wood, he held his breath and fell headfirst through the rattling blue-white ice and propelled himself toward the bed of the river, his hands outstretched before him. He was a small vessel of pain and exhaustion with a fire in its core.

Chiksika and Black Fish and the spectators stood looking anxiously at the hole in the ice. Moments passed. They watched and prayed for the boy down there now unseen under the ice. Chiksika was shifting his weight, thinking how much time was passing, getting ready to dive under the ice himself and get Tecumseh if the boy did not surface in the duration of three more breaths.

Two more . . .

One more . . .

And just as he crouched to leap in, his soul ringing with urgency, he saw something dark move in the greenish water under the broken ice. The dark shape became more distinct, then the ice rattled and a little fist came up, then the head of frozen black hair. Chiksika's love leaped across the space to those wild eyes. He reached down and grasped one icy little wrist and Black Fish grabbed the other, and they pulled the slender brown body out of the hole. It was a moment before Tecumseh could stand. His bones ached into the marrow, and his feet were too numb to feel the firm ice under them. He was gasping desperately. But he was grinning; under the black icicles of his frozen hair, his chattering teeth shone though a triumphant smile. He had done it! His fists were full of debris from the riverbed, too numb to feel what they held. But he was sure he had his *pa-waw-ka:* something was burning through the numbness of his left palm.

It was hours before the terrible ache was out of his bones. He sat wrapped in a buffalo robe by the fire in Chiksika's hut. The news had gone through the village that Tecumseh, the war chief's son born under the sign of the

Panther in the Sky, had completed his ice ritual on the coldest morning most people could remember, and that he was fully well, not sick or even coughing, and that he had found a very good *pa-waw-ka*.

Sometimes the boys would come up with only mud and dead leaves or rotted sticks and gray gravel, and they would have to carry these crumbs and bits in their medicine bags as their *pa-waw-kas*. Even such poor fragments would serve, of course, as means to bring warmth and strength. It was the earning of them that made them powerful. But to find something durable and good to look at while groping blindly with numb fingers in the bottom of the river was a sign of special good fortune. His father's had been a piece of a fox's spine. And what Tecumseh had brought up was such a good thing, a beautiful thing.

He sat by Chiksika's fire, drinking hot broth, very happy, the ordeal being over; he sat under his brother's proud gaze, turning the object over and over in his tingling fingers, feeling the warmth, watching how the firelight limned its facets. It was a stone like a piece of ice. When it was turned to and fro in light, it shifted and rearranged the colors of a rainbow. Black Fish himself had exclaimed in wonderment at the sight of it. It had come a long way from somewhere in the countless years since the Beginning, becoming what it was as it came, and it had taken all of time to place itself there where Tecumseh's numb hand would close over it. And now in his fingers it was full of tiny rainbows. It was an incomparable treasure that he would keep until he died.

It contained the fire that had kept him alive long enough to obtain it.

Star Watcher, her heart full of quiet joy and thanks, made a fine, soft little bag for him to carry it in and sewed tiny yellow-green beads on it in a design like a panther's eye. Turtle Mother said to her, "I have never seen anyone make a design like that. Where did you find it?"

Star Watcher answered, "It was shown to me in my head, while I was praying for him not to die."

# CHAPTER 9

## Near Chillicothe Town
## October 1777

T he deer are a people, as we are," Chiksika said, just above a whisper. "And so they do certain things at certain times, as we do. If you understand them, you will always be able to find them."

Chiksika and Tecumseh were waiting in a dense, shadowy grapevine tangle that had strangled a sycamore tree on the bottomland of a creek. The grapevines made a good hunting blind, as the sycamore stood about twenty paces from a well-worn deer path that wound along the forested bluff and down to the creek's pebbled beach. The brothers had their weapons ready. Chiksika's rifle was loaded and primed. Tecumseh, who did not have a firearm yet, was ready with his new bow. This was no rabbit-hunting bow. It was a powerful, gracefully curved weapon made not from hickory but from the dark, heavy wood of osage, a treasured wood that one had to range far to find. It required strong arms and shoulders to draw it. It was a man's weapon, a bow for killing big animals, and Tecumseh, not yet ten, was one of the few boys who could have used such a bow.

"Now tell me why you chose this place to hunt the deer," Chiksika whispered. "Why not in a meadow where it is easier to see and to shoot?" Both of them kept their eyes on the deer path through the yellow woods. Tecumseh remembered the many things Chiksika had told him and many things he had observed himself.

"They have day paths and night paths," Tecumseh said. "In the night they use their open paths in the meadows and prairies. In the day they use their hidden path in the woods, like this one, because the deer are a shy kind of people. And so to hunt them in the daytime we come to where their day paths bring them to a drinking place or a bedding place."

Chiksika squeezed Tecumseh's arm and nodded. "Good. Already you know better than many men do. Like Stands Firm," he said with a smile. "Right now if Stands Firm is hunting, he is probably lying in grass at the edge of a meadow expecting a buck to walk boldly past him in open light, just because there are fresh tracks on a path there."

Tecumseh smiled. Their friend Stands Firm was a brave warrior and a good-souled young man, but he was not a great hunter. But he *was* a hunter of Star Watcher. He had moved there to follow her.

"If Star Watcher does marry him," Chiksika went on, "she may become a thin woman."

"No," Tecumseh said, taking Chiksika's joke seriously. "If she grows thin, then *I* will bring her meat."

Chiksika gave a hissing little laugh through his teeth. "Tell Stands Firm that! I would like to see his face when a boy tells him that! Ha!"

"Ssst!" Tecumseh was suddenly very alert, looking past Chiksika, scanning the bluff. He thought he had heard a footfall up there somewhere among the fallen leaves. Chiksika, knowing of the uncommon keenness of his little brother's senses, turned to follow his gaze. For a while they stared up the path. They saw nothing yet and heard nothing except the scolding of a squirrel high in the treetops, then the faraway whistling shriek of a hawk in the sky.

These were the best of times for hunting. The bucks were easier to surprise, because it was early in the mating season, and in the rutting time bucks grew foolhardy. Chiksika was home from war for a while, as were most other warriors, to help hunt meat for the coming winter. Much of this year they had been gone, down in Kain-tuck-ee, two hundred warriors from Chillicothe led by Black Fish himself, armed with new muskets and knives furnished by the British, determined to destroy every Long Knife fort and town in the Sacred Hunting Lands. Black Fish and his warriors had swept into Kain-tuck-ee and had gone raiding from one fort to another. They had made daring attacks and had besieged the Long Knives in their forts for days at a time. After four moons they had come back with some scalps. They had made the white people flee from many of their settlements. Hundreds of the whiteface families had retreated back over the mountains. But Black Fish had failed to destroy two of the strongest forts. At those two forts the Shawnees had repeatedly been thwarted by the alertness and the astonishing marksmanship of the Long Knives. The warriors had come back to Chillicothe with awe-inspiring tales not only of their own bravery, but of being hit by bullets from two and even three hundred paces away.

The Shawnees had fought the Long Knives for so long in Kain-tuck-ee this year that they had learned the names of some of them. The war had become very personal. No longer were the white men just a horde of nameless enemies coming closer and closer or burrowed in behind their palisades. Now some of them were spoken of by name, as one would speak of the name of a great chief or warrior of an enemy tribe, and the warriors would describe some of them with such clarity that Tecumseh, wide-eyed and openmouthed by the story-telling fire, could envision them. Plainly, some of these Long Knives were great warriors and crafty chiefs, for had they not resisted Black Fish's invasion? They had killed several warriors, including one of Black Fish's own sons. This had brought deep grief to Black Fish and all his people, and it had hardened the chief's sense of vengeance.

The chief of all the Long Knives' fighting men in Kain-tuck-ee, the warriors had learned, was a big young man with red hair and a voice that could be heard over the loudest battle. He seemed never to sleep. His name, said the warriors, sounded like "Meh-jah Clark." He had been in command at a fort called Harrod's Town, whose village chief was another huge, loud-voiced man, named Harrod. Here Black Fish had conducted a siege for several days until it grew too cold to fight.

There was another chief of the Long Knives whose name was Boone. He was chief of another fort, named after himself, less than a day's travel from Harrod's Town. This Boone was known to be a great hunter and scout. Years ago he had been chased out of Kain-tuck-ee by Shawnees, back before there had been any treaties allowing him to be there. Some of the older warriors had recognized him. This Boone was a quick-minded man and very hard to fool, almost impossible to ambush. It was he who had killed Black Fish's son. Boone had escaped death several times during those four moons and had commanded a defense of his fort that had inspired a grudging respect from the warriors.

One of Boone's amazing escapes had been witnessed by Chiksika, and he had told and retold it:

"Six of us caught their woodcutters outside the fort. We scalped one. Then this Boone and ten of his men rushed out of the fort to chase us. They thought that these six were all of us. It was the only time we fooled this Boone, for when we had led them far outside their gate, a large number of us rushed at them from the woods. They were surprised. But this Boone was quick, and told them to get back in the fort. One of our warriors shot this Boone in the leg, and he fell, and lost his gun. We were almost upon him, and he was helpless.

"But then one of Boone's men did a remarkable thing that I will never forget. This was a giant man with shoulders like a bison. He ran through our gunfire and picked this Chief Boone up in his arms, like a child, and

carried him toward the fort. What strength this man had! Even with Boone
in his arms this man could run like a horse!" Chiksika's voice had been full
of admiration as he told this. "Two of our swiftest ones got ahead of him,
with their hatchets ready. And you cannot believe what he did then! He
threw this Chief Boone at them and knocked them both down! Then he
killed one with his tomahawk and kicked the other one's ribs in, all in a
moment, then he picked this Boone up again. He ran. He ran through our
bullets and got inside the gate, and it was closed against us. What do you
think? Do you believe a man could do this? I tell the truth. And so that
Boone lives."

Tecumseh believed anything Chiksika said. And he would have had to
believe this story anyway, because he had heard so many other warriors
talking about it. His wonderment at that story had turned mostly toward
the giant who had saved Chief Boone. In his imagination this was a giant
like the ones in the red coats and big hats he had seen with Black Fish in
the village two years ago. But no, Chiksika had said. He had not looked
like that at all. "He dressed like a red man. In skins. He wore no hat. His
hair was thick and long, the color of a fawn's coat. After a time we learned
this man's name, too. It is like But-lah. Some of our people already knew
of him. They had fought him before, in encounters in the woods near the
big river. He is the chief hunter for Boone's Town. Someday a Shawnee
warrior will get this But-lah, and such a fame that warrior will have then!"
Chiksika's eyes had glittered as he said this, and it was plain that Chiksika
hoped to be that warrior. All the warriors who had gone with Black Fish
were proud to say that they had engaged in battle against a man like that
But-lah, and each liked to dream that he would be the one to get But-lah,
whose description was now fixed in the mind of everyone who had heard
the story.

"To have a great enemy is a gift from Weshemoneto," Black Fish would
say. "A great enemy makes you worthy." That was something Hard Striker
had used to say, too. It was important among the Shawnee teachings.

But now Black Fish and his warriors were home from war; now they
were hunters. The British whitefaces and the Long Knives were having
their great war in the east, on the other side of the mountains; their big
armies fought each other in great battles with cannons, which were guns too
big for a man to carry. Here in the valley of the Beautiful River there were
not nearly so many people to do such a war, and Black Fish and his warriors
had done the fighting for the English king. They had been glad to try to
chase the Long Knives back over the mountains. They had done what they
could and had put the Long Knives in desperate trouble. But because
Cornstalk, the principal chief of the Shawnee nation, had signed a treaty and

had to stay neutral, there had been no great victory over the Long Knives, and they were still there in Kain-tuck-ee. At least they had been reduced so far that they probably would not dare to come across the river anymore and murder Shawnee hunters. Now it was time for the warriors to be hunters again and prepare for winter.

Thus Chiksika and Tecumseh crouched among these shaggy vines and watched a large buck come down the path through the yellow woods, come stepping slowly and with dignity, upwind from them and not aware of their presence. Tecumseh nocked an arrow and looked at Chiksika, imploring. Chiksika nodded; he would let his little brother have the chance to shoot at it with his great osage bow and would not fire his rifle unless Tecumseh missed.

Silently they stood up. Tecumseh looked through a gap in the tangled vines. He had already planned his shot. There was only a small gap through which the arrow could be shot without hitting vines. This was a disadvantage of hunting from a blind. The hunter might be hidden from his prey, but he had only one good chance with his arrow. A hunter with a gun might shoot right through vines with a chance of killing the deer. But the tough vines could deflect an arrow, so Tecumseh would have to shoot in the moment when the buck was visible through that gap.

So Tecumseh touched his *pa-waw-ka* with the thumb and fingers of his right hand, then he put three fingers on the bowstring, drew just slightly back on the string, and watched for the shape of the deer to approach that short stretch of open path. He could hear its delicate hooves crushing leaves in its path. On the breeze now he could even smell the buck smell. His heartbeat was quickening, but he knew he must not get excited. He could not draw the bow all the way yet; it was too powerful a bow to hold at draw for more than a moment without getting shaky from the strain. Therefore he would have to draw and release very quickly and smoothly just as the buck passed the opening. Chiksika knew this, too, so he eased back the hammer of his rifle, cocking it with a barely audible click, and stood ready to snap off a quick shot in case Tecumseh's arrow missed. Tecumseh heard this little click and with a flush of happy defiance vowed to himself that Chiksika would not have to finish the kill of his first buck.

Head and antlers appeared in the gap; Tecumseh with straining muscles pulled the bowstring back to his nose, sighted over the arrowhead to the buck's left shoulder, prayed for the animal's pardon, and let fly.

For a boy who had once made a running shot to kill a running rabbit, this deliberate shot at a huge, walking target was easy. The arrow went almost to its feathers in the buck's side just behind the shoulder, exactly where Chiksika had always said it must go to hit the heart. The buck sprang awkwardly, reflexively, high into the air and fell dead on the path, at the moment a gasp of amazement escaped from Chiksika.

Usually a boy's first few deer kills were sad and messy, the animal wounded and fleeing far in agony, leaking blood, through miles of forest, or lying down in a covert somewhere to pant its life away and die of pain or thirst or infection, or eventually to be finished off by the hunter himself if he could track it that far, or to be taken off by a wolf. But this, Tecumseh's first deer, was as clean and merciful a kill as Chiksika had ever seen, and his heart swelled with appreciation for his young brother. It was still another sign of a blessed life, for the Masters of the Game did not like to see their animals die in pain and terror.

Tecumseh himself understood all this, as it had so often been explained to him, and he was as grateful as he was triumphant. He felt the buck's swiftness, goodness, and dignity at once enter into his own being, and tears of gladness glinted in his hazel eyes.

The buck was very big, heavier than two large men, so they would carry home only the meat, hide, heart, and brain, not the whole carcass. Under Chiksika's supervision, Tecumseh cleanly removed the steaming intestines, skinned the buck, butchered it, and tied the cuts of meat in the hide. He was nearly choked with strange emotions as he reduced the splendid creature to bloody meat and offal, but he did not try to tell Chiksika how he felt. Then he tied the legs of the hide together and slipped a pole between them. He and Chiksika each lifted an end of the pole, and they set off through the cool yellow woods. They had not come by horse, as horses complicated the hunting of deer, so it was a long, tiring trek of several miles back to Chillicothe with the great, hanging load of flesh. They stopped several times to rest, and at one stop they ate. They built no cookfire. "The heart is yours to eat," Chiksika said. Tecumseh cut out the hole made by his arrowhead and then cut the rest of the firm red meat of the heart into strips and chewed vigorously, while Chiksika ate from a tender strip of venison loin. "We can eat the deer flesh raw," Chiksika said as he chewed, "but remember that bear must always be cooked or, like the meat of the white man's pigs, will make sickness."

The meat of the buck's heart was pure and strong-flavored and without fat, and Tecumseh seemed to feel the life of the buck growing in him as he filled his stomach. To eat the heart thus in silence, with his osage bow lying beside him on the fallen sugar-tree leaves on the sunlit ground, felt like a prayer. He could feel the spirit of the Shawandasse, the South Wind People, running back all the way to the Beginning. He tried to make words and express to Chiksika what he felt, but it was hard to make words that would tell of the profound joy of such a day. He tried:

"Brother?"

"Yes?"

"At this time I think of the prayer words. *Neweh-canateh-pah We-shemoneto.*"

"The Great Good Spirit favors our People. Yes. It is good to be who we are. The blessed People."

"And how good it is that you are my brother."

"It is good for me, too, Tecumseh. I am proud."

"Chiksika! *Tap-a-lot,* my brother," Tecumseh blurted. He knew a man was not supposed to show how he felt, but he had to blink because of the stinging tears on his eyelids. Chiksika nodded, compressing his lips and crumpling his chin, and reached over and pulled Tecumseh's earlobe gently.

"I love you as well. Every day our family grows more and more proud of our Tecumseh. Our father would be very pleased. Now, come. They will be even more proud when they see what you have done today."

Star Watcher put the deer's brain in a wooden bowl and mashed it with a pestle until it was smooth, while her mother stretched the hide between two posts and then worked slowly over the inside of the skin with a scraper made from a shoulder blade, removing all the flesh and fat. "Such a big buck," Turtle Mother said with a sigh. She was not complaining of how big a hide it was to flense. She was very proud of her boy and of how he had killed the buck so expertly that it had not died in pain and terror.

Turtle Mother had a heavy heart on this day. This was the Hunter's Moon, and it had been in the Hunter's Moon three years ago that her husband, Hard Striker, had gone away to be killed because she had yielded to him and not spoken against war in council. Whenever the leaves turned red and yellow she would sigh and feel the loss of him so deeply that she could hardly speak. Her mourning time had ended two years ago, but she had never stopped mourning. And every time she heard of another Shawnee hunter being found dead somewhere in the hunting grounds down near the Beautiful River with white men's footprints around, she would grow more bitter. Her husband's life had been thrown away in a useless battle, and still the white men came over the river, ignoring even their own treaties. Now Turtle Mother did not like even the British, who brought new knives and blankets and kettles for the people and fixed broken guns for the warriors. They were still white men, and it was their conflict with the Long Knives that kept the country full of blood and revenge and cost the lives of warriors every year. Always she expected that Chiksika would go away and not come back. He was like a mad animal against the Long Knives, and from the tales the other warriors told, he was too bold. How often Turtle Mother would remember that autumn three years ago and think: We should have paid heed to Cornstalk. Cornstalk signed a peace with the white chief, and now he does not have to feel his heart eaten by revenge.

Sometimes Turtle Mother thought the best thing would be to leave the valley of the Beautiful River and go where there were no white men.

She scraped the last pink shred of flesh she could find and called to her daughter, "I am ready for that."

Inside the *wigewa* Star Watcher pulled her skirt up to her waist and squatted over the bowl and urinated into the mashed deer brain. Then she stirred it all into a pasty fluid and carried the bowl to her mother. Star Watcher was not unhappy, as her mother was. She was delighted with many things. This excellent kill by her little brother, for one. And there glowed in her a great warmth for Stands Firm, who had come to live in Chillicothe because, she believed, of his love for her. And then, too, this was the harvest and hunt season, and she was aware of the great caches of grain and nuts stored up everywhere in the town and of the great quantities of game meats being dried and salted so aromatically everywhere, all this that would feed the People through the coming winter. The Great Good Spirit and Kokomthena did indeed favor the People, and Star Watcher was always grateful, especially in this bounteous season.

Side by side with her mother she worked; they smeared the acrid, yellow-gray mixture thickly over the cleaned side of the deerhide. Then they untied thongs and took the hide down from the posts and rolled it up with the skin side inward. The hide would be left alone for three days, and the fluid would start tanning the hide. After that it would have to be worked and rubbed and pulled to make it more pliable. A deer had just enough brain to tan his own hide; that was one of the ways Our Grandmother had measured everything out in the Creation.

And then, just as Turtle Mother and her daughter went to tend the fire over which strips of venison were drying, they heard the first of the shouts and wails coming from the east side of the town. The voices were fierce and full of grief.

Even before they heard any words, they knew that something awful had happened. They crouched, Turtle Mother holding her daughter by the wrist, ready to go round up the triplets and flee if this was danger coming.

Within moments all of Chillicothe was in an uproar of yelling, wailing, and drums. The mighty voice of the town chief, Black Fish, was calling everyone to the council house. Suddenly Stands Firm rushed up through the smoke and stopped. Usually he would come to the house shyly, taking care not to look too hard at Star Watcher, and she would lower her eyes. But now he was shaking, and his teeth were bared in a sneer of hatred.

"The Long Knives murdered Cornstalk," he snarled.

Turtle Mother groaned between clenched teeth. "Tell me!"

"That is all I know. The messenger is at the council house! *Pe-eh-wah,* come!"

Black Fish with raised arms quelled the drone of anguished voices in the council ground. He called upon Weshemoneto to give the People strength and courage to bear what was happening to the nation. Then he told them in a voice grim and harsh:

"What has happened in the new Long Knife fort at the mouth of the Kanawha-se-pe we know to be true because our white brother Girty learned of it and sent us the messenger. It is this:

"Hokoleskwah, our beloved principal chief Cornstalk, went in peace to that fort, which the Long Knives have built on the place where we fought our greatest battle three years ago. With him were his son, and his chieftain Red Hawk. Cornstalk went there only to remind the Long Knives of his treaty with them. He went to explain that the Shawnees who raid Kain-tuck-ee are not his treaty signers, and that they only do it to avenge murders the Long Knives have done. He went to protest and to remind them that he was at peace with them. The whiteface captain of the fort took their guns away and made them hostages, and put them in a room. And then many of the Long Knives there went into that room. Cornstalk and his son and Red Hawk saw what was going to happen. They stood beside each other and were praying when the soldiers shot them with many bullets!" Black Fish's hard blade of a face was a grimace as he told this. His chin quivered when the pitiful moans of dismay and the wails of grief rose around him.


They talked low that night in the *wigewa* of Turtle Mother and her children. Chiksika's face had gone stony with hate. "The Long Knives are the spawn of the Great Serpent," he muttered. "They crawled from the sea slime onto the shore of our land. They must be pushed back into that sea slime!"

Turtle Mother's mouth was drawn down in bitterness. "We should not have fought them three years ago. This is more of their vengeance. Now it is too late to have peace ever again. It is time to give up this land and go where there are no white people. There we could live in peace, as in the good days before we ever angered them."

Chiksika looked at his mother with astonishment. And then for the first time in his life he rebuked her. "I cannot believe what words you said! Do you think our father would be pleased to hear that? No! He believed that we must fight to keep them out of our country, as long as one of us draws breath! You know the promises he asked from me, and from Tecumseh. I will not hear those words you said! Our father told me women are strong, that they can bear anything! You talk like a weak woman!''

She took a sharp breath, her nostrils distended, eyes drilling her son's face. Star Watcher pressed her palms over her ears to keep from hearing more, and tears formed in the corners of her eyes. Tecumseh ached to soothe his mother's hurt, though he felt that if either she or Chiksika was right, it was Chiksika.

There would be mourning for Cornstalk throughout the Shawnee nation, and it would go on far beyond the customary mourning time, for Cornstalk had been the greatest Shawnee chief in the memory of anyone, even the most ancient. If he had refused to listen to the whitefaces' lies about treaties and trust, they might have killed him in battle by now anyway, but they could not have murdered him helpless in a room.

"Now the whitefaces have done themselves great harm," Chiksika told Tecumseh as they rode out to hunt more meat for the coming winter. "They murdered a chief who pledged peace with them. Our next chief is one who does not trust them and will never stop fighting them. Our father Black Fish!''

"Black Fish will be?"

"You will see, little brother. When all the voices are heard in the next council, Black Fish will be the one. Some of the gray-hairs who are too weary to fight anymore, they will want a peaceful chief. This is always so. We love and respect our old men, but because of the Long Knives this is a time for warriors to lead. Listen. Some of the old ones say we should sit still and try to be friends with the white people, and share their riches. And some like our mother say we should flee to where there are no Long Knives. Beyond the Wabash-se-pe, toward even the Missi-se-pe.

"Those who wish to do those things can go, and no one will condemn them. But Black Fish says he has not finished what he began in the Hunger Moon. There are still Long Knives in Kain-tuck-ee. He desires to chase them back over the mountains, and the murder of our greatest chief only makes him stronger in his purpose. Listen, little brother. I tell you that Black Fish is great, too. He knows the British officers well. They have told him that they will pay our warriors for every Long Knife we take to them as a prisoner. The British governor-soldier Hamilton at Detroit has sent emissaries to all the tribes, saying that he will buy the scalps of the Americans, too, if they cannot be made prisoners. And greatest of all, the British will lend us some of their brave soldiers and officers to help us in Kain-tuck-ee. You have seen the great British soldiers, in their red clothing. They are said to be the bravest soldiers in the world!"

Tecumseh remembered that the first British Redcoats he had seen had been afraid, but he did not interrupt Chiksika to remind him of that. His brother went on:

"And they have cannons! The great rolling-guns that can knock down a Long Knife fort at once! They have promised Black Fish that they will pull their rolling-guns down to Kain-tuck-ee and shoot down the gates of those forts so we can rush in. Listen! If there had been British rolling-guns with us last spring to knock down Boone's Fort and Harrod's Fort, there would not be a white man still living in Kain-tuck-ee! Black Fish is ready to do this with the British. Black Fish says this is a time for the Shawnee to be brave, not timid. Listen. He will be the principal chief, and he will do things that will make his name as great as Cornstalk's. I am proud that he has taken us as his sons. With Black Fish before us and his British allies beside us shooting the cannons at the forts, we can drive the Long Knives out, and have our land the way it was before!"


And so when Black Fish was elected to be the principal chief, he was strong and eager for vengeance. He said he would not give the Long Knives a chance to rest even in the winter. He had eager young warriors and chieftains who would take raiding parties into Kain-tuck-ee to harass the Long Knife settlers, capture prisoners, kill cattle, attack supply boats, and obtain horses. These raiders would be like wolves in the snow, and they would make life so hard for the Americans that they would flee back out of the country—if there were any left alive to flee.

Black Fish favored several young men as leaders for these raids. One was his foster son, Chiksika. Another was Stands Firm. Another was the hickory-tough warrior Blue Jacket, who was brave and resourceful, who could think as white men think and thus know what they might do. Blue Jacket's hatred of the Long Knives was so strong that it was hard to remember that he had been born a white person. Whenever Tecumseh would look at that splendid warrior, he could scarcely believe that he as a child had whipped him in a blind fury in the gauntlet, only seven years ago.


Snow snakes were strewn far out across the white meadow.

Thick Water, the long-armed, sinewy Kispoko boy who had been such a great hoop roller years ago in Kispoko Town, was looking very smug at this moment, because he had just sent his snow snake hissing and slithering about a hundred paces across the snow, so far that surely even Tecumseh could not surpass his throw. Tecumseh was much younger than Thick Water but was nevertheless the best snow snake thrower known. But that had been before Thick Water had moved to Chillicothe with his family.

Tecumseh's snow snake was a smooth stick of dogwood about six feet long. Its heavy end, which had been the base of the dogwood sapling, curved up slightly. Tecumseh had carved on it the eyes and mouth of a snake and had rubbed the shaft with tallow until it gleamed. It was the snake itself, almost as much as the strength and skill of the thrower, that made it slide to winning distances.

Now Tecumseh walked to the throwing line drawn in the snow, touched it with the toe of his moccasin, and then paced back three long steps. He poised himself, looking toward that farthest stick, the one Thick Water had thrown. All the other boys were quiet, very respectful, though many now believed that Tecumseh could not possibly beat Thick Water's throw. Tecumseh himself knew that he would have to send his stick much farther than he had ever done before if he hoped to win over that.

He held his stick loosely in his left hand in front of him, parallel to the ground. Reaching back, he hooked his right forefinger in the worn notch in its small end.

Loud Noise, standing near the throwing line, began now to cheer and encourage his brother. His face screwed up in a tight grimace. His fists were clenched at his sides, and his body was crouched forward with excitement. And, as usually happened when he grew very excited, that strange squealing began in his throat, that ridiculous, pathetic sound that he apparently could not control, something like the squealing of a big rodent of some kind. He even looked something like a rodent. Other boys sometimes mimicked the sound and the contorted face, but not when Tecumseh was around.

Now Loud Noise began jumping up and down. Not long ago, this would have irritated Tecumseh so much that he might have made a bad throw. But Tecumseh had learned what to do. He turned to face Loud Noise and smile. The child at once stopped making his sounds and turned one way and another to beam at the other boys, as if to say, "Did you see that? My wonderful brother Tecumseh smiled right at me!"

And now Tecumseh announced, "See my snake go! It is the swiftest of them all!" He stepped off with his left foot, made three quick strides, and at the line whipped his right arm with all his strength in an underhand thrust and sent the stick slithering across the snow, a dark streak across the blankness so fast an eye could hardly follow it.

When it slid to a stop finally, five lengths beyond any of the others, Thick Water looked as if he would cry. But Tecumseh turned to him with a pleasant smile and said, "I was afraid I could not throw as far as you did!" Thick Water felt better. He could not dislike someone like this.

But now Loud Noise apparently decided he would do Tecumseh's gloating for him. He began a jerky, awkward prancing in the snow around Thick Water, pointing at him and taunting in a high, nasal voice: "Nyeh-heheh-heheh! Nyeh-heheh-heheh!" Tecumseh grabbed him by the shoulders when he came prancing around and shook him.

"Stop! Stop!" he hissed in his ear. The taunts ceased at once, and the strange, ugly little face was looking up at him in bewilderment. Tecumseh wanted to take the infuriating child aside and give him a talk about being pleasant to people. But he heard something, something in the distance through the snowy woods, and it was something he had been listening for, even when not thinking about it, for weeks. It was the joyous chanting and yelling of a returning war party.

Chiksika had ridden out toward Kain-tuck-ee weeks ago with a war party of more than a hundred young men under the leadership of Blue Jacket, one of the winter raids of Black Fish. They had gone equipped with new guns and knives and plenty of powder provided by the British. These were young men who had been so eager to avenge the murder of Cornstalk that they had exposed themselves to the hardships of winter warfare. For weeks the weather had been miserable and severe, with much sleet and snow, and the women had been acutely worried about their absent sons and husbands. All of Chillicothe had been praying for them and always listening and watching for their return.

The other boys had now heard the distant voices and were all looking that way down the trail, listening, their eyes glittering with excitement. Tecumseh suddenly ran out onto the meadow, snatching up his precious snow snake, and with a wave of his arm to summon his little brother, he raced down the trail through the snow, wanting to be the first to meet the returning band.

The warriors were a glorious sight. They came riding three abreast, their faces brilliantly painted, wrapped in their robes or in red blankets, waving feathered lances and muskets decorated with ribbons and feathers and scalplocks. A hundred warriors made a long and impressive parade coming across the bleak white landscape. And now Tecumseh could see that this war party was even larger than it had been when it had left; as he ran toward them he saw that they were leading a large group of white men, dozens of them, it looked like, ragged figures slogging on foot, led and pulled along by ropes tied around their necks.

Prisoners!

The boys stopped in their tracks and stared in awe. Never had they seen so many white prisoners at once. Usually a war party might bring home two or three or four at the most, sometimes a family, women and children. But these were all men! Tecumseh tried to count them as they came on, and it looked as if Blue Jacket and his warriors somehow had managed to capture some twenty-five or thirty Long Knives!

Chiksika rode with Blue Jacket at the head of the column, and he and Tecumseh recognized each other at the same time. They yelled each other's names and waved.

Now the boys ran alongside the column as it moved toward the town, ran alongside staring and yelling at the white prisoners. These were mostly big men, but they were not elegant soldiers like the British. Their faces were hard, dirty, and stubbly. They were clad in muddy, drab wool, in tattered canvas hunting shirts, in leather leggings wet and mud-spattered to the knees, in rent, frayed woolen hose. Several were limping, some were barefoot in the snow. Most were hatless, their hair matted and wild, their eyesockets deep and dark. Their noses and fingers were red from cold. Most of them looked miserable and hopeless.

But there were no wounds, no bloody bandages, no splinted limbs, neither among the prisoners nor among the warriors. Usually when a war party returned, there were warriors grim-faced with pain, feverish with infections, or sagging from loss of blood. But here there was no sign of anyone hurt. It was a wonder. Except for the war paint, this column looked like a hunting party.

"Tecumseh," Chiksika called down to him, and pointed back toward the file of prisoners. "Look at that man in front! We caught the chief called Boone!"

"Boone! Boone!" echoed several of the warriors, laughing. And the boys responded, shrilling the name of Boone, and they all ran toward that part of the column for a look at the one whose name they had all known since Black Fish's campaign a year ago, the one who had killed the son of Black Fish!

Hearing the name, the first prisoner in the line broke into a wide smile. "Boone!" he yelled in response, then laughed, his head thrown back.

The Shawnee boys were astonished and stared at the prisoner, mouths hanging open. This prisoner seemed to be unafraid—even happy.

He was not the giant he had grown to be in their imaginations. He was not even a big man; he was not any taller than an average Indian warrior and was, in fact, smaller than most of the other prisoners. And his face was not the hard, ferocious devil mask they had imagined. It was instead one of those open, unlined faces one sees rarely and inexplicably likes: a face strong but serene, rugged but kindly. The eyes were like summer sky. And

Tecumseh, despite his fierce excitement at seeing the hated enemy, the killer of Black Fish's son, being brought in helpless, felt merry and friendly when he looked at those light blue eyes. This Boone was not a young man, judging by the gray in his thick, sandy hair; but his face was unwrinkled, his physique, even in the bedraggled wool and leather clothes, gave an impression of spare, sinewy power, and he alone of the prisoners walked along with springy ease instead of trudging. It was as if he were a white man who had a *pa-waw-ka.* Tecumseh could not take his eyes off him for a long time as the cheering, chanting column moved toward Chillicothe. Loud Noise had run up squealing and joined Tecumseh, who now held his hand as they moved along. "That one is Chief Boone," Tecumseh told him, and Loud Noise rolled his strange eyes and wailed, "Wa! Wa!"

Now there were many people running out of the town to greet the homecoming warriors, and Tecumseh's attention was drawn away from the jaunty Boone by a boy's cry:

"Look! Here comes the Man-Eating People!"

"Look!" someone else called. "Here come the Peace Women!"

Tecumseh turned now to watch these two groups race toward the prisoners.

There were only a few of the Man-Eating People in the Shawnee nation at this time. They were not in favor. They were a society, men and women, some of whom were thought to be witches, with their own secret rituals. When prisoners of war were brought in, the Man-Eating People called to each other through the town and raced out, their lips painted red, to claim them. If they could reach and touch the prisoners before the Peace Women did, they could claim them to kill and eat. But if the Peace Women, who were mostly the wives of chieftains, reached the prisoners and touched them first, then the Man-Eaters could not claim them.

"Ha, look!" cried Stands Firm, who was riding near the prisoners. "Here come the buzzards, and they are hungry!" Stands Firm was one of the many Shawnees who detested the eaters of human flesh. "Run, you Peace Women!" he cheered them. *"Pe-eh-wah,* come this way!"

The Peace Women, running so hard their breasts jounced and their moccasins kicked up snow, closed in on the column and swarmed around the prisoners, touching them and screaming with triumph. But some of the Man-Eaters were right behind them, and a few of these sped past to the rear of the file of prisoners and began touching some of them with their sticks, to claim them. Here and there, Peace Women and Man-Eaters began shoving and fighting each other, all cheered on by the laughing boys. And the prisoners, having no suspicion that this struggle was over the fate of their own flesh, just squinted and flinched and plodded on, bewildered by the scuffle around them. The man called Boone was laughing as if all this were simply an uproarious game and he a spectator.

Then Blue Jacket turned his horse out from the head of the column and rode back, his heavy black brows knit, and he was yelling angrily. He rode his mount into the scuffle and forced the people away from the prisoners. "No!" he was yelling. "No! These prisoners are not for you, or for you! No! Get away! These we are taking to Detroit! These we sell to the British chief! Get away!" Blue Jacket's voice was loud and his presence was mighty, and in a moment he had restored order and made the people understand. Then he rode to the head of the column again to lead the procession on into the town, where Black Fish would be waiting to receive Boone, the man who had killed his son.


The prisoners were tied to posts outside the grand council lodge where everybody could look at them. Tecumseh stood ten paces from them and gazed thoughtfully at these shabby, sooty men with stubbled faces. It looked to be as Black Fish had said. These Long Knives were not rich and splendid men, like the Redcoat soldiers who had been in the town before. And yet, though these prisoners did stink in their soiled clothes, though they were prisoners who did not know their fates, Tecumseh did not smell fear on them as he had upon the great Redcoats that long-ago day. They just stood staring straight back at the taunting crowd. These were not cowards. When an ill-tempered warrior, one who had lost his hand at the battle of the Kanawha-se-pe, went close and spat in the face of one of the prisoners, the Long Knife spat back on him.

Boone himself was tied to a post inside the council house, where he remained standing while Blue Jacket told of the capture. Chiksika, who had developed a grudging admiration for Boone, watched him, amazed at his serenity. Several times Boone, turning to see Black Fish staring at him, smiled at him with apparent goodwill. Surely he was not aware that this chief was the father of a warrior he had killed.

Black Fish studied the prisoner and listened to hear how so many Long Knives had been caught without a fight.

It had happened at a great salt lick called Blue Licks, which had been used for ages by red men. These whitefaces had been there boiling brine to make salt for their fort. The one called Boone had been surprised alone one day hunting meat for the salt makers, surrounded, and disarmed. Blue Jacket had questioned him. Boone at first had claimed to be alone, but Chiksika's scouts found the salt makers at the lick, and Boone had admitted that they were his men. Blue Jacket then had convinced Boone that he should per-

suade his men to surrender peacefully, in order to save their lives. Seeing
that the Shawnees were four times their number, Boone had been wise
enough to agree. So the Shawnees had surrounded the salt lick and sent
Boone in, and he had talked to them, and they had given up without any
struggle.

Chiksika nodded his confirmation of details as Blue Jacket related the
story. The crowd in the council lodge murmured its approval. Black Fish
then stood and told the council that Blue Jacket and his warriors had done
an outstanding deed, and that the British Chief Hamilton would pay the
Shawnees richly for such a large body of men. "You have acted wisely.
Some young warriors would have followed the heat of their vengeance and
would have rushed in to kill. Many warriors then would have been hurt,
perhaps killed. And there would have been only scalps to sell at Detroit.
Each of these prisoners alive is worth four times as much as his scalp alone
is worth. Let us all think how well Blue Jacket and Chiksika and Stands Firm
have done this. For his prudent thinking, I recommend that Blue Jacket
should be named a war chieftain."

"Ah-i-ee! Ho! Ah-i-ee!" At the warmth of the men's response, Blue
Jacket seemed to swell up. Black Fish went on:

"I am pleased above all that he caught the chief called Boone, whom you
see here." Boone faced Black Fish when he heard his name and smiled.
Black Fish paused, looking studiously at Boone, then continued. "I recognize this Boone. I saw him shoot and kill my son in battle." There was a
murmur of voices in the room. "I would have the right to kill this Boone
today. But I have been looking at him, and here is what I have been
thinking. This Boone is a kind of man who should be a Shawnee, not a Long
Knife. Look how he has no fear. We have known of this man for a long time.
I have fought against him, and I know he is brave and quick and cunning
in a fight. I know his word is good. He told Blue Jacket he would persuade
his men to surrender, and he went to them and did so, even though he
might have told them to pick up their guns and fight. Look at him now and
you can see that he is cheerful and unafraid.

"Listen: If this Boone would want to become a Shawnee, I would wa t
to adopt him as a son of my own. That is the right of one whose own son
has been slain, and I would choose to do it."

Many in the big lodge murmured in surprise. Many of them nodded.
Many seemed to approve of this idea, especially the warriors who had
captured Boone. In the long march from the Blue Licks they had come to
like and admire him very much. Black Fish continued:

"I now ask Chiksika, who has become one of my sons. Would you like
to have this Boone as your brother?"

"If his heart tells him to join us," Chiksika said, "I would welcome him as my brother. Yes!"

Black Fish's craggy, hard face now, as it often did, melted with the warmth from inside him. Steely warrior though he was, he was also known as a man of the most generous impulses, and this great warmth of his heart had made him the foster father and teacher of many. Though he bore ugly scars and bitter memories from his long conflict with the white men, he was willing to trust and embrace even the one who had killed his son, if he saw just the right thing in his face. He turned to Blue Jacket and said:

"Talk to this Boone. Tell him what I have said. Ask him if he would give his heart to us and be our brother. Let him think about it until he is sure." Boone seemed to be listening with lively curiosity to all this; it appeared that perhaps he was understanding enough of the words to have some notion of what was going on. "Then," Black Fish concluded, "if he so chooses, when you take your prisoners to Detroit, you will not sell Boone to the British chief. You will show him that you have caught Boone. Maybe this British chief will offer you a very high price for Boone, but you will say, 'No, this Boone wants to return to Chillicothe and become a Shawnee, a son of Black Fish.' " He paused and stood very straight and smiled. "That will make a strong impression on the British chief. Probably he would even want to tell his king of England about it."

It was plain that in addition to his warm impulses, Black Fish like many Shawnee had an eye toward his own legend.

And so it followed, early in 1778, that Daniel Boone became a favorite son of Black Fish and thus a foster brother of Tecumseh. As a jocular reference to Boone's quickness, Black Fish named him Sheltowee, which meant Big Turtle.


Some days Big Turtle would sit in the sunshine for hours, wincing, while the children took turns at the tedious task of plucking out his whisker stubble, bit by bit getting rid of his facial hair as the Shawnee men did theirs.

He was learning the Shawnee tongue quickly, and with the help of sign language he told many amazing stories of his adventures, always stating them in a way that flattered the red men, even those he had outfought and outwitted and outrun. Tecumseh and Chiksika and their whole family became as enchanted with this new member as Black Fish had in the beginning. Even Turtle Mother with her great bitterness toward white men would have to smile in fond amusement as this fabled leader of the evil race entertained her three little sons, carved wooden toys for them, played games with them, and told them interesting things about the white people's beliefs.

As winter melted into spring and mild breezes encouraged the leaf buds and the tiny forest flowers to show themselves, Chiksika began to take Big Turtle and Tecumseh with him when he would lead hunting parties down into the rolling hills toward the Beautiful River and westward toward the Whitewater. On these hunting expeditions, Big Turtle showed time after time that he was the equal of the best of the Shawnee hunters and trackers. He could think like a deer and go where he knew they would go, and when he shot at an animal, he seldom missed its heart. He was fast as a rabbit on foot and could lope for hours without tiring. He was as natural a horseman, with or without saddle, as any of the riders. Tecumseh had his own white pony and had already learned to ride so well that he was like a part of the animal. He would guide the pony, even at an all-out run, with the pressure of his knees, with both hands free to use his bow. Tecumseh felt himself fully a man when he rode between Chiksika and Big Turtle, with the sound of a score of mounted hunters coming along behind them. His heart and soul swelled with happiness each time they rode over the crest of a hill and he saw new lands stretching away, meadows of flowers more numerous than the stars in a night sky, forests of enormous hardwood trees in their pale, delicate dress of new foliage, bold, blue-gray stone bluffs above curving river courses, flights of iridescent passenger pigeons swooping through the air, flocks as vast as clouds, their wingbeats like wind gusts; small herds of bison moving slowly along the roads they had trampled out from river to river; roaring tornadoes in which Cyclone Person reached down with black fingers from a greenish sky to pick up trees and toss them like chaff. . . . When the boy saw these wonders he so revered the Great Good Spirit that his breast would swell with joy and tears would fill his eyes.

The hunting parties killed several bison along their great roads and took much meat, so much that they had to build camps and smoky fires and labor for days cutting bison flesh into strips and hanging it on pole racks over the fires to make jerky. "Someday," Chiksika said, "you and I will take a large group of hunters out to the wide prairies west of the Wabash-se-pe for a *big* bison hunt. We will go and visit with our friends the Kaskaskias and the Potawatomi, and with the Shawnees who have a town at the mouth of the Wabash-se-pe. You will meet warriors and chiefs who knew our father. You will see herds of bison so great that you will think Weshemoneto made the world for them instead of for people. And we will hunt them from horseback, chasing alongside the herds as they run. They are so many their hooves sound like thunder, and shake the earth! There is no other hunting that is so exciting to the spirit!"

Tecumseh's eyes were wide. "When can we do that?"

"Not yet," Chiksika said. "When we go back to Chillicothe now, we are going to war in Kain-tuck-ee again."

They were talking beside a campfire at dusk. Their eyelids were red and dry from woodsmoke, and the smell of burnt fat and drying meat filled the cool evening air and permeated their clothes. Off in a grove beyond the camp a grouse drummed its mating message, and meadowlarks trilled in the open. Big Turtle sat near Chiksika, doing what he could to repair a damaged musket with his only tool, a knife. He had become the hunting party's gun repairman. He could adjust bent springs, even repair thumb-screws sometimes, and make serviceable ramrods and gunstocks with his knife. A broken hammer or trigger he could do nothing about, except sometimes by taking a part from one broken gun to repair another, and when he could not fix something he would apologize, saying that if he had the right tools, he could make new parts. Big Turtle was a man of many skills. He had no gun of his own just now; his own rifle had been taken from him by Blue Jacket and not returned. When he went hunting with Chiksika, he would use a gun belonging to some member of the party who was staying in the camp.

Big Turtle did not look up from the flintlock he was working on when Chiksika spoke of the plan to attack Kain-tuck-ee. He seemed not to be listening; perhaps he was too absorbed to try to follow the conversation around him.

Chiksika and the other hunters talked about the planned raids. Black Fish would lead again this spring. One place to be raided was the fort at the Kanawha-se-pe where Cornstalk had been murdered. It might be too strong a fort to destroy, but there would be an attempt to surprise it. Two Canadian officers sent by the British would go with Black Fish and help with strategy. There might even be a cannon, if one could be pulled down from Detroit in time. Black Fish intended to gather as many as five hundred warriors from all the septs. One of Black Fish's best subchiefs, Catahecassa, Black Hoof, would be in charge of a large portion of the Chalagawtha forces. Old Moluntha, chief of the Maykujay sept, would command the warriors of his sept. The main purpose of the war party would be to go down and complete the task that Black Fish had not quite accomplished the year before: the destruction of all the forts in Kain-tuck-ee.

Chiksika, out of respect for his beloved new foster brother Big Turtle, did not mention the forts by their names. One of them was Boone's Fort.

One day late in the spring, while Black Fish and his five hundred warriors were painting themselves and preparing their food and weapons for the raid on Kain-tuck-ee, his newest foster son assembled a rifle from parts he had hoarded as tribal gunsmith and slipped out of the village. He caught and bridled an Indian horse, led it to the edge of the woods, glancing back over his shoulder until he was hidden by foliage, then swung onto the horse's back and kicked it into a gallop toward Kain-tuck-ee. Boone's Fort was one hundred and sixty miles away, by his reckoning, and after his capture last winter he had memorized the return trail.


Night was coming on before his absence was noted, and the news was brought to Black Fish:

"Big Turtle is gone. He stole a horse. His tracks go toward Kain-tuck-ee."

The chief's jaw muscles tightened, and he bent slightly, as if he had just been struck a blow in the belly. In their deep, dark slits, his eyes glinted. Then he stood up straight. A great, warm pool of affection in his heart had just frozen into an icy pellet of hatred. The white man, even that extraordinary and esteemed one, had betrayed his word once again.

"Big Turtle? Big Turtle?" Black Fish replied. "I know no one by that name. Do you mean that white-faced horse stealer they call Captain Boone?"


A crowd of children stood around Loud Noise, laughing at him. But he was used to being laughed at, and the scowl on his face was not one of hurt, but one of defiance. Only *he* had a Thunder-Sucker. No one else had one.

He rolled his eyes and uttered a long string of gibberish, some of that vaguely familiar language that was thought to be Our Grandmother's tongue, and that he should have forgotten three or four years ago but seemed still to remember.

A few of the younger children stopped laughing. Now Loud Noise waved his left hand in front of them. On the wrist was a little bead bracelet with a copperhead's skull hanging on it, a frail piece of bleached bone with the bracelet threaded through the eyeholes. This seemed to intimidate a few more of the children, but some of the older boys were still laughing at him. Now he raised his right hand, in which he held his Thunder-Sucker, which he claimed had great medicine.

Loud Noise was a clumsy boy, who could hardly throw a rock without hitting himself. But he believed himself to have other powers. Most boys played at being war chiefs and great hunters, but he played at being a shaman. It made people remember their old suspicion that he might be a creature of Matchemoneto, the Great Evil Spirit.

His Thunder-Sucker was like a leather bag between two flat pieces of wood. It was something that Chiksika had brought home from the capture of the salt makers and had given to his mother. Blue Jacket said white people used it to help in fire starting, and the name they called it was "bellows." Loud Noise often stole it out of the *wigewa* and took it to use in playing shaman. Sometimes he just blew air out of it and claimed that he had captured the breath of Cyclone Person, the wind spirit. But when a storm was coming, he used it for a more spectacular ceremony. He would stand outdoors with a wild look in his eyes and point it toward the sky, and when thunder boomed he would jerk it open. Then he would say he had sucked in some thunder with it, and that he could release the thunder whenever he wanted to. A few smaller children believed him, and he could scare them or dominate them by pointing it at them and threatening to thunder them with it. Loud Noise was not the kind of boy that other children could like, but he was not one they could ignore, either.

Now Loud Noise held the Thunder-Sucker out in front of him and cried in a shrill voice: "You will see! With my medicine I can take the poison out of the three-leaf poison plant! I can protect myself from all poisons!"

He turned to a thick patch of poison ivy beside the trail, pointed the bellows at it, and squeezed the handles together, making a deep noise in his throat that, with the hiss from the bellows, sounded like a distant storm. Then, to show his contempt for the now harmless plant, he squatted down in it, strained, blew gas in it, and pretended to defecate. Then he tore up a handful of the leaves and wiped his bottom with them. The others were astonished.

It was unfortunate that the strange child's magical powers did not match his imagination. His mother and sister had to treat his bottom with many jewelweed poultices for much of that summer, and he cried almost as much as he had after he was born, and it was a long time before the people of the town stopped laughing about the medicine powers of Loud Noise.


One day during the Raspberry Moon as Tecumseh sat under a hot blue sky scraping at a piece of split hickory, shaping a child's bow for Loud Noise, the breeze in the trees fell still. All the birds stopped singing. A dog leaped up from where it had been lying and ran away whimpering, its tail between its legs. The edges of shadows seemed to dissolve on the ground, and though there was not a cloud in the sky, the daylight was turning a strange yellow gray, then ash gray, and darkening. People were crying out, pointing toward the sun. Heart racing with fright, Tecumseh put his hand up to shade his eyes and squinted under his palm at the sun.

It was not round anymore!

He leaped up and ran home. Other children were hurrying in all directions, scampering, stumbling, squealing with fear.

Turtle Mother tried to soothe the triplets. She told them not to be afraid. It was *Mukutaaweethe Keelswah,* the Black Sun. It came now and then in any lifetime; it always lasted only a short time. Wise men said it happened when the moon got in front of the sun for some reason known only to Weshemoneto.

They were all glad but amazed when the sun was whole again, and there was not a trace of the event left in the sky. The world was as bright as ever. But in the faces of many of the gray-hairs, its gloom remained for a while. For the Black Sun, almost always in the history of the Shawnee nation, had foreshadowed misfortunes in war. And most of the men were now away at war.

"Look, now," Tecumseh said to Loud Noise. "You *must* keep this arm straight." With a sigh, he took hold of his little brother's left arm above and below the elbow and straightened it. "Now you must keep that arm straight like that while you pull the bowstring. Pull it now!"

Loud Noise made one of his awful, mouth-twisting grimaces and tried to pull the bowstring. The bow began to wobble. His fingers on the bowstring began to tremble and spread apart, and the nock of the arrow slipped off the string and the arrow fell to the ground; by then his left arm had begun to quake, and it bent at the elbow again. Now the boy eased the tension off the bow and, making a panting sound, looked down at his arrow on the ground as if he were about to cry.

Tecumseh sighed again in exasperation. Never had he known any person so clumsy and uncoordinated as this poor child. Tecumseh himself had been shooting a bow for three years by the time he was this age. The other two triplets could shoot the bows Tecumseh had made for them. But Loud Noise could just barely do anything that required *one* hand; he could throw a stick or rock, and it would usually land somewhere—not far—in front of him, but not always. Sometimes it would fall behind him or just go up and come down on his head. But anything that called for the use of *both* hands, like shooting a bow or kindling a fire or simply juggling two stones, seemed to be beyond his capabilities. When he had tried to use a rock sling, he had always bruised his shins or gotten the cord tangled around his arm or neck. It was as if he could not think of both hands at once, and anything he attempted usually ended in an awkward, spectacular fumble, followed by squeals or shrieks of frustration. If it had not been so pathetic, it would have been funny.

Tecumseh knew that a boy who could neither shoot an arrow nor light a fire would be helpless in life, so he strove patiently every day to help the poor bumbler overcome his natural ineptitude. He coached him, demonstrated, explained. He wished Chiksika could be here to help him instruct. Chiksika was a wonderful teacher. But actually, Chiksika had never been the kind of a teacher to Loud Noise that he had been to Tecumseh. Chiksika was truly embarrassed by Loud Noise and stayed away from him, and tried to pretend he did not exist.

Besides, Chiksika was not here. He was still away in Kain-tuck-ee with Black Fish and the war party.

After Boone's betrayal and flight, Black Fish had waited a long time before setting out to Boone's Fort; he had waited in expectation of some British cannons. He had known that Boone had gone home to warn the forts, so there would be no surprise, and without surprise it would be important to have cannons. But no cannons had come, and at last Black Fish had led them all away. They had left in a high state of war fever, accompanied by some British captains and interpreters, determined to do great damage to all the white settlements in Kain-tuck-ee even without cannons. But his primary target was Boone's Fort; it was, indeed, Boone himself. Shawnee law decreed that any adopted outsider who betrayed the People was a condemned man. If Boone could be caught this summer, he would be executed instantly—preferably by Black Fish himself, whose heart he had frozen.

"Little brother," Tecumseh said now, sounding more patient than he really felt, "try once more. Listen to me. From the beginning, hold this arm straight. You are strong enough. Draw the string quickly, so you won't tire your muscles. Do not forget to keep holding the arrow between the two fingers so it will not fall. Here. You are ready now. Try to shoot your arrow as close to mine as you can." Quickly he put an arrow to his own bowstring and shot it into a patch of bare clay on the opposite bank of the creek, a mere fifteen paces away. "Shoot at my arrow," he said.

Tecumseh never really saw what Loud Noise did wrong then. Unsteadily the child arched the little bow. His left arm quivered and bent. The bow sprang back; something broke with a loud, splitting sound. The bow and part of the arrow fell, and Loud Noise spun away shrieking and fell on his knees and elbows. Tecumseh leaped to him and turned his face up. A bolt of shock went through him.

Protruding from the little boy's eyesocket was an eight-inch sliver of the split arrow shaft, the feather still hanging loosely on it. The feather was red with blood. Oozing from between the eyelids was a pinkish mixture of blood and fluid from the child's punctured eyeball.

The boy screamed and drooled and writhed.

Change-of-Feathers, the old medicine man of the Chalagawthas, came with two little bundles and squatted in the lodge beside the shrieking child, whom Tecumseh was holding down by keeping his arms pinned.

Turtle Mother was already taking the long splinter out of the eyesocket. Grimly, firmly, her own eyes tearing with pity, she knelt over him in the very face of his terrible wails and pulled out the bloody sliver, not too slowly, for that would have protracted the pain, nor too quickly, either, as that might have damaged the eye even more. It was one of the hardest things she had ever done. The tough integument of the collapsed eyeball came out of the socket with the wood sliver, though still attached inside by its little muscles and cords, and it made her think of the placental sacs and cords that had been pulled out of her every time she had borne children—yes, when she had borne this poor wretch of a child, too—and the thought twisted her heart. Clenching her jaw, she put two fingers against the integument and pulled the arrow fragment out between them, looked at it a moment, shuddered, and then turned and threw the piece of arrow into the fire. Tecumseh watched her do all this and had to bite the inside of his cheek to keep from crying out himself. Loud Noise struggled, but it was easy to hold him down.

Star Watcher was by the fire, boiling a comfrey mixture in a kettle according to her mother's instructions. It was very hot in the *wigewa,* and the women had stripped to the waist and their bodies gleamed with sweat. "Now put the cloth in and take it out and fold it," Turtle Mother said, not looking up from her shrieking child. She was smoothing his forehead with her hand. It was hard to talk over his screeching. He was crying the way he had done all the first days of his life, that pathetic, desperate noise she had hoped she would never have to hear again. Now Star Watcher came around beside her with the hot poultice and gave it to her mother.

Turtle Mother pressed the collapsed eyeball gently back inside the eyelids, bringing forth an even louder outburst of screaming, then she put the poultice over the eyesocket and bound it in place with a strip of strouding. Change-of-Feathers remained beside the pallet and watched all this. He said, shaking his head:

"That eye cannot be made good again. Do not hope for that."

"I know, Grandfather." She had faith in the shaman's healing powers but knew they could not repair that eye. He had more than once restored sight to blind people, but this eyeball was torn up.

"You have done well what you can do," said the old shaman. "Now I will do the rest, with the help of Weshemoneto. All of you go out now." They looked at each other, then Turtle Mother nodded. Tecumseh looked at the old shaman's dark eyes, which were nested in wrinkles. The old man's hair was long and as white as snow. "You go, too, my son," he said to Tecumseh. "He will stay still for me." As he said this, the old man passed his wrinkled, dry-skinned, knobby-knuckled hand a few inches above Loud Noise's forehead, and the child stopped struggling. Even his screams subsided, and he lay whimpering as the women and Tecumseh went out through the low doorway into the late afternoon sunlight. The other boys were sitting on the ground under a tree, their faces streaked from crying. There were villagers standing in the street, waiting to give their quiet consolation.

For several hours the family waited outside. The old shaman's voice chanted softly within, sometimes rising into quavery wails. Odors of tobacco and pine needles, and some unfamiliar smell of rot, came from the house. Tecumseh wanted to go away into the woods and be alone, but he knew he should stay with his family at this time. He wondered if his mother blamed him for this in any way. If she did, she did not show it.

Tecumseh sat trying to remember exactly how it had happened, but he had seen only that instant of the broken tension, and he had seen it only from the edge of his eye. Maybe Loud Noise had drawn the bow too far and caught the whole arrow between the bow and the bowstring, and the tension had split it. But somehow the child had, as always, fumbled what he was doing, and the taut bow had not forgiven his mistake.

Tecumseh's heart was heavy and sick. That sorry child Loud Noise, who from the time of his birth had lacked in everything that grows to make a warrior and a good man, now would have still another disadvantage, still another ugliness. In some tribes he would not have been kept alive. Much misery, his own and his family's, would have been avoided if he had not. But the life of anyone born a Shawnee was sacred. And, as had been said, the child's strangeness probably foretold some special powers. One had to go on believing in the wisdom of heaven.

Eventually, then, at dusk, the shaman called the family in. The inside of their lodge smelled musky and tangy, and the boy lay asleep. The shaman said the bad spirits had been exorcised from the boy and chased from the house, and that the eye wound would not rot, and there would be no fever and no more terror. Then he raised a crooked forefinger, placed it on his forehead above his nose, and said a surprising thing:

"Remember that one eye may see more than two." Then he left.

For a while Turtle Mother sat on the floor with her legs folded under her and gazed at the child, her face full of sadness and deep thought. Then she got up and took a bag of corn out of the *wigewa* and sat down at her hollowed-log mortar, put several fistfuls of corn in it, picked up the heavy stone pestle, and began pounding meal for the family's dinner. Tecumseh walked out in the village and among the domed houses that were silhouetted against the last traces of red in the west. He listened to the murmur of the many voices of the Chalagawthas in and around their homes, smelled their woodsmoke and food, and gazed for a while at the evening star in the darkening sky.

He was watching the evening star when he heard the shouts from out on the edge of town and then that growing uproar of dismayed voices that had already come to mean more bad words about the white men.

The bringers of the dark news this time were three Delaware riders.

First the messengers were given food and water while the people of Chillicothe Town gathered in the council ground in front of the grand lodge. A bonfire lit up the many faces. Star Watcher and Tecumseh had crowded close in front to hear.

The messengers stood with Change-of-Feathers, who translated from their language.

"When the sun went black, an army of Long Knives passed through the lands of the Wabash-se-pe and the Illinois. But none of us who live there saw them or heard them.

"Early in the next moon our brothers the Piankeshaw Miamis saw that the totems of the king of England were no longer on the poles above the forts and towns along the Mother of Rivers. In their place flew the totems of Virginia and the Thirteen Fires. This was seen at Kaskaskia the French town, and at Cahokia, place of the Great Mound, and even at Post Vincennes on the Wabash-se-pe."

Star Watcher groped for Tecumseh's hand and squeezed it in hers.

These were only names that he had heard now and then, places where Chiksika and other warriors had gone sometimes to get gunpowder from the British. He looked at Star Watcher and saw the fear on her pretty face. He looked around at the other listeners, and the dread he saw in their eyes made him tremble. Most of the people in Chillicothe were women and children and ancients. None of the warrior chiefs was here, not even Black Fish was here to hear this threatening news, which made it more ominous. Now some of the old men wanted to know more. What else did the Delawares know of this? asked Change-of-Feathers. Were many people killed in the battles for those forts?

"There were no battles," said the messengers. This answer caused a murmur of disbelief to sweep the crowd, like wind through trees. "Not a person was shot. The Long Knives walked in through the open gates of the forts in the dark of night and surprised and caught everybody while the Redcoats were away at Detroit."

The crowd was jabbering now. It was the kind of coup that every war chief dreamed of, the kind that made a war chief's name a legend. It was the kind of coup that Black Fish had been striving for, season after season in Kain-tuck-ee, without success. Who was this great Long Knife chief, then, who had passed like an invisible wind through the whole Middle Ground and surprised the British? Was it Washington, the principal war chief of the Long Knives? That was the only name anyone knew from the great white men's war in the east. Was Washington himself now standing like a giant between O-hi-o and the sunset? The messengers replied that it was known not to be Washington, though hardly anything else was known. "His name," they said, "sounds like this: Korark."

Suddenly the hubbub started again, everyone talking.

"Clark!" Tecumseh exclaimed to Star Watcher. "That was the name of the chief of the Long Knife soldiers in Kain-tuck-ee. Remember? The red-haired one with a loud voice!"

At once, dreadful imaginings were in every head. If this Clark's Long Knives were in the west, did that mean they had destroyed Black Fish in Kain-tuck-ee before they went? Nothing had been heard from Black Fish for a long time.

And so the next morning the old chiefs sent several riders by different ways to find Black Fish in Kain-tuck-ee and take him this news or to bring back news of him. They sent several riders in case some might fall victim to the Long Knives, for if this enemy had been stealthy and bold enough to pass through the Wabash and Illinois lands with a whole army unseen, there very well might be many of them anywhere in the Shawnee lands now! A deep dread, a fear that almost ached, lay over the Shawnee nation.

It had been proven true again, that the *Mukutaaweethe Keelswah,* the sign of the Black Sun, was an omen of misfortune in war. Now there would be the fearful waiting, the ominous talk in every household. Turtle Mother became one of the most morose of all and began saying again what Chiksika had once scolded her for saying:

"Listen. This has become a lost country, a bad place. When the Long Knives were only to the east of us, they pressed on us from the east. When they went into Kain-tuck-ee, they pressed on us from the south, too. Now they are in the west. Will they not press us from there, too? Are we not like the poor animals in a hunting drive? What way have we to run but to Canada? And they are at war with the British, who have Canada. If they get Canada, then we will be finally encircled and trapped, is this not plain to see? Listen! We should ask our chiefs when they come home, if they come home, we should ask them to lead us out and away. This land is no good anymore!"

No one knew what the Long Knives would do next, and a mystery hung like a haze over all the sunsets.

Loud Noise for several days whimpered about his ruined eye. But the world had changed as much for the Shawnees as it had for him.


Now the Shawnees at Chillicothe yearned even more strongly for good news from the south, for the return of the warriors from Kain-tuck-ee. But days went by and they did not return. The People's anxiety deepened. Now many did believe that Clark's army had met Black Fish somewhere and killed or captured all the warriors. Now the Chalagawthas watched the bluffs and the woods around the town with a dread of seeing Long Knives coming. At night they slept fitfully and woke up listening for sounds. The horses of the town were brought into a corral at the edge of town with a guard, and the men went to sleep with their guns beside their beds. Boys and men guarded the trails and high places around the town and slept out there without fires, to warn if an enemy came toward the town.

And then one night, late in summer when the air grew cool after the sunset, something happened that made them certain that the Long Knives were actually near Chillicothe.

After the middle of that night, the horses began nickering and milling about. The old man guarding the corral rose stiffly in the dark where he had been sitting, slipped his blanket off his shoulders, and began to move along the pole fence, looking in among the horses to determine what was troubling them.

They were growing more agitated, trying to run in the small compound, some whinnying in fear. Their hooves were thudding on the ground, and the poles of the fence rattled and creaked where their big, powerful bodies pressed against them. In the town, dogs began barking, and then querying voices were calling out. The guard, suspecting that a bear or a wolf was prowling close, crouched and hobbled along the fence, trying to make out an animal's shape somewhere.

Suddenly a loud, human-sounding howl tore through the night, coming from the side of the corral nearest the town, followed immediately by the flash and crack of a gunshot. The whole herd of horses, some half a hundred of them, whinnied and thundered off in the other direction. The old warrior raised a cry. *"Pe-eh-wah! Pe-eh-wah!* Horse stealers!" And while he was giving the alarm and trying to see horse thieves in the dark, the herd was thundering out of the corral in the direction away from town. They were out and going away. Either they had knocked down the fence on the far side, or the thieves had torn it down. The entire herd seemed to be getting away, and there was nothing the old guard could do to stop it. For an instant he thought he saw a man running behind the horses, but there was no time to sight a gun on him—if indeed it was a man—and a shot in that direction would have gone into the fleeing herd anyway.

Tecumseh and his family had run out of their *wigewa* following the sound of the shot. They stood outside listening to the distant commotion, the small children clinging to the blanket their mother had draped around herself. Tecumseh's heart was beating in his throat, and his mouth was dry. He expected to hear a great uproar of combat next, a sound he had never heard but had often imagined.

But there was no fighting. The horses could be heard thundering away. Men of the town had rushed out and were talking to the old sentry. After a while it was determined that it had been only a horse theft. Part of the corral rails had been taken down, and a shout and a gunshot had stampeded the horses out. It had not been a Long Knife attack after all. But, said a warrior who had been in the Kain-tuck-ee raids the year before: "That shout that made the stampede, that was the voice of their big man named But-lah. It is not a voice to forget. But-lah stole our horses!" Tecumseh's scalp prickled.

The rest of the night, men and boys lay in watch around the town with their bows and guns. Tecumseh stood watch in a thicket near the place where the trail came down the bluff into the town. All night he imagined the giant called But-lah, who could run like a horse while carrying Boone. It took all Tecumseh's courage to stay by the trail so far from the edge of town. And yet in a way he wanted But-lah to come down this trail. His osage bow was powerful enough to shoot through the heart of the Long Knife. What a great thing he could do for the People if But-lah came by!

As dawn began to bleach the darkness out of the eastern sky, Turtle Mother and Star Watcher, like all the others, crouched by the door with the little children and waited in silent dread. If the Long Knives attacked Chillicothe, it would be at this hour. Loud Noise, a compress still bound over his eyesocket, was so full of misery and fear that he groaned. His mother stroked his shoulders and shushed him.


The sun rose. Tecumseh in his thicket stretched and stood up cautiously. The grass and weeds beside the trail glittered with dew. There was not a person anywhere in sight.

Soon, a few scouts came out from the town. They spread farther and farther out and finally assured themselves that there was no army of Long Knives nearby. Boys who had been on guard were now sent out to round up the stray horses. All but half a dozen were found. In the morning light the men found, amid the profusion of hoofprints around the corral, the footprints of white men. They were moccasined feet, but with that toed-out pattern that distinguished them from the footprints of red men. One set of prints was huge; here a giant had walked. Tecumseh joined the trackers. In the woods a few hundred paces from the town he found a place where iron-shod horses had been tethered. These tracks led away into the woods, along with the prints of several of the Shawnees' unshod horses. Here was where the horse stealers had led the six horses away.

Among the few warriors still in Chillicothe were some good trackers. Five of these men were sent to follow the spoor of the horse thieves, with a warning not to let themselves run into an ambush or an army of white men.

After the trackers had ridden out, Chillicothe settled down to an uneasy but ordinary day. Lookouts were stationed outside the town, and Tecumseh again was one of them. With great willpower he kept himself from falling asleep. When he would begin to slip away into a dream, he would see a giant white man, But-lah, and would be wide awake again.

Turtle Mother and Star Watcher and scores of other women spent the morning in the gardens and corn fields. There were vegetables and beans ready to be harvested; some of the strains of sweet corn were ready for picking. Later in the day, moccasins and clothes and shelters had to be made or mended for the coming cold season. They did this work, but they did it with partial attention. The women in the fields and at their sewing kept raising their heads to watch the bluffs, to watch the road, either for soldiers of the Long Knives or for the return of Black Fish's warriors, or for the return of the trackers, who might overtake the horse thieves at once, or days from now, or not at all.

Star Watcher tried to talk to her mother about the harvest, about the clothing, about the triplets. But Turtle Mother had hardly anything to say. In her face there seemed to be more anger than fear. So Star Watcher finally fell silent and daydreamed, as she worked, about Stands Firm.

The sun went down with everybody still half watching, and the people slept restlessly again that night. The next day was much the same. The day after that there was still no news, and by the next day the tension had eased, and only now and then did the people stop in their work, or the children in their play, to scan the horizons. A cold wind had risen, and the sky was cloudy. There were rain showers for a part of one day, and then the weather grew mild again.

On the sixth day a boy came running into the town from the southeast, running as fast as he could and shouting:

"They come! They caught the horse stealer! He is But-lah! A-hi-ee!"
Shrill, fierce cries answered from the town. "Get switches!" the boy cried,
now jumping up and down in his excitement. "Everybody! They want
everybody to whip the horse stealer!"

The people needed no urging. It was not just another horse thief, it was
the giant Long Knife called But-lah, the friend of Boone, the man who had
saved Boone's life in that long-ago incident at Boone's Fort. They were
going to see for themselves this legendary enemy, and they were going to
get to punish him for coming and scaring their town and stealing horses.
Everyone would be able to tell, from this day on, of striking a blow at the
famed white warrior But-lah! "My club hit him here, on the back of his
neck, and made him stagger," they would be able to relate, even to their
grandchildren, or, "My switch drew blood on his white shoulders!" Or,
"He was a huge man, yes, as mighty as you have heard, but my stick made
him cry out!"

Tecumseh had heard the commotion from the woods north of the town,
and when he ran into the street he saw that several hundred people were
already lined up along the way to the council house, slashing the air eagerly
with their switches and staffs and clubs, laughing and cheering and watching
the trackers come with their prisoner toward the edge of town. They were
in a state of uncommon excitement and were murderously joyous. They had
been worried for a long time about their sons and husbands and fathers who
were away at war with Black Fish. They had been afraid of the Long Knife
army and of its appearance in the west, and they had been outraged by the
audacity of horse thieves who had come near their most populous town.
Now they would be able to vent some of their fear and anxiety upon this
white warrior who was more than just a man, who was a symbol of the most
terrible aspects of the white men. As Tecumseh wedged himself into a place
in line, a fresh-cut switch of limber ash in his hand, he was hearing some
of the details of the capture:

"They tracked them all the way to the Beautiful River!"

"They killed one of the thieves and caught this But-lah!"

"They got all of our horses back, and the horse thieves' horses, too! Ha!"

"They were bold to come here, but they will learn not to do it again!"

"Not to steal Shawnee horses! Ha, ha!"

"Oh! Look at him!"

"Big!"

"There is a man big enough for Tall Soldier Woman! Ha, ha!"

Here and there in this brave joking and boasting Tecumseh could hear
the shrillness and tremor of fear. Sometimes people got hurt in the gauntlet
line. Now and then a mighty warrior or soldier, tormented and defiant,

would strike or kick someone who got too close, even snatch a club from someone and fight back. This one was a mighty warrior. He was a man who had run like a horse even while carrying Captain Boone in his arms. Now he would be coming down this line, which was mostly of boys and old men, women and girls, and he would be passing within inches. Yes. There was some danger that even among these hundreds, this one enemy warrior might be able to hurt somebody. It was just enough of a possibility to make some of the people nervous even in their fierce anger.

The white man was being stripped of his deerskin clothing now. Tecumseh, who was closer to the start of the line than to the finish, was able to see clearly that this was a bigger and more powerful man than he had ever set eyes on before. His shoulders were enormous, and every muscle, from the thick chest muscles to the long muscles on the front of his thighs, was lean and hard under his skin. His face and his huge hands were as coppery brown as an Indian's, but the rest of his body was pure white, except where bruised and reddened with small wounds inflicted by his captors. It was plain that he had not been treated gently on his trip back from the Beautiful River. His hair was long, light brown and sun-bleached. He did not look the least bit afraid.

A drum thumped at the council lodge, and the rangy warrior standing by But-lah swung a staff, striking him so hard across the back that the blow was audible even over the drone of the crowd. And with that blow, which would have felled an ordinary man, the prisoner bellowed, sprang forward, and came bounding up the line with such speed that most of the blows aimed at him missed, and many barely managed to flick his back and shoulders as he shot past. When But-lah, now looking as large as a horse, loomed abreast of Tecumseh, the boy swung his stick with all his might. In that instant he heard the man's breath slumping in his wide chest like the breath of a galloping horse, heard the bare feet pelting the ground, saw the strong teeth bared in a grimace and the ferocious blue eyes slicing into everyone ahead.

Tecumseh's blow did not miss; it connected with But-lah's right arm so smartly that the stick split and stung Tecumseh's palm. And then the boy was standing there with his heart pounding, watching as the man sped on through the storm of whistling switches, his powerful buttocks and haunches pumping, crisscrossed with welts.

A few paces farther along the line something happened with such quick violence that Tecumseh could hardly perceive it. A zealous warrior had stepped out between the ranks with upraised club. He and the white man collided somehow. In the next instant the warrior's senseless body thumped to the ground. A moment later But-lah himself was collapsing under a barrage of blows, and soon his blood-streaked whiteness was lost to sight under the swarm of people who were beating him. Tecumseh remembered the time when the young prisoner who was now Blue Jacket had collapsed and lain under such a punishment and Tecumseh himself had gone blank in the passion of whipping that white skin. The memory, which he had seldom thought of in the years since, troubled him, made him feel a little queasy.

And so when But-lah was brought staggering, bleeding, and gasping back up the line to start the gauntlet all over again, Tecumseh did not like the sight of the bloody white skin. And when the white man ran past a second time, still fast and powerful but less steady, Tecumseh swung half-heartedly at him and was not disappointed that he missed.

But-lah never made it to the council lodge. On this second run he whooped, veered, and crashed through one of the lines, bowling over a woman. But another woman turned and felled him outside the line with a hard blow of a hickory staff. And then the crowd converged on him again, and this time they beat him unconscious and kept beating on him for a long time afterward, as if afraid he might yet rise up.

The great white warrior and horse thief had finally been subdued, and Shawnee women had done it. It was a time for great merriment. But Tecumseh had drawn into himself, feeling a strange shame, an unworthiness. He wanted to be away from the people and stop hearing what they were saying. He wondered if there might be something wrong with him, that he did not rejoice in the enemy's humiliation and pain. All his life his mother had talked to him about being kind and merciful to people.

But that, he had always understood, meant his own people. Surely not the enemy, an awful enemy like the Long Knives.

The battered prisoner was dragged unconscious to a lodge where, under guard, he would be doctored and fed and kept alive until Black Fish and the other chiefs came home and decided his fate.


When Black Fish rode into Chillicothe under a lead-gray sky a few days later, it was not a triumphant return. His huge Shawnee force had failed again to capture Boone's Fort, even with a two-week siege. Thirty-seven warriors had died by the marksmanship of Boone's defenders; everyone in Chillicothe had at least one relative to mourn. Many came home wounded, including Chiksika. Black Fish had been blaming the British, who still had not brought cannons. The failure had been made worse by the word of Clark's victories in the Missi-se-pe and Wabash-se-pe valleys. Black Fish was in a dark, tormented mood.

And so when he was told of the capture of the white giant But-lah, a vicious glitter appeared in his eyes, and it was evident that the lone white horse thief But-lah was not going to find a merciful heart in the head chief of the Shawnees. On the contrary, this prisoner seemed certain to become the outlet for all the pent-up fury and frustration that now boiled in Black Fish's soul. Black Fish wasted no time. Since so many of the nation's war chiefs and subchiefs were already present, he called for a council to settle But-lah's fate. It would be held as soon as the great mourning for the thirty-seven warriors had been done.

When that day came, the huge council house was filled with chiefs and warriors, hundreds of them. But-lah, still naked, tied up, his body a mass of healing wounds, was led out of the lodge and toward the council house by a rope halter. People spat on him as he went. Almost every inch of his body was marked by welts and bruises, but he was still the strongest-looking man they had ever seen, and he still walked unbowed and looked unafraid as he went in. Tecumseh watched him with awe and hatred, then crowded into a place by the door to watch. He saw Chiksika sitting inside, a bloody bandage on the side of his neck.

The council opened. Several chiefs spoke at length, praising the trackers for catching But-lah and recommending that he be burned to death. Almost all agreed, and he was painted black, the symbol of death. Then Black Fish made his recommendations. But-lah should be killed, but not yet. Black Fish said:

"He should be taken from village to village and shown. He should be made to run the gauntlet in every town. In every town there are parents and mates and children of our dead warriors. They should all whip him for their grief. Let this horse stealer, who was too bold, take the punishment for Boone and all the whitefaces in Kain-tuck-ee!

"If he dies in the gauntlets, that will be well enough. But if he lives through them, let him be taken at last to Wapatomica Town, in the heart of our country, where all the people can go easily to see him burned! That is what should come of this man! This friend of Boone! This horse stealer who came here and troubled our women and children!"

That night Tecumseh sat by the fire and watched his mother work silently and gloomily at her duties. Chiksika had come to eat a little, but then with a fever from the wound in his neck he had gone away to his own little lodge by the river, to rest without children around. Star Watcher had gone with him, to clean his wound and make a new poultice for it. Perhaps then she would go by the *wigewa* of the family of Stands Firm and offer them condolence upon the death of one of their cousins, one of the thirty-seven who had not returned from Kain-tuck-ee. Above all she wanted to be near Stands Firm.

Turtle Mother's face seemed to have grown slack and heavy and sagged at the jowls. She muttered as she worked. "War has made Chiksika hard. Did you see? He cared not about his little brother's lost eye. But then he has never cared for the little one."

"Perhaps he is too troubled because so many friends died."

She answered without looking up. "The whitefaces have laid a curse over all our country. They have made the people bad." She worked for a while longer in silence. Then, perhaps feeling Tecumseh's intense stare on the top of her head, she looked up at him and said, "This big man they have condemned to burn. Do you, my son, believe a man should suffer so much?"

Tecumseh hesitated, not quite sure what he really did believe. It was hard to think that Black Fish and all the other great men in council could be wrong or unfair. But then Tecumseh's feelings of the last few days returned, and he slowly shook his head.

"To burn men is bad," his mother said. "But cruel times make good people cruel." She sighed, then set her mouth hard and looked at the fire, and the fire glinted in her angry eyes. "This white man chose the wrong season to come here and steal horses. He should have stayed out of our country. Too bad for him. But will torturing and burning him keep more from coming? It would be foolish to hope so."

A piece of rabbit flesh fell into the fire and began sizzling and flaring. She watched it burn. *"Wapanzo-ah, cut-ta-ho-tha,"* she murmured. "Rabbit, you are condemned to burn up." She sneered and snorted a laugh through her nose. Then she sighed again.

"We should leave this bad country," she said.

# CHAPTER 10

## Chillicothe Town
## March 19, 1779

Turtle Mother stood in mud beside a loaded packhorse in a long line of packhorses and people and looked at her children for what she knew might be the last time. They stood forlorn in the muddy street before her, in front of the *wigewa* that had been their home for more than four years, and her tears blurred their faces. In the days since the terrible decision had been made, her heart had hurt so much that she had hoped it would kill her or grow numb, as other wounds do. But it had not, and she knew it never would. This was the saddest day she had ever lived; it was even more terrible in a way than the time of her husband's death, because then she had been able to draw some consolation from her children and from the Shawnee people. Now neither could console her. For her children would no longer be with her, and the rest of the People, if they could still be called a people, were inconsolable themselves.

Never since the Beginning, when Our Grandmother and Rounded-Side had created the septs and brought them together as a nation, never during all the nation's persecutions and migrations, had anyone dreamed that the nation could be divided or defeated by anyone, not even by the Iroquois or the white men. The Shawnee nation had remained strong enough to endure, simply because of its oneness. Sometimes the parts of the tribe had migrated different ways and lived in places far from each other, but the oneness had not been destroyed. And any Shawnee person had remained strong enough to endure, simply because of his or her inclusion in that oneness.

But the white man's curse on the Shawnee country had at last penetrated and split even that oneness. The nation had separated along that split line, and on this terrible day the broken parts were moving away from each other. Four thousand warriors and women, children, and old people milled among the laden packhorses, their hearts as chilled and dismal as the mud around their feet, and waited for the column to begin moving west, leaving their own lands forever. Most faces were blank. The breakdown of the nation had left many of the people too stunned to think or to talk of anything but the small details of packing and moving. But from every house came sounds of misery.

This split passed through not only the nation, but through the septs and even through families. Twelve hundred residents of Chillicothe were leaving, but not all the Chalagawthas. Twenty-eight hundred people from the other four septs were going west, but some members of each sept—Kispokos, Thawegilas, Peckuwes, and Maykujays—were staying. Every Shawnee adult was free to choose according to the wisdom of the heart, and each had made the choice: whether to stay in the O-hi-o homelands and contend with the problem of the white people or to go west of the Missi-se-pe and help build a new homeland. Over beyond the Great River the Spanish governor had granted them a parcel of land to settle on, in the land near the Missourias. It was not a very large parcel of land, and no one even looked forward with joy to going there. They were not going to something, they were fleeing from something. A trader named Loramie had made the arrangements and would lead them there, those who had chosen to go.

Turtle Mother, bitter, heart-weary of the whiteface threat, had elected to go with the Kispoko sept of her husband. A large part of the Kispoko had voted to leave, along with most of the Peckuwes and the Thawegilas.

But Chiksika had vowed to stay with his foster father Black Fish and resist the whitefaces. Star Watcher would stay also. She was twenty-one years of age and would marry Stands Firm, who like Chiksika had sworn to fight the Long Knives as long as he drew breath.

Tecumseh's choice to stay had most rent Turtle Mother's heart and his own. There had been long, sorrowful talks in their house over the night fires. He had spent days talking with the old grandfathers about what he should do. At last he had come to his mother and said, "I have the sign. I must stay and serve the People."

"But we who go are the People as well. Perhaps you are meant to help the People make a new homeland."

"*Mat-tah,* no," he said. "I was given a promise to keep by my father, and that is not what he wanted me to do."

Loud Noise, who idolized Tecumseh and who had come to depend upon Star Watcher as much as his mother for pampering and comfort, had whined that he did not want to go away. The other two triplets had wanted nothing but for the family to stay here together as it had always been in their memory.

Finally it had come out this way, that the children would all remain together here, foster children of the Chalagawthas, in this familiar land where the Shawnees were accustomed to making a living and getting food, instead of uprooting to that unknown new place beyond the Missi-se-pe.

Out there, for all anyone knew, the migrating Shawnees might starve and sicken with new diseases before they learned to survive. A move to a new land customarily was made only after long study of sites by the shamans, who would note the plants and the animal populations, the quality of the soil and water and the winds, and make a careful divination of the spirits attendant upon those sites. Though the Shawnees had lived almost everywhere on the land between the Eastern Sea and the Mother of Rivers, they had not moved, like this, without preparation. Who even knew how their strains of seeds would grow on that side of the Missi-se-pe?

So now Turtle Mother was parting from everything good in her life. It was not an ordinary thing to do, this splitting of families, but it could not be seen in the way of usual things because never had the Shawnee nation broken apart before, and now there *were* no usual things, there was just this, which was like the ending of their world. It was as if Kokomthena had finished weaving her seine, and her little dog had failed to unravel it.

There had been many big councils in all the Shawnee towns about this, all through last fall and winter. Chiefs and warriors and women had spoken eloquently about what should be done. The young warriors had snarled and shouted of their hatred for whitefaces. The old men had spoken sadly of the futility of fighting a race of men who poured over the mountains and down the river in growing numbers from some inexhaustible source in the east, especially now that the Long Knife chief Clark had taken control from the British.

Some women had cried that they wanted to lose no more of their sons in useless wars against the white men's forts, while other women had cried that the lives of their lost sons and husbands must be avenged in an unending fight here in the homeland.

News of the war between the British and the Long Knives in the east would sometimes come to these councils, but it was hard to interpret what it might mean for the Shawnee destiny. If the soldier chief called Washington had defeated the British somewhere, the councils would tend to be gloomy. If the British won a battle, the councilors might hope that the flood of American white men might yet somehow be stopped. Once in the winter there had been a joyful report that the British chief Hamilton from Detroit had gathered several hundred Redcoat soldiers and Lakes Indians and had recaptured Vincennes on the Wabash-se-pe from the Long Knives, and that he was calling on all the tribes to join a war council in the spring and make plans together to drive all the Long Knives back over the mountains for good. For a while the councilors had hoped that this might indeed end their troubles with the whites, and those who had wanted to stay and fight had rejoiced at the news.

Thus these councils had gone on and on through the winter, with the two factions forming, with hopes rising and falling and then rising again, and might have gone on for years more without any resolution. But only a few days ago some more stunning bad news had come from the Wabash-se-pe, news that made the discouraged ones feel fully hopeless and the angry ones even more desperate to fight.

The Long Knife chief named Clark, instead of running away from the British chief Hamilton, had made another of his surprises. He had crossed the Illinois lands in winter flood time and recaptured not only the fort at Vincennes but also the British father Hamilton himself and all his soldiers and cannons.

"What is the use now?" cried the old men in the councils. "How can we keep fighting the Long Knives when they are all the way around us and the British can no longer help us? Look what the other tribes are doing. Some are leaving. Others have been going to see this Clark and offer him the pipe of peace. Are we the Shawnees the only people stubborn and blind enough to keep resisting an enemy who does such things? Are we so foolish that we will sit here in the middle and wait for him to fall upon our towns with his cannons, and shatter our homes, and turn our women into carrion for the vultures?"

And by crying these questions they had at last made it necessary to decide.

And so the nation had divided itself, and the septs had divided themselves, even families had divided themseves.

So now on this bleak day, that part of the Shawnee nation, four thousand of them with everything they owned, stood in the cold among the steam-breathing packhorses. Their whole history had been one of wandering from place to place; now once again they were going to somewhere unknown, but this time it was worse because they had broken their oneness.

There were low calls and cries. Men and women were beginning to move, pulling the bridles of the horses. People too old or sick to walk rode with the bags and packs upon the horses' backs or lying on travois litters behind them; anyone able to walk was on foot. The farewells were muffled and subdued. Many of the people who were staying would not come out of their houses to watch the others go, because they felt they were being betrayed, yet behind their sulking faces their souls were crying of loss and their hearts were like bullet lead.

Turtle Mother took her lower lip between her teeth and bit hard to make it hurt worse than her heart so that she would not whimper or groan aloud from the heart pain.

Star Watcher stood with the triplets gathered around her. Chiksika was not here; he was near the front of the column, part of an escort of young warriors who would go along and protect the people until they were safely out of the country controlled by the Long Knives.

Tecumseh stood near his sister, tall and erect, his coppery face stoical, looking at his mother. They had all agreed to part with dignity and not make themselves weak and miserable by touching or embracing; they had done all that in the privacy of the lodge a while ago. To weep and wail as a loved one went away would make that one's steps heavy and the way gloomy. They would not do that to their mother. Her journey was going to be hard and dark enough without that. Tecumseh's heart felt as if it were quaking. He wanted to run to her and bury his face against her warm bosom once more before she turned and went away. Turtle Mother with clenched fists and bitten lip crossed her wrists upon her breast and then stretched her arms toward her family, whose beloved brown faces swam beyond a curtain of tears. Then she turned her back on them and led the horse up the street with the other horses, between the familiar houses of gray bark, past the place where the chiefs Black Fish and Blue Jacket and Moluntha stood watching the departure. As Turtle Mother trudged by them, Black Fish put his fist over his heart and looked at her with a glitter in his black eyes. Beside Black Fish was Black Snake, her husband's friend and successor, who had now given up his role as chief of the Kispokos to stay and fight the Long Knives. Black Snake raised his head and clenched his jaw to acknowledge her passing, and she nodded. Then she let her gaze fall to the ground. It had been a winter of almost constant snow, sleet, and cold rain, and the ground was saturated and the rivers high. Turtle Mother trudged along with her head down and watched the horses' hooves step down, squeezing water out of the grass, then rise up, dribbling mud, then step down, disturbing a puddle, then rise up again dripping and step down again and rise up from the mud with a sucking sound, and the hooves of her horse left prints among thousands of other prints slowly filling with muddy water, all leading toward the west.

After a while she raised her head and looked back toward the place where her children had been standing.

All she could see now were more packhorses and people coming along, their hooves and feet squishing the sodden earth of what had been their homeland.

# CHAPTER 11

## *Chillicothe Town*
## *July 10, 1779*

Tecumseh woke up needing to make water and slipped naked out of the *wigewa* into the warm summer night air to do it. He saw the slightest paling of the morning sky in the east. The town, now with so many empty houses, seemed a forlorn place. Everything had been strange and sorrowful all spring and summer, usually the happiest seasons for a Shawnee boy. He kept remembering his mother going away in the gray weather. When he went back into the *wigewa* to lie back down, a figure stirred under a blanket beyond the fire-ring. It had always been his mother who had slept in that place. Now it was Star Watcher. He sighed. Then he turned onto his side and tried to go back to sleep for a little while. But he could not, for But-lah had entered his mind, and now he began worrying about But-lah.

But-lah had escaped. It was a wonder that he was still alive, but he had escaped.

But-lah had not been executed after all. After surviving the gauntlet in a dozen Shawnee towns, he had been taken to Detroit instead of being burned at Wapatomica, and the British had kept him—for as long as they could. Just days ago the news had come to Chillicothe that But-lah had escaped from Detroit.

It was unsettling news. But-lah was one of the few Long Knives who knew exactly where Chillicothe and all the other major Shawnee towns were. Having been taken from one to another of them, he was surely capable of leading a Long Knife army to any Shawnee town.

The towns were weak now, since the division of the nation. Most of Chillicothe's houses had stood empty since then. Chillicothe had been left with only about a hundred warriors who were well and able. And now most of those, Chiksika among them, had gone away to a council in another

134

village. In Chillicothe now there were only about three dozen young men and boys, and some old men, who could help defend the town in case of trouble. Black Fish was here, having been ill, and the chieftain Red Pole was here also. That was all. The rest of the people in the nearly deserted town were women and children. Chillicothe lay almost helpless. It would be terrible if white soldiers came.

Tecumseh was lying awake listening to the first peeps of morning birds and worrying about such trouble when he heard a distant cry:

"*Puck-a-chee,* danger!"

Then almost at once there were deep-voiced shouts east of the village and a sputter of faraway gunshots, then more yelling and more shots and the whinnying of horses. Tecumseh leaped up and put on his loincloth and reached to shake Star Watcher's foot and wake her. She was already rising and pulling on a dress, listening to the banging gunfire. Just then someone ran by in the half-light outside, crying:

"Up! Up! Get up! Long Knives are here!"

Immediately then the town was full of yelling and screaming. In the east part of town there was much more gunfire. It had grown to a storm of noise. Tecumseh, helping his sister rouse the sleeping children, heard a bullet whack against the roof of the *wigewa,* and fragments of bark rained down in the darkness.

Now from the center of town, Black Fish's resonant voice was bellowing:

"*Pe-eh-wah! Pe-eh-wah!* To the council house! Women! Take the children to the council house!" His voice could be heard anywhere in the sprawling town, even over the gunfire that was banging in the east and southeast quarters. Tecumseh was terribly frightened and was angry with himself for his terrible haste and clumsiness. He did not believe he was as brave as he was supposed to be. He dropped his bow twice and had to grope for it. But when Loud Noise awoke enough to begin howling in terror, Tecumseh had to try to be brave, to calm and control his little brother, to help Star Watcher. He was uncertain whether he would be expected to go out and help fight the Long Knives or go with the children to the council house. Maybe only those with guns would go out against the attackers, and he did not have a gun yet, although Chiksika had been teaching him to shoot one and had promised to bring one back to him from the council.

"Hurry!" Star Watcher cried to him. "Help me bring your little brothers!" The triplets were bewildered, having been awakened to such terror, and were stumbling around and whimpering like four-year-olds. Loud Noise in particular was bawling and bumping into everyone, worse than helpless. Tecumseh grabbed his wrist and pulled him toward the door, following Star Watcher, who had just rushed out leading the other two boys, one by each hand. Loud Noise, who would usually do anything Tecumseh urged him to do, now balked at leaving the *wigewa* and going out into the noisy outdoors. He shrieked and tugged. Tecumseh had to yank him out the door, and then to keep him moving along the street he had to jerk his arm with every step. Naked women and children were running, crying, among the houses, stampeding toward the council lodge in the dim gray morning twilight.

Black Fish was outside his lodge near the council house, shouting to the warriors who were gathering around him. With him was Red Pole, the chieftain. Black Fish had been very ill, but that did not diminish the power of his voice. Not knowing whether the town was surrounded, he was directing the women and children into the refuge of the council house, which was built of tree trunks thick enough to stop bullets and had small ventilation holes in the walls through which guns could be fired out.

"Now, come!" Black Fish cried to his warriors. "The whitefaces at last have come out of their forts, and we can get them!"

This was the right thing to say. The warriors gave the tremolo cry, and Black Fish led them at a run toward the uproar of shooting and shouting.

Tecumseh shoved Loud Noise in among the people who were crowding into the big building, then turned and ran after the warriors.

And then he saw the fires.

In the direction of the shooting there was a yellow glow against the dark woods below the dawning sky. Smoke, yellowed by the flames, boiled up. The warriors screamed in their rage as they ran: the Long Knives were setting fire to the edge of the town.

Now the warriors spread out and began moving at a crouch toward the fires, their weapons ready. Tecumseh drew an arrow and, heart pounding, darted among bark huts, trying to stay near Black Fish and watching for the shouting Long Knife soldiers. He was listening for two particular voices: But-lah's and Boone's. He expected to hear those two and was sure he would recognize them. But he did not hear them yet. Now he had reached a place close enough that he could see a few of the soldiers moving in the distant fireglow between houses. Some of them were on foot, some on horseback. They wore long, pale-colored hunting shirts and strange hats. The noise of their yelling told him there were many, perhaps hundreds. There were enough surely to sweep through the weakened town and kill everybody, burn every building. Surely they could just ride their horses straight through the town and set fire to the grand council lodge with all the helpless people in it. Surely Black Fish and his three dozen men and boys could not keep them from it.

Tecumseh saw several warriors nearby aim their guns and fire. Powder flashed and acrid smoke billowed. Black Fish was yelling at them to be strong and fight hard to protect the People. He knew they would fight with their greatest courage now because they were trying to save their own wives and children and sisters and grandparents. They fired their guns and reloaded, shouting and trilling like demons, sounding like many more than they were, and they kept moving closer and closer to the army of the Long Knives, as if they had no fear of them no matter how many they were. Tecumseh got near Black Fish and followed him toward the fires. He had still seen no good target at this distance for his arrows.

"Look!" Black Fish roared in exultation. "Ha! They are going back!" Some of the whiteface soldiers actually were turning and running away beyond the burning huts, running from these few screaming, shooting Shawnees, and Tecumseh for the first time felt exultation instead of fear. Black Fish was howling in fury and triumph, "Make them run back! Kill them! Be—"

His voice was broken by a strange grunt, and Tecumseh glanced aside and saw Black Fish's leg collapse under him. The chief toppled sideways with his eyes squeezed shut in pain and his teeth bared in a grimace, dropping his musket and clutching at his hip with both hands. Tecumseh was so stunned by this that he forgot about his readied weapon, even about the burning houses and the soldiers. He stood for a moment watching his foster father fall to the ground like a great tree, falling sideways it seemed for a long time before he was on the ground. It was one of those strange and awful moments, like the time when he had felt the earth shake; it was terrible enough to see his great chief and teacher fall in pain; it was even more terrible because for a moment the falling man seemed to be not only Black Fish but Tecumseh himself!

Tecumseh knelt at Black Fish's side, and other warriors had come to him, too, their faces in the fire-tinged dawn full of anguish and doubt. The shooting and yelling went on everywhere, and the air was thick with smoke. A few yards away a dry-bark *wigewa,* roaring with bright orange flames, caved in, sending up a high swirl of sparks.

Black Fish had been shot in the hip socket. He could not move his leg. A sheen of sweat covered his contorted face, and though his mouth was working he could not yet make a voice because of the pain. It was a frightful wound. Black Fish had several bullet scars on his body, but never before had a wound hurt so much that he had grown faint.

When at last he could say something, it was, "Bring Red Pole."

And then he let out a long breath and went unconscious.

Tecumseh, still too much a boy to control his sobbing, helped three grim warriors carry Black Fish back toward the council lodge. In the dawn light, dirty gray smoke was darkening the sky over the whole town and drifting among the shabby bark huts. The shooting was still going on back by the burning buildings, but not so much shooting now.

The warriors had brought Red Pole as told to do, but Red Pole was dead.

Now with their chief unconscious and the only present chieftain slain, the warriors and boys had no one to lead them. Those who had been pressing on the Long Knives began to withdraw, following the ones who were carrying Black Fish and Red Pole, retreating into the heart of the town, shooting back as they came. It seemed to them that there was nothing left to do but get into the council lodge and defend their families until the Long Knives burned it down and killed them all. From what they had seen, the whitefaces numbered about three or four hundred mounted men. There was no hope. The rest of the warriors were not expected to return from the council for many days.

"I killed two," one of the warriors was saying as they carried Red Pole's body. "Maybe I can kill ten more before the end of this."

When Black Fish woke up on a bed of blankets in the crowded council lodge, he asked for Red Pole, saying he would now have to lead. They told him that Red Pole had been killed. He groaned. "Then I must continue."

He had to clench his teeth to keep the pain from pulling him under again. He listened. There was no more shooting. He said, "They do not come yet?"

A warrior who had crept back to watch the Long Knives came and told Black Fish what a strange thing was happening. "They burn houses one by one. Before they set the torch, they go in and carry everything out. They make piles of all this and then they burn down the houses."

Black Fish grimaced. "Such a people! But do they come on?"

The scout replied: "When they saw me they threw themselves on the ground behind those piles of things, and some of them shot at me. Maybe we have made them timid. I think they are too busy stealing things and burning houses to come in and fight us. Maybe they do not know how few we are."

Black Fish was keeping himself as steady as the pain would allow. Change-of-Feathers had dressed the wound. The bones of the socket had been shattered. It was a very unfortunate wound, one that could never be repaired. Change-of-Feathers had a secret medicine made from a woods flower that could dull pain, but it also dulled the mind, so Black Fish would not take any now because he had to keep commanding. Black Fish through the hum of pain could hear the voices of the frightened people in the lodge and the wail of babies. From the southeast came the faint yells of the whiteface looters and the rush and crackle of tinder-dry houses burning. Smoke hung like fog in the sultry air of a hot, windless summer morning.

Black Fish raised his right hand and swept it slowly in an arc, pointing to each warrior and boy in the semicircle before him. "Keep watching the soldiers. See if they have surrounded the town. Get the women and children ready to go up the river and out through the ravine, if that way is open. They can flee on to Piqua Town if the Long Knives try to come farther into town. We will fight from this lodge and delay them as long as we can. Where is my gun?"

A warrior said, "I brought it, Father. It is there behind you. I reloaded it for you."

"Good." He winced. The pain was making his breathing very uneven, and he was drenched with sweat. He saw Tecumseh there and smiled. "You came to fight. I saw you near me. Did you shoot any?"

Tecumseh shook his head. "When you fell, I forgot, Father."

"Eh. Come. Sit here by me. Stay with me while we wait and see what that serpent spawn of a people are going to do. What fools they must be, not to come on. Or cowards. Do they have no leader? We have some luck, I say. Whoever their chief, it is not Boone or But-lah or Clark. Those would not hesitate like this." He groaned again, clenched his teeth, and wiped sweat off his face with the palm of his hand. "Now go out and watch all they do. Shoot at them and yell like a hundred if they try to come farther. And always bring me news. Tecumseh, my son. Hold my hand a while. There is no need for you to go out there. You are meant to live far beyond this day. You will be needed enough before we are done with white men."

By the middle of the morning the whiteface soldiers were so laden with loot that they could not even burn any houses. They had loaded their own horses and had rounded up more than a hundred Indian horses. Black Fish listened in disbelief as his warriors told him that the army was leaving the burned part of town and going back the way they had come. Aside from Red Pole, not a single Shawnee had been killed by this mounted army. Only a few of their bullets had hit the council house. Yet they were going away!

Now a murderous smile came onto Black Fish's hard mouth. His eyes, which had been dull with pain, glittered again. He had his two dozen adult warriors summoned to him, and he told them:

"Get horses from the corral by the river. Follow the whitefaces, as wolves follow the bison. Stay hidden. Shoot them in the back. If they turn to fight, disappear. It is a long way to Kain-tuck-ee, and they are loaded with

loot. They will be slow. Follow and kill them. Follow as far as you please.
Maybe only white ghosts will ride home to Kain-tuck-ee. It is good that they
came so stupidly. What did they do after coming so far? They burned empty
houses and did some thievery. I wish I could ride with you and watch them
fall along the trail. Go. Weshemoneto guards you and helps you today
because what you do is right. You are like the bees whose honey has been
stolen. You will go out and sting. Go and do it."

The warriors were stirred, hot-eyed, eager to go after their enemies even
though they were twenty to one. Tecumseh sat and looked at Black Fish's
profile as he told them all this. A shiver of emotion passed down Tecumseh's cheeks when Black Fish spoke of the bees and the honey and the
rightness. Here was truth. Black Fish was one of those great chiefs who
could arouse men to do anything, with true words about right purposes.
This, Tecumseh just now realized, was a great power. It was as important
as strength itself.

By the time the two dozen warriors had returned the next day, they had
made the whitefaces pay with much blood for their honey. The little party
of warriors brought back thirty scalps of soldiers they had killed, and they
had wounded another sixty or seventy soldiers. By following and sniping
as Black Fish had told them to do, they had made casualties of a third or
a fourth of the Long Knife army. These two dozen warriors had done more
harm to these Long Knife soldiers than hundreds of warriors had done in
all their raids against the Kain-tuck-ee forts. Black Fish was pleased. It
would be easier to die now, having won something.

Though he was not bleeding heavily or wounded in any vital parts, it was
a mortal wound. The infection fire had started in his hip, and even if it had
not, this was the kind of pain that eventually would wear a man down until
there was nothing left of him.

In the Hunter's Moon, after having suffered harder and longer than
anyone had been known to suffer, Black Fish died. It was a time of greatest
desolation. The Shawnees had grown to love him even as they had grown
to love the great Cornstalk, and his burial made them feel that the whole
earth lay crushing their hearts. Tecumseh and his brothers and sister were
orphans again for the second time in five years.

The soul of Black Fish did not go into the ground with his body. It flowed
into Blue Jacket and Black Snake and Black Hoof and Stands Firm and
Chiksika and every other warrior and chieftain who had stayed east of the
Missi-se-pe, even into the boy Tecumseh, and there it grew to be like a
thundercloud. When the time came for this thundercloud to storm, it would

cleanse the country of whitefaces, it would rinse out the valley of the Beautiful River with blood. That was the vow they made in their hearts at the grave of Black Fish.

Many more boats were on the Beautiful River since Clark's victory. And so Chiksika and other young warriors took out some of their lust for revenge by going down to the O-hi-o and ambushing flatboats. They did not bother to take prisoners. They killed everyone, looted the boats, and burned or sank them. Their fury over the death of Black Fish had overwhelmed any mercy they might have felt toward the white people.

But Star Watcher said when he came home, "You killed women and children?"

"I did not myself kill any woman or child," Chiksika answered. "I was busy killing the men." He did not look at her eyes.

"But you did not stop the others from killing women and children?"

"I told you, I was busy fighting white men," he muttered.

"I am not proud of you," she told him, and he looked down.

Tecumseh was astonished that Star Watcher had said that.

Most of what the warriors brought back from these raids were only the things useful in hunting and war: guns, powder, lead, blankets, warm clothing, bullet molds, knives, and swords. They also sometimes brought silver money and tobacco and axes and farm tools and seed. Sometimes they found barrels and bottles of rum or whiskey, but they did not bring these home, except in their aching heads and bloodshot eyes and reeking breath.

Chiksika, after scalping a fat white man he had stabbed to death, had brought the white man's rifle home for Tecumseh, who was now old enough for it. It was a much better weapon than the British musket he had brought him from the council. This was a long rifle with a striped-maple stock inlaid with a star-and-moon design of brass. It was a better gun than Chiksika himself possessed, but his first impulse had been to give it to his brother, so he kept his own old rifle and presented this fine one to Tecumseh.

Also among the things found on that boat had been about a hundred of the squarish things the French priests carried around and called *livres*. Chiksika had picked up several of them and examined them, opening their stiff covers and letting their white leaves flutter in the wind, studying the strange, tiny, black markings. He thought Tecumseh might be interested in seeing some of these, particularly those with pictures in them of men and women in strange clothes. But they were heavy things; just a few would weigh down an arm. So he took only two and threw the rest into the river.

Tecumseh found these items very intriguing and laughed with Chiksika at the odd whitefaces in the pictures inside. But of course the gun was of first importance. There was time now for Chiksika to teach him how to use it well. As for the *livres,* Chiksika said:

"Hide them away in your bed. Someday we might take them to Blue Jacket, who knows the language of their talking leaves, and maybe he can tell us about them. They are not important now. But do not let Loud Noise play with them. He would probably tear them up." Chiksika had less and less liking for the little boy now; though he told Tecumseh to protect him and help him, he himself was disgusted with the child's cunning, whining nature.

Lead and gunpowder were always too scarce to be wasted on practice shooting at inanimate targets. The Shawnees hoarded every pinch of powder not used for hunting, so that they would have enough if another Long Knife army came. "The reason we did not defeat the Long Knives at the Kanawha-se-pe," he told Tecumseh, "was because we ran out of powder." Therefore, Tecumseh's first familiarization with the gun involved aiming and snapping the trigger without load. Then Chiksika said, "Now you will learn to measure and load in the powder and ball. And when it is loaded we will ride down the river and see if you can kill some meat with it. Here. You see the little horn tip tied to the big powder horn? That little one holds just enough powder to load the gun one time. So pour from the big horn into the little horn, and then pour it from the little horn down the barrel. Careful. Do not spill any. Good. Now here. Put this patch of cloth across the muzzle hole and then press the ball down into it with your thumb. Now hold the ramrod like this and start pushing the ball down the barrel. Hold the rod in the middle at first, or it could bend and break. Keep pushing. Sometimes it is hard. Keep on. Push till you feel it stop against the powder."

Tecumseh, his tongue sticking out of the corner of his mouth with his concentration, said, "I could shoot ten arrows in the time I need to load this."

"Yes. In that and in quietness the bow is superior. And it is better in my heart to shoot the bow. But some of the white man's things it profits us to use. Iron kettles and axes. And the gun."

"And what about the *livres?*" Tecumseh asked. "What about their little black language on the white rag leaves? Would this profit us to use?" He had been thinking of the books even while learning the use of the gun.

"I think not," Chiksika said after a moment of hard thinking. "It is surely bad medicine to trap words out of the air like birds and imprison them on rags. Maybe that is one reason why the whitefaces are so bad. Because they do that. Think of doing such a thing to words!"

Nevertheless, Tecumseh hoped he would see Blue Jacket soon. He wanted to talk to him about the *livres* and the rag leaf language in them. He could not stop thinking of them.

At a place where a deep creek emptied into the Miami-se-pe, Tecumseh knelt with his new rifle ready. To his left and right were more hunters, some with bows, some with guns, listening to the oncoming cries and clacking sticks of the women and children who were driving the game toward them. Chief Black Hoof had told the men with bows to shoot first, so the noise of guns would not scare the animals back toward the game drivers too soon.

Now the rustlings of the animals could be heard coming closer as they fled before the noise of the drivers. The hunters were very tense. Soon everything would be happening very fast.

Black Hoof, successor to Black Fish, had organized these game drives, in which almost everybody in Chillicothe was taking part, because the coming winter promised to be very harsh and because individual hunters had not been able to bring in much meat. By the deep burrowing of mammals and the early departure of the blackbirds, the old men had foreseen that the cold would come early and be hard and long. Already the leaves were almost all gone off the trees, blown away by north winds, at a time when the hills usually were still cloaked in gold and scarlet.

Between the days of these game drives, boys were out everywhere along the animal paths, setting snares and making deadfall traps, while old men and women fished with hooks and spears and with barb-tipped arrows attached to fishing cord. The harvest of corn, beans, and squash had already been done, and women and girls were foraging in the woods and marshes for nuts and wild grapes, for berries, for arrowleaf and red sunflower roots, for anything that could be preserved and eaten.

Birds were darting everywhere now, stirred up by the oncoming disturbance, their beating and whiffing wings adding to the storm of noises.

A blur of brown showed in the thicket at the upper edge of the sloping meadow. A young buck deer bounded into the open, swift and handsome. Then it staggered and tumbled with three arrows sticking in it. Two does sprang into the clearing almost at once. Tecumseh heard the soft twang of several bows and the hiss of arrows, and one of the does fell. The other darted in a frantic zigzag flight down the meadow with arrows dangling loosely from two reddening wounds, one in forechest, one in haunch. Tecumseh saw Thick Water rise from a hummock of yellow grass with bow already fully drawn and let fly an arrow that went into her flank and made her spin sideways, her nose pointed at the sky. Another arrow from somewhere sank deep behind her shoulder, and she fell to her knees and then toppled out of sight in the grass.

Through all this there had been no gunshots and no voices except those of the women and children driving the game, still growing closer through the woods above the meadow. As they drew nearer, the brush and grass began shaking with the movement of many small animals. Rabbits came bounding through, and scampering squirrels and lumbering raccoons. A bobcat leaped into the clearing and stopped in a crouch, its ears flattened against its skull, turning, seeing or sensing the men along the edge of the trap. Just as it appeared ready to turn back toward the women, the first gunshot banged; the cat leaped ten feet into the air with a yowl and fell thrashing.

That gunshot, and others that now followed it, threw the frightened animals into a frenzy; they were going in every direction, and soon it became easier to club them or catch them barehanded as to get any kind of a shot at them. Tecumseh, still feeling awkward with a firearm and afraid that a shot anywhere would hit some darting hunter, was about to drop the gun and plunge into the melee with a stick, when he heard men yelling, *"Makwa! Makwa!"*

A large, dark form came loping into sight from his left.

It was a black bear. He saw a red tongue and long white teeth, a thick body of dusty black fur. Finding itself in the midst of men and gunshots and seeing the river downslope at its right, the bear veered toward the water, barreling past Tecumseh and behind him.

Heart pounding, the boy spun about and pointed his rifle at the fleeing form. Other guns were banging very close by, and he saw the bear twitch and stagger as it ran. Nothing happened when Tecumseh pulled the trigger, and he realized that he had forgotten to cock the gun. Pulling the hammer back with a shaking hand, he fired a shot that he believed hit the distant bear, and then he ran down the hill after it. Many men and boys had forgotten the small game and were pelting after the bear, whooping and shooting.

The bear died in the edge of the river, his blood leaking out of several bullet holes and staining the green water. No one hunter could boast that the *makwa* had been his kill, but the joy was great, for even a young bear like this would yield much fat meat and oil for the hard moons ahead.


Star Watcher had lived through twenty and one winters and knew the feel of the hard season's approach. But this year a chilling dread began to build in her even before the first freeze. She could see it in the people and the animals. And then came the winter that the People would never forget. It made them remember what the elders had said: that the evil medicine of the white man had made this a bad land. When the snows came they kept falling on old snows and never melted. For three moons the ground was covered. Lakes, then even streams, froze to the bottom. Trees cracked like gunshots in the night. In the daytime the weak sun shone through a violet haze of frozen air and woodsmoke. The snow was carved into sharp edges and curves by knives of wind, and the crust of it squeaked and groaned under the footsteps of wood gatherers and tore up the snowshoes of the hunters. Few hunters could go out, and some who did never returned. Horses froze, starved, or died of thirst. The meat obtained in the great fall hunts had been far too little and was gone soon, and the people grew gaunt. Days would pass when there was nothing but crumbs and husks to eat or leather to chew. That winter even the little glutton Loud Noise grew scrawny and so dull from misery that even his imagination slept. Sometimes an ice-hard carcass of a dog or horse or wolf would be dug out of the snow, and there would be something in the stomach for a while longer. But on many mornings some person too weak to struggle with firewood or tend a hearth would be found in a cold *wigewa,* frozen stiff in bed. Departing spirits were heard moaning in the winds. Medicine bags and *pa-waw-kas* were handled in the cold lodges, and there was an unspoken mourning for the bountiful ways of the Time Before.

Half the Shawnees were gone away to a strange land, and this place seemed to be dying. The sun seemed farther away every day; the very fire of life was ebbing.

One night in the depth of the Hunger Moon, Star Watcher lay in a nest of hides and blankets with Tecumseh and the triplets and watched a star in the cold sky wink and waver above the smokehole of the *wigewa.* They all slept crowded together now, to get warmth from each other, like a covey of quail. Before they had begun nesting together like this, Kumskaka, Cat Follower, had awakened one morning with three toes frozen and a leg so badly cramped that he could not walk for several days. Except for Tecumseh, the brothers seemed to want only to hibernate. Loud Noise was so reluctant to leave the bed that he would lie trembling with bladder full, and then sometimes in the dim margin of sleep he would dream that he was urinating in a rain puddle or on tree roots, and when the others woke they would find themselves chilled, their wet bedding frozen under them. And there would be all the trouble of that.

This night Star Watcher lay awake thinking of two things: of her faraway mother and of the fire in the fire-ring. She yearned for her mother, whose strong presence she now imagined had been the source of the warmth that was gone from this *wigewa*. Though it had been her mother's choice to leave this land, Star Watcher now felt that she herself should have kept her from going, or gone with her. It seemed to Star Watcher now that if she had agreed to go with her mother, the rest of the children would have gone, too, and the family would be together someplace where it could not be this cold. Of course, Chiksika would not have gone. And if he had not gone, probably Tecumseh would not have gone, either. But she and the triplets would now be with their mother, and it would be a warmer place, there where the white man's evil medicine had not yet killed the sun.

But then Star Watcher remembered that most important thing. She was Watcher of the Shooting Star, and Tecumseh was the Shooting Star. It was meant that she would be where Tecumseh was.

Still, it seemed to her that a great wrong had been done when the family divided itself, and that this slow killing cold was the punishment. She had put Stands Firm, a Chalagawtha Shawnee, above her own family, by choosing to stay where he was. Surely this was a great wrong, though she had meant to do no wrong. She lay wondering whether her mother blamed her for this wrong, which she was only now beginning to perceive.

And Star Watcher was afraid to go to sleep now because the fire in the *wigewa* might go out. One other night it had burned out while she slept, and in trying to start it the next morning with flint and steel, she had become so shaky and numb with cold, and her hands so stiff, that she could not make an ember, and she had cried, and finally Tecumseh had gone out into the blizzard to borrow coals from another house.

If I go to sleep and this burns out, she told herself, we can get coals from someone nearby to start it again in the morning.

But, she began worrying then, if everyone thought that way, all the fires in all the houses might burn out while everyone sleeps. And we could all be dead in our beds as hard as ice like those we find. Or we could all be too cold in our hands to start another fire.

She lay thinking this, and the thought grew larger in the night, and it seemed now that she might be the only guardian of the life fire of the Shawnees on this silent, bitter, frozen night. She was very tired. She watched the star through the smokehole, wondering if the sun would eventually shrink to that size and let the earth freeze.

The flames flickered out while she was not thinking of them. Cat Follower moved in his sleep and put his face against Star Watcher's shoulder. With his warm breath comforting her, she went to sleep.

And while she was asleep Tecumseh slipped out from the robes into the frigid air and laid more sticks and chunks of wood on the shimmering coals, and with a slab he scraped up ashes to bank a core of coals alongside the blaze, a core of coals that would still be alive in the morning even if the flames went out. Then he slid back into the body warmth of his family under the robes, and held his *pa-waw-ka* stone, and thought what his father Hard Striker had so often said about life being a fire inside.

# CHAPTER 12

## *Chillicothe Town*
## *Spring 1780*

Loud Noise peered out of the dark *wigewa* toward the fireglow of the stomp ground, hearing the music of the Singer, the drum, and the rattle shaker, and he giggled. He had been mad at his sister at first, but then he had started thinking of how to get even and now was delighted with the idea that had grown in his head. They might make children stay away from the nighttime stomp dances, but he would make them sorry. He would just have to stay awake until the time came.

Oh, it was so funny what he was going to do! Every time he thought of it, he giggled again. Finally his brothers had asked him what he was thinking, and he had brought them in on it.

He had wanted to watch his sister Star Watcher do the frolic dance, because he knew that tonight she intended to get Stands Firm for good. It would have been something to watch her do that. Besides, Loud Noise, like most children, liked to get in on the grown-ups' dances and caper around with them, imitating them. He thought it was unfair that he was not allowed to. When the adults danced and celebrated the return of life in the world, they were happy, happy as children were supposed to be, and he felt it was his right to be happy then, too. But the Mask Spirit Man would come around dressed in his deer suit, wearing a carved mask with bulging eyes and carrying his bag of snakes, and he would scare all the children away from the stomp ground and tell them they had better go home or he would put their hands in the bag with the snakes.

Tonight when the Mask Spirit Man had pranced toward the triplets with his bag of snakes, Loud Noise had done what seemed to be a bold thing. He reached toward the bag and cried, "Give me a snake, then!" While the Mask Spirit Man was standing there surprised with his bugging eyes and trying to figure out what to do about this, Star Watcher came running over,

148

dressed in her lightest, softest dress for the dance, her eyes full of anger, and scolded:

"You three go home and get in bed where you belong, or I'll get a berry switch and scratch your legs!"

Although Loud Noise had learned the interesting secret that the Mask Spirit Man really carried only tobacco in his bag, not snakes, he was afraid of the berry switch, because his mother and sister had used it on him in past times when he was really bad, and Loud Noise feared pain. So he left the stomp ground with his brothers, but not without a defiant parting gesture.

Lalawethika, He-Makes-a-Loud-Noise, had become good at making a very loud noise indeed with his bottom-hole. In fact, he had become a master at it. He was the only boy ever known who could blow sound from his bottom-hole whenever he wanted to. Other boys could make the funny sounds when, by chance, their bowels were full of wind. But Loud Noise's bowels, it seemed, were always ready. Something in his little round distended belly was always at work, some kind of fermentation that produced the smelly winds all day and all night. He loved to eat corn and hominy and beans and breadwater. His belly was always audible, gurgling and burbling and growling and stuttering. Star Watcher once had said that everything he ate turned to beans. He could save up this smelly wind and let it go when there was a proper occasion. It had become like another language. He could modulate it, make it whisper, make it sputter, make it whistle, even make it speak in syllables. He could imitate a dog shaking itself. A grouse drumming. A quail flying away. A baby bird in a nest. Water boiling. A slow woodpecker on a hollow log or a fast woodpecker on a solid log. A horse blowing its lips. Sometimes he would squeeze his Thunder-Sucker while doing it and say he was letting loose some captured thunder. Of course all this was not a language for expressing goodwill or noble or tender sentiments.

So he used it this night at the stomp ground when Star Watcher scolded him. He turned with his brothers to leave, and when his back was turned to Star Watcher and the Mask Spirit Man, he arched his back, squinted tight his empty eyesocket, and blasted her with a raucous, malodorous retort that could be heard by everyone within fifty feet. It made many of the dance spectators laugh, and it embarrassed Star Watcher, which was of course what the boy had meant it to do.

At midnight, unaware of her little brother's plotting, Star Watcher was hurrying around the line of warriors to take her place behind her chosen man. For so long it had been understood by almost everyone who knew them that Stands Firm would be the one for the beautiful Star Watcher. They probably would have been married by now, but he had always been

away at war. Now he was here, and she was in the greatest state of excitement she had ever known. This was the first happiness she had felt since
her mother had gone. It seemed as if new life were starting.

The lines of paired couples shuffled to the drumbeats, heel and toe of
the left foot, then heel and toe of the right, both lines facing away from the
bonfire and a woman behind each man. Not all the dancers would be
selecting mates this night; most were dancing just for frolic. Most of the
people in the lines were already married.

The shell-shaker girl, with little terrapin shells full of pebbles tied to the
calves of her legs, danced at the head of the line, and her chattering sounds
were in time with the drumbeats, while the old man with the drum was also
singing his chant.

*E a le lo we*
*He e yo he ya*

Then the dancers chanted.

*E a le lo we*
*He e yo he ya*

Then he chanted.

*O we a we a o e o*

The dancers' bodies grew warm and moist, and the rhythms moved their
blood. Star Watcher admired the smooth, splendid brown muscles of Stands
Firm's strong back and shoulders, buttocks and thighs and calves agleam
with sweat and oil in the dancing firelight, and she imagined her hands
moving on those hard, shapely muscles. The heavy silver ornaments in his
slit earlobes bobbed and glittered with every step. Stands Firm was wearing
only a short, narrow, bead-ornamented loincloth, beaded moccasins, and a
feather in his scalplock. Every line of every beautiful muscle was delineated
under his fatless skin; she could almost see the muscle fibers themselves
stretch and contract with such graceful power as he moved, and in her loins
a delicious tingle of desire was building. She moved in a way to make the
insides of her thighs slide together at each step, and this hurried and
enhanced the excitement. All her skin was wide awake to every feeling.
When her loose, light doeskin dress swayed around her, it caressed her hips
and the tips of her breasts. The desire in her loins was coming in waves now,
seeming to flow down with every footstep and drumbeat.

Each woman and girl in the line danced with a cloth scarf in her hand. This scarf was the most important accessory in the dance, and the time had almost come to use it. They had been dancing for a long while, so long that each woman was aware of only the man in front of her and each man of the woman behind him.

And now came the Singer's whoop that meant for all the couples of dancers to touch hands.

Stands Firm reached behind him. Star Watcher put her scarf in the collar of her dress, and when she took his hands, her hands were bare, with no scarf between the skin of her hands and his.

This was the sign of acceptance. It meant that their bodies should soon be touching like this, naked.

And so now it was known what her intentions were, and Stands Firm would have to let her know if he intended the same. At another whoop the line of men dancers turned around and faced the women who had been behind them, and the music and dancing continued. Most of the women held the men's hands with the scarves between them. Only a few couples along the line held each other's bare hands.

Stands Firm was most impressive as he faced her now. His chin was firm, his jaws were square, his skull was a beautiful shape, and his eyes were bright. All the muscles of his chest and belly were firm and agleam. He shuffled close to Star Watcher, so close the front of their bodies touched, and she felt an almost overpowering surge of passion as they pressed together their moving bodies. The region of her *massih* was growing very moist. The Singer chanted his syllables, and now, when the dancers were to chant, they spoke words to each other instead of the meaningless syllables. The impassioned couple spoke to each other of their bright eyes and beautiful faces. They took turns complimenting each other on the strength and symmetry of their bodies. Then Stands Firm said:

"I like how your breasts feel against my stomach."

And she replied, laughing:

"Something stands firm against my belly." He laughed, too.

Then they began caressing with their hands. Her palms slid over his hard shoulders and down his chest and belly muscles, and they felt as good as they had looked.

The two of them might as well have been dancing alone now; they were aware of nobody else. The skin between her thighs was slick. The women in the menstrual hut often talked of this. If enough moisture came from your *massih* to drip or trickle down your legs, you could have no doubt that you were really in love with the man who made it happen. Sometimes men understood what this was or could tell by the smell of it that it meant yes.

But there were always a few men who were so stupid about women that when they touched you between the thighs and felt it, they thought you had wet yourself with urine. Some men in fact were so stupid about all this, said the women in the menstrual hut, that their mothers had to come into the nuptial lodge the first night and help their sons get an erection and then help them guide it into the proper hole of the bride. For that eventuality there was even a passage in the Shawnee laws that told in detail about how a mother should help her son if he was naive like that.

It was quite plain that Stands Firm was not naive like that. He touched her in all the places where she told him she would like to be touched, and sometimes he knew where to touch even before she told him. They moved against each other, and it seemed that most of their power had flowed into their loins; here they pressed each other hardest, almost frantically, as they danced, and everywhere else they felt weak, especially in their legs.

And finally, near the end of the dance, very skillfully and at a time when they were shadowed and no one could see him do it, he slipped his hand in under her dress and between her thighs, and when his hand came out slick and wet he said in a voice almost choked:

"*Neewa,* my wife. Come to my house."

And she replied, her heart pounding, her face hot, her knees getting limber:

"*Niwy sheena,* you are my husband. I come."


When the music ended, the lines of men and women stood facing each other in the firelight, breathing hard. Most, who had danced with a cloth between their hands, said politely to each other, "That was a good dance. *Ni-a-we,* thank you," and parted. But the ones who had danced with their bare hands touching went away in the dark. This was not the old way of marrying. But it was more exciting than the old way.

Star Watcher hurried to her family's lodge, and while her warrior stood in the moonlit street outside, his blood rushing with desire, she slipped inside and gathered up a few of her personal belongings. She could see very dimly the beds of the triplets and stepped carefully, not to awaken them. When her arms were full, she went outside, murmured to Stands Firm, and followed him through the moonlit village. Her soul was singing with joy, and her body was aquiver with desire. She did not notice that three stealthy little figures had come out of the *wigewa* door and were slipping along, following her in the darkness.

She went in the door of Stands Firm's lodge, which would now become her own home. He did not waste time building a fire or even lighting an oil wick. The night was warm, and the couple were already burning. Enough moonlight was coming in through the doorway and the smokehole to see each other by. Star Watcher took the silver circlet off the end of her braid, ran her fingers down the braid to loosen it, and shook her hair free while he, almost moaning with each breath, shucked off his breechcloth and slipped out of his moccasins. She drew her dress over her head and laid it on the ground and shook her long black hair again and stood panting, naked, the moonlight gleaming on her forehead and shoulders and breasts, the musky smell of desire rising all around her. She reached toward him, and her hand found his *passah-tih* jutting up at an angle toward her, stiff as hickory and hot. A woman in the menstrual hut once had boasted that she could hang a shirt on her husband's *passah-tih*. Now Star Watcher could believe that. She flung her arms around him, and he held her for a moment like this, almost fainting with his want, almost ejaculating at the touch of her belly flesh on his member. Then with frantic whisperings he eased her down, and they sank in the shadows onto the blanket of his bough-cushioned bed. He got over her on his hands and knees and sniffed her body from her neck to her ankles. Finally in the half-light he touched her in the musky place and, having found it, crawled tense-muscled upon her and pressed the end of his *passah-tih* into her, past the point of pain. Both were moaning now and pulling at each other's hips as if by sheer passionate strength to forge their loins together forever, and they were blind with the inrushing of their passions, making two halves of the world become one, beginning with unspoken hope to rebuild the diminished People, too blind to notice three little figures creeping like lizards in through the doorway from the moonlight outside.

For a few moments the little figures were still, crouching in the darkness near the door, listening to the whispering moans and the quickening groans from the bed.

Then one of the little figures by the door got up and moved toward the bed. He turned his back on it, stooped over, gave a little grunt of his own, then blew open the sweet sanctity above the nuptial bed with the loudest, wettest, longest crepitation he had ever produced, everything from the dog shaking itself dry to the growling bear. By the time it ended and punctuated itself with a few after-stutters and baby birds, all three of the little intruders were giggling and shrieking with uncontrollable hilarity. They barely had strength left to evade Stands Firm's groping hands and escape out the door to race through the moonlit town, laughing and stumbling over each other all the way home.

The boys pounded gently on the green elm log with heavy clubs. Every inch
of the surface they pummeled, then they rolled the log over a quarter turn
and pounded some more. While Tecumseh thumped the log, he did not talk
much. His mind was upon his Vision Quest, which would be soon. His little
brothers laughed and chattered as they worked. Sometimes Loud Noise
would complain to his sister about how tired he was or protest that Cat
Follower or Stands-Between, his brothers, had hit his stick with theirs. For
once he kept his temper and his wind blowing under constraint; he knew
better than to remind her of the prank he had done on her wedding night.

A few feet away, Star Watcher and two other young married women held
a long pole up alongside a row of upright posts, measured it, then laid it
on the ground and chopped it off to the marked length with a tomahawk.

"Now," Tecumseh said, "let us peel the wood." He ran his knife along
the top of the log, scoring it from one end to the other. Then he inserted
the knife point at one end of the cut, working it in under the outermost
annual ring, raised that layer of wood grain far enough to get a grip on it
with his fingers, and pulled up. The wood fiber, softened and separated by
the pounding, peeled off in a long, pliant layer, which he then cut into strips
as wide as his thumb. The young women, wearing only moccasins and short
loin aprons, came and got the wood strips as he made them and strapped
them skillfully, tightly, around the joints where the pole crossed the upright
posts. These strips, made the same way as the material for baskets, were
better than rawhide for lacing a house together, because they dried to make
very rigid joints and because mice did not gnaw at them as they did at
rawhide.

Thus, bit by bit, the skeleton of the new *wigewa* went up. It was to be
a rather large house, because not only Stands Firm and Star Watcher but
also her four young brothers would dwell in it. In marrying Star Watcher,
Stands Firm had at once acquired a large family.

Later in the day, when both side walls were up, poles bent into curves
were laced onto the walls to frame the roof. These curved poles contained
a tension that made the whole frame very strong, so strong that the sweating
women could climb upon the frame as they built it.

They finished the frame that afternoon, but the boys still had to keep
pounding and peeling the log, because more strips would be needed to
secure the bark slabs and woven mats that would cover the frame. Sometimes the young women who were helping Star Watcher would have to
leave to attend to their own chores, but other women, young and old, came
to help. Some brought mats, or reeds to make mats; some brought pots of
food or chunks of maple sugar for the boys to eat as they worked. The
building of a house was a hopeful and joyous thing. And to the house of

the much admired Star Watcher, and her esteemed warrior husband and her star-marked brothers, many of the people wanted to add something.

At the end of that day, Tecumseh went to the river and bathed, sluicing off the pungent wood sap and the wood fiber that clung everywhere on his sweaty skin, and picked minute splinters out of his hands. Then he went up through the town toward the little old *wigewa* where he and his brothers still slept and would sleep until their new house was finished. Clean and tired, he went up the lanes of Chillicothe Town, through the appetizing aromas he had known all his life: stews, Shawnee cake, roast bird and squirrel, fermented breadwater. He knew the various smokes, of maple-wood, hickory, red cedar wood, kinnick-kinnick, and tobacco. The sounds of the hundreds of people were like a comforting music—the sounds of their working and their games, their voices laughing or singing or scolding. To be in the midst of the People was to be secure. Every winter survived made the presence of the People more comforting, and that hardest of all winters, whose memory was still fresh, had made the oneness ever sweeter. Outside, the world was dangerous, harsh, lonely. Tecumseh had never in his life been entirely alone outside the enveloping care of the People.

Soon, though, he would be. When his sister's house was finished, Tecumseh would have to go out alone in the wilderness naked and unarmed on his Vision Quest. It was time. The shaman, Change-of-Feathers, had encouraged him to do it this spring, being certain that special meanings for the People would be revealed in the vision of the boy who had been born under the sign of the Panther Star. This was a most uncertain time for the People; Change-of-Feathers believed that much of the guidance for the Shawnee nation would come through this boy's Spirit Helper.

Tecumseh faced the coming quest with both eagerness and dread. Most boys were a year or two older before anyone urged them to do it. The subtle pressure put upon him by the elders seemed to be a part of that special burden of his, that burden of duty his father had told him of so long ago. Tecumseh walked up through the sunset-flooded town of his People with a bittersweet anxiety in his throat.

When Star Watcher neglected to feed Tecumseh with the other boys this morning, and they all looked so strangely at him with their mouths full and the breadwater drooling from their lips, he had the same feeling of empti-ness on the outside of him as inside. Belly hunger was not a new feeling, but to be alone, to be left out of the circle of care, was something he had never known, and he realized that the Vision Quest would be an even more forlorn ordeal than he had believed.

He could already feel how the black paint on his face set him apart from everyone. It was only soot and bear grease, and he had smeared it upon his face this morning at the beginning of his fast, but, like a mask, it made him something other than he had always been. It was even worse than a mask; when you wore a mask, you became someone you had not been before, but when you wore the mask of black, you became no one. People, your own people, were not to see you. The black told them that nobody was there where you stood, so they would not speak to you or offer you food or water, for who would offer anything to a nothingness?

"I go now," Tecumseh said, his heart chilled and aching. He rose and went to the door, but Star Watcher did not answer him or even look his way. Loud Noise looked at him and started to say something, but she shushed him and said, "Finish, little brother. Our Grandmother says not to waste food, remember?"

"I never waste food!" he retorted, then silenced himself by cramming another spoonful of the pale pulp into his mouth. It was true that Loud Noise never wasted food. In fact, if anyone else left food, Loud Noise saw to it that it did not go to waste. Tecumseh knew that his sister had said that only to draw the boy's attention back into their circle, away from the black-faced nothingness that was setting out from the *wigewa:* himself.

And then the people he passed in the town, who usually had smiles and greetings for this star-favored boy, looked through him, too, and said nothing to him, and by the time he left the edge of Chillicothe to go into the woods, he felt excluded from the bigger circle, the circle of the People, as well as from the circle of his family.

Now he was as empty as a living body could be, empty so that there would be nothing in him to keep the Spirit Helper from approaching. He had no food in his belly, no clothing, no fire striker, no weapon. He was as close to being a spirit himself as a person with a body could be, and if in the next four days a Spirit Helper chose to approach him in the wilderness, it would be as if it came to a nameless, unformed, undressed spirit, a babe. That was the way it was supposed to be, and he knew that was the way it was supposed to be, but he had not expected to feel this way, so utterly outside.

What Tecumseh did not know was that Star Watcher and everyone else who, without looking, had seen him go, prayed that he would be safe in the wilderness and that a very good Spirit Helper would approach him. He only thought he was outside their circle of care.

Tecumseh swam across the Miami-se-pe north of Chillicothe and climbed into the woods on the high bluffs on the other side. Something was supposed to tell him where to go to wait for his Spirit Helper, but for a long time his soul was so desolate that he perceived nothing, and he just walked. He was a lone creature in the woods without family or tribe, and he grew more and more timid, like a deer or a rabbit. Much later in the day when he heard some hunters approaching, going toward the town, he did not want to see them look through him, because that was too painful to bear again. And so, like a deer or a rabbit, he darted into hiding from the hunters. They passed near his hiding place without seeing him, which was what they would have done even if he had not hidden.

The hunters who passed beyond the foliage were his friend Thick Water and a Chalagawtha youth also just coming of warrior age. They were on foot. Thick Water carried a large rabbit, and the other carried a turkey. The dead animals left a musky odor that Tecumseh could smell long after the sound of the hunters' footfalls had faded away. He wondered what Thick Water would think if he knew he had hidden from him and watched him go by. How many animals must watch us in the woods, he thought. Some are probably watching me now. Though I am a nothing.

He stepped out and, for no conscious reason, chose to go along the way from which they had come, to follow their trail backward. For a while he could smell the lingering animal musk. When it became too faint to detect, he went on along their trail, keeping to it by the traces they had left: a moccasin print, a bit of turkey feather, a drop of rabbit blood. It was the first time he had ever followed a spoor in the other direction. He felt as if he were moving the other way on the Circle of Time, that somewhere ahead of him he would find them killing the rabbit and the turkey. It was contrary to the usual way of things, so it seemed to be the way he should go in an occasion like this, when all experience was upside down. There was said to be powerful medicine in all that was contrary. Sometimes the spirit of the Trickster could be heard chuckling among the other sounds of the world. The Trickster was always around, always foxlike and mocking, always making contrary things happen and then laughing at what he had done. Often the Trickster seemed to be inside his brother Loud Noise.

By the middle of the day, Tecumseh had reached the place where the turkey had been shot, a small glade where the ferns were marked by gouts and spatters of dried blood and had been trampled down by the hunters' feet. Here a turkey hen's life had ended. He saw the story of her death in his mind. Then he had to choose whether to follow the turkey's trace backward along the Circle of Time or the hunters'. It seemed he should follow theirs, so he looked about until he found the place where they had knelt to shoot and where they had approached the glade from the west. By the middle of the afternoon he had gone on a curving course through woods and meadows and was on a grassy hill that he knew to be about half a day's walk straight north of Chillicothe. He had come by this hill sometimes while riding with Chiksika between Chillicothe and Piqua. On the other side of the hill, he knew, was the trace between the two towns. Here on this hill he found the place where the rabbit's life had ended: another spray of dried blood, more footprints. He seemed to feel the rabbit's spirit in the air about this place.

If he kept tracing the hunters backward, he would return to Chillicothe, whence they had set out on their hunt. So he crossed the hill and went instead along the road toward Piqua.

At dusk he was in a place he knew well. Hardly aware that he had come so far, he had found the spring near Piqua beside which he had been born. Something had drawn him to the place where his life had begun. He had never heard of anyone standing vigil for his Spirit Helper at the place of his own birth. But had he not been going backward on the Circle of Time? It seemed to him that this was the place where he was meant to come; he had not come here by trying to come here.

The only trace of the hut he had been born in was a weathered post of black locust wood; Chiksika had told him that was the old center post. Everything else had fallen and rotted away in the twelve years of his lifetime.

He sat on the moss beside the spring, and its trickling and burbling sang to torment his thirst. But he was not to drink, though he had traveled all day in the heat. He had crossed creeks, but his moccasins and breechcloth, all he wore, had dried on him. For a while he rested comfortably as the sun went down, its rays peeping through the darkening foliage. But having fasted all day and walked so far, he had nothing in him to fuel his body, and by the time the woods had darkened and the mosquitoes were humming all around, his skin was cold and he began to shiver. He closed his right hand about the little *pa-waw-ka* stone in its tiny bag that hung from his neck, and asked Weshemoneto to fan the fire inside him, and felt the warmth holding in his center. Then he tried to ignore the biting mosquitoes and to empty his mind and calm his heart, so that if a Spirit Helper approached in the darkness, it would not sense a turbulence here and veer away. Change-of-Feathers had advised him of all this.

Through the long hours of darkness he sat, hearing but trying not to listen to the creakings and whirrings of the night insects, trying not to let the assertive hoots of the barred owl or the monotonous whistle of the saw-whet tell him bad things. Now and then, as the world moved around the Circle of Time, a star would show through the high black canopy of treetops, then disappear, and Tecumseh would be tempted to move his head this way and that till he could see the star again. It was something he had done countless times while lying in his bed: looking up through the smoke-hole, trying to watch a particular star while his mind went everywhere, until the turning of the world would move that star away from the smokehole. But now he was not supposed to yield to the temptation of watching stars and thinking; he was supposed to sustain that still, empty readiness that was the prayer for a Spirit Helper.

Through the night it was hard to keep from thinking about his hunger. And it was hard to keep from being alarmed by rustlings he heard in the darkness around him. He had, as a hunter, trained himself to listen to sounds in the woods and concentrate upon each noise until its characteristics told him what kind of bird or animal was stirring nearby. But now he had to unlearn all that, to make himself *not* perceive and identify but instead to listen with his soul only, for something from the Messengers. But it was hard not to be alarmed. When one was light-headed from hunger and weariness in the dark, one heard noises grow closer and louder; a mouse could sound like an opossum, an opossum like a bear. Many a boy who had considered himself brave had broken his vigil and fled homeward in blind panic at the approach of a raccoon. Sometimes, Change-of-Feathers had said, this panic was caused by the Trickster, whose laughter could be heard behind the fleeing boy.

After the middle of the night, or so it seemed to be, Tecumseh thought he was seeing a bluish glow in the corner of his vision. There was no sound, but he thought he could feel some sort of buzz or vibration in the still air. He felt the hair rise on the nape of his neck and tried to look toward the glow. But it seemed to move farther to the right as he looked right. Sometimes it would seem to be moving around in front of him, but then when he would try to see it, it would again move to the edge of his sight, and he could not even be sure he had seen it. It did not behave like anything of the touchable and visible world. Whatever it was, it was of the spirit world.

In his memory of stories and legends there was only one glowing blue spirit: that shape assumed by a Bear Walker when he left his body lying somewhere and roamed through time. Once, Chiksika had told him, once when Eagle Speaker had left his body, people had seen the glowing, shim-mering blue shape of a bear move on all fours in the vicinity. It had passed into the night woods, fading. Before the next dawn, it had been seen returning to the place where Eagle Speaker's body lay. Then it had vanished like an extinguished flame, and when the sun had come up, Eagle Speaker had awakened as from a deep sleep, saying he had been far away on the Circle of Time and that he had seen things that were yet to happen, things

that he could not yet speak of because people were not yet ready to understand them.

Tecumseh, nearly frozen with terror, waited for the shimmering blue
bear for a long, long time. If it were a Bear Walker, and if the Bear Walker
were Eagle Speaker, surely it would not harm him. Nevertheless, he did
not want to see the blue bear glowing close in front of him. A Spirit Helper
was not supposed to be something like that. A Spirit Helper was a Shape
Shifter, but when it appeared it was not supposed to be in a frightening
shape. Change-of-Feathers had told him so.

And so the blue glow remained in the corner of his eye, neither seen nor
not seen, until a moment when Tecumseh suddenly realized that daylight
had come. The sun was already far enough up that its narrow beams were
slanting in through the mist of the woods.

It was the time of morning when there should have been the sounds of
many birds. But he was struck by the silence; it was as if he had awakened
deaf.

And while he was thinking in wonder of that, he heard one sound, one
sound only:

*Coo-ah, coo, coo, coo.*

There not four paces in front of him, as if it had formed itself from the
drifting mist around its own mournful call, was a dove, its left side toward
him, one eye seeming to watch him. But its color was not the dove's familiar
ruddy gray; it was white, the faintly bluish white of snow in shadow.
Tecumseh long ago had dreamed of a white bird. A white animal of any
race of animals was rare and considered to be a chief of that race. This would
be the chief of the doves. When animals spoke to people, it was usually
through their chiefs, the white ones like this. Tecumseh was certain that this
was the form of his Spirit Helper, and he watched it intently waiting for its
message.

But it gave no message. Instead, as he blinked, it became mist again, was
gone. The green leaves and mosses shimmered in the sunbeams, and the
morning sounds returned in a rush: birds twittering, insects droning, the
spring gurgling.

To Tecumseh, this seemed very bad. Clearly the dove had been his Spirit
Helper, but it had told him nothing and had gone abruptly. For a while
Tecumseh sat in deep despair and thought of going home.

No, he thought. I have four days. The dove showed itself to me the first
morning. Good. Before the four days have passed, surely it will speak.

And so he did not move from the place. The sun slowly rose high and
a long time later began to descend. Small animals of every kind came to the
spring during the afternoon, looking at him warily, then deciding he was

no danger. They drank at the spring, preened themselves, went away. A raccoon came and washed a white piece of root in the spring, then ate it while watching Tecumseh with its glinting dark eyes in its black mask.

I too have a black mask, Tecumseh thought toward the raccoon, and it seemed for a moment as if he and the raccoon were laughing together about that, though they made no sound.

Tecumseh could have caught some of these unfrightened creatures with his hands and eaten them, but of course he did not, though his stomach hurt with hunger.

At dusk he rose, his whole body stiff, and went away from the spot to relieve himself, then returned and sat again upon the moss and waited for the second night.

In the night the bluish glow again came and hovered on the edge of his vision. This time it did not frighten him so much. But again it did not become the shape of a Bear Walker.

After many hours of darkness the trees began to sigh. He saw flickerings of light beyond the treetops, then heard the faraway rumble of thunder.

The storm came closer. Cyclone Person began to rush through the treetops. When the eyes of the Thunderbirds would flash their lightning, Tecumseh could see that the trees were waving violently. Twigs and leaves and butternuts began to shake loose from the treetops and tumble, pattering, down through the foliage. Somewhere behind him a great limb or whole tree fell with a loud rushing and crackling, then an impact that shook the ground. A blaze of lightning whitened the whole swaying forest, and immediately there followed a wingbeat of thunder so loud that the earth shook. Then there were more and more of these bolts of light and noise. The entire forest was in a wild dance with Cyclone Person, and bits of blown chaff and bark stung Tecumseh's back and cheeks. At last there came a cold, wet breath of wind, and soon the rain came rushing through the woods, cold, driven rain that soaked his hair and streamed cold down over his naked skin.

Sometimes it was the beating of the Thunderbirds' wings and the falling of trees they knocked down that made the soaked earth seem to tremble. But once, after the flashing and thundering had moved away to the east and only the steady rainfall remained, Tecumseh seemed again to feel the earth shuddering, deep below where he sat on the wet moss.

He was himself shuddering now, gasping and shivering in the hushing, dribbling darkness. He clutched the little wet deerskin bag that held his pa-waw-ka and prayed for the fire in his core not to be extinguished. He remembered the banked coals in the fire-ring at home, thought of Star Watcher and her warmth, thought of his faraway mother and her warmth.

The wet moss chilled him where he sat on it. His hands were cold. It was not, of course, nearly as cold as when he had plunged into the icy river to find his totem; it was summer now. But he had been only moments in the wintry river and exerting himself. Now he had been wet and chilled for most of the night, immobile, and he had eaten or drunk nothing for two days. He was shuddering almost constantly. In his misery he was not aware anymore of the bluish glow, and the image of the white dove, when he thought of it at all, seemed to have been no more than a long-ago dream. Now the discomforts of his body were so great that he could hardly keep the purpose of his quest in mind. Over and over he would try to return to the vacant calm of the prayer, but he was too full of his misery. This made him fear that he was not strong enough in spirit to be all that the elders expected him to be. He felt unworthy, and feeling unworthy made him quake more in his cold and lonely pit of darkness. His mind kept taunting him, asking him why he had not caught something to eat yesterday, why he had not built a brush shelter to squat in, why he had not started a campfire by friction to light and warm the little shelter he should have made.

How he longed for a little campfire! From almost the Beginning, his ancestors had spent their nights gazing into campfires; they had considered their gods and worked out everything they now lived by while talking around fires. To spend a night with no fire was like being in that frightening time before the Creator had provided fire. To sit in the dark without a fire was contrary. How good the smoke of a cookfire would smell now, instead of the dank smell of soaked humus and wet leaves! How good to be in the dry, warm *wigewa,* spooning steamy hominy or squirrel broth out of a kettle, with his sister's smiling face telling him, "Take more, dear brother! You never eat enough!"

The rain stopped near dawn, but for a long time as the forest grew gray and then dull green, the woods were full of dripping, and whenever a part of his skin would become nearly dry, another cold dribble or shower of rainwater would come down from the leaves above and spatter him with a hundred more chills. With daylight came breezes that shook still more cold drops down on him. He hoped the sun would come out and warm the world, but the day was clouded, gloomy, chilly. The woods were full of fog.

At last it was light enough to find the way home. Home was far to the south, and he doubted that he had enough strength to go there. Perhaps he could make it to Piqua and eat there, then go home. . . .

Then he remembered the blackness on his face. Probably it was gone now, after these days and nights, after the rainwater that had washed him for hours and hours. He raised his hand to rub his cheek, gazing dumbly at an oak limb a few paces in front of him.

*Coo-ah, coo, coo, coo.*

There, around the call, the mist again formed the shape of the dove, and everything suddenly was silent again.

The dove sat on the oak limb, its one dark eye seeming to look at him as it had before. The dove did not call again, but from it was coming, instead of sound, something else, something like a pressure in the air. When this enveloped him, Tecumseh suddenly felt warm, and his despair was gone. Then he could open himself again to receive the messages.

They did not come as words or as thoughts or even as images. But they came and filled him with understandings. First, that this was indeed his Spirit Helper. And that it would return at proper times. That it was to aid him with the needs of the People. That it would guide him, that it would alert him to signs, that it would cause him to have dreams in which would lie answers. That he was for the People, and that the white dove was for him. That someday, when the People's needs were most dire, the way would be made clear.

All this comprehension diffused into Tecumseh during the time he sat looking at the dove. He did not know how long that was. It seemed like only a moment or like always. When the dove finally dissolved into mist again, Tecumseh was refreshed and strong. He sat, remembering, in the wet woods. At last he rose to his feet, went to the spring, cupped his hands full of clear water, and drank it from between his wrists. He washed his hands, face, and body in the cold water. And then, grateful but humbled, feeling as weightless as a spirit, he set off down a path for the trail toward Chillicothe, toward food, to the embrace of his tribe and his family.

# CHAPTER 13

## *Chillicothe Town Summer 1780*

Oone day in the Raspberry Moon, Tecumseh, Thick Water, and Chiksika stood together at the riverside south of the town, with most of the residents of Chillicothe, watching the British soldiers bustle around their rolling-gun and waiting for the promised excitement. It was a mild, beautiful morning. The bottomland was full of tiny flowers. The cannon was pointed toward a pile of logs and brush on the riverbank. Four of the Redcoats worked with pails and strange-shaped poles, putting black powder in the muzzle. Their captain, named Byrd, a large, elegant, pink-faced man, shouted words to them.

"So much powder!" Chiksika said. "It is as much as I have used in my life, and they are going to shoot once with so much!"

The people were standing close in bunches of friends and relatives, most holding hands or unconsciously touching. They had never seen a rolling-gun, though they had been promised to them for years, and so now the British captain would show them the power it would have against Long Knife forts, by shooting the woodpile on the riverbank. He had been showing off the cannon in town after town as he moved south from Canada toward Kain-tuck-ee. The power of the cannon had influenced six hundred warriors to join Captain Byrd so far—Ottawas, Delawares, Wyandots, and Potawatomies as well as Shawnees from the upper towns.

Something about the way the British soldiers moved and handled things, something about the shiny brass muzzle poking out from between the tall, spoked wheels, made Tecumseh conscious of the power of it even before it was shot. Most of the people had never seen anything on wheels before, and from the moment yesterday when the big horses had pulled the gun rumbling and rattling through the town, escorted by red-coated British soldiers and Canadian rangers in green, the Shawnees had sensed the awful,

164

waiting force of this white man's object. Obviously it had great importance. But bad spirit seemed to hover around it. It had stood mute all night near the grand council lodge, gleaming in firelight, and people had come around for hours to look at it and speculate. It was said that Captain Byrd had five other cannons in his flotilla over on the Great Miami-se-pe, and that he had nearly a hundred more of these Redcoats and fifty more Greencoats. The cannons, and such numbers of troops, for the first time made the Shawnees really aware of the war between the British white men and the American white men and that they themselves were being made a part of it. It made them feel a little less hopeless about the presence of the Long Knife Chief Clark out west. It was said that Captain Byrd was going to take his cannons down to the Great Falls of the O-hi-o, where Clark had built a fort, and attack him there.

Through the night, the British soldiers had guarded their cannon against anyone's touch. Even though this Captain Byrd said he had brought the cannon for the Indians, they were not allowed to touch it. Tecumseh did not want to touch it anyway because of its spirit. So the people had looked at it in the firelight and talked about what they had heard of the power and noise of such guns. The triplets had kept everyone awake late into the night with their restlessness.

Now on the riverbank no one was talking, except Captain Byrd. Near Captain Byrd stood Black Hoof, the dignified, handsome, graying Chalagawtha who had succeeded Black Fish as principal chief. The bringing of this rolling-gun had been promised and promised during the time of Black Fish, but it had at last come only under the time of Black Hoof, and he, with this great responsibility, was perhaps as nervous as all the rest of the residents put together, though he stood steady and tall and resolute. Near Black Hoof and Captain Byrd stood the wiry, black-haired white man named Simon Girty, who was their interpreter.

Now a soldier put a heavy iron ball in the muzzle, and another pushed it in with a pole. This was familiar to all the Indian men, who knew it was like loading a musket. But each man was thinking of the size of that ball and of the amount of black powder that had been put in before it. They all knew what a ball the size of a hazelnut would do; now here was one the size of a squash! Another soldier stood near the back end of the gun with a small stick of something that smoldered and gave off wisps of smoke.

Captain Byrd said something, which Girty then translated to Black Hoof, and then Black Hoof announced to his people:

"This gun will make a big noise when it is shot. If this noise makes you shut your eyes, you might not see the ball hit that wood down there. He wants you to see it hit the wood because that will show you what it can do to the gates of the Long Knife forts. This is what our friend and ally Captain Byrd has just said to me." Then Black Hoof looked at Girty, who nodded.

Captain Byrd's pink face looked all around now. He made a motion with his hand to some boys who had moved too far forward. Then he looked at the soldier who held the smoldering stick and shouted at him. Everyone was absolutely still. A mockingbird was making its silly songs down by a large tree that stood in the middle of the marsh.

The soldier lowered the burning stick toward the top of the cannon, and Tecumseh could see from the flinching tension in his face that this was the moment. He glanced at Thick Water and saw him blinking, blinking.

The Indians lived in a quiet world, a world of wind, water, and stealthy animals. Aside from the crack of a musket or the thunder of a storm, seldom did a sound louder than the shout of a voice come to their ears.

The cannon bucked and issued a cracking roar so loud, it hurt Tecumseh's head and made him jump and gasp. He felt the shock pass through the soft earth under his feet. A tongue of orange flame and a huge plume of blue smoke shot out thirty feet in front of the cannon. The shock of the blast was so overwhelming to him that he hardly remembered to look at the target.

When he looked, nothing had happened to the wood. But beyond it he saw a spurt of water in the river, no more than that of a big fish jumping.

Tecumseh's ears were ringing. He looked at Black Hoof. Black Hoof looked at Captain Byrd. Captain Byrd's pink face had gone red. His cannon had missed the pile of wood.

Someone in the crowd had recovered enough from the pain of the noise to laugh. It was a young man called Copper Hair, who lived at Piqua Town and had come over with warriors from there to see the cannon. Copper Hair was a white captive who had been adopted into the tribe four or five years ago. Chiksika knew him. When the people heard Copper Hair laugh, they realized that what they thought had happened really had, and they laughed. Now Captain Byrd was almost as scarlet as his coat. He said something to Girty, who was trying not to smile. Girty said something to Black Hoof, who then raised his hand to hush the tittering and said:

"Our friend and ally Captain Byrd explains that he now has tested his gunpowder, and finds that it did not get wet in the recent rains. Now that he knows the gunpowder is good, he will shoot at the pile of wood that we made for him beside the river."

Tecumseh felt Chiksika's hand touch his shoulder and looked up at him, and Chiksika said with a smirk: "Even if they are our allies, the white man cannot say the truth to us."

This time when the soldiers had the cannon ready and had reaimed it, the people put their palms over their ears. The soldier touched it with the burning stick, and it bucked and flashed and smoked again.

And almost at the same time, the big pile of wood down by the river flew into pieces. The people's faces were full of amazement. Logs and branches and bark and splinters twirled in the air and splashed in the river. The people cried out. Captain Byrd said something, Girty spoke, and Black Hoof announced:

"Now our friend and ally Captain Byrd tells us we have seen that no fort in Kain-tuck-ee can stand against the power of this cannon. As for myself, I can see that if they can hit the forts, this will be very useful to us."

And it seemed that in this, at least, was truth.

After the demonstration, when all the people were milling around talking to each other, Tecumseh asked Chiksika to take him to the youth named Copper Hair, the one who had first laughed when the cannon missed.

This young man was very agreeable to look at. His face was red brown like a red man's, but his hair was also dark red, and his eyes were blue. It made him strange to look at. But he was a Shawnee now. Chiksika said to him, taking his hand, "Copper Hair, welcome, if your ears can still hear me. Here is my brother Tecumseh. I have told you of him."

The red-haired one had a pleasant smile, and when he took Tecumseh's hand, Tecumseh saw that his hand had little golden hairs on it. "I have heard much of Tecumseh. They say you were born under a star. Maybe you are going to be a savior."

"I am expected to do something sometime, it is said. But now may I ask you a question, brother?"

"I will answer if I can."

"When you lived with the white men . . ." Tecumseh began. One never said to such an adopted one, when you *were* a white man. "When you lived with them, did you know how to understand the black language on the white rag leaves?"

Chiksika laughed. "I could have guessed that's why you wanted to talk to Copper Hair! You two talk of that, then. I am more interested in this cannon." He and Thick Water went to join some young warriors who were near the rolling-gun.

Copper-Hair looked puzzled. "What did you say?" he asked Tecumseh. "Black language?"

"In the *livres.*"

"Leaves?"

Tecumseh shook his head and grimaced, frustrated. Then he held his left palm open and made over it a motion of turning pages, as he had seen French priests do.

"Ah! Ah, I see! Books!"

Tecumseh tried to repeat the strange word. "Pooks."

"Books. Yes, I could understand books. I could . . ." He said another strange word, having no Shawnee word for it. "I could *read* books."

"Read."

"Read. That means, to look in a book and see what all the words mean. My father had many books. I could read very well. Even my sisters could read."

"Sisters could read?"

"Yes. We were a rich family. My father was a great builder. He made big houses. Council houses. And bridges."

"British? Your father built British?"

The red-hair laughed. "Bridges. They are like wooden roads from one side of a river to the other. But we were talking of books."

"Yes! Books! Brother . . . Ah! What do the words in the books mean?"

"Every book means something different. First, there is the Bible . . ."

There was another word. "Bi-buh?"

"Bible. The Bible is the greatest of all the books!"

"Ahhh!" Tecumseh was feeling a strange excitement from hearing of all these unknown things. "Why is it greatest, this Bi-buh?"

"Oh! Because it is the word of . . . God."

" 'God'?"

Now Copper Hair was getting excited, too. "We call him Weshemoneto. The white men call their Great Good Spirit, God."

Tecumseh stood with his head tilted and his mouth open, absorbing all this. A few yards away, Chiksika and some of his comrades were having an equally taxing conversation with Simon Girty and the Redcoats about cannons, with much puzzlement in their faces and much head nodding. Tecumseh said to Copper Hair: "You had the word of Weshemoneto in a *livre?* In a, a, a book? How can this be? Tell me!"

Copper Hair's eyes were sparkling, and he could not keep his hands still. Something was stirring him very much. "Listen, Tecumseh," he exclaimed. "I would like to tell you all this! But they are taking me back to Piqua Town today. They brought me here to help interpret what the British say. If you can come to Piqua Town someday, with your brother, we will talk for a long time. You ask me things no one has asked me since I have been Shawnee. I want to tell you so much that I remember!"

Tecumseh was looking at Copper Hair now out of the side of his eye. He said cautiously: "When . . . when you were among the white men, did you, ah . . . *like* it?"

"Oh, yes!" Then Copper Hair seemed to draw something down inside

himself, a caution, and said: "It is better being Shawnee, of course. But
. . . but my father, my family . . . oh, they were the best sort of white people. . . ." He seemed terribly agitated, and his eyes were intense on Tecumseh's face. "Listen. If I tell you a secret, will you keep it? On your word?"

"I keep all secrets told to me."

"I've so wanted to tell this to someone, anyone . . ." His voiced dropped
to confide. "It could be dangerous if people knew it. . . . Oh, never mind.
Maybe it is better that I keep still. . . ." Copper Hair looked afraid now;
he was biting his lower lip, as if he should never have said any of this.

"Brother, you do not have to say it," Tecumseh said. "But if you want
to, I will tell no one else."

Copper Hair looked at Tecumseh for some time, plainly very nervous.
Then he said:

"Then I'll trust you. I told you, my family was the best sort. None braver.
None smarter. You . . . you have heard of the Long Knife chief called
Clark?"

Tecumseh shivered at the name. He nodded.

"The one," Copper Hair went on, "who captured all the British forts
and caught Hamilton?"

"Yes. We have heard much of him."

"Listen: I was on a journey with him when I was captured. . . ."

Tecumseh was awestruck. Here was a man who had known the terrible
Clark! Tecumseh had a hundred questions suddenly. But Copper Hair was
whispering on:

"It was Christmas Day of seventy-six, the last date I was ever to know
of for sure. . . . This Clark you know of . . . I was with him. . . . Secret?
Promise? Because he's my cousin!" Copper Hair whispered this urgently.

"Clark is your cousin!"

"Yes! His mother is a sister of my father! We grew up together, all us
cousins, all more like brothers!" Tecumseh was obviously awed. Copper
Hair hurried on, as if this information had been needing to burst out of him
in words: "Oh, what a man he is, cousin George! Whenever I hear of him
I shiver. How I've wanted to speak of him, when I hear tell of what he's
done. But maybe they'd kill me if they knew . . . or put me up as hostage.
. . . But he is my cousin, oh, yes. And there's no finer a man. I just wish
I could come out and *brag!*"

"This Clark, you mean, is *good?*"

"Good? No finer a man! He's a long-seer . . . always keeps his word. And
. . . have you ever known anybody who can talk of a thing so that you want
to jump up and *do* it?"

"Yes!" Tecumseh was thinking of Chiksika. And of Black Fish, especially

Black Fish. Here again was this idea of the power of words, of which Black Fish had made him so aware. Even among the white men, then, there must be people like that. Tecumseh wanted to talk to this Copper Hair for days. It would take days for him to ask all the questions that had come up in his mind in these few minutes. But now Copper Hair's name was being called by someone near the cannon. Some of the warriors from Piqua Town were calling to him and beckoning. They were on their horses.

"I must go now, brother," Copper Hair said.

Of all the questions whirling in his head, Tecumseh felt he had to ask at least one before this man rode away. "Brother, what was your white man name?"

"Ro . . . Rogers. Joseph Rogers. . . ." His eyes looked wild. "Oh, how long since that name's been said aloud! . . . Listen! Come to Piqua Town, and we'll talk! Promise!"

"Yes! I will bring my books!"

"You have books!" Copper Hair's blue eyes were wide open. The warriors were calling him again. They began riding over.

"I have two books, and I will bring them!"

"*Weh-sah,* good!" Copper Hair gripped Tecumseh's shoulder and then turned and ran toward the Peckuwe warriors.

And Tecumseh watched him ride away, so stirred by this that he had nearly forgotten about the cannon.

# CHAPTER 14

## *Chillicothe Town*
## *Summer 1780*

S tar Watcher and her young brothers ran through the town with the crowd, toward the war road. They had heard the returning warriors singing and the dismal drone of the voices of captives. The hundreds came in a haze of drifting dust.

Never in memory had so many prisoners been brought in. They came staggering into Chillicothe, four or five hundred of them, men, women, and children in rags, many naked and hurt, all gaunt and terrified. Their skin was red with sunburn and smudged with dirt and blood. They were loaded like pack animals with useful things the warriors had looted from their towns and made them carry. Many of the Redcoats and the Green-coat rangers were moving beside the prisoners, helping the warriors guide them along. Star Watcher trotted next to the great, long, noisy column of wretches, looking for her husband. At the sight of the scrawny, sooty young mothers leading and hauling their wailing children, she felt heavy with pity.

When she found Stands Firm, riding far back in the column near the slow-moving rolling-gun, she walked alongside him, her hand on his foot in the stirrup. He told her that with the help of the Redcoats and their cannon, the warriors had captured two whole towns full of prisoners, and that they would all be taken to Detroit and sold to the Redcoat chief there. Stands Firm said it was the greatest victory ever in Kain-tuck-ee, but he did not seem very pleased about it.

That evening, when all the hundreds of exhausted prisoners lay groaning and crying mournfully in a field ringed with guards, when the Chillicothe people had grown tired of taunting and tormenting them and staring at them, Star Watcher fed her husband and her brother Chiksika, and the family learned why this great victory seemed so joyless.

171

"No one will want to go to war with this Captain Byrd again," said Chiksika. "He has no stomach."

Stands Firm started telling the story of the campaign. "At first, Captain Byrd was bold. We were going to go to the Great Falling Water of the O-hi-o. With the cannon we would shoot apart the new fort built there by the Long Knife Chief Clark. Clark was said to be still out in the valley of the Missi-se-pe, and all the tribes were eager to destroy his fort at the Falling Waters.

"But then spies came and told us that Clark himself was already at his fort. Therefore some of the chiefs—but not Black Hoof—decided it would be bad to fight there. They said the ghosts of the ancient white giants of Kain-tuck-ee would be against us, because the Falling Waters place is where our ancestors massacred them, as we have heard in the old songs of our people and of the Delawares.

"I was ashamed for those chiefs. Byrd was angry at them. His general had wanted him to strike the fort at the Falling Water place. But Byrd had to go where the chiefs voted to go, as he was only helping us. And so we went into Kain-tuck-ee at the Licking River instead, and up to a new fort called Ruddell's. There, just one ball from the cannon knocked down the gate, and the white men saw how many we were, so they came out to give up. Many warriors ran into the fort and killed about twenty people. Captain Byrd got very mad at us. He told the chiefs he would not help with his rolling-gun at any more forts if the warriors killed people who had already given up. The chiefs said to him, What did we come here for? They said, How are we to fight the other forts of Kain-tuck-ee when we have so many prisoners to guard?

"But Captain Byrd made the chiefs promise that at the next fort the warriors would only kill white people who refused to give up. So we went. It was to a fort called Martin's. They gave up without fighting, and so then we had still more prisoners, almost as many prisoners as we numbered ourselves. The chiefs told Captain Byrd, We must kill these many prisoners so we can go on and fight Boone's and Harrod's forts, as you promised we would do! But Byrd said, No, these prisoners will be taken to Detroit. We cannot strike any more forts till another time. So we had to come back, as you see."

Tecumseh could see Star Watcher listening very carefully to all this, saying nothing as she fed the warriors. Now Chiksika took up the story.

"We were angry. We did not want to come back yet. But what could be done? So we killed the prisoners who were too weak to come, then we started back. Warriors were angry about all these prisoners. When they fell down or got slow, we killed them. Byrd got madder. He told his soldiers not to let us do that. So we are back, as you see. We did more than has ever been done against the Long Knives. We burned two forts and brought home five hundred prisoners for whom the British will pay us, and got much loot. But Boone's Fort is still there, and Harrod's, and some other new forts, and now Clark's big fort at the Falling Water place. We have only forty scalps among eight hundred warriors, and no one is satisfied. Maybe Byrd will have glory in taking so many prisoners to Detroit. But will red men go to war with this Captain Byrd again? No! He has no stomach!"

Star Watcher had been listening to Chiksika with her lips pressed tight shut. Now she smiled, but her eyes were sharp and were aimed straight into his.

"I am sorry there are still Long Knife forts there," she said. "But you know my heart, brother. You know I am glad those white women and their children are alive. They are helpless. For their lives I would thank Captain Byrd, and it sounds to my ear as if the cowards were red men, who would not go to fight their great enemy Clark, but kill mothers and children!"

Chiksika, too surprised to answer, had to swallow her criticism with the food she was feeding him. Tecumseh, despite his adoration of his older brother, found he liked better what his sister had said.


Black Hoof kept one of the prisoners after Byrd went on to Detroit. This was a big, pleasant boy of about twelve years, a son of one of the chiefs of Ruddell's Town. His name was Stephen Ruddell. Black Hoof adopted him into the Chalagawtha sept and named him Sinnanatha, which meant Big Fish. Black Hoof would joke about the boy, saying, "I went to Kain-tuck-ee, and there I caught this Big Fish."

Big Fish was a bold, good-spirited boy, and he quickly took to life in the tribe. As a white boy he had had to work most of the time, but here he could spend his days playing games and hunting. He was a good athlete, and before long he became another rival whom Tecumseh had to strive to beat.

In the beginning, Big Fish knew no Shawnee words, but if he was shown how a game or contest was done, then he could play it well at once. One day in early autumn, Big Fish trounced Thick Water. So the boys of Chillicothe decided that this strong, active newcomer should be pitted against their champion Tecumseh in a wrestling match. Finding himself encircled by spectators and facing this sinewy, hawk-eyed Shawnee boy, Stephen Ruddell presumed that he was about to be engaged in a fistfight, as such an arrangement would have meant in a white town. He was ready. He was accustomed to winning fistfights. "All right, Chief, whenever you're set," he taunted. "I'm about to bust your snot horn."

Tecumseh, understanding none of the words, crouched with open hands and began circling, looking for an opening. Suddenly the white boy snapped out with his right fist. Tecumseh, whose reflexes were so quick he could grab a fly out of the air, caught the boy's wrist in both hands and held him fast, protesting in Shawnee: "No! We do not strike. We wrestle." He let go of the fist, and before he could step back to start again, the boy's left fist shot out. Tecumseh ducked out of its way and grabbed the arm in a powerful lock.

Now the white boy understood. He considered himself no novice at wrestling, either, and quickly broke the armlock in a single heaving motion that flung Tecumseh into the dirt. Tecumseh bounced to his feet, and the two now circled each other with mutual respect, being cheered on by the circle of watchers.

Tecumseh and Big Fish fought in the dust for a long time, straining and sweating, groaning with the pain they inflicted on each other, before Tecumseh finally, with swiftness and surprise, threw Big Fish on his face and bent both of his arms up behind him and locked him in place. Big Fish strained until he realized it was futile, then he nodded. The spectators yipped with delight. When Tecumseh let him up, Big Fish smiled, his face so flushed and dusty that it looked the color of an Indian's, not a white boy's. His smiling face reminded Tecumseh of the young man named Copper Hair at Piqua Town.

And that evening Tecumseh thought:

Now Chiksika is here. I must ask him to ride with me to see this Copper Hair in Piqua Town. We could take the *livres,* the, the *books,* he called them, and maybe he could explain to me how they do what they do to catch Weshemoneto's words and hold them in a book.

Suddenly Tecumseh wanted to do that more than he wanted anything. It might be a bad thing of the white people, doing that to words. But it was certain that Tecumseh would not be able to settle his thoughts until he knew about it. Chiksika knew very well the nature of Tecumseh's persistent curiosity, so he agreed. They would ride to Piqua Town, and they would take the books, and they would talk to this Copper Hair.


Tecumseh came awake feeling a hand around his ankle, the way his family members always woke each other if there was something urgent. The first thing he was aware of was that he was lying not in the family *wigewa,* but on the ground under bright stars. Then he remembered where he was: on the trace between Chillicothe and Piqua Town, with Chiksika. It was Chiksika's hand on his ankle, and his voice, strained with anxiety, was saying:

"Come look, brother. Something is wrong."

The tone and the words made Tecumseh's heart quicken, and he scrambled up from his bed of leaves. "Come here," Chiksika said. By starlight Tecumseh could see him going up toward the crest of the high meadow on whose edge they had made their little camp, and he followed him.

The elevated clearing gave them a wide view of the vast, starry sky and the horizons all the way around. Chiksika pointed toward the south. "The sun does not rise there."

Above the southern horizon was a faint, reddish glow. In that direction lay Chillicothe. Chiksika and Tecumseh had left Chillicothe the day before for their journey to Piqua Town. They had traveled in a leisurely way, stopping here and there to study this beautiful land that lay between the Little Miami-se-pe and the Mad River, stopping again to hunt game for a meal, finally making an early camp halfway between the two towns and sitting up late by the campfire to talk about all matters that were on their minds, from Captain Byrd's campaign to the strange things called books that Tecumseh had brought along. They could have gone all the way to Piqua in three hours but instead had enjoyed this lazy summer trip, a reminder of the old, peaceful days when Chiksika had spent much of his time teaching Tecumseh.

Tecumseh looked at the glow on the horizon, then put his hand on Chiksika's hard arm and felt that it was quivering. Tecumseh said, "Do you think Chillicothe is on fire?"

"We had better go back."

Their horses, hobbled, were a few yards away on the meadow. Tecumseh, tingling with alarm, hurried to get them while Chiksika ran down to gather their guns and bundles from the camp. In a few minutes they were riding back toward Chillicothe as fast as the darkness would allow, their minds full of dread and their hearts racing. They thought of Star Watcher and the three boys and of all the other people who were dear to them. They were less than a mile down the trace when Tecumseh said, "Listen!"

They reined in. Somewhere to the west, some horses were running fast, several horses, going toward Piqua.

"Should we follow them?" Tecumseh asked. "They could tell us what is wrong."

Chiksika paused a moment, considering this, then said, "No. They would be to Piqua before we could catch up. And maybe they are not even our people. Come!" They urged their horses on toward Chillicothe. The stars were fading now as the eastern sky grayed. The sky was still red ahead of them.

Suddenly Chiksika raised his hand and hissed. He guided his horse toward a copse of trees left of the trace. As they rode into the cover, Tecumseh could hear from some distance down the trace the stirring sounds of many people moving: hooves, creaking sounds, low voices, now and then a shout. It sounded like a whole nation moving in the dark. It could be the Long Knife army; that was Tecumseh's first thought. But then he heard the crying of an infant.

"It is the People!" Chiksika said, and they rode out.

Soon they heard Black Hoof's deep voice, and when they were close enough to see him in the gloom, Chiksika rode alongside and Black Hoof grumbled the news.

"The Long Knife army comes. Ten hundred or more. But-lah shows them the way, and the Long Knife Clark commands."

Chiksika made a snake hiss. "Them! They have burned the town?"

"*We* burned the town."

"We?"

"I said to burn the town, to hide everything, to abandon Chillicothe. We burned it to deny it to this Clark. Anything else was useless. But we leave them nothing. . . ." He paused, then added with a choked sound, "Nothing but the crops in the fields." His voice sounded bitterly angry.

"There was time to do all this? How?"

"One of the Long Knives deserted, and came and warned us. Also, our friend Girty, he and his brothers saw the Long Knife army half a day away from Chillicothe and came with the warning in time. We had some hours to prepare. We put the town on fire in the middle of the night and came on. All of us. I hope I will never have to do that again. There is no more a Chillicothe, my son." His face was terrible in the early half-light as they rode slowly on.

"But the families are all safe?" Chiksika looked back as he asked this and could see the long, dark line of homeless people coming along. Tecumseh watched them. He had not felt so forlorn for the People since the nation had split and his mother had gone away west with the others.

"They are all behind me," Black Hoof said. "But how safe are we? If this Clark chief does not stop at Chillicothe, we will have to stand and fight him at Piqua Town. In the log houses and the three-sided fort there, maybe we could make a stand. Some of the Wyandots and Delawares from Byrd might still be in Piqua, to reinforce us; I sent riders to find out. Even then their army is three times the number of our warriors. Listen, my son: If this Clark smashes Piqua Town, there is no hope. And I fear he will smash Piqua Town."

"Why are you sure? Our people will fight like wildcats on our own land!"

"Because"—here Black Hoof lowered his voice—"this Clark chief brings a cannon."

It was terrible to hear Black Hoof talk without hope. Black Hoof was over fifty summers in age. He was one of the greatest Shawnee war chiefs ever. When very young he had helped to wipe out Braddock's British army and had been one of the most active fighters ever since. He was not one in whose voice anyone would ever expect to hear defeat.

By afternoon, scouts came saying that Clark's army had burned and slashed all the corn and crops at Chillicothe and was coming on. Corn, beans, and squash, the three sacred sisters delegated by Our Grandmother to provide for the People. The warriors were outraged by this sacrilege and were clamoring to ambush Clark on the road from Chillicothe to Piqua. Because he was having to cut a road for his cannon part of the way, it was taking him a long time to come.

Chiksika was one of the fiery ones who spoke in favor of the ambush. He argued, "What good can his big rolling-gun do him when we are all around him and he cannot see us in the woods?" So a large band of warriors rode down to ambush him. When they first saw his army, it had already crossed the Little Miami and was halfway to the Mad River, which flowed by Piqua Town. And it soon became clear that Clark would be hard to ambush. All around his army he kept scouts and flankers, and some of the scouts had cur dogs.

Finally an ambush was laid in a good place. But before Clark's army reached that place, a deluge of rain came and forced the army to stop, and Clark put it in a defensive square that could not be attacked. It was as if this Clark had even his God helping him.

At last Black Hoof knew that Clark could not be kept from reaching Piqua Town, so he counciled with the chieftains and warriors on how to defend the town. The most urgent thing was the safety of the families. Like many of the Shawnee towns, Piqua had been planned with routes of escape. Black Hoof pointed to the high stone river bluff behind the town. A ravine through that bluff formed a protected passageway out of the valley onto the high ground to the northwest. "Have the women and children go out by that way and take all they can carry of food and seed and tools. If we fail to stop Clark here, then the warriors will escape by that way later. But I vow that none of us shall flee unless all else is lost."

Black Hoof was realistic. He did not really believe that the Long Knives could be stopped. But he did not intend to let his people be trapped and massacred. He loved his people, and their preservation was his first concern.

Tecumseh still had his books in a parfleche bag on his pony, but now in this desperate turmoil of preparations for defense and flight, he gave the books no thought. He kept watching for the man named Copper Hair, but what he wanted to ask him if he saw him now was not about the books, but one question. At last, near the three-sided fort, Tecumseh heard his name called, and Copper Hair came trotting over to him, smiling. Tecumseh, his blood hot, asked him the question.

"How can you say your cousin Clark is good, when he does this?"

Copper Hair's friendly smile wavered. But then he put a hand on Tecumseh's shoulder and said: "Just as well, how can you say your fathers Black Fish and Black Hoof were good, when they went to Kain-tuck-ee, and burned towns and caught white families?"

The answer to that was quicker than Copper Hair must have expected. Tecumseh said: "This is our country, given to us by Weshemoneto. Kain-tuck-ee was not theirs. They had no right to make towns there."

"But," said Copper Hair, "what if the white man's God tells them He is giving them Kain-tuck-ee? They will believe Him if He tells them that, and they will not feel they do wrong."

This was an astonishing thought. All Tecumseh could say was, "It would be a lie! Does even the white man's God lie? It is not His to give!"

Copper Hair blinked and shook his head. "Do you think a God can be wrong?"

Tecumseh stood before Copper Hair, breathing hard, confused. All around, warriors were rushing, women were carrying things, people were leading packhorses. The air was full of cries, shouts, dust. At last Tecumseh asked:

"In your heart, are you Shawnee?"

A strange, wild, pained look was in Copper Hair's eyes. "Tecumseh," he said in a voice almost choking, "I have been happy among the People. They accepted me, and I have belonged. Yes. You are my brother. I wanted to talk to you. . . ."

"I was bringing the books to you, Copper Hair. That is why I was coming to Piqua Town. I wanted to know . . ." But before he could speak what he was going to say, he suddenly saw Copper Hair with a gray face and bloody lips.

And then the young man reached out and put his hand on Tecumseh's shoulder and said, "Maybe we will have a time someday for the books. Maybe there will not be a battle here. . . . Maybe . . . Listen, young brother. I must go now. They told me to be in the fort. Whatever comes from this day, I am your brother. Remember that. I will watch for you."

These words twisted Tecumseh's heart, because he knew that Copper Hair would be dead. He had seen him dead, and he somehow knew it would be so. But he replied:

"I will watch for you, too."

Early in the afternoon a chatter of drums could be heard down by the fording place of the Mad River, and then the army of Clark was seen coming across the ford, riding through the shallow green water, their weapons glinting, their flags limp in the still, humid air. After the troop of horsemen came an endless line of men on foot, in gray and brown shirts or some only in breechcloths in the Indian fashion, holding their guns across their chests as they waded across. After them came more horsemen and then four horses pulling a brass cannon, whose big iron-rimmed wheels could be heard grinding over the rocky riverbank. The drums chattered ominously, and men's voices shouted commands. When the army was across the river and half a mile from the south edge of Piqua Town, a big man in a blue coat, riding a gray horse, pointed his sword this way and that and shouted in a mighty voice that rolled through the valley, and large parts of the army moved this way and that in orderly patterns, spreading out to make a long double line along the pole fences and the fields of high corn in the rich bottomlands. It was frightening to hear those strange drums, drums that chattered instead of bumping like a heartbeat, and to see men move so obediently, so many of them, as if they were outreaching parts of that horseman in the blue coat, who was surely the dreaded Clark. Tecumseh looked at him in the distance and thought of how it was that he had come here where his own cousin was. Tecumseh had kept his promise and had told no one, not even Chiksika, that Copper Hair was a cousin of this Clark.

Tecumseh was on the edge of the high rock bluff. From here he could see over the bark roofs of the town along the whole bend of the river, and the wide corn fields and bean fields and gardens beyond them, and the Long Knife army forming its straight lines. From this distance they looked like an army of ants lining up. The valley was steamy from the rains, and deep green were the meadows of grass and weeds where the army was. Nearer to the town there was another ant-size army moving, a hundred warriors running swiftly into the corn fields, running crouched down, to make a line that would face the Long Knives' lines. Between the meadows and the town there were several little wooded hillocks. Farther east, closer to the river, another long line of warriors was running crouched along a fence row to make a defense between the town and the river. Somewhere among those warriors were Chiksika and Stands Firm of his own family. In town near the river was the three-sided palisade fort with its hewn-log blockhouse, built by the British not long ago. There were houses on two sides of it, and a field of corn grew almost to its north wall.

Tecumseh was here on this bluff because, though still not old enough to serve as a warrior, he did have a horse and a gun and a pair of the keenest eyes, and he had been assigned with other boys his age to watch and protect the rear of the procession of women and children and old people who had fled up the ravine into the woods on the high ground. Except for a few of the oldest and fattest, who were still clambering up the ravine, most of the people were in the woods now and moving along the path that led north-westward between the forks of the Great Miami-se-pe. There was really no destination for the people now; they were going northward simply because this would take them farther from the Long Knives.

As Tecumseh looked over the valley and watched the warriors and the enemy moving into their positions, he saw a cluster of trees near the Indian lines on his left, a clump of trees where a brooklet ran out and down to a creek, and he knew that it was the place of his birth and of his Vision Quest. Remembering this, seeing the green woods and the corn fields and the curving river and the houses and the beautiful bluffs, he felt such a longing for the peace the People had known before the white men that he groaned aloud. Then he heard a croaking voice behind him. Startled, he turned. An old man stood there, one of the village subchiefs, one who was in charge of the withdrawal of the people, and he was summoning Tecumseh. "Come, my son. We need you with us." And so Tecumseh turned away from the wide panorama of the valley with its little antlike figures getting into their places for battle, mounted his pony, and started following the refugees. He had gone only a few hundred paces when the crackle of gunfire rolled up from the valley, and faint sounds of shouting. It was starting.


Star Watcher carried a kettle and some blankets and a bag of corn and led a packhorse that carried the rest of her household. She had ordered the triplets not to wander far from the packhorse or lag behind.

As she went along she could not see well sometimes because of the blur of tears that would start when she let herself think of what was happening. She kept remembering the bright flames beginning to consume the house in Chillicothe that she had built only that spring. Now that house would be just ashes. And the corn and vegetables that she had planted in the fields around Chillicothe would be just ashes and trampled pulp by now. And the man who had lived with her in that nice new house for those few happy weeks, maybe he would be dead or hurt by now. There was such a thunder of gunfire rolling up from the valley. How could men live long in that?

For a long time through the afternoon the people of Chillicothe and Piqua moved together in their long column, the gunfire growing fainter behind them. Many of the women were weeping voicelessly; the faces of the children were puckered with fear.

Riding in the dust at the tail of the column, Tecumseh kept looking back. He kept thinking of Chiksika and Stands Firm and Black Hoof, who would be always bold and in danger, and wondered if they could still be alive. He thought about Thick Water, who was back there now in his first battle. He thought too of Copper Hair, who had said he would be in the fort. Maybe they had wanted him to be in the fort because they had sensed, as Tecumseh had, that Copper Hair was not a Shawnee through his soul.

After a long time, the battle sounds could hardly be heard through the sounds of the refugees' retreat: the hooves on the ground, the swish of legs through weeds and grass, the creak and drag of travois poles, the blowing of the horses as they plodded through the heat, the whimpering or whining of thirsty, tired, scared children, a little talk, and around it all the dry creak and shrill of late summer insects.

Then there was something else: a thump on the air. Then again. Again. They knew what it was. An old man said:

"May I never hear another rolling-gun. It is revenge for the British rolling-gun that we suffer now."

Star Watcher, like many women whose husbands and brothers were still back in Piqua Town, remembered the demonstration of the British cannon, its great spout of flame and smoke, the woodpile flying apart, and her face crumpled with anguish.

They kept moving on.

And when the sun set red in the haze, and dusk came, they stopped the procession on a high meadow, made a camp without fires, and put boys with bows and guns around the perimeter to guard it. The people ate jerky and cold corn cake and waited, looking back toward the south, looking and wondering and fearing as the stars came out.

And when it was dark, they saw what they had feared to see.

The sky in the south was red. As Chillicothe had burned the night before, Piqua was burning now.


The warriors arrived before midnight. Many were wounded. They brought five dead warriors they had been able to get off the battlefield and the bodies of two who had died on the way from Piqua Town, and they said that another fifteen had been killed whose bodies could not be recovered. The white soldiers had scalped and mutilated those bodies.

The warriors had taken the scalps of about fifteen soldiers and had killed a few more soldiers whose scalps they could not get.

Tecumseh and Star Watcher ran among the grim warriors in the darkness, calling Chiksika's name and Stands Firm's name, afraid they would not be there.

But they were. Both were all bloody but were able to walk and talk. Black Hoof had escaped injury many times, by the protection of the Great Good Spirit. Thick Water was unhurt.

But Piqua Town had fallen. And the soldiers had set it on fire.

Black Hoof said the women should build cookfires to make hot food and broth and poultices. The army would not follow in the dark, he said. They were too busy looting and burning Piqua. And they probably would not come on tomorrow, either, because the battle had lasted until dusk, and the soldiers had not had time yet to destroy the crops. There was of course a danger that the Long Knives would come in pursuit of the People, but if they did, the scouts could give warning in plenty of time.

So, fires were built, small fires which in the midst of the dark woods and meadows made the people feel a little like a People again, and helped them doctor their warriors and comfort their children, and whose smoke helped to keep away mosquitoes.

Stands Firm's face and shoulders were cut and punctured in a dozen places. Chiksika had two wounds on his shoulder and chest. While Star Watcher made poultices in her kettle and cleaned their wounds, Chiksika and Stands Firm told of the defeat. Chiksika said, "No such battle was ever fought on this side of the Beautiful River. To me it was the equal of our great battle at the Kanawha-se-pe."

"Black Hoof was a great war chief today," said Stands Firm. "It was not his fault that Piqua Town fell. The Long Knives were three times our number. And this Clark could turn his army by his voice, so we could never get around his flank. By the afternoon we had been driven back into the houses and the fort. Then his cannon knocked them all to pieces."

"And this," said Chiksika, "was the most terrible thing of all: when the cannon fired those great loads of bullets! It was like a hailstorm of lead balls and splinters, and no one could hide from them."

"All of these holes in me are from one bang of that kind," Stands Firm said, and he tried to smile at the sick look on Star Watcher's face.

Very late in the day it had been discovered that a second wing of Clark's army was coming down the river.

"We heard their bugles and drums coming," Chiksika said.

"Such a sound they make!" Stands Firm exclaimed. "Like mad spirits!"

"Black Hoof tried one more time to turn back the Long Knives before they could catch us between them," Chiksika said. "We all ran straight toward their cannon and rifles. We got so close I could see the face of Clark. I knew him from Harrod's Fort in Kain-tuck-ee. He stood straight up and pointed his sword at us and shouted in his great voice, and there came so many gunshots at once that we could not go on. All we could do then was help our hurt ones get back. Then we withdrew through the corn field by the fort and came under the bluff, and up the ravine the way you came, just before that other part of his army could close on us. And that was all the battle. It was almost dark, and we got away and came. And that is all. And now you see that the sky is red and there will be no Piqua Town anymore."

The story was being told around every fire. Voices were murmuring everywhere amid the twinkling fires, and the women and children and old people were listening wide-eyed, loving the warriors for their courage. Though it had been a severe defeat, there was no shame in the way the warriors had fought for the town, and as long as there were fires and families here and the warriors had nothing to be ashamed of, it was still a People. They could feel it out here in the open, the oneness, even though they were without a place. They had not felt like a People since the nation had divided the year before, but now they did.

Tecumseh noticed the white boy Big Fish standing in the margin of the firelight, a white-skinned boy in Shawnee dress, looking strained and afraid. That was no wonder. It had been only weeks since he had been captured in Kain-tuck-ee, and today the white men's army from Kain-tuck-ee had come and done all this, and maybe he wondered if the People would turn on him and kill him. His foster father Black Hoof was too busy to attend to him now. Tecumseh could almost feel the boy's doubts, just by looking at him. Big Fish gave Tecumseh a feeble half smile and raised his hand slightly to greet him, and Tecumseh raised his hand in reply. Big Fish then wandered away, looking very lost.

Now Tecumseh asked a question that had been on his mind. "Brother, what of the man Copper Hair? I have not seen him here." Star Watcher was now sponging the wound on Chiksika's shoulder with a steaming cloth. He winced, then said:

"Such a strange thing! I was going to tell you this. At the end of the battle he came out from some hiding place and tried to run to Clark, yelling a word in their tongue. And a funny thing happened then."

"What?"

"The Long Knives must have thought he was a warrior attacking. They shot him down."

Tecumseh groaned. He remembered seeing Copper Hair's face dead while he talked to him.

"What, brother?" Chiksika exclaimed. "Do you not think it is funny they shot him while he was escaping to them?"

Tecumseh was remembering Copper Hair's secret. He would have liked to tell them that Copper Hair was Clark's cousin, so they would know how awful this was. But he had promised never to tell—even though it could do no harm now.

Stands Firm said, in a voice without Chiksika's mocking tone: "I will tell you something about that, told me by a Delaware who lay wounded near that place. He saw this before he crept away. He said the Long Knife Chief Clark came down there and held that Copper Hair in his arms. And that he wept on him."

"Poor brother!" Chiksika laughed. "Now who will you talk to about those *book* things?"

# CHAPTER 15

## *A Village on the Upper Miami-se-pe*
## *Winter 1780*

This," said Big Fish, speaking in Shawnee and putting his finger on Tecumseh's nose, "is *watoanee.*"

Tecumseh sighed and shook his head. He said, speaking English: "No. *This* is *watoanee,* mouth! *Watsau-thi* is nose." He touched those respective features of the white boy's face as he spoke them. "And what is this?" He stuck out his tongue.

Big Fish frowned and thought. "We . . . we . . ."

Tecumseh made his mouth round and then stuck his tongue through, unconsciously hinting.

*"Welonee,"* Big Fish cried. *"Welonee,* b'God!"

They had been working very hard at this. Each tried to speak only in the other's tongue when they were having their lessons. Big Fish was quick to understand, but he was also quick to forget. Once Tecumseh had grasped a word in English, he never forgot it. But Big Fish did not remember well without a lot of repetition.

The hard part had been in teaching things they could not point at or touch. They had been hung up for days on such words as "is" or "may" or "was" or "should," until they had managed to catch Blue Jacket and persuade him to sit down with them and explain. He knew both languages so well that he was their best resource. But Blue Jacket could not help them very much. He had gotten married to a whiteface captive woman and was trying to teach her the Shawnee language. Blue Jacket had come to hate his old language, and he told Big Fish that he should forget it and told Tecumseh that it was not a worthy effort to try to learn it, saying, "I would rather we drove the whitefaces so far away that we would never hear their tongue again. It is like an obscenity to speak it." As much as Tecumseh admired Blue Jacket, though, he did not agree with this. He did not argue with Blue

185

Jacket about it, as that would have been disrespectful, but he did believe it would be useful to know the enemy's tongue.

Most of all, he was consumed with curiosity about what meanings lay behind the white men's words. He believed that only in this way could he ever understand why they were so strange in their wants and outrageous in their ways.

Much of the secret of their souls, he thought, must be in their books, especially the one Copper Hair had said contained words of their god. The Shawnee people tried to be such as they thought their own god meant them to be, and surely this would be the same with the white men. But he could not ask Blue Jacket to help him with the books because of the way Blue Jacket felt. Instead, he was going to try to master the white man's tongue, and when he had done that through Big Fish, perhaps he could talk with him about God and beliefs, and perhaps Big Fish could even help him learn what Copper Hair had called "read." It seemed to Tecumseh that the most important word in a language was "why." And he thought the "whys" of the white men must be in that book with the words of their God.

Star Watcher was building a house again. Or, rather, rebuilding one.

The town the Shawnees had come to winter in was an old Peckuwe village on the Upper Miami-se-pe. This town had been almost abandoned when the tribe split apart, and weather and rot had nearly ruined the flimsy bark houses in the many moons since then. Their pole frames had looked like skeletons, the remaining bark slabs like patches of hide hanging on them. Dead leaves had drifted up inside them to cover the broken pottery and utensils; gnawed nutshells and clawed holes showed where animals had sheltered in the ruins.

When Black Hoof had brought his homeless people here, the women had set about repairing the lodges, peeling bark from trees and stacking it to dry with big stones on top to keep it flat. The warriors and boys had at once set out on hunting parties in every direction, hoping to obtain enough meat to preserve a winter's supply. The women had planted some seeds in faint hopes for a late autumn that would allow a few crops to mature and had foraged for nuts and berries and fruits and roots all through the late summer and autumn. Men and boys set snares on every trace of an animal path, and people who were wounded or too old to do anything else fished on the banks of the river. It was going to be a hungry winter because of what the Long Knives had done to the crops. Game was scarce in this place because the Peckuwes had lived and hunted here for so many years before. And the Shawnees had expended so much powder and lead in the futile defense of their towns that they had little left for hunting. And now there had come a rumor that another Long Knife army, of two thousand men, was setting out from Fort Pitt to attack what was left of the tribes.

And so Black Hoof and the other chiefs had resorted to begging. They had a British trader write down a message to Major DePeyster, the new British commandant at Detroit, telling him of their misfortunes at the hands of the Long Knives and of their present state of poverty and begging him to supply them with whatever he could spare. "Father!" the letter concluded. "Here we have determined to make our stand, and wait to hear from you. You must be sensible how you should assist us, having the same enemy as the cause." This message was sent to Detroit along with an eight-string wampum belt to confirm its authenticity. But the trader advised Black Hoof not to expect much. Detroit itself, he said, scarcely had enough provisions, mostly just Indian corn and vegetables, to sustain itself over the winter, and its forces had been much weakened and demoralized by Clark's capture of Governor-General Hamilton. Nothing anymore was the way it had been before the arrival of that Clark in the territory.

Being in fear that he, or another Long Knife commander from Fort Pitt, might strike again, the Shawnee did little to improve the ruined town. And for another reason little was done: this site was to hardly anyone's liking. It was not a beautiful townsite, as their beloved Chillicothe and Piqua towns had been. The people complained of its poor ground, of its windblown flatness, of the unfavorable terrain, of the old Peckuwe spirits that skulked around it, even of the poor quality of the sunlight that fell upon it, or anything else they could perceive or imagine to be inferior to their old homes. Black Hoof was of course wise enough to understand that what was wrong with this place was simply that it was not the other places, that the people were seeing it through saddened eyes and defeated hearts, and that it could therefore never seem right to them, at least for a long while. There was always talk of going back to the old places and rebuilding them, maybe next spring. Matters surely would be better in a year, the people chose to believe, and surely Clark would not come again to attack towns that he had already destroyed. This was the way the Shawnees were talking now. It made Black Hoof sad to hear how low their spirits had sunk, but it was good that they still could yearn for something, even if it was the past.


It was the hungriest of their winters, and the cruel gnawing in their bellies was equaled by the hatred for white men that smoldered in their hearts. The warriors warmed themselves on this. Whenever Stands Firm heard a woman trying to quiet a hungry baby, he clenched his teeth and tensed his fists and dreamed of the joy of smashing a white man's head, and was impatient for spring. The Long Knives had not only destroyed their homes, they had committed the unholy act of wasting corn, beans, and squash, the three sacred sisters.

The hunters' guns leaned useless against the poles of their lodges. There was so little lead and powder, and the British had not yet provided them with any.

A strange thing had been happening for a long time. Many of the warriors and hunters had become so dependent upon their guns that they had lost the stealthy skills needed for bow hunting. Mostly the older men, who had grown up with bows in their hands, and a few of the boys like Tecumseh who had until recently hunted only with bows, could still go out with a quiver of arrows and expect to bring home meat. Many of the young men did not even know how to find good flint or obsidian and knap it to make arrowheads. Once Tecumseh heard Blue Jacket say of this dependency on guns and other iron things: "It is another curse the white man has brought." When Tecumseh heard this he realized how true it was and how sad. It was like the iron kettles and steel fire strikers the women now used: they thought they had to have them, although a few generations ago there had been no such things. If a woman broke or lost one, she would cry and think she could never start a fire or cook again unless she could obtain another one right away. "To me," Blue Jacket grumbled once, "it seems that a woman lives only for the day she can go to the British trading post and buy something the traders have made her think it is necessary to have. She would rather show a red blanket of wool than a beautiful doeskin she has tanned herself," he muttered. The men he was talking to nodded their heads and wondered secretly if Blue Jacket was grumbling about all this because his own paleface wife was asking for too many things. If he hated the whites' things so much, why had he married a white woman? They smiled. There was not much about Blue Jacket that was amusing. So they liked this.

In this winter, Tecumseh and Big Fish hunted together on the snowy plains and in the frosty woods when the early morning air was hazy blue and sparkling with rime. Tecumseh helped Big Fish make a strong bow of hickory, showing him how to shave the white wood down to the right shape and steam and tie it to produce the right curvature, and then taught him to make arrows and to shoot them quickly and accurately. Big Fish was already good with a gun.

Tecumseh loved the bow and took great pleasure in shooting with it. "A bow," he said, "is a beautiful thing, and does not make a noise like a gun that animals learn to fear and move away from. Best, it is not something that white men made and that only white men can repair."

When Tecumseh stood silent in the silent woods, on snowshoes he had made, his feet and calves protected by moccasins and leggings his sister had made for him from the hide of a deer he had killed, his muscles straining to pull the bowstring and a buck or elk just turning its eyes toward him in its last moment of life, he felt that he was like the first Shawnee in the Beginning, and he could almost forget that there were such creatures as white men. Even when Big Fish was beside him, with his strange, pale, freckled face and pink lips, Tecumseh could almost forget the white men, because Big Fish in spirit was becoming the best kind of a Shawnee. He was hardy and bold. He could wade through broken ice in pursuit of fleeing prey and not groan and shake from it. He would not squall in dismay if Tecumseh exuberantly jumped on him and wrestled him down into a wet snowbank; instead, he would laugh and give a fierce whoop or growl like a bear and fight with great energy. In their war games with large groups of boys from the village, Big Fish would always want to be Tecumseh's subchief, but if the sticks fell in such a way that he was on the other side, he would accept that and fall back on his own wily strategies, and the things he had learned from Tecumseh would make him a more formidable opponent.

And even in these cold and hungry times, Big Fish seemed to love being a Shawnee. He was happier than almost anyone else in the town—perhaps, Tecumseh would think, because he does not know how much better it was for us in the other times.


One night in the Hunger Moon, when three mild days had melted all the snow and then a hard cold had come down again to freeze the waters and the ground, and the moon was almost full, high above the bare black branches, sending down so much milky light that they could see their way at midnight, Tecumseh and Big Fish were walking home from a long hunt, walking across the shadow-striped forest floor, their feet rustling the frost-sparkling dead leaves, three rabbits hanging over Tecumseh's shoulder and a raccoon over Big Fish's, and Tecumseh was so stirred by the silvery-cold beauty of the world that he asked:

"Big Fish, do you know anything of the book that has the God's words?"

"The Bible?"

"Yes."

"Of course. We had to read it all the time." He used the white man's word "read" even though he was speaking in Shawnee, because there was no Shawnee word for that.

"You *had* to?"

"My father made us read it. Once, for a while, he thought I might become a . . . preacher."

"What is this 'preacher'?"

"A, something like a shaman, I think. And a little like a Singer, too."

"Did you *like* to read on this Bible you had to read on?"

"Oh, some of the stories I liked. A lot of it was tiresome. Who was whose father and grandfather and great-grandfather and all that."

"This Bible has *stories?*"

"Oh, it is mostly stories. Mostly about Hebrews."

"Hebrews?" Tecumseh shaped the word.

"They were a kind of tribe a long time ago. They moved around a lot, and increased a lot, and fought a lot."

"Ah," Tecumseh exclaimed. "Like the Shawnees!"

"I guess. They had chiefs. These Hebrew men ran everything. Their wives don't get spoken about very much in the Bible." He shrugged.

"Not so much like the Shawnee, then. Our women speak up. We have women who are chiefs. Tell me, Big Fish, why the Hebrews moved around so much. This is interesting."

"Well, there were enemies they had, called Egyptians. These enemies were rich and had big armies."

"Ah," said Tecumseh. "Were these E-zhip-sins white?"

"I don't think so. Anyway, once the Hebrews were sort of their slaves."

"Ah. There should not be slaves."

"One of the Hebrew big chiefs was Moses. He led them out of Egypt, and they got across the . . . the, ah, Great Water, when God made the water separate, and they just walked across on land with a wall of water on either side. That might sound hard to believe, but it's in the Bible, so it must be so."

"Why would it be hard to believe? That is how the Shawnees came to this land. Across a path of land that was made in the Great Water to the west."

"You don't say so! You mean your god parted the waters, too?"

"In some way. Black Hoof says First Man sang on the other side of the water for twelve days, and then the water parted and the People walked over here on the bottom, and when they looked back, it was water again behind them. It is believed that the Great Turtle that holds the land on his back rose up a little and the water ran off and that made the path."

"Great Turtle?" Big Fish exclaimed. "You believe that a turtle holds up the land?"

"I believe what we have been told from the Beginning. We remember it all. We remember it by singing it and saying it. Maybe you remember it by putting it in your God book. Maybe your Chief Moses sang on the other side of the water, and the Great Turtle rose up, but your Hebrews, being white men, could not see the Great Turtle."

"Why couldn't they see it, if the Shawnees can?"

"I don't know why not, Big Fish. But I have talked with Boone, and our warriors have talked with many other white men, who all said that they do not believe things they cannot see. They do not believe the spirits that live in things. But yet you believe your God parted the waters, and you have not seen that."

Big Fish looked out of the sides of his eyes at Tecumseh as they walked in the moonlight. Never in his life had he been in a conversation like this. He said, "What kinds of things have you seen that I've never seen?"

"For one, I have felt the earth tremble under my feet when no one else felt it. Since then I have been able to sense where it starts, which is out there." He pointed toward the southwest. "I have not been to the place where it starts, but if I went to that place, even if nothing, not even a tree, stood there to mark it, I would know I was at the place. This is going to be important somehow, but I don't know yet. That is one thing."

"What else have you seen?" Big Fish asked, and now there was a new tone in his voice, as if he were talking with a preacher.

"In my Vision Quest, I looked at a white bird until it spoke to me, and I could understand what it said to me. Such a bird is one's Spirit Helper. With someone else it might be a rabbit or a squirrel that becomes a small man in a tree and speaks. It was very important what the white bird said. Often a Spirit Helper will tell you how to heal something. Mine told me something bigger than that."

"What did the white bird say to you that you understood?" Big Fish asked after it became apparent that Tecumseh was not going on with his story.

"You could not understand."

Big Fish got a little angry. "I am a Shawnee, too," he said. "I am not a white man anymore."

"I know, brother. But one cannot understand what another's Spirit Helper says. You have to find and listen to your own. And its message does not come in words, so I cannot tell you in words, and so how can I tell you? That is all I can say about it. I would tell you more if I could make you understand."

"What kind of a bird was it, your Spirit Helper? You don't see many white birds. Not in the woods."

"A sort of dove."

"A *white* dove?"

"Yes. Most of them are gray."

"I know," said Big Fish. "The only white one I ever knew of was in the Bible. I mean, I guess it was white. I always see it that way when I read about it. . . ."

"You *see* a dove when you read? Are you talking about the pictures that are in a book?"

"No. No pictures. You just *see* what you're reading about."

"Do I understand this? To read, you look at the black words on the leaves of the book, but even then you *see* the white dove?"

Big Fish thought for a while, then said, "Yes. Sometimes." He had read a great deal in his life, but he had never even thought of it this way, and yet it was so.

Tecumseh thought: Then the white people do have some kinds of medicine power. This was the first evidence he had seen of it. He said, "Tell me of this white dove in the Bible."

"Noah sent it out from the boat in the Great Flood, to see if it could find land."

"So the white man's book has a flood, too? And you say a dove was sent out to find a place to land?"

"Yes!" Big Fish was growing quite mystified, to find that so many things were the same, even though so much was anything but the same. "It rained for forty days and forty nights, and that made the flood. Is that what happened in your story, too?"

"Not quite. It happened this way: that Our Grandmother's naughty grandson, Rounded-Side, who always did what she told him not to do, took his knife and cut open the big stomach of a giant man who had drunk all the waters of the earth, and the water came spilling out, and drowned the earth, and only the good people escaped, in a boat. After a long time Our Grandmother sent a crayfish down in the water to bring up some mud. Then she called a buzzard, and put the mud on his wings, and told him to fly until it dried. When it was dry, the People got on the mud and they live on it because it is the earth."

"A buzzard!" Big Fish exclaimed. "What a story that is! My head is going around! And who is Our Grandmother, anyway?"

"It is a shame Black Hoof is so busy with white man trouble. He knows all this and should tell you, as he is your father. Our Grandmother is the Creator. It is like this:

"Weshemoneto, in the Beginning, lived above the sun. He was invisible, like wind, but in the shape of a man. He made Our Grandmother, Kokomthena, and gave her the task of creating man, and she did it. Rounded-Side helped her, but only because he was not supposed to. Would you like to see Our Grandmother?"

"Can I?"

Tecumseh stopped and pointed into the sky.

"You mean, the moon is her?"

"No. But the moon is near her house, close enough that she can use it for her looking-glass. And if you look at it now when it is round, you can see her shadow in it. You see her cooking over a pot. You can see that she wears a short skirt. Also up there you can see the shadow of her little dog, and of Rounded-Side, and of two other grandsons who are Our Grandmother's Silly Boys."

Big Fish suddenly laughed, looking at the moon. "Silly Boys!"

"Yes. Can you see them all?"

"Not really. We . . . the white people, I mean, look for a man in the moon."

"A man! Who is that man? Is he a Creator?"

"No . . . nobody. Just . . . I don't know. I myself never could make him out. But I sure can't see all those people and dogs, either."

"No. You have to look a while, and we don't have time now. Our Grandmother is through creating things. That happened during the Third Time. We are now living in the Fourth Time, and she does not create anymore. But she does still send messages and wisdom to us when we need to know something."

"How does she do that?"

"Sometimes," Tecumseh said, "she sends it by one of the Truth-Bearers. These are Tobacco, Sky, the Thunderbirds, the Four Winds, Water, and the Stars. *Nilu famu,* sacred tobacco, is the principal Truth-Bearer. When Tobacco is placed in the sacred fire, its smoke goes up, carrying the words of prayers."

"That's strange. White people think tobacco is a thing of the Devil. Some do, anyway. Even people who smoke it admit the Devil's got them."

"If a Shawnee thought Matchemoneto was in tobacco, he would not use it," Tecumseh said with an edge of scorn in his voice. "Anyway, our sacred tobacco we do not smoke in pipes, but put in the sacred fire, as I just told you. The tobacco we smoke is just for pleasure. And I was going to tell you one more way Our Grandmother sends us messages. She tells them to a prophet."

"Ah! Prophets! The Bible has prophets, too!"

"I think," said Tecumseh, starting to walk along again in the crunching leaves, "that my brother Loud Noise is going to be a prophet. He can still speak in Our Grandmother's secret tongue."

Big Fish looked incredulously at Tecumseh. "Your brother?" Big Fish had already observed to his own satisfaction that Loud Noise was only a crazy pest, a cracked-brain, if anything, more akin to the Devil than to the Creator. But he did not dare say this to Tecumseh, especially not now.

"Yes. Someday we will see." Tecumseh could smell woodsmoke now. "The town is just beyond," he said, pointing ahead. "Sometime I would like you to tell me about this Chief Moses. I am interested in how he handled his enemies."

"He had more trouble with his own tribe than he did with his enemies, it seems to me," Big Fish mused.

Tecumseh thought of that. He sensed there would be something important for him in the story of Chief Moses helping his people. Tecumseh walked on in the cold moonlight, watching his breath condense before him. He wanted to say something to Big Fish about the books he had but thought that this was perhaps not yet the time.

But soon, he thought. I waited too long to ask Copper Hair.

"Tell me something," said Big Fish after a while. He had been walking along wrapped in thought about all these things he had heard. "That Grandmother's language your brother speaks . . ." He paused, uncertain whether he should dare to say this. "Is that all that noise he blows out of his behind?"

Tecumseh whooped, popped the white boy on the head with his hand, and laughed so loud in the still night that dogs in the distant town started barking. "Big Fish," he exclaimed when he could finally speak, "you're a contrary!"


In the springtime Chiksika stood on a high place that made his heart feel full of power. Five hundred feet below him flowed the Beautiful River, and the Scioto-se-pe ran into it just upstream. The stone promontory upon which he stood was a sacred place, where the shamans of the ancient tribes had held their ceremonies hundreds of years before the coming of the white men. So often they had made great magic here that grass could not grow near the place.

This great rock projected out from the bluff like the head of a giant raven. Under the overhanging rock there were caves full of the bones and bowls and weapons of the Ancient Peoples. And on the Raven's Head itself stood a crumbling stone tower that had been used as a signal light by the race of giant white Indians whose ghosts now reigned over all of Kain-tuck-ee.

From this high place Chiksika could see so far up and down the curves of the Beautiful River that a boat coming into view with the first morning light would still be in view at noon.

And that was why Chiksika was here. From this height he could see the white men's big boats, those floating houses of theirs that were big enough to carry even horses and cattle and wagons, when they were so far away they looked like dots on the river. And then he could signal to the warriors where they waited along the shores far below, where they waited near their swift canoes, and tell them what they needed to know to attack the boats when they came down. Since the Long Knife Clark had captured the Middle Ground from the British and destroyed the Shawnee towns, white men had been coming down in hundreds of boats, to get Kain-tuck-ee land. And the warriors, with Chiksika up here as their raven-eyes, preyed on the boats. They took scalps and weapons and powder and lead, and tools and grain and whiskey and horses, all to rebuild the strength of their nation which Clark had hurt so badly. Long ago, said the legends in the Delaware picture-stories, the ancestors of the Shawnees had gone down to the great Falling Water place and killed all the arrogant white giants.

When Chiksika stood on this high place, he felt that he might be on the other side of the Circle of Time, like those brave ancestors, and it seemed to him that it could be done again.

This spring and this summer the warriors suffered no defeats, and they wrought much damage on the whites. The Shawnees' spirit began to heal, and most of the tribe moved back down to the old beloved townsites at Chillicothe and Piqua and planted crops in the same fields the Long Knives had burned. Everybody worked, even boys, to rebuild the towns from the ashes. The crops grew well because of the burning of the fields. The world seemed less bad now. Soon the People could resume their games and ceremonies and the dances and story-telling they so loved.

Black Hoof was glad for this happiness he saw returning in his people. His noble face was warm, and he talked to encourage that happiness. But behind his glittering black eyes dwelt the realistic mind. He knew that for every boatload of white people his warriors destroyed, ten or twenty more went on unmolested to Kain-tuck-ee. The places that had been forts two years ago and towns a year ago were becoming cities, and where there had been only solitary cabins, there were now towns that would also become cities. A chief could only guess how many settlers had poured into the Sacred Hunting Ground of Kain-tuck-ee this year, but Black Hoof thought his own guess of five to seven thousand was not too large.

And a place that had so many people, he knew, would be able to raise bigger and stronger armies to fight the red men.

When the Shawnee nation had divided, Black Hoof had been one of the chiefs who had vowed to stay and defend the homeland forever. But sometimes now he would stand at the door of his lodge and look along the street at the little town of a few hundred bark huts, and he would think how few Shawnees there were, indeed, how few red men, and he would think:

What will it be to defend our land next year when ten thousand more whites occupy Kain-tuck-ee, and the next year after that, when a hundred thousand more are there, and there will be thousands of them to the west of us in the Missi-se-pe valley, and they keep crowding into O-hi-o from the east?

And he would sigh. And then a woman and a child would walk up the street on the way to their garden, chatting happily, and they would nod and smile at him, and he would remember how they had looked last fall, crying, fleeing the burning towns. He would smile back at them, as a chief had to do.

Loud Noise was following a tortoise along the edge of a meadow, watching its ponderous, heavy movements, which were rather like his own, when he heard a deep droning sound nearby. Looking up, he saw dark specks darting in and out of a hole in the trunk of a dead oak. Bees. It was a honey tree!

At once he forgot the tortoise. Loud Noise was mad about maple sugar and papaws and honey, honey most of all. He would do almost anything, risk any punishment or censure, to steal a little of it from the *wigewa* of anyone who had some, to dig off a chunk of honeycomb and eat it, even just to stick his finger in and lick it.

Here, he realized, was a tree with probably handfuls of honey in it, and apparently no one else knew about it. He grew so excited looking at it that he started drooling and his body began to tremble. He edged up close to the tree and determined that the hole would be easy to reach into, if he climbed to a thick old limb that stuck out of the trunk about a man's height off the ground.

But as he stood next to the tree, the bees' drone began to sound very menacing. They shot in and out like little bullets and came so close around him that a few times he could feel the fanned air off their little wings.

Loud Noise had been stung by bees and hornets a few times in his life, when he had touched or stepped on them unexpectedly, and once he had sat on a wasp in the *wigewa,* and he could remember all too well the sudden, burning pain of their stings. Quickly he trotted away from the bee tree to a safe distance and stood looking at it, wondering what to do. He was not one of those boys who, like Tecumseh, would bear pain.

And yet one of the worst kinds of pain he could think of would be the pain of knowing that this honey tree was here and that he could not have the honey, and that somebody else might find it and get it.

There were two ways the village boys usually got honey. The most reckless of them would simply tear or chop away the wood to enlarge the hole, then reach in and dig out fistfuls of honey as fast as they could, taking the mad stings as the price of the delicious treasure. More cautious boys would build a smudge fire to stun the bees first. A drawback to this method was that first one must bring or make fire; another was that it was hard to smoke out bees in secret. Anyone who tried to smoke a bee tree usually ended up having to share the honey with many accomplices or onlookers who had been attracted by the smoke. The Shawnees had not had much experience with honeybees. It was believed that bees had come to the land only a few generations ago; it was believed they had been brought by the white men, and that they had escaped and found hollow trees to live in all over the land. Loud Noise knew nothing of all this; all he knew was that he was mad about honey, and that he must devise a way to get it all.

The idea of smoking the bees and attracting everyone's attention to the bee tree did not seem a much better way to get the honey than the first, terribly painful way, which was out of the question. And so it seemed necessary to think of an entirely new way to get honey out of a tree, and he stood thinking and drooling. He thought of the turtle and wondered if he might somehow make himself a shell of bark or something to protect his whole body from stings. But with such a shell, even if he could make one, and even if he could climb the tree with it, his hands and face would still be vulnerable to stings. No. That would not work. He did not know whether bees could sting through ordinary deerskin clothing but suspected that they could and did not want to test it.

At last he gave up trying to invent and thought about his brother Cat Follower, and a plan came to mind. It was a plan by which he might have to share some of the honey, but if he dealt properly with Cat Follower, he might not have to share quite half of it, and maybe even less. Loud Noise turned and headed toward the town to find his brother. He found him near the riverbank with some of the other boys, engaged in a spear-throwing game. He got him aside and whispered something to him, and then, acting very carefree and aimless, the two brothers wandered off. They took a long way around in case the others became curious and tried to follow them.

Cat Follower, of the triplets, was the one who tried hardest to be like their older brother Tecumseh. He was brave and honest. But unlike Tecumseh, he was not especially smart, and Loud Noise often had been able to fool him for useful purposes.

Now Loud Noise told Cat Follower that he had found a honey tree and that he needed help to get the honey because there was so much of it. It would be their secret, and they could have it all to divide between themselves. "I," said Loud Noise, "cannot climb as well as you. I am not fast or strong like you. But I have learned to cast a spell over bees so they will not sting. If you will climb to the bee hole, I will put a spell on the bees, and you can gather their honey."

Cat Follower was not a simpleton. He looked warily at Loud Noise and said, "I remember how you made a spell to keep the poison vine from hurting you, and then wiped your bottom with it."

"I am older now and better at spells, and this of the bees I am very good at doing. Of course I know that you are not afraid of beestings anyway, and you are brave and do not cry. Think of having half of all the honey from a tree! It will be far more honey than you have ever had to eat! But only I know where it is."

Finally, by his flattering appeals and his irresistible descriptions of honey, descriptions that made his own mouth water so that he could hardly talk, Loud Noise persuaded Cat Follower. They went to Star Watcher's house. She was out. They got a kettle with a handle. Then they went to the tree and looked at it and planned their attack. Loud Noise made up some of his nonsensical words to chant and make the spell. Cat Follower stood, holding his *pa-waw-ka* in his hand, hardening his courage. Loud Noise himself had never even tried to earn one, and now he hoped that Cat Follower's token would help him.

Finally Cat Follower felt ready, and he picked up the kettle and climbed up and stood on the big branch. The bees were in a fury over his presence. Taking a deep breath, he thrust his hand into the hole. He found the big combs before his whole hand and arm became numb from stings. He gouged honey out and dumped it in the kettle. The spell was not working at all, but Cat Follower had started this and mere pain was not going to stop him; it would not have stopped his brother Tecumseh.

Bees were drumming around him and stinging his entire body, and in particular his face. Everything blurred as his eyes watered and swelled shut. He could not see Loud Noise, who had hidden himself at a safe distance, but when at last the kettle was full he yelled for him to come and catch it. This was the scary part for Loud Noise, but he lumbered to the base of the tree, caught the kettle, and raced away into hiding. He had not, of course, told Cat Follower that he would go and hide. He wanted some time to eat honey before he had to share it with his brother. Loud Noise exulted. Not one bee had touched him! There were a few in the kettle, but they were bogged down and helpless in honey.

Cat Follower, blind, gritting his teeth but still not crying out, was too full of aching fire from his stings to climb down, so he just jumped recklessly from the limb to the ground, fell, got up, and crashed through the woods in the direction of the creek. He plunged in, stayed under until most of the bees were gone, and then crawled out. Shaking and gasping, he caked himself with soothing mud, and then, unable to see, he groped around, calling for Loud Noise.

In his hiding place, Loud Noise gorged himself on honey. By the time he had had so much of it that he was sick and could eat no more, there was no more left anyway. He lay gasping and sweating and retching in his covert for several hours. He was afraid he was going to die. And he was afraid that if he did not die from this sickness, Cat Follower would kill him for having eaten all the honey.

Loud Noise would not have had to worry about what his brother would do to him.

Cat Follower's body, mud-covered and swollen with stings, his face as big and hard as a pumpkin, had been found in the woods a hundred paces from the creek. His death brought a deep grief to the family. Loud Noise, not wanting to make things worse, decided to tell nothing.


Late in the fall of that year, Simon Girty brought to the Shawnees some news from far away. It was hard for Black Hoof and his people to conceive of what it meant, but their imaginations dwelt on it for a while, and after much thought Black Hoof concluded that the news would probably have a greater effect upon the fate of his people than it had seemed at first hearing.

Girty told the people in council: "The American soldier chief named Washington won a great battle at a place called Yorktown by the Great Sea, and the British chief in the east surrendered his whole army to Washington."

"Does this mean that the war between our father the king of England and the Long Knives is over?" Black Hoof asked.

"That I do not know. There is no peace treaty yet that I hear of," replied Girty.

"But if there comes a peace treaty, many of the whites who have been busy in the east fighting the king's soldiers will not be busy at that anymore. Washington's soldiers will be rewarded with land for their service in the army. What land do you think that would be?"

Black Hoof drew a long breath. His eyes glittered with anger, then he exhaled and looked very tired. He said in a low voice, "Since Clark threw down the British here, the land of the tribes has been filling with Long Knives. If the British give up the war, I am afraid, and I am sure, the Long Knives will claim all the Middle Ground in their boldness." His eyes were bright with anger again. "Therefore," he said, "war against the Long Knives is not over for us. It is just starting."

In the spring of the next year a messenger came from the Delawares, with a tale so horrible that he fell dumb several times before he could finish telling it.

It had happened on the Tuscarawas branch of the Muskingum, two days' hard ride to the east, where a small band of Delawares, sometimes known as the Jesus Indians, lived near the missions of the Moravians. These were people who had accepted the white man's God, forsworn all violence, and raised crops. Most tribes considered them to be harmless dupes and their chief, Abraham, formerly Netawatwis, a soft-headed fool.

A few days ago, the messenger related, a company of Pennsylvania militia had gone to the mission town of Gnadenhutten and, pretending friendship, disarmed the Jesus Indians and tied them up in the mission. Then they had lined them all up facing the walls, a hundred men, women, and children, and, while they prayed to Jesus for mercy, one by one had smashed their heads with a mallet. Then the soldiers had burned the mission down over the corpses. Two boys had escaped to tell of it.

The Shawnees were stunned, then enraged. From that moment on, the red man's war against the white man would be a holy war, to rid the land of a people who were too evil to exist. In Pennsylvania the great Mohawk chief Brant was gathering a large force of warriors to punish the Pennsylvanians. The Shawnees, too, must join with Brant. "We will," Black Hoof vowed.

# CHAPTER 16

## Blue Licks
## August 1782

A s Chiksika and Tecumseh rode their horses into the shallow water of the Licking River at its fording place, Chiksika said: "Right here is where we captured Boone and his salt makers. This very place." He pointed, smiling, along the riverbank. "There, you see, is the salt lick where they were. Ha, ha! That was a good day!"

This was the first cheerfulness Chiksika had shown for several days. That memory of a triumph five years ago was better than this present expedition, which had so far been a dismal failure.

The fording place was full of horsemen crossing the river toward the northeast. Most of them were Old Moluntha's Maykujays and other Shawnees. But there were also British Redcoats and some Rangers in their green coats. The horses splashed through the shallows, the spraying water glittering in sunlight. A few of the warriors and soldiers had bloodstained bandages.

The party, numbering about two hundred and fifty, was retreating toward O-hi-o. They had failed after a two-day siege to capture a fort called Bryant's Station, near the big town of Lexington. Messengers had escaped through the besiegers' lines, and the British commander of the force, Captain Caldwell, had grown afraid that Long Knife reinforcements would arrive. And so this morning he had lifted the encirclement, and the retreat had begun. It had been a sorry campaign, one that had increased Chiksika's scorn for the leadership of British officers.

Tecumseh, though still too young at fourteen to fight as a warrior, had come on the expedition with the camp followers. There were several of them, wives, lovers, and children of the British and Canadians. Caldwell's own wife was an Indian woman, a Shawnee. From hills and woods out of gunshot range, Tecumseh had been able to observe for the first time an attack upon a Kain-tuck-ee fort. It had been thrilling at first, all the shooting and smoke, the warriors darting from stump to stump to get close to the walls, the shouted commands, the vocal taunts between the attackers and the defenders. But nothing decisive had been done, and it had grown frustrating just to watch as the hours wore into days. Tecumseh, eager to see the massacre of the Jesus Indians avenged, could hardly bear to see the attack so mired down. Though his only knowledge of war had been the mock battles of his boyhood and the things Chiksika had told him, he had seen several opportunities not taken: feints, the use of fire-arrows, tunnels. Captain Caldwell had not done any of the bold things that could have been done. And then finally he had fled at the mere thought of enemy reinforcements. It was no wonder Chiksika was so disgusted.

Now as their horses splashed through the shallow ford toward the dark green hills on the other side, shouts from the rear of the column turned their heads. In a moment, one of the trailing scouts came galloping his horse into the river, calling out that Long Knives were coming.

Chiksika's eyes were suddenly flashing. He cried, "Come, brother!" and whipped his horse to speed to the head of the column with the messenger.

The messenger's horse was dancing around as the scout told what he had seen: many mounted militia soldiers, following fast; he had seen them at a distance of perhaps two miles. Captain Caldwell, his worst fears realized, looked scared and confused. But Old Moluntha seemed delighted. So was Chiksika. He pointed up into the ravines ahead, crying: "Up in there! A perfect trap! We should hide up in the woods there and ambush them when they cross the river!" Girty told Caldwell it looked like a good plan and added that there really was no alternative. Gone from the chieftains' faces was the sullen disappointment they had displayed since the retreat from Bryant's Station; they were eager to meet their pursuers. "Now we can catch them outside their burrows!" Chiksika exclaimed, and Tecumseh remembered when Black Fish had said the same thing so cheerfully.

Captain Caldwell, though not so eager, answered yes and acted quickly. He turned and shouted orders to his Redcoats and Rangers. Moluntha, though old and wizened, still had a powerful voice, and he sent his warriors up the ravine to lay the ambush.

"Now, brother," Chiksika exclaimed, gripping Tecumseh's arm, "go up on the ridge. Take the white men's women and children up there out of the way of harm. Hurry them. There is not much time! I think this will be a good day after all! Ha!"

With the English he had learned from Big Fish, Tecumseh was able to herd the camp followers toward the high ridge, leading them up the ravine, which branched and rebranched. Everywhere around them as they went panting and clunking up the draw with their baggage and cooking pots, warriors were dismounting and melting into the terrain. Below, the river flowed over the fording place. The last of the trailing scouts came out of the woods on the other shore and dashed across the ford.

The scene fell into silence. Locust calls spun out. Tecumseh secured his mount to a sapling and clambered up onto a big, mossy fallen log to watch down the ravine. For a while there was no sound but the drone of insects and the anxious voices of the camp followers. Tecumseh lay with his bare chest on the mossy bark. He picked a wood tick off his sweaty arm and flicked it away.

Now he could hear hoofbeats on the other side of the river, and his heartbeat quickened. He watched the place where the road came out of the woods.

Soon the white men began riding out of the trees, their rifles across the pommels of their saddles. They rode to the bank as if to come straight across the ford and up the ravine into the trap, and Tecumseh's heart now pounded against the tree. There were so many of them! They kept riding out of the green woods and onto the riverbank. They were all dressed in gray and brown and tan. In the still, hot summer air their voices and the sounds of their movements rose up from the valley, a great rush of noises: horses snorting, iron-shod hooves on gravel, men yelling questions and replies.

Near the river's edge one of the leading figures, in tan hunting shirt and black hat, had raised his hand and signaled for a halt, and he was scanning the ridge and ravines. Then he yelled something, and Tecumseh recognized the voice at once:

Boone!

Tecumseh felt a rush of confused emotions. At the first sound of that voice his heart had leaped up in pleasure, because this man once had been his foster brother, Sheltowee, the Big Turtle. But Boone had betrayed Black Fish, and thus he was hated and marked to be killed, and Tecumseh was sure that every Shawnee warrior lying down there in ambush had recognized his voice and noted him as a special target. It would be terrible to see Sheltowee killed, but then this was no longer Sheltowee, it was Captain Boone, who did not belong in this sacred Kain-tuck-ee hunting ground and who had ridden out here with all these Long Knives to chase and kill red men. There was no other way to consider it now.

Boone seemed to be arguing with other white men, who were gathering around him on their agitated horses. The horses wanted to go to the water and drink, but the Long Knives were holding them back and having their council with Boone. The whole army was backing up behind them on that riverbank; some were still coming out of the woods on the road.

Tecumseh remembered that Boone was not a man who could be easily trapped. Maybe Boone sensed the danger that lay in the ravines across the river from him.

In half of his heart, Tecumseh now was willing Boone to forget his caution and cross over; in the other half he was remembering Boone smiling at him from across a campfire and wishing he would turn back.

Suddenly one of the white men, a bold-looking figure on a big black horse, snatched off his hat, waved it, broke away from Boone, and rode down into the river, yelling in a loud, snarly voice as he came. Many of the white men then howled and spurred their horses and rode in after him.

They were coming now. Tecumseh gripped the bark of the log. They were splashing across the ford like a hundred unthinking herd animals and riding straight for the ambush.

Boone, on his rearing horse, was shouting angrily at them and waving his hat to try to summon them back, as were some of the others. Then, as if to get ahead of them and turn them back, he kicked his horse and galloped into the ford with them, a young man riding at his side.

For a few tense moments then the white men were swarming noisily across the bottomland and up the ravine, straight into the trap. More than a hundred were across, and a few were still riding out of the woods on the other side, when the wooded hillside exploded in a storm of gunfire and smoke, shouts, tremolo war cries, and the whinnying and screaming of wounded horses. Soon the ravines were full of drifting smoke, through which Tecumseh could barely glimpse flashes of a great confusion. In the bottomland below the ravine, riderless horses were bolting back toward the river, running into the riders still coming up. Men were running for cover or standing and shooting and shouting until they fell.

It went on and on. Of the white men in the river, some were trying to turn their horses and flee while others were trying to rush forward into the battle, and these were colliding with each other, shouting, many falling off their horses and floundering in the water. But it was down in the wooded ravines out of Tecumseh's sight that the uproar was most terrible.

And then after a while—only a quarter of an hour had passed since the shooting erupted, though it had seemed to be a day—the bottomland and the river itself were full of desperately retreating whites, limping, dragging, or carrying each other, bawling for help, trying to catch runaway horses by their bridles, some turning to shoot back up into the woods as they retreated. The war cries in the woods were shrill and triumphant, and pitiful were the screams of the dying Long Knives.

Chiksika's eyes were ablaze. Tecumseh rode beside him along the Warrior's Path toward the Beautiful River in the twilight and listened to him as he told of details of the great victory. Chiksika himself had three fresh scalps at his belt and not a scratch on him. He was nearly bursting with triumph but still seething with anger at the British captain. "We might have chased them down into the river and wiped them out to the last one," Chiksika said. "But Captain Caldwell was afraid still more pursuers might come."

He had called a retreat after the whites had been routed, and the warriors had reluctantly given up their carnage.

Boone had escaped, through hundreds of bullets; his God apparently had put a cloak of safety around him, and he had staggered to safety, carrying the body of his own son. "Now Boone feels what he once made Black Fish feel," Chiksika gloated. "The death of a son. Ha! All things come back around!"

The Shawnees had never had a bigger victory over the Long Knives. They had killed seventy and wounded more than that—all fighting men, no women and children. It was more rich with glory than if they had merely captured Bryant's Station. Perhaps now those poor foolish murdered Jesus Indians could look down from whichever heaven they had gone to and see that for once there had been justice done on the earth below.


Three moons later Blue Jacket galloped into Chillicothe on a spent horse, and his face was full of storm. He took no time to answer the men and boys who ran out in the cold to greet him, so they knew without a word that something was very bad. Blue Jacket rode straight to Black Hoof's lodge and said as he leaped off his horse:

"Clark comes with his big army again."

Black Hoof was not surprised. His face set in sadness, in resignation.

"It has taken me a long lifetime to learn what the old men said at the beginning: Revenge is never satisfied."


Tecumseh crouched behind a boulder and listened to the distant rustling and crushing of dry leaves as the horse soldiers approached. As he checked the priming powder in his flintlock for the fourth or fifth time, he saw that his hand was trembling. He tried to will it to be steady but could not. The awful thing had happened, the thing every boy worried and wondered about as he grew closer to the warrior's age: he was scared, very scared.

Maybe if he had not had to face the enemy until he was sixteen or seventeen, his courage would have matured by then. But he was not yet quite fifteen, and the scarcity of warriors had made it necessary for some his age to help the warriors defend against Clark. Though he had been in the presence of the enemy at Chillicothe and Piqua and Blue Licks, he had not been there facing the Long Knives as a warrior on the line. Sometimes in those past years he had been scared, in a way, but he had been eager to do something. Now he was at the test, and he only wanted to be away from it.

The rustling of the leaves down on the riverbank grew louder. His hand kept trembling, and he was ashamed of it, and he hoped that his brother Chiksika, a few feet away, could not see it. And now as the warriors crouched waiting in the cold, stark woods watching for the Long Knife soldier-scouts to ride into close gunshot range, another part of Tecumseh's body seemed ready to help shame him:

Unexpectedly he felt a powerful need to move his bowels and to make water.

This was a terrible onslaught of betrayals by his own body, this body that had always been so strong and healthy and quick to serve him. He had feared that his will might falter in the face of death but had not worried about the body in which it dwelt. But now this. How could he possibly fight well and shoot straight while having to hold his hands steady and his openings shut?

"Brother," Chiksika's voice said softly beside him. "*Weshecat-too-weh,* be strong! You are now *nenothtu,* warrior!"

Tecumseh nodded. He barely glanced at his brother, not wanting him to see the fear that was surely showing in his eyes. Chiksika was crouched there lithe as a great cat, his cheekbones and chin painted as usual in yellow, the one eagle feather sticking up from his scalplock. Chiksika had fought so many times since that day eight years ago when he had first gone into the big battle beside their father Hard Striker. He had never told Tecumseh anything about being scared.

I am unworthy, Tecumseh thought. He did not want this first chance to prove himself the great warrior of the signs. All he wanted to do was go back to a safe, hidden place and relieve himself and stay hidden until this was over.

*I am unworthy!*
*Weshecat-too-weh!*
*No, I am unworthy and weak!*
*Weshecat-too-weh!*

Now he heard flintlock hammers being cocked all around him, and their sound squeezed his bowels and bladder even tighter. He clamped and squirmed to control them as the first of the Long Knife soldiers appeared in the thick leafless brush by the riverbank below, and his hand shook more violently.

Two horsemen passed below, veering to the left, their eyes darting everywhere. These two were dressed in skins and were lean and hard-looking. Probably these were advance scouts; Clark was known by now to be almost impossible to surprise because of the fringe of scouts he always kept far out on all sides of his army. Those who had just passed were strong-looking men, keen and hawk-faced. But at least neither of them was But-lah, the chief Long Knife scout. And they did not have dogs. And so they seemed not to have detected this ambush. The two rode on up the riverbank among the bare gray trees in the bottomland along the Mad River.

This morning Chiksika's war party had gazed southward to see the enormous smoke clouds rising into the sky where Chillicothe had been burned down once again. There had been no fight at Chillicothe. Once again Black Hoof had abandoned the town and left it to the Long Knives. There had not been enough warriors to defend it.

This time he had also abandoned Piqua Town, and also the upper and lower towns where the Shawnees had wintered after Clark's last attack. This year Black Hoof had moved his people far north and west, clear up to Wapatomica Town on the Upper Mad River, far enough, he hoped, that neither wing of Clark's army could get there in this late season. And to keep Clark from getting to that final stronghold, Black Hoof had sent certain select warriors, like Chiksika and Stands Firm and Blue Jacket and Black Snake, to lay traps all along the Long Knives' route of march, to ambush them, harass them, and then withdraw to ambush them again and pull back again, to kill as many officers as they could until perhaps Clark's column would become too long and disorderly to continue. It was the only kind of resistance the Shawnees had the resources to make anymore.

This was just such an ambush. Chiksika was in charge, and Stands Firm was his second. Now the white scouts had ridden past without detecting it, and soon the advance part of the army would emerge among the dry brown leaves and the gray tree trunks, and as many of them as possible should be killed, and then there would be fewer to fight at the next ambush. Along every river and across every trace between the Shawnee and Miami towns there would be ambushes like this, of a dozen or a score of warriors, who would do all they could to hinder Clark's advance even though there was no chance of stopping it until Clark chose to stop. It would stop only when Clark should decide he had done enough to avenge the losses at Blue Licks.

Now Tecumseh sensed that Chiksika had moved and stiffened. He looked and saw him lay his cheek against his gunstock and close his left eye. Tecumseh looked out over the lichen-spotted boulder, his heart quaking and hand shaking and his sphincter tight, and saw the front part of the army coming, saw clothes and metal through the gray brush, mounted men mostly in tan and gray, with bullet bag and powder horn slings crisscrossing their chests.

"*Metchi,* many!" Stands Firm murmured nearby.

"Shoot the officers," Chiksika said softly. "Now!" And he squeezed the trigger.

The cracking guns and the smoke all around almost made Tecumseh dirty himself in that moment. His gunsight was on a whiteface when he squeezed the trigger, but he knew the gun was unsteady, and by the time he was groping for his powder horn to reload, the horsemen were already coming at a canter, yelling in bold rage and shooting. Chiksika gasped in pain, and Tecumseh in the edge of his vision saw him clap his left hand on his right shoulder. A rifle ball ricocheted off the boulder in front of Tecumseh with a deadly *spannnng!* and his cheek was stung hard by stone grit, and the Long Knives were charging at him as if they had no fear. . . .

The next thing Tecumseh really knew was that he was squatting in a ravine emptying his waste on the ground, moaning like a hurt animal in his fear and shame, and that the shouting and shooting were still going on down near the river, and he was hearing in his head, *I am unworthy I am unworthy,* and he was wondering how he could ever face his brother Chiksika again, if Chiksika still lived. *I am unworthy I am unworthy!*

The worst of all possible kinds of shame was upon Tecumseh. He had lost control of his will and had just cast away his rifle and run blindly into the woods to do this on the ground, this which had seemed more important than living or dying or having honor. And now with shaking hands, and with tears wetting his nose and little strangled sobs in his throat, he was standing here in a stark woods pulling up his loincloth and tying the band around his waist and wondering whether Chiksika was alive and what to do now and wishing that that rifle ball instead of its rock dust had hit him. It was the worst moment he had ever had in his life, and all his tomorrows looked no better than what he had left in the leaves on the ground.

There was no punishment given for such a thing. Chiksika and the warriors did not call him a coward or even look at him with contempt. In fact, they did not look at him at all. It was as if he were painted black for a Vision Quest. They had not been able to see him during the fight, so he must not really be, and so they could not see him now. It was worse than if they had looked right at him and said, "Tecumseh, you are a coward."

Chiksika's war party made no campfire that night. They made their cold camp on a rise of ground north of Piqua. They had no need of fire for light because the flames of burning Piqua Town lit the sky in the south.

Still no one said anything to Tecumseh as the night wore on. They dressed their wounds and ate cold jerky and then got ready to sleep, putting two men on guard and one near the horses.

Tecumseh lay, sick in his heart, looking up at the dull red fireglow on the underside of the low clouds, and felt as if he were alone in the entire world. He was exhausted by fear and remorse. He went to sleep wondering whether he would be able to redeem himself the next day if Chiksika made another ambush, but also wondering if he would be the same again and not be brave enough to redeem himself.

When he awoke before dawn the next day, he seemed still not to exist in the warriors' eyes. The shoulder of Chiksika's tunic was cut open and brown with blood from his wound. The wound was like a reproach. The worst part of what Tecumseh had done was to desert his beloved brother after he had been hit. But in spite of this, there was no scorn in Chiksika's eyes, just a look of sadness. He said to Tecumseh:

"Ride to Wapatomica Town. Tell Black Hoof of our ambush yesterday and tell him we will try to do as well today, if the Long Knives continue to come on beyond Piqua Town, and that we will keep doing it as long as they come. And that if they turn and go back toward Kain-tuck-ee now, we will follow and try to kill them one by one as they go."

Tecumseh nodded. He suspected that he was being sent back so that the warriors would not have to depend upon a coward in battle again. This thought nearly crushed his heart. And then he asked a question that he had been thinking of last night while lying awake looking at the red clouds.

"When I tell Black Hoof what we did, shall I tell him what I did?"

"Ask not me but yourself," said Chiksika. There seemed to be a cold distance between them. "I," said Chiksika, "will not tell Black Hoof. These warriors . . . I do not think they will tell him. After all, you are only a boy."

Tecumseh looked down. It was terrible to be called "only a boy" by someone who had the day before called him a warrior. He looked up at Chiksika's face and said:

"Tell me truly why you send me to Wapatomica. Are you afraid I will fail again? Or are you trying to keep me from harm, as you used to do?"

"To me," Chiksika answered, hardening himself to say the cruelest thing he had ever said to his young brother, "it seems you do well enough at keeping yourself from harm."

Tecumseh turned and ran to his horse. He sped away without looking back, thundering through the thickets so recklessly that the bare branches whipped him as if he were racing through a gauntlet.

He told Black Hoof what he had done.

The great Chalagawtha chief said nothing for a while. Of course he had much else on his mind. But finally, when no one was close by, he turned his intense dark eyes on Tecumseh and said:

"Your father and I were together the first time he was in battle. That was a long time ago, in the war when the English and the Frenchmen fought each other." He was still for a minute, and it seemed that perhaps he had mentioned Hard Striker only to add to Tecumseh's shame. But then Black Hoof went on, looking not at Tecumseh but at the distant treetops. "The first time the white soldiers shot at your father, he ran away."

Tecumseh's heart was in a tumult now. He felt even worse, as if his father's old shame as well as his own now weighed on his shoulders. Black Hoof continued:

"You did not know that."

"I did not know it. Chiksika never told me that."

"No. Chiksika himself did not know it. Chiksika was not there. Chiksika had not even been born. I was there. I saw it. It saddened my heart."

Tecumseh could only look at the ground now. But Black Hoof's rumbling voice said:

"From that time on your father was the bravest warrior I ever knew. I suppose he became a greater warrior than he would have been if he had not run away that first time. I have seen this happen with people who ran the first time."

Tecumseh thought on this revelation for a while. He did not know whether he would ever recover enough courage to face an enemy without fleeing. But at least he knew now that it meant a coward at first was not certain to be a coward forever. Finally Tecumseh took a deep breath and looked at Black Hoof's craggy face and said:

"May I ask you something, Father?"

"Ask me."

"Did *you* ever run away?"

Black Hoof took a sharp breath. Then he said, his voice deep and warm:

"If you dare to ask your chief that question, you surely have some boldness in your heart." He was quiet for a moment, then said: "I never ran away. Most warriors never do. But . . . but many times my feet have run forward when my heart wanted them to run backward. No, my son, I have never run away, but I have often been scared enough. No one is without fear. Not even Chiksika. But one can stay above his fear. That is what one must do. Maybe you thought you would have no fear in your heart, and you were defeated by discovering it there."

"I do not know what happened," Tecumseh said truthfully. He did not mention that about his bowels and bladder.

"Listen, my son. Most of what we learn is to keep us alive. Only one thing we learn is otherwise: to be brave in war. It is not hard to forget that one thing. Only remember this: When you are in war, then you must think first of keeping the People alive, and pray that Weshemoneto will help you in that. He does not like to hear a person pray for himself. But he answers prayers that are for the People."

Tecumseh that winter worked quietly at keeping the People alive. Once again the Shawnees were forced to live on the small portion of their crops that the Long Knives had not destroyed and in hastily made shelters far from their own towns. They moved into the edges of Maykujay Town, and Blue Jacket's Town, and Girty's Town, and Wapatomica, these being the only towns that Clark had not destroyed. The family stayed in Wapatomica Town. It stood on a plateau on the west side of the Upper Mad River. Above it was a high ridge with springs and below it the bottomlands. It was a good place for a town, but it was not a good place to be now. There was little game in the vicinity of these towns. Many of the old people were starving. Many mothers were so hungry they gave poor milk to their babies. The building and repair of *wigewas* was hard because winter is the wrong season to try to strip bark from trees.

And so Tecumseh, as if trying to redeem himself for his cowardice, which he perceived to have been a kind of selfishness, now gave almost all his waking hours to hunting and snaring meat, most of which he gave to families that had no hunters to provide for them or whose hunters were sick or unlucky. And the hides from the animals he killed he gave to the old people or the weak ones, who were poorly dressed for winter or who had gaps in their shelters. A hide could patch a bark hut and keep out some of the wind. The warriors had told no one about Tecumseh's flight from battle, so nobody knew that he was trying to atone for a sin. He had always been thoughtful toward old and weak people. Now when he would appear at the lodge of an old grandmother and give her the first venison haunch or marrow bones she had seen for days, the old woman would not say to herself, "What has come over Turtle Mother's son?" Instead she would say, "Ah, that one has always been so good a boy!"

Even Star Watcher did not know why he was doing all this, but it was what she believed a person should do, and she helped him. Some of every little bit she had, she gave him to give to the hungry and ragged ones. Star Watcher was growing a baby inside. Stands Firm told her not to give so much away, as she herself needed much nourishment for the baby. Then one day Chiksika came and told Tecumseh almost the same thing: "Brother, you do well to share so much. But listen. You must not starve yourself to feed those who do not hunt. I can see your bones under your skin. It is a duty of the hunter to stay strong enough to hunt. Consider the wolves."

"The wolves?"

"The wolves are like us. They depend upon each other. They hunt together and bring food home. They protect their mates and cubs. But though he is for his tribe, the hunter wolf knows he must feed himself. Because if he does not, then he will become another helpless one to feed."

It was so good to have Chiksika telling him things again. Tecumseh felt his heart flush with warmth for the first time in two moons' passing. Chiksika went on:

"You have not had enough chance to watch how the wolves do. Do you remember, I have told you that we will go someday to the prairies near the Missi-se-pe and hunt among the great herds of bison."

"Yes! I remember!"

"I hope that will be soon."

"Yes! I too!"

"When we go there, you will be able to see how the wolves do." He sighed. "Think how much time we would have to ride to new places and find plenty of game, if we did not have to be fighting the Long Knives all the time." Chiksika said this with a warm and yearning voice, and Tecumseh could tell that Chiksika had not mentioned fighting in a way to shame him. Chiksika had come to close the distance that had grown between them. "We lost much of everything again to Clark," Chiksika said now. "When the ice breaks and the white men's big rich boats start coming down the river again, we will have to go to the river as we have done in other years, and see what we can take from their boats to make it easier for our People to live."

"Yes. You will have to do that."

"So," said Chiksika. "Keep yourself strong, my brother. You will be needed to help us."

Tecumseh had to swallow hard to keep his heart from floating up and out.

One night Tecumseh said to Big Fish, "I have something I have long wanted to ask you about."

"What is it?"

Tecumseh went to his bed and reached under a corner and brought out a leather packet. He folded back the leather and held forth the two books he had been hiding for so long. Big Fish's eyes grew big.

"Oh! Where did you get those?" he asked, taking them in his hands. He bent forward and turned them in the firelight.

"Chiksika raided a boat on the river long ago. There were many of these. He brought only these two, the prettiest. Can you read what these are?"

"Yes. Of course. This one is the Holy Bible that we have talked about sometimes."

"Ah! That is good fortune. Most of the books went into the river. This one must have been spared because it is sacred."

"I guess so. . . ." Big Fish had opened the Bible and was looking in it for people's names. He went down the handwritten lists of marriages and births. It was a family he had never heard of before, so he put the Bible down and opened the other book, a small one with engraved pictures. "I know this book. This is *Hamlet.*"

"Is this too a sacred book?"

"I had a teacher once who seemed to think so. But no, it is not a sacred book like the Bible. This is a play." He used the only Shawnee word he knew for play, which was a verb, and Tecumseh was confused.

"This book you mean is like a game?"

"A game? No. How could a book be a game?"

"You said you play this book *Hamlet.*"

Big Fish pinched his earlobe and stared at the title page and tried to figure out how to explain what a play was. He thought about actors and stages, about which he knew practically nothing himself, and decided it would be better to try to explain all that some other time, or never. "It's a story, that's all," he said.

"Ah, a story!"

"About a prince, who—"

"A 'prince'?"

"Ah, a prince is like a young chieftain. His name was Hamlet. . . ."

"Ah! Same name as the book! How interesting that is. Tell me this story."

"I never understood this story very much. Somebody murdered Hamlet's father, by sticking something in his ear, I think it was. And Hamlet wanted to get revenge, but couldn't make up his mind. Nothing much happened in this book. People just talked a lot. To each other and to themselves. And there were ghost spirits in it. And a crazy girl."

Tecumseh thought about his own father, who had been killed by white men, and about revenge, which had become the main thing in everybody's life since the coming of the white men. "Why could not this chieftain make up his mind about the revenge?" Tecumseh asked. "Was he not brave?" He was thinking of everything in terms of what had happened to him.

"I don't know. These people talked grand, and I couldn't understand them much. Hamlet even talks to a, uhm, skull."

"What is 'skull'?"

Big Fish touched himself on the forehead. "The head bone. From a grave that was dug up. Named Poor York, I think it was."

"Oh, yes! In the book is a picture of somebody holding up a head bone. Look, look through the leaves for it!" He gestured with his forefinger, and Big Fish paged through, looking for it. "Yes, there it is," Tecumseh exclaimed. "I thought he dug that head bone up from that grave to steal it, as the Long Knives did when they burned Chillicothe. White men disturb our bones, you know? Girty says they are looking for silver. So! So I am glad this Hamlet was not stealing from this grave, but instead"—he chuckled—"talking to this head bone. Did the head bone answer?" He laughed. "Perhaps it was a contrary's head bone!"

Big Fish laughed, too, then said, "Maybe it was. In that story, only the skull had nothing to say!"


In the Green Moon, Tecumseh was once again with Chiksika and his warriors. One of them was Thick Water, who had already been in a few ambushes against the Long Knives and was said to be very bold. Thick Water had never run from any battles. Tecumseh was glad that Thick Water had not been at the ambush where he had disgraced himself last fall.

Tecumseh knew that if he lost heart and fled this time, he probably would never again get to be with Chiksika in a dangerous place. Chiksika had taken a big step in trusting his brother enough to give him this second chance. Chiksika himself did not want to be embarrassed again. And it was more than embarrassment; a warrior who fled from danger made the danger worse for his fellow warriors.

*Nenothtu,* Tecumseh addressed himself silently. Warrior.

Now at this moment Chiksika was watching his young brother out of the side of his eye as the ten warriors eased down a wooded slope of the river bluff toward the cookfire of the white men from the boat. The foliage on the trees was still light green and half-open and thus did not provide much cover. The warriors were creeping down from rock to rock and tree to tree, careful not to show themselves too soon, careful not to dislodge any stones that might clatter down.

These white men—there were thirteen of them, all well armed—had been spied from the Raven Head Rock, landing on the O-hi-o shore instead of the Kain-tuck-ee shore, near the mouth of the Scioto-se-pe. It was a cloudy, windy day, and the waves on the Beautiful River were rough, capped with white, and probably that was why they had put to shore here. The wind in the trees and along the narrow bottomland was rushing through the new foliage and whiffing over the water. The white men were trying to cook over whipping flames, so they were less vigilant about their surroundings, and the noise of the wind helped cover the little sounds of the warriors' approach. Most of the white men stood with their backs to the wind, but some were kneeling on the other side of the fire, squinting against the blown smoke. Three had left their guns in the boat, which was tied to a large snag at the shore. The others held their guns or leaned on them or had propped them against a willow trunk that stuck up near the fire. These men looked big and bulky and dirty in their long brown coats and three-cornered black hats. There were kegs and bundles and instruments in their big rowboat, which had an awning over the stern. One could only guess what kind of men these were, surveyors or traders, hunters or militiamen. Chiksika had a notion that they were army suppliers and hoped they were because of the things they would have. Whatever they were, they looked dangerous enough, and there were enough of them that they would have to be taken by surprise if this raid was to succeed.

Tecumseh had a weapon he had never used before. Stands Firm had given it to him. It was a war club, made of a fist-sized rock sewn into a rawhide casing that also enclosed the handle, a slender hickory stick as long as his forearm. By a loop this weapon could be hung from the right wrist, leaving the hand free for shooting and loading a rifle.

Tecumseh's heartbeat was going fast, but for once his hands were steady. He did not mean to disgrace himself again, and to prevent it he had done two things before starting this stalking of the whites' camp. He had gone into the woods to relieve himself. And then he had held his *pa-waw-ka* stone in his hand and clenched his fist over his heart and had asked through it for Weshemoneto to keep him brave and steady while he did this for the good of the People. Even now as he edged his way down around a mossy boulder closer to the white men, he could feel the warmth still glowing in his palm, and it was this, he believed, that kept his hand steady now, because he *was* scared, scared of what could happen in the next few moments. An attack like this one could turn out any way; there were more of the white men than of the warriors. Stands Firm had wanted to go up the Scioto-se-pe to the war camp and get more warriors and come back in canoes. But Chiksika had argued: "No. They could get away. This they have is a fast rowing boat, not a float boat."

One of the white men squatting beside the fire rose to his feet, looking toward the slope. He had a sharp, narrow face, dark with stubble. He was staring up at a place on the steep bluff. Tecumseh tensed. If that man had detected a warrior, things would have to be done with no hesitation. Tecumseh cocked his flintlock and aimed it at the man's chest.

The man suddenly began raising his rifle and yelled to the others, who burst from their positions like quail from a covert, snatching up their guns. In that same instant Chiksika screeched a tremolo and fired at the white men. Tecumseh pulled the trigger of his rifle, and several other guns went off at the same time. He yelled at the top of his lungs and sprang out from cover and ran like a deer, but this time he was running down the slope toward the enemy instead of the other way. In the edges of his vision he could see the naked, painted bodies of Chiksika and Stands Firm and Thick Water and others speeding and darting down through the fresh young foliage. Some of the white men's guns were going off. In ten quick strides the warriors were off the slope and onto the muddy, pebbly beach and in among the white men, some of whom were already on the ground. All that happened then was a whirl, and yet Tecumseh's senses were perceiving everything around him, and his reflexes were controlling his every move. He felt almost unbearably alive and vital. He wasted no motion. A big, broad-faced man with blue eyes and bared yellow teeth was aiming a pistol at him, but Tecumseh darted under its muzzle flash, and with the knife he held in his left hand, he stabbed up under the man's ribs. The turning of the man's falling body wrenched the knife out of Tecumseh's hand, and he saw now that another white man was in his way, his rifle barrel in both hands, starting to swing the gun like a club at Tecumseh. Tecumseh sprang like a cat at the man's legs, hitting them with all his weight, and then as he rolled over on the muddy ground, the white man fell with a grunt, his feet in the air. Tecumseh was immediately up in a crouch, and with his own gun butt he crushed the back of that man's skull. All around were yells and thuds and groans and pistol shots, and bodies lurching and turning and grappling. Chiksika was crouched in front of a thick-bodied man; both had their tomahawks ready and were about to strike each other. Tecumseh swung his rifle in a wide sweep that broke the handle of the white man's tomahawk, and then Chiksika lashed out and sank the long, narrow blade of his hatchet through the man's nose and into his brain. Chiksika uttered a triumphant syllable of a laugh for Tecumseh, but the boy had already spotted his next opportunity. Stands Firm had been thrown onto his back, and a white man was on top of him, with all his weight on both hands pressing his rifle barrel across Stands Firm's throat. Stands Firm was flailing and trying to get breath. The tomahawk blow had smashed the flintlock of Tecumseh's rifle, and he cast it aside. Now, with the long war club in his right hand, he leaped close to the struggling pair and aimed a curving side-armed blow at the white man's temple. The velocity of the swinging club head was so great that the man's skull exploded and the scalp burst open and a mass of bloody pink-gray brain matter was protruding when the man slumped to his side on the ground.

In an instant Stands Firm was up and fighting again, wielding the very rifle with which the man had been strangling him. He was exulting but could not yell because of his crushed windpipe.

Momentarily having no foe within reach, Tecumseh stood in a ready crouch, turning on the balls of his feet, getting his first glance at the whole battle. Twenty feet away, Thick Water, sweaty with desperate exertion, having lost or used up all his weapons, was bellowing like a madman and trying to wring the life out of a lanky man whom he held under his right arm in a powerful headlock. Thick Water needed no help.

The narrow-faced man at whom Tecumseh had fired his first and only shot lay on the beach on his back, dead, mouth open, a bloody hole in his gullet. Two warriors were knee deep in the river next to the tethered boat, each pulling one leg of a white man who had gotten halfway into the boat. One of the warriors raised a knife and began stabbing him in the buttocks. The man began screaming, and the Indians laughed and kept cutting his seat to bloody shreds. Elsewhere warriors were kneeling, taking the scalps off the men they had killed, and two warriors were running up the shore in pursuit of a white man who had lost his weapons and was trying to escape into the willows.

Tecumseh's heart was hammering. There were no more white men left to fight! Tecumseh held up his war club and looked at the dark blood spatters on its leather. The warriors were yelling and laughing now, waving bloody scalps, picking up weapons, piling into the boat and ransacking its cargo. The man Thick Water had been strangling had gone limp, and the big youth had dropped him to the ground and stood over him, chest heaving, looking around in amazement. The two warriors up the riverbank were coming out of the willow thicket, dragging by its feet the body of the white man they had chased. Not one warrior had been seriously hurt.

Chiksika came panting and grinning to Tecumseh. He grabbed his shoulders and held him at arm's length and looked into his eyes with open pride. Then he put a knife into Tecumseh's hand and pointed to some of the corpses on the beach.

"Those four are yours. Four!" he exclaimed. "You will want their scalps, my brother, as proof to the people who will be too amazed. Four!"

Now almost in a daze, feeling suddenly so tired he could hardly move,

Tecumseh went to each of his victims, knelt, wrapped his fingers in the hair, pulled up, and made a circular cut in the scalp. The trophies each came loose with a wet popping sound, except that of the man he had hit with the war club. His skull was too fragmented, and it was a mess getting his scalp off. Tecumseh was beginning to feel sick.

The scalplocks were all different. The hair of one was thick and brown and wavy. Another was the color of dry grass in autumn, straight and greasy. Another was thick and straight and black; the last was dark brown with some white hairs in it and sticky with blood. Tecumseh knew he should try to remember which lock of hair had come from each of the men he had killed. But it was too hard to concentrate now. He was swallowing hard.

It would not be good after all this for the others to see him vomit. He wondered if his body would in some way like this embarrass him every time he got into battle. So now his task was to keep from vomiting.

The only white man left alive of the thirteen was the one Thick Water had choked. He was conscious now, looking very miserable, one side of his face red with contusions. He had been stripped naked and tied to a willow tree, and his body was smudged with bruises. He looked like a man without a hope and stayed very quiet in order not to attract the attention of his captors.

Now the warriors, exultant, went about the business of gathering their booty and celebrating.

Much of the boat's cargo was gunpowder, lead, and weapons. Some of the small kegs in the boat contained gunpowder, a great prize. Two smaller kegs contained liquor, also a great prize. Apparently Chiksika had been right; it was a military supply boat. Perhaps all this had been on its way down to Clark's fort at the Falls. It was very satisfying to believe that.

The warriors were exuberant; all this they had done and with no losses of their own to grieve, so when some of them chopped in the ends of the liquor kegs, Chiksika did not stop them. In fact, Chiksika himself put his face down to the rum and sucked up a mouthful and stood up and swallowed it with a smile on his lips and tears in his eyes. Then he shuddered, teeth clenched, and let out a loud whoop. "Brother!" he called to Tecumseh. "You are a man now! You must taste this! Every man should know the taste of this! Here is the white man's most powerful medicine! With this in their veins it is no wonder they are such devils and fools! Hi-hi-*yeeee!*" And all the others of the band, who were rejoicing for Tecumseh's bravery and his remarkable deeds, agreed that he should celebrate with the strong spirit water.

Tecumseh had always done what Chiksika had told him to, so now he stepped up to the rum keg, dropped to his knees, and put his face down to it. The smell rising from it seared his nostrils and made his eyes water and nearly turned his stomach over, and he wondered, How can this be good? The liquor was the color of the gum that forms on the bark of a nicked wild cherry tree, a beautiful color, but the stench of it was like evil itself. Surely the urine of the Great Horned Snake must smell like this. He did not want any. He was afraid of it; it seemed to burn the eyes and nose with invisible flame. The other warriors had already drunk some, and he could see that they were becoming clumsy and looking stupid in the eyes and whooping over anything. But they were all encouraging him to do it, and he did not want anyone ever again to think he was afraid of anything, so he put his face down through the rankling stink and sucked up a mouthful. It burned in his mouth, and he swallowed it at once.

It was as if it did not belong in a person; it tried to turn and come back up. He clamped his throat to keep it down. His eyes poured tears, and everything blurred. The fluid did not come back up, but it boiled and burned in his gullet and guts, and its fumes now came up from inside him to scorch the inside of his nose and the back of his eyeballs. He gasped for fresh air, but the air made it seem even more putrid. His lips and fingers had gone numb, and a wind was singing and hissing in his head. But just as he was making a silent vow never to let another drop of such an evil fluid pass his lips, something in him was beginning to change, and he was starting to feel grand and strong and wise and funny.

Thick Water did not go back for more of the liquor. Tecumseh asked him, "Do you not like that?"

"Not much," Thick Water replied, making a face. "I drank some on another raid, and it made me sick when I drank it, and the next day also." He leaned close. "I pretend to drink some."

The warriors grew clumsier and sillier as they drank the rum and demolished the white men's boat. Everything they wanted to keep they were carrying over to cache under a ledge in the river bluff; they would come back for it in big canoes later. As they staggered and pranced across the beach carrying things to the cache, they laughed at each other's clumsiness and dropped things and laughed because of that, and they laughed out of sheer hilarity from their own thoughts. Then, as dusk deepened, they set to work bashing the boat apart with heavy tools they had found, and this proved to be the most uproarious fun of all. Three of the warriors fell into the river, one of them twice. One of them, pounding on the same plank he was standing on, plunged his leg through the bottom of the boat when it broke loose under his foot. His leg was gashed deeply by a splintery end, but he and the others found it all so comical that they stood helpless with laughter while he bled profusely from the leg that stuck through the bottom of the sinking boat.

By the time they had managed to shatter and sink the boat, though, their drunkenness had taken an ugly turn. Some had taken or thrown overboard things that others said they had already claimed, and these disputes had broken into quarrels. One warrior drew a knife and threatened another, and Chiksika had to take the knife away, getting slightly cut on the arm while doing it. Tecumseh's head was whirling, even though he had not drunk any more after that first draught. When the others had coaxed him to drink more, he had put his lips to it and only pretended to drink. He did not like the feeling of losing control over himself and was determined that he never would again. It was true that the warriors were very funny in the loss of their dignity, but Tecumseh was disgusted when he saw these fine young men fall to their hands and knees and spew vomit onto the ground and then get up and stagger over to drink more from the kegs. When he saw Stands Firm retching into the river, through a bruised throat so sore he groaned with agony even as he gagged, Tecumseh thought of his sister, Star Watcher, and how this would anger her if she could see it. So Tecumseh drank no more, and he was glad when the warriors held up the kegs and complained that they were empty.

By now a large bonfire was blazing on the beach, fueled by driftwood and by broken crates and wooden artifacts from the boat. Tecumseh was kneeling by the fire, bandaging the leg of the warrior who had stepped through the boat. The injured warrior had passed out flat on his back and was feeling no pain at all. One of the warriors whooped and threw an empty liquor keg into the fire, then recoiled and laughed when a *whoosh*ing ball of flame leaped up from it. At once another threw in the other keg, to repeat the fireworks, and they all whooped with joy. Tecumseh cried out:

"No wonder it makes us such fools! It is like gunpowder!" He moved away from the bonfire, pulling the unconscious man after him, afraid that he might blow up if he lay too close to the flames with so much liquor in him.

But his remark about the gunpowder had stirred a reckless notion in one of the others, who apparently had not yet had enough fireworks; this one snatched up a powder keg the size of a man's head and, with a yodel, poised himself to toss it in the fire. Fortunately Chiksika was not too drunk to react, whether to the danger or against the waste of precious gunpowder; he sprang toward the warrior and grabbed the keg out of his hands.

Now that such diversions were over, the attention of the intoxicated warriors began to turn toward the one thing they had not yet destroyed:

the bound captive. He was plain and vulnerable there in the edge of the fireglow, white and naked, his eyes wild with fear.

This image, the frightened eyes in the blanched face, and the ridiculous patches of dark hair on the pallid body, began to work its way through the rambunctious mood of the warriors. This was a white man, maybe even one belonging to the hated Clark who had destroyed their homes once and again. This was a white man who had not only come down the river bringing weapons—weapons no doubt for the killing of red men—but had had the arrogance to land and make a camp on the Shawnee side of the river and build a fire here to cook his disgusting pig meat. He was a symbol of all the things that had hurt and killed and insulted the proud Shawnees for so many, many seasons, and here he was, helpless in their hands and afraid.

The warriors began to go over and visit him one by one. Stands Firm spat in his face, croaking in Shawnee through his bruised throat: "Here is a taste of your spirit water."

The next tugged down his loincloth and urinated on the white man's feet, saying, "Here is more of your spirit water." Most of the others were gathering around now.

Then Chiksika stepped up to the prisoner. He pointed at the patch of hair around the white man's genitals and said, "One should not let hair grow on the *passah-tih.*" Then he clutched a handful of the hair and, with a powerful yank, pulled most of it out. The white man yelped so loudly that his echo came back from across the dark river. And this cry of pain inflamed the contempt of the warriors. The next one stood in front of the captive and drew out his knife. It was a thin-bladed skinning knife, rusty, only its cutting edge shiny from whetting. The warrior held the blade before the white man's eyes and smiled, while reaching down and taking hold of the man's testicles. The prisoner began to moan, tossing his head and rolling his eyes, and only then did Tecumseh, on the far side of the fire still trying not to become sick from the liquor in him, become aware of what was happening. He came around to see what was causing these pathetic pleadings.

The warrior with the knife said, "Let us see if *these* blow up like gunpowder in the fire!" And with a swift motion he brought down the knife and severed the scrotum from the man's body. His exultant whoop and the prisoner's agonized scream were simultaneous and sounded like one wild animal. The warrior spun away and hurled the bloody handful into the bonfire, then, turning an expression of mock disappointment on the shrieking, gasping prisoner, exclaimed: "Oh! They did not blow up! Had they no power? Too bad!"

The warriors, most of them, laughed and howled at this joke, and they were excited by the prospect of making this white man feel still more pain

for the sins of his race. Tecumseh and Thick Water stood nearby, the two
boys among these men, and they were not rejoicing. Thick Water's face was
in a grimace; he was inhaling through clenched teeth in empathy with the
prisoner's pain, probably because he was more sober than the others.
Tecumseh was stunned, too, but his feelings were complex. The dark blood
running down the insides of the prisoner's white thighs brought back that
vague feeling of shame he had experienced at the gauntlets. And in the back
of his mind were many old teachings of Star Watcher, who had always said
it was unworthy of a good Shawnee to inflict pain unnecessarily or to hurt
any helpless creature. And his father, and Black Fish, and Black Hoof, too,
had said that a brave man, even an enemy, should never be reduced to
humility. But these warriors were men, and Tecumseh was only a boy. They
had been in many battles, and he had fought only in this one. His own
brother Chiksika, their leader, was allowing this to happen; how could
Tecumseh dare to object? Maybe this was the true way of war; maybe the
noble and humane things the chiefs taught were only ideals to be told to
boys. But Tecumseh was not dizzy from the rum anymore. The cruelties
being done by his brother warriors had shocked him and cleared his head,
and all that remained of the rum was an ache in his skull and an evil taste
in his mouth.

Now the warriors had begun clamoring around the prisoner. He had not
fainted from the pain, and his wailings had dwindled to gasps and whimpers, and the warriors were not satisfied. One was yelling:

"He is no good for anything now! Burn him! Ha, haaaa!"

"Burn this pale dog! Yes!"

"He should not have come here! He came to burn!"

Tecumseh and Thick Water hung back and watched. For a while the
quiet of the night was broken only by the sounds of frogs and owls and
whippoorwills, and the moans of the bleeding prisoner, and the voices of
the warriors and the cracking of wood as they gathered driftwood to pile
around the willow trunk where the prisoner was tied. They piled it in a
circle around his feet and as high as his knees. Then each warrior took a
long pole and thrust one end of it into the sinking bonfire and held it
there until the end was burning. They were hooting and yipping in anticipation. The prisoner had stopped moaning, and now he held his head up
and began talking to the sky. Thick Water leaned close to Tecumseh and
said:

"He prays, I think. Why did I not just choke him to death while I was
doing it?" He wiped his palms down over his face and shuddered. "Young
brother," he said to Tecumseh, his pained eyes darting to him, "do you like
this?"

"No. I do not believe in this. I will never have a part in this. I wish they would stop."

The warriors picked their long poles out of the bonfire and carried them to the place where the prisoner was praying. They whipped the poles through the air until the burning tips were glowing bright. Then they began poking him with them, pressing the burning ends against his skin in the places where they thought they would hurt him most. Several jabbed him in the groin, and one teased the tip of his penis with his smoking brand. The white man's screams again echoed over the river, one pulsating scream after another, and he thrashed in vain against his bonds. A warrior jabbed his stick into the screaming mouth. Another carefully seared off some of the prisoner's beard and then tried to singe off his eyebrows, but the man's head was jerking too violently. Still another Shawnee went around behind him and stabbed into his anus. Now the man was thrashing as if in a fit, and his screeches sounded as if they would tear his throat out. Tecumseh could smell the burning hair and scorching flesh now, and he turned away, swallowing hard, teeth clenched, fists clenched, and looked out over the darkness of the serene river. Behind him Thick Water was beginning to retch.

Suddenly the screams broke off and the praying started again. The warriors yipped and jabbed and tried to make him start screaming again. One screamed at him, "Just so, the Jesus Indians prayed to the same God while you killed them! Just so! Just so!"

They could not make him scream anymore; apparently he was in such total pain now that no single point of pain even came through to him.

And so now the warriors whipped their smoldering staffs into flame again and put them into the circle of kindling on the ground around him. It caught and went up quickly, with a crackling rush, its light brightening the whole beach and bluff. Tecumseh turned and looked. In the center of the conflagration he could see the skin of the victim's torso and shoulders bubbling and blistering, the hair and eyebrows smoking and vanishing, the mouth a hideous dark hole, wide open in a now voiceless scream or prayer, the head and body still jerking. And then it sagged and moved no more. The flames dwindled.

Something enormous was shrieking through Tecumseh's soul, in the silence where the victim's screams had been, a great storm of outrage and revulsion. He saw the ring of crumbling yellow-red embers and the scorched, blackened, smoking corpse hanging slumped from the willow trunk, the skin of the lower body crisped up in black flakes, and the evil, stupid expressions on the faces of the torturers, and he could no longer contain what was roaring through his soul.

He broke the stillness suddenly with an ear-splitting howl of anguish and fury, startling the warriors out of the stupor of their satiated cruelty. Chiksika turned, wide-eyed, as Tecumseh stalked over and stopped near them. The boy's eyes were afire, and his chest was heaving as he looked each of them in the face and pointed at each one.

"You," he cried. "You! You! And you! Are you creatures of Matchemoneto? Our Grandmother would not have made you, who do *this!*"

Astonished, they stiffened and stared at him, at this boy. He pointed at the charred corpse.

"Look at that! Then you should look at the ground and never raise your eyes again!"

"Brother . . ." Chiksika tried to interrupt Tecumseh for his own good; he moved toward him with his hand outstretched. But Tecumseh shoved past him and stood between the warriors and the corpse and pointed his finger at them, in a sweeping motion back and forth that included them all.

"Look at this disgrace you have made! I did not have any hand in this, yet my heart is stained with shame because I stood back and did not try to stop you! I am ashamed that I was here as it was done, ashamed that it was done by people of my own blood! I am ashamed that my own brother and my sister's husband did this! I say look at what you have done, and never again look up!"

Some of them were muttering drunkenly and scowling at Tecumseh with eyes red-rimmed from heat and smoke and rum. The eyes of some were wavering.

"Our chief Black Hoof says do not burn prisoners!" Tecumseh cried. "Black Fish said do not torture anyone who is helpless. Do you forget their words?"

"You, boy," growled one of the warriors, "this man was our enemy—"

"You," Chiksika snapped, raising his hand toward the warrior. "Close your mouth and hear him."

"Oh, yes, this man was an enemy," Tecumseh exclaimed. "We kill our enemy to keep him from killing our People. I killed four of them today to keep them from killing us, and I helped my brother to kill another. No one of you did so much today to protect us.

"But can our enemy harm us when he is naked and tied to a tree? Were you so afraid of this white man, even as he hung there crying and unable to move, that you had to kill him to protect yourselves? Are you such cowards as *that?*

"Listen! *Listen!*

"It is true I am only a boy yet. And you can say, This boy knows nothing, I do not have to listen to this boy. No, you do not have to heed what I say, but I have to say it or my heart will burst, and it is this:

"Never will I do such a low thing as you have done, Weshemoneto hears my vow. This too I vow:

"Anyone who does this disgrace upon a helpless man from this day on will cease to be my friend or my brother. I will not again stand still and let anyone stain my heart as you have stained it tonight by this cowardice. Someday you might need me, when I am a man. But if ever again you do this, I will turn my back on you forever, and never give you my hand unless it is to strike you! That is what I have to say." He stood now breathing hard, looking from one to another of them with contempt in his face, his eyes both fierce and glimmering with tears. Perhaps he had said too much; he *was* only a boy.

But the warriors were not staring back at him now, not one of them; they were not challenging him with their eyes. Most were blinking and looking at the ground as he had told them to do. The hush of the river and the wind and the voices of the night creatures were all the noise in the black night around this little firelit circle. The wind chilled the sweat on Tecumseh's gleaming skin. His nostrils were full of the smells of rum and river mud, buds and flowers of spring, woodsmoke and burned manflesh and singed hair.

No one moved or spoke for a long time, until Chiksika at last came and stood beside Tecumseh, and he said to the warriors:

"Something has happened that will never be forgotten by our People. One who is a boy in years has proven himself a man in bravery and an elder in wisdom.

"Did you see him? Do you know of anyone of this age in the memory of our People who fought with such quickness and strength that he killed four strong men in moments?

"And did you hear him? What he said was true. He blew the mist of the rum from my eyes so that I can see. Oh! Sometimes I am blind in my hatred. When I hurt that white man whose hands were tied back, I was blind. When you cut him and burned him, you were blind. The Long Knives have struck the spark of hatred in us, and they have fanned it again and again, and it is no wonder we have been blinded by its burning. But the law of our People is *Weshecat-welo k 'weshe laweh-pah,* let us be strong by doing good!

"When I look at the burnt meat of that white man, though my vengeance is satisfied, I do not feel that I have done good. I have helped burn our enemies before, in the passion of vengeance, but when the sun came up again and I saw what we did, I did not feel like a worthy man. I do not feel like a worthy man now, as I look upon this man we destroyed.

"But, my brothers, the mist is gone from my eyes. Now I add my vow to that which Tecumseh has spoken: Never will I do this again. If Weshemoneto gives me power enough and years enough, I will kill white men as long as they come to our land. You know I have sworn to kill a hundred for the death of my father, and a hundred more for each time Chillicothe was destroyed, and a hundred for the Jesus Indians. Yes! I will kill them until I can no longer lift my hand! But never again like this.

"I remind you that my brother was born when the green Eye of the leaping Panther crossed the sky of the night. I myself saw it. I have long known that this boy beside me will be the greatest of us all, and now I see that already he is. Always when he asks me to teach him something, I learn more from his questions than I understood before. This is not the first time my brother has blown the smoke from my eyes. Perhaps it is the first time he has done so for you. So I say this: When he is a man in years, we will need him. When that time comes, I will not want him to walk away from me. And so I add my vow to his. I will not do this evil thing again. *Weshecat-welo k'weshe laweh-pah!*"

"*Weshecat-welo k'weshe laweh-pah,*" some of the warriors responded.

Then Stands Firm came and stood beside them. "Tecumseh is my brother, for I have been favored as the husband of Star Watcher, the best of women. Her kindness I see in him also. This boy is gentle and good not because he is weak or timid. When I was of his age, bold though I was, I would not have been bold enough to speak before men as he has just spoken to us. Nor wise enough to speak so true about this thing. He has made me see, and he has made me feel shame. What we have done was not good for the People. And so I too add my vow to his. I will not do this evil anymore. That is what I have to say."

The other six warriors one by one then murmured their vows and turned their backs on what they had done. They were now as sober as they had ever been in their lives. Then Thick Water, eyes brimming, full of pride for his friend, came forth. He was scared about speaking before all of these warriors. But he said:

"I have never done it, and I never will." Then he cast an almost worshipful glance at Tecumseh and met his eyes. "That is my promise, brother, for I will always want your friendship!"

# CHAPTER 17

## *Kekionga Town*
## *October 1786*

Now he was a warrior, not just a boy thrown into a band for a desperate ambush or a plundering raid, but a warrior with a name for bravery, of warrior age at last and riding with chieftains at the head of a long column of Shawnee warriors, hundreds of warriors, going to join a great war chief to attack the hated army of Clark himself. This, he felt, was what he had been born for; at last he seemed to be under the guidance of his star sign, and his heart was a war drum. Chiksika was beside him on one side and Blue Jacket on the other, young Thick Water and old Black Snake behind. And ahead on the trodden path beneath the yellowing maples and sycamores was Kekionga Town, the place of Michi-kini-qua, Little Turtle, principal chief of the Miamis, whom they were going to join. The night had been cold, and the air was fresh and bracing, the sky clearest blue. Tecumseh was eighteen summers of age now and feared no weaknesses in himself, and he was eager to do this worthy cause.

Here in the Miamis' country the land lay different, and Tecumseh could sense the difference. In all the Shawnee lands the rivers ran southward into the Beautiful River. Now the war party had crossed the high land, and here the rivers flowed northward into the Great Lakes or westward toward the Wabash-se-pe. While the Shawnees had struggled for many years to keep the whites from coming up from the Beautiful River, the Miamis had had peace and trade with the Canadians. Only recently, after Clark arrived in the west, had the Miamis and their allied tribes been forced into conflict with the Long Knives. Now, after six years of conflict, Little Turtle had formed a confederation of twenty hundred Miamis, Weas, and Pianke-shaws, and the worried Long Knives had called on their famed war chief Clark to lead an army against the confederation. Learning of this oncoming

227

army, Little Turtle had invited the Shawnees to join him in a war to stop
it, and Blue Jacket, now the chief of the Maykujay Shawnees, had accepted
eagerly. Many tribes that had been separate for years were now beginning
to join together because they could feel the ring the Americans were
tightening around them.

And although the British had been beaten in their war with the Americans, they were still in Detroit, and still had trading posts in the Great Lakes
region, and still encouraged the tribes to resist the Long Knives. Everyone
knew the Long Knives coveted Canada, too, and none of the tribes wanted
the Americans to close the ring around them in the north.

When Old Moluntha had stepped down as chief of the Maykujay sept
because of his great age and failing vision, he had favored Blue Jacket to
succeed him because of Blue Jacket's insight into the minds of the white
men. Blue Jacket could understand what the Americans were doing in the
east and could explain how those actions affected the red men in the Middle
Ground. Now he was talking about these things as they rode toward Little
Turtle's town.

"In the three years since they threw the king of England on his back, the
Thirteen Fires have been giving land to their soldiers as their reward. And
it has been as Black Hoof told us it would be: the land they give is the land
Clark drove us out of.

"To give land, the white men have to have markings that prove it is theirs
to give. So they called some chiefs of the Ottawa, Ojibway, Wyandot, and
Delaware nations to a treaty council, and persuaded them with rum and
strong talk to mark away lands to the Thirteen Fires. It was easy for those
chiefs to say, 'Take it,' because their people did not live on it. We, the
Shawnees and Miamis and Mingos, lived on it! That is why the Long Knives
did not invite Shawnee and Miamis and Mingos to the treaty. Do you see?
They are cunning that way."

"But," Tecumseh exclaimed, "land belongs to Weshemoneto, not to
chiefs! How can white men mark what belongs to the Great Good Spirit,
and give it to their soldiers?"

"It is a power they believe they have," Blue Jacket replied with a bitter
smile. "Because they can draw lines and numbers and words to describe a
place, they believe they have the power to buy and sell it. It is because of
this power to write words that they think they have the other power. When
I lived among the whites, every man I knew believed he had such a power.
Even," he said after a pause, "the ones who had not learned to write or
read." He snorted a contemptuous laugh.

Tecumseh said hotly, "I learn to read book words some, but it does not
cause me to think I can own land belonging to the Great Good Spirit!" His

head was whirling with this odd and awful idea the white men had. "Then they must believe they can also own and sell the waters and the sky!"

Blue Jacket laughed, tossing his head back, his strong smile flashing. "Young brother," he said then, "they *have* figured out some ways to own the water. As far as I know, they have not yet devised a way to own sky. But if you ever see a white man looking up, he is probably working on a way to do it! Ha, ha!"

"Then," Tecumseh said after a while, "I shall kill any white man I see looking up!"

Blue Jacket grinned at Tecumseh, then at Chiksika, and said, "Better to kill any you see looking at *you,* then. Because in the Long Knife Fire, Virginia, where I was a boy, they buy and sell *people.*"

Then a little way farther, the trail beside the river grew wider, and the smell of cookfires came faintly on the breeze, and the ground in the woods was clear of deadwood. "Now ride proudly and sing," Blue Jacket said. "Up there are the corn fields, and the head of the Maumee. Let us make Little Turtle feel strong-hearted by our riding-in!"

Star Watcher's second baby was a hard sucker. The pull of his little mouth on her nipple was as much an ache as a pleasure. His suckling was so strong, she looked down at his round head with its thick hair and murmured, "Little one, must you try to turn me inside out?" She remembered her mother saying that to Loud Noise, fifteen years ago, so many years.

Star Watcher's first child, a daughter, old enough to walk, was still asleep, only the back of her head visible above the edge of the blanket. Outside the door of the *wigewa* the sun was shining through the bright yellow treetops. The town was quiet. Almost all the warriors had ridden away with Blue Jacket days ago, her husband Stands Firm and her brothers Tecumseh and Chiksika among them, to join the Miami Little Turtle for a stand against a whiteface army that was in the distant Wabash valley. Her younger brothers Loud Noise and Stands-Between were away hunting on the other side of the Mad River.

Star Watcher, usually up before daylight to take care of all those appetites, had slept late in the unaccustomed quiet. She was still sleepy, still sitting naked in bed, and her mind was vague, half given to prayers for the safety of the men, half to the bright-colored patterns of the daydreams induced by the sucking sensations in her nipple.

So when the shouts and screams and banging began in a far part of the town, she had to come from a long way back in her head before she recognized the alarms of another attack. She was hearing the rumble of hoofbeats before she could even move. Women and wailing children were running by outside.

By the time she was outdoors, carrying the baby boy in one arm and hauling the stupefied, terrified little girl by the hand, she could see the dust and gunsmoke and some of the oncoming Long Knife horse soldiers down the street, coming through the town at a gallop, shooting and hacking at the few warriors and boys who had rallied to try to resist them.

Star Watcher ran, at a maddeningly slow pace, up the lanes between the *wigewas,* having to stop again and again to raise the naked little girl every time she stumbled. A number of Maykujay women, not burdened by children, ran screaming past Star Watcher, veering toward the open space of the council ground, and there was a mass of horse soldiers behind them, so crowded by their own numbers that their big horses were trampling down fences and shivering the frail bark huts. Star Watcher could not run fast enough with her children to flee with those women, so she darted aside into a pile of cut brush, like a fleeing rabbit, shoving her little daughter in before her. She crouched there, the brush scratching and gouging her naked skin, hugging the infant under her bosom. Both of the children were howling in terror, but there was no need to hush them, for all the rest of the world was howling, too. Hooves pounded so close by her hiding place that dust and clods were kicked against her face.

And then, peering out, she saw a horror she knew she would never live long enough to forget.

A big soldier swinging a sword overtook the running Maykujay women in the council ground. One by one they tumbled to the ground as he hacked their heads open. She saw him kill seven.

Much later, when the town was roaring with flames and the brush pile was beginning to ignite from the blowing sparks, only then did Star Watcher muffle her children's faces and dash out under the cover of smoke, toward the edge of town. Soldiers were still riding their horses about here and there, like big devil-shapes materializing in the smoke and then vanishing, whooping and laughing, and she had to duck behind something every time she saw one. They were rounding up prisoners, and she was determined that she and her little ones would not be captives of the Long Knives. Between two smoldering huts she saw two soldiers off their horses. They had caught a young woman who was as naked as she was herself. One soldier was holding her bent over with his arm around her head. She was thrashing and struggling and sobbing, but the soldier behind her had a strong hold on her hips and was thrusting himself inside her with hard spasms that shook her whole body.

Star Watcher dared not let them catch her and the children, so there was nothing she could do to help the woman—except throw a rock and run.

The rock was as big as a man's fist. When the soldier with his breeches down around his thighs fell to the ground, his skull was fractured.


Little Turtle was a warm-hearted man and an esteemed chief, but what he told the Shawnees astonished and disappointed them.

He met them in the council lodge of Kekionga Town with great warmth and thanked them for coming to help the confederation. Little Turtle had a kindly-looking oval face, eyes set wide apart, lips usually in a fatherly sort of a smile. He was small, but his physique was compact and graceful. His head was shaved back to its crown, a large, roundish head. With him was a slim, erect white youth of about Tecumseh's age, whom Little Turtle introduced as his son, calling him Wild Potato. This youth had been captured about ten years before in Kain-tuck-ee, and Little Turtle had adopted him. Wild Potato and Tecumseh spoke a little to each other in English, and the young man said his English name had been William Wells. He seemed vain of himself, and Tecumseh did not like him very much after the first few moments.

After the smoking of the pipe, Little Turtle explained why his Miami were at ease in their town instead of preparing for defense:

"It is true that the Long Knife chief Clark was coming here with an army from Kain-tuck-ee, as I said when I summoned you. A large army, maybe twenty hundred. First they went to Vincennes, and stopped there to wait for supplies to be brought up the Wabash-se-pe. I sent Chief Pacane with a white belt to ask why he was coming into our country, but he talked bad to Pacane and sent him back to us with a red war belt. And then he started marching on toward our towns. I got ready to fight.

"But then, a day's march from the Wea towns, Clark turned his army around and marched back to Vincennes. This baffled us very much. But then Clark sent us a white belt and explained that his friends the Frenchmen at Vincennes had come after him begging him to have mercy on us, and to offer us a chance to council for peace. This I thought strange, and I do not know if it is true. But with his army sitting at Vincennes, so close to the Wea towns, I knew we could not leave our homes unguarded and go raid Kain-tuck-ee anymore.

"Until then, at least, we have peace, and we can all hunt and harvest so there will not be a hungry winter. I am sorry, my brothers, that you have come so great a distance for no battle. But you are here, and it is time for the Feast of the Hunter's Moon. Will you come to the Wea towns and join our People for the great feast?"


But the Shawnee warriors were nearly a hundred miles from their homes, and there was much hunting to do before winter, so they started back. Blue Jacket's face was clouded. He had worked himself and his warriors into a mood to fight even the dreaded Clark. Now he felt a little relieved, but more disappointed.

They were not far out of Kekionga Town and going back along the riverbank trace when two hard-riding Shawnee warriors were seen ahead. They came on, yelling, and wheeled their lathered horses around to ride beside Blue Jacket, and they both talked to him at once. Their faces were grim, and Blue Jacket's face grew pale and hard as he heard them.

Clark of Kain-tuck-ee had done another terrible thing. While marching one army up the Wabash-se-pe to intimidate Little Turtle, he had sent another army, of about eight hundred Kain-tuck-ee horsemen, to lay waste to the Shawnee towns again. Boone and But-lah had been seen among their officers. With almost all the warriors gone away to join Little Turtle, Black Hoof had been able to make no defense at all. The Long Knives had burned down thirteen Shawnee villages, including Chillicothe and Maykujay Town and Blue Jacket's Town. They had as usual burned and trampled all the crops at those places.

The Long Knives had killed at least fifteen warriors and boys and that many women, and they had caught thirty-four women and children and old people who had fled too late. Among those prisoners were old Chief Moluntha and his three wives.

And here the worst had been done. Moluntha, too feeble even to consider resisting, had surrendered himself and his wives and had been put under the protection of guards. While he stood smoking a pipe with them, displaying an American flag on his shoulder and an old peace treaty, a loud-voiced officer had ridden up and gone among the guards, and he had asked the old chief, "Were you at Blue Licks?" When Moluntha said he had been, the officer had shouted a curse and chopped the old chief to death with a tomahawk.

Blue Jacket shut his eyes in agony when he heard this; Moluntha had been guide and teacher to him. He ground his bared teeth and groaned.

"What officer did that?" Chiksika demanded. "Is he known to us? Boone? But-lah?"

The messenger replied, "We saw that same man and heard his voice at the Blue Licks ambush. He was the loud-voiced fool on a black horse who charged across the river and led his Long Knives into the trap.''

It was hours before Blue Jacket could speak of this. Then he said through tight lips, ''That officer is called McGary. It was he who caused so many of his soldiers to die, and now it is he who kills our old father in revenge. May that McGary cook forever in white man's hell. May all the men he has killed by his stupid meanness build the fire under him. And may our Moluntha sit above, smiling and drinking cool water, in the green heaven of our Great Good Spirit!''

# CHAPTER 18

## *On the Lower O-hi-o*
## *Spring 1788*

N ow," Chiksika whispered, "watch how the wolves do."
It was a surprise to Tecumseh to see that the bison were not afraid of the wolves. The great, dusty-dark animals grazed calmly on the tender prairie grass, and they seemed to ignore the wolves who shepherded them.

"Sometimes," Chiksika said, "hunters can creep within bow shot of the bison just by putting a wolf pelt on and crawling close. The old men say that before there were horses or guns, that was how the hunters used to get close enough to kill them."

The wolves themselves seemed equally unconcerned about the presence of the bison. They would trot leisurely along the edge of the herd, tongues hanging out, heads low on a level with their silvery-gray backs, seldom even looking at the bison. But of course they were thinking of nothing but bison meat.

"Watch how they move," Chiksika said. "It is a beautiful thing to see."

The wolves seemed to flow without effort across the prairie; under their sturdy, shaggy-coated bodies their legs looked spindly, their feet big. And yet these thin-looking legs and big feet moved them with a sinewy, effortless grace, the feet seeming to kick the earth backward after each step, and though they seemed to be going at little more than a walk, they were actually covering ground as fast as a man could run. "They can go the day long like that," Chiksika said with admiration, "and are not tired. Such a people the wolves are! Now watch this one on the edge. He is up to mischief. Look. He is laughing about what he is going to do."

A bison cow was lying on the ground at the edge of the herd. One trotting male wolf, aware that a bison is not very dangerous lying down, ran up and stopped near the cow's big head and stood there grinning at her. The cow was not alarmed, but she did not take her eyes off the wolf.

Suddenly the wolf danced forward and nipped her black nose. She shook her massive head and snorted at him, and he moved back, as if going away. But instead of leaving her, he went around behind her, darted in, and bit her right on the anus. Bellowing, the cow rose with a heave of her mighty shoulders and spun around to charge at the wolf, her head down. It was easy for a bison to kill a wolf with horns or hooves—if it could catch one. But the wolf, still grinning, trotted away insouciantly, looking back over his shoulder at the angry cow. As he drew her away from the herd, other wolves from around the perimeter suddenly were coming to take advantage of whatever the situation might offer.

In a moment the cow was surrounded by four wolves, and she realized it. With her head down she turned and trotted back toward the herd. Two bulls nearby had noticed what was happening and began trotting out to escort her in. The wolf followed her for a moment, then sprang forward and snapped again at her rump. Her back hooves lashed out in a mighty kick, but the wolf was ready and quick and dodged the kick. Then, still grinning and seeming to shrug, he left her and trotted on around the edge of the herd, looking for another opportunity. The other three wolves had turned and gone off in another direction. Chiksika laughed, and Tecumsch smiled with pleasure and amusement.

Chiksika said, "You see, as I have told you, they are like us. This is the way we do with a Long Knife army. It is too big for us to kill it. But we can nip it on its edges. We can make some of the soldiers come out to chase us, then we catch them. If too many come, we must grin and shrug like that wolf, and go back, and wait for another chance. We can make it nervous and keep it from sleeping, and make it shoot its guns in the dark. When soldiers are nervous and tired like that, they make mistakes. And that is when we get them. It is like the first time their army came to Chillicothe. I was away, but you remember it."

"Yes! When only twenty-four of our warriors followed them toward Kain-tuck-ee and shot a hundred of them."

"We were like the little wolves then, biting the back end of the big army."

"Yes!" Tecumseh nodded, delighted with this.

"While we are here, then," Chiksika said, "study the wolves and see how they do. They have been following and eating the mighty bison since the Beginning, and they have learned things that a Shawnee leader should know. Because the whitefaces are now numerous in this country, big like the bison herds."

"One thing I have learned already: a single wolf cannot pull down and kill a bison. But together they can pull one down. Listen, brother. If the tribes were like the wolves and banded together, they could do more against the whites. Like Pontiac. If the tribes thought together like the wolf pack, the chiefs would never go to the white men's treaty councils and give them the lands we live on."

Chiksika gazed at the bison on the prairie and thought about Tecumseh's words. He said, "Each nation is like a wolf pack. But the nations have fought each other since the time before memory. Now and then they ally with each other for a while. But they never forget the old angers for long. Remember the Grasshopper War. It was a thing that truly happened long ago, but it is a legend to teach us a sad thing about ourselves. Two enemy tribes that had made peace lived in nearby towns. Their children were learning to play together. In a meadow, two children had a dispute over which had caught a grasshopper. They fought. Their mothers came running from both towns. They struck each other's children, then each other. The men came running. Before it was quiet again, many, many had been killed. You see, the tribes are too proud and jealous. Even a grasshopper can be used to break alliances."

"Though that has been so," Tecumseh said, "the nations will have to believe together, or the whitefaces can divide us and do as they please with us."

They went back toward the creek valley where the rest of their hunters were encamped. This limitless prairie made Tecumseh's heart swell with hope and a sense of well-being, for the first time since the Long Knife raids and the death of Moluntha. The sunny-gold grass waved in the warm wind from the west, and the ground under his feet was soft and springy. It was as if the prairie ground were the flesh of the Mother, Earth. There were no rocks or roots in the way of one's feet. There were no trees shadowing the land, except in the creek and river valleys. The sky was vast, piled heaven high with white-gold clouds over the northern horizon, clearest blue everywhere else. The shrilling of insects in the grass seemed to stretch from one horizon to the other. One felt high on this land; to south and west it sloped and rolled down and away to the broad valley where the Ohio-se-pe and the Missi-se-pe flowed together.

And it was a paradise for the hunter. Nearby were the great herds of bison, food, and warm hides in seemingly inexhaustible quantity, visible from miles away as masses of black on the dun prairie, easy to follow and find because of their predictable habits of roaming and feeding and the trampled roads of their migrations. And the prairie land was abundant with lesser foods. Deer and rabbit were everywhere, bear and turkey were in the bottomlands, the backwaters and brushy islands and sandbars were so alive with waterfowl that from a distance sometimes they seemed to shift and tremble. And fish of every kind, up to the great whiskered catfish that would feed a whole family, could be pulled from the waters. There were huge, delicious turtles on the land and in the rivers. In some tributaries, mussels were harvested in such quantities that the houses of the mussel eaters were built upon hills of shells.

It was a paradise for the hunter. But, Chiksika would say, "The Shawnee lands in O-hi-o and Kain-tuck-ee used to be like this. There was more game than we could kill. Now the whitefaces are there, and the hunting is hard. You look at all the bison here and you say, These would last forever. The Sioux and Sauk and Arikara say the herds beyond the Missi-se-pe are so great sometimes that you cannot see to the other side, and you think, These could never be all gone. But, my brother, we used to think that of the animals in Kain-tuck-ee. Until the whitefaces came."

For many moons Chiksika and Tecumseh had been wandering. Since the last destruction of the Shawnee towns in O-hi-o, they had been nomads, hunters, occasionally marauders. In their hearts they longed for the beautiful towns where they had been children, but the towns were not towns anymore. Time after time they had been turned to ash heaps, upon which the patient old Black Hoof and the People again and again tried to make towns. It was too saddening to see the hundreds of charred places that had been houses, to see the little camps of married men with their women and children trying with half-broken spirits to make their country what it had been.

Tecumseh and Chiksika, like many of the unmarried young men, had begun to drift away to other places, places farther from the white man's advance. They had stayed at Miami towns and Kickapoo towns north and west of their old homeland. They had visited among the Potawatomies. Chiksika had taken Tecumseh on long, long rides, to hunt, to raid white men's boats, but mostly just to see the few parts of the country where the red men could still live and hunt and range without having to be on guard against whitefaces. They had stayed in villages built in marshy river bottoms and on windy prairies. They had been the guests of the Miamis at Kekionga, of Kickapoos on the Mississinewa, of Weas on the Wabash-se-pe. They had become friends with young warriors of those nations and of the Sauk and Fox and Ottawa. They had talked and eaten with these young men beside a hundred campfires and had learned many of their words.

They had lived a while with young women of some of those tribes, without marriage. Tecumseh's appetite for women was powerful. These living-ins were not something they would have done in their own nation, which was still more rigid about that matter. Too, the girls of the tribes who would take up with visiting men like that were sometimes girls who had lain with traders or other white men, and there was a danger of getting diseases in the loins. Sometimes Tecumseh would lie awake in the darkness with a musky, warm girl beside him, and, though he would be full of languor and affection, there would be a whisper in his soul, an unhappy whisper, telling him he was taking too lightly something that the teachings said was sacred. Once he had risen from beside a sleeping Miami girl and slipped away from her hut to go and stay by himself beside a small brook and pray for better direction of his life, that direction which had been hinted at so often by the visions, by the Spirit Helper, by his dreams, by the sign of the green Eye of the Panther in the sky. Surely all those signs did not mean for him to expend all his strength in body pleasure.

Thus the brothers had wandered for many moons, these brother warriors who admired each other so deeply. Big Fish had usually traveled with them, and sometimes Thick Water would find them as they passed near home and would join them. They had wandered north to the marshes and the white dunes that bordered the great lake called Mis-e-ken, and there they had walked along the sands with the roar of the surf and the stinging, sand-laden wind blowing away their words as they talked. There Tecumseh had seen tiny cliff swallows darting out of little nesting holes in the steep sand banks, nests right in the path of the strong wind of the lake, and in his wonderment at the immense space of the world, his heart had so swelled with the love of Weshemoneto that he had wept in the wind. And then later that day from the top of a high dune they had looked out and seen on the very horizon of the lake, stark against the gray clouds and gray water, a speck of white. It had puzzled him until Chiksika had realized what it was: the white cloth wings of one of the huge boats of the British. Chiksika had seen one of those once in the mouth of the Maumee-se-pe. "Soon," he said, "we will not be able to look anywhere over land or water without seeing white men."

"Or even sky," Tecumseh said.

Wherever they had wandered, Tecumseh had been able to feel within himself something pointing toward the unsteady place in the center of the earth. When he had walked in the old Shawnee homeland, he had felt that it was far to the southwest. As he walked on the shore of the great lake called Mis-e-ken, he had felt that it was almost straight south but still far away. Now he was close to the place where the Beautiful River and the Missi-se-pe flowed together, and when he walked on this ground he felt that he was almost on top of the center of the trembling earth, as if the heart of the Great Turtle beat deep below his feet. It was not that the earth was trembling; he had not felt that since he'd arrived here. But as he stood overlooking the confluence of the two great rivers, he knew this was the center, as he had always known he would know it when he stood upon it. Now he stopped Chiksika and said to him, "Brother, here is the place I have spoken of. Down deep in the earth, down that way in the Missi-se-pe as if it were far under the water of the river, there is where it is. The place I have felt, the place of which I talked with Eagle Speaker, the Bear Walker." He said this very calmly. Chiksika looked at him with a fearful face.

"It shakes now under your feet?"

"No. But this is the place. The message will come from the earth here." He made a circular gesture, indicating the valley before them.

Chiksika searched Tecumseh's face and seemed to see something in his eyes. "Do you learn what the message says?"

"No. It does not come yet. . . . Look!"

He pointed, down across the huge confluence of waters where the two different colors of greenish yellow and yellow-brown were forever mixing. A white bird had just fluttered over their heads and flown down toward the south. Tecumseh could hear a voice as it flew, but not words. Soon the bird was too small to see. Beyond the place where it had vanished, a wisp of smoke rose over the faraway trees on the western shore of the Missi-se-pe. Down there was a town the Spaniards had built, with fortifications. Even the Spaniards, who claimed the lands on that side of the Missi-se-pe, were wary of the encroachments of the Long Knives.

Tecumseh now stood watching the wisp of smoke for a few minutes, trying to understand what the dove meant. It was like the time it first came to him in his vision: unsaid. Chiksika stood still, waiting for him to explain something. Finally, pointing west, Tecumseh said: "In that way lies the place where our mother went, with our sept and the Thawegilas?"

"That way. Yes. That is the way we will go to see her."

"She is not over there anymore," said Tecumseh.

"Ai! What do you say?"

"She is not that way. She is that way."

The wind was blowing his hair and clothes. He swung his arm then and pointed the way the bird had gone. Far down that way lay the homeland of the Creeks, her people. This perplexed Chiksika. After the buffalo hunting, he and Tecumseh and some fellow hunters from the little Shawnee town at the mouth of the Wabash-se-pe had intended to go across the Missi-se-pe to the place where the Spaniards had given the Shawnees land to live in. Chiksika and Tecumseh had planned to find their mother there and stay for a while with her. After a long time Tecumseh said, "I think she has left the People and has gone to where she was born. It seems to me that it will be a long time before we see her again."

That evening at dusk the brothers sat with the hunters by their campfire and talked about the buffalo. They would ride toward the herd tomorrow and drive them down the bluffs close to the Beautiful River, and there they would kill enough of them for the use of the hunters' town. Women from the town had already come down in canoes from the Wabash-se-pe and had made a camp below the bluffs, where they would butcher the kill, jerk some of the flesh, and clean the hides. By doing this so close to the river, they could then take the hides and meat back up to their town easily in the canoes, much more than could be taken overland. It was all planned.

Now at dusk the wolves began singing. Each voice joined the song in just a slightly different key so that no two were singing quite the same, but their voices were so blended that they sounded like one wolf with many throats. It was a far, haunting song and made Tecumseh's heart ache with a nameless yearning, a yearning to understand the tomorrows. That night he went to sleep thinking of the unseen power of this place.

The ground rumbled with hoofbeats and blurred backward with the speed of his horse. Alongside him ran the herd: a lunging, pounding mass of coarse, shaggy, dusty, blackish-brown hair, dark horns, tiny eyes. Ahead of Tecumseh and behind him, on the fringes of the herd, rode the other hunters, whooping and yipping in a frenzy, secured to their horses' backs by the grip of their sinewy legs. Every hunter was selecting the bison that he wanted to kill first. Some of the hunters were holding rifles, but some, like Tecumseh, had chosen to use the bow. To be able to draw a strong enough bow to drive an arrow into the deep chest of a bull bison and pierce its heart, while clinging to one's horse in a full gallop, was a supreme test of a man's strength and skill and courage, and a bow kill was counted as more commendable. Tecumseh had never killed a bison with an arrow before but was sure he would not fail. The hunters from the Wabash-se-pe town were accustomed to such hunting on the prairie and were masterful horsemen, and they liked to show off for their forest brethren when they came. But it was not in Tecumseh's nature to let himself be outdone, so now he rode with furious speed, guiding his powerful mount with knee pressure and clinging like a burr to its back, riding as close to the thundering tide of beasts as any of the prairie Shawnees were doing. He had already left

Chiksika far behind and was chasing the leader of the herd, a huge bull the rest of the herd was following in its panicky stampede.

The dangers were terribly plain. If a horse fell, it and its rider would instantly be borne down by the awful momentum of the big animals and crushed and chopped to pulp by falling bodies and sharp hooves.

Tecumseh was now ahead of all the other hunters. He yodeled with joy and dug his heels into his horse's flank. The ground was sloping downward here, as the herd tore into the broad valley toward the mouth of the O-hi-o-se-pe. The bison were letting themselves be driven just the way the hunters intended. These men had hunted them here for many years, and such drives seldom failed to turn out just as they were meant to.

His heart high with thrill, Tecumseh now heard a gunshot behind him, then another. Hunters back there were shooting into the herd. Now, the speed of the stampede increasing as it tore down the slope, Tecumseh began his move to cut out the lead bull. He swung leftward, moving across the front of the oncoming herd, riding headlong, hair flying. In a moment he was within five yards of the bull, and he took an arrow from his quiver and nocked it. The bull's massive, surging shoulder, flecked with his foamy drool, drew nearer as the distance was closed by the efforts of the fine horse. The bull's hooves threw up bits of turf even though it now looked as if he were hardly skimming the ground. Tecumseh's heart was big with admiration for the bull. The grass flowed backward, a yellow blur in the narrowing space between predator and prey.

Tecumseh knew that in this desperate last minute he would have to cut the bull aside out of the path of the herd before he shot it, or it would be trampled to carrion. So now he cut in behind the bull, to get on its left side. This was the most dangerous instant. If anything went wrong, he would be down in the path of a thousand hooves. He was aware that this was a greater recklessness than anything he had ever done. It was not necessary to put oneself in quite so much jeopardy to kill a bull bison. But he had selected this chief bull, and he wanted to take it right off the point of the herd, because to do so was excellence, and he was Tecumseh, the Panther-Crossing-the-Sky, and excellence was expected of him—not just by the People, but by Weshemoneto. This he had been growing to understand since his first bravery in battle, and now, here in this place over the Center, where the signs and dreams had been haunting him so strongly, here he had to show excellence.

The bull was aware that his pursuer was now on his left hindquarter instead of his right, so he veered to the right to try to elude him. Tecumseh urged the horse and drew alongside to force him clear out of the line of stampede. The rest of the herd, pressed together in its mass, would not be able to turn this abruptly. Tecumseh glanced back and saw their crazed eyes and flashing hooves and foam-specked forequarters. A little farther and he would have the bull cut out of their downhill path, and he could release his arrow.

But something happened.

Something in the tension of the speeding pursuit snapped, and Tecumseh felt the pony lurch and drop beneath him, felt himself pitching forward toward the blur of yellow-tan grass, saw the blue sky tilt before his eyes and the black wall of bison and then the blue sky again, and then he was on the ground and his left thigh snapped under the weight of his falling horse and there was a lightning flash of pain and an immense black thunder was over him and the ground was shaking. His horse was thrashing and twitching and jolting, shrieking in pain. Many things were striking Tecumseh, striking him hard, making lightning flashes in his head. The herd was running over him. He was in the dusty grass, and the earth was shaking and jolting. He heard a thousand familiar voices at once and yet recognized every one of them in the same instant. In his mind he saw villages falling to the ground and dust and smoke billowing up. He saw a great boat standing in water, piled with great white wings of cloth above it, and men among those wings, tiny men like birds in trees. He saw a stout man in a turban, with a mustache and one eye, and the man was familiar, and his name, Tecumseh somehow knew, was Tenskwatawa, He-Opens-the-Door. He also saw a white man with intense eyes and a small mouth and saw hundreds of huge-headed horsemen riding toward him, silhouetted in such brilliant yellow dust that they were like a herd of dark bison. The pain of his broken leg was all through him. He held the *pa-waw-ka* stone in his hand next to his heart and felt the jolts of the earth coming up from far below. In the thundering noise now he heard the deep voice of a chief he had never heard before and saw his broad, stolid face, a face with faded spots on the skin. Then the dove flew over, and then four wolves went by with the moon in their eyes. He saw himself as a boy standing at the place where he had been born, the spring near Piqua, and trees were falling around him and the spring water was flowing backward, and the bowels of the earth were rumbling and sending up jolts that jarred his teeth together. Only after the rumbling was gone did he see an enormous panther crouched on the horizon. Two rays shone out of its green eye.

Tecumseh was on the ground by the great river. The sun was going down over the river. A woman—he thought it was Star Watcher, her back to the sunset and her face in shadow—was kneeling over him. Chiksika's voice said something nearby, and the woman's reply was not in Star Watcher's voice. This was one of the women from the hunters' town near the mouth of the Wabash-se-pe. Tecumseh smelled woodsmoke and blood and heard many people talking and fires crackling. He looked aside and saw the people butchering bison all around. Horses grazed, hobbled, on the slope. There was one great, fiery pain throbbing up from his broken thigh. It hurt more and more; the bone ends were moving; somebody was pulling his foot and making the broken bone grind and grate on itself within the meat of his thigh, and it was as if he himself were being butchered, being taken apart like all the bison lying around. Hundreds of flies were droning and buzzing. Tecumseh groaned and quaked; he tightened his throat to keep from crying out.

It was Chiksika who was pulling his foot. The woman had her hands around Tecumseh's thigh and was feeling it and looking at it very intently. She said:

"There." Then she wound some strouding cloth snug around his leg. She picked up a large piece of elm bark that had been freshly peeled off a trunk just as big around as Tecumseh's thigh. She pried it open and set it around his thigh and let it close to its natural shape. Then with strips of hide she began tying it shut, binding the bark firmly so that it held his leg stiff and straight. Now Chiksika had moved up and was kneeling by Tecumseh's shoulder, and the sunset glow was bright red on his face. Chiksika said:

"Weshemoneto protects you. The herd trampled your horse to nothing, but you are only cut up, and this leg broken."

Tecumseh released a quaking sigh. In the firm sheath of the bark splint, the pain in his thigh was receding a little, and he could think and remember. "Brother," he said, "tell me: did anyone else feel the ground shake?"

Chiksika looked at him strangely. "The ground shakes under the tread of so many bison, and they ran over you."

"Then," said Tecumseh as if to himself, "no one else felt the ground shake. I have seen more signs, brother. I do not know what they mean."

Chiksika was quiet for a while, a far-seeing look in his eyes as he held Tecumseh's hand and looked toward the sunset. Finally he said, "You had a sign yesterday that you would not go to see our mother. Now that is so." He looked down at Tecumseh's splinted leg and said, "You will not be able to travel on with me."

"Then," Tecumseh replied, "if you find her, tell her I will be along someday." He turned his head and faced the sunset. The red ball of the sun was beyond the heat and smoke of a bonfire, and its image trembled in the heatwaves. Tecumseh looked at the red sun and held his *pa-waw-ka* stone in his hand. He thanked Weshemoneto for sparing his life and for giving him so many important signs.

Then he asked Weshemoneto to tell him, at the proper time, the meaning of the signs.

# CHAPTER 19

## *Maykujay Town*
## *Summer 1789*

I t was early morning. A delicate mist was rising off the creek, tinged with the first rays of the sun. A heron stalked along in the water's edge on its stick legs, looking for something to catch. In the grain fields off to the south, songbirds were starting to trill.

Loud Noise lay on his belly on a robe near the door of his hut with his chin on the back of his hand and watched the path to the creek. His gullet burned with rum.

Loud Noise had built his hut here, in a boggy bottomland, away from the rest of the town, for one reason. It gave a close view of a quiet green pool of the creek banked with flat, mossy slabs of stone, a little above its confluence with the river. The floor of his hut was usually spongy and damp, sometimes even muddy, and everything in the hut was mildewed and muddy. It was a place of mosquitoes and snakes. The hut itself was so carelessly made and shabby that it could have been taken for a beaver house. Star Watcher, a very good house builder, might have helped him build a neat, snug house, even though she had children to take care of, if he had chosen a more reasonable site. She suspected why he had chosen this place, and she called him a twisted-head. And so he had put the rickety, drafty hovel up mostly by himself, as he had no woman of his own to build it for him.

He had no woman of his own, and that was his problem. Loud Noise was a young man now, and he had the appetites of three or four men—in his loins and in his guts. But he was as ugly as three or four men put together. Women and girls laughed behind their hands at him and drew away when his one bulging, evil-looking eye stared at them.

Loud Noise was always conscious of the ugliness of his empty right eyesocket and tended to keep the left side of his face forward and the disfigured eye as obscure as possible, so habitually that his head appeared to be on crooked, and his right shoulder was always aching and hunched. With the prominent left eye he stared at women in rude hunger. Their aloofness angered him, and he hated them even as he desired them.

Girls grew silly and squirmy when his brother Tecumseh was around. Even Stands-Between, ordinary and undistinguished as he was, could cause some girls to lower their eyes and look coy. But Loud Noise, with his great passions and his feeling that he possessed undetected powers and unappreciated wisdom, only repelled them. He was desperately lonely, and angry. Most of the town's people were uncomfortable with his presence, his squinting eye, and his curious outbursts of gibberish and laughter, with his dirtiness and gassiness, so it was fine with them if he chose to burrow alone in the distant bog. People were afraid to offend him directly, because he seemed the kind of person who might retaliate with witchcraft. In his hut he sat up late at night, drank trader's liquor, sang to himself, gorged on food, and grew paunchy. On still nights he could be heard practicing loud belches and windblasts and whooping with drunken hilarity at his more remarkable noises. Unlike most drunkards, he did not wander the town wailing or starting trouble, but entertained himself all night or sometimes tormented himself all night with his strange mind, and slept till midday most days. Hunters seldom took him along because he floundered through the woods and scared away the game. For the great quantities of food he ate, he depended mostly upon his generous sister Star Watcher and her husband. When he did have to depend upon himself, he caught fish, helped himself from gardens or from the tribal corn fields, or sometimes he would trade a drink of liquor for a small hunk of venison or half a turkey from a homecoming hunter. He could eat and digest anything, including unripe corn and vegetables and half-spoiled meat. It was easy enough to get by in a tribe that never let its people starve.

He lived alone with his turbulent longings, and his bed was spotted with old semen, from his dreams and from the self-manipulations he did in the margins of sleep. Too much of this, according to the precepts, was shameful and soul sapping—so he simply mocked the precepts.

It was not for the beauty of the creek that Loud Noise had built his shabby hut here, though he would now and then gaze upon this mossy place with such a poignant appreciation of it that his heart would ache and his tears would blur the scene—usually after he had smoked the seed heads of hemp.

The reason he had built his hovel here was that it was where women and girls came to wash garments and bathe. Here he could lurk in the shadows of his hut, tense and trembling, and watch their naked, gleaming brown bodies in and around the water. With no suspicion that a man was watching, the girls would stoop in the shallows, yipping with shivery voices, and sweep handfuls of water at each other. Long strands of wet black hair would cling to their goosefleshed shoulders and turgid nipples. Women with mature bosoms and powerful haunches would sometimes sit naked on the moss and caress their feet in the water. On hot days there was so much to see that Loud Noise would wish he had ten eyes instead of one.

Star Watcher suspected him of this spying, and that was why she called him a twisted-head. To see a naked woman was not unusual. Though the Shawnee women were modest, there were times in and around a crowded village when their functions would require them to be partly or wholly nude, and on such occasions nothing was to be made of it. Men bathed in the river, women in the creek, and it was considered uncivil to spy. The women of the tribe were, after all, like members of the same great family. Star Watcher told no one else what she thought her brother was doing. It was embarrassing enough having him for a brother with just his *known* aberrations; there was no point in calling anyone's attention to this.

This morning Loud Noise lay looking out, the smell of his burned-out fire rankling in his nostrils. He had awakened from a rum sleep before dawn. To his delight he had found a few swallows of liquor still in the bottom of his jar and had drunk them to get the ache out of his head, and now as the sun came up he lay there just a little drunk, watching for one particular girl whose habit was to come down to the creek early, every other day or so, and bathe before anyone else had stirred up the silt in the creek. This was a Peckuwe maiden of about his age, tall and straight and graceful, and when she came down to the creek in the mornings she seemed like a doe coming down to drink.

Now his heart leaped as a light form approached down the path. It was she!

She glanced at his hut as she passed, but he lay low in the gloom, and if she thought of him at all, she probably thought he was asleep. He followed her with his hungry eye as she went down and stood on the bank.

Now this girl with the fine-boned face stepped out of her moccasins and stood barefoot on the moss, then removed her little headband and laid it carefully in one of the moccasins. Loud Noise lay trembling, his eye as keen and precise as a hawk's, watching her nimble brown fingers braid her black hair. She seemed to glow in the sunbeams. And now she crossed her arms and gripped her doeskin dress at the hips and slipped it off over her head. As she stood folding the garment, humming softly, the reflected sunlight off the water playing over her, his desire became too great at last.

Perhaps if he had been sober, he would have stayed in his hut and watched her, while spilling his seed into his bed. To force oneself upon an unwilling woman was a serious badness, and the family of the outraged one was entitled to take retribution. When Loud Noise was sober, it was fear of retribution, as much as fear of being rejected, that checked his urge to throw himself upon some solitary bather. But he was not sober now, nor was he too drunk to move, and no witness was around, and he knew too that this desirable girl had no dangerous protectors, being the daughter of an old Peckuwe village chief whose two sons had been killed at Piqua Town by the Long Knives years ago.

So when this girl, whose name was She-Is-Favored, was bending over to place her folded dress upon a dry rock, she heard a whisper of motion behind her and at once felt a strong arm encircle her. She gasped and began to struggle. Something rigid was being thrust at her buttocks, and she heard hard breathing and smelled stinking rum breath. Whoever had her was strong. The girl was scared, but more angry than scared. Squirming and twisting to look back, she saw the homely, one-eyed fool, greasy, grimacing with lust, grunting. She was infuriated. If this had been his brother Tecumseh, whom she had seen only once but dreamed of ever since, she might have yielded. It was instead this paunchy stinker.

Loud Noise, though clumsy, had grown up to be strong, especially when in one of his tantrums or frenzies, and people avoided conflicts with him, as he might go out of his head and strike or strangle with incredible power.

But She-Is-Favored, like most Shawnee women, who did hard and heavy work from morning till night, was strong, too. And she was as indignant as he was impassioned. She had learned, in the womanly school of the menstrual lodge, how women held their own in fights with their husbands. One way was by pulling hair. She could not reach the hair of this snorting, grunting man who was trying so frantically to penetrate her from behind. But she could do the other thing. Being bent forward like this with her head down, hissing, clenching her teeth, she reached back between her own thighs and with all the strength of her work-hardened hand she seized his scrotum and squeezed, twisted, and pulled as if to tear it off.

Many of the villagers that morning were jolted out of their sleepiness by what sounded like a wildcat cry down by the creek. As the scream trailed off it was recognizable as a man's voice.

And when the first of the people ran down the path with their guns and knives, they were puzzled to see the crazy hermit Loud Noise, stark naked and doubled over with his hands in his crotch, hobbling in through the door of his hovel, keening and groaning.

The only other person in sight was She-Is-Favored, the Peckuwe maiden, wading into the creek to bathe.

On that same morning, four hundred miles to the south, Tecumseh crouched behind a stump and aimed his rifle at a head in a hat just visible above the pointed log pickets of a small fort called Buchanan's Station. The man in the hat was at the same moment aiming his rifle at Tecumseh. They were fifty paces from each other. Around them at this instant, other rifles were going off, and there was a haze of smoke over the lush spring green of the clearing. To Tecumseh's right just now, Big Fish was lying beside another stump, pushing a ball down the hot barrel of his rifle with a hickory ramrod. His face and hands were sooty with gunpowder. This had been going on all morning. To Tecumseh's left, kneeling behind the trunk of a fallen tree, Chiksika was fitting a fire-arrow to a bowstring. Next to him was a young Cherokee whose task it was to prepare the fire-arrows. He had built a small fire. He had rags and twists of tinder and char cloth and a jar of bear oil. He would bind rags and twists of tinder to an arrow shaft just behind the head, soak it in the oil, then light it from the fire and hand it to Chiksika, who would fit it to his bowstring like this, then quickly rise and shoot the arrow at the wood-shingled roof of the blockhouse of the fort or one of the houses inside the wall.

Chiksika had great faith in fire-arrows. In the six years since the end of the white men's war there had been no more hope of getting British cannons, so the fire-arrow was the only alternative for destroying forts. But fire-arrows had to be used at short range, and the men in the fort were deadly shooters even at long range. It had taken the warriors most of the morning to get close enough to the little fort for Chiksika to shoot fire-arrows at it. Twice they had rushed toward it, dodging from stump to stump across the clearing, and both times their advance had been stopped by the quick and accurate shooting of the men in the fort. Several Cherokees had been badly wounded.

The little fort was near the Cherokee villages in the country south of Kain-tuck-ee, called Tennessee, and the sharp-shooting white men who occupied the fort had bothered the Cherokees a great deal. Chiksika and Tecumseh and their little party of Shawnee warriors had joined with the Cherokees to attack this fort, because they had been visiting with the Cherokees and wanted to help their southern brothers solve the problem of the fort. Chiksika took any opportunity to fight white men.

Chiksika had been fighting with these Cherokee bands for more than a year. He had come down here after Tecumseh's leg was broken in the hunting accident, and when the leg healed Tecumseh had come back with him. Most of the Shawnee warriors, including Tecumseh, were living with

Cherokee girls, and this had bonded them even closer to the tribe. Therefore, although it was a Cherokee matter and the Shawnees would not have
had to join in the attack, they had volunteered eagerly. Chiksika had gained
as great a reputation for killing white men in the south as he had had in
O-hi-o. As he had been doing all his adult life, he was still avenging the
death of his father and the burning of the towns. These fire-arrows would
burn white men's towns. To be the man who rose up and shot the fire-
arrows was to be in especial danger, because the marksmen in the fort knew
where he was, and they tried to fire a volley at him every time they saw him
rise up behind the big log. So far that morning Chiksika had hit the fort with
ten burning arrows. Three of them had started good blazes, two on a roof
and one on the palisade. Men in the fort had extinguished the burning
palisade by pouring water down on it. The burning roof had been put out
both times by a brave boy who had climbed up on it and beaten it with a
soaked blanket. The marksmen in the fort were kept busy pinning down the
Cherokee warriors, but they considered the fire-arrows to be an especial
danger, and just as Chiksika believed that sooner or later one of his arrows
would start a fire they could not put out, they believed that sooner or later
they would hit him when he rose with his bow. The dead tree was full of
holes from their shooting, and Chiksika had wood splinters in his face and
shoulders. The Cherokee who was making the fire-arrows worked on despite the agony of splinters in his eye.

Now Tecumseh squeezed the trigger of his rifle, and when the smoke
billowed away he could no longer see the man in the hat. He yelped with
triumph and quickly reloaded. While he was measuring powder from his
horn, three bullets hit the stump in front of him, and he was stung by chips
of bark.

Chiksika, seeing that one white man had just fallen and at least three had
discharged their rifles, leaped up and drew his bow and sent another arrow
in a smoking arc toward the fort. He dropped out of sight, and several more
rifle balls thudded into the log. He laughed with delight.

Chiksika seemed today, as always, to have Weshemoneto's cloak of
protection around him. But Tecumseh was in a state of the most extreme
dread and grew cold with fear every time he saw Chiksika fit another arrow
to the string.

Chiksika had had a vision three days ago. He had told Tecumseh about
it that night, and it had chilled his heart.

In the vision Chiksika had seen himself fall before the palisade wall of
the fort, shot through the forehead.

Tecumseh could not disbelieve that dream. His father had had a premonition the day he was killed. So Tecumseh had pleaded with Chiksika not
to come into battle at the fort. "You do not have to fight the fort," Tecum-

seh had pleaded. "If you have seen that happen to you at the fort, then do not go to the fort."

"You do not understand," Chiksika had replied. "I have seen it happen, and therefore I know I will be at the fort." Several times Tecumseh had tried to persuade his brother not to join the attack. Finally Chiksika had said, "Brother, I know your heart. Yes. When our father saw that he would die in the battle of the Kanawha-se-pe, my heart was as yours is now, and I wished he would stay back from that battle. But would our father have hung back from his duty as a war chief from fear of such a vision? No. Then would I? No. Listen, my good brother. I have gone into battle many times *thinking* I would be killed. The only difference is that now I know it. The fear is no greater. I think it is less, because what we fear is what we do not know. Now make me a promise, and if you do, I will tell you of another vision I have had."

Tecumseh had lowered his head to hide the grief in his face and said, "I will promise what you ask."

Gazing into the fire, Chiksika had said, "Promise me that when I fall, you will not lose heart for the battle."

"I promise that. If you fall, I will want to fight harder to avenge it."

"Good. Revenge itself is spit in the wind, that comes back, but Long Knives do not belong here, and you must never stop resisting them. The greatest chiefs will sue for peace with the white men. In dreams I have seen even Little Turtle and Black Hoof and Blue Jacket give up and mark treaties."

"No! Not Black Hoof!"

"Yes. Even he. But in my visions, you always refuse. And thus you become the greatest of the Shawnee chiefs, because you do not turn around."

After that talk, Chiksika had seemed serene and almost cheerful. He had repeated the promises their father had demanded before he died and said, "You must promise the same to me. See that our brothers do not disgrace the family or the People. Loud Noise is the dark shadow. He does not have good character. I know I have not been a good brother to him, and I regret. But you have been. Perhaps you have seen something in him that I in my selfishness did not see. He will never be a warrior. He never even tried to earn his *pa-waw-ka.* And he was afraid to go out in the night to find a Spirit Helper. He cares little for his honor, I think. But he loves you and admires you, my brother. Do what you can to help him be an honorable man, no shame to us.

"As for our sister. Always listen to her. She was born wise and grows ever more so. I remember she told me to be merciful to prisoners, but I did not listen until you taught me the same. Tell her I have greater love

for her than it seemed. You already know you have no better ally than Star
Watcher."

That had been their council, the best of all they had shared. And now
they were here in front of the fort. The guns of the men in the fort and of
the Cherokees around the fort were still banging and filling the humid air
with smoke. Chiksika's last fire-arrow had set ablaze something inside the
palisade. Much smoke was rising, and the men inside were yelling to each
other. Chiksika was laughing. He fitted another burning arrow to the
bowstring and stood up, drawing the bow, the long, beautiful muscles tense
in his arms and shoulders, his copper skin agleam with sweat, a fierce, happy
grimace baring his white teeth.

Tecumseh was looking up at him feeling rich with pride when a bullet
from the fort struck Chiksika in the forehead. The fire-arrow flew wild and
stuck in the grass. Chiksika stood swaying. When Tecumseh caught the
toppling body in his arms, its life was already passing out from it. And now
from Tecumseh's heart burst an unbearable dismay, and his cry of lamenta-
tion was heard everywhere on the battlefield, a sound that was never to be
forgotten by anyone who heard it.


For a long while the loss of Chiksika was like a disease in Tecumseh, like
a famine in his spirit. The Cherokee girl would try to embrace him in their
bed and would find him trembling, and he would get up and go away in
the night. By the campfire Big Fish would try to talk to him, about Moses,
about warfare, about heroes and knights in the books that he vaguely
remembered, but Tecumseh would remain silent.

"You do not seem to be listening," Big Fish would say. Tecumseh would
wave his hand as if turning over pages and tell him to go on, but as Big Fish
talked on he would see by the firelight that Tecumseh was listening only
to the echoes in his own empty heart.

The Cherokee warriors to whom Tecumseh had become so strongly
attached during the months of raiding and fighting before Chiksika's death
now stayed back from him. They were polite, but they were abashed because they knew they had failed him. After Chiksika was killed, they had
thought that the death of such a great and invulnerable warrior was a bad
sign, so they had withdrawn their attack of Buchanan's Fort, even though
Tecumseh, with Chiksika's blood fresh on his shoulder, had exhorted them
to stay and charge the fort one more time for a certain victory, to keep
Chiksika's death from being wasted. The fire inside the fort had been
burning hard and most of the men inside busy fighting it, and surely the
Cherokees could have gotten to the walls. But instead they had drawn back

and stood on a hill among the trees looking down on the little fort and the stumps and the dead cattle in the clearing around it. If they had attacked the fort again, he would have let them help him with Chiksika's body. They had wanted to take the body back to their village for the ceremonies of burial. But Tecumseh had not let them touch the body; he had carried it alone through gunfire to a place on the hill, then had furiously hacked out a grave in the thin, rocky soil with his own tomahawk and bare hands and buried him there near the battlefield, as was the Shawnee custom for a great warrior. He had put rocks over the grave to keep wolves from it and had carefully concealed all traces of digging so that the white men would not dig up the body to mutilate it or steal its head bone, and then he had left his beloved brother there on the ridge to look down upon the fort that had killed him. Perhaps he would haunt it forever as it tried to grow into a white man's city.

After a week of struggling silently with his own despair, Tecumseh looked suddenly to Big Fish and the other Shawnee warriors of his little band and said:

"I must go away. I have a promise to keep."


It was in the *Seeminee Keelswah,* the Papaw Moon, when Tecumseh rode into the Creek town of Tuckabatchee far to the south. It was a town of square cabins built of pine logs, with chimneys made of sticks and mud. The town was on a rich bottomland full of crops and cotton fields. The heat of the day was intense, and the sun was so high that Tecumseh's horse stood upon its own shadow. The people who came out of the shade to watch him ride in were a good-looking, well-built people, but some of them very fat. They were almost naked in the great heat, and those who wore clothing were wearing brightly dyed shirts of cloth.

When the Muskogee chief came out to meet him, Tecumseh was jolted by the sight of his broad face. It was one of the faces he had seen in dreams. It looked, he remembered, like the face he had seen that was mottled with pale spots, though this face before him had no pale spots. It was as dark as a deer's liver. Tecumseh dismounted and took the hand of the chief, who said, "You are Shawnee! Long ago we were neighbors of Shawnee. I, Big Warrior, welcome you here!"

They went to the chief's house to smoke and talk, and it was strange. There were many things of white men's manufacture in this house. There were mirrors and other things made of glass. There was a bellows, which made Tecumseh think of Loud Noise and his Thunder-Sucker.

The only times Tecumseh had been in square houses was when he had

raided and burned the cabins of white people. He had never sat in their
stick-seats, which Big Fish had told him were called chairs, and he did not
like this. It creaked when he moved. The chief's chair creaked so loudly
under his great weight that Tecumseh was afraid it was going to break under
him, but it did not. There were roaches on the floor, and a quick little lizard
came in the door and went partway up a wall. Flies buzzed in and out of
the rectangular door, which was blinding with sun glare. After the smoke
and giving of small gifts, Tecumseh explained to Big Warrior who he was
and why he had come, and Big Warrior's face brightened. "So you are
Tecumseh! You are of our blood! We have heard of your birth under the
Panther Star. I myself saw the Panther Star at that time, and I remember
that all the old men said it marked something important. Come, and I will
walk with you to the house."

As they strolled through the big village, through the shade of great oaks
with dusty-looking moss hanging from them, Big Warrior recounted that
he had known Hard Striker as a young man. Tecumseh was listening to the
chief and observing the strange houses and dress and the evidences of the
white men's influence upon the Creek culture—the pigs in the streets, some
mules within a fence, something with wheels that at first he thought was a
cannon but then saw was only some sort of a carrying conveyance—but with
most of his spirit he was yearning ahead and preparing himself. A crowd
began following, looking at him. Finally, near the river, Big Warrior said,
"Now here is the house, and I believe she is here." Tecumseh was happy
to see that it was not one of the square houses but a round one, made of
bowed saplings, like a Shawnee summer house, with woven straw mats that
had been rolled up on the sides to let fresh air flow through. Silhouetted
in the shade within were four people, sitting on the floor. One of them, a
woman, was talking in a soft, low voice, a voice thrilling to hear. The chief
stopped outside this house and said:

"Turtle Mother! Here is your son who has come far to find you."

She turned and rose, her left arm across her bosom, a feather fan held
in her hand, and came out into the sunlight, squinting against its brightness,
and the squinting revealed the many fine wrinkles at the corners of her eyes
now. Her hair hung no more in the Shawnee style with a braid but loose
and cut straight across the brow. There was much gray in it. Her face was
as handsome as ever, but the lines around her mouth showed bitterness,
sadness. She was a Creek by birth and had come home to the Creeks and
now was dressed like a Creek woman, in cotton. Her eyes glittered. She
came toward him slowly, her wrist still on her breast, holding the fan at her
shoulder, looking at him so intently that he shivered.

"Tecumseh!" she murmured. "It is Tecumseh!"

"*Neegah,* my mother!"

Her eyes were brimming, her chin was crumpled and quivering, but she was smiling, smiling with her lips bitten tightly shut, as if to keep from crying aloud. She let go of the fan, which then dangled from its loop around her wrist as she reached toward him with both hands, her palms down, and put them on his forearms. They held each other's arms and stood for a long time, looking deep into each other's eyes as ten years fell away.

"*Weh-sah,*" she said at last.

"*Weh-sah.*"

"A handsome man is my son. I am proud. I hear of you sometimes, even so far. Chiksika told me of your leg. I see it did not heal very straight—" Suddenly she stopped, seeing the strain of grief in his eyes. "What?" she asked.

"I must tell you of a terrible thing."

She shut her eyes, and her eyelids trembled. "It is of Chiksika."

"*Nep-wa,* he is dead." he said softly.

Her hands gripped him desperately as she struggled with her grief. At last she released a long sigh. She opened her eyes and tears flowed down her cheeks, but her face was set firm. "Of course. He was only for war. You must come into the shade and sit with me. There is much to say."

"There is much to say."

"He told me you had promised to come."

"I am here."

Big Warrior, seeing the intensity in Turtle Mother and her son, summoned the other people from the hut, and they walked away with him. Tecumseh and his mother went in under the roof. She gave him water to drink, and then she washed his feet, her head down, tears falling from the end of her nose. After a while, when she could talk, she did not talk of Chiksika at first. She explained that the other people in the house had been distant relatives, a man and his wife and a little girl. Turtle Mother had come to live with them, she explained, because the place where the Shawnees had gone west of the Missi-se-pe was a strange sort of land, on the wrong side of the Great River, and such a small piece of land within such a vast countryside that it had been like being forever shut in a room. To go west, it had seemed to her, was to go toward death. Here in Tuckabatchee at least was the place where she had grown up, and she was more content here, even though, as one who had gone away for a long time, she was a little set aside from the Creek women. The Creeks had not lately had trouble with the whites and did not like to hear her speak of her hatred for white men.

After a while she knelt across from him with her hands in her lap and said: "What does my daughter Star Watcher say of me? Does she curse me for leaving my family? Often I dream this, in shame, and think I should have stayed."

He was astonished to hear this. "No," he exclaimed. "Wipe away that word 'shame.' When we speak of our mother it is only with longing! Often we make ourselves smile in hard times by talking of the days when we were together under your care!"

Turtle Mother's eyes were now glimmering. "This is indeed true? Even Star Watcher does not blame me?"

Fervently, to be sure she knew it was the truth, as she so needed to know, he told her:

"She is so true in her admiration that she tries to be another Turtle Mother. She is beloved by all the People for her goodness."

Tears streamed down Turtle Mother's cheeks. She asked to know everything about her grandchildren, and when that had all been told, she at last braced herself and said:

"Now I am ready to hear about my son Chiksika. It was white men who killed him?"

"Yes. White men."

She took a deep breath and let it out. "So many women would still have our husbands and sons if not for the white men."

"True," Tecumseh said. "And so many white women would still have their husbands and sons if not for Chiksika." He said this with a grim satisfaction.

"Did he hurt long?"

"He was laughing, and then he was gone. He was fighting, and then he was at peace."

"Then Weshemoneto is to be thanked."

"He had foreseen it and was ready."

"Like his father."

They sat silent for a long while, absorbed in thought. The cicadas were shrilling in the bright sunlight outside, and there were the calls and cheeps of many birds, many of them unlike any he had ever heard in the homeland so far away north.

She held both his wrists in her hands now, and with her thumbs she was caressing the bones of his wrists. Though she was grieving, her touch was calming his own grief and strengthening him. He remembered what a different place the world had been when the family had all lived together. He could feel something of that rich, deep inclusion again. But now of course it lacked Chiksika, and there was a gap there in the circle that would never be closed again. Cat Follower too was dead. Chiksika had told her that of the beestings.

Outside the shelter the sunlight hammered down on the yellow grass and red earth, people made their working sounds, the voices of children rang in the distance. He felt as he had felt in the old Kispoko Town when he was a small boy, before he had become aware of the trouble with the whites. He remembered the sunny, droning days, the nearness of a mother, the feeling that there was no trouble in the world.

"My son," she said after a while, "will you stay with me long?"

He shook his head. "Not long. Chiksika led a small band of us. A few Shawnees, a few more Cherokees. We had been active and struck the whites often. We have to do more. Before I came here they chose me to lead them in his place. I have thought of ways to distress the whites by shutting their roads."

She sighed and nodded. "You have a great name among the Cherokees already. The Creeks tell of your deeds. They do not speak of Chiksika without speaking of you also."

"If I am to have a name spoken with his, I shall have to do much to be worthy of that honor."

"You must do the great deeds, it is true. But never be reckless. My heart could not bear to hear again the sadness it heard today." Then, after another deep silence, she said, "Do you understand yet what the shaking earth means?"

"I am more mystified than ever. I have seen more and I understand less. Listen . . ." He told her of the dove, of the wolves with the moons in their eyes, of seeing the face like Big Warrior's, of the houses falling down. Then he was quiet for a minute, gazing out around the village of Tuckabatchee. He said, "The houses I saw falling were not like houses I had seen before. But now I recognize as I look at this town that they were houses like these." She replied:

"When Chiksika came to see me after you were hurt, he spoke of these things you see. I have thought much about them. I do not know, either. The passing of the four wolves means the time of four moons. But from when to when? Not from the time you dreamed them, because more than that has passed. I do not know. You will know when more signs come. You will see things happen that were in the dream, and a little at a time, maybe all at once, you will come to understand. But to understand . . ."

"To understand the signs in time, I must please Weshemoneto and be worthy."

"Yes."

"I know that there will never be any peace for me, as there was none for Chiksika. As long as there are white men in this land I cannot rest. The People and our allies have killed twenty hundreds of whites at least, but a hundred times that many now live where not one lived when I was the age of that boy over there." He pointed at a child who squatted under a live oak. "It would do the People no good to give up and withdraw across the Great River. Though the Spaniards have that land now, they will not be able to stand there when the Long Knives want to cross over for more land. I have heard that a rider can go twenty days and see no one on the plains of the western ground. That sounds like an empty land. But when the whites have filled up Kain-tuck-ee and O-hi-o and all places on this side of the Missi-se-pe, then they will cross over, and they will fill up that great empti-ness as fast as one of Loud Noise's hot stinks fills up a cold house."

She squeezed his wrists and even allowed a fond little smile to pass over the sadness of her face.

He went on: "Is there a way to stop them? No one I hear knows a way. Sometimes I feel that all the signs I have seen are for the purpose of telling me a way."

She nodded. "When there is a terrible need, Weshemoneto sends the People a great man. I know and many of us know that you came through me to be that man." She was rubbing his wrists again and was quiet for a long time. Then she said, "And you know that when Weshemoneto sends a great leader, he sends also a great medicine man to help him. And you know this: the strongest medicine is often found in what is most contrary."

"I have seen in the dreams," Tecumseh said, "a man I believe to be Loud Noise in maturity. And what is there more contrary than he is? Yes! The Great Good Spirit requires something from everyone. Even our poor Loud Noise was marked by a sign."

# PART TWO

# CHAPTER 20

## *Kekionga Town*
## *November 1790*

Star Watcher's world was in a turmoil, her husband was very badly wounded, and she was doing some of the hardest and most unpleasant kind of work a woman had to do, but in spite of all that she could not keep down a silent song of joy that kept bubbling up in her soul.

Half of this town was a ruin of charred poles and heaps of ashes. Kekionga Town and most of the other villages near the head of the Maumee-se-pe had been torched once again by a Long Knife army. From where she stood working, she could see the blackened timbers of the old French trading store. But everywhere among the ashes, new *wigewas* were rising. She herself had just yesterday completed a bark hut big enough for her family; Stands Firm lay on the bed inside it, half-conscious, bound up with poultices, shot through a lung and bayoneted through the face by the Long Knife soldiers. But Stands Firm was a very strong man, and he was making his way back from the edge of death. Every day the seepage from his chest was less bloody, and his cheek was healing. There would be a jagged scar, and the bayonet had also ripped open the elegant loop of his perforated earlobe, leaving a long strand of soft flesh dangling. But he was alive, and he had lived up to his name in the great battle, as one of Little Turtle's subchiefs. The allied tribes had fought savagely on their homeland and had inflicted such severe casualties on the American army that it had turned and fled back to the O-hi-o. The warriors had killed a dozen officers and nearly a hundred soldiers, most of them the Blue-Coat regulars who were supposed to be the bravest soldiers of the Long Knife army, the same kinds of soldiers who had thrown down the British king's Redcoats. Little Turtle's great heart and mind were being celebrated now; he was the chief who had routed the army of the United States. Stands Firm, who had been in charge

261

of a group of Shawnee warriors defending the town, had driven the Blue-Coats back across the river and pursued them along the riverbank in a long, bloody, running battle until the ball through his chest had stopped him. Black Hoof and Blue Jacket of the Shawnees, and Breaker-in-Pieces of the Delawares, and the white allies, the Girtys, had added more to the legends of their names, and for now, at least, it seemed unlikely that the army would ever again be so rash as to try to march into the country again.

But the song in Star Watcher's soul was not the result of that victorious defense: she never rejoiced in the killing of men.

For days she had felt growing inside her a certainty that her brother Tecumseh was coming near, returning after his long absence in the south. It was an instinctive sureness that grew as the hazardous years went by, like the unsaid knowings that animals have. In her heart and dreams she seemed to know when he was going farther or coming closer. And sometimes there would be the hard sudden pulse and want of air, when she felt that he was in extreme danger. Only a few days ago she had felt that, even though he was now not far from home; through a part of a night she had been sleepless and anxious, but finally it had passed.

At this moment Star Watcher was working a new deerhide over the end of a post, twisting it and pulling it and rubbing it, to make it soft and supple. She gripped it with both hands and pulled this way and that with all the strength of her shoulders and back and arms. She would do this for hours, until her hands were so cramped she could hardly open them. It was hard work, but she maintained a kind of rhythm, and her mind drifted with the rhythm and was calm and full of hope. Now and then she would stop and wipe her hands and go in to look at her husband, help him drink water, feed him a little. Her daughter, now six, was playing with a corn-husk doll, the only toy she had managed to hang on to in the flight from the Long Knife army. Her son was out in the town playing with a pack of little ones. It was a cool day, but not raw as the days of this moon usually were, a good day for working outside.

She thought of Tecumseh and of all the things that had happened to him in the south. The stories had come home, season by season, told by warriors of his band who came and went. Star Watcher had long known of Chiksika's foretold death and of Tecumseh's journey to find their mother. And in the year since, there had come story after story of his astounding deeds in the Ten-ness-ee country, in the lands of the Cherokee and Alabamu peoples. In the time since Chiksika's death, Tecumseh had fought the Long Knives as if all of Chiksika's prowess and courage and cunning had passed into his own soul. He had ambushed supply trains and militia patrols everywhere from the mountains to the Missi-se-pe, often attacking even though outnumbered. The warriors who served with him came home full of glory, for he gave them opportunities to do more than they had suspected they could do. They brought home scalplocks and wonderful stories of miraculous triumphs. A young Creek named Seekabo came and told stories that made it seem that Tecumseh could see in the dark, hear through mountains, and deflect bullets; his tales had so stirred Thick Water that he had returned to the south with Seekabo to rejoin his old boyhood comrade. And one of the things these messengers always said that pleased Star Watcher was that Tecumseh never hurt a prisoner. He never killed women or children. Tecumseh might have assumed many of Chiksika's traits, but not his cold vein of cruelty. Even at this distance, and through years of absence, she was still the Watcher of the Shooting Star.

Then she heard the voice behind her: *"Meh Ah' shemah,* my sister."

Star Watcher shut her eyes for a moment. A smile shaped her lips, and her heart felt as if it were being squeezed, then released. She dropped the deerhide, straightened her tired back, then turned to look at him.

*"Meh Ah' thetha,* my brother! I knew you would be here soon!"

The faces around him were a blur; she did not even see who they were. His eyes were, as always, looking in a way that perceived not only the sight but the spirit of their object, eyes that seemed to pull everything into themselves. He was so lean, so tight-skinned, that every bone and muscle in his face and neck was distinct. When she embraced him, he was hard as oak, but as always he gave off great warmth. For a long while they held each other, faces radiant, feeling the long-divided oneness between them closing, becoming again that one dual being: Star and Star Watcher. And finally she drew back, holding his wrists—he remembered how his mother had held his wrists just that way—and she told him, "You must come in and see my husband. The Long Knives almost killed him; to see you will bring him up a long way."

And so it did.

Later Stands-Between and Loud Noise came hurrying. They were of warrior age now. Stands-Between had fought in that long battle by the river. He could not raise his left arm very far; a sword cut was healing along his ribs. "Here is the man who cut me with his long knife," he said, holding up a yellow-haired scalplock and smiling.

But when Loud Noise emerged from the crowd, Tecumseh was shocked. It was the puffy-eyed face of a flabby drunkard, fatcheeked, slack-lipped, a smile more like a sneer. And he stank like a French trapper. Seeing the revulsion in Tecumseh's eyes, Loud Noise suddenly was ashamed and almost afraid. But Tecumseh said, "Brother, I have thought of you very much. They say you did not serve in the battle."

"I am learning to be a shaman," Loud Noise muttered.
"I think that you will need much attention from me."


The next day the story-telling began, between those who had been fighting
in the south and those who had made such a victory here. Old Black Hoof
looked at Tecumseh and remembered that this was a boy who had run from
his first battle. But he was here with a band of young men who had taken
almost as many scalps as the united tribes had taken from the soldiers after
the battle. Black Hoof's adopted son Big Fish proudly told most of the
stories about what Tecumseh's band had done. The listeners were spell-
bound throughout, but especially when he told of a miracle Tecumseh had
made only a few nights ago, after crossing into O-hi-o. Surrounded in their
camp one midnight by about twenty-five white men under command of the
great-voiced But-lah, they had escaped when Tecumseh threw his blanket
over the campfire and created darkness. Then Tecumseh had rallied his
eight to attack the confused white men in the dark, killing twelve of them
and chasing the rest away.

Tecumseh had a curious reluctance to boast and soon told Black Hoof
that he felt foolish for fighting little bands of whites south of Kain-tuck-ee
and missing the nation's greatest victory. "I should have been here instead," he said, and laughed.

Black Hoof told of the cautious and fearful way the American general
had conducted his forces, never making bold moves, never once firing the
cannons he had dragged all the way up from the Beautiful River. The
general's name was Harmar, and he had been an officer in the big war
against the British. But he had not known how to fight warriors in the
woods.

"I am happy that it was not the old Long Knife General Clark, then,"
Tecumseh said. "They would have been wiser to have Clark!"

"Perhaps not," said Black Hoof, his black eyes glittering under his thick,
white-frosted eyebrows. "Girty has heard that Clark is bitter and angry at
his government, that he falls drunk in the streets of their town of Louisville
where he lives. I think we will never have to fear the name of Clark
anymore."

"Ah." Tecumseh pondered on this, with both gratitude and sadness. The
evil of drink was mighty if it could bring down even a great and strong man.
Even an enemy should not be humiliated by it, if he was a great enemy. But
maybe it was more than that. Change-of-Feathers, the aged shaman, said:

"When he built his town in that Falling Water place, among the ghosts
of the old white giants, he was making his doom."

"Now," said Black Hoof, "our nation is joyous and resolute. Surely the white men everywhere are humbled and discouraged even as we rejoice.

"But we have seen that with the white men, even as with ourselves, out of the smoldering ashes of defeat are fanned the flames of vengeance. It is our turn to rejoice, their turn to vow revenge. Before a year is gone, I expect, their father Washington will send another army against us. And surely it will be a bigger army than Harmar's, and surely with a braver general."

"Should this prove to be so," Tecumseh spoke into the thoughtful silence, "then once again we must meet them allied with our brothers from the other nations. Little Turtle, Breaker-in-Pieces, Tarhe the Crane. We must forget old disputes and join together, as you did with the confederation, as we did with our Cherokee brothers. If we are all of one heart, we are all of one people, and however brave their new general is, he will not defeat us. This we must have learned by now."

"Yes," Black Hoof said when he had heard all this. "We must work this winter to strengthen our friendships. What Tecumseh says is true." But Black Hoof's face looked tired and worried as he said this, and Tecumseh thought: Every time, it grows harder for him. As he grows old, he wants peace and rest. How good peace and rest would be. But I hope I shall never grow so old and tired that I would think of peace while the white men come into our country!


It seemed that Loud Noise tried to avoid being alone with Tecumseh.

He was always there in the councils, where there were many people present; he was always there when Tecumseh talked with the family and visited the healing Stands Firm. He always yipped and applauded loudest when Tecumseh was praised and honored, and he even took it upon himself to be a horn and magnify in his own voice the exploits that Tecumseh himself understated. But when everyone else left, he left with them. Yesterday, even when Tecumseh had asked him to stay a while, Loud Noise had murmured that he had something urgent to do and would be back, but he had not come back until today, bringing Change-of-Feathers with him. For a man known as a recluse, Loud Noise had suddenly become quite a crowd seeker. They sat for a long time and talked, and with the old medicine man present, it was not a private conversation. But at last, when the old shaman had grown sleepy and begun snoring right where he sat, Tecumseh turned his full gaze upon Loud Noise and said, "My brother, I sense that you are afraid to talk with me. Why?"

"What!" Loud Noise protested, his eye shifting all around. "How can you think such a thing? I admire and love you!" But he looked away and forced a fake coughing spell, as if hoping to wake up old Change-of-Feathers, who, alas, slept on. Tecumseh reached out and grabbed his brother's chubby chin and forced him to look straight at him, then said in a soft voice:

"When I saw our mother in the south, I had to color my words when she asked me about you, so that she would not have a sorry picture of you. And I thought, Perhaps when I return, the years will have made my brother braver and more trustworthy.

"But since I came back, I am not encouraged. I learn that you did not go to fight the army. I see that you are fat and soft. I hear that you have grown to need liquor, and that when you drink it you bully people, and take things that are not yours, and that you try to force women to lie with you. I think these are some of the reasons why you have been afraid to face me alone. You were afraid I would speak to you of these things."

Loud Noise tried to turn his eye away from Tecumseh's probing stare, but the strong hand still held his face. He murmured through twisted lips, "People make more of things because they don't like me. I do not drink very much. I have not stolen, only borrowed things. And no woman has lain with me unless she chose to." Now, though his head was still locked in place, his eye was rolling, trying to avoid the needles of Tecumseh's gaze, which seemed to penetrate right into mind and heart. Now Tecumseh let loose of him.

"I told our mother I expect you will become a great shaman, that the signs say it will be so. But, my brother, hear me: You cannot become one just by pretending to be one. You have to become worthy of any gift, or you will not receive it. You will not learn to heal just by following Change-of-Feathers around and talking with him. You cannot force a woman to want you. And above all you cannot draw the power of Our Grandmother down from the moon to help you when you are so drunk you see several moons."

Loud Noise, despite his great discomfiture, almost smiled at that. If Tecumseh joked even a little with you, you knew you were not out of all favor. Loud Noise lowered his face and gazed wistfully into the fire. The old Shaman snored on. And now Tecumseh went on in a quiet voice, "If you do not believe you can be a real shaman, then you cannot be. But anybody can be good, even one who does not believe he will be great. Our father charged Chiksika not to let us become a shame to the family. He did this as he died in my arms in battle. Now Chiksika has died in my arms, and he passed this same charge on to me. Tell me if our family means nothing to you."

"Brother," Loud Noise whined, "our family is important to me."

Tecumseh gazed at him for a long time. After a while Loud Noise grumbled, "Who tells you I bully and steal?"

Tecumseh did not answer that. Instead he said, "Tell me, brother. In your own heart, how do you esteem yourself?"

Firelight flickered on the walls of the lodge. Outside in the winter night the sounds of the village, voices, crying babies, were faint: the sounds of the people. In Tecumseh's eyes Loud Noise was a shapeless lump with hair and earbobs and a feathered turban on top, abjectly looking down and away, his face hidden. Tecumseh suddenly remembered that long-ago day when the bow had sprung and the split arrow had pierced his little brother's eye, and the memory stabbed him in the heart. He reached and put his hand on his brother's shoulder. He felt him take a deep breath, and then the ugly face turned to him, the one eye glittering with a tear, but a kind of angry resolve showed in the set of the fleshy lips. Loud Noise began speaking.

"I am more than anyone thinks I am. No one knows the things I see. No one knows what I have thought. All the earth and the sky and the waters have been clear in my mind. It is true that I am not ordinary, and the people do not know how to see me or hear me. Being as they are, being afraid, they think I am a witch, but that is not so. If I am different, it is because I am more, not less, than a usual man."

Tecumseh nodded and squeezed the shoulder, and this little pressure of affection seemed to move Loud Noise as if it were a light from heaven. In his eye suddenly burned such an intense love and gratitude that Tecumseh seemed to feel it in the smoky air, and he said to his brother, "That is what I have always hoped to believe. I have said it to Chiksika and to our mother, even when your conduct could have caused me to doubt. I am happy that you believe this of yourself.

"Listen, my brother. The signs are a great gift. But a great gift is a great burden. One who has it cannot live only for his own pleasures. For us it will be hard. And hardest of all is to understand it.

"Promise me one thing," Tecumseh went on. "I have never asked you for a promise, have I? Now I ask it."

Loud Noise almost cringed, as if afraid he would be asked to do something courageous or inconvenient. "Promise me that you will try to master your appetites. All of them. This is the first thing a man must do if he is to deserve the gifts given to him, and if he is to be of good to his People."

It was as demanding a promise as Loud Noise had feared it would be. But he nodded and said, "I shall try."

"*Weh-sah.* Remember: We belong to the People."

The defeat of the white general Harmar had given the red men great heart, and many went down to the O-hi-o to raid boats. But a hard winter came early and froze the rivers and made it hard and miserable to live in war camps far from home, so most of the warriors returned to their villages to hunt and try to keep their families alive through the frozen and hungry moons. The distance they had been pushed northward from their old towns had been far enough to make the winters harder. Up here the wind blew hard and cold. Harmar's army had destroyed many crops before its defeat, so food was scarce again.

During this time, Tecumseh worked all his waking hours to help the people survive, and to help solidify the tribal alliances, and to harden himself for the great conflict that he felt would come in the next year. With his band of select followers, which now included Stands-Between, he wandered the upper Wabash and Maumee country both as a hunter and emissary, among the Wyandots, the Miamis, the Weas, the Kickapoos, and even the Ottawas, firming the bonds of friendship among the young warriors of those tribes, talking to the chiefs of the sacred duty of preserving the homelands from further invasion of the whitefaces. Tecumseh made himself known to the British Indian agents McKee and Elliott and renewed his acquaintance with Simon Girty, knowing that British guns and supplies probably would be needed to resist the Americans. The city of Detroit, though in American territory since the war, was still dominated by Englishmen who were eager to keep the tribes under British influence.

And to toughen himself for the coming trials of his life, he resumed the daily ordeal that he had followed periodically since boyhood. Every morning, except when the river ice was too thick, he broke it and plunged into the river to strengthen his inner fire. Loud Noise lived in dread that Tecumseh would force him to start strengthening himself in that way. It was all he could do—indeed, more than he could do—to curb his appetites as he had promised. When Tecumseh was close by to watch him, he would resist his gluttony and would feel pious about the growling of his half-empty guts. He would not drink liquor any time when Tecumseh might detect it. But as soon as Tecumseh would leave for a while, his resolve would melt; he would gorge himself with breadwater and succotash and any kind of meat he could get, and he would scheme frantically to obtain whiskey somehow without his family's knowledge. Then, after such binges, he would wallow in guilt or would rationalize that Tecumseh was a fanatical, unreasonable taskmaster.

Thus Loud Noise would suffer under Tecumseh's discipline when they were together. But only when he was suffering like this did he approve of himself, only when Tecumseh was protecting him from himself. He could not control himself without Tecumseh's will imposed upon him.

And so as the winter passed into spring and summer, his need for Tecumseh grew to be as strong as it had been when in his boyhood he had trailed him everywhere. And to his great relief, Tecumseh never insisted that he bathe in the icy river.


The smell of baking filled the warm air as the Bread Dance ceremonies began.

Twelve women, the selected cooks, sat in a circle in a lodge. Star Watcher was one of them. In the center of the floor lay a hoop made of a strip of split white oak. This hoop was the Round of the World, the Circle of Time. In the center of the hoop lay a leather ball, made of two pieces of hide sewn together, stuffed tight with deer hair.

One by one the cooks rose and knelt by the hoop and tied little packets of seeds along half of the circumference of the hoop—the female half. The seeds were of red corn, white corn, large squash, small squash, brown beans, red beans, melon, cucumber, and pumpkin. These seeds were prayer offerings to Our Grandmother the Creator for abundant crops. The women smiled and sometimes hummed happily as they made these offerings. Our Grandmother liked prayers to be sincere but not solemn, because she liked the People to be happy. The packet Star Watcher tied on was the white corn. These were most important seeds, being the corn used for Indian flour.

Then the cooks left the lodge and went away to the earthen ovens outside to finish baking the ceremonial bread, ninety small breads and three large ones.

Twelve men, the selected hunters, filed into the lodge. They arranged themselves around the hoop. They tied on the male side of the hoop small patches of skunk fur, raccoon fur, and deer hair, and Stands Firm, now recovered from his wounds, tied on a turkey feather. These were the offerings for plentiful game.

When the sacred hoop was thus prepared, it was taken by a very old woman and held over the shoulders of the man who would be the leader of the Bread Dance and the other dancing after the ball game. He carried the hoop to a tree at the edge of the stomp ground. There, with everyone watching, he hung it by a thong from a limb of the tree. It would be left there and never bothered again. Sometimes a person looking through the hoop could see the tomorrows.

No woman who was impure with her bleeding moon, no man who was impure from drinking liquor in the last four days, could attend the ceremony. For this latter reason, Loud Noise was not on the ceremonial ground, and he was sulking in his lodge when he heard the cheering in the town and knew the ball game was about to start. He was disgusted with himself, and he knew that Tecumseh was disgusted with him.

All the hundreds of people on and around the ball game field were concentrating on the leather ball, which the game starter held high above his head in one hand.

Tecumseh had won the position of leader of the men's team, by tossing a small hickory hoop over the top of a sapling pole twenty feet high. The women's team was led by the young Peckuwe woman named She-Is-Favored. It was at this time that Tecumseh first became fully aware of this graceful young woman, although Star Watcher once had pointed her out to him as one who was thought to have defended herself against Loud Noise's drunken lust two summers ago.

This girl now stood opposite Tecumseh in the middle of the ball field, an arm's length from him, like himself in a half crouch waiting for the ball to be tossed into the air above them. All the women fit to play, young and old, were massed behind her, ready to snatch the leather ball if she could bat it to them, and behind Tecumseh were all the men, waiting for him to bat it into their midst. The men were confident that they would have the first chance at the ball, because Tecumseh was so quick he could catch flies out of the air.

It was a moment of tense excitement, this pause before the frenzy of action. All the bets—scarves, bracelets, mirrors, paint bags, and a hundred other treasures—hung colorful and glittering on a pole at the edge of the game field.

But the biggest stake of the game was the wood gathering. The side that lost would have to gather all the bonfire wood for the days and nights of the ceremonial, a very big task, and they would have to do it cheerfully, because Our Grandmother liked everything in the ceremony to be cheerful. Spectators stood all around the grassy field, almost silent, holding their breath for the moment of the jump. It was a time for full concentration, and Tecumseh had no leisure to study the look of the girl, but in this instant he was aware that he was next to an uncommon presence; he could feel the emanations of her vitality. Her body, stripped down for the game to a pair of short aprons, before and behind, was deep-chested and lean, and her lithe muscles were delineated under the oiled, tawny skin. He was aware too of the boldness of her eyes; here was a girl who considered herself second to no one. And despite the tension of the moment, she was smiling with confidence. She and Tecumseh, and everyone else, were watching the ball in the game starter's hand. The ball was the size of two fists held together. Just as it had been the center of the sacred hoop, it seemed the center of their world now. Tecumseh looked at the brown leather ball against the blue sky, and at the game starter's hand, watching for that first tiny tensing of muscles that would precede the throw. The jump was crucially important in a man-woman game, because the men had to propel the ball strictly by kicking or batting it, while the women were permitted to carry it and to pass it to each other by hand.

The game starter's hand shot up, and the ball turned in the air ten feet up. Tecumseh sprang straight up, right hand outstretched for it. He saw her hand coming up against the blue sky, too, and her torso smacked against his, knocking him off his aim, and she flipped the ball in among the women. And as the crowd's cheer burst over the field, an older woman caught the ball and with powerful legs bounded straight toward the center of the men's team, with three quick young women in front of her to break a path. In a moment all the players were storming toward the men's goalposts. Shrieks of joy came from the women's throats as they saw which way the rush was heading.

Tecumseh, astonished that the toss had been taken from him, was at once bounding like a buck after the ball carrier, even hurdling over those who blocked his way. The men were yelling to each other and trying to plow in through the guards and knock the ball from the woman's hand, and men and women were colliding and falling all over each other. Ten paces from the men's goalposts, Seekabo managed to fight his way through the defense and smack the ball out of her hand. There was another mass of collisions as the players veered and milled about, and the ball tumbled on the grass. A few on both teams were knocked silly when their heads banged together as they dove for the ball. At once Tecumseh was at the tumbling ball and gave it a mighty kick back toward the other end of the field. But it was not in the air ten feet before She-Is-Favored had sprung into its way and caught it in her left hand, and she was sweeping around the edge of the milling players with the bounding steps of a doe, carrying it again toward the men's goalposts. The field was only seventy-five paces long, and she had less than half that distance to go, and in the duration of two breaths this fleet young woman had darted around the chaotic mass of wheeling, falling, screaming players and pitched the ball past the bewildered goalkeeper into the space between the men's goalposts. A shrill cry of triumph went up from all the women both on and around the field, and She-Is-Favored sprang up and down on her toes, laughing, thrusting her fists over her head. The men were laughing ruefully but with admiration. The scorekeeper at the edge of the field stuck a sharpened wooden peg into the ground on the women's side of the line drawn before him on the ground.

They went back toward the center of the field. Tecumseh whispered something to Seekabo and Thick Water as they took their places. The game starter held up the ball again. She-Is-Favored crouched to spring and gave Tecumseh a big, triumphant smile. He smiled back at her and said, *"Weh-sah!"*

The ball shot up. Again as they leaped she slammed her flank against him. But Tecumseh was ready for the impact this time and compensated for it, and he slapped the ball out of the air straight to the place where Seekabo stood. And the moment Tecumseh touched the ground he sprinted toward the women's goalposts, bowling girls and women over as he went. When he was through the mass of them, he looked back and up and, as he had anticipated, saw the ball flipping through the air toward him from Seekabo's powerful kick. Tecumseh sprinted to it as it fell, in the corner of his eye seeing the women now stampeding toward him like a herd, all bobbling breasts and shrieking throats. The moment it touched the ground he caught it with a running kick of his right foot and sent it arcing toward their goalposts and bounded after it. The ball tumbled to a stop ten paces short of their goal, and as he sped after it he was spacing the strides so that his right foot would be already moving to kick it the instant he was upon it; the women were at his back now, and he would not have an instant to spare. He felt fingers touch him and slide off his oiled skin; he felt feet kicking at his legs; he even felt a hard tug at his midsection: some pursuing woman had grabbed the flying tail of his breechcloth and was trying to hold him back. Bounding forward even harder, he felt the waistband break, and the garment came off in the woman's grip. His stride was not broken, though, and his foot caught the ball with a thud and propelled it between the goalposts just as half a dozen women smashed into him from behind and bowled him over, tumbling upon him.

When at last he had squirmed out from under them, stark naked, bleeding from both knees and his nose, his head ringing, players and spectators alike were in a frenzy of cheering and hilarity. This was one of the funniest things they had ever seen in a ball game. Everyone was overjoyed, knowing that Our Grandmother and her grandson Rounded-Side, in whose honor the game was always played, would be wonderfully amused, and that being so pleased, they would bestow good things upon the People. Laughing so hard that he could barely see what he was doing, the scorekeeper now stuck a peg in the ground on the men's side of the line, while the woman who had jerked Tecumseh's loincloth off handed it to him. It was She-Is-Favored, and she was laughing harder than anyone else, with a raucous, naughty throatiness in her laughter. Seekabo and Big Fish were hooting and pointing, almost doubled over with hilarity, as Tecumseh tied his cloth back on. He himself was laughing breathlessly. He was as amused by the spectacle he had presented as he was exultant about the incredible goal kicking he and Seekabo had done. Never in anyone's memory of the games had a score ever been kicked in so quickly and surely as that, which made the comedy of it even more wonderful. And when Tecumseh and She-Is-Favored faced each other at the center line for the next start, and their eyes met for one instant, there was something crackling in the air between them, not just the fiery respect of formidable competitors, but something like the tense attraction of lightning for the thing it is about to strike. The game ended nearly an hour later when the men, scratched, aching, and exhausted, achieved the winning score of twelve pegs. But the women were only one peg behind, and their champion was the amazing She-Is-Favored. Standing before Tecumseh, smudged with dirt and sweat, breathing hard, bruised on her ribs, grass-stained on her knees, one eye swelling shut from its contact with somebody's elbow, she smiled at him with bloodied lips and said boldly:

"We will play again. This is not the last for us."

And Tecumseh thought: How rare this woman is, and bright and bold. She could be a woman chief such as we have not seen since Tall Soldier Woman.

She could be another great gift to the People.

But for the rest of this day she would be one of the wood gatherers.

# CHAPTER 21

## *At the Head of the Maumee-se-pe*
## *October 1791*

t dawn the Singer, sitting at the edge of the Stomp Ground
between the Second Singer and the Third Singer, facing south
with the water drum between his knees, dipped his wet finger
into red pigment and began to draw the Four Winds on the wet
hide drumhead. Inside the hollowed log of the drum was a small piece of
charcoal in a small quantity of water. These represented Fire and Water, the
drum itself the Earth. In a continuous line, without lifting his finger, the
Singer started at the south and drew the line in a circle along the edge of
the drumhead all the way around the perimeter and back to the south, then
continued another quarter circle until at the east, then straight across to
west, made another quarter circle to south again, and finally drew his finger
toward him all the way across to end at north.

A quarter of a mile away, in a glade beyond the village, Tecumseh and
some of his warriors, painted for war and dressed in full regalia, knelt around
the hide-wrapped War Bundle and watched as the bundle keeper untied the
thongs. Tecumseh trembled as the sacred contents were dimly revealed.
Even at arm's length from it, he could feel its power, like a vibration, and
hear, though not through his ears but in his head, the hum of its being. A
redbird had started to sing near the edge of the glade, but when the wrapping
of the bundle was laid open on the grass, the bird fell silent.

Some of the small parcels inside the bundle were the original *Mesawmi*,
gifts from the Creator, and were set aside. One of these Tecumseh knew
to be full of the flesh of the Great Horned Serpent, still fresh and bloody
even though it had been put in the bundle in the Ancient Time. But for
the war dance on this day, certain sacred relics were to be worn and carried
by the Kispoko warriors. The war for which the nations were preparing
now would be the greatest resistance ever made against the whites.

The white chief Washington had sent still another army toward the Shawnee lands, exactly as Black Hoof had prophesied. This, according to the spies, was a well-trained army mostly made up of Blue-Coat soldiers, not just the woodsmen and farmers who usually took up arms to invade the towns and destroy them, but real soldiers, who obeyed their commanders and whose duty it was to die fighting rather than run away. With them were coming many cannons.

The soldiers' chief was another famous general from the American war against the British, a very important man who was not only a war chief, but the governor of all the vast O-hi-o land the whites had so far taken from the tribes. This governor-chief's name was St. Clair, and he was expected to prove himself a wiser and braver man than Harmar, for the chief Washington certainly would not send one cowardly fool to avenge the failure of another. Since the spring of this year, Tecumseh and other warriors scouting the Beautiful River had watched army boats full of supplies and soldiers come down to St. Clair's huge new fort, called Fort Washington, at the big new white men's town called Cincinnati, which in a few short years had sprung up opposite the mouth of the Licking River. Hardly a day had passed since the spring without some sign of the gathering war clouds. And the tribes, understanding this fully, were preparing themselves with urgency. Chosen to lead the united tribes was the same great war chief who had defeated Harmar: Little Turtle of the Miamis. Second under him would be Blue Jacket of the Shawnees. Allied with them were the Delawares under Chief Pipe and Breaker-in-Pieces, the Wyandots under Tarhe the Crane, the Weas and Mohawks led by White Loon. Warriors and chieftains also from the Kickapoo, Ottawa, Potawatomi, Piankeshaw, and Mingo tribes had come to fight. The Indian towns where the Auglaize flowed into the Maumee-se-pe were like anthills, swarming with the three thousand warriors who had gathered. For weeks there had been councils to plan the defense, to arrange for the feeding and arming of this huge concentration of warriors. The British agents McKee and Elliott worked night and day to obtain enough powder and lead and knives and meat and flour to supply so many.

This biggest war would require all of Weshemoneto's powers as well as the special powers of the sacred War Bundles. The bundle keeper now lifted out an old, old tomahawk and gave it to Tecumseh. It had a dark, slender wooden handle a foot long. Its stone head was shaped like a trefoil leaflet. Then he unwrapped four clusters of long plumes, made of split feathers. Tecumseh was to carry the sacred old tomahawk in the war dance and to wear one of the plume ornaments, which were made from the feathers of the Thunderbirds.

In his hand the old tomahawk was warm, like his *pa-waw-ka* stone, and, like it, emanated force, which he could feel flowing into his arm.

Now Tecumseh attached the plumes to a bone tube socket on the crown of his roach headdress. The roach was like a redbird's crest, made of two erect fringes of tufted, red-dyed animal hair, running from his brow down to the middle of his back. Usually only one feather, an eagle's feather, was worn in the socket at the crown. But now as Tecumseh and his three selected Kispokos mounted their decorated horses, the elaborate clusters of Thunderbird plumes bobbed with their movements. Then they rode two abreast toward the Stomp Ground, where the water drum was already sounding its deep, reverberating announcement of their approach.

Four times the warriors rode around the ceremonial ground, their weapons held upright, the deer-hoof rattles and silver bells on their legs chattering and jingling as the horses trotted along the edge of the crowd. Tecumseh held the sacred tomahawk high. The people were standing in the chilly morning air all along their route, watching them, silent, as the sun rose and touched the treetops, where the last red-and-yellow leaves still hung against the clear sky. As he rounded a quadrant of the Stomp Ground, he saw She-Is-Favored standing in the crowd looking at him. Her eyes looked sleepy, as if she had only just gotten up from bed, and she smiled at him as he rode by. His impulse was to smile at her, but the feeling from the ancient tomahawk kept him solemn.

The column of warriors now halted and dismounted, and their horses were led away by boys. The people parted to make a way for the warriors, and they walked two by two into the grassy space of the Stomp Ground. Each warrior's face was painted with red lines across the temples and blue dots between the lines. Tecumseh led them to the middle of the ground, where a post stood, painted with blood-red stripes. The warriors formed a semicircle here, facing the Singer. When they were thus stationed, the drum stopped and the warriors gave one tremolo cry.

Now the drumbeats began, a hard beat, three softer, repeated, repeated; the helpers beside the Singer joined his tempo, one with a tortoise shell rattle full of pebbles, the other with a small silver bell. The Singer began his chant.

*We ya-a we ya-a*
*Ho-i ya . . .*

His voice was flutelike, sung through a tightened throat. The warriors responded, their voices deep and open.

*We ya-a we ya-a*
*Ho-i ya . . .*

They sang the war chant four times, while doing a toe-heel, toe-heel step in place, which shook the deer hooves and bells on their legs in time with the drum. The warriors were as colorful as male birds.

Then a faster beat was struck up. As the warriors toe-heeled faster, they added a quick ankle turn with each step, which gave their leg rattles and bells a faster, shivering sort of double-beat sound. Their faces began to look trancelike, and they chanted faster, their eyes glittering, their plumes bobbing. Tecumseh suddenly stooped down, sweeping the sacred tomahawk an inch above the ground, then sprang erect, high in the air with the tomahawk over his head, and dropped back into the crouch. The other warriors leaped high.

Tecumseh now began dancing in a curved course toward the Singer, turning and whirling, springing and crouching, as he went and singing of an exploit in his battles against the Long Knives.

*Many white men came like hunters*
*Many came*
*In the night they came creeping*
*To catch the Panther sleeping*
*But the Panther's eyes are open*
*His eyes are always open*
*His ears are never still*
*The Panther knows that they are coming*
*He knows how many come*
*Even in the dark he sees them*
*Sees where they are*
*His claws and teeth are sharp and long*
*Sharper than long knives*
*The bones of twelve now lie there*
*Where the Panther was not sleeping!*

He sprang high in the air with a whoop and then danced back in a curving course toward the semicircle of warriors, rattles shivering and chattering, every muscle tense and agleam with sweat even on this cold morning, and the people's eyes were fastened upon him as he took his place. And then the second warrior leaped high and went forward to sing of another victory.

Never had the people seen more splendid dancing than this, never had they been so stirred by the daring spirit, as they heard these songs. The air around the Stomp Ground was charged as with the coming of a lightning storm, and the people's hearts were strengthened for the coming of another Long Knife army. In these quick, strong, handsome young men burned the spirit of the Shawnee People, and like the Panther, it would not be caught and killed.

In the edge of the crowd of watchers stood the young Peckuwe woman, She-Is-Favored. She was trembling. Her eyes were upon Tecumseh. She saw nothing else.

Near her in the crowd stood Loud Noise. His eye was upon her, and he saw how she was watching his brother. He sighed in misery.


The white men's army was deep into the country again, moving like a huge herd, and Tecumseh and his warriors were around them like wolves.

It was late in the year, cold, and the clouds were dark and heavy with snow. The Long Knife war chief St. Clair had sat in his fort on the O-hi-o two moons longer than expected, getting his army ready, and the tribes for once had had time to harvest their crops so the soldiers could not destroy them. This was a good fortune, and a sign that even this new white war chief might be stupid, too, and gave heart to the people. They began to feel strong and were not awfully afraid even as the army came toward them.

Tecumseh had been selected to lead the scouts and the harassing parties, to watch the army and to nip at it and see that it got no rest. He was to observe when the army was least vigilant and when it was on ground most favorable for attack.

This time, as with Harmar's army the year before, Little Turtle wanted to strike the Long Knives out in the countryside and not let them come and burn the towns, not if he could possibly stop them.

Almost as soon as St. Clair's army marched out of Cincinnati Town, Tecumseh had observed another clue that this general was perhaps stupid: he did not keep a company of scouts out in advance of his army. It was plain that this was another of those eastern generals who did not know how to move in the red man's country. Tecumseh and his scouts had no trouble getting close enough to the army to study it in detail, to circle around it like wolves, to catch its stragglers and to disrupt its sleep many times every night.

At once Tecumseh began to notice other weaknesses in this army.

For one, it was not the disciplined army all of Blue-Coat soldiers that the spies had warned it would be. Though perhaps half of it was Blue-Coats who moved in an orderly fashion, the other half was composed of the usual unruly farmer soldiers with their strutting colonels and captains, their slow and noisy and straggly way of marching.

For another, the army seemed to have hardly enough of a supply train to feed it more than a few days. Tecumseh looked at the packhorses, which were laden with tools and boxes and bundles and powder kegs, and he calculated in his head, and it seemed to him that there could not be enough food here to supply such a mass of men very long.

Still another weakness of the army was that it was followed by a great crowd of women, many of them with children and baggage, sorry-looking horses, dogs, tents, trunks, and kettles. Watching them in their evening camps, Tecumseh could discern that many of these followers were the soldiers' wives and children, while many of the women seemed to belong to no one in particular. Tecumseh knew already that the white men's armies usually had some camp followers, but this noisy mob of tagalongs was nearly a fourth the size of the army itself, and it was plain that it would cause big problems for the Long Knife general. It either slowed down the army's pace or fell behind; on most days it did both. The camp followers were miserable in this weather, just as the soldiers were miserable, and Tecumseh at night, prowling near the enemy's camp, could hear the men and women quarreling and the children whining. It was easy to guess that the war chief St. Clair must dislike having this mob following his army into the Indian country, for not only would he have to feed them from his army's supplies, he would have to protect them.

And so the Long Knives rumbled and grumbled and bawled into the old Shawnee lands, moving just a few miles a day through the leafless, cold, wet woods, then setting up its squalid, noisy evening camps. Every evening it would build around itself a barricade of dug earth, brush, and deadwood and set out a ring of sentries, which was the only sign Tecumseh could see of any wisdom in this general. During the nights, then, Tecumseh and his party would make noises in the darkness, make birdcalls that deliberately did not sound very much like birdcalls, so that the white sentries would know there were warriors close around them. Sometimes they would creep close to the army's camp and, like mockingbirds, do enough yelling to sound like hundreds and would shoot their guns and create a panic in this herd of an army, only to vanish suddenly and then repeat the disruption somewhere on another flank. These alarms would take hours to die down, and at once Tecumseh's men would create more. Sometimes in these disturbances the army sentries would shoot at each other in the dark, and when this happened the warriors would laugh aloud. It was a fine game. Without rest the soldiers weakened and grew surly and disobedient, and many began to fall sick from the cold and wet and exhaustion. It was just as Chiksika had taught Tecumseh about the wolves and the bison. A wolf can hardly kill a healthy one, but sick, tired ones can be brought down at the edge of the herd.

A few days out of Cincinnati, the chief St. Clair had stopped his army to build a fort on the east bank of the Great Miami-se-pe, a fort with three blockhouses and with a dug well inside the palisade. Tecumseh had watched the construction of this fort with interest and noted that when the army moved on, twenty soldiers were left to garrison the fort.

Then, late in the Hunter's Moon and nearly fifty miles farther north, the army stopped and built another fort. Here something happened that filled Tecumseh's heart with more hope for his people.

It was a windy, moonless night, cold and dank, the woods full of the rustling of dead and fallen leaves. Tecumseh stood near a huge oak tree on a rise of land between the confluence of two small streams, looking down on the fireglow in and around the new fort, when he heard from his left the call of the *andakwa.* Immediately he slipped off through the woods in that direction, knowing that something very important was happening. He had designated this bird's call as an urgent summoning signal because the raven is seldom heard at night.

He found Stands-Between there on the slope above one of the two creeks and at once knew why his brother had summoned him: he could hear the movements of many people along the bottomland of the creek. They were moving back down the trail along which the army had come, and it seemed they were trying to go in stealth; there was no talking, just whispers and the rustle of many footsteps in the fallen leaves, the bumping of equipment, and now and then the whimper or cry of a small child, quickly muffled. Tecumseh marveled at this and wondered what was happening. Stands-Between told him as much as he had been able to observe of it.

"These are the militia soldiers whose camp was at this end of the fort. As I watched them I saw some of them picking up their things and leaving their fires. Then more did the same. I could see their camp standing almost empty, but their fires still burning. So I came this way. I found them down there by the creek, all whispering and murmuring. I think there are four hundred or five hundred of them, soldiers and women and children. When they began to move away along the creek, I called for you."

Tecumseh smiled in the dark and thanked the Great Good Spirit for this. "So the unhappiest ones of this unhappy army have chosen to desert their war chief and sneak home! Ah, this is good!" He squeezed his brother's arm. "Listen, brother. Will you take Thick Water and follow these and watch them? I will send Seekabo up to tell Blue Jacket what you have found.

Use Thick Water as your runner to come and tell me what these deserters do as they go down the road. Tell him I will not be hard to find because I will always be where the general's army is. Ha! This St. Clair will be a mad chief when day comes to show him that a fourth of his army is gone! Now, my brother. I am pleased with you. Go after them now, guard your life, and may you see with the eyes of the Panther!"

It was almost daylight, and Tecumseh stood wrapped in his blanket against the gray morning cold, watching the smoke drift off the dying fires of the deserted part of the army camp, when he heard a sentry soldier cry out and knew that the desertion had been discovered. He smiled and shook his head. It had taken the Long Knives seven hours to learn that their farmer-soldiers had deserted, because for once Tecumseh had let the exhausted army sleep. He had let them sleep so that the deserters might be far away into the south.

There was a huge uproar around the fort, and one of Tecumseh's scouts up in a beech tree said he could see the Long Knife general limping around waving his arms at other officers. Then there was a long period in which nothing seemed to be happening. And then at last one of the Blue-Coat officers rushed out of the fort into his part of the camp, where he shouted and waved *his* arms, and then to Tecumseh's great joy this officer's whole regiment, an entire half of the Blue-Coat soldiers, formed up in lines and started back down the trail in pursuit of the deserters.

At once Tecumseh sent another runner to Blue Jacket, to tell him that St. Clair's once feared army, already a half as numerous as it was supposed to have been, now was further split into halves and now sat here with less than two thousand fighting men, still burdened with two or three hundred sick and hungry camp followers, with no supply train coming yet from the south. Let us see what this poor Long Knife chief will choose to do now, Tecumseh thought. Will he march on toward our towns or hide here in his fort until things get better and the weather gets worse? We already know he is a fool. Now let us watch and see if he is a coward as well. Whatever the general chose to do now, he was surely defeated in his purpose, Tecumseh was certain. If he stayed and waited for his army to reunite and for supplies to arrive, winter would come and hold him in place. If he tried to march on with this divided army, Little Turtle and Blue Jacket would meet him with nearly an equal number of well-rested, well-fed warriors, hungry only for another victory over the American army. Tecumseh was so exhilarated about the anticipated deliverance of his people that he had to force himself to withdraw from the view of the fort and get the sleep he needed.

It was not long before the general made it clear that he was a brave fool, not a cowardly fool. He marched his army away from this new fort and headed northward, going toward the headwaters of the Wabash-se-pe. At once Tecumseh sent runners ahead to tell Blue Jacket. Then with his remaining scouts he began once again to play wolf around the army herd. He and his warriors played more boldly now, letting themselves be seen, making a show of their confidence, revealing themselves on high places almost within easy rifle shot of the Long Knives, swiftly crossing and recrossing the army's path to leave as many tracks as possible, making themselves seem more numerous than they were. Once Tecumseh turned grinning to Stands Firm and joked to him, "Brother, tell me whether I look like a wolf or a mockingbird, because I am being like both and don't know which I am."

"To my eyes," Stands Firm replied with a quick laugh, "you are still a panther."

Snows came while Tecumseh's young men were thus harassing the soldiers. It fell and melted, then fell and stayed, and now the dispirited soldiers and their pack animals and their six heavy cannons struggled on ever more slowly, leaving as their trail a rutted, pitted road of mud-brown slush, dotted with discarded equipment. Coming along this road, Tecumseh picked up one of the cloth bags that lay in the mud and examined it. There were a few grains of cornmeal in its seams. It was the sort of bag in which the militiamen carried their rations of meal, and, he knew, they would not throw these away unless they had given up hope of getting more rations. It was a good sign of the army's desperation and misery, and Tecumseh welcomed it. If this St. Clair believes he will arrive and plunder food at our towns, Tecumseh thought, he will learn another hard lesson.

Thick Water came at night from the south, sent by Stands-Between with messages. He stood with Tecumseh in the darkness outside the fireglow of the army camp to tell him what was happening down there. "Those deserters went past the fort on the Miami-se-pe. The Blue-Coats who went after them still did not catch up with them. And the supply train still is not in sight. Surely it could not catch up for days."

Tecumseh gazed toward the enemy's campfires, and they glinted in his eyes. "Now," he said, "is the time to strike. I am going up to see Blue Jacket."


The war chiefs were surprised to see Tecumseh when he appeared in their camp. He gave his account.

"The Long Knife army is camped now on the bottomland in the place where the Wabash-se-pe headwater crosses the trace. The soldiers are less than half as many as they were. They are hungry and fatigued and afraid. Their feet are wet. You hear them coughing in their camp, and they sound like a lot of geese. They are too sick even to fortify themselves. They have lined up their six cannons and left them with no breastworks in front. All they are doing is making big bonfires to warm themselves. All their powder and arms boxes are in stacks. The Blue-Coats who went after the deserters surely will go on down to protect the supply train from them, instead of coming back up. The soldiers are dull and least brave now. There will be no better time."

Blue Jacket's eyes glittered in his rugged face, and he breathed fast, staring out the door of the lodge into the dusk. "Ah," he said. *"Weh-sah. Weh-sah!"*

"There is no question," said Little Turtle. "We must go and get around them tonight, for they surely will start to fortify at daybreak."

"Now what will you have me do, Father?" Tecumseh asked. "We who have been wolves around the herd are ready to rush in before light and kill the old sick bulls."

"No," Blue Jacket said. "You are our eyes. Your seeing has served us as well as ten hundred warriors. In the morning we will see the face of our enemy and destroy him. I ask you to go back around and be the eyes at his back. Stay on the road between the army and its forts, and watch for the return of the Blue-Coat soldiers who went down, so they cannot surprise us. The Eye of the Panther is keen, and we need it still."

"Then," Tecumseh said, hiding his disappointment, "I will do that if it serves us best."

Blue Jacket gave him a grim smile and squeezed his arm and said, "My son, you already have more scalps than most of us will get in our lives, so now I ask you to stand back and let others get some. Ha, ha!"

"All the People owe you much," Little Turtle told him.

"The Great Good Spirit favors our People," Blue Jacket breathed.

"Let us be strong by doing what is right," Tecumseh whispered, going out into the darkening cold.


Tecumseh and his scouts heard the distant shooting begin at daybreak the next morning. Low, dark, ragged clouds covered the sky. The low hills were covered with patchy, wet snow.

The noise from the north started with a stuttering of gunshots and then began to swell like the faraway coming of a storm. Soon there were so many shots that they were not distinct from one another and sounded like a steady thunder roll. Now it would die down a little to sputtering, then swell again to a muted roar. After a long time there came two or three thuds that might have been cannon shots. Tecumseh and Big Fish looked at each other, grim-faced. In such a storm of gunfire, they knew, men on both sides must be dying. Tecumseh wondered what Big Fish could be thinking. In an army of that size there probably were relatives and people he had known when he was Stephen Ruddell. But of course Tecumseh did not ask, because he knew that Big Fish was fully a Shawnee in his spirit.

By the middle of the morning the shooting had dwindled. Tecumseh sent riders down the rutted, muddy army road to look for sign of the other Blue-Coat regiment coming up. No report of them came. Tecumseh with Thick Water and Stands Firm, Seekabo and Big Fish, set up a vigil on a bluff overlooking a fording place where the army road crossed a shallow creek, about halfway between the battleground and the army's upper fort. On that bluff stood a huge oak tree, from whose high branches the road could be seen for miles in both directions. Tecumseh said, "In Kispoko Town I remember there was a boy who was sometimes called Squirrel for the way he could climb trees." Thick Water nodded with a slight smile, slung his gun on his back, and soon had climbed to a high fork. It was cold up here in the wind, but he could see over most of the treetops and rises of land for such a distance that he took deep breaths and smiled with his love of the country. When he looked down to the others, their horses looked the size of little dogs. The treetop swayed in the cold gusts and rocked him. Thick Water tied a thong around his waist and a limb, hooked his elbow over a branch, wiggled his feet until they were as comfortable as possible, and looked up and down the road. Far to the north a smudge of pale smoke against the lead-colored clouds showed him where the battlefield was. Because of the wind around his ears he could hardly hear any gunfire now.

Late in the afternoon Thick Water called down. He could see the remnants of the American army starting to come down the valley. For a long time they were mere specks on the far snowy meanderings of the road, coming singly or in little clusters, in no sort of order.

As they drew closer he could hardly believe what his eyes were seeing. He took every detail into his memory, as if he might need to confirm with others that this wretched sight was what they too had seen.

They came in knots and clusters, in ones and twos, stumbling and staggering, some without weapons, some helping badly hurt comrades hitch along. Some fell and remained in the snow. A few were on plodding horses, and some of the horses sagged and fell and lay in the road. Figures were strung out for miles. They were no army anymore.

When the first of them were within half a mile, Tecumseh called for

Thick Water to come down out of sight. And then from cover they watched them.

Some of the soldiers were wild-eyed, some dead-eyed. Some would run a few steps, moaning and gasping, as if demons were after them. Almost all were black with gunpowder and reddened with blood. As they moved down across the ford, they turned the snow red. Their voices were a dissonant chorus of pain and misery. Tecumseh and his scouts hovered almost invisible in thickets along the road and watched them pass by.

Only a few of the Americans who went by were officers on horses, and most of these were bloody and white-faced, slumped in their saddles. One humped, thick-bodied old man came by on a bony, feeble horse. This old man wore a three-cornered hat and was cloaked in a capote stained with mud and blood, his eyes cast down, his scabbard empty. He was on down the road a way when two officers rode up to speak to him, and suddenly Thick Water turned and asked Tecumseh:

"Is that not their general?"

"That is St. Clair. Yes."

"Should we not shoot the old general?"

"No," Tecumseh said. "We are here as eyes, not as teeth, to watch, not to kill. And you know what I have said. I will not kill helpless men. What honor is there in killing men whose hearts are already dead?"


The next morning Tecumseh and his scouts went up the army road toward the battleground. The snow of the road was brown with mud and red with blood, littered all the way with hats, buckles, broken ramrods, bayonets, bullet bags, blood-soaked bandages, shreds of blanket, boot soles, and broken guns. Frozen corpses lay where they had been hastily buried in snow; some of them had already been partly dug out and gnawed on by animals.

But even this pitiful trail of death and defeat did not prepare Tecumseh for what lay on the bottomlands of the Wabash-se-pe.

In the river bend, the entire valley was dotted with scalped, mutilated soldiers and dead horses. Every foot of ground was a trampled, bloody slush, strewn with smashed objects. Wagons with broken wheels, crates, and kegs lay broken and smoldering with dirty smoke. Some bodies lay over each other, in places where soldiers evidently had grouped and been surrounded. There were black smudges where gunpowder had been spilled. A shoeless, scalpless corpse lay curled on its side, both hands frozen around the haft of a lance that had gone clear through it. Buzzards were settling and hunching on bodies, picking out eyes or tearing at wounds, shaking their beaks. Town dogs skulked around the edges of the battleground, gorging themselves on the half-frozen human carrion. Indian boys from nearby villages were working over the field, harvesting brass buttons and buckles and gorgets. Every corpse had been scalped, most had been stripped of their shoes and blue wool coats. There were no guns in sight; all had been gathered up already. A cold wind drifted snow up against the dead.

There were nearly six hundred dead soldiers on the battleground, Blue Jacket said. Tecumseh told him of the many he had counted on the road and of the old general going by. Blue Jacket was marked by many blows but not badly hurt. "We could not kill that old general," he said with awe. "Whenever he tried to mount a horse, we killed it. Whenever he spoke to an officer, we killed the officer. All morning he tried to make his soldiers stand and fight, but we killed them. Many stood together and cried, and we killed those, too. He tried to make his cannon soldiers shoot, but we killed them after a few bangs. We killed his camp followers. But we could not kill him, though he was in plain view all the time. I think this means he was meant to take defeat back to their nation himself. Oh, he was a brave old man! But not smart enough. Young brother, listen! For two years we have defeated their whole army, yes, twice Little Turtle has beaten America! If the tribes always fight together, we can do this any time they dare to come again. Perhaps we can preserve the rest of the lands the Great Good Spirit gave us, after all!" His eyes were red, his bruised face aglow. "Think what we have done! Think what we can do if we stand together!"

"The Great Good Spirit favors our People," Tecumseh murmured. But he remembered Chiksika's prophecy that even this Blue Jacket and Little Turtle and Black Hoof would mark peace treaties under the force of the white men.


Loud Noise again had managed to stay out of battle by proclaiming himself not a warrior but a healer and medicine man. There was indeed much healing for him to do, for more than two hundred warriors had been wounded in the battle. Loud Noise had learned enough from Change-of-Feathers about herbs and poultices that he was able to help mend some of the severely wounded warriors.

But in the orgy of celebration right after the battle, Loud Noise was caught up in the sanguinary madness, and he did something he had often thought about with fascination during his lonely, rum-soaked reveries in his old hut in the marsh.

Tecumseh came looking for his brother and sister in the uproar of the village after the battle. The people were in a frenzy of feeling. There was dancing, there was boasting, fueled by kegs of army liquor that had been taken at the battleground, and fresh scalps were being exhibited every-where. But amid the rejoicing there was also the keening of mourners, for the sixty-six warriors who had died in the attack. All the people were pouring out their hearts either in warlike exultation or grief or in both. Tecumseh, with Stands-Between at his side, moved through this firelit pandemonium with a bittersweet heart, loving and pitying the People, asking this crazed face and then that one where Loud Noise might be found. At last he found Star Watcher. She was standing in front of a small lodge, very rigid, her face set hard and eyes glinting with tears. She pointed at the lodge and said, "He is there. With them."

Tecumseh turned back the door flap and stooped to enter. He glanced around the circle of men and women who sat facing a fire in the dense smoke within. They looked up at him with glazed, red-rimmed eyes. Their mouths were painted crimson. There was a stench of liquor in the close air. Strips of flesh hung on a spit over the fire, and the people were eating with their fingers. There was an air of awful tension in the lodge, as if some terrible excitement had just been interrupted. Even without the red-painted mouths to explain the scene to him, Tecumseh would have known what was being done here. He knew well enough from war the peculiar smell of seared human flesh. He knew that the meat over the fire had been brought from the battleground, where it lay in such profusion.

And there beyond the fire, his one eye bulging, his lips and mustache smeared with red paint and the grease of the meat, a bowl of liquor on the floor beside him, sat Loud Noise, who had promised to subdue his appetites and do honor to his family and his destiny.

Tecumseh stared at him, face drawn with loathing, and it seemed a long time before the cloud of Loud Noise's stupor cleared enough for him to realize that this was his own brother standing in the firelight glaring at him. He grinned drunkenly, and there was half-chewed human flesh in his teeth. When at last Tecumseh could speak, he said in a sad, low voice:

"So now you have even come down like one of the vultures."

And then he was gone, leaving only the contemptuous echo of his words and a draft of the winter air.

# CHAPTER 22

## On the Upper Maumee-se-pe
## Winter 1792

L
ike a silent, invisible revenge for their defeat, a disease of the white men swept through the Indian towns that winter. Warriors who had dodged a thousand bullets and bayonets were brought low by burning fevers. Their bone joints ached until they could not move, and their lungs filled up. Women and children and old people fell into whimpering, sweat-soaked sleeps from which they never awoke.

Loud Noise boiled roots and barks to make bitter teas. He burned pinecones and nut shells to make healing smokes. He wore a wooden mask, shook a tortoiseshell rattle, and sang prayers. His decoctions made people sweat or shiver or vomit, made their bowels spew dark fluids, made them urinate almost ceaselessly in their bedding. Many of those he treated died without relief, some more miserable than the disease itself would have made them. When they were in their graves they did not say he was a poor medicine man. Some got well, because or in spite of his remedies, and these were glad to praise his medicine. So when the epidemic had run its course, there were a few people who would say he was a healer, and therefore he was. There were many people who still did not like him or trust him enough to turn to him for medicine. He was still a drunkard and a loud mouth with crazy ways. It was known now that he had eaten manflesh with members of that unpopular society, a society that old Black Hoof and most other leaders termed evil, and many members of the tribe shunned him for that reason. But some of the Shawnee secretly believed that manflesh eaters and other contrary people were in touch with special kinds of magic. Maybe it was the magic of Matchemoneto, and if a person grew desperate enough, he might eventually turn to the Evil Spirit for help. If an illness or pain was believed to be caused by a witch, extreme cures were needed. Thus it was that Loud Noise began to have a small following, and he studied hard with

288

Change-of-Feathers to learn all he could before the ancient shaman should die and take his knowledge to the grave with him. And so Loud Noise, once useless, now had a way of making a modest living and no longer had to depend entirely upon the generosity of his family. Now he spent much time in the woods digging for roots of dogbane and sassafras and mayapple, drying and grinding them, stripping out the inner bark of elms, making feather fans and bone rattles, grinding mouse bones to powder, rubbing tobacco down to dust, and, as he had always done, talking and chanting to himself.

Beginning to fancy himself a substantial member of the tribe, Loud Noise set his mind on getting a wife. Once this would have been his most hopeless task. But his medicine had cured some men and women who had daughters, so now as a suitor he had some choices. His first choice was, of course, She-Is-Favored. But when he approached her she looked at him with a wary and defensive gaze that brought back to him the memory of the worst pain he had ever felt—his testicles seemed to have a memory of their own—and Loud Noise simply nodded to her and passed on by. And when he took a wife it was instead a round, placid, pretty-faced girl who seemed unlikely ever to twist her husband's balls, even if he deserved it. Loud Noise had long since decided that he was not by nature a fighter, so why should he bring a fighting woman under his own roof?

Loud Noise was no sooner married than he began suggesting to Tecumseh that he, too, should enter that state so natural to man.

They sat in Loud Noise's clean, orderly new lodge, which his bride had recently built. It was the first time the brothers had visited with each other since the night Tecumseh had found him among the manflesh eaters, and it seemed as if Loud Noise were advocating this natural condition of marriage in order to make himself seem less unnatural by it.

Loud Noise exaggerated the bliss of his marriage. Though his new wife was a calm and gentle woman who kept a good house and never raised her voice, she did have annoying ways of expressing her dislike of her husband's personal shortcomings. She would wrinkle her nose at the smell of his breath when he had had a little whiskey. A garment he had worn too long she would hold at arm's length between her thumb and forefinger as if holding a rotten fish by the tail. These silent expressions would irk him more than if she had complained aloud, and he would glower at her and get heartburn. And when she saw his angry expression, she would cringe about in the lodge, her eyelids trembling as if she anticipated being hit— which he understood to be an allusion to his notorious bullying of women in the past. Yes, this woman looked like an ideal wife. But she would not let him sleep the day away as he sometimes would have liked to do. She would not let him nest in his own squalor as he had used to do. And when he vented his gases with his usual loudness and virtuosity, she would not laugh but instead would get up from whatever she had been doing and go outside and make a great show of breathing fresh air, inhaling until her big breasts were as high as her chin. Furthermore, she had a passion for such costly white men's things as iron kettles and steel awls and needles and mirrors and tin cups and silk cloth and glass beads. People would say she was a perfect wife. But without a word of complaint or nagging, she had made it clear from the beginning that she did not have a perfect husband, nor a good provider.

Loud Noise was not as happy a husband as he pretended to be. And perhaps his reason for urging Tecumseh to get married was that he thought someone else in the family should be as miserable and exasperated as he. So he discussed with Tecumseh the idea of marriage, saying, "You're going to be an important war chief. You should have a woman and children, so people won't shake their heads and moan about you."

"I know," Tecumseh replied. "You are not the first to give me such counsel. I have heard it from Black Hoof. And from Stands Firm, and certainly from our sister. And from Blue Jacket. Even from Little Turtle, who is not even of our tribe." He smiled with patient amusement and said, "The next American general who comes into our country will probably send a messenger, saying, 'Tecumseh, you should have a wife and children.' Ha! And I will answer, 'Why? If I had children, you would burn down the house they live in, and destroy the food that was raised for their mouths, and chase them off the ground they play on, and then drive them into a corner and chop them with your long knives.' That is how I would answer. No, brother. I do not want to put children onto this earth until I am sure that they will not be like leaves before the wind." He drew from his pipe and looked at Loud Noise, then at his woman, who was moving a piece of bark to enlarge the smokehole in the roof—her silent way of saying that she did not like all this tobacco smoke in her lodge, even if it was being produced by one of the tribe's most renowned warriors, her esteemed brother-in-law.

"But if you *were* to marry," Loud Noise persisted, "you would want a woman of this kind. . . ." He nodded at her with a smile, speaking clearly so she would hear every word. "A perfect and obedient wife, not one of those ball pullers."

Tecumseh smiled at this. "Of course," he said.

"May I ask who would interest you, if you were interested?"

Tecumseh sighed. How could he make it clear to a misty-brain like Loud Noise this important conviction he had reached? He tried to say it in a way that would not offend the woman on the other side of the fire:

"The Messengers tell me that my life will be used up in fighting the white men. They tell me that I alone of the Shawnees will stand against them when all the other chiefs have put their marks upon their treaties. Until there are no more white men coming against us, I cannot divide my spirit between this task and the needs of a family. The Shawnee are my family, and I must be free to take care of them. And so, I am not interested in a wife yet. Even though . . ." He smiled and inclined his head toward his sister-in-law, who pretended not to be listening as hard as she was. "Even though a good wife does give her husband strength as well as comfort, as I am sure."

Loud Noise seemed to have been listening well to all of this, and he sat puffing smoke and gazing into the fire. But then he said, "If you do try to get a wife, you would not want to get one like the Peckuwe woman, She-Is-Favored. You would not want a troublesome woman, one of those ball pullers." He feared the maiden might tell Tecumseh of his assault.

Tecumseh sighed. Then he tilted his head and looked with mock reproach at his brother. "Why do you call that one troublesome? You know it is one of the worst offenses to say untrue gossip about a person."

Loud Noise, suddenly afraid of being censured again, raised his eyebrows and shrugged like an innocent. "Oh . . . I know nothing! She just *looks* bold, like one of those who would not be afraid to grab you."

Tecumseh smiled. He did not know the painful memory Loud Noise had of being grabbed by the Peckuwe girl. He himself was remembering when she had grabbed his loincloth off in the ball game. He smiled at the memory of that hilarious moment that seemed so long ago. "It is true," he said, "that one would not be afraid to grab you."

But, he thought, who would want a woman without strong spirit?


Whenever Tecumseh made a hunting camp, whether he was near enemy country or not, he chose the most advantageous spot he could find and walked all around it, memorizing the terrain, noting where gullies and thickets and approach and escape routes lay. Chiksika had taught him this, and several close escapes in the south had affirmed the lesson.

Now, as the campfire burned orange and low between the two shelters of his hunting camp north of the Beautiful River, and droplets from the day's drizzle pattered in the woods, Tecumseh sat wakeful and tense, a hide robe over his shoulders. He had started this hunting trip in the Green Moon with ten men. But this morning, while they were rounding up horses, one of the hunters had vanished without a trace. Most of the day had been spent hunting him instead of game.

Now his remaining hunters, including Big Fish and Thick Water, were asleep in the two army tents they were using as shelters. The horses were hobbled in a small meadow below the camp. The fires under the jerky racks were out, but the ashes were still warm, and in Tecumseh's nostrils lingered the smell of meat grease and ashes. He had been awake wondering about the missing hunter. Then his wakeful mind had wandered over the signs and dreams that guided his life and from there to wondering what the American great chief Washington would do next—whether he would again this year try to avenge the defeat of his army.

Tecumseh knew by now that those two things in his life were bound together: the signs and the doings of the white men. This was plain to him, and it was seldom out of his waking thoughts—or even his dreams, when he could sleep. This night he apparently was not to be allowed to sleep; his thoughts had been clamoring. Because of the disappearance of that one hunter, he had a persistent intuition of danger. Probably the hunter had gotten in a long pursuit of something and would find his way back tomorrow. Tecumseh had not seen or smelled or heard any sign of enemies near the hunting camp, even while lying awake in the stillness. But something, like a tiny sharp point, stayed at the base of his skull and would not let him relax his vigil and sink into sleep. Because of the snoring of Big Fish he could not listen well enough to the woods.

At last he rose from his bed of boughs and, still wrapped in his robe, carrying only his war club and sheath knife, crept out behind his shelter to sit leaning back against the big tree trunk, in the warmth of the ashes of the jerking fire but out of the campfire glow. Here he could keep a keener watch and determine whether there was any real cause for his uneasiness.

For a long while he sat and heard nothing, and at last the middle-of-the-night weariness overwhelmed him. In his dream he saw Eagle Speaker, who was telling him about the day when the bed of the Great River would heave and its water would flow backward.

He awoke, heard nothing, and tried to go back to sleep, hoping that perhaps if the same dream continued, Eagle Speaker would reveal more about the meanings.

But in this dream, Tecumseh was a boy and was standing in a line of the gauntlet with a whipping-stick in his hand, and the big Long Knife they called But-lah was running up the line toward him. But this time But-lah came running not naked and unarmed but carrying a rifle.

Tecumseh started out of his sleep, fully alarmed. There were men moving between him and his sleeping hunters. He could see several of them outlined by the glow of the little campfire. They were white men. They were aiming their guns at the two tents.

Just as Tecumseh sprang to his feet, a warning cry rising in his throat, a big voice at the south edge of the camp yelled, "Now!"

In that instant, as fifteen or twenty rifles roared and flashed in the night, Tecumseh recognized that voice.

*But-lah!*

Tecumseh was on his feet in the smell of their gunsmoke, leaving his robe behind him, and in three quick strides he was beside the nearest white man, and his stone club crushed the man's skull. "Big Fish!" he shouted, his voice carrying over the outburst of the white men's yelling. "Long Knives! Take them on the river side! I have these!"

Now the white men were crashing about, some into the firelight, some getting in each other's way as they tried to turn on Tecumseh, others away from him, and he leaped among them, shoving men down, thudding against their moving shapes with his deadly club. Men tumbled in the dim, fire-tinged smoke, and he leaped over them to strike at more.

At that moment Big Fish darted out from the doorway of his tent into the firelight with his rifle at the ready. Several white men charged into the firelight brandishing guns and tomahawks. The one closest to Big Fish was a huge, leathery-faced man in deerskins, whom Tecumseh at once recognized as But-lah.

Someone just then rushed toward Tecumseh, who turned and felled him with a blow of the club on his chest. The man dropped to the ground, wheezing and gurgling. When Tecumseh glanced back to the tents, he saw Big Fish's gun pointed straight at the broad chest of But-lah, who was so astonished that he had stopped in his tracks, knife in one hand, gun in the other. The flintlock of Big Fish's rifle sparked and flared, but the night-damp powder fizzled. By then But-lah had sprung off into the darkness. And now the other warriors were boiling out of their tents like hornets. Big Fish and Tecumseh gave war whoops then, and Big Fish yelped, "Ai-hee! I made But-lah run!" As Tecumseh charged hard on the heels of several white men into the woods, the rest of the warriors took up the cry, and soon the camp was a vacant, firelit place surrounded by a ring of invisible conflicts in darkness.

The white men fleeing from Tecumseh dispersed noisily into the underbrush, and soon they were still, not running anymore, perhaps trying to find each other and regroup. Tecumseh crouched with the night cold on his sweaty skin and listened. He heard someone disturb the foliage a few paces away. He could smell the man. In the distance, down toward the river, he heard voices and rustling sounds.

Thinking of English words Big Fish had taught him, Tecumseh whispered in the direction of the hidden white man:

"Come here."

The man started edging toward him, murmuring something in a querying tone.

Suddenly another voice close by whispered something that sounded like "Boone." Then the other man whispered, "Boone." Tecumseh cocked his head. And from a few feet away still another voice murmured, "Boone."

Tecumseh's scalp prickled at the belief that not only was But-lah among the attackers, but also Boone.

But on hearing all these voices saying "Boone" to each other, and no answer in Boone's voice, Tecumseh began to suspect that they were using Boone's name as a password to find each other in the dark. So, with a grim smile and his arm ready, he called softly:

"Boone."

"Boone," whispered a voice nearby, and a figure moved toward him.

"Boone," Tecumseh murmured again, and this time when the name was repeated, the voice came from less than two paces away, and Tecumseh could sense just where he was. He swung his club. It hit something soft, and with a grunt the man fell.

"What's that?" a voice hissed, close by. "What happened?"

"Boone," Tecumseh called softly.

"Boone," said this voice, revealing the location of its speaker. Tecumseh swung again. The club whipped through some twigs, but it landed a glancing blow on another man, who bellowed in pain or surprise and blundered away, now yelling something that Tecumseh could not understand. In a moment he could hear the bustle of many men hurrying off, mostly toward the south and east.

"Boone!" Tecumseh shouted after them. His laughter followed them into the darkness.


The white raiders' bullets had riddled the tents and even made holes in some of the warriors' robes and blankets, but by Weshemoneto's protection not one of the hunters had been hurt worse than a nick. As the woods grayed with the approach of morning, the Shawnees spread out cautiously from camp. They found the man Tecumseh had killed with his club, and Tecumseh scalped him. There were no more bodies but plenty of blood spots on the grass and leaves. The traces indicated that the attackers had numbered as many as twenty or thirty and that they had stolen up on the camp from two sides. The warriors felt good. That many enemies, led by the dreaded But-lah himself, yet they had foiled them and chased them away! It was like that other time But-lah had tried to catch him sleeping.

But if there were that many white men, there was still a danger that they might regroup and come back. It would be wise to take the meat and break camp.

When they went down to round up the horses, they found that several had been stolen, including Tecumseh's own stallion. The footprints of a white man with small feet led down to where the horses had been, then hoofprints led away toward the southeast.

Tecumseh, eyes full of indignation, picked Big Fish and two other warriors to go with him and told Thick Water to break camp. Thick Water begged to go with him. "We will be enough," Tecumseh said, and led the three out.

It was easy to follow the trail. The sun was just coming up. The ground had been damp overnight, so the hooves had made deep, distinct tracks in the humus of the woods and the short grass of the meadows. Tecumseh was able to keep his eyes on the tracks even without slowing his swift, silent running pace. The pale young spring foliage, dappled with sunlight, blurred as he sped through it. Deer and squirrels bounded away as he came into their view with his three warriors in a file behind him.

Now and then Tecumseh would stop and scan the way ahead. He must not run headlong into an ambush, particularly if But-lah and the rest of his Long Knives might have rejoined this horse stealer. So far there was no sign of them.

The Shawnees ran on for several miles like this, silent except for their shallow breathing and the pad of their moccasins on the soft earth.

Suddenly Tecumseh raised his hand and stopped. He smelled smoke and meat cooking. One of his warriors, tired and clumsy, almost ran into him and made a rustling in the brush.

Directly to Tecumseh's left off the path, a white man squatted by a small fire, holding a piece of meat on a stick. The man had heard the warrior's noise and turned. His face was pale and dirty and stubbled, his eyes were wild. Quick as a deer the white man dropped the meat, grabbed his rifle, and sprinted into the woods. Tecumseh leaped forward in pursuit. His warriors sped after him, refreshed by the prospect of catching a single white horse thief.

Down the shimmering green valley they raced, following flickering sunlit glimpses of the white man's coat. He was a good runner, and he was fleeing for his life. Little by little, though, the distance between the prey and predators closed. Big Fish was abreast of Tecumseh now, his steps bounding, his teeth bared in the fierce joy of pursuit.

Suddenly the white man stopped and spun about, bringing his rifle up to sight on his pursuers. The other warriors darted aside off the path into cover. But Tecumseh did not pause.

His warriors saw him sprint on across the space and straight into the blast and smoke of the white man's rifle. Then they could see only the bluish smoke drifting in the green woods, and they ran forward.

When they came up panting, they found the white man on his back on the ground, wheezing desperately for the breath that had been knocked out of him; his discharged rifle lay a few feet away. Tecumseh was straddling the white man, smiling coldly down on him, his rifle pointed at his eyes.

Tecumseh was in a hurry now to get the stolen horses rounded up and return to the rest of the hunting party, worried that But-lah and his band might surround them again or even that they might have done so already. Big Fish had startled the big white man badly last night, but But-lah was not the kind of man to be scared away.

The horse stealer sat on the ground, wrists tightly bound behind him, studying his captors furtively. "We must round up the horses," Tecumseh urged them. "Come."

"Let us rest a moment, brother," one of them said. "How you ran us this morning!"

Tecumseh hopped up, impatient. "Then I will go get them. Come, Big Fish."

They sped off up the trail toward the place where the white man had been cooking. The horses, hobbled and still bridled, were grazing within a few hundred paces of the little cookfire. Tecumseh made a chirping sound, and his horse came toward him.

In a few minutes they had all the hobbles off and the horses strung together and went back down the trail to get their captive. Tecumseh was satisfied with the day. Except for his anxiety about the hunters back at the camp, he was in a happy state of mind, ever more convinced that the luck of the Long Knives was running out, that the superior courage and cunning and the moral righteousness of the red men would finally prevail. We-shemoneto seemed to be rallying his powers and all the lesser spirits to help his children, while the white men's God seemed not to be helping them at all. In the Blackberry Moon last year, American emissaries had come to the confederated tribes to negotiate peace. But the red men were full of confidence after defeating St. Clair and had replied that they could promise peace only if the white people removed themselves entirely to the other side of the O-hi-o-se-pe and stayed there. Of course there had been no such agreement, but there was hope yet; surely the Great Good Spirit was stronger and more righteous than the God of the whites. How could he not be?

Thinking this, Tecumseh rode upon a sight that blew out the flame of his pleasure.

Lying on the trail before him was the mutilated body of the white captive. Tecumseh's horse shied at the smell of blood.

The fresh spring foliage all around the body was spattered with red, as if it had rained blood here. The head was gone from the body. And a short way down the path stood the two warriors, grinning, smeared to their elbows in blood. Above them on the end of a pole, still dripping blood, was the head of the white man, frozen by death into an eyeless mask of agony.

The grins faded from the warriors' faces as Tecumseh dropped to the ground and advanced on them, his eyes alight with wrath, his voice rankling with disgust.

"Oh, you are slinking dogs! You were too tired to help your brothers collect our horses, but not too tired to butcher *my* prisoner, the man I caught and made helpless! Stand away from me! You stink with cowardice! You! Never will you ride with me again! Not to hunt or to war! Since you have done this, you are no longer my brothers." His mouth was a bitter sneer. He glared at them until their eyes fell. He wanted to tell them how they had befouled the good and honorable thoughts he had had about the righteousness of the red men. But he could say no more to them; his throat was clogged with loathing and remorse.

And so he turned and swung onto his horse and led Big Fish and the string of animals back up the trail at a fast trot. Those two could come back on foot, if they dared to come back at all.

"So they were too tired," he snarled to Big Fish. "Good. Maybe they will never catch up with us."

But his heart ached as he rode. His heart ached for the weaknesses and the meanness of his People, who so needed now to be strong and good.

# CHAPTER 23

## *Fallen Timbers*
## *August 19, 1794*

T hat one, the big soldier sitting outside the big tent, is General Wayne," Blue Jacket said, and he handed Tecumseh the English spyglass. "He-Who-Never-Sleeps."

Even without the telescope Tecumseh could see him, a man of bulk seated beside a map table outside a white tent among many other white tents on the weedy bottomland of the Maumee-se-pe. When Tecumseh put the piece to his eye and brought it to bear on the man, he could see the general's florid face and his elegant blue uniform all edged in gold braid. The general was moving his lips, talking to an officer nearby. Though portly and jowly, the general gave an appearance of strength and confidence.

"The word on his flag," Blue Jacket said, "is his own name. Wayne. He thinks highly of himself."

It was strange to be seeing the American general so close, as if standing a few paces from him, watching his lips move without sound, while hearing Blue Jacket's voice right at his ear, even though the general was far off. It was like being in two places at once, like a Bear Walker. Tecumseh raised the tube slightly and looked at the flag on its pole near the tent. It was of alternating red and blue stripes, with the general's name across the top. Tecumseh had been seeing that flag come farther and farther into the Indian country for weeks.

At first it had seemed that this general would make all the same mistakes that had ruined Harmar and St. Clair. He had moved his great legions of Blue-Coat soldiers slowly along in straight, visible lines with their cannons and wagons and baggage and beef cattle. He had stopped at intervals to build forts and left whole companies of men to live in them and guard them. At first he had seemed to be the same sort of general, and Blue Jacket had

298

predicted: "In a few days his army will begin to get out of order, and the time will come when they are weak and dull and uncomfortable, and we will strike them and destroy them, as we did the other armies."

But this general was not like Harmar and St. Clair. He was more like Clark, except slower and more deliberate. He had kept a whole company of swift, skillful scouts out at a distance all the time and built a fortified camp at the end of every day's march, so he could never be surprised. His soldiers were tough and well trained and high-spirited and did not straggle. Some of them even dressed as Indians and moved in parties to nearby villages, where they terrorized the women and children. This army thus had moved much farther north than any American army had done before and was in fact now within a day's march of Lake Erie, threatening the new British fort and trading post at the foot of the Maumee-se-pe rapids. This General Wayne crept along like a cold serpent but never closed his eyes or stopped flicking his tongue, and Blue Jacket was growing desperate.

Blue Jacket was the war chief of the united tribes now. Little Turtle had voted that they should not try to strike another Long Knife army, that it was useless to try to stop an aggressive people who kept coming in numbers too great to count. Feeling this way, he had not been elected the main war chief this time, though he was here as the leader of his Miami warriors. So for the first time in years, it was a Shawnee who led the confederation of defenders. It was Blue Jacket, a man who had been born as white as General Anthony Wayne.

Tecumseh lowered the spyglass from the red-and-blue flag to look again at the American general. The general's image in the telescope was wavery in the heat waves rising out of the meadow. It was now the Plum Moon, the hottest of the year. There was no wind, hardly enough to make the general's flag flap lazily about its pole. The sun beat down on the valley of the Maumee-se-pe through a steamy haze, and high, slow-moving rain clouds were piled along the western sky far away.

The general was now wiping his face with a cloth. His lips were still moving. Tecumseh wondered what he was saying and to whom he was doing all this talking. Surely to another chief, he thought, and he moved the spyglass over to look at the other officer.

When he saw the face, he felt a chill. He had seen this face. His mind raced. He had seen this face. . . .

Yes. In the dream when the bison were running over him!

This man standing in the circle of glass was lean and narrow-shouldered. And he was very young, with dark hair. His face was homely, big-nosed, but with a certain intensity in the eyes that made it remarkable. It was such an extraordinary face that Tecumseh had remembered it from a dream of six years ago. This young man appeared to be listening to the general; Tecumseh saw him nod once or twice, but he was looking all about like an eagle as he listened.

For a long while Tecumseh found himself unable to take the spyglass off this young officer's face.

Once it seemed as if the officer's scanning eye had come to rest upon Tecumseh himself. He stared in this direction for a long moment. No doubt he could see this warrior with a telescope watching him from the edge of the woods. And Tecumseh sent a concentration of thought toward him.

*You cannot see my face as I see yours. But mark me well, for I am my People.*


Lieutenant William Henry Harrison had been listening to Mad Anthony Wayne talk about tactics when suddenly he had an intense sensation of being watched.

". . . savages get confused when they have to wait for action," the general was saying. "I've heard they'll just walk off and go home if something doesn't pop right away. Believe me, my boy, I'm making good use of our time. Who knows how many of them are straying off while we stand here seeming to do nothing? I know there are impatient elements among the officers. I know they call me 'Big Turtle' because my method isn't rash enough to suit them. Heh, heh!" He wagged his head. "I'm used to nicknames. In the war I got to be known as 'Mad Anthony' for what they saw as too much rashness. But I always know what I'm doing, and why. Caution's the word, my lad, way out here where we are."

Lt. Harrison, who was Wayne's aide, nodded and said, "Yes, sir." He had heard the "Big Turtle" nickname used by a certain cadre of self-styled wits among the legion's officers. He had also heard Wayne referred to as "that cumbrous body" and as "Mars." But Harrison had no quarrel with Wayne's method and was learning many valuable lessons from the old campaigner. Harrison was, like Wayne, a scholar of Roman campaigns. He liked it that Wayne called his army "the legion," and he liked the strong discipline and order that Wayne demanded. Wayne was the kind of man to tame barbarians and civilize a wilderness, like a Caesar. Young Harrison considered himself quite lucky to have obtained this position as the old hero's aide-de-camp, though he knew it had been more than luck. The young officer's father had been one of the Virginia signers of the Declaration of Independence and a personal acquaintance of President Washington. That connection had enabled the young man, after his decision to forsake a medical career for a military one, to get a personal audience with

Washington and thus a commission and a brisk start upward in the military hierarchy.

During the long months of training and then the slow, methodical advance into the Indian country, Harrison had grown used to feeling watched. He had thought with constant wonder that among all the trees and brushlands along the route, there were always savages watching. Often the Indian scouts had been visible. Harrison had sometimes wondered how their primitive brains perceived as they watched this great legion. He could fancy that their savage heads were full of the same sort of brute fear and dark cunning and murderous anger that the ancient tribes of Huns and Scots and Levantines must have known centuries ago as the gleaming legions of civilized Rome moved into their unruly domains.

But just now, while listening to his commandant, he had felt the eyes upon him with such an intensity that he had felt compelled to scan the woods at the edge of the clearing.

"How singular," he remarked into a pause in the general's discourse. "Sir, have you ever seen an Indian scout use a spyglass?"

Wayne chortled. "Well," he said, "I'll wager it's got a British trademark on it."


The warriors had purged themselves and fasted to purify themselves for the battle, and then the battle had not come that day. Instead the Long Knife general had moved his army around for a while in the valley and then settled in one place. And the warriors, waiting in the woods for his attack, had eaten nothing for a second day, thinking he would attack on that day. The warriors prayed and lay in wait, and their bodies felt lighter and more pure, and their heads hummed like the mosquitoes in the wet summer heat. Their sight grew terribly clear, and for a while they could see every detail of the army in the distance, the white tents, the blue lines of men, the many mounted soldiers in the lush green valley. Sometimes drums would rattle and a regiment would form up and start to move toward the bluff, or a bugle would call and a troop of the horse soldiers would mount up and ride about with the plumes on their shiny helmets shaking in the air, and the warriors would grow tense and the thin blood in their veins would quicken. But then the regiment or the horsemen would go back into the camp, and the hungry waiting would go on.

Then the warriors' vision grew more dreamlike as they lay hungry, and sometimes these moving parts of the army would seem like phantoms drifting this way and that in the distance.

A heavy rain poured all night on the hungry and unsheltered warriors, and they were cold and wet and could not sleep, and on the morning after that night they were feeling weak and could not see well, and when the sun rose behind clouds of mist and heated the wet air, the warriors grew drowsy.

Loud Noise was on the line for the first time as a warrior and was having a very hard time with this fasting. Hunger to him was almost as bad as death, and to be starving half to death while waiting to be killed by Long Knives was simply the most dreadful plight he had ever imagined. He was scared and famished and kept dreaming up errands on which he might be sent back to the rear, where there was food and comparative safety. Tecumseh would look at him, raise an eyebrow, and shake his head with a sigh. "No," he would say, "I need my brother here." And so Loud Noise was here. But somewhere he had obtained a bit of whiskey, to bolster his courage, and he staggered and stank, and it was doubtful that he would be of much service.

There had never been a chance to surprise and attack Wayne's army like St. Clair's, and the confederation of tribes had been on the defensive for a long time. Blue Jacket on this morning had concentrated his thirteen hundred warriors in an enormous tangle of dead trees where a tornado had blown down a grove. This fallen forest made a natural barrier across the valley, from the bluffs down to the river, in the path of the Long Knife army. Here the warriors could hide like poisonous snakes in a brushpile, and if General Wayne meant to move down the valley, he would be bitten terribly in the tangle of the fallen woods.

Two miles downriver from the fallen timber, the new British fort called Fort Miami stood on the river bluff. It had been built by the British to stand in the way of Wayne's slow march toward Detroit. This fort was full of Redcoat soldiers and surrounded by high palisades and ditches, with its cannons pointing all ways and out on the Maumee-se-pe below. In that valley were hundreds of Indian houses, and orchards, and vast fields of corn and hay, and Alexander McKee's British trading post. A large island at the foot of the Maumee rapids was growing in tall corn, and on the other bank of the river stood the big town of Chief Pipe, principal chief of all the Delawares. The valley was a rich place, full of food, with the British allies standing ready to feed and aid the warriors, and all of it was protected by this splendid natural obstacle that the Great Good Spirit, through Cyclone Person, had thrown down in the way of the Long Knives. It was no wonder the American general hesitated so long before this. It was hard to imagine that white soldiers, even three thousand of them, would have enough courage to enter this huge, deadly maze.

Blue Jacket finally decided that the warriors who had fasted so long must eat, or they would have no strength to fight. He was content that Wayne would not attack this morning, if ever. So he arranged for one-third of the warriors to go back toward the British fort, where the agent McKee and the English major Campbell in charge of the fort would distribute food. Some of the warriors did not want to break their fast, famished though they were, because they did not want to face the army's bayonets with their bellies and bowels full. Others accepted Blue Jacket's judgment that the army would not move that day, so they left their hiding places in the edge of the blowdown and moved back through the jumble of trunks and dead limbs toward the fort to get rations.

Tecumseh and his warriors lay and knelt behind logs at the top of the bluff. To their right was a band of Ottawas commanded by Turkey Foot, and to their left the ground sloped steeply down to the bottomland meadows a hundred feet lower. Down this slope too and into the bottomland the debris of the tornado was strewn, almost to the river, and everywhere in that great tangle were hidden Shawnees and Wyandots, Delawares and Miamis. Also among the Indians were about seventy of Colonel Baby's Canadian militiamen from the vicinity of Detroit. Down by the river at McKee's house, the Indian partisans Girty and Elliott had established a command post.

Suddenly there was a rush of activity in the Long Knives' camp. Distant bugles blew. Horsemen mounted. Blue-Coat soldiers ran with their guns and lined up.

The warriors still on the line in the timber murmured to each other, checked their weapons, held their medicine bags or *pa-waw-kas* in their hands, and prayed for strength. Tecumseh moved along the line encouraging his warriors to stand firm and be brave. He slipped and squirmed over and under great splintered limbs and roots and through underbrush whose foliage was still beaded with water from the rain. His brothers Stands-Between and Loud Noise trailed after him, and Thick Water was as close as his shadow.

Tecumseh ran hand and foot up a slanting poplar trunk to gain a higher vantage point and watch the army. He saw the blue lines of troops moving on the green meadows below, and some of the troops were being marched westward up the slope of the bluff, carrying their flags with them, as if they were not going to fight here. He saw also a troop of the horse soldiers from Kain-tuck-ee, riding in that same direction, and much of the remaining army was also lining up as if to march that way.

To Tecumseh now it looked as if they might intend to go around the right flank of the Ottawas, pass through the woods west of the fallen timbers, and perhaps try then to swing northward, either to get behind the warriors or simply to march straight at the British fort. It was a surprising move, one that could endanger Blue Jacket's well-prepared defense.

On the ground below the tree, someone called Tecumseh's name. It was a runner from Blue Jacket, saying that the Shawnees should be ready to move to the west with the Ottawas, to help them extend their line in that direction if the Long Knives did try to go around their right flank. The hot, steamy air was tense with expectation and doubt. Tecumseh came down from the tree. He told the runner to go back to Blue Jacket and say that he understood and was ready. Loud Noise stood visibly trembling, his one eye wild with fear. But he was drunk enough not to panic and run away.

As the troops in the distance moved up the slope, they vanished into draws and defilades and could not be seen from where the Shawnees were. The regiments still visible in the meadows below were going slowly in that direction.

Suddenly an excited murmur swept along the Indian lines from the right. The Ottawas were pointing and crouching to move. Tecumseh looked toward the southwest and was astonished to see the mounted Kentuckians coming along the slope, strung out in a skirmish line, rifles, hunting shirts, black hats, straight toward the Ottawas' position as if they did not even know they were there. Perhaps they did not know. If they did not, it would be a stroke of good fortune.

They came on, riding at a quick walk, straight toward the ambush. The warriors, naked and painted and greased for battle, crouched and slithered in the shade, moving to the best vantage points in the edge of the woods for good shooting. The horses were so close now that even in the rain-soft ground their hoofbeats could be heard, and the rattling of guns and gear.

Then a loud cry spun out on the air, and one gunshot, then a hundred, and the quavering war cry from hundreds of throats. Soldiers fell from their saddles. Horses fell or reared. The remaining horsemen stopped in disarray, raised their rifles, and returned a ragged volley into the woods, and some of them were already riding away in disorderly retreat.

It was too much of a temptation for the Ottawas and Wyandots and many of the Shawnees along this front. With a howl they burst from the woods in pursuit of the fleeing Kentuckians. Thick Water was among those rash ones.

Tecumseh sprang up in alarm. He shouted, "No! *Pe-eh-wah,* come back!" It had looked too much like a decoy trick, those troops riding up so close while the main army was maneuvering around on the slope. But not many warriors heard his warning cry over the noise, only those nearby. Some who heard his voice stopped and came back, but not many. Warriors from up and down the line were darting out from their hiding places and running out to get the scalps of the fallen horsemen, ready to rush on to another great victory. Was not this just the way St. Clair's militia had turned and run? Was not this just the way the defeat of St. Clair had begun?

Tecumseh watched, still shouting, as the hundreds of warriors rushed screaming across the open slope in pursuit of the horsemen. And then what he had feared began to happen.

Army drums, faint and dull sounding because of the damp air, thudded in the distance, down toward the river, and two cannon shots reverberated in the valley. Shouts relayed along the slope.

And then the whole Blue-Coat army, on that signal, suddenly was coming into view, moving not to the west, but straight toward the timbers. A double line of them three-quarters of a mile long had flanked right and was coming on at a very fast step. Some of them were hidden by the gunsmoke of the skirmish, but it was plain that the whole line of Blue-Coats was in a full charge now, that it would simply overrun the warriors who had rushed out into the open and would be here in the edge of the timbers within minutes. Never had Tecumseh imagined that so many hundreds of men could move in such unison. They came swiftly, the weeds and tall grasses soaking their legs, their long guns and bayonets held on a slant. This was an attacking army, coming on hard, not an army moving away in confusion.

Now these oncoming lines let the retreating horsemen pass back through to safety and closed again, still coming. The warriors who had run after the horse soldiers were now hesitating, right in the path of these hundreds and hundreds of Blue-Coats. Many of the warriors turned and raced back toward the timber; others stood bravely shooting at the ranks. Tecumseh saw Thick Water load, fire, then turn back toward the timbers.

Tecumseh clenched his jaw in dismay and in frustration, because now his warriors in the woods could not shoot at the Blue-Coats without hitting their own people, those who had been rash enough to be decoyed out. The warriors had been deceived by one of their own kinds of ruses, because they had not expected one of these marching generals to use a decoy trick.

The lines of Blue-Coats began a deep, droning cry, a monotonous bellow of fury from a thousand throats, as they clashed with the warriors in the field. Some of the warriors shot or hacked at soldiers before they themselves were speared by the bayonets or trampled by the oncoming lines. The flurry of fighting out there hardly slowed the soldiers. Down by the river the mounted dragoons were charging forward in front of the walking soldiers, who now were charging as if with lances instead of guns, and they were almost at the edge of the woods now. The warriors floundering back into the covert were in the way of those who tried to shoot at the soldiers.

Tecumseh's heart was torn with chagrin. The chance to mow down the soldiers with arrows and bullets from this covert was lost. So swiftly the advantage had been swept away! The only hope now was that the mass of fallen trees would slow the tide of Blue-Coats enough that clubs and knives and hatchets would suffice to stop them. Tecumseh could see the soldiers' faces now, the young, pink ones, the craggy, leathery ones, the blue-eyed ones, their faces pouring sweat, their mouths open with their hard yelling and hard breathing, could see the teeth in their mouths, could see the sheen of daylight on the sweaty planes of their faces, and he screamed in desperation to his warriors, "Be strong! Kill them now! Brothers, be strong!" He discharged his rifle into the face of a gaunt soldier who had reached the woods. Then in his haste to reload, he tamped a ball down the muzzle without a charge of powder, thus rendering the gun useless. With a curse for white men's iron inventions, he cast it down and drew his war club from his belt with his right hand and his knife with his left. *"Pe-eh-wah!"* he cried, and sprang forward. His great voice rallied some of the warriors, and they screamed their battle cries and flung themselves at the countless soldiers who came crashing and bellowing into the deadwood. Tecumseh flailed at black hats and ferocious faces, and he parried away thrusts of the long bayonets. He was desperate; his blood was full of fire. He could not bear the thought that a white army might once again win a battle in his land.

For a few moments then the close wet air was a din of blows, screams, curses, crackling twigs, commands, groans, a few pistol shots. The warriors fought in a way that surely would have stopped any other army that had ever come against them. Even Loud Noise in his desperation was standing his ground and hacking away with his great strength, drunkenly brawling to defend his life.

But these soldiers were not scared. They did not stop pushing their way into the woods. It does not take long to determine whether an enemy is just obeying orders or is truly strong-hearted, and these men had the spirit that Clark's soldiers had had. They ducked under and clambered over trunks and branches to get into the combat, crunching ever forward with their deadly steel spikes probing the way, as eager as hungry bear hunters closing in. Tecumseh saw his warriors being impaled and twisted to the ground. He saw them being slammed back against the dead trees and clubbed to death with rifle stocks. The long bayonets on the long guns outreached tomahawks and clubs and knives. And when a Blue-Coat soldier fired one shot into the massed warriors, several could be hit by the mixed load of ball and shot.

Tecumseh had a glimpse of Stands-Between fighting beside him, and when the youth glanced toward him, Tecumseh saw that his eyes were filled with the most terrible desperation Tecumseh had ever seen in a life of conflicts. There had never been soldiers like these. Tecumseh was sore with bruises, and though the leather of his war club was soaked with soldiers' blood, his own blood seeped over his skin from many places where the probing steel or buckshot had gouged him. It was impossible to go forward against them; it was impossible to stand still in front of them. The woods were full of the blue coats and white belts now. If the warriors had been here who had gone back to get food, there might have been enough to stop the army. But there were not. And the mass of fallen timber that was to have been the warriors' defense was proving to be their death trap. As they fell back they were blocked by it and pinned against it. And in their hunger these frantic exertions were weakening them quickly. Tecumseh found it hard now even to swing his club. He was gasping for air and squirming and dodging and twisting for his life. Loud Noise was out of Tecumseh's sight now. Stands-Between was still at Tecumseh's right hand and was fighting without flinching, his arms covered with blood. He struck a soldier in the face with his tomahawk. When the soldier fell, the bloody-slick tomahawk handle was wrenched out of his bloody hand. Another soldier thrust at Stands-Between, who grabbed the long bayonet with both hands and strained to tear the gun from the soldier's grasp. As they struggled, Tecumseh lashed out with his club and knocked the soldier into the other world.

"Back, brother," Tecumseh cried. Stands-Between, holding the gun by its bayonet and barrel, cocked it back to swing at an officer who was coming forward with a pistol in one hand and a sword in the other. The officer fired his pistol point-blank in Stands-Between's face. Tecumseh glanced at his brother in that moment and saw part of his head pop open, felt flying bits of his flesh and drops of his blood. As Stands-Between swayed on his feet, Tecumseh screamed in outrage, leaped at the officer, yanked the smoking pistol from the officer's hand, and cracked his skull with the butt of it. When he turned to his young brother, Stands-Between was already on the ground. His body was still twitching, but his face had a hole of torn meat and gristle where his nose had been, with grains of gunpowder still smoking in it.

Crazed with grief, Tecumseh knelt and grasped Stands-Between under the arms and raised him up. Sobbing, straining, his throat burning from thirst and smoke, he cradled him in his arms and stood up. Then he turned his back on the Blue-Coats and began staggering deeper into the fallen woods. To his left and right, warriors were fleeing into the thickets, many of them bleeding and limping. The soldiers could be heard close behind, still yelling, still crashing and crushing through the deadwood like a herd of heavy-footed animals, still sending ball and buckshot snapping through the foliage. Flying splinters stung Tecumseh's back. There were still blows and screams of pain back there, as a few warriors fought on. But the battle was lost. The thick, damp woods were blurry with smoke, and among the fallen trunks and split limbs flitted the forms of the retreating red men.

Tecumseh staggered on with his burden, gasping for breath, stumbling, his heart torn apart by grief, his feet and legs being scratched and gouged by briers and broken branches. Twisting dead limbs reached out like hostile arms trying to wrench Stands-Between's body away from him. He fell to his knees, and the body slipped from his arms. Panting, hardly able to breathe the close, smoky air, Tecumseh carefully gathered up the youth, lurched to his feet, and staggered on. There was no movement in the body now. Another brother was dead. He could still hear the shouts and uproar of the advancing army a few paces back. He was not afraid of being shot in the back. It did not matter now whether he lived or not. But he could not lay his brother's body down, he could not leave it where the Blue-Coats would scalp it and skin it and take fingers and ears and genitals as trophies. He must keep going, as the rest of the shattered tribes were going, back through to the far side of the fallen timbers and up the road into the safety of the new British fort.

Yes! he thought. Yes! When we come out of these woods, our British friends will take us in through the big gate, and then their cannons will boom and blow these Blue-Coat soldiers down. The fort will stop them!

"My brother," he gasped to the bloody-faced corpse in his arms, "it is not lost yet!" And he floundered on with the great dead weight in his sweat-slick arms, its bloody head hanging and bobbling with every step, and he tried to hope even as the last strength of his body wore down.


Loud Noise came lumbering through the brush, his body fat quivering with every step, exhausted but trying to run to Tecumseh. He was wet with blood from many small wounds. His face was smeared with sweat and blood and war paint, and he was totally sober. When he saw his dead brother in Tecumseh's arms, he clenched his jaw and groaned.

Hundreds of warriors were moving around them, going down the river bluff toward the British fort. Many were carrying or supporting wounded ones. Thick Water, whom Tecumseh had given up for dead, came limping. More of Tecumseh's warriors saw him now and came to gather around him. "Let us help you carry your brother," Seekabo said, and quickly they grasped his arms and legs, and the four of them carried the corpse. But Stands-Between's death was no lighter on Tecumseh's heart, only on his arm. As they moved on toward the British fort, Big Fish joined them, then Stands Firm, face set in bitterness. He kept looking back, watching the warriors emerge from the timber. He looked down at the body, and his face set still harder.

"Turkey Foot they killed," he said. "I saw him down. Many chiefs are dead because they rushed out of the woods for the decoys." Thick Water, hearing this, looked abashed.

Now they could see the British flag ahead, and soon they emerged onto a clearing at the top of the curving bluff, full of stumps where trees had been cut to make the fort. Tecumseh spoke now of his hope.

"When the Long Knives come out of the woods, the cannons in the fort will shoot them and turn them around. We have not lost this day! The British soldiers will help us, as they promised, and we will destroy the enemy!"

They limped on in the hot sun. Then Stands Firm said, "Look below! McKee, in a boat!" Several men in a vessel were rowing fast, downstream, and the Indian agent was among them. They swept down the current of the river, and soon they were close offshore from the landing wharf below the fort. McKee was standing up in the boat, shouting something up to the fort, but his words could not be heard from this distance.

Now as the warriors thronged up the road toward the gate of the fort, Tecumseh saw that something was going wrong there. Hundreds of Indians were crowded around the outer gate where the road passed through an abatis of sharpened limbs. They were roaring in anger, shaking weapons and fists. Up on the wall of the fort within, the British commander Campbell stood silent with some of his officers, using a telescope to study the distant woods where the Americans were. The warriors were all shouting up at him, but it seemed as if he did not hear them—even as if he could not see them. The cannons' black muzzles pointed over the river and toward the woods, and there were many Redcoat soldiers up on the parapets, but both the outer gate and the inner gate were shut, and no one in the fort was moving to open them.

Some of the warriors began to pound on the abatis gate with their gun butts and hatchets.

"Father," a mighty voice bellowed over the clamor. It was Blue Jacket's voice. He was pointing at Major Campbell. "Father! You have promised to help us! Your children need you now! You see us! We come in great trouble! Many are hurt, many dead!" He swung his arm and pointed up the river toward the fallen woods. "You see the Americans coming. You must shoot your cannons at them! You must let us come in. Father, can you not hear our voices? Can you not remember your promise?" He was calling all this out in Shawnee. The officers on the high wall did not reply. They did not look down. It was as if the Indians were not there. Now Blue Jacket, who had often said he hated the white man's tongue and would never use it again, began shouting at the British officers in that language, using many words Tecumseh had never used before. He was calling Campbell a traitor and a coward and a son of something.

And now Tecumseh understood what was happening, and his heart went bleak and cold and hard inside him.

The British were afraid. They had not expected the Long Knives to get through the fallen timbers. They were too afraid to help the warriors. There was nothing that could be done to persuade them to help. They were so ashamed, they could not even look at the huge crowd of desperate warriors, their allies who had fought to hold the Americans away from the fort. In the last war the Americans had knocked down the English king, and now the British were afraid to be in another war with them, regardless of their many fervent promises to the tribes. Tecumseh looked up at the British in their splendid scarlet coats, and disdain swelled within him. He stood straight, taking a long, deep breath, his arm still holding one arm of his dead brother, his brother who had died trying to keep the Americans from reaching the fort. And then Tecumseh shouted over the uproar:

"Brothers! Come away! These are not allies! They are whitefaces! They are cowards! They are as bad as the Long Knives! Come away! We must care for ourselves!" And, face drawn in a sneer, shaking his bloody war club toward Major Campbell, he turned off the road, saying to Loud Noise, "Come. We must go down the river and find a place to bury this brave warrior, our brother."


And so the Blue-Coats of General Anthony Wayne infested the rich, beautiful valley of the lower Maumee-se-pe. They yelled and whooped and slashed all the crops, and girdled the trees in the orchards, and burned villages, and plundered McKee's store and burned his house, and destroyed all the crops on the beautiful island at the foot of the rapids—all within view of the British in the fort, who made no effort to stop it. The three sacred sisters, corn, squash, and beans, were cut and smashed and burned, and this sacrilege demoralized the Shawnees even more. The soldiers scalped and skinned or mutilated every body they found. They went into a burial ground and dug up old corpses, and took items from the graves, and drove stakes through the bodies. Soon the beautiful valley lay under a pall of smoke and stench. The British stood in their fort and watched all this and did not move.

The defeated warriors of the confederation went down the river past the fort to the place where Swan Creek flowed into the river, five miles down, and made a camp there and prepared to defend the women and children if the Long Knives came on down. Tecumseh buried Stands-Between, the second of his brothers to die in his arms. Then he went back up the river to a place from which he could watch the Americans, his heart cold and bitter. He saw that Wayne was building a fortification within view of the British fort. He saw the desolate, smoking valley, all wasted.

While he was watching, General Wayne and his young aide rode out from their fortification and rode close to the walls of the British fort, within a pistol shot of it, then rode insolently around the fort, looking at it as if it were nothing, defying the Redcoat cowards inside to shoot. Tecumseh looked long at the young officer. This man, he knew, had something important to do with the signs. Tecumseh felt nothing when he looked at the old general, nothing but hatred and regret. But when his eyes went back to the young officer, he could hear the wind whispering something to him, though there was no wind blowing, and he could feel the earth grumbling beneath his feet, though nothing moved.

In that dark head and slender figure of the distant young officer on a war-horse, Tecumseh saw the evil for which the spirits had always been preparing him. He could not stop looking at him.

There was no doubt of it. That was the one.

Four weeks later, in the Papaw Moon, a Shawnee woman came down to Swan Creek. She had been caught in the summer by General Wayne's scouts, and now they had sent her back so that she could carry a message to the tribes from General Wayne. Captain Elliott, the Indian agent, translated it to the red men.

> Brothers:
> The President of the United States, General Washington, the Great Chief of America, once more speaks to you thro' me, his Principal Warrior Major General and Commander in Chief of the Federal Army, and Commissioner Plenipotentiary for settling a permanent and lasting Peace with all, and every tribe or tribes, nations or Nation of Indians, north of the Ohio.
> Brothers, summon your utmost powers of attention, and listen to the voice of Truth and Peace. . . .
> The United States love Mercy and Kindness more than War and Destruction. . . . Be no longer deceived by the false promises and languages of the bad white people, in the fort at the foot of the Rapids. . . .

You preferred War; and instead of the Calumet of Peace, you suddenly presented from your secret Coverts the Scalping Knife and Tommahawk; but in return for the few drops of blood we lost upon that occasion we caused Rivers of yours to flow. I told you that the Arm of the United States was strong, you only felt the weight of its little finger. . . .

The British had neither the power nor the inclination to protect you, you have severely experienced the truth. . . . Be, therefore, no longer blind to your own true interests and happiness; but listen to the Voice of Peace. . . .

Brothers, appoint a number of your Sachems and Chief Warriors, bring with you some of your most Confidential Interpreters, and I hereby pledge my Sacred honor, for your safe return, & for your kind treatment while with me.

Open your minds freely to me, and let us try to agree upon such fair and equitable terms of Peace as shall be for the true interest and happiness of both the white & red people; and that you may in future plant your corn & hunt in peace & safety, and that by an interchange of kindness and good offices towards each other we may Cement that Brotherly love and affection as shall endure to the end of time....

You shall receive a sincere Welcome from your friend and Brother

Anty. Wayne

Matthew Elliott had been issuing three thousand rations a day to the defeated warriors and their families at Swan Creek, and there was a fear that if the tribes remained here, neither fighting nor at peace, supplies would be exhausted early in the winter. So even Captain Elliott did not try very hard to discourage the Indians from going to hear General Wayne.

The chiefs sent no answer to General Wayne's letter right away. They had much talking to do among themselves. They were still licking their wounds, and Wayne had built a chain of strong forts clear through their country, from the O-hi-o-se-pe to the western end of Lake Erie. His words sounded kind, the chiefs said, but he *was* a chieftain of Washington, and he was in control, so it was doubtful that the terms of peace would be good for the tribes.

"What will we do?" Tecumseh was asked by Big Fish, and by Seekabo, and even by Stands Firm, who once had been like a father to Tecumseh but since had become like a son to him.

Tecumseh had not smiled since Stands-Between's death. He finally did smile, a grim, wolfish smile.

"My brother Chiksika told me, before he died in the south, that even when Black Hoof and Little Turtle put their marks on the white man's treaties, I would refuse. My brother Chiksika always said the truth."

"Would you not even go to listen to the Long Knife chief?" asked Seekabo. "You would not have to put your mark on his treaty."

Tecumseh put his hand to his waist, palm down, and swept it over the fire, as if throwing something away. "I prefer to hear truth. All the treaties of the Long Knives have been made of lies. This one will be also. I would rather go away and sit in the woods alone and hear the truth of silence than sit in a square room with white men and hear false promises. No, brother. If I do not go to a treaty, by the law of our People, I am not bound to live by that treaty.

"And you have heard me. I would never live by a treaty of lies. This Long Knife Wayne has not defeated me. He has not made me afraid to fight on. I do not have to go when he calls."

Many young warriors believed as Tecumseh did and chose not to go to the treaty council. They gathered around him and made their own council. The future of their nation was now hanging in doubt. No one knew what sort of boundaries the white general would try to draw now, but these young men chose to stay as near the old Shawnee lands as they could without being bothered by the Long Knife army. And so they agreed to go with Tecumseh to a place where he had often had hunting camps. It was in the valley of a stream called Deer Creek, a tributary of the Mad River, about a day's journey northeast of the ruins of old Chillicothe Town. To this place many of the younger Shawnees went, and in council they chose Tecumseh as their chief, and here they built a small, orderly town of *wigewas* set in two rows along the creekside, with a council house on a hillock. Wives and sisters and children of the warriors came, and also some young Wyandot and Delaware warriors who had become attached to Tecumseh during Wayne's advance. And also among Tecumseh's followers was Star Watcher, and there was also the Peckuwe maiden, She-Is-Favored.

It was too late in the year to plant any crops, so the women worked hurriedly to build the huts and forage for wild foods, while the warriors went out and scoured the forests and plains for game. Much meat would have to be got and preserved to make up for the lack of corn. To arouse the hunters' best efforts, Tecumseh proposed that the hunt be a contest, with each hunter accumulating the skins of all the deer he killed. Showing their first happy eagerness for anything since the tragedy at Fallen Timbers, the young men spread out into the countryside, each determined to do the greatest good for the new little town and gain renown as well. The time of the contest hunt was set at three days.

And so they hunted with uncommon skill and attention. Even the least successful of the hunters brought in three hides; several came with four to six; a few even came in with ten or twelve hides. The women became very busy drying venison as the contest went on.

Tecumseh himself ranged the faint but familiar paths along the creeks and the meadows, hunting as Chiksika had taught him, praying for help from the Masters of the Game, thinking as the buck deer thinks and as the doe thinks, standing motionless among the falling yellow leaves, sniffing breezes, kneeling to examine deep tracks in the creek banks, armed with both bow and rifle, sending off arrow or ball with the quickest reflexes, thinking at every moment of the needs of these people who were now *his* responsibility, and his fortunes in the hunt were far better than any he had ever enjoyed. When the period of the contest was over, Tecumseh had obtained for his band enough venison for many, many pounds of jerky and no less than thirty deerskins for his people's clothes and shelter. She-Is-Favored looked at him as the people celebrated him, and it was plain that she wanted to be chief's wife.

Tecumseh saw what was in her eyes, and he considered. Star Watcher, who seemed able to read his thoughts, hurried to tell him: "A chief should have a wife. He should have a wife not just to care for his needs and warm his bed and give him pleasure and children, but also because it has always been so, since the Beginning. The wife of the chief is the leader of the women's council, and speaks for them in the open council. You know how important she is in the Bread Dance and Green Corn Dance." Then she added, "Her father surely would bring many of the warriors of his village to live here and strengthen us."

Tecumseh knew all this. An unmarried chief was not traditional, and he did hope to keep the old ways strong in his band, even though the whites were scattering tribes and changing everything. "Yes, my sister. A chief should have a wife." But in his heart he did not yet want a wife. He had his destiny signs, and a wife could distract and limit him as he searched for the meanings. And he had told himself often that this time of war and terror and moving was not a good time for children to be born Shawnee. So he agreed in principle that he needed a wife but did not yet move toward marriage. In this small village he saw She-Is-Favored almost every day. He thought of the qualities he had seen in her that made her seem a gift to the People. And whenever he looked at her he could not help thinking how it would be to lie with her and could see that she too was thinking such thoughts. It was like a force that could be felt between them, and the dwellers of the town could sense it. But it was not time yet.

Better, he thought, to wait and see what our world will be after the big treaty council next summer with the Long Knife general. After that, we might not even have a place to lie on.

Chiefs and warriors of twelve tribes went to conclude the peace treaty with General Wayne the next summer. He stood straddling their lands and all their waterways and main trails, and they knew he would not wait forever for them to decide. He could go and destroy every ear of corn in the Middle Ground this summer if he grew impatient. He had built a huge fort on a branch of the Stillwater River, named Greenville in honor of his old commander in the war. The main Shawnee chiefs who went to Greenville were Black Hoof, Blue Jacket, and Black Snake. Little Turtle went for the Miamis, with his adopted son Wells, the Wild Potato, as his interpreter. Breaker-in-Pieces and Twisting Vines went for the Delawares and Tarhe the Crane for the Wyandots. Tecumseh sent Big Fish to attend and listen and to bring back a true report of everything.

Big Fish never returned.

In the Plum Moon, Blue Jacket rode to Tecumseh's town to tell him what had happened at the council. In his eyes was the look of a whipped man. Tecumseh called a village council to hear him.

Blue Jacket told in detail of the exchange of white peace wampum between the chiefs and the American general. He told of the long days of talk and ceremony and of the measures of whiskey the Americans had given out to mellow the hearts of the embittered chiefs and warriors. He described the enormous fort with its gardens and the general's huge log house inside, and the great council house outside the fort, where all the talking had been done. He made it clear that such a place could have been built only by much wealth and power. Finally he told of the treaty terms. From the first words, Tecumseh had to clench his jaw to keep from crying out.

"We who marked that treaty," Blue Jacket said, "promised never to raise the hatchet against the white men again. We promised never again to dispute the Long Knives' control over the old homelands. What were Shawnee lands are now white men's lands. Even this town you have just built is on land now owned by the Sixteen Fires. Only on the other side of the Auglaize River is still the red man's land.

"In return for those lost lands, the chief of each tribe will be given one thousand dollars each year for his people. Dollars are their kind of wampum. It was not easy for our chiefs to understand the value of those things called dollars, but we were warned that we would need these dollars if we are to live in a country run in the ways of the white men, and I am afraid that is true.

"It was agreed also," he went on, his eyes dull, voice growing tired, "that all captives held on both sides are to be exchanged. They made your brother Big Fish go back to his native race, and his name is now Ruddell again. But," Blue Jacket said over the dismal murmur of his listeners, "he told me that he will come back to us some way, that the Shawnee are his people. We who marked that treaty were Black Hoof, and Black Snake, Tarhe the Crane, and Leatherlips of the Wyandots, Twisting Vines and Breaker-in-Pieces of the Delawares. And Little Turtle, who defeated the Long Knife army two years, spoke for peace at last and made his mark."

As Blue Jacket told all this, he began to fade, and Tecumseh now saw him as he had first seen him four and twenty summers ago: on his elbows and knees in the line of the gauntlet, bleeding under the blows of switches but not crying out. Tecumseh, heart aching, remembered whipping him in his frenzy.

Beyond that Tecumseh could not listen.

The great chiefs Blue Jacket and Black Hoof and Little Turtle suddenly had become, in Tecumseh's mind, men who were no more. There was no reason any longer even to listen to them. These tired men had given away to their enemies everything. They had made the whole Shawnee world a world that was no more.

Tecumseh, nearly strangling with remorse, thought of the towns—of beautiful old Chillicothe, embraced in a curved bluff beside the green river; of Kispoko Town, where his father had been chief a generation ago; of Piqua Town, his own birthplace, where he had made his Vision Quest so many years ago, that place where these same chiefs had fought so hard and long against the Long Knife Clark; he thought of the deer trails and the hunting grounds whose every hill and valley and spring he had known, of the meadows where he had sat in silent moonlight or watched fireflies twinkle like drifting stars, of islands in the rivers, of the mounds of the ancient fathers, of bottomlands where he had gazed into cedarwood fires or smoked meat into jerky, of particular caves and trees where Chiksika had sat with him and taught him the Shawnee way; he thought of the great numbers of dome-shaped *wigewas* that had filled the old towns and remembered how they had looked to the returning hunter, all soft gray in the gloaming with fires gleaming warm everywhere; he remembered the smells of Shawnee cake and meat cooking and the murmuring voices of the people who had felt safe and happy in those old towns, a people happy because they were the ancient and great Shawandasse, the South Wind People, the free People. He remembered the drumbeats and singing and the chatter of deer-hoof rattles at the Bread Dance and the Green Corn Dance and the roaring laughter at the Frolic Dances and the ball games. He remembered the feel of mud under his feet at the river's edge in his childhood, and the sacred mud on his feet in the ceremonies of the spring council, and the old chiefs scattering the sacred tobacco around the ceremonial ground and the altar, and he remembered the power and the spirit whisperings discernible in the mild night air at those ceremonies, back when his People had been strong and proud and happy because they were living as Weshemoneto wished them to live, free, on the land where he had placed them.

And now so quickly all that proud and happy world was gone. That dark-eyed, bitter-mouthed old man Black Hoof had thrown it to the white men in return for a worthless and unholy something called annuity dollars, in return for some peace and safety.

All of it gone! Everything Tecumseh had ever known, everything that had fed his soul! Black Hoof had given that all away! Black Hoof had given away his own soul, but worse, he had given away the soul of his People! Tecumseh's father and two of his own brothers had died readily and without fear to keep it from being lost. But Black Hoof had given it away!

What would the People become now? Without these things they would be dead even though they kept walking around!

"But not I," Tecumseh said, interrupting whatever Blue Jacket had been saying. "I signed no treaty, and by the law of our People I am not bound by what you promised the whitefaces. The land and the way still live in *my* heart! These things will keep on living, if I have them in me. I will take them someplace else, and I will keep them alive, somehow, and if the white men come to that place, I will fight them as long as I have a breath, and I will never grow so old and tired that I will lean back and say, 'White man, it is yours.' *Never!*"

And then, unable to bear any longer the sorrow and shame of the defeated chief, Tecumseh did what he would never have done before.

He stood up and turned his back on him and walked out. Outside the council house, the wind was warm, and clouds were moving past the face of the moon, where Our Grandmother bent over her cooking pot. In the wind there were voices.

Star Watcher went outdoors and gazed at her brother, but he did not see her; he was seeing things from his life dreams.

He remembered the wolves passing with the moons in their eyes. The white dove. The earth trembling. The one-eyed face of someone called Tenskwatawa, Open Door. The young officer beside the Long Knife general, the young officer whose name, Blue Jacket had informed him, was Harrison. *Harrison.*

All these things were yet to be. And if they were yet to be, the fight was not over, the Shawnee were not yet dead. Not all of them would stay with Black Hoof and be walking dead men.

Once again it was necessary for the Shawnees to divide, to follow their hearts in two different directions. Tecumseh felt the cold of death coming from where Blue Jacket sat. But no, he thought, taking his *pa-waw-ka* stone in his hand and feeling its heat. No!

I am still alive. I am still Shawnee. All the past of the Shawnees is gathered in my head and my breast. Those who go with me will be given all I have of it, and they will still live, and they will still be Shawnee.

He did not yet know what he would have to do. But it was he who would have to do it. His aching heart pumped his defiant blood as he prayed, despite the tragedy he had just seen:

*"The Great Good Spirit favors our People."*

# CHAPTER 24

## On the Whitewater River
## Spring 1797

Star Watcher and her littlest daughter were weaving mats for the floor of their house in Tecumseh's third new town when he came and sat down nearby, as he did often at this time of afternoon. He watched them work and seemed lost in thought.

Star Watcher was twisting the pairs of fiber strands that laced the rows of cattail reeds together, while the girl sorted the reeds and handed them to her one at a time. She would place one reed small end first, then the next one large end first, the next small end first. "If we do not turn them this way and that," she explained to the little girl, "then the mat would be longer on one side, or it would bulge here and draw up there and not lie flat. Remember?" She had already woven one little bad example to show the child how not to do it. Taught in this way, she knew, the girl would always remember just how to do it.

It was almost dusk and would soon be too dark for any more weaving. It was a time of day Star Watcher loved. The last meal of the day had been eaten and most of the work was done, and the children were tired enough to be most calm and affectionate, and this was true in most of the families, so the noises of the village were low and cheerful.

This was Tecumseh's third new village because the first, on Deer Creek, had been inside the white man's imaginary treaty lines, and the second, though west of the line, had proven to be too close; the Long Knife hunters and liquor sellers and spies had come around almost immediately. To them, it seemed, the line was to keep red men out, not to keep themselves in. Tecumseh had told the liquor sellers: "It is only you white men who say there is a line on the earth. If you are the only ones who can see this line, why are we the only ones to obey it?" Then he had fed them and sent them away, telling them that if they came near his village again, he would spill their liquor on the ground, and that if they came back still again, he would spill their blood on the ground.

Star Watcher understood that the treaty made by Wayne and the old chiefs two summers ago was a promise of peace and brotherhood by both sides. But, like her brother, she sensed that it was just another time like that twenty-five years ago when the line had been a visible one, the Beautiful River, and the whites had started coming across. It would not be long, she was sure, before all the old troubles would build up again. Everything goes around and comes again; like sunrise and sunset, summer and winter, seed and harvest, birth and death, there would likewise be peace and war. She was thinking this and tying off the fibers at the edge of the mat when Tecumseh startled her by saying:

"I have thought long on your words and the words of all the others, and now I am ready to have a wife."

Such a bittersweetness swelled in her that she did not have any words at first and brought him into the house to give him a tea of sassafras root and maple sugar so she could get her thoughts together. She had expected to be very happy if he ever made this decision. What she could not understand was why she felt sad, too, and even a little angry, but not angry at him. Soon she realized that she was angry at the woman who was to be the wife. Her heart was saying, *This is our chosen one. You cannot care for him as well as I have done.*

Star Watcher was sure the woman would be She-Is-Favored, though Tecumseh had not said so yet. Always she had thought that She-Is-Favored would be the best mate he could find. But now all at once she could think of things she did not like so much about her. The young woman was like a bird egg, so full of herself that there would be room for nothing else. She seemed to be as her name implied, so favored that no one was good enough for her.

When I was that young, Star Watcher thought, I was as beautiful as she is, but I do not think I was so full of myself. I do not *think* I was. I hope I was not.

"Is it to be the Peckuwe woman?" she asked finally.

He smiled. "You will be pleased that it is. The things you have said in her favor are true, as I have seen, too. She is strong of heart and quick in her mind, and will be a good women's chief."

"A little lazy, perhaps," Star Watcher said, letting the words slip out before thinking better.

He frowned. "Why do you find a fault, you who have praised her to me? You and Loud Noise always say I should have a wife. When I choose to, you tell me she is lazy. And Loud Noise tells me she is a ball puller! Do you not know your minds?"

"Just a *little* lazy," Star Watcher said, looking down. "Not enough to bother you, perhaps."

"Ha! And I suppose just a *little* of a ball puller, not enough to bother me? Our brother is small in spirit, to say such things he does not know."

She shrugged. She thought about telling him her suspicion that the maiden had once pulled the balls of Loud Noise but decided not to retell an old tale that made Loud Noise seem even sorrier than he did already. "Brother," she said, "I am very happy that you choose to do this. I will be more pleased than you can imagine, to see you with a wife and children. And I do believe that She-Is-Favored is the right woman." She was looking up at his eyes now, and her own were shining, and the little wrinkles of smiling radiated from their corners. She put her hand on his wrist and said, "What has made you decide to do this now?"

He looked at the metal cup in which his tea was steaming. It was an army cup, from the battleground where Little Turtle had destroyed St. Clair's army six years ago. It was a good and durable item, one of those white men's artifacts that made a woman's chores easier, and she treasured it for its usefulness, but he still somehow did not like to drink or eat from metal. He thought for a while, then said, "I have thought of many matters since the chiefs marked the treaty and turned themselves into dogs in the white man's yard. Now, I see, only we are the true Shawnees, we who came here to keep the old ways.

"And so, if we in this band are the only true Shawnees anymore, should we not multiply and grow? Oh, as I have told you many times, this is not a happy world for children to come into, and I still say so. But should I not have sons and daughters who will grow up as proud and free as our People used to be? Should there not be more of us who are *not* under the foot of the white men?"

She smiled. "That is so, my brother. I am glad that you are at last looking at it from this side."

He nodded. Then he said, "I have also decided that the wedding will be in the old manner. Not like yours, a mating after a frolic dance."

She compressed her lips. Rarely, but sometimes, her brother could make her angry. Like this. Once he had decided something, he talked as if anything else could not be right. In her mind, her marriage to Stands Firm had been as sacred as the old manner, for the tribe had come to accept that as a way of marrying. And it had been a good marriage in all ways since. She thought of mentioning the girls he had lived with unmarried here and there. But she did not retort, because she too believed that it *would* be good to resume some of the customs from the old days, those times before the coming of the whites had unsettled the People and loosened their morals. She understood why Tecumseh wanted to change back to those very spiritual customs. It was just that he had not said it in a very good way. So she told him, "It will be good to see you wed as our father and mother were. And I will pray to Weshemoneto that your marriage will be as long and good as has mine, which came from a mating dance."

She saw in his face that he was abashed, as he deserved to be, and with a rush of tenderness she understood why she had felt the sadness and anger at first. There were words for the two kinds of love. *Tap-a-lot* was the love between adults and children, between brothers and sisters, between members of the tribe and relatives, between great friends, even between leaders and followers, like that which Tecumseh had had for Chiksika, like that which Thick Water had for Tecumseh. Like that which she herself had for Tecumseh. It was the biggest kind of love in the world. *Soos* was the kind of love men and women have for each other, in which they yearn for each other and get their bodies together. *Soos* was just a little part of *tap-a-lot*, but at times it could seem greater and stronger, as when you danced with the person you wanted and gave him the signal of your bare hand and did not care who saw or what they thought. And sometimes your *tap-a-lot* for someone was so great and so complete that you did not want anyone else to give him *soos.*

That was how she had felt, she understood that now.

Change-of-Feathers, believed to be the oldest man in the nation, he who had seen the coming and going of more than a hundred summers, sprinkled tobacco dust on the bed of embers in front of the beautiful young man and woman. As the smoke curled upward around his silvered head toward the vent in the roof, he prayed in a voice dry as husks:

"Weshemoneto, Master of Life, father of Our Creator, of all the sky and waters and world! The smoke of the *nilu famu* carries our prayer to you. Weshemoneto, who create by your thought, bless what we do here and make this one of the best days in the whole time of the South Wind People!"

The folds of skin over his eyelids were so creased and loose that his eyes were almost hidden. His face, once so round and grandmotherly, was gaunt, sunken by toothlessness. From the jutting cheekbones his skin hung in wattles. A heavy necklace of bear teeth and a breastplate of quills looked as if their weight would drag him to earth. Loud Noise, formerly his student, looked at him from behind Tecumseh and wondered if he would ever die and make a place for another shaman.

Star Watcher knelt on the floor near the place where the bride stood, and as she looked up at the old medicine man her heart quaked with reverence. It was said by the Singers that the Master of Life was so old that, if he were not invisible, he would be beautiful. Change-of-Feathers was almost beautiful in his great age like that, she thought.

The voice of the ancient grew stronger and more resonant in the Great House of Tecumseh's town, where the old man had been brought on a travois to perform this marriage. "Here is Shooting Star, whose destiny you have foretold to us. You see him. You know the good he has done. You direct the good he has yet to do. He is worthy. Here beside him is She-Is-Favored, a maiden who is good to her old father. You see her. She is worthy. These two are worthy of each other. We ask that you find them worthy of your blessing.

"Now witness, Great Good Spirit. He will cover her against the cold and draw her to him, to show that she will be only for him, and that he will protect her against all harm."

Loud Noise unfolded a fine-tanned deerhide, soft and pale as a morning cloud, and gave it to Tecumseh, who then draped it across his own shoulders and hers. She was trembling, this bold and quick woman who once had challenged him on the field of play combat; she was trembling, and her eyes were wet with joy. His heart was suddenly so swollen with his feelings that he groaned to keep from weeping.

"You are my wife," he murmured in her ear.

"*Niwy sheena,* you are my husband!" she gasped.

Loud Noise, who could remember how she looked naked by a stream in the morning sunlight, sighed with miserable envy. His bandanna was tied low over the right side of his face to hide his empty eyesocket. Now for a moment in the midst of this sacred beauty he felt so ugly that his heart hurt. He had a lewd thought, that this woman might someday yank her husband's balls. This made him smile, a lopsided smile rendered more lewd by his stringy fringe of mustache. Loud Noise was the only man in the village with hair on his lip. He could not bear to pluck the hairs out or let his wife do it; it made his face twitch and his nose run and his eyes water and caused fits of sneezing, so he had a mustache—just another one of his strangenesses.

He became aware then that Change-of-Feathers was looking at him—or seemed to be; his eyes were hidden in pouches of wrinkles—and the old one did not look pleased. Surely he sees inside my head, Loud Noise thought, and knows what I was thinking about. He squirmed and tried to assume an expression of piety and happiness. He wondered if he would ever have the power to see into people's souls. His doubt made him sigh again.

Star Watcher was looking up at her brother and his bride. Light from the roof seemed to shimmer on their glossy black hair. Inside the soft deerhide together, they were in their *soos.* She was excluded from that, as she knew she should be. But she could feel the greater love, the *tap-a-lot,* surrounding all the People in the Great House and the village around it. It was as if the Great Good Spirit held a vast, warm, soft robe around everybody, and Star Watcher, a woman of nearly forty summers of work and grief and giving, felt young and happy. *She is always happy,* her father had used to say of her. And that had been true, it seemed, despite the troubles of her People. She was doing well at watching over her brother the Shooting Star, so she was happy in his happiness.


There were said to be—so women would giggle as they talked in the menstrual hut—there were said to be a few fortunate women who carried such passion in their loins that they could start coming down inside just by thinking and flexing. And She-Is-Favored was one like that. Since she had fallen in love with Tecumseh, she had had those moments of inner brightness several times while sitting alone, dreaming of him and rocking on her hips.

Now there had come a time when there was no line between what was dreamed and what was touchable, and on the bed in his lodge by firelight they coupled again and again, anointing each other with musky juices and sweat, slowly at first and then quickening, with the cries of excitement clamped in their throats, galloping finally into the joyous spasms. She felt as if she must turn herself inside out upon him. Again and again they became a single being. Behind his eyes he saw glowing, warm, shapeless dreams.

At last, her hair wet with sweat, sweat drying on her copper skin in the night-cooling air long after midnight, she went to sleep.

Tecumseh lay with his head propped on the heel of his hand, leaning on his elbow, feeling the flames of their *soos* diminish to coals in his tingling groin, wondering and glad, watching her sleep with the little pout on her lips, watching her brown, small-nippled breasts rise and fall with breathing, watching the dim light gleam along the length of her naked body, feeling reverence for the creator of man and woman. Lying there wakeful but languorous, he remembered how his mother would tell that story: *And this time Our Grandmother remembered to give them their genitals, which they found to be very interesting.* He smiled, remembering those words. At this moment he

was happier than he had ever been since the dreamlike days of his childhood. He was complete now; he was one with a woman who was as beautiful and fertile as Earth the Mother.

Soon his eyes were not seeing and his head dropped forward, awakening
him. Somewhere out in the darkness, where before only the barred owl had
been screaming, people were screaming.

Wide awake at once, he rose and put on his breechcloth and slipped his
feet into moccasins. Several people were screaming out in the night. In an
instant he had primed his rifle, snatched up his war club, and sped out into
the night, as swift and silent as a breath of wind. People were stirring in
the doorways of their *wigewas,* their voices querying as he went by. Could
the Long Knives be coming? The Treaty of Greenville had said there would
be total peace forever.

Tecumseh had not roused the village because he did not think it was
Long Knives coming. The disturbance was down near the stream, beyond
the ceremonial ground. And there were no white men involved in it—only
the white man's curse. Tecumseh could smell the whiskey in the air even
before he reached the screaming people.

A knot of them were screaming like demons, staggering and shoving
each other around in the light of a bonfire. A whiskey keg sat open. In the
mud and grass a few men, and two naked women, lay unconscious. One of
the women was asleep under a sleeping man. Some men simply sat in the
grass, their faces stupefied, shrieking for no apparent reason other than their
drunkenness. A few warriors in the milling mob were waving knives at each
other. Near the edge of the stream Loud Noise lay facedown in his own
vomit.

With an angry bellow, Tecumseh charged into the clearing, knocking
men down as he came. He went straight to the keg, and before the bleary-
eyed men could gather their wits, he kicked it into the bonfire and a
*whoosh*ing flame billowed up, getting the attention of even the wildest
screamers.

"No!" he roared, spinning to face them. At a flick of his arm, his war
club knocked a knife from the hand of a swaying, whining, slobbering
young warrior.

He cried to all of them: "This is the white man's poison to make us weak
and stupid! Look at each other! Are you not poisoned? Where did this come
from? Do you think we want this poison here?"


It was several hours before everything was back in order. Some of the men
had to be carried to their homes. Two who had been cut with knives had

to be patched up. One very young man was found unconscious in the woods, where he had fallen down a rocky bank and broken some ribs; he stank, and his breechcloth was full of his own waste. It was the first time this youth had ever had whiskey, and it had hit him exceptionally hard. The women were wives of two men who were away hunting, and they had drunkenly fornicated with three or four of the revelers before passing out, and then many others had lain upon them while they were unconscious, so there would be much trouble ahead about that. The whiskey, he learned, had been bought from several white men who went from village to village with kegs loaded on their packhorses.

"I told those white men," Tecumseh warned, "that I will kill them if they try to sell their poison again near our town." There would have to be a discussion of this problem in the next council, of course, and Tecumseh knew it would be a delicate matter to judge over, particularly since his own brother was one of the worst of the addicts. The council could decree that anyone who wanted to drink whiskey should be sent away to one of the towns of white men's Indians. But for several reasons he did not want that solution. First, it would mean banishing his own brother, who was the shaman of this town; second, there were so few warriors left who were not under the treaty chiefs, and Tecumseh did not want his core of followers decreased by this kind of trouble. The way to strengthen and purify the true Shawnees was to make them spurn the whiskey poison, to make them yearn for something better, not to make drunken outcasts of them.

And so these were the worries he had as he returned to his lodge before dawn, exhausted. When he stretched out in the gloom with a long sigh beside She-Is-Favored, thinking she was asleep, she startled him with a light slap on his mouth, and he sat upright, slightly angered by this slap because of the problems on his mind. She complained, in a voice that sounded only half-teasing:

"Bad husband! You left your wife still hot in our bed."

"I am sorry. I had to go. Some of the people were in trouble with whiskey."

She was quiet for a moment, then said: "What did you do?"

"I threw it in the fire."

"Oh! They'll not like you for that!"

"I did it to help them. Are you saying I should not have done it?"

"Whiskey costs them much, and you threw it away."

He looked at her silhouette in the gray light before the dawn, and he was not pleased to hear what she was saying. *"Neewa,"* he said, "you did not see how they were hurting themselves and each other, nor the fat women doing adultery in their stupor. Maybe you do not understand how bad whiskey is."

"Husband, is it so bad for the People to enjoy themselves that you must leave your new wife alone and go out to stop their pleasures?"

Tecumseh gasped. "Cutting each other with knives is not pleasure! Screaming with your head full of devils is not enjoyment! Listen! My People are weak and foolish about whiskey, and my People are in my hands. You were asleep from a better kind of pleasure. Why should you complain that I went to help them?"

After a pause of silence, her voice came softer. "I woke up wanting you to do it to me again. I was sorry and afraid because you were not here."

Those words, even as exhausted and upset as he was, at once made his *passah-tih* start to harden and his heart to soften, and he looked at her dark eye-sockets and started to reach with his hand to touch her belly. But she said:

"I am cold. Put a blanket on me."

He sighed, gathered his weary legs under him, and got up to get it. Perhaps if he had not been so tired and unsettled, he would have known better than to sigh at a woman's request. When he got the blanket and spread it over her nakedness, she did not thank him. He was still too warm for the blanket, so he lay down outside it. Outdoors, some of the dawn birds were starting to chirp, and in the distance a dog began to bark. He could hear voices here and there in the village. Already people were waking up, and no doubt they were talking about the whiskey trouble and about their chief's wedding night and about other things that concerned him. It was not likely that he would get to sleep any before morning, and he felt weak, drained by their excess of abandon the night before.

And although She-Is-Favored seemed not to want to copulate right now, apparently she did not want to sleep, either, for she began talking into the rushing of the fatigue in his head.

"Who were the women doing the adultery?" she asked.

No, he thought, groaning. I pray that she is not one of those women hungry for bad gossip. Gossip about other people was one of the most despicable offenses against Shawnee law.

"Why do you make that groan?" she demanded. "I only asked you something."

"I do not wish to talk about who it was. It will be dealt with when their husbands return. I need to sleep now."

She let out a sharp breath. "These People of yours took you out of our bed for their silly problems," she snapped. "I deserve to have your attention now."

He sat up suddenly, appalled. *"Neewa,"* he said, keeping his voice low so his neighbors would not know he was angry with his bride already. "Whiskey is not a *silly* problem. It is one of the worst of the many evils the whitefaces have brought. It is as bad as the coughing sickness they give us.

It is as bad as burning our towns and destroying our grain. Let me advise you, *neewa,* not to be selfish with my time. You are just one of the People who are in my care!" This, he realized at once, was a hard statement, even though a truth, so he added, "You are the most important of them. But they too are mine, and their care will need my time." It crossed his mind that some people called her a spoiled woman, as her name implied. For one tired, exasperated moment he wondered whether he should have followed his own wisdom and stayed unmarried. Then he chastised himself. He reminded himself of the truth that if a person says and does wrong, it is because of a lack of understanding. And so, patiently and with tenderness returning in his heart, he said, to help her understand:

"We in this village are the last hope of the Shawnee People. We must do good. We must be strong. We must not let the white men make us corrupt. These People of ours are good. They were brave to come here with me. You yourself were brave to come here with me. We must keep our People pure. They have weaknesses, and we must help them conquer their weaknesses. We must pray to Weshemoneto and ask him to see us as good and strong and pure People. That is because what Weshemoneto sees is what is. If he sees us pure and good and strong, we will *be* pure and good and strong. All this you know from before, but now there is also this you must know:

"I am my People. And since you have chosen to be my wife, you are these People, too. Just as I must care for their needs, so must you. You are the women's chief now. As my time and strength and wisdom belong to the People, so do yours. You are not alone anymore. You cannot think only of yourself. Listen to the people out there." Outside the bark walls there were all the sounds of a village stirring to life. Someone was breaking dry wood for the breakfast cookfire. Someone was soothing a fussy baby. Someone was whetting a knife on stone. Someone was laughing. Someone was grinding corn in a wooden mortar, humming. They were the beautiful sounds of peaceful life, and among them were the hushings of a light, mild wind in the leaves and the songs of birds. This was the peaceful music of life that he had heard as a child in his mother's lodge so many years ago before the white men had started coming, and it filled his heart with caring. "Hear them," he said to her softly. "Those are our children." He smiled at her. Her eyes were closed as if she were listening carefully and thinking deeply. "You have been a married woman only one night, and already you have hundreds of children!"

He had thought she would laugh or at least smile at this joke. Instead, a soft snore came from her throat.

She had fallen asleep.

As the next few months passed, Tecumseh spent much of the nighttime lying awake beside his sleeping wife. She seemed to need twice as much sleep as he did, but she did not want him to sit up by the fire or go out while she slept. He tried to please her by going to bed when she did, and often she would go to sleep with their *soos* juices seeping out of her *massih* and a smile on her face. Then she became pregnant, and even after they stopped copulating she still insisted that he must always be beside her when she was in bed. For a while this great needing of hers charmed and flattered him, and he would lie beside her feeling tender about her *tap-a-lot* for him and for the baby inside her. But he could not think about those things all the time, and sometimes he would think that this way of hers was a little selfish.

So now Tecumseh could not go out and seek solitude for thinking, as he had used to, not unless he wanted to hear her complain about being abandoned. And so these nights he lay beside a sleeping pregnant wife and tried to ponder on his dreams and his destiny.

All the dams against the flood of the Americans were broken, now that the old chiefs and the British had given up. Somehow, according to the signs of his own destiny, he was to build another dam. But how? He was only a warrior chief, of twenty and eight summers, chief of his own village only. He was Kispoko by birth, and by the old law of the People, only a Chalagawtha or a Thawegila Shawnee could be chief over the whole Shawnee nation.

He did not yet have his answer. But since he had started thinking about floods and dams, he had been considering the Beaver People and the way they dammed a flow. The answers to many things were in the ways of the animals, and even animals that were not one's Spirit Helper could teach.

No single beaver builds a dam. But many beavers, working together as if with a single will, build a dam that holds back a large and powerful stream. The answer lay in that single will of the many.

When Tecumseh was wakeful at night, his wife breathing softly beside him, he would lie looking into fire, or at stars beyond the roof, hearing the river's liquid song and the owl in the tree and the whippoorwill in its covert, and he would ponder on what needed to be said to make the many wills of the many tribes become the same—permanently the same, as the Beaver People are permanently the same in will—so they could build a dam and stop the flow.

He could think deeply of these things only at night now. As he had feared, having a wife kept him too busy to think, until she went to sleep.

Sometimes during the days, Star Watcher would come and try to talk to

She-Is-Favored about some of the little things the chief's wife should be thinking of and doing for the women. She was appalled when She-Is-Favored would say she had no time for this or that, that she was pregnant and too tired, or when she would lean toward Star Watcher with a languid smile and say, "Sister, could you do that for me instead?"

After this had happened a few times, Star Watcher began to fear that she had served her brother ill by approving of this woman. She began to notice that Tecumseh spent less and less time among the People, that he could not sit by the fire with Stands Firm or other subchiefs in the evenings, that those with problems could not find him out in the village and talk with him.

She thought: Perhaps he will grow wiser about handling this woman now that she is pregnant and cannot put his will to sleep with her pretty bottom. Maybe he will never make her a good chief's wife. But he must become a good chief again.


The next spring Breaker-in-Pieces came to Tecumseh's town, on his way home from a visit to Black Hoof's town at Wapakoneta.

"You would be sad to see him and his People," the Delaware chief said to Tecumseh. "Some of them wear white men's clothes. The men are plowing the ground." Breaker-in-Pieces was a fierce-looking warrior chief with a terrible scar and a missing ear on one side of his head, a man famed for keeping his word. He and his People were under the Greenville Treaty, too, but at least they had not yet begun to live like the white farmers, because they lived farther west, where there was still game.

Tecumseh shook his head slowly and looked down into the fire. After a while he said, "Do they like being white men?"

"They have little heart for it. But they try. They still believe Black Hoof when he says it is the only way for them. They try to be white. But for one thing, they do not know how to control whiskey like the white men yet, and there is much whiskey. I think the whites do not eat the corn they grow, I think they drink all of it."

Tecumseh looked over at him with pain in his eyes, and the Delaware went on: "They are crazy for it, and they are crazy from it. Anything they have, they give for it. Then they drink till it is gone. They vomit and scream and beat their families, and try to stab their brothers. Then they pass out. They wake up sick, in their own filth, and have nothing left but pain. Then they go to the trader store to get something to live by for a while, and the trader makes them promise him their tomorrows." He sat quiet, looking down in sadness.

She-Is-Favored waddled into the house to get a bowl and went out, saying nothing. She would be having her baby soon, and she was not happy with carrying its weight, or the shape of her body, or all the silly talk all the women always had about babies. And she was worried; women always warned her that having a baby hurt worse than anything. Also, she could not understand why the other women did not admire her more than they did, for she was the women's chief.

The main reason they did not admire her, even as much as they had used to, was because they could see that she troubled their chief. She nagged Tecumseh about the time he spent with the People's problems and because he gave to them so much of what he had. "You are the chief, I am your wife," she would complain, "but almost anyone in our town has more nice things than we have."

"What do you need that we do not have?" he would ask her, and she could not name anything they needed, though she could think of many things she wanted. Then she would get angry at him because he could point out the difference between needing and wanting. So she was sullen, even in the presence of their guest. Being of hot spirit, she gave off sparks from her eyes, not tears.

Breaker-in-Pieces said nothing to Tecumseh about her demeanor. It annoyed him, but it was none of his concern. Now he said, "I am glad my town is farther from the white man's roads. They do not come so close with their whiskey. Though even there, it disturbs us sometimes. A few of my young men have come to need it."

"We have had some trouble with it here," Tecumseh said.

"Yes. One day, I fear, it will ruin us all. But I have some distance from it, and from their hunters. Listen. Many of the chiefs have trouble already with the white men who come across the new treaty line and hunt in their country. The whitefaces kill more game than their own hunters kill. Then they leave much of the meat lying for the carrion birds." He shook his head.

"And so we see once more," Tecumseh said, "what the boundaries of a white man's treaty mean to a white man."

The Delaware put his hand on Tecumseh's arm, and in his scarred face there was an earnest light. "My son, what you do here, we think often of it, we who were pressed down to mark the treaty of Wayne. . . ." He paused, as if remembering something, then went on: "My villages on the Wah-pi-ha-ni, near the Great Mound—you know the place—this is a good land, my son, fertile, easy to defend, and not so close to the white man's roads. My People would be pleased if your People came to live nearby. . . ."

Tecumseh felt a great warmth. To receive an invitation like this, from another tribe, was an uncommon honor. He lowered his head. "Thank you.

My People revere our grandfathers, the Delawares. And you know my belief: we must all be united together as red men, or the whites will scatter us until like dust we will no longer be seen nor be able to see each other. In council next time I will tell my People what you have said." He paused, then said something he had not thought he could say. "I understand, Father, the great weight that pressed you down when you went to treat with Wayne. I know that many who put their marks on the treaty withheld their hearts."

The old chief nodded. "We grow sick now as we watch the white men come like a flood into the old lands. The boundaries are being forgotten already by the O-hi-o governor. St. Clair has made a new division he calls Wayne County, named for that general, and as I hear this land described, it is far outside their boundaries and into the land of our brothers, even the Auglaize, even to Mis-e-ken, I hear."

Tecumseh clenched his jaw. This was no surprise to him, but it churned him inside. For nearly half his life he had been fighting to hold back the white intruders, but it was apparent that the fight had only begun. And now the Delaware was saying:

"Here is another thing about Wayne. I hear that his aching sickness brought him down and down until, in the last Hard Moon, he died, in a fort in Pennsylvania, on his way home. He was a great war chief, even we whom he harmed must say he was great, but it would have been better if his aching sickness had taken him two years sooner, before he struck us at the Fallen Timbers."

"Ahh!" Tecumseh nodded. He sat quiet, remembering what a force Wayne had been in the fate of his People. Wayne had crushed the confederation "under his little finger," as his boast had said, then had forced the British to withdraw from Fort Miami, then out of Detroit into Canada. The British had been cowardly, and Tecumseh did not feel sorry for them. But their departure boded ill for the red men.

Wayne had done all that, and now Wayne was no more. His body lay dead in the earth somewhere, but what he had done was still here, and would continue, and in this way his spirit would never leave the red men in peace. "He, like Clark, was a mighty enemy, and he still hurts us," Tecumseh said. "May there never be another so great." But as he said this, the other officer's face came into his mind, the young one who had always been at Wayne's side. When Tecumseh thought of him, he felt a chill.

Then Breaker-in-Pieces, as if he had seen into Tecumseh's mind and glimpsed the young officer's face there, said, "Wayne's young chieftain, the one named Harrison. He grows very fast in importance for a man so young. He is now the chief of Fort Washington, by their big town of Cincinnati.

He has married a daughter of one of the biggest of the land buyers. This one man, called Symmes, has bought all the land between the Little Miami-se-pe and the Great Miami-se-pe, all the way up to Fort Hamilton."

Tecumseh remembered that area well from many hunting trips, and he gasped. "One man buys for himself a whole hunting ground!"

"Yes," said Breaker-in-Pieces.

"And then he says all of it is his!"

"Yes. And all the white people have to believe him."

"And then what does he do?" exclaimed Tecumseh, hardly knowing whether to laugh or cry at such a grandiose illusion. "Does he then tell the Great Good Spirit, 'You must get off of my land'? Is that what he does?"

The old chief's brutal face softened and creased with amusement. "Yes, that is what he says. And from what I have seen of white men's land, Weshemoneto does leave it. And he takes with him all his creatures, and all that made it good."

The two chiefs laughed at this. But their laughter was not light and pleasant. A deep foreboding loomed, and in its deepest shadow lurked the man named Harrison. There was something ominous in this: an ambitious white chieftain, rising fast, and associated by marriage with one of the great land-taking devils. The workings of the white man's society were an unimaginable mystery, but even from the outside this seemed to portend the worst sort of trouble.

And then Tecumseh said something that made the Delaware's eyes widen with surprise. "But the Great Spirit will come back with his creatures and make it a good land again," he said in a soft but certain voice, "when we return and make the white men leave it."


One day Star Watcher met She-Is-Favored at the spring, where both had gone for water.

One was not supposed to meddle in another's marriage, but Star Watcher put herself in the way of She-Is-Favored and made her meet her eyes and said, "Young sister, there is a cloud over your house. I see my brother drawn tight like a bow. This must not be. Are you the wrong woman for our chief?"

To Star Watcher's surprise, She-Is-Favored did not shut her out but looked as if she were hungry for a chance to speak of her troubles. "He stays away from the house, with the People, too much," she said.

"Yes. Is he not the chief?"

"Am I not the chief's wife?" she snapped.

"Listen. Some think you do not act like it. To both the chief and his wife, there is only the health and happiness of the People. Tecumseh gives all to that. You must, too."

"What of *my* health and happiness?"

"Sister, you have good health. You have all the food you need, for your husband is the best hunter. You wanted to be the wife of the chief, and you are. You wanted to have babies, and you are going to. If you are unhappy, it must be from holding everything to yourself." She reached for her hand and told her the old teaching: "When you give from your heart, your heart grows lighter. I hope you will learn the joy of giving from your heart to the People. As the wife of the chief, that is what you are for."

But the face of She-Is-Favored did not show that she understood.


When it was agreed in the next council that it would be good to go farther from the white men and become neighbors of the Delaware, Loud Noise was sent to locate a favorable townsite on the Wah-pi-ha-ni, which was the Delaware name for White River. The shaman was always the one who determined whether the medicine of a place was good. The tribe would move after the harvest.

Through all this planning, She-Is-Favored grew closer to her term and ever darker in spirit. She complained that she did not want to go farther away west from her home country.

"Just so do we all feel," Tecumseh exclaimed, "but the whites move us despite our wishes. Do you not remember that half the nation long ago had to move beyond the Great River? Compared with what they had to do, this is not far, to the White River."

But she argued and was still arguing when the baby started to come down. Then she stopped complaining long enough to groan with the labor. Tecumseh sent for Star Watcher to help her. His sister acted very happy for him, then told him to go someplace else. "For once she will not want you right here," she said. "So go, and enjoy your freedom to walk around." He went, but his mind was in a turmoil.

She-Is-Favored had ruined for him the proud, tender anticipation of fatherhood. Their marriage had become a relentless, unwanted burden because of her selfishness, her unwillingness to give any time or attention to the People. Many spoke of her as a nosy-mouth, which was their word for a gossip. She had not had a smile for him in months. After a hunt she would insist that he not give so much of the meat or so many of the skins to the old people. But she would not even tan the skins he did keep for her. She was a spoiled woman who would not listen to teaching and seemed not to want to understand anything important, and Tecumseh feared that their child would grow up in a house of silent thunder and become unhappy. Maybe she would choose to leave him and return to her Peckuwes. Probably that would be the best thing. But then what about this baby?

While he was pondering this problem, he was also beginning to watch for any sign of the baby's *unsoma.* He watched the sky and birds; he listened for sounds. As the wait went on there was nothing remarkable. The day was oppressive and still; nothing moved or announced its singularity. The sky was overcast but with no feel of rain, and thus there were not even any shadows to make suggestions.

At last an old midwife came to tell him the child was born and well, and was a boy, and She-Is-Favored was also well.

When Tecumseh went into the *wigewa,* the room still full of the moist musk of childbirth, she actually smiled at him, and he wondered if mothering might soften her, make her more giving, as motherhood tended to do. Perhaps his worries about the marriage had been unnecessary. She lay bared to the ribs, the dark, almost purple, animallike little creature squirming on her arm. Her breasts were swollen large. Tecumseh knelt and put his hand on her forehead. Her hair was damp. He looked closely at the baby, smiling with tender wonderment at all its tiny perfections: jointed fingers no bigger than flower buds, ears no wider than a man's thumb, the little sprig of a *passah-tih* between his legs. Here it was as from the very beginnings, and for this moment Tecumseh did not worry that it was not a good time to be born. The baby outfaced all portents. The pungent room was a sacred place.

"Thank you for what you have done," Tecumseh said.

She let him press his cheek against hers and felt the wetness of a tear.


When the time came for the baby to begin suckling, Tecumseh was there watching. Having seen no *unsoma* sign yet, he had been idly thinking that somehow the infant might acquire a name associated, like his own, with the Panther.

It was night. Now the child, as if suddenly finding the milk-turgid breast beside him for the first time, squirmed violently, grabbed for it with both hands, and tried to stuff the whole mammary into his gaping mouth.

Tecumseh laughed. "He should be called The-Panther-Seizes-His-Prey!"

And so that—Neh-tha-weh-nah or Cat Pouncing—became the baby's name.

Soon the maternal languor wore off, and She-Is-Favored began using the baby to put more pressure on Tecumseh. Now that she had gone to such effort to bear him this perfect baby, she did not feel obliged to do much of anything else, even though she was up and about. And she mentioned many pretty little things she had long wanted from the white men's store near the Auglaize: a new mirror, a certain kind of earbobs which, she thought, would delight the baby as they dangled from her ears above him . . . The list of wants grew every time she spoke.

"The white men's store is an evil place," Tecumseh said. "It is the place of whiskey and debt. Look, the gifts our own women make are more beautiful."

She clamped her mouth shut and glowered at him. "Do you mean to say we will never trade at the white men's store?"

"Only for true needs," he said. "And then it will be a British store, not the American. Their goods are better, and their cost is more fair. And though they amount to little as friends, at least they are not enemies."

She-Is-Favored expected all the women of the town to come and pay homage to her now that she had borne the chief this wonderful son. But those who did come she found tiresome, because they wanted to talk about their own mothering as much as hers. And two women had had the effrontery to suggest that she should change the down in the baby's bundle sooner and more often. Soon her laziness became so great and her tongue so abrasive that one evening Tecumseh lost his temper and grabbed her by the shoulders. He did this to make her look in his eyes, because it was time to blow the mist from her vision and make her see clearly. She reacted not as a mate in a quarrel, but as if she were once again, as of old, out on the ball ground. She clenched her teeth, shook her hair, and kicked Tecumseh hard on the ankle. Astonished, he tightened his grip on her shoulders and shook her. "Listen to me!" he hissed.

But she was not going to listen. Suddenly, teeth bared, she snatched with a quick, strong right hand at his genitals, grabbing the knot of them and his breechcloth and starting to twist and pull.

The pain was blinding, but Tecumseh shoved her to arm's length so powerfully that her grip was torn loose, and he held her there while his vision came back and he gasped for breath. She struggled against his iron grip until she was too tired to move, then slumped there, hair disheveled, glowering at him, panting, sneering. And he said:

"Woman, you chose me as your husband. I have tried to be a good husband. I have never hurt you, even when you were so insolent that another man would have beaten you. Our People need a women's chief, but you are too selfish to serve them. For a long time you have shown that your heart is not with mine. Now you have shown me that you want to hurt me." He paused, to let her deny this if she would. She simply glared, her lips drawn, and tried to shrug off his hands. He let her loose and stepped back. "This being so," he went on, "I will spare us any more pain and anger. I give you whatever you want from this house. You are free to go. Since I am not the husband you want, I am not your husband." And, with a long sigh both of disappointment and relief, he said, "I will still provide for our little boy. If you grow even too lazy to tend to him, I will put him in my sister's care." He stood staring at her firmly, showing neither his anger nor his regret. Her angry expression was dissolving into disbelief, as if she had thought he would take any abuse she gave and now had learned, too late, that she had pushed him beyond the limit. He said, "Tomorrow I will load horses for you and have someone ride with you to your Peckuwes on the Auglaize. You may explain this to people in your own way, but be truthful. As for me, I will not speak of it to anyone. It is just one of those lessons one learns as he makes the round of his lifetime. *We-pe-the,*" he said.

Go.


Here it stood, Tecumseh thought, stopping his horse among the weeds and sumac and berry brambles and looking around, then down at the mound of ashes and blackened stones. Exactly here.

He dismounted among the scarlet leaves and dry weed stalks, his rifle in the crook of his arm, knelt at the old fire-ring where he had warmed himself so many hundreds of cold nights in his boyhood. There was nothing left of the bark or poles of his mother's lodge. They had long since rotted away into the ground. The lodge was whole and intact in his memory, every detail of it, but it did not exist here anymore. The air was hazy with woodsmoke, but no longer from the cookfires of old Chillicothe. The white farmers in this beautiful valley used fire to burn slash and to kill the big trees as they cleared land for their farms. In the distance Tecumseh could hear an axe chopping, and its echoes returned from the bluff beside the river. Years of rains had dissolved much of the ash in the old fire-ring and washed it down. He picked up a stained, blackened shard, and he could remember the bowl it once had been, from which he had eaten a thousand times. And here was a piece of stag horn his mother had used to drive with a mallet to split firewood. There, where the little boys had slept, was pale bone: a copperhead's skull that Loud Noise had found, treasured for years, then lost. It was packed full of dirt. Probably it had been pressed into the ground under the bedding long ago, then slowly uncovered again by rains after the *wigewa* rotted away. Tecumseh smiled wistfully, remembering how Loud

Noise had cried and cried after its disappearance. It had been one of his shaman toys. I shall return it to him, he thought, palming it. Then he stiffened.

Someone was behind him. He heard leggings brushing through weeds. It would be a white man, of course. His nerves grew taut, and he prepared himself to move fast.

Turning his head slightly, he caught the figure in the corner of his eye: a man in a hat, perhaps thirty paces away. Pretending not to have seen him yet, Tecumseh cocked the hammer of his flintlock, easing it and muffling it with his hand. He calculated that if he whirled to his left as he rose, his horse would be between him and the white man. He tensed to jump up. But at that moment the man's deep voice spoke: "Hello?"

The tone of the voice was pleasant, and Tecumseh knew that was one of the friendly words of the white man's tongue. He paused, then stood up instead of jumping up, but when he turned, his rifle barrel was aimed at the man.

But only for an instant. The man held a rifle, too, but it was cradled in the crook of his left arm, and he was holding his right hand up, palm forward, the sign that he would not strike. Tecumseh uncocked his rifle, lowered the muzzle, and looked at the man, who was big and solid, a man in his prime years, with a rugged brown face. He was somebody Tecumseh had seen before, he was sure of that, someone he had seen long ago. If the man had been a red man, he might well have been a chief; there was something unusually strong and calm and wise about his face. This man did not look like Boone; his face was more round, chin more pointed, but there was something about him that seemed like Boone. He and Tecumseh looked at each other for nearly a full minute, and in that time Tecumseh put the face where he had first seen it: one of the scouts of Clark, riding past the ambush place, on the day when Tecumseh the boy had run from his first battle. The memory of that awful day whirled through his mind, and he was surprised that he remembered a face from a moment like that.

Now the white man began moving his hands for a greeting in sign language. But Tecumseh said, "I know your tongue."

"Ah!" The man's face brightened with a strong, gap-toothed smile. Then he came to Tecumseh and extended his right hand. Tecumseh did not take it and still showed nothing in his face. The white man lowered his hand, but despite this rebuff kept a pleasant expression and said, "My name is Galloway." Then he raised his hand again, to sweep it over a part of the overgrowth that had once been Chillicothe, and said, "This is my land."

"Ga-lo-weh," Tecumseh said. Then he pointed over the same field. "My name is Tecumseh. This is *my* land." And he smiled, his teeth a startling white in his russet face. It was a brilliant smile, but the eyes were not smiling. Though this white man made an admirable impression and seemed unafraid, he was, after all, a white man, specifically one of the old invaders, and he had been audacious enough to call the old Shawnee homesite *his* land. He could not have said a worse thing to Tecumseh at any time, and particularly now, when Tecumseh had just been revisiting the old town in his soul.

Perhaps the man realized it now; his eyes fell for an instant, and he bowed his head slightly. He said, "I am sorry, Tecumseh." The man looked him in the eyes, then let his gaze wander over the field. "It was a beautiful place for a town, a beautiful town. I'm sure you were sad to leave it. I came back because I had never seen a better place."

Tecumseh looked hard into the man's eyes. "You saw Chillicothe sometime before."

The man sighed, and there was long remembering in his eyes as he looked. Then he said, "Do you know the name of Clark?" He saw the Indian's eyes flash, the single curt nod. Tecumseh picked up the explanation and finished it:

"You were one of the scouts in front of Clark."

The man's blue eyes widened in surprise. "Yes. In eighty-two, the second time he came here. How did you know?"

"Once you rode past my gun. I could have shot."

"Thank the Lord ye didn't!" He was still for a moment, then said, "Your people had left the town burning."

"Yes. Cata-he-cassa."

"Cata-he-cassa?"

"Black Hoof. Was chief in that time. Said burn towns." Tecumseh had not spoken the white man's tongue for several years, since Big Fish had left, and it was hard to remember some ways of saying things. Now the white man replied:

"Black Hoof. Yes. He is still your chief, isn't he?"

"Not my chief. For some Shawnee, Black Hoof is chief. For the others . . ." He touched himself on the chest. "Tecumseh chief."

"Ah, I see," the white man said, obviously intrigued by this statement. "Then you don't live at Wapakoneta?"

"That way, far," Tecumseh said, pointing west. Then he decided he was telling more than he needed to tell this white man.

"Well, then," Galloway said, "if you came a long way, you might be hungry? Thirsty? My house is over yonder." He pointed toward the yellowing woods, toward the river. The axe was still striking wood there. "Would you come to eat with my family?"

Tecumseh hesitated. It was hard not think that he was talking with an enemy, and the enemy was inviting him to come into his lodge. But finally he said, "Tecumseh might. When will Ga-lo-weh's family eat?"

A smile spread on the white man's face. "Before the sun goes down. You'll hear a bell."

"Bell?" Tecumseh remembered bells, little brass or bronze or iron bells the traders sold, to hang on horses' necks or on dancers' legs.

"I'll ring a bell to call my sons in from work, and then you come, if you will. I'll be proud to have you at table. I'll be proud to have you meet my family." He paused. "If your family's with you, bring them."

"No family of Tecumseh." With a twinge of remorse, he thought of She-Is-Favored and the baby Cat Pouncing. But he did not mention them.

"Please do come," Galloway said, and he extended his hand again.

This time Tecumseh took it, and in spite of himself he liked its warmth and strength.


For the rest of the afternoon, Tecumseh had sat among the trees on the riverside, studying the house of the man called Ga-lo-weh. It was a strong house of thick, hewn logs, two stories high. The house stood a few hundred paces from the river, in a clearing studded with tree stumps. Tecumseh had seen a woman come out of the house once and carry a pail inside. He had seen a tall, muscular boy come in from a field south of the house, carrying an axe. The boy had put the axe down. Then he had gone down the path to the river's edge and washed himself and returned to the house and gone inside. Two or three times a little yellow-haired girl of about six or seven years had come down from the house to fetch water. One of those times she had been singing, and Tecumseh had heard her voice faintly over the distance. Tecumseh had watched the house so carefully because he was having a very hard time deciding what to do about Ga-lo-weh's invitation.

Now the man came in from somewhere. He too went to the river's edge and washed his face and arms. Then he went up into the house, and after a while he came back out and put his hand under the iron bell and made it clang. The noise startled Tecumseh and hurt his ears. It did not sound like the little bells of the traders. It had a loud clang, which rang on in the ears after every stroke. Tecumseh winced at its harsh noise. But he could understand the use of such a strong iron voice. Surely it could be heard for miles.

Before long, then, three more boys came in from the distant fields, carrying tools. The youngest of them seemed no more than ten, but he looked as if he too had been working very hard. On a breeze Tecumseh could smell meat cooking.

All the afternoon, Tecumseh had been thinking that he should not go and eat with the white people, who were here, wrongly to Tecumseh's mind, on Shawnee land. In earlier days, in the south with the Cherokees, he had watched families from cover like this, and sometimes he had shot the men and boys, and then with the warriors he had gone down and killed their cattle and taken their horses, and set fire to their houses, and tied the terrified women up and taken them to the Cherokee towns. It was strange to be watching them like this and not attacking. These people were intruders not on the distant lands of his Cherokee brothers, but on the very land where his own town had stood. This very man had been one of the scouts for the dreaded Long Knife Clark. This man had had a part in the destruction of Chillicothe and Piqua. Tecumseh was now the chief of the Shawnees who were still hostile to the Long Knives, and he wondered why he even considered going to their house to eat. And yet . . .

And yet, now for the first time in many years, the smell of cooking and the sounds of family voices, singing and talking, drifted over the vacancy where Chillicothe had been. This man and his family were making lives and foods grow here. This man Ga-lo-weh seemed somehow to believe that he had a right to be here and thus was not doing wrong in his own mind. It was therefore hard to blame him as a man.

Now the man appeared in the doorway of the house, his face ruddy in the late afternoon sunlight, one hand on either side of the jamb, looking around slowly. Tecumseh knew the man was looking for him. The man really was expecting him to come.

After a while the man shook his head and went back into the darkness of the doorway. Tecumseh withdrew to the thicket where he had tethered his horse and swung onto its back. He kneed the animal and rode westward into the woods, away from the log house, relieved that he had not gone there but for some reason a little sad, a little lonely, even.

He was not far into the woods when he heard the bell again.

And he knew that the man Ga-lo-weh had rung it for him.

Tecumseh reined in his horse. He gave a little puff of air out through his nostrils, both a sigh and a voiceless laugh, and shook his head.

Then, to his own surprise, he turned the horse and rode back toward the log house.

The white woman and boys at first were wide-eyed with awe and seemed frightened. They hung back behind Ga-lo-weh as he told Tecumseh their names. The oldest son was named George, after his grandfather, the second James, after his father, the third William, and the fourth Samuel, after other relatives, and the yellow-haired girl was named Rebekah, after her own mother. She was missing some front teeth. Except for her father, the girl was the only one of the family who did not seem to be afraid of Tecumseh. She simply stared at him, her sky-colored eyes full of admiration. Tecumseh repeated each name and smiled as the introductions were made.

James Galloway seemed very proud to have brought a genuine Shawnee chief home to supper. He was making quite an impression on his family. They had seen Indians before, of course. Formerly from Pennsylvania, they had settled in Kentucky during the war. They had never had a chief as a guest, however, nor seen one who gave such a pleasing impression or one of such graceful power. His tunic and leggings were of clean, soft, fringed deerskin. His moccasins and the edging of his breechcloth were decorated with delicate quillwork in red and white. These garments had assumed the shape of his physique, so the depth of his chest and muscularity of his shoulders were very evident to these people who did their work by muscle. Now just a little over thirty, Tecumseh was all force and dignity. His hair, unbraided, parted in the middle, raven black, hung to his shoulders. Around his head he wore a red silk band, on whose left side was attached a swiveling bird-bone socket into which a single eagle feather had been inserted. In the septum of his nose was a small silver ring from which hung three tiny silver crosses; to this little piece of jewelry the family's eyes kept straying. In his simple but beautiful garments, with his erect posture and candid gaze, Tecumseh looked to these people as graceful and elegant as a lord. James Galloway's father had been Speaker of the Pennsylvania Assembly, so he and his wife were familiar with fancy and important men, but no one in their memory, in velvet or lace, had so drawn the eye. Except for a crooked thigh that made him look a little bow-legged, this Shawnee was perhaps the most beautiful specimen of a man the family had ever beheld. And there also hung about him the aura of the dangerous savage. Sheath knife and blood-darkened war club were part of his costume. He was of another world, heathen and frightening.

They watched him as he gazed about the big room and took note of the unfamiliar interior: the huge fireplace at one end with its kettle arms and oven, the trestle table with its chairs and pewter, the hewn-log joists so low overhead that he tended to stoop as he moved under them.

And then he saw the shelves of books, and a look of childlike incredulity transformed his calm countenance. He turned, all but gasping, to Galloway, and exclaimed, "So many of books! I never did know there are so many!" An entire corner was filled with shelves of books.

Galloway beamed with more pride. "Probably the best library this side of the mountains, that's what. They've been a load to carry about, but I'd not go anyplace without my books. Even Gen'l Clark didn't have such a library, and how *that* man loves to read."

"What is this, 'li-ba-lelly'?" It was a hard word to say.

"Library is . . . well, many books in one place we call a library. So you know books, even?" Galloway was becoming more and more intrigued with his Shawnee guest.

"I know Bible. I know of Hamlet Prince and the"—he quickly searched his memory for Big Fish's word—"the skull."

Galloway's eyes were wide. "Skull? You mean . . ."

"Ah . . . skull from Poor York."

"Alas, poor Yorick!" Galloway exclaimed, posing as if talking to a skull in his outstretched hand. "I knew him . . ." Galloway's face was glowing with excitement, and his children were covering their smiles with their hands.

"You knew this York?" Tecumseh asked in amazement, and the children laughed out loud. And while Galloway was trying to explain what he meant, Mrs. Galloway was shaking her head.

"Mercy!" she said. "I'll never get you two gents apart now!"

And thus Tecumseh began one of the most interesting evenings of his life, as did Galloway and his family. The family prayed before eating, then sat respectfully for another minute as Tecumseh prayed to Weshemoneto in his own tongue. During the dinner, Galloway fully explained to Tecumseh the tenets of his Scotch Associate religion, after which Tecumseh told of the Shawnee cosmology. He then spoke of the nation's elaborate moral code, of which Galloway had never heard or even suspected, though he had known and fought Shawnees for years. These plainly were no soulless savages after all. Galloway was impressed by the degree to which the Shawnees' reverence pervaded all their mundane activities.

Then Galloway spent an hour telling of the fervent revivalism that had lately been sweeping through the frontier: of Shakers, of Baptists and Methodists and evangelists of many kinds, of great gatherings of men, women, and children falling, rolling, flopping, and shouting with religious frenzy. "The bloodiest sinners are being turned into lambs of God," he exclaimed. "These are portentous times. Many, many are preparing for the end of the world!"

Tecumseh then told an astonished Galloway of some of the religious upheavals and witch hunts and spirit societies that had swept through various Indian nations in recent decades, since the approach of the white men into the Middle Ground. Only as he talked of it did Tecumseh begin to realize how much of it must be due to the disruption of the old ways. He did not say it to the Galloways, but he understood that the white men were the reason for most of the spiritual confusion of the Lakes tribes, that this was another evil that swept in ahead of the white people.

As the evening wore on and the discussion ranged over the whole frontier, Galloway told Tecumseh more about Clark, whom Galloway still deemed the greatest white man west of the mountains, despite his penchant for strong drink, and Tecumseh had the strange experience of seeing a demon of an enemy transformed in his own imagination to a noble, God-fearing warrior of great vision and humanity.

They spoke then of Boone and But-lah. Tecumseh told of his acquaintance with them, and the Galloways were astonished at some of the coincidences—that Boone had for a time been Tecumseh's own foster brother, that Tecumseh had fought But-lah's raiders at least twice in night raids and survived. Galloway told Tecumseh many good things about those two men that the Shawnee found easy to believe. But their appraisals of another well-known frontier figure were far different: Simon Girty. Girty's name had become like a profanity among the Americans of Ohio and Pennsylvania and Kentucky, and Galloway was astonished to learn what a staunch and generous friend of the Indians he was. James Galloway was a man of many scars, and one, a bullet still lodged in his neck, had been fired at him point-blank by Girty during a skirmish. Girty had shouted words Galloway could still recall after some fifteen years. "He yelled at me just as he pulled the trigger, 'Galloway, you son of a bitch, I've got you at last!' Well, he'd got me, that's true, and I was mighty surprised when I woke up alive. And now this ball in my neck—feel the lump back there, Chief. . . ." Tecumseh touched the white man's neck with no revulsion and could feel the lead ball move strangely in the flesh. "It hurts like the devil when there's a change of weather coming. But that makes me a better farmer. Ha, ha! For the good Lord puts some redemption in anything He does. I guess even through a bloody Tory renegade like Girty, He did a bit of good. Yes, the Lord be praised!"

Tecumseh then politely inquired how the white man's God could let his children break so many of their promises and treaties, and when Galloway asked for examples, Tecumseh astonished him with his detailed knowledge of past treaties. Galloway shook his head and looked down in embarrassment when Tecumseh recounted how each treaty had been violated by the white men.

Later, Galloway explained to Tecumseh how a frontier becomes a territory, and a territory a state, and how the Ohio Territory was on the verge of becoming a state. He described the territorial legislature as a council.

And then he described the way in which a representative from the territory would go to the grand council of the United States, called Congress. In his opinion, he said, the man most likely to go to the Congress from Ohio was a very young man, already secretary of the Ohio Territory. When Galloway mentioned this man's name, Tecumseh grew rigid.

"What's wrong, my friend?"

"This is Harrison who was chieftain of Wayne?"

"Aye, the very one. William Henry Harrison. Goes from one high place to the next one up, quite regular. Knows presidents personally, they say. He's a man bound to get important, mark my word. Don't tell me you know him, too!"

The name had cast a chill over Tecumseh. But of course he could not explain to Galloway and his family his dreams, his signs, or his premonitions about this man Harrison. "Only have seen him in battle," he said.

The meal had been of venison and squash and a kind of cornmeal bread very familiar to Tecumseh. To turn the talk away from Harrison, Tecumseh began telling Mrs. Galloway how good the food had been and asked her what the white people called this kind of bread.

"Why, sir," she replied, "we just call it johnnycake."

"Aha," he said, raising a brown forefinger, "you say wrong!"

She touched her throat. "Sir?"

"Not say it right. *Shawnee* cake! My people teach your people to make this, but you forget our name! Ha, ha!"

Everyone laughed at this welcome levity. "Shawnee, Johnny! They sound the same!" the yellow-haired girl Rebekah piped up. "Is that really true, Mister Tecumtheh Chief?" Her blue eyes were enormous with the excitement of speaking directly to this glorious man. With her missing front teeth, she could not pronounce a hard *s,* so her pronunciation was closer to the lisplike Shawnee pronunciation of the letter.

"I say only truth always, Ga-lo-weh's girl. And you, you are first white person who ever say my name right. Te-cum . . ." He elaborately formed his lips for the soft sound, and she watched minutely from across the table, unconsciously shaping hers the same way, like a little kiss.

"Ftha!" he said.

"Ftha!" she said, and then in embarrassment covered her toothless smile with both hands.

"Ah! Ha, ha!" Tecumseh laughed, and his eyes sparkled with genuine enjoyment. "Say right! I like this Lebekah!"

"And I like you, Mister Tecum . . . ftha!"

"We all like you, Chief Tecum-*fa!*" Galloway exclaimed, trying to make the sound. He spread his arms. "By heavens, it's been a long time since I've felt so good inside, without whiskey! Ha! Now, sir, I would like you to know that I am your friend, and my door will always be open to you!''

"I am your friend, Ga-lo-weh," Tecumseh said, surprised that the swelling of his heart had caused him to say such a thing to a white man who now ripped up the earth of Chillicothe. "Whatever come, be sure in your heart that no people of mine ever hurt anyone of family Ga-lo-weh!''

And they all felt so warm that they did not even consider what he might have meant by "whatever come."

Riding homeward through the hazy, golden fall days, Tecumseh decided to veer north up the old trace to Piqua and then on toward Wapakoneta. He had to see with his own eyes what Breaker-in-Pieces had said about Black Hoof and his People.

The trace was a road now. Wagon tracks scarred the soil. Columns of smoke leaned into the blue sky, marking the clearing of land, and wherever an old Shawnee town had stood there were log houses and white men's towns being built. Tecumseh would turn off the road and wait at a distance whenever he heard a wagon or horses coming. He did not care to have any unnecessary confrontations with white men who now considered this their land. He would sit on horseback and look at forts from afar. Near the forts there were white men's towns, and near those towns there were shabby little Indian camps—Shawnees, Delawares, Miamis, all mixed together—and in those camps many of the People wore ragged white men's clothes and were sickly and stupid with drink.

Arriving at Wapakoneta, Tecumseh was shocked by the circumstances of the main Shawnee tribe. Some were living in square houses, of poles chinked with mud, houses lined up along straight dirt streets. Pigs ran in the streets, those ugly little creatures of dirty meat, whom the Masters of the Game had given no souls. This meant the Shawnees now were eating foods without spirit. There were pole fences around the houses. Long-eared dogs lay in the yards.

Black Hoof came out with a gathering crowd to greet him, and the old chief was a spectacle to make his heart sink. He wore a black wool frock coat with long tails, dusty with dried dirt, and a stained white stock, gray knee breeches, and muddy boots. His silver hair was lank and unkempt, his craggy brown face ever more deeply lined and careworn. He was fully a white man's Indian now, a farmer; the hand that took Tecumseh's was hard with thick calluses.

Black Hoof talked long and hopefully about the new life of his tribe, of the wonderful ground-cutting plows they had been promised by the government, of the government men who were to come someday soon and teach them how to harness mules and cut ground with the plows. Black Hoof admitted reluctantly that the People had been waiting longer than they had expected for these promises to be fulfilled and were still farming with hoes. Whatever plows arrived, it seemed, the white people got them.

"Ah, yes," Tecumseh said. "For the white men's promises, I hope you will live a long time, Father."

Black Hoof frowned. He said that was not a good way to think of the white men's nation. He said he was worried that Tecumseh and his followers might have much trouble with the white men because of their hatred, and he said he would be happier if Tecumseh had signed the Greenville Treaty so there would always be peace.

"What, Father?" Tecumseh cried. "Are you not happy, in your heart, that some of your People are still free, to hunt and fish in the way of our grandfathers, to strike back when someone hurts us? In your heart, do you really want us to be tethered by our necks, as these of yours are, tamed and helpless like the Moravians, eating pig meat and drinking whiskey and getting the white man's sicknesses? Do you really in your heart want us all to be dead in our bodies, grabbing for what the white man's government throws us, waiting forever for plows to come so our proud hunters may stoop and sweat in the fields? Does my father Black Hoof the renowned warrior really believe his People should live like this? Would it not be better to die quickly under the white man's gun than slowly under his boot?"

Black Hoof sat and took this tirade, his mouth downturned and his eyes glittering wet, and finally all he could say was:

"My son. You know already that it is a hard thing to be chief of a People even in the fairest of times. For many years I have been their chief, in the worst time we ever knew. Finally one cannot bear to hear the women and children cry in fear anymore, or cry for their fathers and brothers and sons who do not come back from battle. That, my son, is when a chief says, 'No more tears, no more blood. Lay down your treaty and show me where to mark on it!' " His voice quavered. "It grows too hard after a long time, my son. The chief must protect his People from harm."

"Father," Tecumseh said, "you are a great man, and I always loved you and listened to you. Never has any chief had to lead his People through a worse time; what you say about that is true. But do you think your People will not cry anymore when they live like this? Maybe you do not see tears on their cheeks. But inside their breasts they cry without sound, and all their grandfathers and grandmothers back to the Beginning cry for them. But the old ones do not have to cry for *us,* for *my* People, who still hunt and fish and dance. My free People. They do not weep for them."

"Perhaps not," said Black Hoof. "Not yet."

Tecumseh dined with Black Hoof and slept in his house that night and by morning felt lice on his body. As he mounted to ride out of Wapakoneta, Black Hoof reached up and took his hand and implored:

"Avoid trouble with the whites if you can, my son. Do not hate them so much that you fight foolish battles you cannot win. Do not let hatred blind you. Remember that white people are not really the spawn of the Serpent, but only a people, who believe they do right. Some of them are good, though you may find that hard to believe."

Tecumseh thought of Ga-lo-weh and his family, and he was able to say, "Yes, some of them are good. But their way and our way cannot be, in the same land. Some wrong voice has told them they can have this land. But, Father, you remember my signs. My signs tell me that I will be the one who will wipe away all these lines they have drawn on Weshemoneto's land, and put them back even across the mountains. Look," he said, pointing southward. "Coming up this road I saw them putting their plows in the ground where the bones of our fathers lie. Is the Great Good Spirit pleased with that? Do you think he means for us to let them plow up the graves of our ancestors? No, Father! No! In my head and my heart I am still learning the way to push them back!"

For a moment in Black Hoof's eyes there flickered the fierce spirit of old, as he heard these words. But then it died, and the fear and worry were there. Black Hoof had been standing on the ground by Tecumseh's horse all this time, looking up at him, and was still holding his hand. Now he gave it a squeeze and released it and said in a low, soft voice, "Beware." Then he stepped back and held up his hand in the old farewell, and Tecumseh left him standing there among his sorry People, an ancient red man in the white man's clothes, in the dirt street of an imitation white man's town.


Tecumseh rode down the valley of the Auglaize until he was alone in wilderness and dismounted at a sandy fording place. Though the day was cold, he stripped off his clothing and carried it into the river. He washed and wrung it to get rid of the lice, then hung it on branches to dry, went back into the water, and scrubbed himself with sand until his skin was tender. Though he had declined to eat any pig meat at Wapakoneta, even the corn and beans he had eaten there had been cooked with pig fat and felt unclean in him, so he drank his fill of water and then vomited to cleanse himself inside. The air was cold on his nakedness, but the autumn sun was still warm. Only the birds and squirrels, and the dry leaves in the breeze, and the trickling and gurgling of the river, covered the profound silence, like a thin skin of noises over a swollen stillness. He sat by the river until his skin and hair were dry, listening. He sat with his face to the sun and his eyes closed, and inside his eyelids swam the red-and-orange light.

After a long time something white, but shapeless at first, moved through the red-and-orange glow, swooping up and around and growing smaller until it was a dot. Then it swerved around and grew larger, as if coming toward him, and it was the white dove, flying toward him. It came closer and grew larger until it filled his mind and all was white.

And then this whiteness became the white hair of Old Change-of-Feathers, the shaman. Change-of-Feathers' head of white hair grew smaller, as if he were moving away. Tecumseh saw the old man walking away along a path that led into a thorny thicket. The old man sat down beside the path in front of the thicket. Then he spread a blanket on the ground and lay down on it and crossed his hands over his chest and shut his eyes. Another man, a big young man, walked up the path to where he lay and stood over him, and when this man turned, Tecumseh could see the right side of his face. It had a black scarf pulled down over the right eye, and on the lip was a mustache. It was Lalawethika, Loud Noise, his brother. But when the young man spoke his name, it was not Lalawethika, but Tenskwatawa, which meant He-Opens-the-Door. And when he said the name, the old man's hands lifted, and the white dove flew out of his chest and into the chest of the young man. The young man then walked away, into the thicket, which parted to let him walk through, and old Change-of-Feathers lay on the ground lifeless until he dissolved.

Then the young soldier called Harrison came. He wore a blue coat with gold decorations. With a disdainful look on his face, the officer picked up a dead stick and tried to bend it with both hands. It snapped in two, and he cast the pieces down. Then he cut a green stick and bent it, and it did not break, although he bent it almost double. The young man kept bending the stick back and forth and twisted it until its bark came off and the limber wood frayed into splinters. He kept twisting it until the last limber fibers gave way and the green stick was in two pieces. Then he cast them down.

Then Harrison picked up a bundle made of dead sticks tied together. It was very rigid and thick, and he could not break it. So he put his knee against the bundle of dead sticks and gripped the bundle at both ends and strained with great strength. Sweat stood out on his face. He pulled harder, wincing. And at last the whole bundle of dead sticks crackled and broke, and he threw the pieces down, smiling.

Then the young officer picked up a bundle of green sticks and tried to break them but could not. Even with his greatest effort, he could only make them bend a little. He tried everything to break them, even bending them around a tree, but they would not break, and at last he fell down exhausted.

The vision faded away, and there was only the red-and-orange billowing behind Tecumseh's eyelids, and the sound of the river bubbling over its shallows, and the cool wind in the leaves, and the squirrels chattering and scolding and gathering food. Tecumseh opened his eyes and was still sitting there naked, and the sun had moved a long way in the sky. His clothes were dry. He put them on and mounted to ride the rest of the way back to his People. He had seen something very important, and he needed to ride now and think of what it meant. He rode westward now, feeling light and pure and strengthened, out of the land called O-hi-o, toward the land they were now calling the Indiana Territory, meaning the Land of the Indians, where, as a neighbor of Breaker-in-Pieces, the Delaware, he would make a new home for his People, his few hundred Shawnee who were still free.

# CHAPTER 25

*White River Mounds, Indiana Territory
Spring 1805*

S omething dreadful was going to happen. Loud Noise knew it.
He was sober for once. He never liked the feeling of being sober,
for his stomach would quiver and his hands would shake and his
mind would scream silently. And when he was sober, the world was
a stark, harsh place, and he could not hide from himself the truth that he
was a fraud and a failure.

But now on this evening as he filled the stone bowl of his long pipe, as
his trembling fingers spilled shreds of tobacco on his lap, as his fat wife sat
sullen beyond the fire with still another squirming baby at her breast, Loud
Noise felt something worse than his usual profound misery, worse than his
usual desperate craving for whiskey.

Something monstrous was trying to get into his soul. He could sense it
hovering outside and above him; he could almost hear something, though
not with his ears, some woeful moaning or wailing. His heart quaked and
fluttered. The fear was worse than the awful fear he had felt before the
Battle of the Fallen Timbers, for he had been able to see what threatened
him then: soldiers. Now he could see nothing to explain this fear. Perhaps
a witch was working against him.

Yes, very likely it was a witch. Anybody might take up his personal
medicine bag and invoke its powers against someone he did not like, and
Loud Noise knew he was disliked by more people than anyone else in the
tribe. Many suspected what he secretly knew: that he was no real master of
medicine, though he worked with the herbs and incantations and sometimes
just by chance his patients recovered, that their bodies healed their own
sicknesses. One of the white men's diseases just weeks ago had run its
course in the village and had taken away many of the people during the
winter and had left many others too weak to hunt or to plant or to repair

the damage the winter had done to their *wigewas*. Change-of-Feathers had died among the first, leaving Loud Noise as the only healer in the village, and though Change-of-Feathers had taught him many of the remedies and rituals, never had Loud Noise truly felt the power, never had he had so much as a vision. The appalling fact was that Lalawethika, He-Makes-a-Loud-Noise, who claimed to be Change-of-Feathers' successor as the tribal shaman and prophet, did not even have a *pa-waw-ka* or a Spirit Helper. He was in truth more poorly equipped to be even a minor medicine man than just about anyone in the tribe, and he was addicted to whiskey as well, and though he boasted and made claims about his powers, many people knew what a great lump of nothingness he really was, and they had good reason to do witchcraft against him. Often lately he had kept a wary watch on the doings of animals, for he knew that witches sometimes assumed animal shapes to disguise their evil deeds. Once Loud Noise had seen a dog, a dog he had never seen in the village before, looking steadily at him with its yellowish eyes from behind a tree. Once a kingbird had flown down and struck at his head. And once, as Loud Noise had staggered drunkenly out to the sugar maple grove where Tecumseh and a group of people were making sugar, an owl, one of the chief omen birds, had silently flown three times across his path.

Yes, he feared, it could be someone working witchcraft against him.

He sat gazing with a blank eye into the fire, unable to think. He had forgotten even that he was loading his pipe. In his mind he saw the dog's eyes, the kingbird, the owl floating swiftly through the forest. A witch usually assumed the disguise of only one kind of animal. Could this mean that several people were trying to bewitch him at the same time? That was a frightening thought, and his dread grew almost unbearable.

He would have liked to get some whiskey right now. But now was when he needed it, and now none was at hand. Tecumseh had made it hard to obtain whiskey in his town, by putting all the whiskey sellers in fear of their lives. Only when Tecumseh went away, on one of his trips to talk to the chiefs and young warriors of other tribes, was it easy for Loud Noise to make deals to get whiskey.

Loud Noise knew what his brother was doing on those frequent and far-ranging trips. He had told Loud Noise about a dream, a dream of the white soldier Harrison and a bundle of sticks. Tecumseh believed that the dead sticks meant old chiefs and the green sticks meant young warriors. He believed that the dream was a message that while the old brittle sticks could be broken, or any single green stick could be broken, all the green sticks in the bundle were the young warriors of all the tribes united together.

Loud Noise still loved and admired his brother, but sometimes he was unsettled by his zeal. Loud Noise could remember all too clearly the burned towns and the devastated crops that the People had suffered almost every year while the war hatchet was up. And he could remember all too vividly the sight of Wayne's Blue-Coat soldiers rushing toward him in the Fallen Timbers with their terrible spikes and their roaring war cry. Loud Noise had decided that one can accomplish more alive than dead, so it was a major inclination of his spirit to remain alive. He dreaded war as much as he dreaded witchcraft and failure, and, as all those hovered near him, his burdens were terrible.

And sometimes the most shameful thought of all would get into his head and bother him so much that his heart would hurt. Sometimes, when he saw or tasted honey, he would remember his brother Cat Follower dying of beestings while he gorged himself on that honey. Sometimes he feared that Cat Follower's ghost was near and was waiting to take revenge. This night he had thought of his dead brother that way. Loud Noise, pondering all this now, found his pipe in his hand with tobacco in its bowl, and he searched the fire-ring for a twig with which to light it.

Sometimes Loud Noise thought that Tecumseh made too much of the white man's evil, that he was too rigid. Loud Noise himself could tolerate white men when he was among them. The ones who sold whiskey were a smiling, friendly sort of people; certainly they treated him more respectfully than most of his own people did. They made him feel he had some importance. Tecumseh hated and feared whiskey, so he deemed whiskey sellers evil men of the worst sort and would not even talk to them, except to threaten them. But they were really not that bad—at least not if you needed whiskey sometimes.

And then there were the Shakers.

These people recently had made a profound impression upon Loud Noise. Though they called their God by a different name, they had, like the Shawnees, a moral code of behavior that pervaded all the hours of their lives. Like the Shawnees, they believed that the divine spirit was released in people by dance. Loud Noise had witnessed some of their agitations in O-hi-o, where they recently had settled; he had seen them seized by such ecstasy that their bodies convulsed and twitched in a strange, frantic dance, and he had felt that he was seeing true holiness. Like the Shawnees, the Shakers believed that God is not only man but woman as well. The Creator of their sect, like Kokomthena of the Shawnees, had been a woman. And their moral code itself, calling for truth and trustworthiness, generosity and kindness and gentleness, was like an echo of what the Shawnee code had been, back in the happy days before corruption. Though Loud Noise himself was one of the most corrupt, he had become poignantly aware of the code when he recognized it in the Shaker teachings. If all white men were like the Shakers, Loud Noise suspected, there never would have been trouble with them. Loud Noise thought very often about the Shakers, in a wistful sort of way.

But of course he personally could never have been much like a Shaker; they were against liquor and copulation, which were to him about the only things that made life worth living—until afterward when the hurting head and the crying babies came.

Loud Noise sighed and picked up a twig with his trembling hand and held one end of it in the fire until it was burning, and he looked at its flame as he lifted it to the tobacco bowl and put the stem of the pipe in his mouth. All these things continually flowed through his head, like a muddy river, but they came to nothing and only added to the misery and foreboding that pressed down on him. His heart was huge in his chest and twisted with anxiety, and he could hardly breathe. It felt as if the spells of witches were crushing him from all sides.

The fire on the end of the twig burned bright over the pipe bowl. It grew brighter. It grew blindingly bright like the sun.

Then a terrific roaring scream exploded in his head.

Loud Noise's wife heard him grunt. She looked up at him.

His eye had rolled back till only the white showed. The pipe and burning twig fell from his hands. A great sucking noise sounded from his throat.

And slowly he toppled to his side and lay curled up like a stillborn.


Thick Water with a racing heart watched Tecumseh begin to weave his spell again through the semicircle of warriors and chiefs seated before him in the Delaware council house. Thick Water had traveled to villages throughout the Middle Ground with Tecumseh in the last three years and had heard him say these truths over and over, and they seemed more powerful each time.

"The white man's trap closes upon us!" Tecumseh cried. "Already you know that the white men's chief Jefferson has bought from the French father those sunset lands that lie beyond the Missi-se-pe to the Shining Mountains. Already you have seen two Long Knife captains lead soldiers out into those lands. Do you believe just because they go far away that their going will not bother us? Listen! I will tell you what they are doing!" Tecumseh stretched his arm to point to the west. His listeners were taut with attention. He had been talking to them for an hour, and his voice was like thunder, his reason like lightning.

From the constant and bewildering movements of the white men, only Tecumseh seemed able to deduce just what they were really doing at any time, and why, and Thick Water was convinced that this was the truth and that it was the most important truth the red men could learn.

Tecumseh went on:

"I have traveled far. I have talked with the Sioux, and their neighbors who live beyond the Great River, who were called to council with those two captains. They told me what those captains said to them. Those captains told them that American traders would soon follow them up the Missouri-se-pe, bringing them goods that will make them happier and make their days easier, and that the Sioux should trade with them, not with the British traders. Those captains put their flag up on a pole and said the Sioux must now live under it. They said that if they would be good red children of the white father Jefferson, and would be friendly to the whites who followed, then the white father would smile on them and send them many desirable things. In council they gave the chiefs a taste of whiskey. Maybe that is one of the 'desirable things' the white men will take to the Sioux. Ha!

"But they said if the Sioux would *not* give their hand to the white men, the white father Jefferson would send into their country more white soldiers than they could count, to make them behave!"

Tecumseh paused and looked in the faces of his listeners and saw many of them clench their jaws, saw their eyelids harden. They had heard just such warnings themselves in the past, and the white armies had come, and come again, and again. It was the familiar story, and now it was happening to People far in the west, the Sioux and others beyond the Sioux. The Sioux were not especially liked by the Indians in this council lodge, for they were arrogant and pushy and perhaps deserved to be pushed themselves. But it was not good to hear of this being done to any red men, even remote and alien nations like the Sioux, if it was the white men doing it.

"Now hear what I say," Tecumseh went on. "I have learned the names of those captains. One is named Clark." He paused, and they murmured that familiar name. "Yes. 'Clark.' Is that name an echo in your ears? This Captain Clark is a young brother of the great old enemy General Clark. I tell you this is so!

"Do you remember what happened to us after General Clark appeared in our country? Were we not scattered and driven out of our homelands? Did we not lose everything when the old Clark came into our country? Remember. Remember!

"And now if this young Clark does the same to all the land in the west, where will we withdraw ourselves when they grow too thick here? I remind you that we are surrounded by white men, and they tighten their trap

around us even now. There is no place to go, except Canada. And the Long
Knives covet Canada, too.

"And do you think the Long Knife government means to let us keep
these lands we now inhabit, between O-hi-o, which we have lost, and the
Wabash-se-pe, which we are losing? Oh, we sit here now, yes. But in the
west, we no longer have a path to the Missi-se-pe. In the south, we have
only a narrow path to the O-hi-o-se-pe. And in the east, white men have
been coming across the lines of Wayne's treaty for all the ten years since
that treaty was made, and they kill much game in our lands, so that our
women and children are hungry. They bring whiskey across the line and
sell it. And they have murdered many of our people, and the treaty forbids
us to punish them for those murders. Do you remember the murder of our
brother Waw-wil-a-weh, who was killed even though he had embraced the
white man's ways? And so many others? The white men say there has been
peace ever since Wayne's treaty, because we are forbidden to kill white
men. But they shoot our hunters as if we were the hunted!

"Listen! I warn you of something very close to us:

"Here where we now live, the whites now call this the Indiana Territory.
This word means 'Land of the Indians.' But what is a territory? Just before
they drove the Shawnees from O-hi-o, they named O-hi-o a territory, and
put a governor over it. St. Clair. You remember St. Clair. And thus two
years ago O-hi-o was changed from a territory to what they call a state. It
is now the Seventeenth Fire of their nation. Even a young man remembers
when that nation was the *Thirteen* Fires!

"Now, my brothers, heed this: This Indiana Territory where we live,
*it* now has a governor. Yes! The white chief Jefferson has put a governor
in Vincennes, in the heart of 'the Land of the Indians,' a governor who can
decide on land treaties. Does this not warn you of what the white chief
intends? If they truly believed it is the 'Land of the Indians,' why would they
put a white governor here?"

Now his voice took on an edge that made their scalps prickle:

"Beware of this governor! I have seen him in dreams, long before I saw
him riding beside General Wayne on the battlefield, learning from old
Wayne how to invade lands! That day Weshemoneto pointed to him and
told me this will be our greatest enemy, worse for us than the old Clark or
Wayne! Listen:

"In only two years, this governor has stolen from the red man by treaties
more land than Wayne took from us by war!

"Listen! Two years ago I could ride three days south from here and six
days west from here, on our lands. Now I can ride only one day south and
three days west. Do you remember as I do? Two years ago at Fort Wayne

this governor made a treaty with foolish chiefs, which gave him land reaching two days' travel all around Vincennes. Two moons later at Vincennes he made another treaty, which took from us ten times that much more land, from the Illinois-se-pe south to the Beautiful River. Last year he took all the land south of the great Bison Trace as far west as the Wabash-se-pe, and then all the land between the Illinois-se-pe and the Great River! Think of this! And at this moment he calls *more* chiefs to him at Vincennes, for *more* such treaties! Before this year ends, old fools living on annuity dollars may give him the land upon which you are now seated!

"Unless! Unless we all join our hands and tell him with one voice: 'No! Red men will not move back anymore, will never sign another treaty! The Great Good Spirit put *us* here!' We must show this governor we all have the same heart, that no red man will ever sell another handful of ground to him, ever! We must make our old chiefs see they are killing their own people with their treaty marks, and that if they mark again, we will kill *them!*

"Brothers, I say: Beware this governor who sits beside the Wabash-se-pe at Vincennes. Refuse him anything he asks! Take nothing he offers! Do not provoke him, for that would give him an excuse to strike us. But refuse him! Any red man who takes that governor by the hand and marks another treaty is a traitor to all our race, and ought to be put to death for killing our life!

"Go warn your old chiefs that they had better not go when he calls them! Warn them that we are tired of feeling the trap tighten on us! Beware of this governor, whose name is *Harrison*!"

Their response swept through the council house as one great, breathy voice. And Thick Water was more moved than any of them.


As he rode home up the river with his little group of chieftains and bodyguards, Tecumseh knew he had as usual stirred his listeners deeply and had given them a look at the truth that they had never seen very clearly before, and that it was a truth that would not easily go to sleep in their minds. Hundreds throughout this territory had heard his warnings and his explanations of what was happening, and they discussed them in their own councils after he left. He carried in his soul the sound of their cries of affirmation, the sight of their glittering eyes.

And yet this seemed a task that would never be finished. There were still important chiefs who resisted Tecumseh's words and undermined his warnings. Many of those who had signed the Treaty of Greenville thought Tecumseh was a dangerous upstart. They feared he would bring the Long Knives' might down upon them again. Black Hoof was against him—his own elder chief, the true chief of the Shawnees. If his own chief was against him, how could other tribes follow him? Black Hoof, Little Turtle, and Tarhe of the Wyandots were three of the greatest chiefs the Algonquian nations had ever had, and in their age and wisdom they had chosen to take the white man's path. They honored the treaty despite the white man's violations of it, and they lived on the annuity the white man's government gave them. They had grown to need the white man's tools and goods and were bogged down in the white man's credit, as in quicksand. They had to agree with what the white chiefs wanted. They were not themselves anymore. It was too late for them to go back to the old ways and to walk the old warpaths again. They had been tamed and put in invisible harness. And so these old, tamed men feared Tecumseh, because he was not tamed. He was a great warrior with a mighty voice, who somehow understood what the white men were doing and how they did it, who excited the young men and made them proud and defiant, and who traveled tirelessly to towns everywhere with his message of resistance. But being a Kispoko, he could never rightfully be the chief of all the Shawnees. And if he was not the true chief of his own tribe, how could he imagine himself the chief of all the Indians? Who had ever even heard of a chief of all the Indians? The Indians were not all one people. Why did he keep talking to them as if they were?

Tecumseh knew that was how people felt, and that was why it was an endless task. Even when he swayed some leaders, others would weaken and fall away from him, some through fear of the white government, some simply because they decided he was assuming too much power. Or his old allies would die. Breaker-in-Pieces, war chief of the nearby Delawares, had seemed to believe in Tecumseh's cause, but he had died last year of a white man's sickness, and the Delaware king Twisting Vines was the old man who had exchanged wampum belts with Wayne at the Greenville Treaty: he certainly was not for Tecumseh. And there were some tribal chiefs who would not stand beside Tecumseh simply because others did. This jealousy between tribes was the oldest and firmest obstacle to his dream. Each tribe thought of itself as the People and set itself above the others. And while some might make temporary alliances in the face of a common crisis, such as Pontiac's and Little Turtle's and Chief Brant's confederations, it was beyond their minds to envision themselves as one red People.

But, Tecumseh knew, somehow they would *have* to. Only if they would unite as a single council of all the red men would they become a force so powerful that the white chief Jefferson and all his ministers and agents and generals would be unable to play tribe against tribe or make land treaties with this old chief or that old chief. If all the red men were of one heart, the white man's government then would have to council with a body as strong as itself. In the face of such strength, the white men would have to stop where the red men told them to stop.

It was a magnificent notion, this of Tecumseh's; it had grown out of a lifetime of signs and hard thinking, and he had planted the seed of it in the minds of many red leaders and warriors. He had traveled to more towns and spoken to more councils than any other Indian had been known to do. He knew it would be a task of years. He was ready to spend his life at it. He knew it was what the Great Good Spirit had assigned to him. But sometimes his heart would grow heavy, and he would think, I do not have a lifetime to do it in! Unless this Harrison is stopped, the rest of our lands might be gone from us by the next season! Oh, my poor, many-headed People! You are like that tribe of Moses that Big Fish spoke of: enemies to yourselves! Will you never allow yourselves to be saved? Is there no way to bind your many hearts into one unbreakable bundle?

And that was what he was thinking now as he rode in the dusk past the ancient mounds of a once great Indian nation, returning to his little town, when a youth came running down the river path crying for him.

"*Pe-eh-wah! Pe-eh-wah!* Hurry! Your brother dies!"

Loud Noise's wife and children were crying. He was on his back beside the fire. The people were already talking about the arrangements for burial and mourning. When Tecumseh entered his brother's crowded lodge, he could only wonder if he had killed himself by drinking, but he did not say this, with the wife and people there. No doubt they were already thinking it themselves.

He knelt beside the pudgy body. There seemed to be no breathing. Here lay this dissipated lump of flesh which, though such a strange and wretched nothingness of a person, was his last blood brother, from the same womb. There would be those who thought he was better off now. Yet Tecumseh was dismayed as well as aggrieved. His signs had seemed to say that Loud Noise would have a part in the events to come. This went against the signs!

A stink of rot rose, as if he had been long dead.

Then someone cried, "His mouth! Look!"

Loud Noise's lips were moving. His mouth was open. The smell of rot was his breath.

Tecumseh arched over him, staring. The eyeball was moving behind the closed eyelid. Tecumseh called to him. "Brother! Brother! Wake and be well! Please come to us!"

Loud Noise began whimpering, and his chest began to rise and fall with his breathing. Even before his eye opened, it was trickling tears. His sobs and whimpers were pitiful. His wife lifted his head onto her lap and stroked it and murmured passionately to him as if he had been not a source of misery and embarrassment to her for years, but instead an esteemed lover and provider.

He wept and groaned for a long time. When he opened his eye it was flooded with tears. His face was contorted. Little by little his strength seemed to return, and he could raise his arm, which he laid across his forehead. When he tried at last to speak, he broke again and again into abject weeping. When his wife asked him where the pain was, he touched his chest over his heart.

Late in the night Loud Noise was sitting up and sipping broth. It was the longest he had ever gone without food; he had been gone for two days. He sat with a robe over his shoulders. With hesitation and stammering at first, then with an eloquence growing beyond any he had ever revealed before, he told his amazed listeners where he had been while he was dead.

"Two perfect warriors came down from the sky for me," he said. "They took my arms and pulled me out of my body. I looked down and saw my wife lay the baby down and hurry over to my body where it had fallen. Then we rose out through the roof, into the evening sky. The warriors who flew me up, they wore dark blue breechcloths and moccasins decorated with glittering stars.

"Never had I seen the land from so high! Not even as a boy when I climbed a great oak so far that its little branches bent! In the dusk below I saw the White River twisting through the woods and meadows. I looked one way and saw the *wigewas* and smoke of the village, and in the other direction the ancient mounds, and farther down the town of the Jesus missionaries. The western sky was the color of squash, and in the blue above it was the evening star.

"We went higher and higher until things on the earth were too small to see, except the rivers and the Great Lakes. Up there, there was no smoke in the air, no bird song, no voice of tree frog or cricket. It was a perfect silence, the only perfect silence I ever heard. We came onto the Road of Stars and kept going upward. A long time later we passed through the Roof of the Sky and onto the Parallel World above. When we passed through, the sky felt like spring water, and then at once it was bright daytime.

"There the road forked. To the right it went on as a road of stars, but to the left it was a road of dirt, like a bison trace. The star road led toward a green and misty land of meadows and corn fields, and elm trees and blue streams, where herds of bison and elk stood in grass as high as their shoulders. Birds flew everywhere, more than could be counted. Happy men and beautiful women were hunting, fishing, planting, playing games, and dancing. Oh," he groaned, tears flowing, "the sound of their laughter made me weep!

"But the other road went through a wasteland. Trees stood dead and leafless in bogs. Their bark was gray and always falling off. Everything there was rotten, and there were green bubbles in the thick water of the swamp. There were hovels by the roadside, and at their doors were sick, snarling people, with hogs running among their legs and knocking them down!"

The listeners' faces were grimacing as they envisioned this place he described. Star Watcher and Tecumseh looked at each other across his shoulders.

"I tried to ask the sky warriors which way they were going to take me, but they answered me not. And then as I had feared they took me down the road to the left, away from the heaven I had seen. They took me to a smoky, scorched lodge, hundreds of paces long, which was Matchemoneto's house. They made me go inside. Oh! The heat in there seared my skin! I watched blisters come up! I was choked by the thick, brown smoke!

"The crowds of sinners in there were sooty, and their eyes were red. They went in three lines. One line of them walked wailing into the heart of the fire! There they twitched and blistered, they grew black, they turned to ashes. Those were the Worst Sinners.

"Another line of people went only to the edge of the great fire. They had to stick their hands and feet into the flames, and they were screaming almost as loud as the roar of the fire. These were the Lesser Sinners.

"The sky warriors put me in the third line. This went not to the fire, but to a great smoking stone, where iron ladles steamed. In them was molten lead, as when musketballs are made, but it smelled like whiskey. We in this line were drunkards. I recognized people I knew had died of drinking. Do you remember Crooked Hand, who died in our town at Deer Creek? He stood there and greeted me. His lips were all burned. From his mouth came stinking smoke, and red flames, and flakes of burned-off skin. . . ."

A screech of horror came from a woman among the listeners. It was Crooked Hand's widow. She gasped and sobbed as Loud Noise talked on.

"Crooked Hand offered me one of the iron ladles. 'Drink some!' he told me, and more flakes of burned skin floated out of his mouth with the words. I was afraid. 'Come, drink,' Crooked Hand told me. 'You love whiskey! Look! I drink! Oh, it burns me inside! Oh, but the burning is exquisite!' Crooked Hand poured it into his own mouth. It was terrible to see him drink it! More flesh burned off his lips, and he dropped the ladle and clutched his arms over his glowing belly, and made a bubbling scream!"

Crooked Hand's widow screeched again and fell in a faint. Loud Noise went on, his voice quaking and curdled with horror.

"Hundreds of other drunkards were doing the same. Their screams were like the roar of a great waterfall. They drank and screamed, they fought with knives for more to drink, they fell, they rose and drank again, burning their insides worse each time! Smoke came out of their noses, and ears, and navels, and from their behinds squirted a boiling froth of melted metal, blood, and runny excrement. Many of them were screaming to me, 'Come! Drink!'

"I began to drool! I wanted to seize a ladle and empty it in my mouth, even though I knew the pain would be too much to bear! My hands shook. I reached for a ladle, beginning to cry for it!"

His listeners were moaning, aghast. Almost every one had had a relative who had died from drinking or from the troubles of drinking.

"But the sky warriors saved me from that. They had only wanted to show me. They took hold of my arms again and took me out the door, and we flew up again, into the cold. We came near to the moon, and stopped at Our Grandmother's house. They threw me inside. There she sat! I have seen Kokomthena! She is huge. Her face has the wrinkles of thousands of years. Her hair is white, in a long braid. On her cheeks are red dots. She reached out toward me! Her hand was bigger than I! There were sparks in her eyes. Her mouth was down in anger. Her voice sounded like brush burning. I was afraid. She asked me a question." When Loud Noise related the question, the voice sounded not like his own, but like the one he described, crackling and rushing. No one had ever heard such a voice. "Her question was: 'How are you getting on with the task you were to do?' I did not remember any task. She said to me:

" 'You were born under a strong sign. Two others were born from the womb with you. You have been told that you have a sign, and thus a great good task to do. But you have done nothing good!' Then she did this to me:

"She reached out and pinched my mouth off and held it before my eyes! It was lopsided and sticking out in all directions. She shouted, 'Is it for this that I created your mouth, to lie and deceive and mock and gossip?' Then she slammed my mouth back on my face and yanked off my ears and showed them to me. They were all hairy and twisted and clogged with dirty wax. 'Is it for this that I created your ears, that they will listen to anything bad, but not to truth and law?' Then she slammed my ears back on so hard that I heard my head crack, like a hazelnut between two stones! Then the worst thing she did: she plunged her fingers into my chest, fingers as big and hard as logs! And plucked out my heart to show me! And Our Grandmother shouted at me:

" 'Is it for this that I created your heart, that it is full of rot and lust and corruption?' My heart was furrowed and stained and moldy! She shoved it back into my chest, and she told me:

" 'You have been permitted to come and see the World Above, the past and the future. You saw the heaven where your father and your dead brothers now hunt in happiness as in the early days. And also you saw the house of Matchemoneto, where drunkards and sinners suffer for what they have done. Many more of the People go to that house now than before. They have been made weak and confused by the troubles the white men brought, *but their sins are their own*! They will not be strong and happy again unless they return to the old ways. I have brought you here to tell you how to make them pure again. You will go back as a messenger. You will have to help your brother do his great work.

" 'Now listen well,' Our Grandmother told me. 'I have cleaned the wax and dirt out of your ears so you can hear the truth from me. Here are the things you will tell all the red people, not just the Shawnees, but all . . .' "

The people crowding into and around the house of Loud Noise cast dubious glances at each other, to see if others were believing or not. There was much reason to suspect that the crazy shaman had simply come up with another elaborate sham to make himself seem more than he was. Tecumseh himself listened most skeptically. Though happy beyond measure that his brother was alive after all, he as well as the others had little reason to believe that Loud Noise was telling the truth. And this afterworld of Match-emoneto's that he had described in such horrible detail sounded less like the Shawnee underworld than like the hell in the white people's religion that Big Fish had used to tell of in their talks. Tecumseh wondered if Loud Noise had borrowed it from what he had overheard in those talks or perhaps from one of the various other Jesus religions he had become fascinated with lately.

Tecumseh was in fact ready to believe that this whole episode was a trick, by which his wretched brother meant to improve his sorry reputation as a medicine man, when Loud Noise said something that went through him like a lightning bolt:

"Our Creator told me, 'You will go back as a messenger. Your name will be Tenskwatawa, He-Opens-the-Door.' "

"Brother!" Tecumseh gasped. "She said, 'He-Opens-the-Door'? She said you will be called . . ."

Turning his head like a man in a trance, Loud Noise said in a soft voice: "Yes. Tenskwatawa."

"He-Opens-the-Door!" Tecumseh repeated, suddenly full of shivers. It was the name of the one-eyed prophet in his own dreams! Then he quickly tried to remember: Had he ever told Loud Noise that name, ever told him that the Shawnee prophet would be called Tenskwatawa?

He was sure he had not.

So now Tecumseh sat stunned, having to believe that the same name had been given in his own vision and his brother's. Yes! This did go with the signs! Tecumseh's heart was beating fast, and he inhaled as if he had been running. At last something was coming by another way to confirm the signs that had for so long been only in himself!

Now Loud Noise—or Open Door—was shaking and weeping openly as no grown Shawnee man would do in the presence of others, and between spells of sobbing he poured out confessions and vows. "Yes! I have sinned every day of my life that I can remember! There was no law I did not disobey! There was no sacredness that I did not spit on! I have stolen from my people, I have hurt the weak. I have hidden from danger. I have done things in secret for which others suffered the consequences! I have spied on women and forced myself upon them. I have ridiculed the good that people do! I have lied for no other reason than that I scorned truth telling. I have eaten manflesh, only to seek deeper for revulsion! And, oh, my beloved people, I have said bad things, untrue things, about every one of you. . . . I have . . . only now do I understand it . . . I have been like a disease among my own people. I have been a slave to whiskey for half of my life. I have gone cackling and dirtying everything, thinking the whiskey made me wiser than the wise men. . . ."

The people in the lodge, family, warriors, womenfolk, at first grimaced and squirmed with disgust and embarrassment at hearing this outpouring, as if they were watching someone eat his own vomit. But as he went on purging himself, their eyes began to glitter with pity, their faces began to glow with compassion as if they were seeing something holy happening before them in this transformation. Some of them began to tremble with him now, realizing that he had had to go face to face with the Creator to be so shaken and wrung out in his soul. Some of them were wondering how they could face the Creator with their own little sins drawn out from the secrecy of their hearts; imagine going with Loud Noise's load of sins and standing before Our Grandmother, who knew them all! And here was a man who had died and been returned to life! Of course he would have appalling things to say! And how blessed they were to be here and hear it from his own mouth!

The word was spreading in the village, and dozens, then hundreds, were crowding in the night outside his dimly lit lodge.

"Never! Never again," he bawled through contorted, drooling lips, "will a drop of that white man's poison enter my mouth! I vow this from my purified heart! My people, how I have suffered to pass through this door and learn what I know at last! Our Creator ripped out and held my own corrupt heart before my eyes to teach me the lesson. And now I have been sent back to guide our poor People out of the pain and confusion they live in. I am the Open Door! And through me you must pass to find the narrow road to paradise!" He was trembling violently now, and many of his listeners were, too. Tecumseh watched and listened with utmost concentration for gestures or words that would reveal how this miracle was to interweave with his own.

"I am tired now," Loud Noise intoned with sighs. "I have traveled as far as anyone travels, and returned as well. I must rest. Tomorrow let us gather under the sky in front of the council lodge, men and women and children. And then I will reveal to you the way to purity, as Our Creator decreed it to me. My children! Cry your thanks to the Great Good Spirit, for telling us how to save ourselves from doom, and how to find the joy we knew in the earlier times!"


When Open Door went out in the morning, there were more people, many more, waiting in front of the council lodge than there had been crowding outside his *wigewa* the night before. There were, in fact, more people than the population of the village. Many Delawares, and some Shawnees and people of other tribes who lived with the Delawares, had heard of this miracle and had come to hear what he would tell.

People had never looked at the man who had been Loud Noise the way they looked at him now that he was Open Door. Their gazes followed him with awe, or reverence, or at least with intense curiosity, as he made his stately way along the edge of the crowd under the trees to the front of the council house. Never had Loud Noise moved in a stately way before. Never had he enjoyed being looked at before. He was a changed one. Though he was still the stout, one-eyed man with the hairy upper lip that he had been—for the Creator had not remade his physical body or visage—he now walked erect with his head high and his face straight forward, no longer edging obliquely along with a stoop and one eye leading him.

And he was no longer unkempt and filthy in half-rotted, grease-darkened skins. For this occasion he had borrowed from Tecumseh a clean, soft, beautifully tanned hide robe which he wore like a toga; his bare left arm was encircled at wrist and bicep by wide silver bands. Under his nose hung a silver ornament in the fashion of three leaves. Tooled silver earbobs the size of white men's dollar coins hung by thongs from his earlobes to the base of his neck, and with the motions of his measured steps they clinked against the silver gorget that curved around his throat. His hair for once was clean and untangled, and around his head he wore a patterned silk bandanna of scarlet, orange, yellow, and green shimmering like a songbird's plumage. A silver scalplock tube with a lock of his hair pulled through it hung over the bandanna from the crown of his head.

He walked with a long staff decorated with a quarter circle fan of feathers, and he was as resplendent and serene as a king. The staff was in his left hand; in his right hand, held up before him, was a short, slender stick decorated at its upper end by a small plume of delicate, flame-colored oriole feathers that trembled in the breeze to give an appearance that the stick was burning. On a string from the other end of the stick dangled the fragile copperhead skull Tecumseh had brought him from the ruins of their home in Chillicothe. He carried this stick as one would carry a torch at night; indeed, even in the bright, sun-dappled glade he seemed to be lighting his way with it.

Those who had come to ridicule the biggest fool of Tecumseh's town held their tongues, for the moment, anyway, for they were impressed by the profound change in his demeanor. He had not said anything yet this morning, either foolish or wise, but for the first time he did not bear himself at all like a fool.

Most of the people had not come to mock. Through the night they had been thinking of him and of what he had said, or what they had heard he had said, and had felt a strange tension in themselves, like being pulled between eagerness and dread. Somehow for many of them his miracle had come as an answer to a question they had not known they asked. Through the dark hours as they thought of him, they had become aware of a kind of buzzing empty place in their souls where some lost hope or faith belonged, and his words had started to fill that empty place. All sensed, whether they ever said it or not, that the spirit of the People had been weak and unhappy. Except for a few like Tecumseh and Stands Firm and Seekabo, there seemed to be no exciting warriors anymore. Many now and then would do an act of boldness when necessary, but there were few of great repute. Deep in their hearts the People suspected that their spirit had been weakened by the white men and their liquor; some thought the Great Spirit was displeased with them, some thought there was witchcraft being used by many against many. And somehow they sensed that what the one-eyed medicine man had encountered might raise them from their lethargy, might restore new power to their spirit. Here seemed to be a true messenger at last. Though few could have explained it in words, they had drifted to the council lodge yearning for hope. They filled the shady space, seating themselves on their blankets and robes, murmuring to each other, watching him, their hearts beating a little faster, a People nervous but wanting. Their chief Tecumseh, the dominant and most beloved figure in their lives, stayed in the background, standing quietly under a great, mottled sycamore off to the side instead of at the door of the council lodge. Tecumseh felt that he did not need to preside in this. He himself was so impressed by his brother's confident new demeanor that he was willing to let him hold his own show. Tecumseh had thought often during the night about his own dream of five years ago, in which the white dove had flown from Change-of-Feathers's breast into Tenskwatawa's. And as his brother, who *was* now He-Opens-the-Door, took his place before the council house and faced the multitude, straight and glittering and grave, he who before had been afraid to look one person in the eyes and now dared to do so with hundreds, Tecumseh felt an unusual compassion for this odd, star-marked person, and he sent a thought to him on a warm impulse of his heart.

*Speak well, my brother. We will listen well.*


For minutes after the crowd fell still, Open Door stood silent before them, still holding his staff in his left hand and his short stick in his right, turning slowly from one side to the other to look at them all with his good eye. The crowd waited, looking at him. Then they began to look around, at Tecumseh, at each other. Tecumseh grew alarmed that the poor man was suddenly tongue-tied in the face of so many.

It was awkward. Unlike a council, which began with a pipe ceremony and then opened with general discussion of old familiar matters and proceeded to new, this was simply one man standing before a crowd, which expected him to start without preamble and tell them something from beyond experience. Small wonder it was that the people were beginning to squirm and the would-be mockers to smirk, and Tecumseh thought now that perhaps he should not have let his brother plan it this way. What confidence he had summoned might be blown away forever if he made a fool of himself now.

Loud Noise had witnessed some of the white men's religious gatherings and had been impressed by the drama that was created when one man stood apart and above, gazed at the people for a while until they were uncomfortable, and suddenly opened up in a loud, emotional voice with a message from God. To him, this tense pause before the beginning was a rare and pregnant moment. And just now, by happy chance, a lark's song trilled through the village from someplace, like a signal from the Great Good Spirit.

Now he took a deep breath and thrust his arms up. The colorful feathers on his stick and staff were held high above the heads of the sitting crowd and trembled in the breeze. Then, when they had feasted their eyes long enough upon this commanding gesture, he opened up with a tone of voice he had sometimes practiced in his solitary monologues when he was a drunkard living in a bog. It was an eerie, flutelike tone created by a tightened throat, and he measured out his phrases so they were like a chant.

"My brothers! My sisters!"

Their scalps prickled as the strange, quavering sound wove through the space under the trees, so unusual a voice that it might well be coming from Weshemoneto through him, as a musician will express his music through a flute.

"I have been given a great power. I have been told by Our Creator to use this power to save you.

"My name is He-Opens-the-Door. I have been shown how to open the door that has shut us out from happiness.

"I died and went to the World Above, and saw it. I had done every sin, against my people and myself. You knew me! I was a sinner, I was a drunkard! I had another name then. That name is so smeared with the filth of my old sins that my mouth will not utter it, for my mouth is now pure! Tenskwatawa, Open Door, has never spoken a lie or an obscenity, and never will. I have come back cleansed. I am as we were in the Beginning! In me is a shining power!

"In the Beginning, we were full of this shining power, strong because we were pure. We moved silently through the woods. With a silent arrow we killed the animals and ate their pure meat. In silence the fish swam in pure rivers, and we caught them in silence and ate them. In silence our corn and beans and squashes grew from the earth, and those we ate. We drank only clear water, after the milk of our mothers' breasts.

"I have heard that lost silence. You have not heard it because you have not been dead." He pointed up with his small stick. "Up under the roof of the sky, there is that pure silence!"

He let them imagine that high silence. Then he went on:

"In the Beginning, our People broke that beautiful silence only to pray to the Great Good Spirit, or to speak wisely in council, or to say kind words to our children and our elders, or to give the war cry when we avenged wrongs.

"Our Creator put us on this wide, rich land, and told us we were free to go where the game was, where the soil was good for planting. That was our state of true happiness. We did not have to beg for anything. Our Creator had taught us how to find and make everything we needed, from trees and plants and animals and stone. We lived in bark, and we wore only the skins of animals. Our Creator taught us how to use fire, in living, and in sacred ceremonies. She taught us how to heal with barks and roots, and how to make sweet foods with berries and fruits, with papaws and the water of the maple tree. Our Creator gave us tobacco, and said, Send your prayers up to me on its fragrant smoke. Our Creator taught us how to enjoy loving our mates, and gave us laws to live by, so that we would not bother each other, but help each other. Our Creator sang to us in the wind and the running water, in the bird songs, in children's laughter, and taught us music. And we listened, and our ears were open, and we saw, and our eyes were clear. Our hearts and stomachs were never dirty and never troubled us."

Tecumseh listened, and his heart ached for the time when the People and the world had been so good. In the eyes of the listeners he could see the same yearning. Surely his brother had been purified, if a mouth that had only lied and profaned and gossiped could now evoke such pictures of goodness.

"Thus were we created," Open Door went on in that strange voice that was now beginning to sound beautiful because of what it said. "Thus we lived for a long time, proud and happy. We had never eaten pig meat, nor tasted the poison called whiskey, nor worn wool from sheep, nor struck fire or dug earth with steel, nor cooked in iron, nor hunted and fought with loud guns, nor ever had diseases which soured our blood or rotted our organs. We were pure, so we were strong and happy.

"*But!* Beyond the Great Sunrise Water, there lived a people who had iron, and those dirty and unnatural things, who seethed with diseases, who fought to death over the names of their gods! They had so crowded and befouled their own island that they fled from it, because excrement and carrion were up to their knees. They came to our island. Our Singers had warned us that a pale people would come across the Great Water and try to destroy us, but we forgot. We did not know they were evil, so we welcomed them and fed them. We taught them much of what Our Grandmother had taught us, how to hunt, grow corn and tobacco, find good things in the forest. They saw how much room we had, and wanted it. They brought iron and pigs and wool and rum and disease. They came farther and drove us over the mountains. Then when they had filled up and dirtied our old lands by the sea, they looked over the mountains and saw this Middle Ground, and we are old enough to remember when they started rushing into it. We remember our villages on fire every year and the crops slashed every fall and the children hungry every winter. All this you know."

Tecumseh was surprised that his brother's sermon had picked up his own theme of the white men's evils. He had not suspected that Open Door's mission had to do with the problem of the Americans. But now he realized that somehow their two voices were conveying the same complaint. Of course, he thought. Our messages are from the same heaven!

"For many years," Open Door was saying, "we traded furs to the English or the French, for wool blankets and guns and iron things, for steel awls and needles and axes, for mirrors, for pretty things made of beads and silver. And for liquor. This was foolish, but we did not know it. We shut our ears to the Great Good Spirit. We did not want to hear that we were being foolish.

"But now those things of the white men have corrupted us, and made us weak and needful. Our men forgot how to hunt without noisy guns. Our women don't want to make fire without steel, or cook without iron, or sew without metal awls and needles, or fish without steel hooks. Some look in those mirrors all the time, and no longer teach their daughters to make leather or render bear oil. We learned to need the white men's goods, and so now a People who never had to beg for anything must beg for everything!"

Much of what Open Door was saying now, Tecumseh recognized from his own harangues. It was good that he was saying these things. Open Door went on:

"Some of our women married white men, and made half-breeds.

"Many of us now crave liquor. He whose filthy name I will not speak, he who was I before, was one of the worst of those drunkards. There are drunkards in almost every family. You know how bad this is.

"And so you see what has happened to us. We were fools to take all these things that weakened us. We did not need them then, but we believe we need them now. We turned our backs on the old ways. Instead of thanking Weshemoneto for all we used to have, we turned to the white men and asked them for more. So now we depend upon the very people who destroy us! This is our weakness! Our corruption! Our Creator scolded me, 'If you had lived the way I taught you, the white men could never have got you under their foot!'

"And that is why Our Creator purified me and sent me down to you full of the shining power: to make you what you were before! As you sit before me I will tell you the many rules Our Creator gave me for you. I will tell you how I went to the World Above. When I tell you of the punishments I saw, they will terrify you! But listen: Those punishments will be upon *you*, unless you follow me through the door that I am opening for you!"

The hundreds of people sat like children before a storyteller as he related again his travel through the sky. Their faces were soft with longing as he described the paradise he had been permitted to see but not to enter. And then as he described Matchemoneto's house of smoke and torment, they winced and moaned. Some covered their ears because they could not bear to hear of it but then uncovered them for fear of missing some words that would save them from it. When he told of the Worst Sinners who went clear into the fire, or those Lesser Sinners who were only burned on their limbs, the people were wondering to which fire their own departed ones had gone or were wondering which fire they themselves deserved. When he described the punishment of the drunkards, many people rocked to and fro and wept, because, as he had said, everyone had some relatives who faced that punishment.

As the sun rose to midday, Open Door went on and on with the story of his journey. Even the few people who still doubted him were afraid; whether he had seen it himself or only learned of it some other way, the afterworld surely was as he described it, and everyone was eager to learn how to take the right road and avoid the left one.

Tecumseh grew ever more amazed at his brother's speaking powers. In this great oratorical flight he recognized many elements. Much of Tecumseh's own doctrine was in it, and some of the fables told by Black Fish and Black Hoof were there and some Bible things he must have overheard from Big Fish and perhaps the Shakers, and probably there was more than a little of his own strange imagination. Tecumseh, who knew Loud Noise as well as anyone had, could almost point to the origin of each phrase that came forth. But he did not doubt that his brother had dreamed in his trance or that his spirit actually had been taken away and inspired. All these recognizable embellishments were, like those a child puts on the retelling of a dream in the morning, no less a part of his true soul, or they had come through Tecumseh from the same divine source and thus were true. The spiritual force Open Door was creating here would not remain confined to this crowd of listeners; it would spread like light in darkness, from village to village, from tribe to tribe, from nation to nation. Tecumseh could not doubt it: his brother's miracle was a part of the great design that had been coming in signs since his own childhood. However Open Door might color the words, he was surely a Messenger.

Now Open Door held up his short stick with its fire feathers on the end and passed it before him in a half circle and cried in that strange, flutelike voice:

"Here is what Our Creator told me we must do, to be happy and strong and proud as we were before we listened to white men. Listen well! Here is the way to stay out of the house of fire and go to the beautiful country I saw at first. Some of it will be hard for us! Now listen to me with all the power of your attention:

"No red man must ever drink liquor, or he will go and have the hot lead poured in his mouth! You know I have been a slave to liquor since first I tasted it. But never again will I take any! If ever you saw me taste it again, you would know that what I tell you is false!"

Tecumseh and Star Watcher looked at each other across the crowd, both amazed at the conviction in his statement. Surely their brother knew what he was putting at risk by promising to curb that appetite for liquor! If he had had any doubt about his dream, that would have been the last thing he would have forsworn.

"This also Our Creator told me:

"No red man shall take more than one wife in the future. No red man shall run after women. If he is single, let him take a wife, and lie only with her.

"If any wife behaves badly, her husband may whip her. But then they shall look each other in the face and laugh together, and have no more ill will.

"Any red woman who is living with a white man must return to her people, and must leave her children with the husband, so that all nations will be pure in their blood.

"Our Creator told me there are too many doing witchcraft, and using their medicine bags for false beliefs. All the People must gather together to destroy their personal medicine bags, in the presence of all, for all our medicine now is in the shining power I have been given!"

A murmur of astonishment swept through the crowd, because in their medicine bags the People kept the sacred things that protected them and healed them. "I tell you what I was told!" Open Door's voice carried over this hubbub. "We cannot save ourselves from corruption by doing only little, easy things! Listen! And when you destroy your medicine bags you will make an open confession of all the bad deeds you have done, and beg forgiveness. You heard me confess all my sins, which were much worse than yours, and I did so because it is required by the Great Good Spirit! Only light will cure moldiness; only light will purify your spirits. Soon I will call us all together for this cleansing, and anyone who wants to follow me through the open door to goodness will have to do this, or else be doomed!"

When these words had cowed the crowd back into silence, Open Door resumed. "Now hear what I was told about dealing with white men! These things we must do, to cleanse ourselves of their corruption!" Many of the listeners seemed relieved that he was directing himself away toward that race. Few of the men or women really had any direct association with whites.

"Our foods are sacred. Our Grandmother taught us how to hunt and raise these foods, to select seeds and continue the best strains. These foods are for us only. Never sell any of our food to a white person. If a white man comes to you hungry, give him a little, only to give him strength to go away!

"Do not eat any food that is raised or cooked by a white person. It is not good for us. Eat not their bread made of wheat, for Our Creator gave us corn for our bread. Eat not the meat of their filthy swine, nor of their chicken fowls, nor the beef of their cattle, which are tame and thus have no spirit in them. Their foods will seem to fill your empty belly, but this deceives you, for food without spirit does not nourish you."

Tecumseh remembered the food he had eaten with Ga-lo-weh and his family in his visits over the years. Sometimes it had been game and corn, but often beef and wheat. The things Open Door was saying pointed at everybody in some way.

"There are two kinds of white men," Open Door went on. "There are the Americans, and there are the others. You may give your hand in friendship to the French, or the Spaniards, or the British. But the Americans are not like those. The Americans come from the slime of the sea, with mud and weeds in their claws, and they are a kind of crayfish serpent whose claws grab in our earth and take it from us."

Tecumseh recognized that as one of his own figures of speech that he had used in anger once long ago. This was good. Tenskwatawa, the Open Door, could not have said anything more in harmony with Tecumseh's purposes than this.

Open Door, who had been talking for almost three hours, went on with his commandments.

"Wear only clothing that you have made from skins and sewn with sinew. I see here wool garments and hats made by white men. Give those back to the first white person you see.

"In our towns there are dogs of the white men's kind, those whose ears hang down. I saw such a dog watching me from behind a tree with white men's eyes, and I knew: these are prowling our towns with the white man's spirit in them. And there are cats that you got from the white men. These are bad animals. Often a witch takes the shape of a cat. You must kill these cats and dogs, or else take them to a white man's town and leave them there."

This commandment was heard with almost as much dismay as that of the medicine bags. The white man's kinds of dogs were more trusting and amiable than the wolflike Indian dogs, and many people had grown attached to the ones they had. Some red men had learned how to use the long-eared dogs to help them hunt and thus found them useful. Some of the big dogs could pull almost as much baggage on a travois as a pony could.

And the cats were liked by children and helped keep rodents out of the grain. "Yes! I told you! Some of these steps to purification will be hard!"

The next was hard indeed:

"The fire struck by white man's steel is not sacred fire. You must put out such fire in your lodges and kindle a new fire using the old way, and this will be a sacred fire." Most of the women groaned and gasped. Making fire without flint and steel was very hard and tedious. "You must never let this sacred fire go out, for it is your reborn spirit, beginning now, and if it goes out, so will your life go out. When you move from place to place you must bear sacred coals with you, as we did in the ancient times, and rekindle the fire when you arrive.

"And now listen:

"The Great Good Spirit wants our men to hunt and kill game as in the ancient days, with the silent arrow and the lance and the snare, and no longer with guns."

Here again was more of Tecumseh's practical thinking that he had absorbed sometime; with game growing more scarce every year, gunshots drove animals away from a hunting ground. But another practical reason for this was as Open Door now said: "If we hunt in the old ways, we will not have to depend upon white men, for new guns and powder and lead, or go to them to have broken guns repaired. Remember it is the wish of the Great Good Spirit that we have no more commerce with white men!"

It was evident from the expressions in the men's faces, though, that this would be a hardship. So many had lost, or never even had, the skill needed for stalking and killing game with a bow. But these were commandments brought to the People from heaven, and they must be obeyed. Many of the men sat in humility, almost in despair, wondering if they would even be able to feed their families. As if seeing their thoughts, Open Door told them: "It will take us a while to become such hunters again. We may keep our guns, and if we need to defend ourselves against American white men, the guns will kill them because they are a white man's weapon. But arrows will kill American intruders, too! You must go to the grandfathers and have them teach you to make good bows and shape arrowheads, and you must recover the old hunting skills. That is what the Creator instructed me to tell you.

"And now listen, for here is the most important message I bring you:

"The Great Good Spirit will call me from time to time and teach me more to help you. Our Creator told me that all red men who refuse to obey these laws are bad people, or witches, and must be put to death. Anyone who does not wish to live in a way that pleases Weshemoneto must want instead to please Matchemoneto, and such a person must be a witch.

Witches should be killed, for they divide the People and weaken their spirit." This was a chilling announcement, but the people were quick to nod agreement to it, because many did believe that witchcraft was a cause of much of their anxiety. To live in the midst of a witch-hunt was a frightful ordeal, as anyone could be accused and tried. But it had been done before in the People's past, and after the hunts had come light and freedom from fear.

"Hear me, my People," Open Door intoned, raising his stick and staff and holding them as he had in the beginning of this long and disturbing oration. "All red men will soon know these messages I have brought. They are hungry for guidance from heaven. I will tell the people I see, and you will tell those you see. But I warn you: Our Creator thundered and said that anyone who reveals these laws to any white men will die at once, and never be shown the right road!

"The Great Good Spirit will appoint a place to be our holy town, and at that place I will call *all* red men to come and share this shining power. For the People in all tribes are corrupt and miserable! In that holy town we will pray every morning and every night for the earth to be fruitful, and the game and fish to be plentiful again. We will no longer do the frolic dances that excite lust and make us silly. Instead, the Great Good Spirit will teach me the old dances we did before the corruption, and from these dances we will receive strength and happiness!"

*All red men!* Tecumseh shivered at the sound of that. Open Door with his appeal to the yearnings of all the miserable red men must be the way to bring the tribes together despite their many-headedness! Open Door truly must be, then, an instrument of Weshemoneto's design! *All red men!*

"Now I, Tenskwatawa, He-Opens-the-Door, will go and be alone for a while, to learn more of what we must do. I have told you everything I know, but soon I will know more. You will go and tell what you have learned here, but tell it to no white man, or to anyone who would tell it to a white man. Get rid of cats and long-eared dogs! Make good bows! Put out your fires made with steel, and kindle an everlasting fire by wood on wood. Turn your backs on the whiskey sellers and the traders, and do not listen to the Jesus missionaries!

"Look among yourselves for witches, and note who they are, and they will be judged soon. How will you know witches? I will tell you: They will be doing commerce with Americans, and going to their treaty councils, against the warnings of Our Creator.

"And they will start whispering to you that Open Door is not a true holy man or prophet! *That* is how you will know witches!"

Tecumseh, who had been absorbed in his brother's declarations, suddenly felt eyes upon him. He turned his head and saw, among the hundreds staring at Open Door, one pair of eyes again turned his way. Star Watcher's eyes met his. They stared at each other across the crowd, their faces full of questions.

They, above all others in the nation, knew the strange powers of their brother's mind, and each could see that the other was impressed by the cunning in those last words.

# CHAPTER 26

## *Vincennes, Indiana Territory*
## *April 1806*

G overnor William Henry Harrison put his hands on the edge of the table and rose, leaving most of his breakfast on his plate. "Please excuse me, my dear. I must finish a letter. The messenger is waiting."

Anna's morning smile faded. She pointed with her pert little nose at his plate. "You've eaten hardly a thing!" She was annoyed. He never had time to sit through a breakfast with her. He was always in his office, meeting with Indian agents or Indian chiefs, or with traders or politicians, or with Mr. Stout, editor of the *Indiana Gazette.* Or, if he was alone, he was always writing, writing, writing his countless and interminable letters. In the eleven years of their marriage, she estimated, he must have written as many words as there were in the Bible. It was hard for her to understand why a man who was always succeeding at everything he undertook should waste so much time and ink *explaining.* She had always thought that unsuccessful men were the ones who needed to explain. He wrote long letters explaining his doings even where no explanations were even asked for and often would send the same explanations to various government officials who could not possibly have any interest in them whatever.

In these last few months, she knew, he had been fretting terribly over some so-called Shawnee prophet and his mumby-jumby, which, in her secret opinion, was not even any of his business, being outside the Indiana Territory, back in Ohio. He was so preoccupied with it that he lost sleep as well as his appetite.

Anna Symmes Harrison sighed and excused him. She would just have to stroll in the garden alone. Again. He had built this handsome mansion and estate, called Grouseland, the most impressive place north of Louisville, but never allowed himself time to enjoy it. The only time he used the lawn and veranda was when he held councils out there with Indian chiefs. He would drop everything to spend a few hours with any bushloper or trader or missionary or half-breed who could confirm his fears with more distressing tales of that faraway Shawnee prophet and his cult. And he was always muttering that the British must be behind it. British indeed!

She almost snorted into her teacup at the silliness of her husband's concern. After all, the whole frontier was in the throes of revivalism, wild, trembling, screaming revivalism, with shrill-voiced evangelists whipping hundreds at a time into a frenzy; why shouldn't the poor savages do the same? But of course she never expressed these opinions to him.

Governor Harrison shut his office door, sat down at his desk, and pulled out from a pigeonhole a rolled sheet upon which he had begun writing before dawn. He had been thinking about writing such a letter for a long time, but this latest horrible news had made it an urgent necessity. The influence of the Shawnee named Tenskwatawa had grown to alarming proportions in just a year, but now, with the news of the burning of witches, it was time to undermine that charlatan before he became too great a danger.

For months the rumors and reports of strange happenings had been trickling in. Along every Indian trace there were hundreds of warriors, women, and children traveling. And as all roads once had led to Rome, they all seemed now to lead to the Shawnee prophet's new village near Greenville in Ohio. There, near the ruins of the fort where Harrison had assisted in Wayne's great treaty, this mysterious Shawnee had built a town of some fifty or sixty cabins, many *wigewas,* and an enormous meetinghouse reported to be 150 feet long. The man called Tenskwatawa had proclaimed himself successor to the old shaman of the Shawnees. Moravian missionaries among the Delawares in eastern Indiana last summer had reported that their large congregations of hard-won Christian converts had suddenly shrunk to a handful. A few months later, large numbers of Ottawas, Wyandots, and Senecas had been seen on the trails, despite the harsh weather of early winter, and Harrison's informants had told him that these people were going to hear the Shawnee preach. Traders along the way had reported the surprising news that they could not sell their liquor to very many members of those tribes anymore. Indeed, their sales of many items—ammunition, clothes, and tools—had mysteriously declined.

Then, two months ago, according to Governor Tiffin of Ohio, three Ohio militia officers had discovered a large council in progress on the headwaters of the Great Miami River and had been turned away when they went to investigate it. The Shawnees there had shaken hands with them in a very cool manner—and with their left hands only. Eventually Governor Tiffin had been assured that the gathering was only a ceremony of worship, but the officers had remained suspicious because of the many painted feathers being displayed and a war post visible in the camp.

These distant activities, even though in another governor's domain, had haunted Harrison's sleep, for he did not like any secretive Indian activity that might somehow hinder his grand progression of land acquisitions.

But only now had he been shocked into action, by some very chilling news: a witch-hunt among the Delawares.

The details of it were so grisly that he had not even mentioned them to Anna. A group of Delaware warriors, who were disciples of this mysterious Shawnee prophet, had rounded up and confined a dozen Christian Delawares and old people in the town of Wah-pi-kah-me-kunk, charging them with being witches, then had summoned the Prophet himself to come from his town and judge them. After looking each in the face and allegedly seeing into his heart, he had named three as true witches.

The first was a Christian convert called Ann Charity, a favorite of the Moravian missionaries because she was, in every respect but the color of her skin, like a clean, devout, industrious old white woman. The witch-hunters had tied her to a pole over a bonfire, burning her feet and legs for four days until she had screamed her confession. Then they had lowered her into the blaze and burned her to death.

Next condemned had been Twisting Vines. This aged Delaware chief had been a leader in the treaty ceremonies with General Wayne at Greenville and in the decade since had been a model government Indian. Twisting Vines had been a Christian convert, though lately he had drifted away from it. Accused and tortured, the chief had confessed to poisoning people's minds. Then he was tomahawked and burned while the missionaries were forced to watch.

The third condemned one had been a Christianized Mohawk called Joshua, whom Twisting Vines had implicated during his own confession. Joshua had been the missionaries' carpenter and organist. The Moravians had pleaded desperately that this beloved and useful man be spared, but of course their pleas had only strengthened the witch-hunters' suspicions, and Joshua had been sentenced to burn at the stake. The witch-hunts, according to reports Harrison received, continued to this day in the Delaware towns, though the Shawnee prophet had returned to his own village. Even in his horror, Harrison could perceive quite clearly what these three victims had

had in common: they all had been special favorites of the whites. In this lay
the true basis for Governor Harrison's alarm. And so he was writing a letter
to the chiefs of the Delawares.

>    My Children:
>    My heart is filled with grief, and my eyes are dissolved in tears at
> the news that has reached me. You have been celebrated for your
> wisdom above all the tribes of the red men who inhabit this great
> island. . . .
>    From what cause, then, does it proceed that you have departed
> from the wise counsels of your fathers and covered yourselves with
> guilt? My children, tread back the steps you have taken, and endeavor
> to regain the straight road which you have abandoned. The dark,
> crooked, and thorny one which you are now pursuing will certainly
> lead you to endless woe and misery. . . .
>    Who is this pretended prophet who dares to speak in the name of
> the great Creator? Examine him. Is he more wise and virtuous than
> you are yourselves, that he should be selected to convey to you the
> orders of your God? Demand of him some proofs at least of his being
> the messenger of the Deity. If God has really empowered him, He
> has doubtless authorized him to perform miracles that he may be
> known and received as a prophet. If he is really a prophet, ask of him
> to cause the sun to stand still, the moon to alter its course, the rivers
> to cease to flow, or the dead to rise from their graves. If he does these
> things, you may believe that he has been sent from God. He tells you
> that the Great Spirit commands you to punish with death those who
> deal in magic, and that he is authorized to point them out. Wretched
> delusion! My children, do not believe that the great and good Creator
> of Mankind has directed you to destroy your own flesh. . . .
>    Clear your eyes, I beseech you, from the mist that surrounds them.
> No longer be imposed upon by the arts of an impostor. . . . Let peace
> and harmony prevail amongst you. Let your poor old men and women
> sleep in quietness, and banish from their minds the dreadful idea of
> being burnt alive by their own friends and countrymen. . . .
>    Let me hear by the return of the bearer that you have determined
> to follow my advice.

There, he thought, reading back over it, more than just a little pleased
with his composition. It was straightforward, impassioned, and adorned
with the figurative language the red men so loved, but not too much of it.
He read it through still another time, so pleased by it that he forgot it was

an urgent message of life and death and that a messenger was waiting to
take it to the Delawares. Then he took a deep breath, shook his head once,
and signed it.

Your friend and adviser,
William Henry Harrison
Governor—Indiana Territory

Then he summoned the messenger.


Tecumseh and Galloway sat on chairs near the shelves of books after supper
to smoke a pipe and talk. Galloway's sons sat nearby, listening, while his
wife and daughter scoured pots at the fireplace in the other end of the room.

Tecumseh had not meant to stop here. Much was happening now in the
world of his own race, so much that he and Open Door were always on the
move, and the brothers were so absorbed in matters of the deepest importance to all red men that he felt almost guilty about veering down to visit
this white family again, to step across into the white man's world he so
deplored. But now he was at ease in the family again, being treated as an
old close friend, as he had been each time he had come in the past years,
and he was glad he had come. It was good to look at the site of Chillicothe
and believe that through his efforts it might someday become the Shawnee
capital again. And this was like a refuge from the tension of responsibility,
from the strain and work of their sacred mission.

Open Door had had several more visions since his first one a year ago,
and his religion had grown more elaborate; more rules and commandments
had been given him, and he had developed new rituals and ceremonies and
dances, while revising many of the old ones.

His religion had caught like a dry-grass fire, spreading among people
who had been desperate for hope and pride. Doubters had been swept away
by the fervor. The new village at Greenville now had more than seven
hundred permanent residents, and there were always hundreds of visitors
who had made their pilgrimage from distant tribes. By now four or five
thousand had come, listened, then carried the word back to their homes.
Always the drums beat, and there was singing and dancing. Mass prayer
meetings morning and night filled the People's hearts with joy and unspeakable understanding.

But for the chief and shaman of such a town there was not a moment's
rest, ever. To feed the inhabitants, and the great numbers of pilgrims who
always arrived hungry and exhausted by their hasty travel, was a great task.

And then there were matters that, by the very nature of the movement, required the greatest sort of tact and wisdom. With the people came their chiefs, who were often jealous of the importance being assumed by the Prophet and Tecumseh. These chiefs had to be persuaded, convinced, sometimes flattered—especially when they began to realize that this movement was not simply religious in nature. Tecumseh had to determine just how much information he could entrust with any chief at any time. Some of the chiefs were hungry for the spiritual guidance but were treaty-bound to the Americans. Tecumseh and his brother had conferred secretly with each other for hours on end about their signs and what the whole aim of Weshemoneto really was. Open Door himself had had to be persuaded that his own great transformation, his sudden prominence, his miracle, was only a part of the movement. He found it hard to stay humble.

"The Great Good Spirit wants to make the red men all one, so they will all agree not to give up their lands anymore," Tecumseh would explain to him. "He has put you here to make all the red men one in heart, to turn them back to the old pure ways in which they did not need the white men. When they are all this way, then they can unite their minds also, and learn how to stop the white man and put him back where he came from. Weshemoneto has chosen us, my brother, to do this together. Each of us has a part to do that he does better. But," he had added as an important caution, "until we are united, no one must know what the end of it is to be. Jealous men would set us against each other or betray us to the whites. The whites would grow scared and try to scatter us before we were strong enough. Therefore, my brother, we must stay at peace with the white men until our strength is complete. Maybe we will have to bear their insults sometimes. Maybe we will even have to profess brotherhood with them for a while, so they will leave us alone. This we can do if we must. We owe them a hundred hundred deceits."

This white man Galloway was aware that something extraordinary was stirring among the woodland tribes. His house being on an important road, the old Bullskin Trace, he was visited by travelers on every kind of business—soldiers, traders, judges, and government men as well as migrants and settlers—and the activities of the Indians were always discussed. Though there had been a general peace here for more than a decade, since Wayne's treaty, the slightest rumor could cause a wave of fear to sweep through the settlements. James Galloway was aware of the recent alarm about the Indians at Greenville, and he was aware too that his guest Tecumseh was involved in the secret councils in some important way. But he did not ask. Tecumseh had not mentioned anything, so Galloway knew better than to probe. He did not want to drive away his friend. Instead they would talk of books and stories, of how technical things worked, of their deep personal beliefs. Tecumseh remained most interested in the stories of Hamlet and of the chief in the Bible called Moses. He was intrigued with the story about Jesus, the son of the white man's God, and he pressed for explanations of how the white men of that day could have put to death the son of their own God. To him this cast a doubt over every aspect of the white men's religion, and Galloway would squirm and frown as he tried to explain it in a way that would make sense. Once again Tecumseh was having a good time. He camped near the site of his mother's old *wigewa* and stayed several days, meditating on his duty in the daytime, watching for signs, and visiting the white family in the evenings. No bodyguards were with him.

The girl Rebekah, who had already read nearly every one of her father's books and spoke with the precise grammar of a schoolteacher, was not shy about correcting Tecumseh's awkward English. In fact, she used this task or anything else as an excuse to stay near him and get his attention. Of the dozens of men who passed through or sheltered here every year, this good-humored, musky-smelling, naked, brawny chief with his beautiful, smooth copper skin, sparkling hazel eyes, brilliant smile, and probing intelligence was by far the most splendid. He drew her like a magnet, stirred strange yearnings in her.

"I have," she would drill him. "He has. They have."

"I have. He has. They have."

"I will have. He will have. They will have."

"I will have. He will have. They will have."

"I have had," she would intone, secretly admiring the delineation of muscles on his shoulder or the hard, gleaming contour of his hip where it was bare between his belt and the top of his legging, muscle as solid as that of a running horse. "He has had. They have had . . ."

She had breasts now, swelling in the cotton front of her dress. She was becoming a woman, and feelings stirred in her lower belly sometimes, and she had had—indeed, was now having—her monthly flow, with its sensations that made her confused and ashamed. When she was this close to this half-naked, vibrant man, the feelings would unsettle her, she felt the discomforts of her condition, and she had to concentrate to keep her mind on the phrases she was teaching him.

Tecumseh was no stranger to the admiration of young women or to what the moon did to them, and now as he repeated, "I have had, he has had, they have had," he was surprised suddenly by the moist rutting scent in the warm closeness between them. He drew back slightly. He did not allow himself to think of it. This was the child of his friend, and besides that, she was of the white race, a different kind of people. There was supposed to be no connection of that kind between the races, according to the admonitions brought by his brother from the Creator.

Yet for a moment, as his gaze passed over the form of her body in its concealing dress, he wondered what certain portions and junctures of it must look like. He shivered. "Enough, Ga-lo-weh girl," he said. "My head is tired of who has!"

"Mister Tecumftha Chief," she scolded, feeling flushed and giddy, "I *do* have a name, which you should know by now after seven years, if you're as bright as you seem. Please do me the courtesy of calling me Rebekah, if you will."

"Courtesy?" He pronounced it carefully. "What does mean this word, Rebekah Ga-lo-weh girl?"

And later that night, when Rebekah and her mother had gone up the steep stairs to the sleeping rooms, and Tecumseh could hear the creaking of the floor above him as they moved about, and he and James Galloway sat talking about the things of the world, Tecumseh looked at this solid, happy man and wondered if he was aware that his daughter was under the moon and, if so, why she had been allowed to be here in this room with men, handling food, talking with the guest, not hiding her face or shutting away her odor. The white people had so much knowledge stored in their books, and such a fine, difficult tongue, and a grave, mythical religion. And yet they were so lax, or ignorant, about the taboo.

Galloway was saying: "Have you ever seen an eclipse?"

"I do not know. Have I? What does mean this word, my friend?"

"Eclipse. It's when the moon passes over the face of the sun, and makes it dark."

"Ah! When the sun is black!"

"Well, yes, it looks black."

"Our elders know much of the Black Sun. They call it *Mukutaaweethe Keelswah.* It is a sign of war trouble. Once when I was a boy I saw it happen, and less than one moon later, the Long Knife Clark was in the valley and had thrown our British allies down. Have you seen a Black Sun in your years, Ga-lo-weh?"

"I saw the one you speak of. In June of seventy-eight it was. But seems we will see another one soon enough. There's to be one this year on June the sixteenth. Several gentlemen from Harvard and the government have been through here, going west to set up stations in the prairies for watching it. President Jefferson's quite a scientist, you know."

Tecumseh's brain was humming. Suddenly he had a dozen questions to ask. Putting a hand on Galloway's wrist to slow him down, he asked first, "What is 'thsi-enisht'?" It was a hard word to say, and likewise it proved a hard word for Galloway to define.

"A scientist is a, ah, a man who studies the things of earth and heaven, who watches them to see how God governs them . . . how they move and grow . . . how man can use them. . . ." He grasped at the air with both hands, trying to pull out the right words for his meanings. "Scientists watch plants and animals, they watch stars, they watch clouds and rain, and the earth. . . ."

"Does not all white men do this?" Tecumseh asked. "All Shawnee does this." But without waiting for the reply, he hurried on to the question that loomed largest in his mind. "How does this scientist *know* this will happen on the day you told me? Is scientist a prophet?"

This question precipitated a long explanation with slow, sweeping movements of the hands, showing where the sun moves and the earth and the moon, until finally, beyond his depth on certain details, Galloway turned to his bookshelves and drew out one that was illustrated with diagrams of circles lined up within circles, this one called Earth, this one Sun, this one Moon, this one Mars, and so on. When these diagrams had been fully explained, Tecumseh for the first time since he had learned of books began to suspect that some of them must be as full of wrong ideas as were the heads of white men. If the white man could believe that the earth was a ball that spun around another ball, the sun, staying up forever with no Turtle under it to hold it in place, and believe it so strongly as to put it in a book and thus misguide other men, then it would not be wise to put as much faith in books as he had tended to do. So, shutting his mind to these absurdities to keep his head from spinning off like another ball in the sky, he asked simply:

"But can you promise me, Ga-lo-weh, on your heart as my friend, that on the day you said, there will be *Mukutaaweethe Keelswah?*"

Galloway chuckled. "Absolutely! At high noon. Harvard says so. Nine professors can't be wrong."

"Then you promise, Ga-lo-weh? I can stand in front of my lodge on that day and know you say truth?"

"Ha, ha! Yes, my friend! I promise." But now Galloway himself looked just a bit dubious, to find himself making a promise it was out of his personal power to keep. "I, uh, I can't say it won't be a cloudy day, but mark my word, it will be dark at noon."

Tecumseh slapped both hands down on his knees and laughed. "Good! I will stand outside in the middle of the day, and I will see. How many days do I count before this one you call June the sixteenth, Ga-lo-weh?"


When Tecumseh returned to the town at Greenville, Open Door greeted him with important news. Young Wyandots in villages on the Sandusky in northern Ohio had sent messages down. They feared witches in their towns, and they wanted their prophet to come and reveal them as he had in the Delaware town. He was very pleased with this request. Though he did not have many followers yet among the Wyandots, this meant that the ones he did have placed great faith in him. He would go and help them.

Tecumseh was not so pleased with this request. The hunting of witches and execution of nonbelievers was an aspect of Open Door's code that he did not like. It went against all his personal convictions about merciful treatment of captives and the helpless. In particular the execution of the woman Ann Charity had disgusted him. But if the Prophet's followers sought help in this unsavory way, he obviously would not deny them, as he had first called for it.

"Beware, though," Tecumseh admonished him, "of the Crane, Tarhe. He is a friend of the Americans, and he is jealous of your power. Be careful what you do there."

Then, while Open Door was preparing to leave for the Wyandot country, a delegation of Delawares arrived from their White River towns. They brought a letter that had been written to them by the governor named Harrison at Vincennes. Tecumseh read it in silence. He recognized most of the words. Then he translated it for Open Door, who was at first amazed that his brother had learned to speak the marks on paper. He knew he had been taught some by Big Fish, but he did not know of all the help that Tecumseh had gotten from Ga-lo-weh and his daughter.

Then as he got the gist of the challenge in the letter, Open Door began to look stricken. Tecumseh turned to the Delawares. "Did you reply to this?" They said they had.

"We told Harrison this. We said, You white men also try your bad people, and you kill them if they are guilty. We only do among ourselves what you do among yourselves. These witches were guilty of bad things."

"A true answer," Open Door said. *"Web-sab."* But he looked worried, and then he said, "What did you tell him about . . . about proving me?" This, plainly, was worrying him.

Their leader looked almost apologetic. "We told the Governor Harrison, 'The Prophet may choose to prove himself. We will not demand it.' " But then the Delawares looked at Open Door expectantly, as if a miracle would be very welcome. Open Door glanced at Tecumseh. His pleasure at the prospect of going witch-hunting among the Wyandots apparently was being overshadowed by Harrison's challenge, which seemed to hang in the air. It was one thing to have visions. But even if one understood and believed them, it was another thing to prove oneself by making a miracle.

Open Door knew in his heart that he was not even a very good healer. He had not the slightest faith in his ability to make miracles on call.

But as the Prophet's face darkened, Tecumseh's brightened. Extending his hand to the Delawares, he said, "You have come far to bring us your letter. Thank you. The white man Harrison must esteem the Delawares highly to show fear of what you do. Now, rest in our holy town, and eat, and we will talk more about miracles after a while. We do not have to satisfy this land stealer, but we do want you to remain firm in your faith and friendship. Maybe my brother will decide to do a miracle to teach this Harrison not to be so smug."

In the privacy of Open Door's lodge, Tecumseh leaned toward him, looking very happy and playful, and he chuckled and said, "Brother, the white governor gave you many suggestions for miracles in his letter. What would be the best miracle? Oh, let us think hard. . . ." He put his hand on top of his head and shut his eyes and grunted as if thinking very hard. Open Door scowled at him as if he resented being teased about something this serious. "Ah!" exclaimed Tecumseh, opening his eyes and pointing upward. "Let us have a miracle that is easy for all to see. Let us have, ah, a *Mukutaaweethe Keelswah!*"

"A Black Sun?" Open Door was looking at him as if he were a crazy man.

"Yes! A Black Sun. Of course you could darken the sky right now or at any time just to show the Delawares, but maybe it would be better to do it one or two moons from now, so that people can come from far away to see you do it. Think how that would make an impression in their bosoms! Think how your fame would spring up then! Yes! We could summon people from far away, and hundreds from many nations could be here to see you do it!"

"Brother," Open Door groaned, "if I were to call upon the sun to grow dark, I would not want hundreds to watch it refuse. I would not want one!"

"Ah, my brother! You lack faith in yourself! How can all red men have faith in you if you have no faith in yourself?"

"But I have never promised them I can make the sun go dark!"

"Then do! Ha, ha!"

And then he told his miserable brother about the scientists who were moving into the prairies of the Illinois country and into the Iowa land west of the Missi-se-pe, to watch what was called an eclipse, on a day that would be called June the sixteenth.

Open Door wanted to believe there was such a splendid opportunity, but after a moment's thought he had the very same question Tecumseh had had. "Can we be sure of this?"

"Listen," Tecumseh said. "These scientist men always know when it will happen. Not by magic, but just by a way of writing down and counting up. They are right every time." He recited from his memory of Ga-lo-weh's book all the times they had been right.

"Then can you promise me," Open Door said dubiously, "that on the day you speak of, there will be *Mukutaaweethe Keelswah?*"

"At the middle of the day," Tecumseh replied, smiling, remembering how Ga-lo-weh had convinced him. "Har-vard cannot be wrong."

"Who is Har-vard?"

Tecumseh shrugged. "Someone who cannot be wrong."

Open Door's eye began to twinkle. "What a great thing that would be!" He rubbed his palms together. "It is not that I would want to fool our people. But it would take such a smugness out of Harrison! I must trust you, then, my brother. We will have a Black Sun. Let us call for the People from many nations to come and see my powers!"

So they sent forth the word of the miracle, and the People looked amazed. Then Open Door went away north to the Wyandot towns to hunt witches. Tecumseh sent Thick Water and some other bodyguards with him, both to protect him if he needed it and to bring back their own version of whatever he might report.

But then Tecumseh began to worry. Despite Ga-lo-weh's confident promise, Tecumseh realized how rashly he had staked everything on some dubious white man's information. Can you hang the fate of your brother and your People, he chided himself, on a book that says the universe is a handful of balls rolling in the air?

Star Watcher soon noticed how worried her brother was. She sensed that it had something to do with the prediction of the Black Sun, so she caught Tecumseh alone one day and probed until he told her the story of the prediction. Her eyes widened. She put her palm on her throat and took a long breath. "My brother! Have I ever told you that you did a foolish thing? I think I have to tell you now! This was you who did this deceit? Such a thing I would have expected only from your brother!"

He confessed his shame but expressed his lingering hope that the books would prove right. To strengthen her hope and his own, he told her everything about his friendship with the white family and his faith in the mind and heart of the man Ga-lo-weh.

"Then, my brother, you had better pray many times every day until that day that for once the white men's knowledge will be right. Of course I will pray with you. You know that what has happened to our brother has saved him from the worst misery. If this caused the many People to lose their faith in him, he would fall to a lower place even than he was before!"

"Yes. And the spirit of the People would fall with him. It would be the worst thing ever. I am ashamed. I will pray. I would give my life to keep this from failing!"

And his faith grew ever fainter when he realized that in his dreams there had never been a Black Sun with the other great signs. He was nearly at the point of weeping. Star Watcher, seeing the fear and remorse in his face, did as she had not done for nearly thirty years. She put her arms around his neck and held his head to her shoulder as she had done when he had hurt himself in child's play. She held him this way until he was calm, and he prayed.


Less than a moon after Open Door had gone away to the Wyandots, he returned, seething with indignation. He would say hardly anything about what had happened, so Thick Water had to relate it.

"Of the suspected witches," he said, "your brother pointed to four. They were women who dressed and acted like white women. His followers in the Wyandot tribe started to get them ready to burn. There were many in that town who did not approve of this witch-hunt, but told me they remained silent for fear of being accused themselves.

"But then their chief the Crane, who is no timid man, called councils and shamed people. He spoke against Roundhead, who is Open Door's best follower there, and shamed him. The Crane was so firm that the accused women finally were turned free."

Tecumseh did not say so, but he was glad it had turned out that way. He could see that Open Door was seething with hurt pride. But that, he thought with a gloomy heart, would be nothing compared with the downfall that might lie ahead.

Thick Water sat in Tecumseh's lodge and told him all this about the witch-hunt, and there was a strangeness in his eyes, a vagueness in the way he talked. It was so strange that at last Tecumseh perceived it, even through his own despair. He put his hand on the shoulder of his rangy friend and said, "Be open and tell me what is in your heart. Does it trouble you, this accusing of witches? It is a strong and terrible thing, but perhaps it will help rid us of the ones who go and give our land away. I do not know if it will. You can say it to me, for it darkens my heart, too."

"I should not have gone," Thick Water said. "Killing of women and feeble old men should not be. Please, do not send me with your brother to hunt witches anymore. I am meant to stay by you."

"You will stay by me, then."

Thick Water nodded and looked pleased, but there was still something unsaid. He lingered, looking uneasy. Tecumseh coaxed, and finally Thick Water said, "Yes, there is another thing. Please do not be angry." He braced himself, seeming to fight down embarrassment. "When we were in the Wyandot town . . . There is a young woman there. . . ." He looked down and seemed unable to go on.

Tecumseh leaned back and smiled for the first time in many days. "Look up in my eyes," he said. "Now tell me this: Is she a white woman? Or a half-white?"

"No! No! She is Wyandot!"

"Then"—Tecumseh laughed—"be bold and happy! Bring her here as your wife, if that is what you want! Ha, ha! Bring her here to stand with you and watch my brother make a miracle to ridicule the white governor!"

Or, he thought, to watch us die in ridicule.


On the last day of the counted days, on the day the white men called June the sixteenth, the sun rose in a clear blue sky. Bird songs trilled in the meadows and glades. The dew on the grasses sparkled in the sunlight and vanished.

In hundreds of Indian towns throughout the Middle Ground, from the Allegheny Mountains to the plains beyond the Missi-se-pe, the People kept unusually quiet, aware of the sun climbing in the eastern sky. Shawnees, Delawares, Wyandots, Mingos, Senecas, Miamis, Piankeshaws, Potawatomies, Ottawas, Ojibways, Kickapoos, Winnebagoes, Sauks, Foxes, Oneidas, Munsees, Menominees, Kaskaskias, Michigameas, Peorias, Arikaras, and Sioux, all in their towns or hunting camps or at the salt licks or at fishing camps beside the Great Lakes, all knew this was to be the day of the Black Sun predicted by the Shawnee prophet. They prayed for the safety of their brothers who had journeyed to the Prophet's holy town in O-hi-o to attend the miracle.

And in little tent camps on the prairies of the Illinois and Iowa country, government astronomers and university professors sat on chairs and adjusted instruments. When Indians from nearby villages wandered close and inquired what they were doing, they explained that they were going to watch the sun go dark at midday. The Indians were speechless with awe; even these white government men knew what the Shawnee prophet was about to do!

On a pretty tongue of land between two tributaries of the Great Miami-se-pe, in a crowded town made of hundreds of *wigewas* and lean-tos, the people prayed fervently, then at midmorning began to move toward the glade in front of the enormous council lodge of the town. They looked for their leaders, the Prophet and Tecumseh, but these two had not yet been seen. The People seated themselves and sat waiting, hardly daring even to whisper to each other. Few of them had ever experienced such a press and crowding of bodies; there were tens of hundreds, people who spoke all the known tongues, people who had ridden weeks to reach this important place. There were people in this crowd whose tribes had long been enemies, but they sat near each other, and they grew more and more quiet as the sun moved toward the center of the sky. Men and women now and then shaded their eyes with their hands and squinted up for a moment at the blinding orb; then they blinked, half-blinded by its intensity; they felt the heat of it burning down on their heads and shoulders, and they grew ever more amazed at the audacity of their Prophet, who meant to command such power. They began to gaze toward Open Door's lodge, whose door flap was shut. Over his house hung a dense stillness and an air of mystery. Some even imagined that they could see the roof vibrating.

Perhaps it was, for inside, both the Prophet and his brother were praying so desperately that their heads were buzzing and they were nearly faint from it. Both had the unutterable fear that nothing was going to happen in the sky. As Open Door prayed he drew a necklace of varicolored beans through one hand. Once in Wea Town, so long ago that he did not really remember it, he had seen one of the French Black Robes do this with a string of beads while praying, but now he believed the Great Good Spirit had directed him to make the string of beans as a prayer helper. Tecumseh, kneeling on the other side of the fire-ring, gripped his *pa-waw-ka* stone in his sweaty right hand as he prayed. In the fervor of their prayers, they had let the sacred fire die out and had not even noticed.

At last, exhausted by the concentration, Tecumseh opened his eyes in the hot, brown gloom. A ray of sunlight coming in through the smokehole shone almost directly in the fire-ring, which meant that it was now midday and that the sun was still shining. A fly buzzed loudly, passing back and forth through the dust motes in the sunbeam, and outside there was the vast, buzzing murmur of the waiting crowd. Tecumseh looked at his brother, who was still pulling his beans through his fist, his eye closed, his lips moving. Open Door, despite the intense heat in the closed lodge, wore a long robe, and over the black bandanna that covered his bad eyesocket he wore a headdress made of a raven's skin and feathers, the wings outstretched. On his lap lay his short medicine stick with its fire feathers and copperhead's skull.

"Come, brother," Tecumseh told him in a soft voice, nearly choked with dread and desperation. "It is time. They are waiting for you." Oh, what a delightful joke on the white governor it had seemed at first, so many weeks ago. But now, it seemed, his poor, strange brother, who had spent his whole life as an object of ridicule and for just a few seasons had risen above that to a position of power, was about to be hurled back down into even more ridicule, and all because of Tecumseh's own rash acceptance of a white man's absurd idea. Oh, my poor brother, Tecumseh thought, what have I done? And then with a great pang in his heart, he decided something:

*I shall take the blame onto myself for the failure of this prophecy.*

To do so surely would damage his own reputation severely. But he knew in his heart, by the Shawnee code of fairness and honor, that he could never let his brother suffer the ignominy for this great folly.

Now Open Door opened his eye, and the first thing he saw was his brother Tecumseh sitting there, handsome and perfect, gleaming with sweat in the light from the sunbeam, this brother of his who had always been favored by everybody, by Chiksika and Star Watcher and their mother, by Black Fish and Stands Firm and by all their playmates, and Open Door looked at him, hopeless, angered beyond words by what Tecumseh had done to put his fame in such jeopardy. And Open Door thought of what he had decided to do:

*I will just go before the People and tell them the truth, that this was Tecumseh's prophecy, not mine. Let him look like the fool for once!*

They rose like condemned men and went to the door, pushed the flap aside, and stooped out into the sunshine, Open Door going first. They kept their eyes down so the sudden brightness would not hurt their eyes or make them sneeze. To sneeze now would be ridiculous upon ridiculous. The sun was blazing down as it always did.

The crowd had left a narrow pathway open between Open Door's lodge and the front of the great council house, and as the brothers moved along shoulder to shoulder between the masses of waiting people, Open Door felt as if they were marching to the stake. Maybe Twisting Vines and the other accused witches had felt this way. The sun was at its greatest height, and they were walking upon their own shadows. The presence of the People was like a terrible, yearning pressure.

Tecumseh was watching his own shadow moving along the beaten earth in front of his feet when he noticed the strangeness of its outline. The shadow seemed to have three edges, not just one.

His heart surged. He remembered the eclipse he had seen, in his boyhood nearly thirty years ago, the *Mukutaaweethe Keelswah* that had augured the coming of Clark, and he remembered that the first sign of it was this blurring of shadows. Praise to the Great Good Spirit, he thought. It is happening!

Maybe no one else had noticed it yet; the crowd seemed to be intent upon the brothers only, moaning and murmuring for them. As they came to stand before the council house, Tecumseh said softly but urgently in Open Door's ear:

"Brother, command the sun! Now!"

Open Door in his forbidding raven headdress looked out over the masses, startled by Tecumseh's intense words, and he saw that the daylight was strange, that the faces in the crowd were graying. He heard that all the bird songs had ceased. His heart blossomed with joy. At once he thrust his medicine fire stick above his head, pointing it toward the sun, and in his eerie flute voice he cried:

"That white man at Vincennes has been so saucy as to challenge your prophet! He told the Delawares, 'Make this prophet prove his powers by commanding the sun.' Therefore, my children, so that you will never again heed the words of white men, who are all liars, I have commanded the sun to be dark at midday, and now see! It obeys me now!"

A moaning, wailing noise arose from the mass of people, who were just now noticing the ominous change in the daylight. Hundreds dared to glance up at the sun from under their hands and saw that it was no longer round, that it was being eaten away from one side. Women hugged their bosoms and looked down at the ground in terror, watching their own shadows dissolve. Men who had been standing dropped to their knees. Even those who had seen this happen before were fully awed, because they had heard with their own ears and seen with their own eyes that it was this time the doing of their prophet!

The world was hushed, perhaps ending, some feared; the great one-eyed shaman stood grim and mighty before them with his fire stick pointed at the sun and making it die above their heads; their souls quaked.

In a few minutes the world was in a deep, shadowless twilight. The sun was black, with a shimmering halo around it. Though it was noon, stars could be seen. The people saw some bats flutter back and forth over the glade, drawn forth by what seemed to be nightfall. The Prophet stood pointing at the hideously beautiful phenomenon with his stick until his shoulder ached, but his spirit was soaring with gratitude. He knew that every place where there were red men, not just here in this holy village, but across the land, their souls now must be turning to believe in him. Tecumseh stood beside him, exhausted but serene and humble, his soul like a clear pool. All that marred it was his knowledge that it was a trick, that it could not have been done without the white man.

And in the garden of Grouseland estate at Vincennes, with his wife, Anna, and a few guests of the local society whom he had invited to have refreshments and watch the scheduled eclipse with him, Governor William

Henry Harrison made learned statements of his knowledge of eclipses. The darkness, he told them, would remain for about seven minutes, after which the moon would pass from the face of the sun and continue its orbit. Some of the guests were looking at it through pieces of smoked glass the governor had prepared, exclaiming, making witty or profound comments, their glasses of whiskey momentarily forgotten on the linen cover of a lawn table. It was a pleasant diversion; for once the governor was thinking not at all about the problem of the Shawnee prophet.

At Greenville, where his hundreds bowed terrified before him in the still dusk, Open Door's voice called out again through the glade:

"Do you believe me, my children? Are you ready to see the radiant sun again? Then I shall ask the Master of Life to remove his hand!" He lowered his medicine fire stick.

And when the stars faded and the treetops began to fill up with light again, and the birds to sing, and then it was a normal noontime, the people slowly stood up, blinking, looking around, gaping at the Prophet. Their hearts were shaken. Their souls felt drained, empty, thirsty for the wisdom and strength and faith that only their prophet could pour into them.

And in scores of other Indian towns, from the eastern mountains to the headwaters of the Missi-se-pe and beyond, the hand of Weshemoneto had scarcely released the sun before councils were called, to select more delegates who would journey to the Prophet's village in Ohio, for there, plainly, the power of God dwelt in a man, a man who must be heard, a man whose word must be proclaimed everywhere.

And was this prophet not the brother of the great warrior Tecumseh, who had already come to these towns before, appealing for a true brotherhood of all tribes?

Yes, the men said in their councils. He is the one. And we should have listened better to his words before.

In the legends of most tribes, the best things had been done when the Master of Life had joined a wise sachem and an extraordinary warrior chief together and given power to them both, like Hiawatha and Dekanaweda many generations ago, like Pontiac and Wangomend one generation ago. Now here were two, and they were brothers, both born under great signs, and their words had come in a time of great troubles. This prophet had said that these troubles were omens of the great final darkness, and that only those who gathered around his eternal light would be guided safely on the good road.

There is not much time left, they said in their councils. We must go and hear him, and learn how to be saved!

# CHAPTER 27

## *Prophet's Town at Greenville*
## *Spring 1807*

T hick Water went away to the Wyandot town near the end of Lake Erie after the last snow, to get his young woman and bring her to the Prophet's town.

Star Watcher was out on the edge of town, with Tecumseh's son Cat Pouncing, digging with a mattock to gather sassafras root. When She-Is-Favored had died in an epidemic in her town, Tecumseh had gone to get his son and bring him to his own town. Naturally much of the boy's care and upbringing had been taken over by Star Watcher, and the boy became as close to her as if she were his real mother instead of his aunt. The boy, now approaching his ninth summer, was a supple, tall, healthy child, beautiful of face, shy, and polite. Tecumseh would look at the boy and wonder why he had in him the fire of neither parent. When Tecumseh had time from his duties in the busy, crowded holy town, he would try to teach him some of the hundreds of tricks and secrets of hunting. The boy learned well but seemed to have no spring-forward of his own. He seemed to be the kind who could keep up but never darted ahead or lunged forward. But the demands of the village and its endless hundreds of pilgrims did not leave many opportunities for teaching the boy or inspiring his energies. The lad seemed content to follow his aunt around and help her gather sassafras or cattail or red sunflower root.

Now Star Watcher looked up from the black earth and the pungent orange roots where she was digging and saw the tall figure of Thick Water coming up the road on a small horse, the warrior's legs so long his feet brushed the grass. Behind him rode a woman, on a pony that was also pulling a travois. Star Watcher straightened up, slowly; she was nearly half a hundred now, and though she was as strong and healthy as a young man, she was usually tired in the back and feet because of her ceaseless labors

395

for the holy town. She went out waving and smiling toward the road to greet the couple.

She had not known what kind of a woman to expect, and as she drew near she could scarcely believe the beauty of the young woman. Thick Water was not the sort of a man who would make women's hearts race, as was Tecumseh, nor was he even a chieftain, but somehow he had won for himself a woman of extraordinary comeliness and physical grace.

When they went into the town, Shawnee warriors who had known Thick Water since boyhood looked intently at him as if trying to see if there might be something special in him that they had never noticed before. All they could presume was that this spectacular Wyandot maiden liked a big man, for Thick Water was certainly big. Or maybe she had presumed that he was very important because of his closeness to the Shawnee prophet and the chief. But it was plain that she adored Thick Water, and after a few days in the town, staying in the great House of the Stranger where the pilgrims were lodged, she was serene and happy and full of the good religious fervor of the place and was eager to be married.

The wedding was performed by Open Door in the old way, and Tecumseh was deeply moved as he saw his dedicated bodyguard standing, as he himself had just ten years before, with a most beautiful bride, holding the symbolic deerhide across their shoulders. And Tecumseh thought:

I do not want this to end for him as it did for me. So he summoned Thick Water to talk with him a few days after the wedding. He said, "My brother, I see great happiness on your face."

"That is true." Thick Water's face was glowing.

"Your wife is good to you and to others?"

Thick Water nodded, his eyes full of wonder at his own good fortune. So Tecumseh said then, "Brother, you are one of the very good ones of our People, and you have given me many years of your life. I wish your happiness to continue, and pray that your marriage will be fruitful with many beautiful and happy children. Because I wish that, I want to tell you something I think about marriage." He was remembering his own brief and troubled marriage to She-Is-Favored, who had been this beautiful a woman to look at, and he said, "To be a good husband, and a father and teacher to his sons, and a bringer of meat and hides, is much for a man to do. It is hard for him to do something else besides. He must be near when his family needs him."

"Yes."

"That is why I want to advise you to stay by your wife. You have traveled much of this land being my friend. If you tried to go on with me as you have done, you could not be the best sort of husband, for the work I have ahead of me will pull me along many roads, for many seasons, maybe for the rest of my days. I have been given this to do, and because of it, I was not meant to be a husband.

"A man should be all he can. You are a kind of man who would probably soon become a subchief or a chief of a town, if you ever stayed in a town. You should . . ."

He saw the alarm dawning on Thick Water's face, and the tall warrior quickly protested: "Wait! I respect your advice, and always do what you ask. But please do not forbid me to go on as I have with you. It is my duty! I have seen that it is!"

"To have you with me is good," Tecumseh assured him. "But as you know I have others, enough others, who choose to go with me and watch my back for me. They do not have beautiful and kindly wives to provide for, or children to teach. Your wife would not understand. You have placed the cape across her shoulders, and drawn her to you, and that is your promise to protect her and be by her side."

"No! She understands already! I have told her what my duty is, and of what you have to do, and the years it may take. She knows this!" Thick Water's eyes pleaded.

"She knew this before she said yes to marriage?"

"Before I brought her here. Yes."

"Brother, as you know, a chief cannot forbid a man from doing what he feels is right, but can only request and advise. If you go where I go and guard my back, I will be glad you are there.

"But I ask you: pay attention to how your wife acts. And if her eyes start to tell you that you are not a good husband, be wise enough to stop traveling and stay with her."


The town of the Shawnee prophet had become like a great hive, swarming with people whose prayer chants could be heard droning among the trees from a mile away. The road leading down the grassy plain to the wooded point where the village lay between converging creeks was a road wide and hard-packed from the passage of thousands of hooves and moccasins. Always there were people on this road coming or going, usually in tribal groups. Never had so many kinds of dress and decoration been seen in one town—tattoos, mussel-shell earbobs, badger skins, bison-horn hats, seashell wampum, eagle–feather bonnets, moosehide moccasins. Never had so many languages been heard in one place. Sometimes the Prophet's words had to be translated through four or five tongues before they could be understood by a particular band from far away, and even then it would have to be aided by hand language. But everyone had patience and paid the greatest attention. Weshemoneto could not fail to make his words understood.

Many of the people were hungry when they arrived and remained hungry all the time they were there. Though the land was rich and the villagers worked hard and cheerfully to raise enough food, and the hunters ranged far for meat, there was scarcely enough at any time to feed this multitude more than a few bites a day. If they had not been fed such rich spiritual food as they received, their empty stomachs would have caused serious trouble. But most were so enraptured by the hope and brotherhood and the palpable presence of the Great Good Spirit that they were little interested in food for their physical bodies. Their bodies were light and thin, and their souls were afloat on rapture. Open Door encouraged fasting, of course.

Still, the Prophet was not such a fool as to believe that his children could subsist on his words and inspiration alone, so he and Tecumseh, and their hunters, and in particular the women of the town, exercised every resource to obtain and provide food. When garden crops and corn were not ready for harvest, the women and their children prayed early in the morning, then spent their days foraging and gathering in the woods and meadows and bottomlands for miles around, bringing in roots, berries, wild greens, tubers, bird eggs, milkweed, seeds, even the inner bark of elm—all of the many things they knew were nutritious or just filling. All fished the river and the creeks. Boys shot or made snares for anything that walked, climbed, or flew. Families shared their meager rations with the endless procession of sojourners and felt happy because they believed they were helping them along the Good Way. Always a generous people, the Shawnees in this holy town were now selfless to the point of sacrifice. Even if they had themselves eaten no more than a spoonful of succotash in a day, they would rush out to greet and embrace another new band of hungry Menominees or Potawatomis coming up the road.

Now, as Star Watcher and Cat Pouncing were returning to the town, carrying between them a blanket full of foraged roots, milkweed flowers, and watercress, they saw three white men riding along the beaten road, all dressed in black coats and hats, leading a laden packhorse. They were skinny, hunched men, who in their black garb looked like buzzards on horseback.

Cat Pouncing, chilled by the sight of them, looked as if he might run back into the woods. "No, stay," Star Watcher soothed him. "Look, they have no weapons!"

This was most surprising: unarmed white men riding straight toward a large Indian town. The white men reined in their horses for a minute to gaze across the creek at the great rotting pile of Fort Greenville's block-house, then rode on toward the droning village. Warriors came trotting out; there was sign language, and then the warriors led them into town.

"Come," Star Watcher said, "let us see who these strange people are. Maybe they are traders, with their goods on that horse. Or what if they are spies?"

They did prove to be spies—but of an open, welcome sort. They were Jesus worshipers, Open Door explained to the People in council before that evening's prayers, but a good sort of Jesus worshipers that he had known before. They did no violence to any red men. They found inspiration in a kind of dancing. They were called Shakers. They had come to look at the holy town and had brought some seed for the town's fields and gardens. They were, said Open Door, the one kind of white men who were welcome here. "Love them," he cried, "and show them how joyful and peaceful we are in this blessed place!"

Star Watcher wondered what Tecumseh would think, if he were here, about white men being in the holy town, watching.


James Galloway took the pipe tomahawk from Tecumseh and held it across both his palms, admiring its beautiful craftsmanship and decoration. Tecumseh had brought it to him as a gift, saying that it would be the pipe they should smoke together whenever they met. Galloway felt quite solemn about this gift. Nearby sat Rebekah, shaking her head slowly and looking down in disbelief at the treasure Tecumseh had brought to her: thirty delicately tooled little brooches of pure silver. He had brought gifts for the rest of the family, too, but this wealth of silver ornaments, he had explained, were for all the time she had spent helping him with the language and the reading and writing. But Rebekah in her own secret mind fancied that they were a love gift. She wanted to believe they were, and the tenderness in his beautiful eyes as he gave them to her had made her sure. She kept glancing between the silver and Tecumseh, her heart in a turmoil.

Rebekah Galloway was certain that this intriguing and stimulating man wanted to marry her. This was how Indian suitors announced their intentions, she had heard: by bringing very valuable gifts. And the pipe with her father . . . Oh, there was no doubt of it.

She wanted him. Oh, she wanted him!

But he was of another race! Her father was becoming one of the leading men in this growing part of the state. He was enjoying the highest form of respectability. He was important in church.

And though he liked and admired their guest Tecumseh as much as most any man he knew, surely he would be aghast at the thought that this chief wanted his daughter!

She could never live in an Indian village, of course. Now as she gazed at the soft sheen of the silver, she envisioned a hut with a fire in the center, a pallet on the floor covered with animal hides, naked children squatting around the smoky fire eating half-raw meat with their fingers, drums beating outside, and herself there pounding corn, slowly forgetting the joys of reading and writing. . . .

No. If by the wildest vicissitudes there could chance to be a marriage between Tecumseh and herself, he would have to adopt the dress and ways of a white man. After all, with his qualities, could he not be a remarkable man in any society? There were Indians in Ohio now who wore suits and hats and raised livestock. Surely Tecumseh could do that, and do better at it, too.

But he was of a different color! Wouldn't that bring shame to her father in the eyes of his fellow citizens? She had heard travelers here talk contemptuously of "squawmen," who were white men who had married Indian women. And treated most contemptuously were those white women who in captivity had married Indian men, then had been returned to white society in prisoner exchanges. If she married a red man of her own free will, what would her father's and mother's associates think of them then? Especially those in the church? They would be scandalized!

But she wanted Tecumseh. Oh, how she wanted him!

She had spent so many of her lonely hours in the past year remembering how Tecumseh looked, how his voice sounded, even how he smelled. And sometimes in bed at night, remembering him, she had sighed and tossed, making the cornshuck mattress rustle until her mother's voice would come out of the dark from behind the privacy curtain: "Becky? Are y'all right, dear?"

"I'm hot," she had whimpered, throwing off the covers, then lying there feeling the air on her sweat-damp nightdress. Once she had pulled it up around her waist and had lain there in the dark that way, growing excited in the loins, until she had remembered that God could see everything, even in the dark, and had covered herself, heartsick with frustration and shame.

She looked up from her silver at him, gazing long and wistfully, seeing his white-toothed mouth as he smiled.

Almost with reverence, her father now lit the silver-trimmed tomahawk with a coal from the hearth. He and Tecumseh then shared the pipe for a while, and then they resumed old conversations as if they had been together only yesterday, though it had been more than a year.

From time to time Galloway would notice a strange, droll expression on the chief's face, as if he were trying to keep himself from laughing. Finally Tecumseh said:

"Your promise was good, my friend Ga-lo-weh."

"My promise?"

"Yes. The Black Sun was when you promised it to be."

"Oh, yes! The eclipse! You saw it, then, did ye?"

"As I told you I would do. I stood outside and saw it come. I was eager, and I thanked you in my heart." He was still trying to swallow his smile.

"Don't thank me." Galloway chuckled, leaning back in his chair, which creaked under his strong, heavy body. "Thank G . . . the, the Creator."

"That I did, too, Ga-lo-weh." Now Tecumseh leaned back, too, from his customary erect perch on the front of the chair seat, and laughed loudly. How he wanted to tell Ga-lo-weh the magnificent joke about Governor Harrison's taunt and Open Door's use of the Black Sun! But of course he could not.

Galloway was bursting to talk about something that had been the topic on the frontier for months. "Chief," he said, "did ye know that the Corps of Discovery came back alive? That they'd got all the way to the Pacific Ocean, and home safe?"

"Ah. The Captain Clark and the other. Yes." He had heard things about this from many sources—from bands arriving from the west, from Girty, from British traders and agents out of Canada. It was bad news for the red man. But of course he could not say that to Ga-lo-weh, either.

"Cap'n Clark aims to set up a fur trading company in St. Louis, so I've heard," said Galloway. "He claims there's so much beaver and otter and mink out there, it keeps you hoppin' to empty your traps. And on the far side of the mountains, seals and sea otters, the finest fur in the world, bar none. Why, that could just about put Britain out of the fur business on this continent. . . ." He paused, remembering the long association between the Shawnees and the English.

Tecumseh said nothing about this yet, only nodded. What had troubled him most deeply was what the western chiefs had told him: that the Long Knife Captains Lewis and Clark had gone peacefully all the way to the Western Sea and back, making strong friendships with tribes that had never been exposed to Americans before, building their trust and making them eager for trade. Some of the chiefs from far up the Missouri-se-pe were traveling to Washington to see the white chief Jefferson. Tecumseh wanted to catch these naive fools and warn them of the treacherous ways of white men. Now that Americans had made a white man's trail out there, hundreds of hundreds of hundreds more would rush up that trail and fill up that country and kill the game, even the bison, who were so many that they made thunder when they ran. Tecumseh no longer had any delusions about limitless space and inexhaustible game. The white men, he believed now, were capable of overrunning all the land in the world and making farms out of it. So to him, the news of the success of the explorers was the worst possible news, enough even to overshadow the good thing that had happened about the Black Sun. There had also been another American journey, almost as ominous; another American army captain named Pike had explored all the way up to the beginning of the Missi-se-pe, and he had reported the richness of land and the plentiful fur animals up there, which would soon mean the ruin of another quarter of the red man's world.

So all Tecumseh could say, out of the sense of foreboding these explorers had created in him, was, "Those captains were strong. Their father Jefferson must be proud."

"Aye, is he ever! What I hear is, he's making Cap'n Lewis governor of the whole Louisiana Territory, and Clark the Indian agent and militia commander. Now, I don't know Lewis, but that Clark lad's the spirit 'n' image of his brother, the best soldier I ever served under. . . ." He stopped, seeing in Tecumseh's face that all this talk was anything but delightful. Sometimes with his friend he simply forgot that he was talking to a red chief, who had reasons aplenty for seeing things otherwise. He saw a hardness in Tecumseh's face and asked, "What's wrong, my friend?"

"What is wrong? Oh, Ga-lo-weh, this: When there is a governor of a territory, I know, as you have explained to me, and as I have seen happen with my eyes, there will soon be more states. You like many states, for they are your people's states. I do not like many states, for they swallow the lands of my people. You are good, Ga-lo-weh. I suppose some other white men are good, like you.

"But, Ga-lo-weh, you face me from one side, and I face you from the other side. And that is what is wrong."

Galloway nodded and was quiet for a while, his enthusiasm suddenly clouded by the signs of Tecumseh's sadness and distress. Galloway sat fingering the lump of Girty's bullet in his neck, absently. And Rebekah nearby, though little more than a lovesick girl, was perceptive enough to feel the widening of the chasm between the races even more poignantly. As she rubbed one of the silver brooches between her thumb and forefinger, she was looking at the silver ornaments in Tecumseh's nose and was now more deeply aware of the space between their two worlds, and for the first time that evening she was not so sure that Tecumseh was there to sue for her hand. She grew frightened, troubled by a premonition of loss.

James Galloway had warned himself time and again not to jeopardize his friendship with Tecumseh by prying into his affairs at the Greenville town.

But it was hard now not to say something that had been much on his mind. So he said it:

"I should tell you this, as your friend, because we are, as you say, looking at each other from different sides. There are people around here, powerful people, who want the government to move your tribe away. They don't know what you're doing, and they're scared because they see so many coming and going."

"Yes, Ga-lo-weh, the white people are always scared when we do something they do not control." Tecumseh's voice was low and even, but his lips were hard. "What we do there is worship. We learn not to drink liquor. Not to be violent. Not to breed with white people. Not to steal. Only to do good and keep peace. I think many white people do not like it because we worship *our* Great Spirit instead of yours. Listen, Ga-lo-weh! The white people would rest if they believed how good our people are in that place, but to trust is not their way. That is all I want to say about it, Ga-lo-weh. It is ours, what we do there. Not of your powerful people around here."

Galloway took a long breath that hissed in his nostrils and decided to say just a little more, since he was at it, for Tecumseh's own sake.

"One of those people is General Kenton. He looked at your town, and he believes you're preparing for war."

Tecumseh's eyebrows went up. "Ah! Let us speak of this, then, yes! This general and some other militia soldiers with him came to my town, while my chiefs and I were away. He said he is General Kenton, but some warriors see he is But-lah! I have been angry about this. Is this a true man, then, to come and pretend he is another name, not our enemy? This is deceit—"

"Oh, wait! Wait!" Galloway said, holding up his hand. "You are right. Kenton *is* Butler. He called himself Butler, back in the war, because . . . well, for his own reasons. But he uses his real name now. He wasn't trying to deceive you. He is as honest a man as ever was. And people *listen* to him, my friend, because he *is* honest. He's a friend of mine, you know; he was a scout for Gen'l Clark, just like me. He's a fine man! But here's what he told me. He said you chiefs were gone to the British when he went to your town. And he said your people wouldn't give him their right hand, but only their left. That, I reckon, stuck in his craw most. . . ." Galloway suddenly realized he was revealing the private notions of one friend to another and stopped. There was a moment's silence, and the words seemed to hang in the air.

Finally Tecumseh said, simply, "They gave their left hand only because they thought this man was lying his name. That is interesting, about But-lah's name. It is good to learn there is an honest man. Thank you for clearing my eyes on his name. My people, too, may change their name. If their life is not good under one name, perhaps it is a bad name and it will be better under a better one." He was thinking of his brother Loud Noise, now Open Door.

But Galloway was not ready yet to lapse back into general conversation. They had at last spoken of the tension created by the Indian town, and Galloway wanted his friend to be aware. "They're saying, my friend, that your town is inside the treaty lines, and that you have no right to be th—"

He stopped. Tecumseh's face had suddenly flashed anger as clearly as a bolt of lightning. It passed, but everyone in the room remained electrified for a moment. Tecumseh stood up quickly. His expression was kindly again, but his eyes were now troubled, even as he smiled at the members of the family, and he was strung very tight. Galloway had risen halfway out of his chair, a hand outstretched, hoping to calm and detain him, deeply sorry that he had said too much and caused this unpleasant moment, the first unpleasant moment they had ever had in Tecumseh's presence.

"I have sat here too long," Tecumseh said, "as it pleases me to do with my friends."

"Tecumseh," Galloway said earnestly, now standing before him, "please know that it's not *I* who question your right to be there. . . ."

"I know, Ga-lo-weh. Thank you for that. Good-bye."

And then he was out the door into the night, stalking through the fresh air toward his little camp by the riverside, breathing hard, his jaws clenched and lips open in a grimace as he tried to control his fury.

*No right to be there!*

He wanted to howl like a wolf, to ease the fiery pressure in his heart. But he must not let this family hear such a sound.

He heard a voice calling his name, footsteps behind him. He stopped and turned.

The girl Rebekah was hurrying along the path, thrashing in brush as she came through the darkness, calling in soft urgency, "Please! Wait. . . ."

She ran against him in the dark, bumping hard, and as if to catch herself, she reached around him and sagged against him. He held her upper arms, gently, steadying her, pushing her away. But she clung to him, panting against his chest, shaking her head in confused desperation, making little sobs in her throat, and trying to talk through them. In her hair was the particular musk of her, and the trace of tallow soap and of the woodsmoke from the cooking hearth. Tecumseh's anger was still in him but going away like a muttering thunderstorm and confounded by the tenderness he had felt for her since she was a child.

Five of Tecumseh's bodyguards lay on their blankets around a little camp-fire by the river, at the place where he had always camped when he visited the Galloway family. In the old days he had camped here alone, but as the importance of Open Door's movement and the white people's nervousness about it had grown, the bodyguards had grown more concerned about Tecumseh and would no longer let him travel alone. These bodyguards were very anxious for him while he was alone in the house with the white family and did not easily understand why he visited white people like this. He had told them the truth, that it was an old friendship with a good and sober white man who gave him useful information and helped him under-stand what the white settlers were doing and why they did it. The body-guards accepted this to a degree, but they were uncomfortable and nervous here, and none of them wanted to be near the white family or to eat with them. So they would just wait in the camp, the horses tethered nearby ready for quick flight, and watch the dim glow of the distant light in the window of Galloway's house and listen for any sounds of trouble there until he would walk back down the path into camp or until the fireglow and the murmur of the river put them to sleep.

But one of Tecumseh's bodyguards never slept while he was here. Thick Water sat facing the little dim rectangle of the lighted window and listened, all the time his chief was in that house. His thoughts were often with his young and beautiful Wyandot wife back in the holy town, where she had become one of the selfless helpers in the struggle to feed and care for the pilgrims. But even while he was thinking of her and of what she was doing, he was on guard for any indication that Tecumseh might need help. Some-times Thick Water would have an urge to go near the house and look in, but Galloway had several long-eared dogs that barked loudly at the ap-proach of any red man except Tecumseh.

Suddenly now Thick Water leaned forward and cupped a hand behind his ear. It seemed he was hearing voices and movements, very slightly audible over the gurgles of the river, somewhere between the camp and the white man's house. He held a half breath and concentrated. It seemed to be on the path by the riverside.

He rose silently and picked up his musket. He considered waking the others but decided not to stir them until he felt there was a reason to. His joints hurt a little at first as he stole out of the circle of fireglow. Thick Water was forty-two years of age, and many winters of exposure had cost him some of his suppleness. But he was keen, and a little alarmed, and he moved now as smoothly and silently as a wildcat stalking—a few steps, then stopping to listen, a few more steps, a stop . . .

Thick Water shivered. Though he saw nothing, a few paces ahead of him he could hear a woman's voice talking in the English tongue with, it seemed, urgency and great emotion. He was recently enough married that he was reminded of the talk his wife made in *soos* with him. And on the cool night breeze he now detected the faint odor of soap and a woman's musk. Perhaps this was the white farmer's pale, strange-looking daughter, whom Thick Water had seen from distances.

He presumed from her impassioned tone that she was with some man in the dark beside the path, though he did not hear a man's voice respond to hers, nor did he smell the usual dense smell of these men who never bathed their bodies.

Amused, smiling now, near to laughing aloud, Thick Water thought for a moment of creeping closer and startling these people with a war whoop. But no. The consequences of a prank like that could be anything. The white man in the house might jump up at the sound of a war cry and try to kill the nearest red man—Tecumseh. This man had been one of the scout-warriors of the old Long Knife Clark, Tecumseh had said.

Also there were now several white men's cabins in this valley within the sound of a shout, and all the white men in these lands were very nervous now about red men. And they probably knew of Tecumseh's camp on the riverbank.

So Thick Water, who seldom thought in terms of pranks, let that prankish impulse pass and turned to go back toward the little camp, walking back as stealthily as he had come.


Tecumseh stood holding the girl's wrists to keep her white hands from clutching at him and listened with bewilderment and pity to her entreaties, hardly comprehending them. He was used to hearing her speak her tongue with clarity and precision; now she was mumbling and gasping and whimpering. She seemed to be saying that despite the troubles between their races, he must not leave her. Had he not brought her a dowry? "What is 'dowry'?" he asked, and she spoke of the silver brooches. "Yes," he said, "those dowry are for you."

His feelings were in turmoil. He wanted to soothe her, but knew not what words to use. He could hear voices at the house, her father's, her mother's, talking to each other, calling low for Rebekah, anxious voices. Then he saw a little glimmer of a lantern moving. She turned her head toward the voices.

"Maybe they be afraid I hurt you," he said. "Go make them calm." He was impatient now, and his anger at the presumptions of her race still

seethed inside him, yet he did not want her or her family to have any
distress. And he was confused by the musk of desire that rose from her
clothing. He remembered with shame how he had daydreamed of her
womanhood before.

The girl's face was just an oval not quite as dark as the darkness around
it. She turned and started to move toward the floating spark of the distant
lantern. Then she stopped a few paces away and spoke to him in a tremulous
voice.

"Will you come back soon?"

"I . . . Yes. . . ." He was not sure he was telling the truth.

"You spend all your time talking to Papa. I want . . . I want to be with
you a bit now and then. . . ." Then she went toward the house.

When she appeared in the light of the tin lantern, her father blew a
breath of relief. "Are you all right? Whatever possessed you to run out here
in the dark? Did ye talk to him? Is he angry at me? What—"

"He . . ." She looked back toward the darkness, shaken to her soul,
feeling moist between her thighs, remembering what he had said about the
silver. "He wants to marry me, Papa."

She believed that was what all this meant: the silver gifts, his promise to
come back soon.

"Oh, Lord God," Galloway moaned.

Down the path, Tecumseh stood in the dark listening to their faraway
voices talking and wondered if Ga-lo-weh would come and follow him. He
felt as if he had betrayed his own deepest beliefs, the trust of his people,
by entering the bosom of that white family as he had done. He felt as untrue
and as unworthy as when he had tricked the People with the Black Sun. He
felt as low as he had felt on that day so long ago when he had run from his
first battle . . . the same day he had first seen this same white man! His heart
felt dark and foul, and the night was ominous. Such intimacies as he had
know with the enemy would disturb the spirits.

It had made a mockery of his brother's inspired teachings, about drawing
back from white people, about sharing with them no more. His heart was
squeezing down with regret. He thought of how Star Watcher would be
ashamed if she knew of this. He was angry at the strange white girl for
coming after him with her yearning, but he was much more angry with
himself for causing her to do it. A woman knows if you even think of her
with yearning, he thought. That is why she came running. Most of all he
was afraid of the displeasure of the Great Good Spirit.

Thick Water had just put a few sticks on the fire and sat back to amuse
himself with the thought of white people having *soos* on the path when he
heard a whisper of motion beyond the fire and saw Tecumseh striding into

the firelight. Thick Water was about to ask him if he had not found white copulators underfoot on the path—surely he must have stepped right over them on the way from the house—when he noticed the stricken, angry look on his face. He presumed that he had, and that it had disgusted him.

Tecumseh hardly glanced at him and stopped to lay his knife and club on a log near the fire. Thick Water sat with his mouth open. He watched, stunned and confused, as Tecumseh went back out of the firelight, this time down the riverbank. Then he could hear water swishing and splashing down there.

In a short time Tecumseh emerged again from the darkness, wet from head to foot, water dribbling from his hair and his loincloth. As he stood by the fire sluicing water off his limbs with the edges of his hands, the other warriors began opening their eyes, sitting up. Tecumseh said very quietly, "Let us break the camp and ride away from here." At once they were all wide awake and moving. One rode at night only if there were danger or urgency.

Despite his muddled feelings, Tecumseh was now becoming alert to a possible danger. Rebekah's father might have supossed anything from her agitation, and instead of coming out alone to confront Tecumseh, knowing he had bodyguards camped here, he might have set out to gather neighbors to attack the camp. Tecumseh was ready and willing to face Ga-lo-weh, but he did not want to draw danger down on his men by this problem he had caused. No. It would be good to get his companions out of this place. Sometime later, when he had had time to weigh all this in his soul, he might come back and face Ga-lo-weh. Now it would be wise only to leave.


The road was easy to follow under the stars. He looked down toward the site of old Chillicothe as he rode away and could see a few patches of soft light, from the doors of the white men's cabins in the old Shawnee main town. It was *they* who had no right to be here! Did they not know that?

Perhaps they do know it in that kind of knowing that will not speak, he thought. Perhaps that is why they are always afraid of us: they know they are wrong. To know you are wrong makes you afraid of those who are right.

No matter what hard things happen to my People, he thought, how good it is to know we are not wrong about who should be here.

But he was afraid now in a part of him, because he knew *he* had been wrong. To have given so much warmth to those whites was against the teachings of Weshemoneto as brought by his own brother.

Tecumseh felt terribly unworthy now, and in many ways. He had come only to bring gifts of gratitude, but the visit had revealed the great division, the boundary, between their races, and the girl's confusion had made him realize that he had overstepped the boundary.

They rode a long time before the soft noises of the unshod horses and the monotonous motions of riding calmed his thoughts; the stars made the troubles smaller and more remote.

The girl had acted like a desperately lonely person.

Maybe that is why white people are the way they are, he thought. They live in solitary houses, far from their tribes. No wonder they are afraid and suspicious. And lonely.

A girl of her years should be among other young women. She should have plenty of young men around, to tease, to choose from. She should have grandmothers, to teach her about her people, about the moons.

Her only grandmothers are books, he thought. No wonder she is confused and reaches out to her father's friend! Tecumseh was now nearly forty summers in age. This girl could be no more than fifteen or sixteen. In the tribe, a girl of that age knows much and is ready to become a wife and mother. But this white girl is like a child in her heart and like an old man in her head, he thought.

I should not have made her so warm.

He remembered how her body had interested him even though she was of that race. He had not suspected that she would be perceiving those private thoughts and growing warm. He thought that if he had not taken things out of his town to give to white people as gifts, they would not have presumed so much.

Tecumseh had decided many moons ago to abstain from connection with women until such time as his task might be completed. His first notions of celibacy had been simply to avoid problems in the holy town. He had all the troubles a chief could deal with, in a town full of hungry worshipers, all speaking different tongues, all with their various tribal codes and morals. There were tribes in which parents offered their daughters and men offered their wives to esteemed friends, and there were women of some tribes who thought it was proper to offer themselves. But Tecumseh was watched by the visiting worshipers, almost as closely as the Prophet himself was, and he was especially watched closely by his own Shawnee People, whose one criticism of him was that he was not married. "Not all women are like She-Is-Favored," Star Watcher would say to him sometimes. "You should consider marrying again. You need a wife to help you with the People."

Being so watched by everyone, he had come to understand that to accept the favors of a woman of one tribe could create envy or contempt among other tribes. Only by taking a Shawnee woman could he avoid those troubles. But if he took a Shawnee woman, he would, by his brother's code and by the old Shawnee tradition as well, be expected to marry her. Long ago, with She-Is-Favored, he had learned that he could not be such a good chief when he had a wife scattering his thoughts and draining his strength. And then, little by little, he had come to believe what it was convenient to believe and what seemed true to him in his own heart: that he could be a purer, stronger helper of his People if he contained himself and kept himself above desire. It was one of the few beliefs of the French Black Robes that made sense to him. He had looked at the faces of the Black Robes he had seen in his life, and he had seen in their faces a peculiar quality which, it had seemed, must please their God.

And since in his own visions and dreams he had never seen a wife at his side, he suspected that the Great Good Spirit did not mean for him to expend half of his powers upon a wife. Maybe his celibacy did not satisfy the People, but he believed it satisfied his Creator.

Still, he was a strong man nearing his fortieth summer, and his soul and hands and loins had their memories of the pleasures of women, and he would see one now and then whom he desired. But when one turned his head that way, he would remind himself of what had to be done for his People, and he would pass her by, or look away, or remember the misery of that year with She-Is-Favored, and he would not let himself be tempted. He could not control the beauty or appeal of a woman, but he had been learning all his life the many ways of controlling himself. Anger, fear, pain, and lust all could be controlled if a man had learned to rule himself.

But he had not ruled his own head closely enough, and thus he had misled that lonely white girl. She had not even really been one of the women who had turned his head. For years she had been more like a strange little sister. She was an alien. She was rather odd-looking to him, with her light-colored hair, her pale skin that grew red in patches in hot weather or when mosquitoes made her scratch, with her long face and strange, lonely eyes. Probably she would look quite good to a white youth; her smile was interesting, her large blue eyes were very lively, her voice was rich, and her body was strong and well shaped. But to Tecumseh she looked odd and unhealthy, as most white people did.

She did have a remarkable mind, though, and he did like her very much. He had liked her since he first saw her as a child. He had liked certain white people very much—uncommonly much.

It was a strange thing to him, an unsettling thought, that several of the people he had liked most in his life, those to whom he had been most drawn, and those whose thoughts and words were most intriguing, were white people. He thought of Rebekah and her father, then of Boone, whom he had liked and admired intensely. He thought of Big Fish, who once had been, and now was again, Stephen Ruddell. He remembered, too, how strongly he had been drawn to Copper Hair, Clark's cousin who had been killed at Piqua. His feeling for those people had not been the same as his love for the people of his family or for Black Fish, his foster father. But what pleasures he had known in his hours with those white people. How they had pulled at his soul! And, in a way, But-lah. Or Kenton, as his real name was. He had not known But-lah in the same way he had known those other white people, but he had admired and feared him for a long time.

And even after all these years he could remember how violently he had hated and loved the white youth who had become Blue Jacket when he was whipping him that day in the gauntlet.

And then suddenly in the eyes of his memory, Tecumseh saw another white person who he knew was more important to him than all the others: the slender young officer whom he had seen at the Fallen Timbers through a spyglass, beside the Long Knife General Wayne.

*Harrison.*

He remembered how his eye had been drawn to him, how his spirit had whispered to him of that man's place in his fate, how he had dreamed of that man and the bundle of sticks. And it was all turning out to be so.

And Tecumseh thought: I have cared much for most of the white people I have known, even though they are my enemy. And even the one who is marked as my chiefest enemy, this one for whom I have no love at all, yet I think of him more than I ever thought of anyone I loved.

He was thankful that his warriors, riding so close around him, could not hear his thoughts.

But he knew that the Great Good Spirit could hear them, and that knowledge troubled him. He wondered if prayers could ever bring him to terms with Weshemoneto after this.


When Tecumseh returned to the holy town, he had no time to retreat into prayer, because the Shaker white men were there and many more chiefs of bands from the northwest to be met. And then a half-breed named Anthony Shane rode in with his unwelcome message from the white men's government. Shane had grown up as a Shawnee in old Chillicothe but now was attached to the Indian agency at Fort Wayne. Shane said:

"I bring to you and your brother a very important message from Captain William Wells, the Indian agent. I am to read it to your men in council."

Tecumseh's eyes hardened. "Captain Wells still believes he is very important, if he expects us to call a council to hear his message." Because of his knowledge of the tribes and his close connection with the vanquished Miami chief Little Turtle, Wild Potato had been appointed Indian agent at the important post of Fort Wayne. Wells had grown rich and was now married to one of Little Turtle's daughters, and the old chief lived in Wells's home. Tecumseh knew that Wells was much under Little Turtle's influence, as well as Harrison's, and that he had been a big voice in stirring up the white men's animosity toward the Prophet's village. Now Tecumseh said to this messenger, "Shane, we will interrupt the good things we are doing, and will call the council as you ask, and hear whether this message from Captain Wells is as important to us as it is to him."

Soon the huge council house was filled. Shane smoked the pipe, looking around timidly at the huge crowd of warriors and chiefs, many of whom wore garb such as he had never seen before. Then he was invited to stand and speak his message.

It was a demand from Captain Wells that the Prophet and Tecumseh and two of their chiefs come to Fort Wayne, where Wells would read to them a letter from their great father, the president of the United States.

Tecumseh and Open Door looked at each other, eyes flashing. Tecumseh rose to his feet in one swift motion and stood before Shane, his jaw tense.

"Go back to Fort Wayne," he said, "and tell Captain Wells that Tecumseh has no father who is called 'president of the United States.' The sun in the sky is my father, and the moon is my mother, and I know no other. Tell Captain Wells that my fire burns on this place appointed by Weshemoneto and that he must come here if he wants to tell me something. I think six suns is enough time for you to go back to Fort Wayne and send him here. I shall watch for him to come up the road with his letter from President. Now with a prayer to the Great Spirit, we close this council, which was not as important to us as you thought. You may eat with us and rest before you go back."

The women gave Shane a dab of pulp in a pan, a gray blob that was hominy cooked with cattail roots. "It is not to insult you," Tecumseh said. "This is all we have to eat at this time. Game is not so plentiful as it was before your white men came."

Open Door's word had spread far west into the Illinois country and up into the lands between the Great Lakes, to the Potawatomis near Lake Mis-e-ken, to the Ojibways and Ottawas from Saginaw Bay to Michilimackinac, to the many Ojibway towns on the dark evergreen shores of Lake Superior. The Ojibways especially, whose villages along the lakes were chaotic with drunkenness and plagued by witches, were seized by the fervor for salvation. One whole village of them, incited by an eloquent disciple, held a ceremony of the Prophet's rituals, threw all their medicine bags into the lake, then, as the little relics bobbed away on the waves, packed everything and set out down through the Wis-con-sin and Illinois lands, picking up some Menominees on the way, and headed east across the Indiana Territory toward O-hi-o and the Prophet's village. Their trail led them through Fort Wayne, where their passage in such great numbers added to William Wells's alarm. These Ojibways would buy no whiskey at Fort Wayne. And more amazing, they would not drink any even when he offered some free to their chiefs, as he did in hopes of getting them to talk about why they were going to Greenville.

When the Ojibways reached the Prophet's town, they were welcomed very warmly. At once they arranged themselves in a half circle outside the council house, with interpreters, to hear the Prophet, to gaze upon him, and to ask him questions. They looked on in awe as he came out from his lodge carrying what appeared to be a corpse wrapped from end to end in strips of cloth. He carried it as effortlessly as if he were carrying an empty basket; if it was a corpse, then it appeared that their prophet was also a man of uncommon physical strength. He leaned this against a tree beside him, and it stood there stiff and ominous. The visitors looked their famous prophet over long and reverently, remembering that this was the shaman who had once darkened the sun, but they could not quite ignore the mummy, either. They had many questions to ask, but they felt afraid to ask what it was.

"What," some wanted to know, "did the Great Good Spirit look like? We have heard you saw him even though he is invisible."

"On one side his hair is gray," Open Door replied. "On the other side it is white. For the rest, his face and arms, he is a red man of great age and strength. Words cannot tell it. He is so old that the age itself is beautiful and shiny." They were convinced; that was how the legends described the deity.

Since his early visions, Open Door had gone back to the other world several times and had received instructions for making the sacred paraphernalia of his office. Now in addition to his medicine fire stick and his strings of sacred beans, he had picture sticks to give to the chiefs of the bands who came to his town. When his followers returned to their homes, they would be able to look at the images carved upon the sticks and remember his recitations. The sticks were uniformly made, of smooth heartwood cedar slabs as long as a man's forearm, tapering from the width of two fingers at the base to one at the top. The markings carved on the sticks depicted all the things important in life between the family and the house of Heaven: Earth, Water, Lightning, Trees, the Four Winds, Corn, Animals, Plants, Sun, and Sky. "All these," said the Prophet, "are in me."

Each of these sticks he presented wrapped in a bundle of smaller, unmarked sticks, like that bundle in Tecumseh's dream of unity. Thus each bundle was the Prophet, with the unbreakable unification of tribes gathered around him. With such talismans as this, the People could not forget even when they went away.

The most prominent of the Prophet's totems was the life-size effigy of himself, this large, hollow doll made of hoops and reeds, as lightweight as basketware, concealed from end to end in its wrappings of cloth. Sometimes the Prophet kept this near him while he was preaching. But when he was needed in two villages at once, his disciples could carry to one town this effigy, in which his spiritual power could be transported. Thus many of his converts in distant villages, though they never saw him in the flesh, could attend his presence in the effigy. With this effigy standing nearby, they would draw the strings of beans through their fists, and in doing so they were shaking hands with the Prophet. Open Door had begun training disciples who could carry the word, the totems, and the rituals to far places and thus reach people who had not yet been able to come to his holy town.

And as the red people kept coming and going, the apprehension of the white settlers grew. They began petitioning Governor Kirker of Ohio to raise the militia.


On the sixth day after Anthony Shane had been sent back to Fort Wayne, lookouts saw a rider in white man's clothing coming down the road from that direction.

But it was not Captain Wells. It was once again Shane. Tecumseh knew at once in his heart that Wells had been afraid to come. Wells was aware of the executions of the witches, and he was known to be a cautious sort of man.

Shane himself plainly did not relish being put in this spot a second time, and he could see at once that both Tecumseh and Open Door were insulted that Wells had not come. To add to the insult, it happened that the letter was not really from the president of the United States, as Wells had said; it was actually from the secretary of war, Dearborn. However, Shane assured them, it expressed the wishes of the president. The council was convened again to hear this letter.

The message reminded them that the land around Greenville was now American land, part of the state of Ohio and within the boundaries set by the Treaty of Greenville. The message read:

> Just as the Great Chief of the Seventeen Fires loves his red children
> and will not suffer his white children to interrupt his red ones, neither
> can he suffer his red children to come on the land of the United States.

When this was translated, the indignant mutterings that filled the council house made Shane break out in a sweat. And when he turned and saw the fury blazing in Tecumseh's eyes, he wondered if he would get out alive.

Tecumseh leaped to his feet. He thrust out his arm to still the hubbub of voices, then he filled the room with his own voice.

"Hear my answer to this: Tell Captain Wells, tell President, tell any white man:

"These lands are ours! No one has a right to remove us! We were on these lands from the Beginning. The Great Good Spirit above appointed this place for us on which to kindle our fires, and here we will remain! As for boundaries, the Great Spirit above knows no boundaries, nor will his red people acknowledge any!"

He stood directly in front of Shane, the whites showing all around the irises of his eyes, his deep chest rising and falling with his breathing. Even after they were spoken, his words seemed to resonate among the pole rafters of the long council house. He pointed at Shane's chest and said, "If the president of the Seventeen Fires has any more to say to me, he must send a great man. I will have no more talk with Captain Wells!"

And then Open Door rose beside him. Raising both arms, his medicine fire stick in his right fist, he faced the People and called in that flutelike voice, so startling a sound after the deep roll of Tecumseh's:

"This Miami squaw-man Wells has displeased me more than he can ever know! As mean a man as he is, he sends a still smaller man to talk to me. To *me!* Am I not the Prophet? Am I not a holy man, acclaimed by all the tribes? Why does not that president send to me the greatest man in his nation? If he would do this, maybe I, Tenskwatawa, would talk with him. *Maybe* I would!" Now he pointed his stick at Shane and shrilled, "I can bring darkness between him and me. More, I can bring the sun under my feet! What white man can do this? Tell me, you! What white man can do this? *Tell me!*"

Shane, afraid to speak, stood looking down, the voices of the hundreds in the council lodge roaring in agreement around his head.

And when he rode out of town, the half-breed's face was as pale as that of the purest white man. But a grim smile began to grow on his face as he galloped along the road toward Fort Wayne, passing one band after another of pilgrims. After what Captain William Wells had put him through, there would be a delicious, malicious satisfaction in telling him what had been said about him!

Shane laughed.

Now Open Door was feeling very confident in every way. Two moons had passed with no more words from Captain Wells at Fort Wayne.

The numbers of pilgrims had been swelling with every week. Even Sauk and Assiniboines had come, from lands northwest of the Missi-se-pe head-waters. Some food was being harvested from the village gardens, but not enough. The three Shaker ministers who had visited the holy town had been so impressed with the godliness in the place and so appalled by the hunger that they had supplied twenty-seven packhorse loads of provisions from their nearby settlement. Though Open Door had preached against the acceptance of white men's food, he accepted it eagerly and managed to justify it by clever talking.

And then some very welcome and unexpected help had come from Blue Jacket.

Though bound by treaty not to fight the Americans, he had come to the town and expressed to Tecumseh his secret support of the religious work. He then worked out with the brothers a scheme to get more food for the village—from the American government itself. At first Tecumseh had objected to the idea. But after Blue Jacket explained that it would be a trick rather than begging, Tecumseh saw its appeal. Blue Jacket himself, who was known by the whites as one of the treaty Indians, would go up to the American fort at Detroit and, talking with an oiled tongue to the befuddled old commander General Hull, would get some provisions or annuity money and give it to Open Door's town instead of the treaty Shawnees, who were already getting annuities. He went, and he did it.

Roundhead, a Wyandot village chief of great stature, had broken away from the Crane. He brought his people to come here and live permanently, this bringing still more prestige to the Prophet.

And news came that far away in the eastern sea, some British warships had shot their cannons at an American warship. There was much talk then of a new war between the two white nations. Such a war would mean, of course, more solicitous attention from the British, perhaps provisions, too. Maybe even the Americans would be more careful in their actions, so as not to drive the tribes into a war alliance with the British. Always the white nations had used the red men in their wars against each other. This time the red men, wiser in the wiles of the the white men's governments, and more unified than they had ever been, might be able to use a white man's war to their own advantage.

In fact, one of the British traders from Canada, a man named Frederick Fisher, was in the village now, seated across from Open Door on a cattail-rush mat, talking in veiled terms about these very matters. A British trader on the prowl in O-hi-o had to be very careful what he said and how he said it in these times. He had to hint at England's need for red allies in case of war but at the same time not make any overt invitation. England was bogged down in a distant war with Napoleon and could ill afford a conflict on this continent. England's fur trade with the Indians was depressed by that same war, and thus the old commercial cohesion between British and Indians was eroding. And in the minds of most Algonquian tribes there was also the bitter memory of the battle at Fallen Timbers, where the British commander had shut the gates of Fort Miami in the face of the routed Indians. That being the only battle Open Door had ever fought in, he was particularly bitter and skeptical of any British promises, either straightforward or tentative. Therefore he was, in his present euphoria of self-confidence, making light of both the Americans' threat and the friendship of the British.

"You do not know how strong and pure the red men are now, Fisher. We do not fear the Blue-Coats, and we do not need the Redcoats. Ha, ha!" Open Door had blossomed as a man of words and enjoyed exercising his wit in a conversation like this. He could not give way to much levity when talking to his flock; that was always dead serious. So now Open Door smiled slyly, thinking in jokes. That had been a good one about Blue-Coats and Redcoats, he thought.

Open Door had eaten only vegetables and beans and roots for days, game being so depleted in the vicinity, and his intestines were bubbling in him like a brine kettle. He could feel some of his older sort of eloquence coming down, that particular kind of mocking language he had used to use, back in the days when he was a boy underdog, to get the last word in. So now he stood up slowly, saying as he rose from his mat:

"Do you know, Fisher, the white man is so little to me now, Long Knives or British, that I can tell you in one word what they all mean to me. Here, Fisher, is that word."

Turning to put his ample behind close to Fisher's face, bending over, biting his lower lip and raising his right foot off the ground, the Shawnee prophet pronounced his singular word.

The word started as the drumming of a ruffed grouse, increased to the growl of a bear, and then, as its last syllable, finished with the loud, wet sound of a horse blowing its lips. Fisher recoiled, his head enveloped by the fertile scent of the Prophet's last word, and Open Door skipped about, helplessly carried away by his own cackling hilarity.

Since the Shakers were the only white men who had been permitted to see into all the doings of the Prophet's village, they were asked by the governor

of Ohio to write a report on their sojourn there. Profoundly impressed by
the prayers, the sobriety, and the selfless sharing of meager rations in the
crowded town, they wrote:

> Surely the Lord is in this place! Although these poor Shawnees
> have had no particular instruction but what they received from the
> outpouring of the Spirit, yet in point of real light and understanding,
> as well as behavior, they shame the Christian World.

The hearts of the Shakers had been won, and when, a few weeks later,
Open Door sent to ask them for more food, the Gentle Believers again
ransacked their own larders and granaries and sent another pack train to the
hungry Indians.

Soon thereafter, the Shaker settlement was disturbed by shouts and
hoofbeats. The visitors were militia officers. They were slit-eyed and white-
lipped with anger, and their language was un-Christian. They charged the
Shakers with sustaining "a goddamned Shawnee charlatan" and even accused them of encouraging him in his preparations to make war on the
settlers. The Shakers were dumbfounded by the allegations and tried to
convince the officers what a good and sober and devout place the Prophet's
town was. "Surely the Lord is in that place," they insisted.

The militia officers retorted by threatening to put the Shakers to the
sword for treason. And so the Shakers ended their brief association with the
Shawnee prophet.


In the summer, Tecumseh was pulled away from his duties at the holy town
by an incident that threatened to fan the settlers' fears into another Indian
war.

The decomposing body of a white man named Myers had been found
under a congregation of buzzards on a trailside near a new settlement called
Urbana on the Mad River. Though most of the skin was gone, those who
found the body had perceived in particular that it had no scalp.

At once the settlers were seething with fury and fear. There was only one
explanation, in their opinion: this must have been the work of some of those
transient Indians who were forever going to and from the town of the
Shawnee charlatan! Surely this was only the beginning of a bloody uprising.
The news went like the wind, and within days militia companies were
mustering everywhere and standing by for orders, and farm families were
moving into the safety of forts and towns.

For a few days more the situation simmered while Ohio leaders planned some approach that would calm the fears and meet the danger. At last they decided upon a big council, to be conducted by a commission of militia officers, for the purpose of questioning the Indian leaders and producing an Indian to hang. Only this, it seemed, could ease the tension and prevent a panic or a large-scale, indiscriminate retaliation.

Word was sent to tribes in and around western Ohio to bring their leading men to Springfield, a new settlement in Clark County near the ruins of the old Piqua. Black Hoof at once alleged that Tecumseh's followers must have killed the man. Tecumseh asked, "Why does no one say it was Black Hoof's?" The militia general Simon Kenton, who now lived near this town of Springfield, was put in charge of the commission, which comprised Kenton, Colonel Robert Patterson, and three other officers. The council was convened outdoors in an open field near an inn. Old Black Hoof and Blue Jacket arrived with 170 warriors. Tecumseh came with 130. Two parties of Wyandots came, Crane's and Roundhead's, and these two watched each other sullenly. It had been agreed in advance that all armed warriors would remain off the council ground, each faction to one side, and the white spectators on another part of the field, that only the chiefs and shamans would come onto the council ground, and that they must stack all their weapons off to the side before entering. Waiting for them there were the commissioners with a large body of interpreters, clergymen, and other white men of the sort who feel that nothing important can be well conducted without their presence.

General Kenton, once known as the dreaded But-lah, no longer dressed like an Indian. But at fifty-two years he still gave the appearance of a man of extraordinary physical power, and his face was benign and good-humored and shrewd.

Black Hoof, silver-haired, dressed in a wool coat, and the solid, middle-aged Blue Jacket, led their chieftains in. Black Hoof was more than eighty years old now, but still erect and stately. He was a chief of great stature among many red men, and whites, too, for he had twice been to Washington and seen the Great White Father there. He had gone to plead for the plows and the agricultural advisers for which he had been so long awaiting.

Black Hoof now watched with masked emotions as Tecumseh and a score of his sinewy chieftains approached. Suddenly Black Hoof pointed and exclaimed about something that the white men themselves had just noticed: Tecumseh's men had not divested themselves of their tomahawks or knives.

Kenton at once called to him, in Shawnee, and reminded him that all parties on the ground were to be unarmed. Tecumseh replied:

"I remember what happened to Cornstalk when he went unarmed among your people at Fort Randolph."

Kenton drew up stiff momentarily. Then he said in a cordial tone, "There will be no trouble here. Please do not try to bring your hatchets into this peaceful council."

Tecumseh held up his tomahawk and pointed to it. As white men crowded in close on him, he said, "But this is my pipe as well." It had a tobacco bowl in the head and a hollow handle. "I might need to use it during this meeting." Then he added, flashing a big smile: "One end or the other." There were some chuckles among the Shawnees.

At this, a tall, long-jawed clergyman stepped toward Tecumseh and proffered a deacon's pipe, a long-stemmed pipe of white clay now very thumb-smudged and blackened by use. "Maybe," he said, "the chief might smoke for peace with this instead."

Tecumseh took it but gave the parson such a hard look that he backed into the crowd. Then Tecumseh looked at the filthy object, sniffed the bowl, and made an exaggerated grimace of disgust. Then he flipped it back over his shoulder onto the ground. A roar of laughter went up around the council ground. White men and red alike howled at the parson's discomfiture, and Tecumseh's own warm, infectious laugh overrode the rest. Suddenly the tension was gone out of the air, and when Tecumseh and his followers moved on in to take their places, no more effort was made to disarm them. Black Hoof still looked miffed, but Blue Jacket was rocking with voiceless laughter.

Then the council was opened with the customary passing of a ceremonial pipe, and as the interpreters came forward and took their places, one of them, a big minister in a black frock and deerhide leggings, signaled toward Tecumseh with a big smile on his face. When Tecumseh saw him, the light of recognition flashed across his face, and he raised his hand in a salute. He wanted to cry out to him, "Big Fish!" But the pipe ceremony was too solemn to be disturbed by an outcry, so he and Stephen Ruddell simply stared at each other with sparkling eyes, their faces almost breaking with grins, nodding, shaking their heads. Even old Black Hoof was beaming. He, too, remembered the brotherhood of Tecumseh and Big Fish and their escapades in those long-ago skirmishes and battles. Tecumseh nodded toward Kenton and made a motion of holding a rifle, and Ruddell grinned and nodded, remembering the time his rifle had misfired at Kenton's chest. Ruddell was now a Baptist missionary and had come to work in Black Hoof's town. As promised, he had returned to the Shawnees.

In the preliminary statements of the council's purpose, Ruddell proved a skillful enough interpreter, and the council proceeded to its subject, the murder of Myers. The white commissioners said it was beyond doubt that Myers had been killed by an Indian. They demanded that whoever the killer was, he must be identified by his own chief and turned over to the white authorities for retribution. The Crane was the first chief to respond. He stood up and asserted that none of his Wyandots could have had anything to do with it. He spoke of his acknowledged friendship with the Americans, and his mark on their treaty, and his strong desire to keep this chain of friendship intact.

When the Crane finished, Tecumseh rose gracefully and was asked to speak. As he moved to the front of the council, the Indians all leaned forward, and the white men all noticed the intensity of their attention. The commissioners and spectators all had their eyes on this striking warrior chief who, even in unadorned deerhide, made a finer sight than either the white men's Indians in their dark suits or the garish, befeathered warriors. Some of the whites knew this Tecumseh was a legendary warrior and the brother of the notorious Shawnee prophet; others had no idea who he was but could sense his importance, not only by his bearing, but by the expectancy that had fallen over the other red men. It was feared by many that he who had at first warmed the council with laughter might now fan it to flames by accusing Black Hoof's people of the murder.

Tecumseh faced the crowd and looked them over. It entered his thoughts suddenly that he ought to see Ga-lo-weh here, since he was an important man in the vicinity and his home was scarcely ten miles away. But there was no Ga-lo-weh among the spectators. Tecumseh did see some familiar white faces, men he knew he had fought years ago.

The breeze hushed in the foliage, and birds were singing in the sunlight. Stephen Ruddell cleared his throat.

Tecumseh could have made his statement in English, for the edification of the white commissioners. But his real audience, he knew, was this gathering of red men. His oratorical skill was greatest in his own tongue, and he did not mean to let the white men think mockingly of his imperfect English. He began, and at first the white men, not understanding his words, were captivated by the sheer power, tone, and inflections of his voice, by the grace and power of his gestures, by his imposing stance—and by the intense concentration of his red audience.

"The Great Good Spirit has brought us together so that we may speak and hear the truth about a death that has happened. We red chiefs are expected to point at one of our people and say, 'Here is the man who killed your Myers; take him and hang him up to die.'" The Indians nodded and muttered.

"I do not know who killed that man," Tecumseh said. "Ask Black Hoof.

Perhaps he knows." At once there was an uproar. Black Hoof rose to his feet with a swiftness amazing for a man of his years and shouted that Tecumseh was a liar. His chieftains formed around him, facing Tecumseh's followers. For a few minutes the armed men around the field hesitated and milled, readying their guns, while the commissioners shouted for order. Black Hoof was yelling that Tecumseh's renegade Indians at the Prophet's town or the many visiting Indians there must have killed the white man. For a moment a great fight seemed imminent, and the town of Springfield had its first big scare. At last the hubbub died down. Tecumseh and Black Hoof stared at each other. Black Hoof had broken the protocol by interrupting a speaker, and at last he sat down, realizing that he had acted like a white man. Then Tecumseh resumed, in a mild voice:

"No, I do not truly think even Black Hoof knows. I do not believe that anyone here knows.

"If I did know the name of a warrior who killed that man, would I deliver him to you white men, for you to hang him up? Would you be able to prove he had done it? Would you even bother to try to prove it? I do not think so. You do not seek justice. You seek a red man whom you can hang up, to satisfy the cries of your people.

"Why do I say you do not seek justice? I can remember many times since the Greenville Treaty when red men and women were killed, and though you had the murderers in your hands, your judging councils turned them loose, as if justice were of no importance to you.

"I remember when an Indian family gave shelter to three white men, who killed the family in their sleep. Those three white men were not hung up.

"I remember when a white man made a red man drunk and killed him after he went to sleep. You had that white man and you knew what he had done, but you did not hang him up. Earlier, I remember when your Captain McGary killed the old Chief Moluntha with a hatchet, while the chief stood prisoner, holding a peace treaty and your flag, and many soldiers stood and watched him do it. But was McGary executed?

"Still more seasons back, our great Chief Cornstalk, his son, and Chief Red Hawk were murdered while unarmed in a room at Fort Randolph, where they were visiting on a peace mission."

Whenever Tecumseh paused and let Ruddell translate, the commissioners grew more gray and grave. And Tecumseh went on, his voice now harder:

"I remember when all the family of Logan the Mingo were murdered by Greathouse, whom they had trusted. Was Greathouse executed for that? No, not until the Shawnees caught him seventeen years later on the Beautiful River and made their own justice.

"I remember when your militiamen went to Gnadenhutten and put one hundred Jesus Indians, men and women and children, into a big room and smashed all their heads even while they prayed to your Jesus Christ. Were any of those militiamen ever executed? No.

"If you wish to hear of more, I am able to talk for a long time without tiring, or without repeating any names, or running out of such stories.

"But you brought us here to talk instead about the death of a man called Myers, who you say was murdered, although you do not really know if he was killed by a red man who had to defend himself against this Myers. Or maybe he was killed by a *white* man." There was a rumble of consternation among the spectators at this suggestion. Tecumseh waited till it subsided, then went on. "Maybe this Myers was killed by an Indian woman whom he had molested. Your white men seem to like to bother our women, when there are no warriors around. If you want to hear of such cases, I can recite them for a day or two." This conjecture made the commissioners squirm, and the men writing down the words of the council did not even put their pens to their paper. It was not the kind of allegation that should be written on a record.

The commissioners looked as if they might like to cut Tecumseh off here, but in a council with Indians every speaker was allowed to talk until he was through. At each of Tecumseh's pauses, the congregation of red men nodded and made throaty noises of agreement.

"So," he went on now, "maybe your Myers was killed because he was doing harm to a red man or a woman, as your lawless people think they can do. If so, then justice has already been done in this case. No one will ever know what happened, because Myers cannot speak anymore, and the person who took his scalp, whether it was a red man or one of the many white men who also take scalps—did you not know that?—that person has surely passed on out of the country. I do not believe any of our people did this killing of Myers. A warrior takes a scalp for one reason only: so that when he tells a story of a victory, he can show that his story is true. Would a *secret* murderer take a scalp and come home and boast to me that he had killed a helpless white man? No. Because all red men know that in my town, the Prophet teaches against violence. He teaches for peace. Every morning and every night in my town, all the People pray that we will not have violence with the whites. And so a man would not come there to brag of such a thing, so why would he take the scalp?

"I do not know how it is in Black Hoof's town; maybe they do not pray for peace." As the old chief's eyes flashed, Tecumseh added: "But Black Hoof's people are under a treaty not to fight white men, and red men do not violate treaties." Black Hoof's momentary look of anger passed, and he nodded in agreement. It was plain that Tecumseh's line of talk now was pleasing all the red men present. And the red men were, after all, the audience he cared about. In fact, his voice had such clarity and carrying power that even the three hundred warriors waiting in the distance off the council ground could hear him. That included Black Hoof's followers and the Crane's Wyandots, any of whom Tecumseh knew might be swayed to his cause.

Now Ruddell had translated the statement about treaties, and Tecumseh moved ahead in that vein:

"My mind is confused about what a white man means by the word 'treaty.' When the white man makes a treaty with us, we think he is giving us his word. Maybe our trouble is that we do not understand what whites mean by 'treaty.' Perhaps some white man here is a great explainer, and could tell us what a white man thinks a treaty is for. The long and sad story of treaties on this land, from the first when your ships came to the shore of the sunrise, make me think that a treaty is not what the red man believed it to be. Maybe the red man has a mist of trust before his eyes, and cannot see what is really there. From what I have seen and studied of all the treaties from that day, I come to believe that a white man with a treaty is like a dog who wants permission to put his nose in the doorway and smell the meat cooking inside. 'Only my nose,' this dog promises, and he waves his tail to show he is sincere." The Indians in the council, even a few of the white men, were getting the drift of this and smiling, already thinking ahead to the dog's next move, and then the next and the next. Tecumseh said:

"I will begin with the first treaty made with the English white men, by Chief Powhatan in Virginia, who did not think any harm would come from a dog's nose in his doorway. And then I will tell how with each treaty the dog got farther inside the doorway and closer to the meat, until all the meat was inside the dog."

The Indians laughed aloud. Even those old chiefs who had signed treaties with the white men nodded and smiled grimly because they had seen the terms of their treaties diminished little by little, either by the individual white settlers who simply ignored them or by the government officials who regularly brought forth new treaties that overreached the old ones. It was evident in the faces of the chiefs that they were eager to sit here and hear a long story full of righteous grievances.

Tecumseh set forth on his narrative of treaties and deceits. He spoke of old names like Samoset and Massasoit and of tribes and treaties the educated white men could only vaguely recall and the uneducated ones had never even heard of. The terms of each treaty he described in detail, and then he related all the specific violations by which each had been destroyed or nullified. He related how whiskey and rum had been used to confuse the red men at treaty councils and how it was brought into towns and sold to make the people more weak and confused so that they would go blind into new treaties. On and on he went, his voice rolling forth, pausing only to let his words be translated. Stephen Ruddell was sweating with the effort of remembering so many names and details long enough to translate them into English. Another interpreter, who was translating from Shawnee to Wyandot, was having even worse trouble and sometimes simply stood gaping, his mind unable to correlate so many unfamiliar things. The white people were astounded that so much information existed, and more so that it had been compiled and arranged in one aboriginal mind; they were appalled that he was standing here in a council to which they themselves had invited him and serving up this long, compelling indictment of the perfidies of their race. The red men in the council were like an empty cup that he was filling up with vitriol.

Nearly two hours later, as Tecumseh was reaching the present day in his history of broken trust, condemning Governor Harrison's awesome series of land treaties and the corrupt chiefs who had signed them in return for promises of more annuity money, the commissioners were almost numb with the weight of their mistake and had whispered an agreement among themselves that perhaps the case of Myers's death should just be dropped, not even mentioned again in this council. Its importance seemed to have shrunk down very small. And one other thing was being whispered guardedly among the old implacable Indian fighters who made up the commission:

That this Tecumseh was a dangerous man, perhaps as dangerous as his brother the fantastic shaman, and that it might not be a bad idea, at some propitious time, to kidnap or kill them both.

By now all the red men were leaning toward the speaker as leaves stretch toward the sun, and their eyes glittered and their faces were intense with indignation. The commissioners were not sure whether the whole body of them would rise up and leave in defiance or even rush for their weapons. The interpreters were now merely stumbling along, translating a phrase here, a sentence there, left behind by the arrow of his narrative.

Suddenly he paused and looked over his shoulder at the commissioners and said:

"This is why I expect neither truth nor justice in your councils, and this is why I will never mark your treaties, and this is why I discourage all my red brothers from putting their mark on them.

"But we in our town by Greenville do not talk for war against the whites. We only say, Here is what the white men did when they got close to us;

let us forever keep at a little distance from them. This is what you white men want, too. Your treaties always tell us, move off a little farther.

"Brothers, we cannot move any farther. You are all around us and tightening in. But in our hearts we can be pure and peaceful and sober, and depend upon ourselves and each other, and leave the white men alone. We would only do ourselves more harm if we attacked white people, or likewise if we listened to any more of their promises.

"And therefore I, Tecumseh, who value my people's freedom more than my own life, I assure the commissioners here that in my camp we do not incite our people to war with the whites; on the contrary, we teach and plead for patience, and truth, and wisdom, and each morning and night we pray for these. This is the word of my heart, and I tell it to you, because you have been so busy trying to find out what we do there. I will assure your highest chiefs of it: ours is not a war camp, and we do not go about murdering white men."

Then he walked to his place and sat down, and it was plain that all the red men thought that everything worth saying had been said.

With few more words, none about Myers, the commissioners closed the council, and it dissolved in apparent good spirit. The three hundred warriors and chieftains elected to remain at Springfield for three more days, to engage in sports and competitions of skill. Stephen Ruddell and Tecumseh had a warm reunion, but a certain distance separated them because of Ruddell's attachment to the faction of Black Hoof, who was his adoptive father, and because of his obvious antipathy toward Open Door's religion.

The white men who observed the ensuing games noticed that Tecumseh, though nearly twice the age of many of the competitors, won nearly every contest.

What the white men did not notice was that while he was winning athletic victories on the sunny field, he was also winning hearts and minds at the little fireside councils at night. By the time the red men left Springfield, many young men of Black Hoof's Shawnees and the Crane's Wyandots had come to believe that his way was better than the way of their old tame chiefs and had pledged to come and join him at the village in Greenville.

The proper place for Open Door's soul was on the Road of Stars between earth and heaven, he felt, either going there alone to receive more divine instruction or leading the red people there by his words. Therefore he did not like having to deal with the earthly problems of running a crowded town or making the kinds of decisions the white men required. Those matters he liked to leave to Tecumseh or, if Tecumseh were absent, to his own wife, who was becoming an able women's chief, or to Star Watcher, who seemed to know how Tecumseh would have handled something.

Now Tecumseh was gone, and a white man had come with an important message. This was a big, shrewd-eyed man in fine clothes. Open Door peeked out the door of his lodge and recognized the man. He was John Conner, who with his brother William ran a trading post in the Indiana Territory. Open Door had known him in the days of Tecumseh's village near the Delawares.

Open Door guessed that Conner had come with a message from Harrison. He came out to meet him. Conner looked at him indirectly and asked to be taken to the chief and head man of the Shawnees here. He said he had a letter for them from the governor of the Indiana Territory. Open Door said, "I am here before you. You may read the letter to me."

Conner looked confused. He had not expected this well-known drunkard and fool to be the head man. When the warriors and chieftains assured him that Open Door was indeed the principal man, Conner had no choice but to begin reading the letter, and it was at once apparent why he had not wanted to.

The Prophet's expressions went from anger to exaggerated imitations of hurt feelings as he listened.

The letter scolded the Shawnees for listening to a fool whose words were not truly the words of the Great Spirit, but of the Devil and of British agents. The letter ridiculed and abused Open Door openly. It accused him of summoning tribes from far away in order to mislead them, and it told the Shawnees they should send him to the lands beyond the Great Lakes, where he could hear the British more distinctly. Sheepishly, Conner finished the letter and waited for the worst.

Open Door stalked about for a while, swelling up and looking furious, then shaking his head and looking pitiful. It was plain to him: Harrison simply could not believe that this movement had grown among the Shawnees themselves, out of their own needs, that this was purely an Indian refuge from the troubles the Long Knives had brought. Harrison, like all the Americans, had to blame it on the Americans' old enemies, the British.

Open Door did not reply the way he would have wanted to. He wanted to call Harrison the real fool and taunt him about how he had answered his stupid challenge to make the sun stand still. He wanted to curse him as a thief of the red men's lands.

But Tecumseh had warned time after time: "Do not provoke this Harrison. He is dangerous, and we are not yet ready to defy him. We must play with him and confuse him so that he knows not which way to move."

So Open Door, cooled from angry to crafty, directed Conner to write a reply:

> Father,
> I am very sorry that you listen to the advice of bad birds. You have impeached me with having correspondence with the British, and with calling and sending for the Indians from the most distant parts of the country, "to listen to a fool that speaks not the words of the Great Spirit, but the words of the Devil." Father, these impeachments I deny, and say they are not true. I never had a word with the British, and I never sent for the Indians. They came here themselves to listen and hear the words of the Great Spirit. Father, I wish you would not listen any more to the voices of bad birds; you may rest assured it is the least of our idea to make disturbances, and we will rather try to stop them.

When John Conner rode out of the Prophet's town with this surprisingly mild reply, he was almost singing, he was so surprised to find himself alive.

"This Harrison hears his own conscience and thinks it is the voices of the British!" Tecumseh cried when he returned and heard about the letter. "He never admits the great crimes his treaties are, but blames the British for troubling us! Though we are not even in his territory, he cannot leave us alone!" Then he put his hand on Open Door's shoulder. "It is good how you answered his insults, without anger. Listen. The matter of the dead man called Myers is settled. The governor in O-hi-o is going to send his farmer-soldiers home.

"But the settlers who live close to us will not lie easy. If a horse wanders or a hog is killed, it will be blamed on us. Black Hoof will never stop complaining to his white fathers about us. He learned how Blue Jacket got annuity money for us from Hull at Detroit, and screams that we do not deserve it because we are not treaty markers. Ha!"

Now Tecumseh made a statement that astonished Open Door. "It would be better for us if we did move from this place."

"But . . . my brother! This is the place the Great Good Spirit sent me to! This is the place my poor People know! Look at them, how happy they are here!"

"Yes. This has been a good place for its time. But I feel that the Great Good Spirit may soon send you a sign to move elsewhere. Surely he does not want us in conflict with the white people now as you create peace among the tribes. But we are on land within the treaty boundaries, and they will not let us rest here long."

"Boundaries? Is this my brother Tecumseh who speaks now of boundaries? You said you know no such thing as boundaries!"

Tecumseh put a calming hand on his arm. "I still do not believe in boundaries. But I do see that those lines do exist in the white men's minds, and on their sheets of paper, and they feel these lines give them a cause to molest us. That is why I say we should move into land they do not yet even claim. From there we will be free to watch the boundaries, and if a white man puts his foot over, we can put him back. There, we can build our nation of all red men, without so many spies and soldiers and nervous whitefaces coming to the edge of our camp. And there we can better avoid more treaties."

Open Door frowned, thinking hard. "West would be closer to Harrison. Besides west, there is nothing but Canada."

"The closer to Harrison, the better we can watch and confuse him."

Open Door cocked his head. "If we were west, true, my followers from the northwest would not have to come so many hard days."

"And thus would not be so hungry when they arrived."

"Where would this new town be?"

"Will not the Great Good Spirit tell you?" Tecumseh replied. "Some sign will come, pointing to the place."

In the autumn there came to the good town a man whose glory was in being bad.

Main Poc, Withered Hand, of the Potawatomi rode in from the northwest with a large bodyguard of warriors, his arrival creating a great stir among the Ojibways and Sauks and Menominees in the holy town. Open Door had never met Withered Hand before, but Tecumseh had visited him often in his own travels.

Withered Hand was a brawny, ugly giant in his middle years, respected and feared throughout northern Illinois and west of Lake Mis-e-ken. His influence extended beyond his own tribe and into the Winnebagoes and Sauks and Ojibways. His favorite pastimes were drinking liquor until he was full of thunder and striking like lightning across the Missi-se-pe against the Osages. Main Poc's name referred to his left hand. He had been born without fingers or thumb on that hand, and he boasted that this was his special sign. Though he could not shoot with a bow, he could use a musket with his right hand alone and was said to have killed Osages with the stump of his left, as with a war club. Withered Hand was both a chief and a shaman, which was permitted in his nation but not in the Shawnee. He was a member of the Wabeno, or Fire Handler Society, and possessed such medicine that bullets and arrows could not hit him. That he had come this great distance to see the Shawnee prophet increased Open Door's prestige even more.

But Withered Hand was not the kind of man who comes to look up at another man. He had come as an equal, to meet another great shaman and orator like himself, a prophet of whom he had heard much from the Ojibways passing through.

When the two came face to face, the people looking on saw their strong medicine passing both ways between them. They not only respected each other, but liked each other at first sight. Each recognized the other's disfigurement as a special gift of the Creator. Withered Hand said he had come to stay for a long while. From what he had heard, he had come to believe that Open Door was a great man who had been delivered to the red men because one was needed. Withered Hand, without any humility, said he was here to learn the Prophet's doctrines with his own eyes and ears and to go home and spread them deeper into the north and west. Some of the warriors he had brought with him, he said, he had selected because they too showed promise of being effective disciples.

Tecumseh had long foreseen that Withered Hand's wide influence and his bravery could be important in the confederation of red nations. That was why he himself had gone so often to talk to Withered Hand. The Potawatomi chief had welcomed Tecumseh and had accorded him much respect but had not shown any enthusiasm for the unification of tribes. To Withered Hand, intertribal warfare was natural and traditional. It was the way a warrior and chief found glory and proved his tribe's superiority. Tecumseh had tried to convince him that there was greater glory to be found in fighting the red man's common enemy, the Americans, than each other. But until lately Withered Hand had been remote from the white man's evil and had never engaged in such great struggles as the war with Clark or St. Clair's defeat, so his mind had not yet been turned in that way. Lately, though, the Americans were becoming more of a bother up and down the Missi-se-pe valley and near Lake Mis-e-ken, and he was starting to think more about them.

Now, as the two ugly shamans conferred with each other day after day, Open Door began to realize that Withered Hand would probably never give up liquor. He loved liquor and stated over and over: "If I quit making war and quit drinking whiskey, I would become a common man. This the Great Spirit has told me. He has spoken to me, as well as to you." Most of the other tenets of the Prophet's teaching, however, he found good, so their bond of friendship grew stronger as his visit extended over the next two moons.

And when, in the Hard Moon, Withered Hand and his warriors rode homeward, he left Open Door with an invitation:

"On the Wabash-se-pe, where the Tippecanoe flows into it, there is a valley so rich and pleasant that tribes have been living in it since the Ancient Times. It is sheltered from the strong winds off the prairies, and it is far from Fort Wayne and far from Vincennes. It is in the center of the Indian lands. My own ancestors were in that part of the valley for many years. You should move to that place and make your holy town there." He told the Prophet that it would be especially easy to move there, to carry everything by raft and canoe. Not far north of Greenville rose the headwaters of the Mississinewa. One could float down the Mississinewa to the place where it flowed into the Wabash-se-pe, then down the Wabash-se-pe a little farther, and there the Tippecanoe flowed in, and there was the place. It was not far above Weatanon, the old French trading post and the home of the Wea tribe of the Miami nation.

Tecumseh had seen the place often. He remembered the wide, fertile bottomlands, the wooded bluffs rising to the prairies above. "Yes," Tecumseh told his brother, "he speaks true. It is a good place."

And after Withered Hand had ridden away with his warriors into the wet, leafless woods, Open Door slept a night and told Tecumseh the next day:

"I dreamed. Weshemoneto spoke and said that I should lead our people to the Tippecanoe on the Wabash-se-pe, when the ice breaks in the springtime."

"Good," Tecumseh said. "I was confident that the sign would come." He smiled. It was always good to let Open Door think an idea was his own, for only then would he dedicate himself to it.

# CHAPTER 28

## *Near Old Chillicothe*
## *July 1809*

Tecumseh and Thick Water looked at each other with pain and sadness in their faces when they gazed down from the bluff over the site of the old Shawnee town. There were square houses and dirt roads in every part of the valley. Fields were separated from each other by great, shaggy windrows of rotting brush and stumps. In sloping places, eroded bare earth showed like gashes through the weeds and scrub. Giant hardwood trees, their bark girdled by the settlers long ago, stood gray, rotting from the top, or lay broken, the cornrows plowed around them. Smoke rose from brushpiles and chimneys everywhere in the valley. Pigs wandered all about, dogs barked from horizon to horizon. The corn was not very tall and looked parched and spindly in the dusty fields. Brambles and tall horseweeds choked every unplowed corner.

Tecumseh urged his horse forward and led his five bodyguards down the slope toward the river. They rode in among the sycamores and willows and dismounted at the old campsite not far from Ga-lo-weh's house. Much had happened in the last two years to keep Tecumseh from coming back to face the troubles he had made here. The holy town had been moved to the place on the Tippecanoe; Open Door had gone to meet Harrison in Vincennes and, it seemed, had at last convinced him of the harmless and strictly religious nature of his following.

A fine holy town had been built on the north bank of the Wabash-se-pe, and it was thronging with worshipers. In the same time, Tecumseh had ridden hundreds of miles in every direction with his retinue of splendid young warriors, spreading his fervent message of intertribal unity. He was now returning from deep in the south, and the road once again had brought him to this place of memories. In his breast he was agitated as he had not been for a long time.

Tecumseh advised his bodyguards to be peaceable and polite if any of the white settlers of the vicinity approached them, and then he set out on foot toward Ga-lo-weh's house.

He looked at the place on the path where they had paused in such confusion, and it was like stooping in the vanishing ruins of his childhood home: so much had happened there that it seemed wrong that there was no trace of it. He stood remembering, how she had grown from a little girl to his teacher: recalling *I have he has they have,* in her voice and his for hours, in facing chairs, reading to each other for pleasure and practice, remembering her gestures and expressions in moments when their minds would converge from the farthest points of their respective worlds, remembering how the air between them would seem to glow in those moments of comprehension. It had been more like a friendship than anything he had ever known with a woman; it was like a part of his friendship with her father, and thus her desire had simply ambushed him.

Now he hoped she would have forgotten all that, that in two years she might haved married and would not be lonely now.

He heard something fall.

He looked up the path toward the house.

She had stopped a short distance up the path, a wooden pail fallen by her feet, and she stood there with her hand at her throat, looking at him.

She began walking slowly toward him, her hand still at her neck, and she looked so strange, all her colors so pale—hair, face, eyes, limbs, homespun dress, bare feet—it was as if she were a spirit only, mist in the shape of a girl. And what he remembered was true: he did not desire her, did not even want to touch her. Yet his spirit reached for her spirit, as it always had, and he smiled.

She stopped more than three paces away. She was not smiling. Her eyes were full of tears and doubt; she looked as if she suffered. At last she said, "I knew you were here." Her voice was weak and small. He took a step toward her, but when she looked as if she would turn and flee like a fawn in the woods that has never seen a person before, he stopped. She was very much changed. Now she said:

"You told me you would come back."

"I come. You see me here."

She raised her hand from her throat and covered her mouth with her fingertips. Between her brows there was a knot of agony. She made her hand into a fist and pressed the knuckles against her mouth and shut her eyes as tears began flowing.

"You came too late!" she sobbed, then whirled to turn her back on him. She stood with her head bent forward, shoulders shaking with sobs, little strangling, high-pitched sobs. Tecumseh was stunned by this, confused and swept by pity. He raised his hands as if to take her shoulders, though she was several paces away, and then he dropped them to his sides. He did not know what to do and did not know what she meant.

And so he stood at this distance, feeling that to go and touch her would make her run. There was no sound but the breeze in the foliage and her little throat sounds. It was several minutes before she stopped sobbing. Quietly then he moved toward her and went around to stand in front of her. Her hands were down by her belly now and twisting at each other; her head was still forward, and he was looking at the parted hair on top of her head, the pale line of skin. Her yellow hair was in two braids. Strands were loose, stirring in the breeze, gleaming in the sunlight that winked through the blown foliage. In the quiet he said, "Why do I come too late?"

For a while she neither wept nor spoke and just seemed to be looking at the ground under his feet. Then, her face still down out of his sight, she began talking, slowly, pausing, as if to keep from weeping.

"You said you would come back soon. You wanted to ask Papa for my hand . . . We waited and waited . . . All troubled . . ."

For a moment as these words whirled in his head, he had that same wild impulse to run away that he had felt in his first battle. It seemed like something too awful to be really happening to him. The Great Good Spirit did not want red people marrying white people. And it had brought suffering to this good white girl. Then he thought too of his friend, her father. So much must have happened in this family since that night!

At last he asked her, "You told your father such a thing?"

She nodded slowly.

He started to speak, but was bewildered, then angry, and could not think of words. Then he said grimly, "You should not have told him such a thing! Why did you think to tell him that?"

Now her eyes were full of disbelief, "You gave me a dowry!"

He barely remembered that word. "Just silver things. They make this happen?"

She was sobbing again. He looked down on her and then reached out and cupped her face in his hands and felt her shudder at his touch and felt the wetness of her tears on his palms. She would not look up at him. "My . . . Rebekah Ga-lo-weh girl. I do not understand this. Tell me all of this."

They sat down on a fallen log beside the path, and little by little she told him the story of it, sometimes stopping to cry or for long silences. Sometime during this she had let him take her hand, and he held it as she told him.

That very night she had told her father that Tecumseh wanted to marry her. "I thought that was what you meant . . . the silver . . . you telling me it was a dowry . . . so, yes. . . . I told him, 'Papa, Mister Tecumftha Chief will come and ask you for my hand.' I thought you would! I really thought that was what you wanted!" Saying this, she slumped and wept again for a long time before she could go on.

After a while her father had started asking her if she really wanted to be married to a man who was not a Christian. Often he had assembled the family to pray for guidance. They had prayed about the problem for many days before they could talk practically about it. Her father, looking like a wounded man, had spoken over and over of the troubles to be expected in a mixed marriage, but she had known he was mostly worried about the shame. She had protested that Tecumseh was a perfect gentleman by anyone's reckoning. Her father had replied that however much a gentleman he was, the brethren in the church would not accept him. A year passed in this doubt and misery, then another, and Tecumseh had never come. Had Rebekah not told several people about the proposal, the crisis would have passed in the family. Her father felt embarrassed.

After a long silence at the end of her story, Tecumseh said, "Your father was my good white friend, but he would not want me to be your husband."

She thought, then said, now looking down at his hand holding hers, "He would not want it, but he would bless us. He still . . . he's dubious, but he still esteems you very highly. He knows you wouldn't hurt us on purpose."

"And you know that, too?"

She nodded, swallowing and swallowing. "Yes. But . . . did you never mean to ask me that?" She shut her eyes and bit her lip and trembled after the question.

Deeply, sadly stirred by all this, he answered in a gentle voice:

"Since I first saw the little Ga-lo-weh girl you have been very big in my heart. But I had never thought of it. I did not know dowry meant that kind of a gift. Ah! No!" They sat enveloped in their confusion and regrets for a long time, still holding each other by the hand, and eventually he said, "I must go and speak to your father and tell him I did not know this." He wondered if her father would try to attack him. It was a dismal possibility. He just did not know how a white man would be about a matter like this. Tecumseh was less afraid of being hurt by Ga-lo-weh than of having to hurt him. But Rebekah shook her head.

"Papa isn't here. He's gone up with gentlemen to Fort Wayne, for the treaty council."

Alarm prickled in the back of Tecumseh's head. Trying to keep his voice calm, he said, "I know of no treaty council. Tell me."

She looked up at his face for the first time, and in her eyes was hurt, even anger. "Is that more important to you than I am?"

"Just tell me of it!" His voice was urgent. If it was in Fort Wayne, it would be Harrison's council, and that could be more important than any- thing.

She looked down and shook her head. "All I know is, it's with some chiefs, about some land in the territory. . . . But what about—"

He stood and pulled her hand to make her stand with him. "I must go. You give me too much for my head. I must think."

She held his eyes with hers, and hers were full of the fear that he would stay gone forever if he left now. Desperately she blurted out: "Are you going to think of . . . us being married?"

"Because you have asked, I will have to think of it." He thought of the holy town and all that was being done there and what it was being done for, and of the Prophet's pronouncements about white and red people marrying. "My friend girl," he said, "you could not come and live among my people."

"I know," she said, having already given that much thought. "But you could come here and live like us. . . ." Her chin was trembling, her wet eyelashes were blinking. She saw the sudden hardening of his expression, then at that moment saw beyond him five warriors approaching. She gasped. The warriors, seeing her and Tecumseh, stopped and stared, ten paces away.

Tecumseh squeezed her hand and released it. "Forgive me for your hurt. I am always your friend and your father's. Your family will be safe whatever comes. You are very big in my heart, but I am my People. Be strong. Do not look for me anymore." He was almost choking. *"Tanakia,"* he said. Farewell.


Tecumseh rode hard for the first five miles or so, so that he was always out ahead and his mystified warriors could not see his face. But after he had firmed himself against his feelings, he slowed to a walk. They had scared several white people off the road riding hard like that, and it was not good for a small band of red men to be racing through this part of O-hi-o, even as desperate as he was to learn more about the treaty council as soon as he could.

After they had ridden a few more miles, Seekabo said, "Father, we saw you shake the hand of the white hag." Thick Water, who had his memories about the white girl on the path from two years ago, stared ahead and pretended to be disinterested.

At first Tecumseh was astonished and almost angered by Seekabo's use of that word. But then he realized that to them, with her pale coloring and yellow hair and distraught face, she must have looked strange and ugly, as he himself had thought she looked until he had gotten used to her and to the goodness in her spirit.

"She was afraid," he said. "I took her hand and promised her that no harm would ever come to her family. Remember my promise."

They passed and frightened two white men who were riding big-footed draft horses. The farmers looked as if they were ready either to shoot at the Indians or try to lumber off in escape, so Tecumseh rode out to them with a hand up, told them who he was, and explained that he was only passing through in peace, going to his home in the Indiana Territory. He asked, "Do you know anything of the council at Fort Wayne?"

They probably knew more than they were willing to tell an Indian. One said, "Gov'nor Harrison's buyin' some land, is all I know."

"Which chiefs?"

"I don't know who they are. Little Turtle's the only one I know of."

Tecumseh completely masked his screaming anxiety. "I thank you. I must pass on now."

When the Indians had ridden off up their westering road, the white men rode on, much relieved, their heartbeats gradually subsiding to normal. One of them said:

"So *that's* that Tecumseh! Pretty uppity Indian, ain't he? Talkin' English and all. Y'know, don't ye, Jim Galloway says that redskin p'posed to marry his girl Becky. Heard about that? Man, that takes some uppity Indian! Pretty, well-raised gal like her! Man!" He shook his head angrily. "Galloway said she turned him down good and proper, but nice-like. Said she couldn't be no squaw." The man's face was in a sneer.

After a while the other replied, "That's somethin' all right. I'll tell you, I wouldn't mess with no daughter of old Jim, even if I *wasn't* a redskin. Which I ain't."

Riding hard at the head of his bodyguard, his mind seething with rage and remorse, Tecumseh sped through the sunny, tall grass of the prairie, toward the line of green treetops that marked the valley of the Wabash-se-pe. Above the trees in the pearly blue sky hung the smudge of smoke that marked the site of Prophet's Town. He galloped headlong down the slopes as the valley opened to view. Such homecomings from their long journeys were usually rich with joy and relief. But Tecumseh was full of bitterness now. It had been growing in him at the thought of Harrison's greed.

They thundered down into the upper streets of Prophet's Town. Open
Door had built a good and beautiful town here. It was made up of orderly
rows of *wigewas,* first filling the bottomlands below the Tippecanoe's
mouth, then spreading up these slopes onto the prairie. On a low rise next
to the river stood its largest structure, a wide, long house of logs and bark
called the House of the Stranger, the shelter for visitors and pilgrims. In
a clearing on the bluff at the other end of the town stood a large, traditional
council house and next to it a smaller structure that was Open Door's
medicine lodge. It was toward this building that Tecumseh rode now. He
waved and answered the greetings of the many villagers who came running
and cheering him along the street, but really he hardly saw them, hardly
noticed how crowded the town was with pilgrims.

Open Door, intense and worried, greeted him at the door of his medicine lodge, and the two went inside at once. Open Door said, "You know
of the council at Fort Wayne?"

"Only that it will be. Tell me what you know."

"That Harrison is as cunning as the thieving fox. He kept his treaty
council from me as long as he could, for he knows we would oppose it. He
does not imagine we know of it even now. He has summoned all his faithful
red dogs. Little Turtle and Pacane of the Miamis. Of the Delawares, Beaver
and Cracking Noise. Winnemac and Five Medals of the Potawatomi. And
others, but, of course, none who live on the land he wants. Not us."

"What land is it, my brother?"

Open Door described the boundaries, and Tecumseh's blood grew hot-
ter at every word.

It was a vast area of woods and prairies north and east of Vincennes, in
the Wabash-se-pe and White River watersheds, from the Greenville Treaty
line near O-hi-o all the way across to the Wabash-se-pe and even across it
into the Illinois lands. Tecumseh knew very well these lands that were being
coveted by Harrison now; a dozen tribes had villages in them and depended
upon their hunting grounds for their food. And if Harrison got it, the
American boundaries would reach within two days' march of the Prophet's
town!

"While you were gone," Open Door said, "I did what you told me to
do to keep the white men at ease about us. I went to Fort Wayne and
Vincennes to assure the Americans again that we are peaceful. There is a
new Indian agent at Fort Wayne, called Johnston. Wells is gone. Annuity
dollars had been sticking to his fingers while he counted them, they say. I
got on well with this Johnston. He believed what I said to him, and I
thought he would not alarm Harrison about us as Wells was always doing.
But when I went to Vincennes in the next moon, Harrison was cold to me.

He had changed his manner since the first time I visited him. He accused me of harboring troublemakers here. I assured him that I discourage any talk of troubling the Americans. But I could not make him believe me.

"And while I was there he did not tell me he was calling this big land treaty council! Brother, is this not a man of two faces?"

"As we have long known!" Tecumseh exhaled sharply between clenched teeth and pounded his thigh with his fist. "Do our friends in those tribes now have enough voice to keep the old traitors from marking a treaty? Do you think so?"

"I *think* so," Open Door replied. "Have we not warned them again and again that Harrison will try to do what he is now trying to do? Will they not believe it now by seeing it, and speak up in time? And are not the old chiefs aware by now that if they mark another treaty, they will be known as witches?"

Tecumseh nodded, then shook his head, brusquely, angrily. He did not like this killing of "witches" and had stopped Open Door and his zealots before, when they had been executing suspects too enthusiastically. But still the fear of such witch-hunts was very strong, and it had kept some of the government chiefs humble. "So, then," Tecumseh said at last. "The Miamis and the Delawares and the Potawatomies will go to Fort Wayne to meet with Harrison, and there is nothing we can do to stop them from going. To try to threaten them or stop them by force would ruin the wholeness we have been trying to build here. So they will go. Many of them probably have gone already, hoping the kegs will be opened early. All we can do is encourage our people in those tribes to talk against marking it, and send a few hawks to sit in the crowd and keep a watch on them. . . ." His voice trailed off, then suddenly he clenched his fists until they shook and ground his teeth together. "Think, brother!" he hissed. "Think of how much land he tries to grab this time! No; rather, think how little it will leave for all the red people if he does take it!"

He sighed. Suddenly he yearned only for someone whose presence could calm the great tightness these vexations had drawn in him. "I am hungry and tired," he said. "Let us go over to Star Watcher's house. I long to see my sister. And my son."

# CHAPTER 29

*Fort Wayne, At the Head of the Maumee*
*September 30, 1809*

L ittle Turtle limped into the council house, with fourteen hundred red men watching him, their feelings a mixture of curiosity, respect, and annoyance. Though he was the most honored war chief here, it had been nearly fifteen years since he had given up to the Long Knives; he was wholly a white man's Indian now, doing everything he could to help his people adapt to the white man's strange and demanding ways. And though he lived closest to Fort Wayne, he had taken days and days to get to the council house because he suffered from gout and had been unable to come forth. But at last he was here, and the council could begin.

During that long wait, the Potawatomies of Five Medals and Winnemac had begged Governor Harrison to open the whiskey kegs. But he had held them off. And many of these thirsty red men were now blaming Little Turtle for keeping them thirsty this long.

The massive two-story blockhouses of the fort overshadowed the council house. From his table, Governor Harrison could see out the door to the old Miami town that General Harmar had attacked two decades ago before Little Turtle had trounced him.

Now the tribes asked for whiskey again.

But Harrison wanted these important and long-awaited talks to go quickly, and he believed it was more effective to hold out the whiskey as a reward than to get the Indians confused with it in the beginning, so he kept the kegs locked in the fort.

Now all the chiefs at last were on hand, and Harrison began his speech. He told them why they should be willing to sell the land between the Wabash and White rivers. This land had little game anymore, he said. Although the chiefs knew this was not true, they did not interrupt him, because whiskey was waiting. He told them how important the annuity money was to the support of their people, because the cost of goods would always be going up and because the war in Europe was depressing the values of their peltries. "It is better to raise pigs and cattle for their meat and skins than to hunt game," he said. "They are easy to keep, need little land, and they increase, while game, on the other hand, always decreases." He gave such reasoning for two hours.

When he felt he had convinced the Indians that the land was of little value to them, Harrison then showed a map of the piece the white people needed. It looked small on a map. But the map was a meaningless picture of a country to the eye and mind of the red man, who does not see land as lines on a flat parchment surface, so some explaining was necessary. "If," he said, "you stood at the place where Raccoon Creek pours into the Wabash, in the middle of the morning, ten o'clock exactly, and looked toward the sun, that line between your eyes and the sun would be the northern boundary. The southern boundary will be where the northern boundary is now," he said, "above Vincennes."

Now they understood. Most of them in their lives had been at the place where Raccoon Creek flowed into the Wabash-se-pe. They told the governor they would go to the Delaware camp beside the fort and hold council among themselves and give him their answer as soon as they agreed upon it. Several of the chiefs indicated that a drink of whiskey would help them think. Harrison suggested that it would be better to have the drink as a celebration for agreeing.

Among Tecumseh's friends who sat in the council and watched the opinion form were Seekabo the Creek and Billy Caldwell, a half-Irish Shawnee who had been schooled by Black Robes and could write. The council took a long time, as there were three tongues to be translated, and many misunderstandings to be labored through, many kinds of fear and eagerness.

The Potawatomies were most eager to have the whiskey kegs opened; they were slavering at the thought of it, so they recommended the sale at once. After all, they did not even have any claim to the land south of that ten o'clock line and thus nothing to lose, but whiskey to gain. The Delawares were thirsty, too, so they agreed, although more reluctantly, as they did use some of that land.

But Little Turtle was not ready. Something was bothering him, and he had to go and talk to Harrison in private. He limped away, taking his interpreters with him.

Little Turtle had to know whether the dismissal of his son-in-law Wild Potato, William Wells, from the Indian agency was going to diminish his own position in the favor of the Seventeen Fires. Harrison smiled and assured him that he would be esteemed as he had always been. So the old Miami smiled and said he would do all he could to advance the treaty, and he limped back to the Delaware camp.

Then there followed a long squabble over the annuity dollars. In the evening the Miami chiefs sent word to Harrison that their young men were thirsty, and that if they could have a little whiskey, they would leave the chiefs alone to decide about the dollars. With a sigh, Harrison agreed to ration out a little: only two gallons for each tribe, until the rest of the agreement was done.

With that as an appetizer, the rest of the haggling was concluded very quickly. Winnemac came to Harrison after dark, but his smile was enough to light the night. He said, "I thought our father Harrison will sleep better knowing we have agreed to accept your offer."

Of course Harrison was too exultant to sleep for a long time. For ten thousand dollars he had bought three million acres of the land called Indiana, meaning "Land of the Indians."


Tecumseh sat, his eyes smoldering, his stomach churning with disgust, as Seekabo related what had been done at Fort Wayne. Open Door sat beside him, huffing and gnashing his teeth.

"After the chiefs agreed to say yes to the treaty, there were many arguments over this and that. Harrison gave the chiefs a little whiskey now and then to make them mellow. When all was settled, he called everyone together and spoke a long time about the British. He said the British were the cause of all the red men's woes, that the Americans are the red men's brothers."

"Hear that," Open Door said through his teeth to Tecumseh. "Hear *that*!"

"The chiefs who put their marks on the treaty were Cracking Noise, Beaver, Winnemac, Five Medals, Little Turtle, and Pacane."

"Hear those names and remember them," Open Door said just above a whisper. "They are probably witches and should all be killed."

"After that," said Billy Caldwell, "Harrison rode away to Vincennes with his piece of paper. The kegs were broken open. For several days there was much drinking in the Indian camps. Several warriors were killed having fights with knives. It was a bad time. There was much anger, and the whiskey made it worse. Not many were pleased with what their chiefs had done. Many Miami warriors who have always been faithful to Little Turtle now say that he is too contemptible to speak of, that to say his name makes them vomit. There are Potawatomi warriors and Delaware warriors who told us even before we left Fort Wayne that they should have listened to your warnings, that what you said was true, but before now they could not see."

"Listen," Tecumseh said when the awful report was over. "Here is what we believe, and here is what we must say to anyone, even to the Americans:

"Those chiefs did not have a right to sell that land, which belongs to all red men. Therefore Harrison's piece of paper means nothing. White men will never occupy that country. When they come in with their instruments to put lines on it, or with tools to cut the trees or plow the ground, they will risk their lives.

"The chiefs who put their marks on that treaty have betrayed all red men. These chiefs are now in danger; they deserve to be killed for what they have done. Listen:

"Harrison surely feels full of satisfaction now, for the success of his crime. But I foresee this: It will cost him more than the few dollars. It has opened the eyes of hundreds who have been blind. Now they know that we have told them the truth from the beginning, and I say that they will be coming here to join us by hundreds by the time of the next planting. I foresee that from this time the government chiefs will be losing their hold upon their people. Warriors, and all men who can think, will see now that Harrison means to take the very land they stand on, and that if this is permitted, there will not be a spot of ground anywhere for them to step back on. You know that he bought the Illinois land five years ago. There is no place for them to step back.

"At last they can see this! At last they must come to us here and say, 'Brothers, how can we unite and keep this from happening anymore?' In the next summer they will be of one heart with us. I will go to the south then and embrace the Five Nations also. Brother! Today we are closer than we have ever been to standing all together, and how funny it is that it is Harrison himself with his greed and his cunning who sweeps us into each other's arms!

"We must guard our old boundaries, for in our eyes this new one does not exist. And we must entreat the British agents for more supplies, my brother, for this place soon will be swarming like an anthill with people whose eyes are open wide!"

William Henry Harrison had just held a great banquet at Vincennes, with territorial officials and prominent settlers in attendance, to celebrate his latest remarkable land acquisition, when a letter was brought from Prophet's Town by a messenger.

The letter was from Open Door. It was short and direct. It made no overtures of friendliness or politeness. It warned Harrison not to send surveyors into any land north of the old boundary. It read:

> Your people should not come any closer to me—I smell them too strongly already.

With the green of springtime began the swarm that Tecumseh had predicted. Warriors riding in small bands appeared on the distant prairies, coming from north, west, and east. They were Miamis and Delawares. They came, saying they had quit listening to their old chiefs.

A large group of men with their families, bringing their belongings on travois poles pulled by horses and dogs, came into view one day, and when they rode smiling into Prophet's Town they were recognized as the Kickapoos from the Vermillion and Sangamon river towns of Illinois. They were yearning for the favor of the Great Good Spirit. They were troubled by the closeness of the new white settlements. They had been eager all winter to pack up and come.

After them came a messenger from Shabbona, the Charcoal Burner, a subchief of the Sauk Chief Black Hawk, saying that he would come soon with many of his people.

"Black Hawk is a great one," Tecumseh said with delight, "and Charcoal Burner is no less. How pleased I will be to have them live here!"

Another large body of families soon came into sight on the prairie and proved to be all the Potawatomies of Withered Hand, with their giant one-handed chief riding at their head. He had not had nearly so many people on his first visit. But scores had turned their backs on Winnemac and Five Medals after the treaty and had come with Withered Hand.

What Tecumseh had predicted was happening.

By now even Black Hoof's eyes might have been opened to the white man's treachery, Tecumseh believed, so in the Raspberry Moon he rode to the Auglaize.

Wapakoneta now looked much like a white man's town, cabins and a mill surrounded by corn fields planted in rows instead of hills, pigs running everywhere, milk cows grazing within fenced fields.

Tecumseh asked for a council. Black Hoof and a few of his old men would not come, but most of the warriors had been shaken out of their lethargy by news of the Fort Wayne treaty, and they came. Black Hoof sent Stephen Ruddell to attend as an observer and as a calming influence. Also present in the edge of the crowd was Johnston, the new Indian agent from Fort Wayne.

A little council fire burned in the semicircle where Tecumseh spoke. He poured out his heart and mind to the Shawnee warriors. Never had he spoken so well. He was talking to his own people, in his own tongue, without the need to pause for a translator. Interpreters usually were unable to convey the stunning figurative language or the logic that marched forth from him, but on this audience nothing was lost. When he told them how they were being changed from a proud, free people into slaves of credit and livestock, they knew he was right, and they were pained and angry. It hurt to hear stated outright what had been eating their hearts for so long. When he invited them to leave this unnatural condition and become free men, warriors and hunters as Weshemoneto had meant them to be, the longing shone in their eyes, and for the moment, even in their drab and muddy farmers' garb, they looked like Shawnees again.

"All the American promises are two-tongued," he told them. "The white men drove you to this place and told you to live here. When Black Hoof went to Washington and asked for a title to this place, did the government give him a title? No! They put him off, because they want no red man to have a written title to anyplace! If he had a title, it would be harder to chase him off. They have never given a red man a title to any piece of land—even his own!—because they do not mean to let him stay anywhere! Is this not plain to you now? When white men make a treaty, it gives them title, and tells them where they can stay, but for the red man it only says where he can *not* stay! How long do you think you will be here before they want this place and write a treaty to put you out?

"Come, my brothers! Move your families to the Prophet's town on the Wabash-se-pe at Tippecanoe. There is a land from which the red man will never let himself be moved. There live a thousand warriors now with their families, and more come every day, from all nations, and there they live in harmony with each other, favored by the Master of Life, sworn to allow no white government to push them back any farther.

"The white people there are afraid. Because they see that we are strong and free, the white people stay at a distance. They are afraid we are preparing to attack Vincennes. The governor calls together his militia and sends to Washington for Blue-Coats. He blames the British. He blames everyone but the guilty one: himself! Now we tell this governor only the truth, which he will not believe: that we are not planning to make war, but that we prepare ourselves to stand together against him if he tries to take more of our country. Is our town a war camp? No. It is a home of free people. But if a people mean to stay free, they must be strong and ready. It is not true that we plan to attack Vincennes. We mean only to keep a place where we can stand, and burn our fires, to live as we were created to live. Brothers! Do not stoop at the plow like white farmers! Do not eat the flesh of filthy hogs! You are red men! You are greater than hog eaters!''

When Tecumseh had finished, the Shawnee men clearly were stirred. Their voices were an excited buzz in the council ground. And, seeing this, Stephen Ruddell came forward to speak, to try to warn them of the trouble they would be in if they went to the Wabash with Tecumseh. Ruddell had never thought he would be opposing his old friend, but it was apparent to him that Tecumseh was trying to lead them away from the path preferred by the one true God.

Ruddell stood before them now and drew from his pocket a piece of paper. They all knew what it was. Black Hoof had had him read it to them many times. Ruddell cried:

"My children! Give me your best attention! You see what I hold here. Warrior Tecumseh tells you that Governor Harrison is not your friend. But you know the kind words Harrison wrote in this letter to Black Hoof. You remember how he praised him, and you, for your peacefulness, for your industry, and for shutting your ears to the bad birds of the British! You remember his good words. Brother," he said, turning to Tecumseh, "you need to read this letter, too, to hear how kind Governor Harrison is, how he loves the red—"

As Tecumseh, eyes flashing, snatched the paper out of his hand, Reverend Ruddell remembered with pride that it was he who had taught Tecumseh how to read.

But Tecumseh did not read it. He did not even look at it. He flipped it contemptuously onto the fire. All watched in silence as it flared up. Ruddell stood blinking, astounded.

"Listen!" Tecumseh cried, pointing at the ashes. "If Governor Harrison were here, I would serve him in the same way!" And then, with a scornful glance at Stephen Ruddell, who had once been his good friend Big Fish, Tecumseh turned and walked away.

And when he was ready to return to the Tippecanoe, many of Black Hoof's young warriors were ready to go with him.


Open Door was called from his medicine lodge on a hot, dry day by an excited runner. The Wyandots were coming!

Although he was already swollen with pride and confidence about the thousand warriors in his town, the Prophet was thrilled by this message, and he hurried out to greet them.

Roundhead was at the head of their column, which was so long and wide that it made a dust cloud on the dry prairie road. Roundhead was one of Open Door's favorite disciples; he had already proven himself as a witch-hunter, and he was a respected war chief, too, one of Tecumseh's best aides. He held high in one hand a long spear decorated with a fan of hawk feathers, and in his other hand he held up the Great War Belt.

Open Door's chest heaved at the sight of the Great Belt. It had been the symbol of Indian unity in the old days of the defense of O-hi-o. Now these Wyandots had brought it with them, which meant that they were here as their nation, not as a dissident fragment of their nation! The Wyandots were venerated by the western tribes for their strength and wisdom, being called uncles by all the tribes, and it was to them that the Great Belt had been given for safekeeping after Wayne's conquest of O-hi-o. The arrival of the Wyandots nearly doubled the size of the warrior contingent, and the Great War Belt carried enough medicine to equal still another thousand. Round-head dismounted and handed the Great Belt to Open Door, and the people cheered.

They called a council. Here Roundhead explained why the Wyandots had come.

"For a long time," he said, "under the power of the Crane and old Leatherlips, the Wyandots stood apart from the Prophet's movement. Only I and a few others believed. But the rest of my people finally saw that the whites were ignoring their own boundaries from the Greenville Treaty and creeping ever deeper into our tribal lands. Then last year many were shaken out of their sleep by the Fort Wayne Treaty. Then early this year, Harrison made threats that all Indians had better behave, and this angered us. And, finally, this spring, the disciples of your prophet came with this challenge: 'How can the mighty Wyandots, keepers of the Great War Belt, sit idle on that great token while the white men keep stealing land from all the red men?' All this at once cleared our heads. Now these of us have denounced the Crane and Leatherlips, and mounted up to ride here."

Furthermore, he recounted, as his procession had moved past the Missis-sinewa with the Great Belt, they had paused for a conference among the Miamis there and had shamed Little Turtle for allying with the whites against his own race. At this, still more Miami warriors had spurned Little Turtle and left him and were now following the Wyandots to this place!

Open Door stood beaming and praised Roundhead for all this. He reminded the whole council of the prediction that Tecumseh had made last year after the Fort Wayne treaty: that the old traitorous chiefs would lose their hold upon the warriors, that hundreds would see the truth and come swarming to Prophet's Town. "And now!" Open Door cried. "See us! We swarm like an anthill, just as he said! We have been favored at last with good crops! We have new hunting guns and provisions from the British, who help us because they believe our cause is right! The Great Good Spirit favors our People!''

Star Watcher was worried because there was hardly any salt. With the fall hunts beginning, there was not enough salt in Prophet's Town to preserve meat for winter.

Of course, she thought, with so many people here, the meat might not last long enough to need to be preserved. Nevertheless, salt had become precious since the arrival of the white men in Kain-tuck-ee and O-hi-o; they had not only killed off the game and cut down the woods, they had also taken over the salt licks. They had barred the red men from those places where, since the Beginning, they had made the salt they needed. There were few salt licks in what remained of the Land of the Indians. So now if the Indians wanted salt, they had to buy it from the white traders, whose price was high. But some of the tribes whose leaders had signed land treaties now got part of their annuity payments in salt. Because the Shawnee leaders Tecumseh and Open Door had signed no treaties, salt was always scarce in their village.

One day while Tecumseh was still away in Ohio, a large *voyageur* canoe came up the river from Vincennes, its crew made up of French paddlers. They stopped on the shore and said they had some barrels of annuity salt on board that were for the Kickapoos, due them under the terms of the treaty their old chiefs had signed before the Kickapoos had moved here. The Kickapoos refused to accept it. To take it would imply that they supported the treaty, which they did not. The Frenchmen in the canoe, however, had been told to leave it here. They had more salt for other bands up the Wabash and did not want to paddle all this Kickapoo salt upstream just to take it back down to Vincennes. Open Door was called down to the riverbank to deal with the problem. The salt was very valuable. But what would Tecumseh say if it were accepted? Open Door had a head full of big matters and small details already, being the spiritual leader of a town of hundreds and hundreds of people, and he did not know what to decide. Finally he told the Frenchmen to leave it on the bank. If it was still there when they came back down the river, they could load it and take it back to Vincennes. "No one will touch it," he said. "My people do not steal." He would let Tecumseh and the Kickapoos decide the matter when his brother returned. After all, it was not a spiritual concern.

So the Frenchmen shrugged, left the salt barrels on the riverbank, and resumed their journey against the current.

The women, desperate for salt, looked at the barrels every day, but none took any, which made Star Watcher proud of them.

When Tecumseh returned from the Auglaize with his new Shawnee followers and found Roundhead there with his huge party of Wyandots and the Great Belt, there was much celebrating and talking to be done.

Then one day the big canoe returned down the river and slid to the bank. The crew had delivered salt annuities to Miamis and Delawares upstream and were back, and they were surprised to see the salt barrels still there, untouched. Indians gathered on the bank, and soon there was a hubbub.

Tecumseh emerged from the crowd, saw the salt and the white men, and looked angry. Open Door explained what had happened.

To Tecumseh, the salt annuity was one of the American government's great insults to the red man. It symbolized the hated dependency into which the Indians had been forced, as well as the theft of the salt that We-shemoneto had given the People.

He strode down the riverbank toward the head boatman, who was an arrogant-looking, deep-chested, black-bearded man wearing a scarlet *voyageur*'s cap, its floppy crown hanging jauntily down over his left ear.

Tecumseh stopped in front of the startled man, snatched off his red hat, and threw it in the river. As the man opened his mouth to bellow a protest, Tecumseh grabbed his thick hair above his ears with both fists.

"Are you an American dog?" he yelled into the man's grimacing face. Then with all the force of his sinewy arms, he shook the man by his hair until he was screaming for mercy through his clashing teeth. When Tecumseh released him, the man was cross-eyed and staggering to stay on his feet. Tecumseh turned to the others, who cringed and backed away. He pointed at the kegs and the canoe. "Take it back to Harrison. Tell him Tecumseh says we will have nothing from him."

Star Watcher did not want to criticize what Tecumseh had done about the salt. She understood why pride was more important than salt. But she did tell him how little salt there was and asked him what might be done.

"There are small salt springs in the lands of that treaty," he said. "No whites will keep us from going there to make what little salt the springs will yield, my sister, because as I have said, that treaty means nothing to me or our People."

"Then," she said, "I will get some women and go to those springs, and we will work hard to make salt. You must give me some warriors to protect them. And now, come home with me and eat. My husband and your son have not seen you for a long time."

He looked at her for a moment, at this sturdy, good-faced, graying woman who had seen half a hundred years of strife and hunger and had given the People everything she had but was stronger than ever and had more than ever to give, and his tension and anger about the treaty and the annuity salt just melted away. And he thought:

How much of our strength comes from such as she!


When the boatmen returned to Vincennes with the rejected salt and told of their rough treatment at Tecumseh's hands, the governor expressed his regrets absentmindedly. Then he went back into his office and sat down. He picked up a quill pen and gazed out a window, his face pale, grim.

The treatment of the Frenchmen ordinarily would have provoked him to take up his pen and issue still another ultimatum to those insolent Shawnees at the Prophet's town.

But just that day Harrison had talked with a group of twenty Iowa Indians, who told him that they had recently encountered on the Illinois River a large band of Sauks, Foxes, and Winnebagoes who were on their way to the Prophet's town on the Wabash. That in itself would have been no unusual matter; warriors were always, it seemed, traveling to and from that damned place. Winnemac's recent report of two thousand warriors there was, Harrison had thought, probably exaggerated, but still there were too many there. When Harrison had asked the Iowas what numbers they meant when they said a large band, their answer had made him step back with a gasp.

There were, they said, eleven hundred.


A cry came down from the prairie into the town: Many people were coming! They were in the dress of western tribes.

Tecumseh rode out to greet them, and as he rode toward the drifting dust of their coming, he was astonished at their numbers. Then their head rider separated from them and came galloping with a spear held high, and a smile of joy spread on Tecumseh's face. There was no mistaking those massive shoulders, that wide, happy face. It was Shabbona—the Charcoal Burner—Black Hawk's second chief and a man Tecumseh had grown to love like a brother already. And here he came, as he had promised, face aglow with happy triumph.

They halted their horses together and clasped each other's hands, grinning as if their cheeks would split. "So many!" Tecumseh exclaimed, waving toward them.

"Yes! When we heard of the treaty of that white governor, many said, 'Unless we unite and go with Tecumseh, they will overrun us!' We see their

Fort Madison there in our own land, and we grow harder inside. And so I bring more than you expected. Two hundred and forty strong young men. And their families, with some older men who can fight if they are needed. And these are only the ones who come to stay. Black Hawk's warriors will be ready when your great sign comes and you call them."

Two weeks later, when their lodges were standing on the prairie near the upper end of Prophet's Town and the families of all of Charcoal Burner's warriors were deep in the ceremonies and teachings of Open Door, Tecumseh sent the two hundred and forty warriors up to visit Matthew Elliott at Fort Malden in Canada. "He is our friend. He has many new British guns and much powder that he is eager to give you," Tecumseh said. "Get them and come back, and may the Great Good Spirit smile along your way."


Open Door was alone for a change, sitting in his medicine lodge, just himself and his effigy, which stood against a pole opposite him beyond the fire-ring, as if it were the Prophet's guest—or as if the Prophet were its guest. Perhaps the Prophet was the guest, he was thinking, idly pulling a string of his sacred beans through his fist; the hollow reed man lived here in the medicine lodge almost all the time, while Open Door was forever busy among his multitudes, seldom alone, seldom with a moment for meditation.

Of course it was good to be so important to so many people, to give them spiritual food where they had been empty and hopeless for so long, and when Open Door was preaching to their upturned, rapturous faces, all was well, and he was joyful that Weshemoneto had made him the messenger for this great upsurge of love and power in this critical time.

But the people had so many nonspiritual needs and problems, too, and were always entreating him for some little thing or other. They had their little disputes and jealousies, being from so many different tribes; they had their particular rituals and manners, and he and his wife and Tecumseh were constantly called upon to make judgments and decisions. The followers always had to be supplied with food, which sometimes had been an unfulfillable task, but for the present anyway was being met. Kokomthena at last had helped the women bring in bountiful crops, and the British had been generous, and the hunters, by traveling far south toward the White River country, had been able to bring in adequate meat. Open Door's wife had turned out to be the best sort of a village queen, able to administer and oversee the women's part in ceremonies and food preparation even on this enormous scale. She was, he had admitted to himself at last, a great blessing

to him after all. Before he had gone to Heaven and acquired this importance, she had been a scornful, nagging woman, a curse and a burden upon
his life. But she had grown with the rise of responsibility, as had he, and
now she was a helpmeet of immeasurable value, as well as a good mother
who kept their children from becoming tyrants as the children of important
chiefs sometimes become. In her own spirit she had become great and
powerful, and her hatred and distrust of the whites was as keen as his. She
felt a holy duty to keep the women and children safe. Yes, all was most
favorable, in general. Open Door felt that he himself was a miracle of the
Great Good Spirit's wisdom and power. From a drunkard and an object of
ridicule esteemed by no one, he had been transformed into the most revered red man of his time, perhaps of all times. He was a miracle, and he
carried the race of red men upon his shoulders.

But lately, in these rare moments of solitude, when there was time to
reflect, Open Door had found himself troubled and frightened now and
then. Subtle changes were taking place, and even in the midst of the great,
humming, throbbing spiritual power of this sprawling village—no, it would
be better to call it a city now—Open Door would look at the effigy standing
over there beyond the rising smoke and would feel that the big reed doll
was substantial while he, Tenskwatawa, its creator, was hollow.

It had been three years since he had had a vision or even a dream of any
significance. Nothing came to him that could be read as a prophecy. Though
he might pull his string of beans through his hand like this, or chant prayers,
or pass the sacred sticks through the smoke of the sacred tobacco, no ecstasy
visited him, no more messages came in the roaring silence of the voice of
the Master of Life; even when he looked out the smokehole at the moon
where he had once gone, it looked like nothing but the moon, a ball in the
sky as the white men believed it to be; Our Grandmother never talked to
him or showed her beautiful wrinkled face. She still had never revealed
anything special to him about medicine or cures, beyond what he had
learned from Change-of-Feathers; the truth was, he was just as mediocre a
medicine man as he had always been.

When Open Door would think of the moon, that was when he would
feel most hollow and afraid. His one great triumph of prophecy, the day
he had made the moon cover the sun, had been a fake. Though he reminded
his followers of that miracle over and over, and his fame rested largely upon
the world's memory of that day, the awful and shameful truth of it was that
he had got the information of it from Tecumseh, who had got it from some
white man. Sometimes Open Door convinced even himself that the Great
Good Spirit had told him of the eclipse; sometimes, carried away by the
flights of his own preaching, he even recalled that he had simply com-

manded the sun to go dark and it had done so. If a whole People believed something, did that not make it so? But then he would remember how it really had happened, and he would grow afraid, because he would wonder if he really was the hollow one.

And there had been other things that had made him feel hollow.

Some things he had had to do simply because of the way life was on this lower world: despite his preaching against hog meat and cattle meat, there had been many times when nothing but British salt beef or the arrival of a stray pig had kept the People alive. There had been times when he had let his own fire go out, and his life had not ended as he had predicted would happen to anyone who neglected the sacred hearth fire. . . .

Or had it? He pulled the beans through his fist—though they were sacred beans, they grew moldy in these humid summer months—he wondered if the visions had stopped because he had failed to keep the fire kindled now and then. Oh, it was frightening to think!

Sometimes when he was thus troubled he would feel that there were still witches working against him. Only this spring he had learned that Leatherlips, the ancient Wyandot chief in O-hi-o, had been poisoning people's minds, denouncing the Prophet, and using witchcraft against him. To defend himself against it, Open Door had sent Roundhead and five warriors to find Leatherlips, try him and kill him. They had found the old man in his camp on the Scioto-se-pe, had tried him in council as a witch and a traitor to his people, and had found him guilty. They had made the old white-hair kneel at the edge of his grave, then struck the blade of a tomahawk into his brain. Leatherlips had jerked about and fallen partway into the grave but had not died right away. For a long time his blood had oozed onto his white hair and his body had perspired, which had proved that he was indeed a witch.

Open Door also believed that Winnemac the Potawatomi was using witchcraft against him, as well as spying for Harrison. Winnemac was without doubt an American dog, who had helped Harrison make the terrible treaty last year, and the only reason Open Door had not openly accused him of witchcraft was that he was related to so many important Potawatomis that to kill him would likely drive some of them from the alliance.

The alliance! Yes, the alliance itself was one matter that whispered always over Open Door's shoulder. Of course the alliance was a good and necessary thing. He understood perfectly well how important the alliance was, and he supported it in every way. Tecumseh had explained over and over to him that the alliance of all tribes into a red nation was Weshemoneto's larger plan, and that the Prophet's religious movement was just one part of it.

But Tecumseh was the maker of the alliance, and that part of the miracle was growing more and more important.

Open Door was aware that his city was becoming as much an armed war camp as a holy place. He knew that hundreds of the warriors and dozens of the chiefs were here because of their dedication to Tecumseh rather than to his own spiritual power. Withered Hand was an example. He was here not because he wanted to stop drinking and become a good man, but because he wanted to be a great victor when the war against the Long Knives came. Withered Hand believed his own medicine was as great as the Prophet's; in fact, it probably was as great, if not greater, Open Door would have to admit, though with awful chagrin and only to himself. Withered Hand looked across to Open Door as an equal shaman, but he looked up to Tecumseh as a superior war chief. In fact, almost all the chiefs, when it came to such matters as dealing with the British, talking back to Harrison, or planning hunting trips and diplomatic journeys and the ultimate tactics of the whole red nation, looked to Tecumseh for guidance and judgment, not to Open Door. Why, even the Prophet himself had fallen into the habit of letting Tecumseh decide things. And not just big things. Like that matter of the Kickapoos' annuity salt. Open Door could well have made a decision about that at once; it was, after all, *his* town. But he had been preoccupied with spiritual things, with rituals, with dances, with morals, so he had let Tecumseh handle that of the salt. And then he had envied Tecumseh the pleasure of shaking that American dog of a Frenchman by the hair. How the people had liked that—how they had laughed and cheered Tecumseh for it—when it could have been Open Door himself receiving that applause.

He sighed. Then he scowled across at the silent effigy.

I am the holy man! I am the Open Door for the red people, Tenskwatawa suddenly and silently cried within himself. Weshemoneto, why do you not reveal yourself to me anymore? Why is it Tecumseh who has the dreams and the signs of the shaking earth and the moon-eyed wolves and the bundles of sticks? Why did you show me a glimpse of Heaven so long ago and come to give me all these things to do, and then retreat into silence and invisibility again? Why do you not visit me with guidance anymore? Why have you put all this upon my shoulders and then gone away?

A great, bitter, swollen ache gripped his heart; he was afraid, as he had always been as a child, afraid that somehow, sometime, he would be ridiculed again, that no one would respect him, that no one would believe him, that no one would need him, and that he would be scorned. His heart hurt, an exquisite pain.

Oh, how glorious it was to be needed! What a power it created in one's being! How terrible it would be to lose that! He shut his eye tight and moved his head slowly from side to side.

And then, just as he thought Weshemoneto was about to respond to the cry of his yearning heart, someone outside the lodge called for him. Some-body needed something again. With a groan he rose to his feet, hung the necklace of beans around the neck of the reed doll, and went to open the door flap.

A messenger, they said. Another Frenchman from Harrison. Probably another American dog of a spy, Open Door thought. It sometimes seemed to him that Harrison sent messengers only in order to look around Prophet's Town. The governor could not bear not knowing what was happening here.

Open Door composed his morose visage and went out. This Frenchman had a round face and wore the little eye things they called spectacles. Around his head was a blue bandanna covered with silver brooches.

This man's name was Toussaint Dubois. He had a message from Harri-son that he wished to read in council. Open Door sighed with impatience. Did the white governor think the people here had nothing better to do than sit in councils listening to his arrogant letters? But of course he acquiesced. It was always good to hear what the enemy was thinking, what he was worried about. Open Door wished Tecumseh were here. The letter would require an answer.

The message from Harrison was first an inquiry and then a warning. The governor wanted to know about the Shawnee prophet's "hostile prepara-tions and enmity." There had been incidents. Horses had been stolen from settlements near Vincennes. Cattle had been killed. The white people on the frontier were alarmed, they had heard that the Prophet was planning to attack Vincennes, and they were calling on the governor for protection. Open Door smirked as he listened to all this.

But the smirk faded away as Dubois read the warning part of the letter. Harrison said that militia soldiers both in Indiana and Kentucky were preparing for service. He said he had called for more Blue-Coat soldiers to come from the east to help defend Vincennes. These soldiers were not coming to attack Prophet's Town, Harrison said, but they would have to do so if it became clear that the Prophet was hostile.

Open Door saw the alarm in the faces of the people. This had frightened them. They had come here to be happy and peaceful. But if the white governor made up his mind that they were hostile, or even just pretended to believe they were, he would come up the river with his Blue-Coats and attack, even though he had no right to march into the Indian land. Vin-cennes was not very far away.

And so, though Harrison's message outraged him, Open Door gave a
polite answer. He repeated that he had built this town on the instructions
of the Master of Life, and that the many people who were here had come
for the good of their spirit. He said that he was angry about the treaty of
last year, that it had cheated the red men and was not valid, but that even
this treaty was not provoking him to hostilities. Open Door made a long
issue of the illegality of the treaty, because it was one of the things the
people could not hear too often. But, he insisted, he had no idea where
Harrison had got the notion that he was planning to attack Vincennes.

Finally, when he had finished, Dubois suggested that the Prophet might
visit the governor at Vincennes and discuss his grievances with him.

Open Door gave Dubois a haughty look and replied:

"Tell Harrison I will not go to visit him, because when I went to see him
last time, he treated me ill."


It had been a hot, still morning in the Blackberry Moon. But suddenly
people were running and crying in the village.

"The Blue-Coats! The Blue-Coats are here!"

The panic spread through the town. It had been one moon since the man
called Dubois had come with the warning about Blue-Coat soldiers, and the
people had been buzzing with anxiety and anger all that time. Some had
wanted to leave Prophet's Town to keep their women and children out of
the way of harm. Many of the warriors, on the other hand, had begged for
a chance to go down and destroy Vincennes and the arrogant governor.
Open Door's own wife, surprisingly, was one of the most angry. She had
wanted her husband to kill Dubois for coming here with a threat. She
thought her husband should let the war chiefs go down and burn Vincennes
before the rest of the Blue-Coats got there.

But Tecumseh had returned in time to put a stop to that kind of agitation.
He had reminded the warriors that there must be no conflict with the Long
Knives until the alliance was complete and all the red nations were one and
the great sign came.

But now a white man had been seen riding toward Prophet's Town on
the road from Vincennes, and the people, fearing that he was an advance
scout for the Blue-Coats, were running and screaming, and the warriors
were grabbing up their weapons to defend the town.

Then a lookout came in and said that the white man was alone. There
was no army anywhere behind him. Tecumseh and Open Door sent the
chiefs through the town to settle the clamor and calm the people, and a party
of warriors was sent out to escort the white man in.

It was not Dubois. But it was another messenger from Harrison, wanting to see the Prophet again. "Bring him before me," Open Door commanded, and he climbed onto a platform he used to preach to the multitudes. Upon it was a kind of thronelike chair, and Open Door seated himself upon it. He was furious about the disturbance this man's approach had created. He was sick of this constant parade of intruders from Vincennes, and his anger was like a black cloud on his face. Tecumseh stepped inside the door of the medicine lodge, to observe.

The white man was brought ungently into the clearing and made to stand in front of the Prophet, who scowled at him for a long time. He knew this man; his name was Barron, and he had come to the Prophet's town before, with Conner. Finally Open Door spoke:

"Barron, for what do you come here? All the white men who came here have been spies of Harrison. Now you have come. You, too, are a spy." He thrust out an arm gleaming with silver bracelets and pointed to the ground at Barron's feet and screamed suddenly:

"There is your grave! Look on it!"

The people around Barron yelled at him and edged closer to him, ready to kill this white man who had frightened them and made their children tremble. Barron stood trying to look unafraid, but his tanned face was paling.

Now Tecumseh came out from the medicine lodge, naked except for breechcloth and moccasins, his sinewy body gleaming like burnished copper. When he walked into the center of the clearing and placed himself in front of Barron, the hubbub died and the crowd stood quiet. With no warmth in his expression, Tecumseh said, "Your life is not in danger. Why are you here, Barron? Answer."

Barron swallowed, licked the inside of his dry mouth, and gave the expected reply: "Governor Harrison sent me, with a letter to read to you and the Prophet."

Tecumseh glared at him for a moment, then stepped back. "Read, then."

From his kit bag Barron drew out a sheaf of papers. "It's from William Henry Harrison, governor and commander-in-chief of the territory of Indiana, to the Shawnee chief and the Indians assembled at Tippecanoe. It says:

" 'Notwithstanding the improper language which you have used towards me, I will endeavor to open your eyes to your true interests. Notwithstanding what white men have told you, I am not your personal enemy. Although I must say that you are an enemy to the Seventeen Fires, and that you have used the greatest exertion to lead the Indians astray. As I am told, they are ready to raise the tomahawk against their father. Yet their father, notwithstanding his anger at their folly, is full of goodness, and is always ready to receive into his arms those of his children who are willing to repent, acknowledge their fault, and ask his forgiveness. . . .' "

Tecumseh raised his eyes toward the sky and took deep breaths to control the rising storm of fury in his breast. How sick he was of these white leaders, men of an inferior, clumsy, greedy race, always talking as if they were gods and the Indians were their poor, senseless, foolish sinners! And this Harrison was the worst of them for sounding like a god. Tecumseh yearned for a chance to grab this Harrison by the neck and stuff his mouth with the dirt from a bear wallow. But he kept still and glanced aside at Open Door, whose eye was glittering with a similar scorn. Barron read on:

" 'The little harm done may be easily repaired. The chain of friendship which united the whites with the Indians may be renewed . . . the destiny of those who are under your direction depends on the choice you make of the two roads that are before you. The one is large, open, and pleasant and leads to peace, security, and happiness; the other, on the contrary, is narrow and crooked and leads to misery and ruin. Don't deceive yourselves. Do not believe that all the nations of Indians united are able to resist the force of the Seventeen Fires. I know your warriors are brave, but ours are not less so. What can a few brave warriors do against the innumerable warriors of the Seventeen Fires? Our Blue-Coats are more numerous than you can count; our hunting-shirts are like the leaves of the forest or the grains of sand on the Wabash. Do not think that the Redcoats can protect you; they are not able to protect themselves. They do not think of going to war with us. If they did, you would in a few moons see our flag wave over all the forts of Canada.' "

Barron paused to let the red men think of these words and become properly intimidated. They well knew the destruction the Long Knife army could bring; the Shawnees in particular had suffered their storms of fire time and again, in the long and violent years before the Greenville Treaty.

But there were many of the older warriors here, too, who had chased Harmar out and slaughtered St. Clair's army, and they were not likely to be as cowed by Harrison's mighty talk as he expected them to be. The tribes had been at peace for more than fifteen years since Wayne's victory, but that time of peace had not been a time of security and happiness like that implied in Harrison's letter. No. They had been years of drunkenness and restriction and shame and frustration and dwindling boundaries.

The next words Barron read from the letter were so outrageous that Tecumseh wondered whether Harrison was simply blind or so practiced a liar that he did not know how to tell the truth anymore.

" 'What reason have you to complain of the Seventeen Fires? Have they taken anything from you? Have they ever violated the treaties made with the red men?' "

Tecumseh's jaw dropped when he heard those questions. What! his mind screamed within him. They have taken *everything* from us! They have violated *every* treaty!

The people saw the incredulity on Tecumseh's face, and they murmured ominously. Barron looked around but read on:

" 'You say they have purchased lands from those who had no right to sell them. Show that this is true, and the land will be instantly restored. Show us the rightful owners. I have full power to arrange this business; but if you would rather carry your complaints before your great father, the president, you shall be indulged. I will immediately take measures to send you, with those chiefs you may choose, to the city where your father lives. Everything necessary shall be prepared for your journey, and means taken for your safe return.' "

The Prophet's eye had opened wide at this last. It was a flattering thing to be asked to go see the president of the Seventeen Fires in the city of Washington. Any red man who was invited was obviously esteemed as a very important man by the white men, as Open Door well believed he should be. And any chief who went there was considered by his own people to be a very awesome and interesting man. Withered Hand was an example. He had gone once. Another example was Black Hoof, whose long-ago visits to the president named Jefferson, to beg for plows, had given him a stature that even his abject attachment to the white man's way had not diminished very much. Open Door began to see himself traveling on a big boat to the great capital city of the Americans and sitting in council with the president, talking as an equal with him: the most important chief of all the white men and the most important shaman of all the red men, sitting on thrones, wrapped in their finest robes, smoking together, facing each other in an unimaginably big house, discussing the fate of the red men. Open Door could envision himself spurning the offer of a drink of whiskey and the president's surprised but respectful expression. Surely this president must be a more reasonable man than the outrageous liar Harrison; surely his eyes could be cleared! This was what was whirling in Open Door's head, and he was thinking that he might accept.

But in Tecumseh's mind something else was uppermost. It was what Harrison had said about returning the lands if the red men could prove that the chiefs had had no right to sell them. Tecumseh wondered about that proof. He did not have much faith left in Harrison's word, but if the governor hinted at such a thing, it must mean he was sincere. Did this mean there was some chance that Harrison could be persuaded to back down from the Fort Wayne Treaty and *not* settle those lands between the Wabash and the White rivers? If there was any chance of this, Tecumseh should seize it. And, suppressing the fury he had felt earlier, he said politely to the messenger:

"Barron. I do not intend to make war, as this letter accuses. But I cannot be a friend of your country unless you give up making settlements closer to us than they were before that treaty. I cannot be friendly with your seventeen united states unless they will say to me, 'You are right, the country is the land of all the tribes in common.'

"Listen to me," he said, his voice becoming deeper, louder. "The Great Good Spirit gave this island to his red children. He put the whites on the other side of the big water. They were not contented with their own, but came to take ours from us. They have driven us from the sea to the lakes. We can go no farther.

"They have put it in their minds to say that this piece of land belongs to the Miamis, that one to the Delawares, and so on. But it is not so! The Master of Life meant it to be *all* the land for *all* the red men. Our father Harrison tells us that we should not be upon the Wabash, that this place belongs to other tribes. He does not understand! The Great Good Spirit ordered us to come here, and here we will stay!"

Suddenly he dropped his voice to a less impassioned tone. "The governor's letter makes me believe that he might listen if I went to him and explained. Maybe I will decide to do that. Now, Barron, you have come a long way. Eat with us, and stay with us, and we will talk about this, and tell you what we will do. You will leave the council now and let us decide."


A surprising thing came up in the council. Usually it was women who called for peace and kindness when the men were hot for war. But this time the women wanted killing. It was not war they wanted, but many of them wanted Barrow to be executed for the panic he had caused by riding in, for the terror he had caused the children. Open Door's wife, as the village women's chief, was most ardently for it. And even when Tecumseh reminded them that by Shawnee law a guest is safe, and the council voted not to let Barron be hurt, the women then held a secret council of their own and plotted to kill Barron while he slept in the House of the Stranger. It was Star Watcher who came to Tecumseh in the evening and revealed the plot. Tecumseh squeezed her hand. Then he invited Barron to stay in his own lodge, and he prepared a pallet beside his own fire for him.

Tecumseh had another motive for doing this. He needed to talk to Barron.

That night as the white man sat and smoked in the small, flickering light from the fire-ring, the soft drone of village life and the creaking of crickets and katydids filling the night outside the lodge, Tecumseh asked the question that had been in his mind. "What does your governor mean when he says, 'Show us the rightful owners of those lands'? In our eyes, Weshemoneto is the only rightful owner, but he put us here, *all* of us, not just Miamis and Delawares and Potawatomis, to use it. What does he mean, 'show him'? Tell me truly, as my friend and guest."

Barron's face twisted up with the implications of this question, and finally he shrugged and said, "A rightful owner, by law, is someone who has a deed. You know of 'deed'? Of 'title'?"

"A white man I know once showed me his deed. They are on paper, yes? They have words and lines on them."

"Yes, that's right, I reckon."

"And so a land treaty, such as the one made at Fort Wayne, is a deed or a title?"

"Well . . . yes, in a way. . . ."

"But then a deed or title is something a white man would have but a red man would not have?"

"Umm . . ." Barron shrugged and nodded.

"And only one who has a deed or title to a land can sell that land?"

"Well . . . I suppose that's what the governor means, yes."

"Then, Barron, since Little Turtle and Cracking Noise and Winnemac are red men—at least on their skins—and had no deeds and titles, then they could not sell those lands to him. I believe this is what you have been saying."

"Umm . . ." Barron waggled his fingers, as if trying to pull some kind of refuting argument out of the air.

"So, then," Tecumseh said with some satisfaction, "I told my people in the council today that I will go talk to Harrison at Vincennes. I have just proven to you that those chiefs could not sell him that land. I will go then and prove it to him just so, and he will have to burn up the paper treaty and leave us the lands, as his letter said he would do if I proved."

Barron looked at Tecumseh with genuine appreciation in his eyes. But he smiled on one side of his mouth and shook his head. "Chief," he said, "you can try that on Governor Harrison. But don't be surprised if he disagrees."

"But how can he disagree? I have proven."

"Nevertheless," said Barron, raising his eyebrows and bobbing his head, "he might disagree."

Now Tecumseh's eyes hardened. "Then you say now that these things he said in the letter are only words, and that he does not really mean to give the land back to us, no matter what we prove. That when your governor writes his word in a letter, it is like a treaty, not to be believed."

Barron fidgeted and tried to smile, but he could not look in Tecumseh's eyes.


The next day Tecumseh told Barron, with Open Door standing by:

"Tell Harrison that we will meet each other in one moon from now, at which time I will have decided whether to go and see President. You can say it will be the first time I have looked upon Harrison since he was beside Wayne at the place of the Fallen Timbers, where he stood beside Wayne's chair and listened to him talk, outside their tent near the flag. If his memory is as clear as mine, he will recall that day. Tell him that Tecumseh will come to help him understand the owning of land and to prove the truth. That I do not mean to attack his town, as the bad birds have told him. And that when I prove to him about the false treaty, I will expect him to burn it in the fire. Tell him I will bring some of my principal chiefs and, perhaps, too, a great many of the young men who like to be present on such occasions. Perhaps a hundred. Now, Barron, let me escort you to the road, with some warriors who will protect you until you are a good way along."

"Pr-protect me?" Barron looked at the half-dozen armed warriors Tecumseh had summoned. Suddenly he was afraid.

"They will protect you until you are safe from our women. Go, Barron. I will take your hand again at Vincennes."

And Open Door stood sullen as the messenger was escorted away. He glanced out of the side of his eye at his brother.

So, it was to be Tecumseh again going to do the big things.

It was not that Open Door would have wanted to be bothered with another trip to Vincennes, to face Harrison again. But to sit in the palace of the president!

And again he felt that bitter ache. He seemed to lose as Tecumseh gained.


Before it was time to go to Vincennes, runners came to Prophet's Town from Harrison. Their only message was that Tecumseh should come with just a very small party, in order that the town of Vincennes should not be alarmed.

Once again Tecumseh's blood grew hot. Did not Harrison understand that the number of people traveling to council with their chief was a sign of their support for him, an acknowledgment of his importance to them?

"Beware," said some of the chieftains. "This governor wants you to come with few warriors so that he may seize you or kill you!"

Tecumseh decided to take with him only a select retinue of two dozen, made up of his bodyguards and his tribal chiefs. "But," he added, "if any more choose to follow us, that is a matter of their own hearts. And if they wish to bring their wives and children, to have a look at the white governor's town, I will not stop them. The presence of women and children would ease the white people's fears that we are a war party."

# CHAPTER 30

## *Fort Knox, Above Vincennes*
## *August 11, 1810*

hey're here, Cap'n," exclaimed the orderly. "They just showed
up round the bend, and they're some spectacle!"

"Well, then, let's go have us a look at this spectacle," replied
Captain George Rogers Clark Floyd, commanding officer of the
little fort overlooking the Wabash. Captain Floyd was a nephew and name-
sake of the old Long Knife general and bore himself with an authoritative
posture and self-confidence befitting the name. He professed to be in awe
of no man, nor afraid of any, and he was hard to impress.

But after that day, he wrote home in a letter:

> The four hundred Shawnee Indians have come; they passed this
> garrison above Vincennes in eighty canoes. They were all painted in
> the most terrific manner. They were stopped at the garrison by me,
> for a short time. I examined their canoes, and found them well pre-
> pared for war in case of attack. They were headed by the brother of
> the Prophet—Tecumseh—who perhaps is one of the finest-looking
> men I ever saw—about six feet high, straight, with large, fine features,
> and altogether a daring, bold looking fellow. . . .

Tecumseh made his camp near a Shaker village between Fort Knox and
Vincennes. All the warriors and women had been exhorted to make their
best appearance, to be polite but reserved with any whites who came around
the camp, to accept no presents, especially liquor, and to get into no trouble.
The Shakers hosted and helped them.

Barron came out to greet Tecumseh the next morning. It was a Sunday,
and the tones of a church bell came through the sycamores and willows from
Vincennes. The bell made Tecumseh think of Ga-lo-weh and Rebekah.

Now here he was, again visiting white people in their own place. But such a difference in the circumstances now! There with Ga-lo-weh he had been a private friend; here it seemed that every whiteface west of the mountains was looking on, and not in a friendly way. The town was full of Blue-Coats walking in ranks, dragoons in helmets riding the streets, white women in voluminous dresses and sunbonnets that hid the shapes of their bodies and almost hid their faces as well, and all the officers and Supreme Court judges of the territory. They were all waiting for the council to proceed, and Harrison had called for it to begin the next day.

But Tecumseh had come as an equal and was not going to have his schedule dictated. He wanted time for the Shakers to look over the town and be sure that no tricks or traps had been arranged.

On Monday he decided to let Harrison fidget and sweat for another day and sent Barron to inquire whether Harrison would be attended by armed men in the council. Soon Barron came puffing and sweating back into Tecumseh's camp with Harrison's reply that the matter could be at Tecumseh's choice. So Tecumseh sent Barron puffing back to say that the men ought not to have muskets and rifles on the council ground, but only side arms. To Tecumseh that meant only knives and tomahawks, which his warriors always kept at their sides to defend themselves against treachery. At last all that was settled, and Tecumseh believed Harrison should be well aware by now that a Shawnee chief was not one to be hurried or shoved around. Just to make sure Harrison understood, though, he did not hurry over to the town on Tuesday morning, either; in fact, while the guests and dignitaries waited and milled around Harrison's veranda and under a canopied arbor, sweating in the muggy heat of an overcast day, Tecumseh stayed in his camp until afternoon, praying with his people, pondering on his speech, and making sure the companies of Blue-Coats were too confused and weary to plan any treachery. Even at that, it required courage and faith for the two dozen warriors and chiefs to walk down the road into the heavily armed town of their enemy, leaving their guns behind.

Still, they were fierce and formidable enough to make the onlookers draw back to the edges of the streets as they walked in, in a double file, with Tecumseh at their head. They were all lithe and erect; all wore only breechclouts and clean, fringed deerskin leggings and beaded moccasins; all were naked from the waist up, and their bodies and faces were decorated with red paint. All had shaved or plucked their heads bare except for the scalplock. Tecumseh himself was shirtless and wore over his shoulder a long scarlet cape that billowed as he walked. His black hair was still long, hanging to his shoulders, bound around by a colorful headkerchief decorated with one eagle feather. Barron showed them the way onto the grounds of Harrison's estate, through a grove of trees on level lawn.

As they approached the mansion, Tecumseh saw that an arbor by the veranda had been covered with a canopy to give shade for a large number of chairs. Behind the elegantly dressed white people stood a platoon of honor guards, with pistols in their belts. He saw the figure he took to be Harrison and saw also among those people the contemptible Winnemac, dressed in a light cloak, and he saw the young captain named for Clark who had stopped him at the fort.

Suddenly a prickling of caution was set up in him by the sight of this arrangement; he felt as if he were walking into a trap. His warriors were like animals being funneled into a dead end during a hunting drive.

So he stopped in the grove of trees, a hundred paces from the veranda, and his warriors stopped behind him. Barron, unaware, went on a few more steps until the chuckles of the spectators stopped him. He hurried back, red-faced, perspiring. "What now?" he asked.

"Tell Harrison we will talk here."

Barron made an exasperated motion toward the elaborate arrangement on the veranda. Tecumseh said:

"My people talk in the council circle, where no man is higher than the other. I will not go before that . . . *thing* they sit on, and look up to Harrison. He may come out here."

"But, Chief," Barron now pleaded, "you're to sit up there with him!"

"And my people on the ground looking up? No. Let him come out here. I have traveled many days to see him. He can come off the side of his house."

Barron looked as if he might explode. "It would be so much trouble to move all those chairs! Be reasonable, Chief!"

"Barron, only the white men's chairs need be moved. We do not require chairs."

So Barron bustled back and forth two or three more times, and finally the arrangements were modified and all the white men's chairs had been brought out into the grove. Harrison stayed on the distant veranda until all this milling around was done and then at last came down and walked toward the grove with his dignitaries behind him. Tecumseh's eyes flashed.

"Barron! Those men, and all those soldiers, they have pistols in their belts! I do not like this! I said sidearms, and he agreed!"

"Sidearms," Barron answered with a sigh, "means pistols, to them."

"You did not tell me that!"

Barron had had enough. "Is the chief afraid?"

Tecumseh's eyes froze on him. "I saved you from angry women once, Barron. You owe me a life, and I might take it, for what you have said. Now stand away. I want to have a clear look at this governor."

Harrison came with his retinue. He wore an elegant frock coat with a high collar despite the close heat, and a shiny ceremonial sword hung at his left side from a silken sash. He was hatless, and his short hair was combed forward on the brow and temples. There was a strange, barely perceptible lopsidedness about his eyes, which, as Open Door had said, made his penetrating stare hard to look at. Though his physique was not imposing, there was something in his carriage that suggested uncommon strength, and in the hard, arrogant look of his visage, no timidity was revealed. He shook hands with Tecumseh, looking him over quickly, then went to the biggest armchair a few feet away and stood in front of it. Then he pointed at the chair next to it and said something to Barron. Barron told Tecumseh:

"Your father says for you to sit by his side."

Tecumseh, head high, looked at Harrison for a moment, then suddenly raised a brawny arm to point at the sky, and his strong voice filled the grove.

"Father? The Great Good Spirit is my father! The earth is my mother, and on her bosom I will recline!" He seated himself on the ground, and all his warriors immediately sat down in a semicircle behind him.

Harrison puckered his lips. Then he began:

"Well, if our guest is finally satisfied with everything, we can begin at last. As you know, it is my desire to discuss with Tecumseh the relations between my people and his . . ." A damp wind suddenly turned the leaves of the trees underside up, and drops of rain sprinkled cool on heated faces. A rushing, hissing sound was coming from the river, and the finely dressed white people murmured and stirred. Harrison hurried on, glancing up: "And to give him a chance to carry his grievances to the president, if he so desires it. . . ."

And then suddenly a deluge of summer rain came hushing across the estate, and the white people were scurrying toward the canopied arbor and the porch, and Harrison, his caesarean hairdo plastered wetly to his head, his shoulders so hunched that his coat collar covered his ears, shouted the obvious fact that the council was adjourned and slogged off after his guests toward the canopy.

Tecumseh and his warriors walked unescorted back through the town to their camp in the downpour, convinced that Weshemoneto had not meant for them to talk with the governor on this day. When they came into their camp, the women cried out in alarm; the dissolved paint running down their bodies had made them appear blood-soaked.

A week had gone by with weather and other influences postponing the council, but at last the chief and the governor were face to face again in the grove, under a clear sky, and it looked as if the council could proceed. Now there was a table in front of Harrison's chair. Beside him sat old John Gibson, secretary of the Indiana Territory, a gray-haired man whose face was so long that he was known to the Indians as Horsehead. Gibson, who had been married for decades to a Mingo woman, understood the Shawnee tongue. He, like most of the white men, wore a pair of pistols. On the other side of Harrison was Captain Floyd from Fort Knox. On the grass between Harrison's table and Tecumseh sat Winnemac the Potawatomi. Harrison had chosen him as one of the interpreters, which had annoyed Tecumseh tremendously. But Tecumseh was not going to let an unpleasant detail like that prevent him any longer from saying what he had come to say. He stood looking at Harrison and began:

"Brother . . ." He noticed the flicker of anger that crossed the governor's face because he had not called him "Father." "I wish you to give me close attention, because I think you do not clearly understand. I want to speak to you about promises that the Americans have made.

"You recall the time when the Jesus Indians of the Delawares lived near the Americans, and had confidence in their promises of friendship, and thought they were secure, yet the Americans murdered all the men, women, and children, even as they prayed to Jesus?"

This immediate mention of the Gnadenhutten massacre made Harrison set his face hard. But Tecumseh had not come here to please Harrison with sweet words. He went on: "The same promises were given to the Shawnee one time. It was at Fort Finney, where some of my people were forced to make a treaty. Flags were given to my people, and they were told they were now the children of the Americans. We were told, If any white people mean to harm you, hold up these flags and you will then be safe from all danger. We did this in good faith. But what happened? Our beloved chief Moluntha stood with the American flag in front of him and that very peace treaty in his hand, but his head was chopped by an American officer, and that American officer was never punished.

"Brother, after such bitter events, can you blame me for placing little confidence in the promises of Americans? That happened before the Treaty of Greenville. When they buried the tomahawk at Greenville, the Americans said they were our new fathers, not the British anymore, and would treat us as well. Since that treaty, here is how the Americans have 'treated us well': They have killed many Shawnees, many Winnebagoes, many Miamis, many Delawares, and have taken land from them. When they killed them, no American ever was punished. Not *one*.

"It is you, the Americans, by such bad deeds, who push the red men to do mischief. You do not want unity among the tribes, and you destroy it.

You try to make differences between them. We, their leaders, wish them to unite and consider their land the common property of all, but you try to keep them from this. You separate the tribes and deal with them that way, one by one, and advise them not to come into this union. Your states have set an example of forming a union among all the Fires; why should you censure the Indians for following that example?

"But, brother, I mean to bring all the tribes together, in spite of you, and until I have finished, I will not go to visit your president. Maybe I will when I have finished—maybe. The reason I tell you this: you want, by making your distinctions of Indian tribes and allotting to each a particular tract of land, to set them against each other, and thus to weaken us.

"You never see an Indian come, do you, and endeavor to make the white people divide up?

"You are always driving the red people this way! At last you will drive them into the Great Lake, where they can neither stand nor walk."

Tecumseh watched Harrison keenly for some kind of response, but the governor's face was stolid. He sat with his hands enfolded in each other on the table, his eyes never moving from Tecumseh's.

"Brother," Tecumseh went on, "you ought to know what you are doing to the Indians. Is it by the direction of the president you make these distinctions? It is a very bad thing, and we do not like it. Since my residence at Tippecanoe, we have tried to level all distinctions, to destroy village chiefs, by whom all such mischief is done. It is they who sell our lands to the Americans. Brother, these lands that were sold and the goods that were given for them were done by only a few. The Treaty of Fort Wayne was made through the threats of Winnemac; but in the future we are going to punish those chiefs who propose to sell the land."

He paused and gave Winnemac a murderous stare, forcing him to look down, and suddenly cried out, "There sits the black dog who makes lies and tells them, to cause white men and red men to hate each other!" Then he turned his eyes from Winnemac, leaving him to writhe in fury, and continued: "The only way to stop this evil is for all the red men to unite in claiming an equal right in the land. That is how it was at first, and should be still, for the land never was divided, but was for the use of everyone. Any tribe could go to an empty land and make a home there. And if they left, another tribe could come there and make a home. No groups among us have a right to sell, even to one another—and surely not to outsiders who want all, and will not do with less." And now his voice rankled with sarcasm.

"Sell a country!" he cried. "Why not sell the air, the clouds, and the Great Sea, as well as the earth? Did not the Great Good Spirit make them all for the use of his children?"

Suddenly his whole visage changed. He turned an expectant expression upon Harrison and said: "Brother, I was glad to hear what you told us. You said that if we could prove that the land was sold by people who had no right to sell it, you would restore it. I will prove that those who did sell did not own it. Did they have a deed? A title? No! You say those prove someone owns land. Those chiefs only *spoke* a claim, and so you pretended to believe their claim, only because you wanted the land. But the many tribes with me will not agree with those claims. They have never had title to sell, and we agree this proves you could not buy it from them. If the land is not given back to us, you will see, when we return to our homes from here, how it will be settled. It will be like this:

"We shall have a great council, at which all the tribes will be present. We shall show to those who sold that they had no right to the claim they set up, and we shall see what will be done to those chiefs who did sell the land to you. I am not alone in this determination; it is the determination of all the warriors and red people who listen to me. Brother, I now wish *you* to listen to me. If you do not wipe out that treaty, it will seem that *you* wish me to kill all the chiefs who sold the land! I tell you so because I am authorized by all the tribes to do so! I am the head of them all! All my warriors will meet together with me in two or three moons from now. Then I will call for those chiefs who sold you this land, and we shall know what to do with them." Now he pointed straight at Harrison's face and said slowly in a sharp voice: "If you do not restore the land, you will have had a hand in killing them!"

As this was translated, and the white people began to understand that he was seriously threatening to kill other Indian chiefs, they began turning to each other and buzzing to each other their horror and consternation; it was as if they only now realized how much in earnest he was about all this. Harrison, still not showing a trace of emotion, simply raised a hand and held it up and looked around at them until this fearful clamor subsided. Then he turned again to Tecumseh, who was beginning to wonder if his logic was making the least impression upon the governor. Tecumseh was not used to using the unadorned language this subject and this audience required. When he spoke to his own race he spoke to their emotions, with figurative language that made them see glorious or terrible pictures in their heads and feel joy or remorse in their hearts, and he yearned to pour out the familiar oratory of the heart. Suddenly, then, he cried out:

"I am a Shawnee! I am a warrior! My forefathers were warriors. From them I took only my birth into this world. From my tribe I take nothing. I am the maker of my own destiny! And O that I might make the destiny of my red people, of our nation, as great as I conceive to in my mind, when

I think of Weshemoneto, who rules this universe! I would not then have to come to Governor Harrison and *ask* him to tear up this treaty and wipe away the marks upon the land. No! I would say to him, 'Sir, you may return to your own country!' The being within me hears the voice of the ages, which tells me that once, always, and until lately, there were no white men on all this island, that it then belonged to the red men, children of the same parents, placed on it by the Great Good Spirit who made them, to keep it, to traverse it, to enjoy its yield, and to people it with the same race. Once they were a happy race! Now they are made miserable by the white people, who are never contented but are always coming in! You do this always, after promising not to anymore, yet you ask us to have confidence in your promises. How can we have confidence in the white people? When Jesus Christ came upon the earth, you killed him, the son of your own God, you nailed him up! You thought he was dead, but you were mistaken. And only after you thought you killed him did you worship him, and start killing those who would not worship him. . . . What kind of a people is this for us to trust?" Most of the white people were now gasping and muttering, some even putting their hands over their ears, but Harrison still sat expressionless.

"Now, brother," Tecumseh went on, "everything I have said to you is the truth, as Weshemoneto has inspired me to speak only truth to you. I have declared myself freely to you about my intentions. And I want to know your intentions. I want to know what you are going to do about the taking of our land. I want to hear you say that you understand now, and will wipe out that pretended treaty, so that the tribes can be at peace with each other, as you pretend you want them to be. Tell me, brother. I want to know now."

Then he billowed his cape behind him with a sweep of his arm and in a graceful motion sank to sit cross-legged on the ground. The eyes of his chieftains were on him, glittering, full of pride. But Harrison still sat with his hands before him on the table and no expression. He was angry. He had brought these Indians here to chide them for creating tension on the frontier, but instead he had been challenged and accused and put on the defensive by Tecumseh.

After a moment he stood up and walked out from behind the table, his left wrist resting on the silver guard of his ceremonial sword. He stood in front of Tecumseh, looking down on him. At his feet Winnemac reclined like a faithful dog, his cloak draped over him.

Harrison made no preamble but headed straight to the point, as Tecumseh had.

"I do not see how you can say the Indians are one nation. It is absurd to say the red men are all one people. If your Great Spirit meant this to be, why did he give you different tongues?

"Listen to me, my children. I am going to tell you why the Miamis had a right to sell us their land. When the white people came to America, the Miamis lived in all the country of the Wabash. At that time the Shawnees lived in Florida and Georgia. Since then they moved from place to place, and only lately did they come near the Wabash. The Shawnees never lived in this part of the continent. . . ."

Tecumseh stiffened. Either Harrison was lying to advance his coming argument, or he simply did not know. The ancestors of the Shawnees had lived in this O-hi-o watershed, building mounds and living in walled towns long ago, long before being forced to the south. In fact, there was hardly any place east of the Great River where the Shawnees had *not* lived. The old fathers and the Singers knew every detail of the Shawnees' history, back to the Beginning, and Tecumseh had learned it from them. Harrison was ignorant or lying deliberately, and he continued:

"The Miamis have been here since before the memory of man. And now recently they thought they should sell some of their land to increase their annuity, which has long been of the greatest benefit to them, and which has always been paid promptly to them by the United States, in honor of its promises. So I say, this has *always* been the land of the Miamis, to do with as they saw fit. And the Shawnees have no justification to come from a distant country and try to control the Miamis in the use or disposal of their lands. . . ."

Tecumseh had been too angry for too many years, and now, hearing Harrison throw this accusation at the Shawnees, he lost his self-control. As if his blood had boiled over into his head, he sprang to his feet, his face a snarling grimace, pointed his finger into Harrison's face, and cried in Shawnee:

"Oh, this man is a *liar!* What he says is false, and an insult! It is not the *Shawnee* who tries to keep this land, it is the *race of red men!* Hear him even now try to divide us up! He is a *liar!*"

At Tecumseh's first move and outcry, the council had been thrown into fearful confusion. Two men who understood his Shawnee words, Secretary Gibson and Winnemac, drew pistols, Gibson from his belt, Winnemac from under his cloak where he had been holding it concealed. Gibson shouted for a lieutenant to bring up the honor guard, and twelve soldiers came running with their pistols. Captain Floyd drew a dirk, and Harrison himself unsheathed his sword. At this move, Tecumseh snatched out his tomahawk and raised it, and his warriors leaped to their feet, whipping out their tomahawks and knives. They formed a defensive circle and stood fiery-eyed, ready to defend him, to do whatever he called upon them to do.

"He called you a liar," Gibson told the governor.

Harrison scarcely heard him over the slamming of his heart. The alarm had spread beyond the council ground, and the bellowing of sergeants and the tramp of running feet could be heard all around. Some of the men in the crowd were drawing pistols and daggers and unsheathing sword canes, others rushed to the governor's kitchen house woodpile to grab billets of wood, and some caught swooning ladies in their arms.

For a minute that seemed to be forever, the Shawnee chief and the governor stood poised with their steel to strike each other, their eyes locked, glittering with hatred. An awesome, tense, wordless stillness rang in their ears. Tecumseh's arm, thick with tense muscle and sinew, banded with silver, held his polished, silver-mounted tomahawk high. Harrison had never in his life felt death so close, seen so vividly this much swift power coiled to strike directly at him. His heart was hammering, and his face was pale, but he would be damned if he would show fear before this insolent savage.

Tecumseh heard Seekabo whisper behind him to the others: "*Weshecat-too-web,* be strong. I will take Winnemac myself." And the Potawatomi, who had not dared to stir from the grass where he lay, cocked his pistol, a ghastly sound in the stillness.

Harrison had to do something. This deadly situation had erupted in his own backyard. Though there was no doubt that Tecumseh and his few warriors could be killed by the hundreds of soldiers in the town, it was plain that much white men's blood would be spilled, probably including his own, before they were dead. And then there were many more warriors outside of town, who might rush in if they heard gunfire.

So, slowly, in order not to set off Tecumseh's arm, which was cocked like a hair-triggered flintlock, Harrison took a deep breath, made his facial muscles relax, and lowered his sword. He slipped it into its scabbard with a metallic sliding sound, stepped back a pace, stood straight, and raised a calming hand toward Gibson, toward the guards and officers. Then, still not taking his eyes off Tecumseh's, he swallowed and said:

"I see no reason for this to go on. Gentlemen, this council is adjourned. Let's all retire peaceably."

Finally, when he saw Tecumseh lower that terrible tomahawk and heard him breathe some words to his warriors, only then did Harrison dare to move, to step out of that dreadful radius. Once out of it, he walked quickly toward his house, face and ears aflame, and the guests and dignitaries followed him, leaving the warriors in their little circle, the vacant chairs by the table, the soldiers standing awkwardly nearby. Some sheets of paper were lifted from the tabletop by a breeze and floated to the ground. Winnemac had slithered back a few feet and now rose with his pistol still in his hand and trotted after the governor. Barron stood in the distance looking at Tecumseh but seemed afraid to come close and had no idea what to say or do. This momentous council in which he had been forced to play such a thankless part had turned into a debacle and nearly into a disaster.

At last Tecumseh slipped his tomahawk into his waistband and turned to his warriors.

"You have been brave and good," he said. "Come. Let us try to go back to our camp. But be ready. All the Blue-Coats are in motion, waiting for orders, and I do not trust Harrison."

Tecumseh asked to be left alone when the warriors were back in the camp. He sat in the midst of his buzzing encampment and smoked and went back over the incident in his mind, and his heart cooled. He began to be angry now at himself, for losing control. Here was this opportunity to make Harrison and his officials aware of his viewpoint, and even though Harrison seemed impervious to reason, Tecumseh knew he should have remained patient and reasoned with him as long as possible. How often had he himself counseled his followers not to let themselves be provoked, told them even to suffer lies and insults, if necessary, to keep peace until the alliance was completed? And now he who was supposed to be their wise leader had let himself be provoked; perhaps Harrison even now was deciding that councils were useless, that it was time to attack Prophet's Town.

Tecumseh sat with his fists clenched, and now he was as angry with himself as he had been at Harrison. Even poor Open Door, volatile and foolish as he was, could not have handled this any worse!

Barron came up to the Indian camp in the morning and was brusque. He said Harrison wished to know what Tecumseh's plans were. Was he going to stay encamped so near to the town with all his warriors, or would he be going back up the river to Prophet's Town? The governor would like to know, so that his people and soldiers could return to their normal pursuits.

Tecumseh's reply surprised Barron.

"Go and tell the governor that Tecumseh makes an apology for that anger which happened yesterday. We rose only to defend ourselves because the soldiers came running with their guns. Say that I have no wish to give personal offense to him, that this should not be one angry man against another, but a talk of principles between two peoples, a talk that should be finished, so each understands the other. Tell him that I would welcome him in my camp if he wants to visit me here, and that no harm would come to him here." It had occurred to Tecumseh that Harrison might be more reasonable if he did not have to put up an appearance of strength and firmness before crowds of his own white people. "Or," Tecumseh added, "if he wants me to go there and explain my thoughts to him, I will go."

Harrison rode into the Indian camp that afternoon on a great, light gray war-horse. He made a brave appearance; except for Barron, he was alone, though companies of soldiers and dragoons had quietly taken places all around the Indian camp.

In the midst of the camp, surrounded by the aromas of cedarwood and hickory smoke and baking Shawnee cake and roasting meat, Tecumseh offered Harrison his hand and showed him a place where they could sit to smoke and talk as man to man. It was a large section of a log two feet thick and ten feet long, the top side hewn flat to serve as a bench. They smoked from the pipe in the head of the same tomahawk that Tecumseh yesterday had held ready to strike Harrison, which the governor noted with a strange feeling in his breast.

Now Tecumseh felt pleasant and expansive. This was the proper way for two strong men to start building an understanding, if such a thing could possibly be done. Tecumseh was satisfied that Harrison was in his own way quite a strong man. And the governor had shown a certain nobility in accepting the invitation to come to the camp so soon after what had happened between them. As a man, if not as a representative of a policy, Harrison had risen a bit in Tecumseh's esteem.

Harrison had surprised himself by agreeing to come. He had spent much of yesterday evening in a turmoil of novel feelings. He had been drained to exhaustion by the fright and the anger, then tormented to distraction by the yammerings of praise and sympathy and advice that his wife and staff and officers and guests had poured upon him for the rest of the day. He had cursed himself for not taking the war secretary's suggestion and seizing Tecumseh—but then had cursed himself again for even considering such a treacherous recourse. Upon retiring finally and lying in the dark, he had found one image in his mind: that of this splendid savage standing ready to strike him—with this very pipe-tomahawk—and he had felt that never in his entire life had there been a moment of such exquisite dread. For that instant he had felt what the prey must feel in the claws of the predator.

Harrison had lain in the dark remembering. He could hardly recall having drawn his sword, more a decoration than a weapon. He had apparently done that by reflex alone. He could vaguely remember that he had held it for some time pointed at that deep, wide, muscle-girt chest, that heaving, red-painted, dark-oak barrel of a chest, and only by the old conditioning of the fencing school had he managed to hold it steady. He had lain thinking of Tecumseh's eyes, which he had plumbed for so long, those curiously light, hazel-colored eyes, and recalled that he had looked through them as if into a long tunnel that stretched back through all time, back through the leafy silences of the wilderness, back to the dire beginnings of man, back even to the panthers and the wolves. . . . That incredible notion he had had, and then he had marveled that from this aboriginal soul with its deadly passions and dark superstitions there had come such a formidable line of reasoning, such an accurate recital of pertinent grievances. Harrison well knew that some of the grievances were valid. He was all too aware of the overbearing, lawless behavior of the white roughnecks who did the actual breaking through on the frontier, and he knew that those complaints of Tecumseh's were, alas, justified. Late into the night, then, strangely, despite the requirements of his own principles and the doctrines of the administration toward the Indians, Harrison had come to admit to himself that this Tecumseh might be as brave and incorruptible a man as he had ever met, as perfect a man, in the natural sense of the word "man." Here in this chief—not in that magnetic but murky-headed and vainglorious shaman Tenskwatawa, but here—was the Moses of the poor bewildered savages, and Harrison had regretted that such a wall of bitterness and hatred had built up between Tecumseh and himself. Some things had come to him only in retrospect, as he had lain in the dark alone with his mind: how he had loved the sound of this man's voice and the rich music of the Shawnee tongue played in that voice—the lisping consonants, the orotund vowels. And how fearless the chief and his warriors had been, armed only with steel, two dozen of them in a town full of hundreds of armed troops; every one of the chieftains had looked as if ready to die to protect their chief—and most of them were not even Shawnees!

Oh, it was strange to Harrison, this succession of feelings he had had last night; he had tried to think of some parallel in his readings of ancient history. He had thought of Vercingetorix the Gaul, that nearly unconquerable foe of the Roman conquerors. Thus, full of admiration for his adversary, troubled by the early failure of the council, afraid that it might drive the Shawnees into an even tighter partnership with the British, Harrison had been delighted this morning when Barron had come to the mansion bearing Tecumseh's apology and invitation, and he had spent little time wondering about the safety or advisability of it but quickly made arrangements to come. And now he was glad he was here. This Tecumseh in a friendly mood was as warm and charming a fellow as Harrison had ever met.

As they sat side by side on the log talking, Tecumseh told Harrison in general terms about the anxieties created by the land-buying policies of the American government. "It is like a mighty river coming toward us," he said, and as he spoke he edged closer to Harrison until their shoulders were touching. Harrison moved away slightly. "It threatens my people like a high flood of that river," Tecumseh went on, once again scooting close enough to Harrison that their shoulders were touching, and once again Harrison moved a little away. "It is like a flood of that river pouring over the banks and making the people move to higher ground," Tecumseh went on, once again pressing against Harrison, who again moved. "I," said Tecumseh, scooting toward him again, "am trying to build a dam, to stop this flood before it rises to cover and drown all my people, all the red people."

By now Harrison was sitting on the very end of the log, and Tecumseh was pressing more firmly against him.

"See here, Chief," Harrison interrupted him, "if you keep crowding me over, I'll fall off."

Now a great smile spread over Tecumseh's face, and in his eyes there was both delight and mockery.

"Aha!" he laughed. "Now *you* feel how it is to be pushed off!"


They agreed to resume the council the next day, in the grove as before. This time all the soldiers had rifles, but now Tecumseh had no anxieties about treachery. Tecumseh and Harrison shook hands. "Remember the end of the log," Tecumseh whispered to him, and the two actually smiled at each other. While everybody was getting settled in for the resumption of the council, Tecumseh became aware of being watched very intently from somewhere off to his left and glanced over to find the dark eyes of one of the townsmen upon him. This young man held a writing board with some paper on it and was alternately staring at Tecumseh and then making marks on his paper. There had been a few men writing at the first part of the council, writing down the things that were being said, but now this young man seemed to be writing even though nothing was being said. This made no sense. But then the young man let his writing board tip forward for a moment, and Tecumseh saw that he was not writing but drawing a picture. So *that* was what he had felt: the young man was taking some of Tecumseh's

image off of him. Tecumseh did not like it; the youth had not even asked
if he could take some.

But that was the way of the white men, it seemed, and as the council was
about to reopen, he decided not to make any protest about it.

When Tecumseh stood and resumed his argument about the Fort Wayne
Treaty, he took a new tack, which surprised Harrison.

"Two years from now, brother, you will no longer be in the office of
governor. You will be replaced, I expect, by someone who is a good man
and a true friend of the Indians."

Where the devil, Harrison wondered, did he learn anything about our
politics? Tecumseh continued: "I have learned that many white people do
not agree with you that it was necessary to make that treaty and get more
land. Just to see for myself, I sent some of my own men toward the O-hi-o-
se-pe not long ago to look at the land between here and there, the land you
got from us in earlier treaties, and, ha! They reported to me that those lands
are still quite empty, not filled with settlements at all, and so your white
people do *not* need the lands you bought with the Fort Wayne Treaty, as
you are not using what you already have. So, brother, not all your white
people agree that you should have made that treaty, which was an illegal
treaty, as I have proven already. Further, the chiefs of all tribes agree with
me that it was an illegal treaty, and that you had better not step onto those
lands." He sat down and Harrison rose, saying:

"Brother, you tell me that chiefs of all the tribes support you in this
question. This I do not believe. Can you prove it to me?"

Tecumseh held up his hand, smiling. He said something. One by one,
the warriors behind Tecumseh stood up, and each in turn—Wyandot,
Potawatomi, Winnebago, Ottawa, Kickapoo—made a speech, stating that
he was the representative of his own people, and that they had united as
red men with Tecumseh as their chief and Tenskwatawa the great Prophet
as their shaman, and that they agreed with Tecumseh and would follow him
in all these matters. Secretary Gibson compressed his lips and shook his
head, but Harrison only nodded as the last warrior finished his testimonial
and sat down. Harrison said to Tecumseh:

"Then tell me this, as I need to know what your true intentions are: If
I send surveyors into the land obtained by the last treaty, will the Indians
interfere with them?"

Tecumseh nodded and replied solemnly: "I am determined that the *old*
boundary will continue."

Harrison, his lips firmly closed, took a long breath through his nose. "I
also want to know whether the Kickapoos will accept their annuities due
them by the treaty they made."

Rising to stand before Harrison, Tecumseh replied, "Brother, when you speak to me of annuities, I look at the land and pity the women and children. I am empowered by my Kickapoos to say for them that they do not want the annuities, and will not receive them, for you would then say they accept the treaty. Brother, we want to save that land. We do not want you to take it. It is small enough for our purpose. If you do take it, you must blame yourself as the cause of the trouble between us and the chiefs who sold it to you. I want the present boundary line to last. Should you cross it, I assure you the consequences will be bad. I would not want to make war upon the United States. I would not want to go with the British. The red people no longer wish to be set down between the white nations as you set dogs to fight in a pit. We would rather be at peace with the Seventeen Fires. However, if your president does not agree with what I have asked here, this would oblige me to take the side against him."

Harrison stood for a long time looking into those amazing hazel eyes, at that resolute copper face. Then he sighed. "I will tell the president what you propose. But I am sure I can say there is not the slightest probability that he will accede to your demands."

Tecumseh nodded once. "So, then. As your great chief is to decide this matter, I pray that his God will put enough wisdom in his head that he will direct you to give up that land. It is true, he is so far away that he will not be injured by the war. He may sit in his town and drink his wine, but it will be you and I who will have to fight it out!"

# CHAPTER 31

## *Vincennes, Indiana Territory*
## *November 12, 1810*

Governor William Henry Harrison stood before the legislature of the Indiana Territory and spoke of what needed to be done toward gaining statehood. Though the territory now had nearly twenty-five thousand free white residents, three gunpowder manufactories, thirty gristmills, and about an equal number of distilleries, it still had one big obstacle to its statehood: Indians still owned the central portion of the land. Harrison, his voice echoing in the high-ceilinged room, felt akin to a Caesar in the Senate of Rome as he informed the assemblymen:

"Although much has been done toward extinguishment of Indian titles in the territory, much still remains to be done. We have not yet a sufficient space to form a tolerable state. The eastern settlements are separated from the western by a considerable extent of Indian lands; and the most fertile tracts that are within our territorial bounds are still their property. Almost entirely divested of the game from which they have drawn their subsistence, it has become of little use to them; and it is the intention of the government to substitute, for the pernicious and scanty supplies which the chase affords, the more certain support which is derived from agriculture and the rearing of domestic animals."

Most of the legislators listened with proper respect. Harrison had acquired the stature of a hero in the eyes of many, for having held off at the point of his dress sword the murderous intentions of more than a score of painted savages. The hero continued:

"Are then those extinguishments of native title, which are at once so beneficial to the Indian, the territory, and the United States, to be suspended on account of the intrigues of a few individuals?" And now he concluded his argument by paraphrasing the reasoning of President Madison: "Is one of the fairest portions of the globe to remain in a state of nature, the haunt of a few wretched savages, when it seems destined, by the Creator, to give support to a large population, and to the seat of civilization, of science, and of true religion?"

At the same time, three hundred miles to the northeast, Tecumseh was standing on the parade ground of Fort Malden in Canada, presenting to British officers a beautiful old wampum belt that had been given to the Shawnee as a token of neutrality at the end of the Seven Years' War. Standing with the British officers were Matthew Elliott and James Girty of the Canadian Indian Department. Girty was writing with a pencil. Behind Tecumseh sat more than 150 proud, tense warriors of the Potawatomi, Winnebago, Sauk, Fox, and Ottawa nations. The parade ground overlooked the sparkling, broad waters and wooded islands of the mouth of the Detroit River. Nearby towered the masts of huge ships being built or outfitted at the shipyard of Amherstburg. Off Lake Erie came a steady, fresh, chilly wind that was stripping the last red-and-yellow leaves off the great maples and poplars and sending them tumbling along the ground to drift up in moats and at the foot of bastions and barrack walls. Around the edge of the parade ground were several hundred ragged, spiritless Indians, looking on. On the islands and around the fort and the town there loitered a thousand or more Indians of other tribes, living in any conceivable kind of shelter—scrawny, hollow-eyed Indians with pinched faces, their threadbare blankets and tattered hide robes clutched around them against the winter-hinting wind. There were always at least a thousand, it seemed to Elliott, and each autumn their numbers swelled, as they gave up hopes of supporting themselves through the cold moons in their distant towns and came crowding in for food, for blankets. Fort Malden was like a great kitchen, a great commissary, funneling thousands of rations a day into the mouths of desperate red people from around the Great Lakes. Last winter Fort Malden had supported five thousand destitute Indians. It was a dismal, perennial task, and Elliott was growing old and tired under the responsibility of it. His heart was huge with its capacity for pity for the Indians. He had lived most of his life among them; his own handsome, solid wife was a Shawnee woman of great character. He, like the Girty brothers, had deserted the colonial cause long ago and allied himself with the British because of the American policy toward Indians.

These Great Lakes tribes, who had for generations been assimilated into the white man's fur trade economy, now were helpless and impoverished because of changing circumstances they could scarcely understand. First, the Napoleonic Wars had depressed the European market for furs; then an embargo placed by President Jefferson's government in 1808 had all but finished off the fur trade in this region. Having been made almost fully dependent upon it, the Indians had been thrown rudely back upon their own resources—only to find their resources gone. The winters in Amherstburg were terrible times. In the squalid huts and lean-tos, Indians died daily from cold, hunger, and disease. When Erie froze solid and the supply ships could not come from Niagara, Elliott and the other Indian agents often had to clean out their own pantries to provide even a mouthful for some of the wretches who came trekking through snow to the door. From two to four thousand new blankets were issued every winter, and even then some Indians froze to death because they could not obtain any.

So here now was another winter coming on with its imminent drain on the resources of the Crown, and to add to the trouble, here was Tecumseh of the independent Shawnee band, up from Prophet's Town on the Wabash, not only seeking more food and munitions for his distant following, but seething with such hostility toward the United States that it would be a wonder if he did not precipitate a war.

Elliott was on a delicate line. He personally was inclined to give the Shawnee everything he wanted. But Elliott knew full well that Governor-General Craig, and England herself, did not want to be drawn into a costly, hopeless border war with the United States by supporting the Indians too openly. It was already known that American governors, William Henry Harrison foremost among them, were obsessed with the notion that British Canada was fomenting a war against the States. A coterie of young congressmen, known as "war hawks," constantly chanted for the invasion of Canada. Governor Harrison apparently did his best to keep the American Secretary of War in a high state of excitement about "the British threat." In fact, as Matthew Elliott well knew, Canada was ill prepared for a war with the States, and the Crown itself wanted no conflict on this continent.

But on the other hand, the British officials knew that if the States *did* precipitate a war, only the ready assistance of the tribes could protect Canada's undermanned posts against a swift invasion by the American hordes, and therefore it was necessary to feed and arm the Indians. But of course this in turn convinced the Americans even more firmly that Britain was inciting the Indians.

And now Tecumseh was here, presenting this wampum belt and asking for British backing, because he was convinced that the council in Vincennes had not altered Harrison's thinking in the slightest degree. Tecumseh was trying, in the brief time left before the closing in of winter, to obtain promises of British provision for the confederation of tribes and of weapons and ammunition with which to hunt for meat for the many people of Prophet's Town. Indians were hard on guns and had no facilities to repair them, and thus were always short of workable firearms.

The British officers were fascinated with Tecumseh. Here was one red man they did not treat with condescension. Not only was he an appealing specimen at first glance, he was good-humored, amiable, and charming. He could speak clear English and was one of those rare natives who had some concept of European culture and military strategy. So the officers were attentive as he presented the wampum belt, and they heeded his words respectfully.

"Father, we have a belt to show you, which was given to our chiefs when you laid the French on the ground. Here it is, Father. On one end is your hand, see; on the other, that of the red people. Both hands are in white wampum, but the Indian end of the belt is darker than the other, and in the middle you see the hearts of both. Father, our old chiefs have been sitting on this belt ever since, keeping it concealed and running our country. But now the warriors have become the chiefs, and have turned their faces toward you, never again to look toward the Americans. We the warriors now manage the affairs of our nations. We sit at the border, where the contest will begin. Father, I discovered this belt and took it out from under our chiefs. Take it and look." He handed the belt to the senior British officer, who passed it on for all to see and touch. Tecumseh went on:

"Your father has nourished us, and raised us up from childhood. We are now men and think ourselves able to defend our country. In our cause you have always given us active help and advice." Tecumseh restrained himself from mentioning the British officers' cowardice at Fallen Timbers; this was a diplomatic mission. "Now we are determined to defend our country ourselves; we expect that you will forward to us what may be necessary to supply our wants.

"Father, I intend to go toward the midday to summon the southern nations into our confederation, and expect before I see you again next autumn, that that will be done. I ask you to be charitable to our women and children. The young men can more easily provide for themselves than they.

"Now, Father," Tecumseh said, the wind from the lake buffeting the feather in his turban and whipping his cloak around his legs, "I thank you for what you can do for us. I want you to believe that when the Long Knives try to come to Canada, my warriors will never quit their father or let go his hand."

My God, Elliott was thinking as he watched James Girty write all this down. What a stir this is going to cause up the line! These Shawnee brothers are like sparks around a powder keg!

# CHAPTER 32

## *Indiana Territory*
## *April 1811*

T he Shawnee hunters in the wet woods heard the sound coming down from the north like a windstorm and saw the treetops and underbrush beginning to shake, but wind never had sounded like this, and they cringed down, looking up in terror toward the high branches.

The wind sound was full of chattering and squeaking, so loud it was painful in the ears, and dark things could be seen moving, coming from that northerly direction, as if it were a wind full of crazy birds. It came on, and the dark things were so numerous, they darkened the woods with shadow, and the treetops shuddered with the agitation of their coming, and the shrieking grew louder. Suddenly one of the hunters, his eyes wide with disbelief, cried out:

*"A-ne-quoi!"*

Squirrels!

This was not a wind rushing through the treetops or a cloud of birds, but a horde of squirrels, hundreds of hundreds of squirrels, leaping from branch to branch or bounding along the ground, chattering and squeaking as they fled southward.

It was a sign. Squirrels lived in small families, not herds or packs. But under some direction of the Great Good Spirit—or perhaps of the Evil Spirit—they were fleeing in hordes, countless squirrels moving with one common will.

Now as the cloud of squirrels passed over, leaf debris and insects, even some squirrels, rained from the treetops onto the warriors below. For a long time they knelt with their heads bent down and prayed as the squeaking multitudes went over and around them and rushed shrilly onward toward the O-hi-o-se-pe.

When their din had finally faded to silence, there were injured squirrels squirming on the ground and dead squirrels by dozens, all for the gathering. These men had been hunting in the woods for many days, for food for Prophet's Town, and had found hardly any game. It was as if all the animals had left the place, frightened off by the strangeness of the season, and the hunters were hungry. But they would not touch the squirrels that had fallen at their feet. These animals, acting in this frightening and desperate way, must be full of bad medicine and should not be eaten.

Tecumseh nodded when hunters came in and told him of the great flights of the *a-ne-quoi*. Bands of hunters in several places had seen such flights. It was happening all over. Most of the squirrels drowned when they reached the flooding O-hi-o-se-pe and tried to cross it. Tecumseh remembered one other time when this strangeness had swept through the squirrels. It was when he was a very young boy. It had been followed by the troubles with the Long Knives, by the war between the British and the Americans, and by other strange signs. Tecumseh sat and thought of the signs. Since the melting of the deep snows this spring, all of the world had been troubled and full of omens.

Rains had come early, days and days of rains heavier than anyone could remember. With the melting snows these rains had fed the rivers until they were yellow-gray and swift and high, and then they had flowed over their banks and covered the bottomlands. These floods, to Tecumseh, were like the flood of white men coming ever into the country, as he had told Harrison. Tribes along the Wabash-se-pe and its tributaries had moved their camps up onto the hillsides and prairies, and the rains had kept falling, and the days were dark, the nights cloudy and moonless. Waters of the turbid Wabash came up within inches of the House of the Stranger at Prophet's Town, and only by praying and using his greatest medicine was Open Door able to stop the river from rising far up into his town.

This stopping of the flood had been Open Door's first demonstration of power for many years—since the Black Sun, in fact—but he had little time to bask in the glory of what he had achieved before a greater evil fell upon the People, one against which he seemed to have almost no power at all. It was a terrible new disease. Children and adults grew feverish and could not swallow and declined into states of weakness. Something like dirty gray skin grew in their throats, bloody mucus poured from their noses, their necks swelled, their hearts skipped and fluttered, and dozens quickly died. Many who did not die could not move their hands or feet for weeks, and some were left with uncontrollably trembling hands, others with an overpowering weakness. Open Door with all his chants and remedies had been able to cure only a few, and some of those had suddenly died after they thought they were well, so his powers as a healer came under doubt.

And then when at last, in the Green Moon, the rains stopped and the sky cleared, another awesome sign redoubled the People's fear:

There was something in the sky!

It was bright like a star but was not a point of light like a star; it was long, a streak. It was in the northern sky, in a place where usually no major star was. It reappeared on every clear night, just perceptibly higher, as if it were moving slowly across the sky toward the south. All the red people watched it and wondered at it and turned to their shamans for answers, but in virtually every Indian town it was thought to be connected with the Shawnee prophet, who, five years ago, had made the sun go dark. Nobody could look at the bright streak in the distant sky without thinking of the Shawnee prophet or of the great sign predicted by his brother, the sign that would come when the alliance was ready and the red men would turn back the white men. To Tecumseh, who had been born under a shooting star, it had to be a part of his pattern of signs. One thing he knew: he must go to the southern tribes. This year the oneness would have to be completed.

Thus for those who were committed to the Shawnee brothers, the bright thing in the sky was a speck of hope; for the others it was a troubling omen of a conflict they did not want.

Being one or the other, it unsettled everyone, and people began doing strange things. All over the frontier, things began happening that should not have happened. The world was unsettled this year, and the People began behaving from the darker side of their souls.


The Spaniard Bazadone, innkeeper and trader in Vincennes, a man known to have a penchant for trouble, was in one of his dark moods when the knock came at his door. It was very late at night, and he had been poring over a huge portfolio of papers that always put him in a bad mood.

A quarter of a century ago, when General George Rogers Clark had been to Vincennes on his campaign against Little Turtle's confederation, Clark had seized a boatload of Bazadone's goods to help provision his troops. Bazadone had begun a lawsuit against Clark, a lawsuit that had by now moved into its second generation of lawyers and still was not settled, even though it had helped substantially to bring the old general to financial ruin and transform him into a bitter old drunkard. The litigation had taken its toll on Bazadone's soul, too. Now at the knock on the door, he slapped down the papers and went to open it, holding up a lantern.

There in the night stood an Indian, a Muskogee far, far from home, to whom Bazadone had sold some rum earlier in the day. The Indian was now quite drunk, grinning crookedly, swaying, and asking for more rum. Bazadone knew the Indian had nothing left with which to pay for any more rum, so he told him to go away.

The Muskogee, weaving this way and that like a tree about to fall over, began to plead, and Bazadone slammed the door in his face with a curse. When the Indian began knocking on the door again, Bazadone grabbed down his flintlock, which was loaded with bird shot. He flung open the door and discharged the gun point-blank into the Indian's abdomen, spewing blood and innards all over the yard.


Withered Hand the Potawatomi was always very sensitive to signs, and when he was unsettled by those this spring, he interpreted them to mean that he must do something to stop the white men who were spreading out from Kaskaskia into his hunting grounds in the Illinois country. Withered Hand considered himself the most important ally of Tecumseh and Open Door, but he also considered himself their equal in judgment and ability, and he did not feel bound to sit and wait for their signal to resist the white men. In the spring, as soon as there was sufficient grass to feed horses, he rode out with a band of warriors and began raiding isolated farms. Settlers began deserting their homesteads and fleeing to Kentucky and Kaskaskia.


A party of government surveyors up from Cincinnati, in black hats and greatcoats, with their supplies and instruments on packhorses, moved up the Wabash, past the mouth of Raccoon Creek to a meadow surrounded by budding hardwoods. They unloaded their equipment, made a camp, built a fire, and marked the point that was to be the western end of the Ten o'Clock Treaty line according to Governor Harrison's treaty of 1809. They were cold and hungry. They would rest now and begin their survey the next morning.

"Look," one whispered, raising his head from a canvas-wrapped transit he had just set down. "Injuns right yonder."

The warriors, clad in plain, unadorned deerhide clothing, had appeared in the moist young grass of the meadow without a sound. They were three or four times the number of men in the surveyors' party, and they carried muskets. They had on no war paint.

The party's guide, a hunter from Vincennes, calmed the surveyors with a chuckle.

"Them's Weas," he said. "Friendly little fellers from just upriver, never gave anybody a bit o' trouble. Heh, heh! Fact, they help keep th' gov'nor informed o' what mischief them Shawnee scoundrels is up to. Ready to share with some guests, gents?" And he got up and started walking toward the Weas with his right hand up and a big smile on his stubbly face.

But the warriors walked past him as if they had not seen him and went into the camp. Without a word they snatched up all the surveyors' gear, their guns and provisions. They dumped some of the instruments in the fire, threw some in the creek, and broke others by hurling them against rocks. They emptied the priming powder out of the white men's guns. When one big surveyor tried to shove away an Indian who was reaching for his powder horn, three warriors converged on him and threw him to earth. Then the first yanked off his powder horn, breaking the strap.

When the whites at last were thoroughly disarmed and stripped of their possessions, one of the Weas pointed southward and said in English:

"Go that way. Go past Vincennes very fast and not stop. If your faces are in our country again, you will not be happy we see you."

Governor Harrison could see the pattern beginning to emerge. Horses were being stolen from farms in the border areas. Potawatomis known to be under the influence of the Shawnee prophet were raising hell in Illinois. Pacane, a Miami chief who had signed the Treaty of Fort Wayne, had now turned around and balked at receiving annuities, protesting that he had been forced to put his mark on the treaty. A party sent out to survey the Fort Wayne Treaty lands had been threatened and chased out, just as Tecumseh had warned him they would be.

There was no doubt of it in Harrison's mind: the Indians under the leadership of the Shawnee brothers at Prophet's Town were commencing their hostilities. The governor had been fretting all winter about the vulnerability of Vincennes, which could be reached in a few days by canoe from Prophet's Town.

Indians who were jealous of the Shawnee brothers' influence brought rumors of all kinds to the governor: that Tecumseh was plotting to murder him; that British agents were at Prophet's Town, inciting the brothers; that Tecumseh was going to attack Vincennes in force with British help. Though Harrison understood the motives behind such tales, he could not shake from his head the notion that they might have some basis in fact. He began writing long letters with great frequency to the War Department. He requisitioned five hundred new rifles and asked for better swords, saying that the presently available swords might do to split the bare skull of a savage but not the helmeted head of a British dragoon. In his many personal letters to the secretary of war, he began suggesting that he should perhaps be authorized to march a strong force up the Wabash toward Prophet's Town and at least intimidate the Shawnee leaders. He requested that the federal authorities build a strong new fort close to Prophet's Town, to guard the way to Vincennes.

In the meantime, he was having Indian troubles right in his own town. The innkeeper Bazadone had killed an unarmed Muskogee, and Harrison, in an effort to soothe Indian resentment, had compensated the Muskogee's friends with goods and had ordered Bazadone put on trial. Two trigger-happy white ruffians had shot and wounded two Weas without provocation near Vincennes, then had been killed in turn by avenging Potawatomis. The entire population was getting very nervous about any and all Indians. Settlers were leaving. Immigration into the territory, which was needed to bring the population up to the minimum for statehood, was slowing because of the scare.

Harrison began to examine from all angles the idea of marching an army against Prophet's Town. Of course, as he well knew, he had no legal right to send a force into country still claimed by the Indians. But by broad interpretation of the laws governing territorial defense, he might get away with launching a *retaliatory* campaign—if he could find something in the Shawnee's doings big enough to retaliate for.

Once he had got the notion of invading, it began to grow. He wanted the Fort Wayne Treaty lands surveyed and sold and settled as quickly and easily as possible, and the only recourse he could see to clear the way for it was by scattering that nest of red militants and fanatics who dwelt at Prophet's Town and defied him at every turn.

Then, in the midst of these ponderings and plottings, he would remember that most vivid of all memories: Tecumseh poised to strike. And he would feel the delicious chill of dread. What an enemy that man would be! Sometimes in his reveries of the invasion he would see himself and Tecumseh, in the great, sprawling chaos of battle, seeing each other and going straight at each other with naked steel. It was a rather frightening image, and he would have an uncanny feeling that that was just how it would happen: that Tecumseh would find him and attack him face to face.

But then Harrison would remember the maxim:

The greater the enemy, the greater the victory!


Bazadone went to trial for the murder of the drunken Indian. Harrison desperately hoped the Spaniard would be sentenced to severe punishment.

He was aware, as Tecumseh had pointed out to him in their private talk, that not once in the years since the occupation of the Northwest had any white man been convicted for killing any Indian, though there had been hundreds of murders. If the Indians could see just one white man punished for such a crime, Harrison knew, one of the worst grievances of the red men would be eased, and incalculable benefit surely would come of it. So he brought the prosecutor to his mansion and talked to him for a long time about the importance of this matter. He said:

"Bazadone is known to be guilty. There is no doubt! You will do the greatest service to this capital and the territory by making the clearest and strongest possible case against the murderer. Do so, sir, I implore you!"

The prosecutor did so.

The jury, made up of white men haunted by the specter of warlike Indians, acquitted the Spaniard without deliberation.

The news traveled swiftly through all Indian towns in the territory.

Once again it had been proven that by the white man's law, the life of a red man was of no importance at all.

By midsummer Tecumseh and his bodyguards and dancers were ready to go to the south. Their canoes were loaded with weapons, ceremonial objects, red sticks, and paints. Now Tecumseh went into Open Door's medicine lodge and sat with him for the most urgent and serious talk he had ever had with him in all the years of their mission. This time he did not sit on the opposite side of the fire-ring but close beside him, and he put his hand on the back of Open Door's neck, to speak to him as an older to a younger brother, as he had in their childhood.

"My brother," he said, "I am going to explain some very important things, and I am going to ask for your sacred word of promise. Everything we have done in the past six years, and everything we are about to do to complete our great work, depends upon your attention to what I tell you now. There has never been a time like this, and if you do not give me your word, everything could be undone; as quick as a thunderclap, the fate of our People could be made dark."

Open Door, his eye glittering with fervent sincerity, said, "Brother, you know you can depend on me. Our mission is my life!"

Tecumseh hoped he could. Lately Open Door had shown some of his old foolish, spiteful traits. He had seemed to grow more distant from Tecumseh, more resentful of his suggestions. It was not hard to understand why, of course. For a while he had been adored and respected as the spiritual father of all the People. But then the realities of the white invasion had required more than mere religious leadership, and Tecumseh had had to assume more and more of the command. It was clear that Open Door felt his own stature shrinking, that he resented being second to his brother as he had always been in childhood. But for these next few critical moons, there must be complete concurrence between them.

Now Tecumseh said:

"As I leave for the south, I am going to stop at Vincennes and try again to soothe Harrison's fears. He is like a child needing some more attention, but he is like a dangerous child with many knives in his hands. I understand him. He wants to come up here and scatter us because we will not do as he demands. He looks for any excuse to do so. I will try to put him at ease so that he will sit where he is until I come back from the south. When I return from there, the alliance will be complete. It is not quite, yet, and nothing must happen to shake it down until I have put the top on it. Harrison must be given no excuse to march against us. None! Do you in your heart understand how important this is?"

"I understand. How could I not understand?"

"I have told you that this will be the year of the sign. It will be the year when the nation of red men is complete. The long star is in the sky, going toward the south. The squirrels listened to the Master of Life and fled toward the south. Everything on the earth is getting ready. All creatures except the white men know that this year the red men are to be as one, and that the president of the Seventeen Fires will then have to be honorable with us, and stop what he is doing. This is the most important thing that ever shall have happened among the red men. Not Cornstalk, not Chief Brant, not Pontiac, not Little Turtle in their old greatness ever did a thing that was this important to the red people. You, my brother, have become the greatest of all the leaders. As such, you will have to show more patience and wisdom than any red man ever has, and you probably will be tested very hard by Harrison while I am gone. Listen:

"It will surely take me six or seven moons to do what I have to do in the south. In all that time, everything we have here will rest in your hands. I feel that Harrison will seek an excuse to destroy it while I am gone, and if I did not have to go to the south now, as the signs direct me, I would not leave this place. When I go to see him, I will try to put him at ease. But if in my absence he demands anything, you might have to give it. If he gives you an insult, you might have to eat it. And listen, now: If he does come up the Wabash-se-pe with his army, you must not fight him, but take the people up the Tippecanoe and hide them until it is safe. Remember, my beloved brother: If he burned this town, we could build another. But never again could a confederation like this be rebuilt. Do I have your sacred promise? Will you live up to my trust, knowing that the fate of all the red people depends upon doing so?"

"My brother, you have my sacred word."

"*Neweh-canateh-pah Weshemoneto,* the Great Good Spirit favors our People."

"*Weshecat-welo k'weshe-laweh-pah,* let us be strong by doing right."


Then Tecumseh went to see Star Watcher and Cat Pouncing. He told his son, "While I am away, I want you to go and seek your Spirit Helper. It is a hard and frightening thing to do, but your life will be blessed when you have done it. Promise me that you will try to do that, and I will be happy as I travel."

Looking frightened, the boy replied, "I promise, Father, I shall try."

Then Tecumseh said to Star Watcher, "Good sister, great love I have for you. I will be away from here for as much as half a year, and this is a terrible time to be gone because of the Long Knife Harrison. He wants any excuse to blow us away like leaves." She nodded her graying head, then looked straight into his eyes, her face resolute. He told her of the promise he had extracted from Open Door, then said, "Our brother has become a great man, and we know he has done much good for the People. But he is like a stone house built in a marsh, so great a weight upon a character of muck. I wish my trust could rest with him as easy as it does with you. How I wish his heart could be as strong and true as yours!

"Our brother listens to your wisdom as to no one else's. Help him stand by his promise to me. If Harrison provokes him and he swells up, remind him of what I said to do. Use your voice in the women's council to hold this town safe.

"Now here is something I have done. I asked Charcoal Burner to stay here and be a second chief in my absence. I beseeched him to use all the same cautions, and to be a steadying hand. Charcoal Burner wanted to go to the south with me but said he will stay here and do this. He gave me his pledge that he too will always counsel Open Door to restraint. With you and Charcoal Burner on either side of our brother, I have less fear of leaving. Now, listen:

"I am going to stop at Vincennes on my way down the Wabash-se-pe, and will try to put Harrison to sleep. I will tell him the truth of my going, so that he will know I am not here planning war. I will ask him again not to let white people move into the treaty land until I have talked to the president of the Seventeen Fires, and I hope he will grant me that promise."

"Are you going to talk to the president, then?"

"When the five southern nations have joined us, I think, it will be a good time to go and talk to him. Then we will be so strong that he must listen to us. We shall see. The tomorrows are in the management of the Great Good Spirit, who will tell me what to do. This is the year of the great sign. We must all do the best that is in us, and thus we can turn the fortunes of our race."

She gripped his hands in both of hers. Her hands were work-hardened and as strong as a man's. Then she spoke of something he had known she would say. "When you are among the Muskogee, you will see if our mother is well?"

"I will find her."

"Do you think she would want to come back and live her last years among us?"

"I will ask her that. She was bitter when I saw her last. And what made her bitter has grown much worse since she left us. But with the years she may be serene in her heart and say yes."

Star Watcher drew his hands toward her and put her cheek against them and was silent for a while, and they could feel goodness and strength flowing between them. "I wish," she said, "you could take your son with you, so that she might see him."

"I will try to bring her back here to see him, and to see your own children. Going there will be too dangerous a trip to take a boy. We will pass through many whites, and then among many red peoples who have been our enemies. I hope to make them our friends."

"Then," she said, "until you have won them, may the Great Good Spirit shield you with his hand."

Governor Harrison watched with satisfaction, even with delight, Tecumseh's departure down the Wabash with the twenty-four elegant warriors of his bodyguard, their canoes filled with weapons and ceremonial objects.

And the populace of Vincennes then watched with great relief as the rest of the Indians, in canoes, on horseback, and afoot, struck their camp north of the town and started back up the Wabash toward their own village on the Tippecanoe, their dust and their voices lingering in the hot summer air after them.

The governor's second council with Tecumseh had been mere formality. Neither had said anything new, and neither had conceded anything. Harrison had not let himself be disarmed by Tecumseh's personality this time, but neither had there been any anger shown on either side. Each had been merely playing for time.

Harrison was delighted not only because the Indians were gone and the townspeople could breathe easy, but because he knew the most formidable opponent of his plans would be far out of the way in the south for a long time, which would make everything so much easier. He could not have asked Tecumseh to do anything so convenient. And now Harrison penned another letter to Secretary of War Eustis, reporting on the council and stating his own intentions:

> The implicit obedience and respect which the followers of Tecumseh pay him is really astonishing and more than any other circumstance bespeaks him one of those uncommon geniuses which spring up occasionally to produce revolutions and overturn the established order of things. If it were not for the vicinity of the United States, he would perhaps be the founder of an empire that would rival in glory Mexico or Peru. No difficulties deter him. His activity and industry supply the want of letters. For four years he has been in constant motion. You see him today on the Wabash, and in a short time hear of him on the shores of Lake Erie or Michigan, and wherever he goes he makes an impression favorable to his purpose. He is now upon the last round to put a finishing stroke to his work. His absence affords a most favorable opportunity for breaking up his confederacy. I hope, that if I can move against Prophet's Town before his return, then that part of the fabric which he considered complete will be demolished, and even its foundations rooted up.
>
> I remain, Sir, Yr. Mo. Obt. Svt.,
> William H. Harrison

The sunlight gleamed on Thick Water's muscular shoulders as he stroked tirelessly with his paddle. The green water of the O-hi-o-se-pe gurgled under the bark hull of the canoe, and a warm breeze came pouring up the wide river between the far, dark green bluffs, into the faces of the paddlers of the three canoes.

Tecumseh's heart was high with joy and eagerness and with the sheer thrilling spaciousness of the broad river. Through the canoe's bark and its frame wherever he touched it, and through the paddle with which he stroked the water, he sensed the life of the water and its relentless, seeking flow, and the invisible ooze of its bottom, and all the slick and scaly and shelled creatures that lived in it, the watersnakes, eels, mussels, turtles, the fish, from the tiniest minnows to the great barbeled fish the size of a man. For now his mind was clear of the tense, imageless, spiritless kind of thought one had to use when arguing or dealing with white men, and everything was alive, round, full of the Great Good Spirit. This warm wind blowing in his face was the very breath of Weshemoneto; this river was a flowing vein of Weshemoneto; the sun over his head was the eye and mind of Weshemoneto. Tecumseh himself was a part of the Being; there was no boundary, his skin was no boundary, between it and himself; he was as dissolved in the universe as a drop of his sweat would be in this river; to be was to pray; to exist was to understand everything. Soon this great vein called the O-hi-o-se-pe, or the Speh-ley-weh-se-pe, in his people's tongue, would flow into that greater one, the Missi-se-pe. He knew that when the canoes turned southward around the next bend, the Missi-se-pe would lie open and vast before them, and the water would be more yellow and full of dangerous currents and powerful swirls where the two great waters rushed together; he could see it already as he had seen it from up on the bluffs when he was a younger man. He looked up to the bluffs on the right and saw the place where he had recklessly chased the bison when he was half the age he was now. Yet he was the same young man still. Years did not pass but rolled around to the same place, and all times were now; as he looked up at the bluff there thundered the same herd still, and there rode Tecumseh still, swiftly among them. The rumble of their running and the yipping cries of his fellow hunters were in his ears, the dust and musk in his nostrils, the surging motion of the horse between his knees—and the sudden falling and the snapping pain in his thigh. . . .

And the great shaking!

Even in the smooth-gliding canoe now he could feel that shaking of the earth, the hint of the great sign to come. Now he was seeing in the other direction across the Round of Time, as if he were in its center looking first toward the arc called Yesterday, now the other way toward the arc called Tomorrow, as if he were, as he had felt before, over the very center of the Round of Time, and he saw the earth shaking, saw the trees falling, houses tumbling; he saw dust and heard roaring in the sky; he felt the flow of the river reverse itself and go the other way; he saw the long-tailed star in the sky, but now it was in the other quarter of the sky and going away, and it was also the white dove flying away across the river, as he had seen it go once before when he had stood upon that bluff.

Then he could see it no more, just the water swirling where he had lifted his paddle, just the curving insides of the canoe, the parfleche bags, the guns, the folded blankets, Thick Water's muscular, gleaming shoulders and shaved head and feathered scalplock right in front of him, and the paddles of the other warriors dipping. And now Thick Water turned with a happy smile on his face and cried:

"There!"

The others all cried out and laughed, and excited cries came from the other canoes. Before them now, between the bluffs, spread so vast an expanse of water that the land beyond it was a line that looked as thin as one hair. The Missi-se-pe!

The banks of the O-hi-o-se-pe widened and widened and then slipped away behind the swift canoes. Here the wind was stronger; here the waters roiled and mixed, and the surface was dimpled with little whirlpools. Dark, dead trees bobbed and moved swiftly in the flood, coming down on the muddy water. The canoes went skidding with the powerful confluence.

Tecumseh remembered when he had been a boy and had put dry seed pods of the bean tree into the swift waters of a brook and watched them go sliding down the current between the stones, the seeds like little men in a canoe. It was like that now. And the warriors laughed and exclaimed about this swiftness, and paddled hard, and watched to avoid the floating trees that could tear up the bark of their frail vessels. Such a water! So vast and wide and deep, flowing down the very middle of the land! For a while it was too great upon Tecumseh's senses, and he could not think well yet upon what he had just seen in his soul. But this boiling confluence under the canoes, here above the Center of Time: he could feel the canoes drawing still closer to the Center; he could feel the great sign waiting far below the ooze of the riverbed, and he knew that he would soon understand it all; all the signs of his lifetime would soon reveal their meanings to him. For three and forty summers he had been as worthy as he had known how to be, and now the long star was in the sky somewhere, and surely the Great Good Spirit would let him know! Surely his few transgressions would have been forgiven, and Weshemoneto would deem him worthy of the great knowing!

That evening Tecumseh's canoes came ashore on a brushy, silty bank on the east side of the Missi-se-pe below the confluence. Two miles away, on the dusky west shore, a wisp of smoke could be seen against the afterglow of the setting sun, smoke from the place that had been a Spanish town the last time he had seen it but was said to be an American town now. A few faint, distant lights glowed over there as the dusk deepened.

When the canoes were on the shore and the camp was being made, Tecumseh went around the perimeter as he always did, noting the best areas for defense and flight in case of an attack. The white men controlled this river now. The Shawnees who lived near the mouth of the Wabash-se-pe had said they saw a white men's boat as big as a council lodge float down the O-hi-o-se-pe three moons ago, not one with the white wings on it, but one with a chimney that gave off a great amount of smoke. That boat had made a strange, ugly noise and had churned the water white. It had scared the children.

A little way below the confluence, Tecumseh's canoes had passed the dark mass of a ruined fort, a fort that the Long Knife Clark had built during the war between the Long Knives and the British. It was abandoned now, rotting and overgrown with brush, and Tecumseh had thought:

Someday, if the Master of Life helps us to finish this great work, all the places of the Americans will be like that, empty and rotting, even their cities, and there will be no more smoke boats or wing boats on the lakes or the rivers, and our People will hunt happily and freely over all this land which was ours, and will forget the fear and sadness we have known for a generation. There will be only raccoons and chipmunks and snakes living in the forts that Clark built.

*Clark.*

Tecumseh looked across the river to the darkening sky over the western country and thought:

Now the governor of that land over there is named Clark. The young brother of the old Long Knife Clark. The Clark who is the governor there now is the one who crossed the Shining Mountains six years ago and went to the Western Sea.

The Long Knives had truly crossed this whole immense land. There were some living over there now. Not many yet, but a few, trading furs, making treaties. . . . Boone, it was said, lived in a big house far up the Missouri-se-pe now; But-lah Kenton, it was said, had bought a great piece of land right over there, somewhere near those distant lights. . . .

There were Shawnees over there, too, those who had left O-hi-o thirty-two years ago to escape from Clark's Long Knives, and now another Clark was the ruler of the lands where they lived. . . .

"Great One," Tecumseh murmured, raising his eyes to the sky over the great river, "guide me. Show me what I must do to stop the intruders, to turn them back before they fill up the world! Reveal to me now the meaning of the great sign, so that I shall be ready and know what to do!"


That night he slept on the riverbank over the Center of Time, and in his sleep all the things passed again: the white dove crossing the sky with thundering wings, the face of He-Opens-the-Door, the four wolves following in the shadow of the dove with moons in their eyes, the green eye of the Panther in the Sky, the bundle of red sticks, and then the great shaking and jolting of the earth straight below, the river flowing upstream, the dust and smoke rising over the whole Middle Ground, the horsemen coming toward him through yellow light . . .

When he awoke the sky was growing light. The Missi-se-pe gurgled and whispered a few yards away. The long canoes lay on the shore. All was still. His warriors were sleeping in their blankets all around, except for Thick Water, who sat on guard with a blanket across his shoulders and a rifle on his knees, a gray sentinel in the river mist.

He smiled at Tecumseh, seeing him awake. Tecumseh smiled at him and sat up.

"We must move now," Tecumseh said. "We have to go to all the towns of the southern nations before the sign comes, and it will come sooner than we had thought. We have only four moons in which to do all we have to do!"

Thick Water's eyes widened, and the other warriors, hearing this, sat upright. "Wake, and hurry!" Tecumseh told them with a thrilling urgency in his voice. "At last it has all been told to me, and I know!"

Thick Water leaped up, heart pounding. He understood and was amazed. Weshemoneto's revelation of when and how he would shake the world had happened in the soul of his leader during the night, and most amazing to Thick Water was that he himself, sitting guard, had heard nothing but the gurgle of the river and the cooing of a dove, had seen no light but the stars above and that Long Star of the Year of the Sign!

# CHAPTER 33

## Vincennes, Indiana Territory
## September 26, 1811

The drummer boys of the Fourth United States Infantry Regiment began a long, chattering roll on their instruments. It was a brave, thrilling sound to the ears of the people of Vincennes, who for three years had lived under the imagined threat of an Indian massacre. The crowds lining the street shivered at the sound, and when General William Henry Harrison rode up on his light gray mare alongside the columns of troops, wearing a fringed calico hunting shirt over his uniform, glanced left and right with those piercing eyes, drew his sword—not a ceremonial sword this time, but a big, curved, razor-edged man-killer of a cavalry saber—and raised it in front of his face in a salute, the crowd broke out in huzzahs, their eyes shining with exultation.

There were shouted commands. The legs of the infantrymen, in tight, buttoned leggings of gray wool, began stepping in unison, and the regiment moved forward: tall, cylindrical black hats with huge eagles over the visors made the soldiers look tall as giants. They were splendid in their dark blue woolen coats with high collars and brass-buttoned cuffs, sheathed bayonets, black cartridge bags and light blue wooden canteens dangling at their hips. These were disciplined, firm-jawed soldiers, mostly New Englanders, sent down from Pittsburgh by President Madison, commanded by Colonel John Boyd. The senior officer under Boyd was Major George Rogers Clark Floyd, and Boyd's aide-de-camp was another nephew of the old Long Knife George Croghan. Here were men with war in their blood and officers with glory in their heads. General Harrison watched them with the pride of a Caesar watching his legions go forth. There were four hundred of these Blue-Coat Regulars, the cream of the American army, and they in themselves looked invincible—yet they were but a third of the force General Harrison had at his command.

499

Up ahead were the mounted regiments: the Kentucky Dragoons of Colonel Joseph Daveiss, in their blue coats and beaver hats, and a troop of mounted infantry militiamen, called the Yellow Jackets because of the yellow facings on their blue coats; these were under the command of Captain Spier Spencer, a tavernkeeper from the frontier town of Corydon. There were six hundred Indiana militiamen in total and more than a hundred Kentucky militiamen furnished by Governor Scott. Supply wagons rolled by then, following the army, and a herd of beef cattle was being held north of the town to be driven at the army's rear.

The last time such an army had been seen in Vincennes had been exactly a quarter of a century ago, when the Long Knife General Clark had marched up the Wabash against Little Turtle's confederation. It was like a repetition of history for some of the citizens who were old enough to remember. Back then, too, the threat had been a confederation of Indians up this same river; it was as if only the names had changed. That time it had been General George Rogers Clark against Little Turtle; this time it was General William Henry Harrison against the Prophet. Harrison, combining lessons learned from Clark and Wayne, and a whole age of Roman generals before them, meant to move steadily but cautiously up the Wabash, building forts and supply blockhouses as he went and keeping out a screen of scouts commanded by his old spy Dubois. If all went as he meant it to, the followers of the insolent Shawnee brothers would be scattered and cowed before this year was out, and then the acquisition of the rest of the Indian lands could continue without opposition, and Indiana would become a state.

To be the father of a state! How Harrison's soul fed upon that notion!


Open Door ran his string of sacred beans through his fist and gnawed inside his lip, his eye fixed on the hollow man without seeing it, his heartbeat fast. He was scared and angry.

The white governor Harrison was coming very slowly up the Wabash-se-pe with his big army. His army crept slowly, but he was coming; there was no doubt that the Prophet's holy town was where Harrison was coming with his big army!

At the present time, the army was stopped on the banks of the river at a place halfway between Vincennes and Prophet's Town, and there they were building a fort. The place was called High Ground, Terre Haute by the French, and was a favored camping place for red men traveling up and down the Wabash-se-pe. In the long-ago war against the Iroquois, a battle had been fought there, and it was a sacred place to the Wabash tribes. Now the Americans were there cutting down trees to make a fort, on that sacred place. Worst of all, it was within the lands of the Fort Wayne Treaty. Tecumseh had asked Harrison not to move into that country until he had come back from the south and talked to the president, but Harrison had come into that country now and was building a fort. Moreover, it was clear that he intended to come farther with his army. He had not gathered eleven hundred soldiers just to build a fort.

Open Door sighed and sighed. On learning of Harrison's approach, he had sent messengers in all directions, asking warriors to come to Prophet's Town. Then his messengers had learned that Harrison also had sent messengers, to all the friendly and neutral tribes, telling them to stay out of his path.

The beans slipped through his palm. They were shiny like old wood from being pulled through the hands of hundreds of his followers and from being pulled through his own when he was worried like this.

He heard Charcoal Burner's voice calling to him from outside and a flurry of excited voices in the distance. Open Door was silent for a moment, scowling. He admired Charcoal Burner and was glad to have his help in Tecumseh's absence. But in a way he resented him, too. It was as if Tecumseh had not thought the Prophet could manage matters or make wise decisions in his absence and had set Charcoal Burner beside him as a watchdog. On learning of Harrison's advance some weeks ago, Charcoal Burner had come to Open Door and said, "Remember. We are not to fight them. Tecumseh told us not to let ourselves be provoked. Everything depends upon it."

"I remember that," Open Door had said, irritated. "I do not mean to be provoked." But at the same time, he had resented it.

Now he called for Charcoal Burner to come into the medicine lodge. As the door flap opened, Open Door could see the yellow-and-red leaves of the trees in the valley. Harrison, like all the Long Knife leaders before him, was coming before the approach of winter and no doubt meant to burn Prophet's Town and destroy all its foods and leave the people hungry and homeless in the face of winter.

Charcoal Burner said, "Some Miamis have come. Harrison sent them with a message for you."

"So. Then let us go and see these faithful dogs of government, and hear their message."

The message was that if the Prophet would disperse his warriors and surrender all of his followers who had been involved in the raids in Illinois, and all who had stolen horses or otherwise troubled the whites this summer, Harrison would not attack Prophet's Town.

"What do you want to reply?" asked Charcoal Burner.

"He is still far down the river, building his fort," Open Door answered. "I do not believe he really dares to come into our lands and attack us here."

"I," said Charcoal Burner, "believe he dares."

"If we send our warriors away and leave our sacred village to the white soldiers," Open Door hissed, "do you believe they will not come and burn it down? What will become of the People's faith? Have I not told them this town is protected by Weshemoneto, and that anyone who tries to hurt it will die or lose his mind? Do you doubt this? Do you want the People to think I doubt my own words?"

"Father, listen to me," Charcoal Burner said, leaning forward in earnestness. "I believe in you. I believe the Great Good Spirit will favor us. But I have watched Harrison's soldiers come along the river. I do not think they are harmless or afraid. I have seen them shoot squirrels out of the trees from the backs of their moving horses."

"You are afraid."

All the kindness went out of Charcoal Burner's face. "Draw those words back into your mouth, Father, for they poison the air between us."

"I draw the words back into my mouth," Open Door apologized impatiently. "But I tell you, I do not want to cower before this snake's dung of a white man!"

"Tecumseh did not advise you to cower. Only to keep the People safe until his return. Not to do battle."

Open Door scowled past Charcoal Burner. His hands, now mindlessly pulling the string of beans again, were shaking. "I am not a warrior, I am a holy man," he said as if reminding himself. "I will call Weshemoneto for guidance."

"Yes. But what will we tell the Miamis?"

Thoughts raced behind Open Door's eye. "That I will meet with Harrison and discuss his demands. Only that. That we do not understand why he comes into our country with an army, that he insults our hearts. I will go and talk with him, if it will keep him from my town for a while." He thought of the large supplies of food and the new British guns stored in the town. How could the people flee ahead of Harrison's horse soldiers with all that? No. Harrison must be delayed, and perhaps words would delay him.

But in the meantime, Open Door would send to the Kickapoos and Potawatomis for more warriors and have the people make a hiding place in the woods for all the food. He suspected that talk would not stop the Long Knife governor for very long.

The thousands of Choctaws were full of fire when the drums stopped.

Tecumseh stood naked except for breechcloth and moccasins, his skin gleaming from the exertions of the war dance; his warriors stood ranked behind him, breathing hard, eyes wild. The dance had had a powerful effect on this enormous crowd of Choctaws, evoking yips and howls from the warriors and moans of admiration from the women. Much of the Choctaw nation was here, eager to hear him. Many of them had heard him first when he had addressed them in their own towns, then had followed him here to Moshuletubbe's Town to hear him again.

For weeks Tecumseh had been in the Choctaw country, crossing and recrossing the Noxubee River to go from one town to another, dancing the Shawnee dance with his agile warriors, giving variations of the same speech, exciting the young men of his audiences until they were ready to take up their weapons at once and follow him to the north. Except for one problem, he would have had hundreds of Choctaws pledged to his cause by now, but because of that one problem, he was not sure he had even one.

That one problem was Pushmataha, the principal Choctaw war chief.

Pushmataha towered over the village chiefs who now stood nearby on the knoll at the roots of the giant council tree. He wore a white cotton robe that draped from his broad shoulders to his feet. On his head was a turban decorated with long, curving plumes. His face was wide, almost black from sun, and his eyes were glittering, fierce as an eagle's.

Pushmataha had first opposed Tecumseh at Hoentubbe's Town, and in the weeks since then he had taken it upon himself to go everywhere Tecumseh went in his nation and to follow every one of Tecumseh's speeches with a rebuttal. As principal war chief of the nation, he threw a powerful weight of discouragement over the passion Tecumseh was creating.

So now, here again in Moshuletubbe's Town, in a wide, sloping draw that allowed everyone to see the dancers and hear the speakers clearly, thousands sat ready to hear the final round of the traveling debate between Tecumseh and Pushmataha. Tecumseh knew he would have to try to stir the people's souls to such heights that Pushmataha's cautions would not even reach their hearts.

Unfortunately, there was a white man seated among the chiefs this time. He was a prominent settler named Colonel Pitchlynn, a friend of the village chief Moshuletubbe. The colonel's curiosity had been aroused by all the stir Tecumseh's presence had created in the region. Tecumseh did not want to talk with an American in the audience but would have offended Moshuletubbe if he had insisted on his removal. And so the white man sat listening. The Choctaw chiefs stood before the great tulip tree on a rise of level ground in the center of the natural amphitheater, and Tecumseh and his dancers stood before them facing the listeners, who were so many they were crowded together. Even at Prophet's Town at the spring and fall gatherings Tecumseh had never seen so many in one place. If only all these could join him!

He held his right hand high. In it was his war club. In his left was a bundle of the red sticks.

"Brothers and sisters of the great Choctaw nation, hear me! I am Tecumseh, born a Shawnee but now war chief of all tribes north of the O-hi-o-se-pe. The long star you have seen in the sky is mine. I was born by the light of a shooting star—your fathers here remember that star—and now that star has returned to warn you of the time of greatest danger. I am Tecumseh. Following my signs, I have united tribes who once were jealous enemies, so that they might stand together and resist the enemy of all red men: the Americans! The Americans are at this moment plowing up the graves of my ancestors. Tomorrow they will be plowing up the graves of *your* ancestors! Brothers! I have been given signs that tell me when and how to stop them! There is little time left. Before three moons, all red men must join hands to do this!

"Brothers, hear what has been done to the red men in my land! It will be done to you as well, unless you will take my hand!"

He looked up and spread his arms, looking bewildered, and cried:

"Where today are the Mohican? The Narragansett? The Pequot? The Pocanoket? And the other old and once powerful tribes?" He left the question hanging in the firelight. Then he said:

"As snow vanishes before the sun, they have melted. They died of disease, of poverty, of drunkenness. Of trying in vain to fight alone against the spawn of the Serpent, the white man!

"Look toward their country, that once was so wide and beautiful. What do you see? Stumps and fences! Muddy roads! The fertile earth gone, washed away, the graves of their ancestors plowed up, the elk and the deer gone, only dark smoke and noise remaining, where once the air was clean and the lark sang! So will it be with you the Choctaw."

He cried out fervently: "This great tree under which I stand!" He turned and spread his arms toward it, reaching like a growing tree. "In its shade you played in your childhood. You rested after the hunt. You listened to the words of the councils. This very tree, which was already a growing tree before the white men even found our shores, will be cut down to make fences, to keep you out of lands which you now call yours, but they will soon call theirs! Soon their wagon roads will pass over the graves of your fathers, and the place of their rest will be blotted out forever, horse dung will drop on it, iron wheels roll over it.

"When a people has no place anymore, it is no longer a people. Think not, mighty Choctaw, that you can sit idle and passive while the ravages of the white men go around you and destroy someone else! No! They will not go around! You, like all the rest, will be uprooted! You too will be like fallen leaves and smoke before the wind! It has happened to the Narragansett, the Mohican, the Pequot. It will happen to the Choctaw, the Creek, the Chickasaw, to all red men—unless we become one in our heart, unless we see clearly together, act wisely together, stand bravely together.

"Sleep no more, O Choctaw! Stop dreaming that the Seventeen Fires will favor you and not hurt you! Your chief, Pushmataha, keeps saying that your fathers went up and shook hands with the first white chief Washington, and you remember that, but the white men will not remember it! Every year, my brothers, every year the white intruders turn against the tribes who were friendly to them. Every year they grow more arrogant, more greedy, more numerous. If you bleed, they care not. Your life is nothing to them. You are only in their way. They have never punished the murderers of any red man. They have murdered our great chiefs, even in peacetime, and gone unpunished. They have cheated us of our hunting grounds, and paid us with empty promises, with salt they had stolen from us, with kegs of rotten meat that make us sicken and die.

"Before the white men came, we could follow the game animals anywhere, we could put seeds in any ground that felt rich between our fingers, and any red man could speak what was in his heart, and had to ask no one but his Creator for anything. But how is it now? Those who were the greatest chiefs must beg for everything. They must beg before agents who are liars and thieves and spies. They must beg before governors, who look down on them from high chairs, and insult them, and threaten them.

"Now we are hungry every winter. Every new season, hundreds of our people die of diseases bred in the unclean ways of the white people. Every year hundreds go crazy from their whiskey, and every day we have to ask the white man for permission to stand up!"

Hundreds in the audience were grimacing now, and many were crying out in anger and astonishment. Now was the time to tell them how the desperate tribes had regained the favor of the Great Good Spirit.

He told them how his brother had been changed at once from a drunkard into the greatest force for sobriety. He told how the inhabitants of Prophet's Town had come from over the horizons in every direction to live with their great shaman, how they had cast off their dependence on the white men, and how they now labored to do only good in the eyes of the Master of

Life and to save the lands he had entrusted to them. He made the Choctaws laugh and cheer when he told how the white governor there had for six years been unable to intimidate or debauch them. He spoke of Prophet's Town as a haven of brotherhood and morality in a sea of white man's corruption, of the united warriors as a brotherhood of brave and strong men surrounded by drunkards and weaklings. The Choctaws listened to this, and he could see in their faces a yearning to be like those brave and united people.

Then he told them that the Choctaws and all the other southern tribes *could* be like that, living in harmony with each other, standing in an indestructible circle against threats, deceptions, and corruptions. He spoke against the horrors of intertribal warfare and the way it weakened the red men just when they needed to be strong against the invaders. He pleaded for mercy and pity for the women and children, who always suffered most in war. He denounced the cowardly practices of torturing and killing prisoners. He praised the bravery of any warrior who fought only for right and told of the great power Weshemoneto reserved especially for such warriors. And the holy cause for such warriors, he said, was to preserve Weshemoneto's land from the plows and pastures and pigs and cities and rats of the American white men.

"O Choctaw! Will you lie on your backs dreaming of ease and safety, while they plow up the bones of your fathers and turn their graves into hog wallows?"

"No! *No!*" they were howling.

"Then come with me and take my hand, my brothers and sisters! No one red nation can resist their numbers. All the red nations together can hold them back, can even drive them back into the sea where they were spawned by the evil Serpent! It must be now, now! Or tomorrow they will be all over your sacred land, and you will lie under their hooves and wheels, dreaming too late of all you lost: your lands, your freedom, the honor of your Choctaw name!"

When he saw that their eyes were glimmering with dismay at the prospect of such loss, he told them of an opportunity that was coming. He did not want to mention this with the white colonel present but could do nothing about him.

Soon, Tecumseh told them, the Americans and the British would be at war with each other again, because the Americans wanted not only this land bounded by the Great Northern Lakes and the Eastern and Southern seas, even the Western Ocean, they wanted even Canada, they wanted even Mexico. The British would be in a right cause in that war, he said, because they would be trying to save the land of the Canadian red men from the

Americans. And so, not only would the red men all be united in this right cause, the British would be helping them with food and weapons from their own rich supply houses.

And at last, deep in the night, he called upon the Choctaws to give him their hands and their hearts.

"In three moons," he cried, "when all the red men are brothers and ready to join in this right cause, there will come a great sign from the earth that all is ready, that it is time for us to take hold of our fate and save ourselves! It will be such a sign that will rouse even the blind and deaf!

"I will give to your chiefs these bundles of red sticks." He held one up. "They will throw away one stick each day, and after the last stick is gone, the sign will come. At that time, all must come and put your hand on the tomahawk with mine, ready to resist the white intruders!"

Many warriors leaped up, yelling, after his last words had been translated. Everywhere in the crowd prevailed a turmoil of talking and crying. This went on for several minutes, while Colonel Pitchlynn sat trying not to reveal his anger and alarm, and it did not grow quiet until Pushmataha rose and stood where Tecumseh had stood before. As always, the Choctaw chief looked like a giant warrior in the garb of a holy man. And as he had begun each time, he now raised his mighty arms and cried:

"You know me! I had no father, no mother! The winds blew howling, the rains poured down, the thunder shook the world, the lightning flashed down and split a pine tree, and then, out from the splinters and smoke stepped Pushmataha with a rifle in his hand!

"Thus made, I fought our enemies and made them afraid. I have gone alone into their towns, and when the banging and screaming were over I came forth, Pushmataha, with handfuls of scalps. But I have killed women and children, and I have thought later that this I should not have done. These words of Tecumseh the Shawnee have touched my heart, and I believe he is right. I, Pushmataha, will never hurt a woman or child again. I have thought of this myself! Nor will I harm a prisoner. It is true what he says, there is no glory in hurting a man who is tied up.

"What Tecumseh told us about peace among the tribes is true also. I have often thought what a bad thing it is that good men die in wars among brothers. To the west of us are the Chickasaws, and farther that way, the Osages. I have fought them. I have made their blood pour out. The Osages now leave us alone and stay beyond the Great River. The Chickasaws now grow their gardens and hunt pecans and pick fruit, and make war on the mighty Choctaw no more. To the east are the Muskogee Creeks. Sometimes they still fight us, but it is better when they are at peace with us. Often I have thought how good it is to be at peace with neighbors."

Tecumseh knew which way Pushmataha was going with this. The Choctaw had seen that his people liked these ideas, and being a chief who was jealous of power, he was pretending that he had thought of them himself.

"My people," Pushmataha said now, "I think the Shawnee Tecumseh has many of my thoughts. But!" He pointed at Tecumseh. His voice grated. "I am not with Tecumseh in going to war with white men! The Choctaw see no reason to like British better than Americans. Did not the Choctaw help the Americans against the British king in their great war a generation ago? Did not our fathers go up into the east and take the hand of their first chief, Washington, and promise to remain his friends always? This is a sacred promise! Even though the chief Washington is dead now, our promise to him lives! No! We must never shed the blood of Americans! To break this promise and go to war against our friends, *that* is what would end in the ruin of the Choctaw nation! We must not make our friends into enemies by taking the talk of Tecumseh!

"Tecumseh tells you that Americans are the spawn of the evil Serpent, and he asks you to take hold of his war club with him. I do not stand here to deny what Tecumseh says happened to his people up there. The Shawnees surely have been hurt by the Americans, by fighting against the white men. Surely their troubles began when they shed white men's blood!

"But I am leader of a people who have not spilled the blood of Americans. We have not had such troubles! We are not starved because of the nearness of white men. We have commerce with the Americans, and some good things have come of it. If they have done harsh things to other members of our race, I am sorry to know of them. I well know that causes often arise which force a people into hard places. But, my Choctaws, these causes are not upon our nation. We have not been pressed to a hard place.

"Think, then, without fire in your souls! Remember, the Americans think well of us! Would you cry to avenge acts you have only heard about from this talker who has come among us? Were you thinking of raising your hand against Americans before he came and asked you to? No!

"My people, you know that we and our neighbors have in the past fought the Shawnees. It was long ago, but once we suffered at their hands. We have never suffered at the hands of Americans. How come you then to cry out with an old enemy for the blood of an old friend?

"Listen! To war against the Americans would commence the destruction of our nation! They have more land, more men, more horses, more guns, more wealth, than we have—yes, even more than that of all the red nations together!

"Listen to the voice of prudence, my Choctaw, before the exciting words of our Shawnee guest make you leap up and do a terrible thing you had never until now even thought of doing!

"But do as you may, know this before you act:

"If such a war begins, I, Pushmataha, will stand on the side of the Americans. And if any Choctaw warrior follows Tecumseh to such a war, when he returns, I shall kill that warrior!"

Tecumseh saw a look of joy and relief on the face of the American colonel Pitchlynn. His own heart smoldered with hatred for Pushmataha and contempt for his short vision. But he did not let these feelings show. He had seen that many of the young warriors had been stirred. It was not unusual for the old chiefs to resist his pleas for action, for change. He was used to that. The same had happened with the Chickasaws, the nation he had visited before this one. When in the Hard Moon the great sign would come and all the earth would shake, the warriors would remember what he had said, and some would forget Pushmataha's threat and would pick up their weapons and go to meet him in the north. Tecumseh was disappointed by Pushmataha's advice, but not crushed. He had done what he could with the Choctaw. It was time to move eastward among the people of his mother. There were still hundreds of miles to go, many Creek towns ahead, Alabamu towns, Seminole towns, Catawba towns, Cherokee towns, and then west to the Osages and Missouria-Otoes and the Iowas . . .

There was so far to go, and so little time left in this Year of the Signs!


Star Watcher could not persuade Open Door to prepare the town for flight from the Long Knife army. "Our harvest," she would insist, "should be carried up the Tippecanoe and cached there. Just enough should be kept here to feed us a week or two. When the army arrives there will not be time to flee ahead of them with so much grain. They would catch us and hack us and destroy the corn, and leave us hungry for another winter!" He would grimace and protest:

"I do not want to abandon this holy town!"

For days Open Door had been turning over and over inside. His warriors and war chiefs kept him always in councils. What was he going to do about the Long Knives' army? It had completed its fort on the High Ground and resumed its march up the east bank of the Wabash-se-pe. At Big Raccoon Creek it had crossed from the treaty lands onto the lands of the Weas and was now in Indian country to which the Americans did not have even any pretended claim.

"There is no doubt anymore!" the war chiefs hissed at their prophet.

"They do not come close just to frighten us, they are coming clear to your town to destroy it! Father, they will fall upon us in days! You must let us go out and strike them before they come closer!"

But Open Door, with Charcoal Burner at his side and Star Watcher's entreaties in his head, would reply: "We are not to be provoked! You know it is our plan not to fight the Long Knives until my brother returns from the south with the warriors of those nations!"

The war chiefs argued:

"Provoked? What is this you say, Father? They do not provoke! They invade! They come to destroy this very place!"

"We are not ready to fight their army," Charcoal Burner would argue.

"Do we fear their army?" White Loon cried. "I do not fear this army! They put on war clothes to come into our country, but they are not warriors. They are only calico peddlers and farmers!"

"Then they are calico peddlers who shoot from horseback and knock squirrels out of the trees," retorted Charcoal Burner, who had been so impressed by that sight that he mentioned it over and over.

"We could lay an ambush at any creek and kill them as they tried to cross," growled White Loon. "They are slow with their wagons and their cattle. They could be treated as they were treated at Blue Licks, long ago before we signed treaties and became timid. Father, we must decide what to do. There is little time!"

"There is more time than you imagine," Open Door replied. "I sent the Miamis down to talk to them, and tell them I wish to parley with them."

"Aha! Where, then, are the Miamis? Why have they not come back with his reply? The Miami who were here are friends of the Long Knife governor. They are traitors. They came only to confuse us. If not, they would have come back with his answer whether he will stop along his way and talk with you. He means to make you believe he will stop, but no! He will be upon this town suddenly, and we will have to fight him in the open fields, with the women and children nearby and in danger. We are fools to stand and wait!"

We are not fools!" Open Door cried. "His army is not near us yet! Have our scouts come to say they have seen him close by? No!"

"Maybe our scouts are dead," a war chieftain retorted. "Maybe they were shot like squirrels by the long guns of the army."

Open Door chopped across the air with his open hand. "This is enough dispute among us!" he cried. "Even if he came this far, how could he surprise us? He is on the other side of the river. Do not press upon me like this! Have I not told you that our town is under the protection of the Great Good Spirit, and that anyone who tries to harm it will be struck dead or crazy? Now cease these alarms. I go now to the medicine lodge, where I will call again to the Master of Life for the power that has always protected us." Even as he spoke these words, his heart quickened and felt lighter, as it did when Weshemoneto was listening and ready to respond. Yes, he thought. Weshemoneto, I need your answer. I need your guidance now!

Without Tecumseh to guide him, he was woefully aware, he needed desperately to hear from a messenger of the Great Good Spirit, who had said nothing to him for so long. Weshemoneto was sparing with his signs, of course. He had not spoken before now because there had not been such a crisis of danger before now. But now, Open Door was sure, now the answers would come. Weshemoneto would not have made Loud Noise into He-Opens-the-Door and put him into this crisis only to abandon him.

In the medicine lodge that night, Open Door sat before a cedarwood fire, his eye closed, and tried to open his soul to the messages from above. He had asked his wife to come into the lodge with him, to aid his concentration by guarding the door against intruders and to hand him the sacred artifacts he might need as he communed with the Messenger Spirits. He still had true faith and was sure he would be guided in time.

Open Door long ago had learned that trying to force messages to come only drove them farther away. So he pretended that he was not trying to force them to come, though in fact by his mental straining he was. As he sat facing the fire, he seemed to hear with his mind the marching feet of Harrison's army. But this was not a real sound. Outside there was only the quiet noise of the village, the rustling of the last clinging oak leaves in the night wind. Harrison's army would not be marching at night, and it was after all on the far side of the river. Open Door told himself he must calm his imagination, or he would never perceive the messages when they did come. He murmured his chants and tried to draw the voice of the Great Good Spirit down to himself.

After a while, eye still shut, he spoke softly to his wife and asked her to bring him his sacred medicine fire stick and the beaded bag that contained the *nilu famu*, sacred tobacco. He felt them being put into his hands. He laid the stick upon one thigh, opened the neck of the bag, and pinched out a bit of the powdered tobacco. Then he rubbed his thumb and forefinger together, dusting the tobacco into the fire before him. He smelled it burning and knew its sacred smoke was now rising out of the smokehole into the night, and he put his prayer into the smoke, that it might be carried to heaven.

Again now he felt his heart growing quick and light.

Yes! Soon he would know! At last the Messenger was about to visit him again with wisdom and guidance!

Open Door saw a light growing in the darkness. It was an irregular, shifting light, darkening now and then as if something were passing before it. Open Door breathed slowly to soothe his soul so that the image would form.

And after a while he saw that the light was a white tent gleaming in the light of a great bonfire.

Now Open Door saw that it was an army tent, of the sort he had seen at the Fallen Timbers.

In the image the tent was among big trees. There were people lying in blankets on the ground around it and many bonfires burning. The people in the blankets were soldiers. Many of them were not moving, not even breathing; others lay with their eyes and mouths wide open, turning their heads upon their necks like madmen, rolling their eyeballs.

Now, as if he were walking toward the tent's door, he saw it grow closer. But it was not himself going toward the tent. He felt himself to be far back behind the person who was moving toward the tent, yet seeing it through his own eye looking through the eyes of the one going there.

Now the person was inside the tent, and there upon a bed lay Harrison the governor, asleep.

Open Door heard a rapid heartbeat. He felt in his hand a handle. It was not the fire stick he actually held in his hand, but a handle made of horn from an antler. It was the handle of a knife.

In the light that diffused through the cloth of the tent, he saw Harrison's eyes open, those strange eyes that were so hard to look at, and the eyes saw the knife.

Suddenly with a surge of power and a grunting breath, the carrier of the knife struck at Harrison's breast with it. The knife went through the blanket and between ribs and into the heart. His mouth opened to emit a cry, but only blood came forth.

Open Door felt a hand on his shoulder shaking him hard. He opened his eye and saw his wife's fat face before him, full of alarm.

"What, woman?" he exclaimed. "Why do you disturb me?"

"You cried out."

"Woman! Leave me alone!" he groaned. He was furious. At last he had been permitted to glimpse the event, but this stupid woman had disrupted it.

She looked very hurt. "I was afraid you were going to fall and . . . and go away as you did the first time. . . ."

"I was! I was! I was away! I meant to be! Go," he whined. "Go home!"

He tried then, late into the night, to return to the vision, but We-shemoneto did not let him see any more.

But Open Door was heartened. The Great Good Spirit had told him a very important thing: that Harrison could—and surely would—be killed in his tent at night. And that the soldiers around him could not protect him because, it seemed, some were dead and the rest crazy!

First it was one distant cry in the drone of afternoon, then more voices spread the cry of alarm, and in a few seconds the cries were shrieking down through Prophet's Town:

"The Long Knives! The army is here!" The people were stampeding. The town was in a turmoil.

From his medicine lodge, Open Door, dismayed, could now see them coming. They were more than a mile away yet, and only the Leathershirts scouting in advance of the main army were clearly visible, but, yes! The army was in sight, the lines and masses moving slowly in the hazy distance through the gray, leafless woods, and the horror of it was that they were not on the other side of the Wabash, but on this bank! Charcoal Burner's scouts had discovered only this morning that the army had apparently crossed the river somewhere far down and had been coming unseen along the north bank for days. There was nothing between Harrison's approaching army but the mouth of one narrow, shallow creek and a mile of marshes and harvested corn fields!

As the war chiefs gathered around Open Door, he had all he could do to mask his fright and despair. No wonder was it that the Miamis he had sent down with a message to Harrison had not returned with a reply. They had missed the oncoming army entirely. And the time Open Door had hoped to gain by parley was lost. Now the enemy was here. The dark lines of troops could be clearly seen coming out of the cottonwoods and sycamores and the willow thickets into the fields: horsemen first, hundreds of them, then the twin lines of Blue-Coat walking soldiers, at this distance seeming hardly to move, yet coming into view across the gray-brown landscape. There could be no parley with them at a safe distance from the town, no way to persuade them to stay down the river, no way to stall them until more warriors could come from Illinois or Mis-i-ken, no way to ambush them from the woods at some creek crossing, no way to slip into Harrison's camp and kill him in his bed. . . . They were here, marching upon his sacred town, and Open Door had no plan, now. His head was full of a silent scream.

But the vision! Weshemoneto had shown him what to do; had even Weshemoneto tricked him?

Why? he cried in his heart. Is our cause not right?

I have tried to be the best of all holy men!

I have been sober and have sacrificed myself for six years for my People

and kept them out of conflict and given them hope and happiness! Have
I not been worthy?

Now the American army was changing shape to the sound of drums and
shouted orders from the distance, forming into ranks and marching straight
toward the holy town with flags and bayonets, stepping in unison, coming
closer and closer. The people in the town were weeping and rushing about,
gathering their children, seeking their loved ones, bundling things up. Star
Watcher stood near her brother, watching him.

"Father," cried a warrior beside Open Door, "what will you have us do?
Tell us!"

The Prophet hid his hands beneath his robe and wrung them to stop
them from shaking. He must think of something now. He had never meant
for war to come right into his town! He had always believed that Harrison
would stop and talk. . . .

Charcoal Burner came riding up from the river, shouting for the people
to get out of the way of his excited horse. He reined in, staring at Open
Door, eyes wild, his whole being demanding some answer, some guidance
at last, and finally he said, "They mean to attack now. They must be delayed,
Father, they must be delayed until we can move the people to safety!"

Delayed. Yes. Suddenly Open Door braced himself. Had not the Great
Good Spirit shown him that Harrison *would* die in his bed? Therefore it
could *not* end here this way!

Quickly Open Door pointed out six chieftains and one who could speak
English. "Go and show your hand for parley. Tell the Long Knives we are
surprised to find them here, and our feelings are hurt. Tell them they must
come no farther because they put our women and children in danger. That
we would like to know what they want. That we invite them to camp near
us in peace, and will parley with them tomorrow and find out what they wish
us to do. . . ."

"Now! Parley now, not tomorrow!" Star Watcher urged.

"I have a reason," Open Door replied, then said to the messengers,
"Tell them I sent Miamis many days ago to ask them this, but they came
up the wrong side of the river. Charcoal Burner, what say you to doing this
to halt them where they are?"

"Yes," said Charcoal Burner. "There is hope in this. Perhaps it is not
too late even now to get the people away. If Harrison can make his soldiers
stop. If he *will!*"


Tecumseh was painted black; his war club was painted red. He wore only
his crane feather headdress, loincloth, sheathed knife, and a pouch. He

walked, very erect, toward the pole in the center of the council ground, before which a small fire burned, and his warriors, decorated in the same way, followed him in a single file.

Smoke from the fire rose toward the stars. In the sky stood the long-tailed star, now grown so long and big that it cast light like that of a full moon.

Thousands of warriors of the upper Creek nation stood on the edges of the field and watched, lit by bigger bonfires around the perimeter of the field.

From one side of the field now entered their principal chief Big Warrior, to meet Tecumseh by the fire. He carried a pipe, and a warrior behind him carried a bowl of coals. Tecumseh remembered when he had first seen Big Warrior, many years ago when he had come to Tuckabatchee Town to find his mother. Tecumseh here found another dream manifest. Something, maybe a disease in the years since Tecumseh had seen him, had caused his skin to fade in spots, as Tecumseh had seen. His nose was broad and flat, his jaw wide and square as a box.

They lit the pipe from the fire carrier's bowl and smoked to the Four Winds. In the silence of this ceremony, Tecumseh could feel the power and even the mood of Big Warrior beside him. Big Warrior was not very pleased with Tecumseh, who had come here more than a week ago to address the full autumn council of the Creeks, then had postponed his speech day after day because two white men had been present. At last one of the white men, the Indian agent Colonel Hawkins, had grown tired of waiting and left. But the other, a frontiersman named Samuel Dale, seemed to have nothing else to do but wait around, and at last Tecumseh had decided that he must go ahead with his plea anyway, even if a white man did hear it. Dale sat among the chiefs on the other side of the field now, and Tecumseh could feel his presence waiting. But white man or no, Tecumseh was going to talk war. He could not dally any longer; there were still hundreds of miles to go.

These Creeks were his mother's people. Tecumseh had fame among them, and they were not so bound to the whites as the Chickasaws and Choctaws were. In the Revolutionary War they had fought against the Americans. Big Warrior was on good terms with the Indian agent Hawkins but only pretended to like him. The danger of holding his war council while Hawkins was here would have been extreme, for the agent was a friend of President Madison; Tecumseh had learned that Madison and Hawkins had been something called classmates at someplace called Princeton. Whatever that was, it surely meant that Hawkins would tell the president if he heard Shawnee war talk in the great fall council of the peaceful Creek nation. Tecumseh expected to talk to Madison himself after the confederation was complete; he did not want him to know anything yet. This man Dale would probably report to Hawkins and Hawkins to the president, but there was nothing Tecumseh could do about it now.

Big Warrior laid the pipe across his arm, nodded once to Tecumseh, and then turned and went off the field.

Now Tecumseh and his warriors went to one quadrant of the field, and there they took crumbled tobacco and sumac leaves from their pouches and sprinkled it on the ground. They went on around the circle, doing this at each quadrant to sanctify the ground and keep bad spirits out of the council. Then, as the hushed crowd looked on, they returned to the pole in the center, went around it, and then shook the rest of the tobacco from the pouches into the fire. When they had done this, they were standing in a small circle around the pole, with the small fire smoking in their midst, large bonfires around them, the dense circle of Creek warriors around the council ground, the sprawling town of Tuckabatchee nearby, and the Tallapoosa River flowing deep and quiet nearby with the long star reflecting off its misty surface.

Suddenly this hush was rent by a pulsating shriek. Tecumseh's war cry then was magnified by the tremolo voices of his two dozen warriors, a chorus more fierce and primal than that of a wolf pack at twilight. The drumbeats began pounding like a great heartbeat, and the warriors leaped into the stalking posture. They moved in unison, following Tecumseh: a toe pointed and placed delicately upon the earth, then the heel set down, while the muscular bodies moved slowly in exaggerated postures of stealth, eyes darting left and right. Then the other foot, toe down, then heel down, arms slowly moving as if parting the foliage of a place of ambush, and the only sound the heartbeat pulse of the drum. In the circle they stalked their enemy, and the Creeks were with them in their hearts, feeling the tension build, hearing the tempo of the drumbeat gradually quicken.

Then the tremolo cry again, and at once the drum was pounding rapidly, taking the people's heartbeats up with it, and the dancing warriors were springing, crouching, whirling, swinging their clubs, and stabbing with their flashing knives. No warrior who had ever surprised and attacked an enemy, no youth who had ever dreamed of doing it, could fail to respond to the sight of those postures, those gestures, to imagine themselves this swift, this powerful, this fearless in the attack. The dancers yipped with every sudden move; they sprang shoulder high from the ground and landed crouched, grimacing, their eyes mad and mouths wolfish; they bounded forward, grappling with imaginary foes, stabbing them, then spun about to kill enemies behind them. So swift and hard were their strokes that the dance had had to be rehearsed and coordinated and practiced over and over, or these dancers with their flashing, naked blades might have hurt or killed each other in performance.

Firelight gleamed on their sweating muscles; they turned and leaped upon their own shadows. The Creek warriors looking on were wild-eyed now as they watched, and their own limbs twitched, their own hands clutched spasmodically, as their souls moved in battle with the dancers' souls. *Ai! That is how I would spring upon my enemy! Ai! So strong is my own arm! Ai! Now I stoop to take your scalp, you who were a great warrior but not so great as I!* The dancers now were in a crouch, and their knives flashed this way and that, and finally with an ululating cry of triumph they all leaped far off the ground and landed on the balls of their feet at the last thump of the drum, and stood with weapons in their right hands, their left hands thrust upward, and though their upraised hands were empty, the spectators for a moment saw scalps in them, blood dripping.

Then Tecumseh stood alone in the firelight, his chest heaving from the intense exertions of the dance. All his warriors had filed out from the circle. Of them only Seekabo remained on the council ground. He stood between Tecumseh and the chiefs, to translate. Here he would be at his best, the Muskhogean being his native tongue, the Creeks his own people. Seekabo waited, looking at Tecumseh.

Alone, a black-painted figure on the ceremonial ground of Tuckabatchee in the homeland of his mother, his shadow thrown in all directions by the bonfires around him, Tecumseh waited for his silent immobility to affect the thousands. His heart was fire, honey, and salt because of what he had learned here.

On arriving at Tuckabatchee he had inquired about Turtle Mother.

Ah, they had told him. Your mother has gone. Great in age and wisdom, she should have lain down in peace to sleep with a serene face. But some whites were here, and when they left, many people died of a disease which was like drowning out of water. She like many of the old and weak was among them. Come, we will show you where she is buried.

Now he stood alone in the middle of the council ground just as he had stood at her grave and remembered her face as he had seen it so long ago, beautiful but bitter with hatred for white men, and he remembered the warmth and comfort of her arms. The white men had killed his father, Hard Striker. They had killed his foster father, Black Fish. They had killed his beloved brother Chiksika in Tennessee and his brother Stands-Between at Fallen Timbers. They had driven his mother out from the Shawnee land into a lonely exile among the Creeks from whom she had grown so different, and at last, thirty years later, they had killed her with a disease instead of a bullet. All this was in Tecumseh's heart now as he began to speak:

"O Muskogee, my kin! People of my mother's blood!

"You have seen how the Shawnee strikes his enemy! You have seen his quickness, his strength! My warriors have shown you.

"Thus in the years of my youth I roamed through the south, and struck at white men who were doing wrong things. I made my knife taste their blood because they had taken the Sacred Hunting Grounds."

He spoke with nearly as much motion as he danced. His arms swept and arced as if with weapons. He coiled tight like a snake and then sprang forward to hurl challenges and taunts from his mouth. He reached for the sky and shook his arms as if creating the thunder in his own voice. The Creek warriors strained forward to watch and listen when he lowered his voice to hisses and whispers; they yipped when he shouted in passion.

"Once our people were many. On all the land from the sunset to the sunrise our campfires shone like stars rained out of the sky.

"Then the whites came. Our fires have dwindled; everywhere our people have passed away, as the snow in the mountains melts in the spring. We no longer rule the forest. Yes, brothers, our campfires are few. Those that still burn we must combine into a great fire!"

It was nearly daybreak when Tecumseh had finished. The Creek warriors were nearly in a frenzy; their hearts were twisted with sorrow and anger for what had been done on the land of the Great Good Spirit by the invaders from the slime of the Eastern Sea. Never had their souls been blown so high and low by words, so thrown about by gestures. The white man Samuel Dale had made himself as inconspicuous as he could, and his own head was spinning with the comprehension of what he had seen happen here. He had remembered everything so that he might report it to Hawkins and show what a danger was being created here, but he wondered if he would get out alive to report it. Such a passion these people were in!

And he knew he would never forget one particular sight: Big Warrior's own hand clenching his knife handle. Big Warrior himself!


But by the time of the council next day, something had turned inside Big Warrior. It was as if he thought he had been moved further than he should have been. He knew now that Tecumseh's night of oratory had made the Creek warriors eager to follow him into a war whose consequences he had not allowed them to think of. Big Warrior himself, who had to think of consequences for his people, had nearly leaped up in accord with the emotions Tecumseh had aroused in every man. But Big Warrior had thought much since then, and he had grown indignant about the influence this visitor had exerted upon his warriors, and he had talked in secret with

Dale and with cautious old chiefs. And now Big Warrior faced Tecumseh before the gathering and said:

"You are a bad man. I will not encourage my people to follow you to ruin."

Tecumseh drew his head back. His lips and eyes narrowed. For a long time he said nothing. Then he pointed his hand at Big Warrior's mottled face and cried for all the council to hear:

"Your blood is white! Even your skin is growing white, to show it! You have taken my talk, and the sticks, and the wampum, but you do not mean to help the red people! I know why. You do not believe that the Great Good Spirit wants this done. You do not believe that he has sent me on this holy mission!

"You shall know! When I return to the north I will stamp my foot on the ground, and here in Tuckabatchee you will feel the earth shake!"

Now Big Warrior once again felt himself being jarred, almost intimidated, by the boldness of Tecumseh's words and startled by the fire in Tecumseh's eyes, which looked as intense as if Weshemoneto's own eyes were drilling into him with contempt. The council had become a hum of awed voices at those last words.

Tecumseh knew that whether Big Warrior finally condoned or condemned him in the council, many of the Creek warriors had perceived the truth and importance of his plea and were eager to join in resisting the white men. When the earth trembled and the dust rose and the river ran backward, it would shake them loose from all fear and doubt, and they would take up arms against the Americans!

# CHAPTER 34

## *Tippecanoe*
## *November 6, 1811*

I expect nothing whatsoever to come of this parley," General Harrison said to the officers standing around his little field table. "That humbug is only stalling."

The officers nodded, their elegant bicorn and beaver hats bobbing up and down. They all wore capes and cloaks against the raw, misty cold. Nearby, mauls thudded on tent stakes, soldiers yelled and grumbled, axes thudded, and saws rasped as the army set up officers' tents and gathered deadwood for bonfires. The aroma of beef boiling in kettles for the evening mess was already spreading in the dank air. There was a rustle of heavy canvas as a team of privates grunted and raised Harrison's white marquee tent a few yards away. The general went on:

"Here is what I mean to do, gentlemen. We will meet with this Shawnee prophet tomorrow as he has requested. We will restate our demand that he disperse his warriors now and forever. I do not expect him to comply. He will probably plead for more time, more councils.

"But he won't get them. If he doesn't yield to our demands tomorrow, we'll wait till they've gone to their huts, then fall upon the town and destroy it. Burn it down, and burn their harvest."

Colonel Boyd, commander of the regulars, cleared his throat. "Governor, sir, I've been thinking we'd do better to strike them now."

"Aye!"

"Aye! My thinking, too!"

"Now! Yes!"

"Why let them ready themselves, Gov'nor?"

The militia officers were eager. Harrison held up his hand, tilted his head, and lightly shut his eyes and waited for their clamor to stop. A cavalry troop was noisily setting up its camp on either side of the staff officers' compound. "Gentlemen," he said, raising his voice to be heard over the noise, "no one is more eager than I to break up this nest of banditti. That's why I brought you here. But the president and the secretary of war both have urged me to do it without force if that's at all possible. So we shall try that by talk. If talk doesn't work, as I expect it won't, we'll treat them to buckshot and bayonets. Your boys will have their chance to do what they came here for."

Actually, Harrison well knew in his own mind, the president probably would have apoplexy if he knew the army was here. Harrison had been authorized to march his army only to the edge of the treaty lands as a show of force. By coming into the heart of the Indian lands like this, he was committing just such an act of aggression as the old Greenville Treaty forbade. But the president was too far removed from the Prophet's establishment to understand what a Damocles' sword it was over Vincennes, what an obstacle it was to settlement and statehood, what a vipers' pit of British intrigue it had become. Harrison figured that he knew the situation and its remedy better, and that the national administration would, after he had solved the problem quickly and neatly, admit that the end had justified his means.

Dusk settled early over the Wabash valley, under the gloom of low, drizzling clouds. Charcoal Burner's scouts watched Harrison build his camp on the narrow, wooded plateau a mile west of Prophet's Town, and they noted every detail. The plateau was covered with an open oak forest, among whose trees the army had set up a defensive perimeter in somewhat the shape of a footprint. The long east side of the elevation looked over a marshy, grassy bottomland that stretched along the Wabash toward Prophet's Town, and along this side, for a distance of three hundred paces, were posted a large part of the Blue-Coat regulars, interspersed with units of the Indiana Hunting-Shirts. At the south end, or heel, of the encampment, the Yellow Jacket militia could be clearly seen setting up their tight salient, their horses tethered inside. In the woods at the wider north end of the camp were the Beaver-Hats, also with their horses tethered inside. The west side of the plateau dropped off abruptly twenty feet into a willow-thicketed ravine through which gurgled a fast, rocky-bottomed creek on its way to the Wabash-se-pe. This long side of the camp was guarded by a small body of Blue-Coats and a long line of Indiana Hunting-Shirts. In the heart of the camp stood the officers' white tents, protected by horse soldiers. Supply wagons were also inside the perimeter, the beef cattle were grazing in the lowland beyond the camp of the Yellow Jackets, and there were

sentries stationed everywhere outside the lines. Charcoal Burner noticed
that although the soldiers were cutting a great amount of wood, they were
not building breastworks with it but only making big stacks of firewood.

Charcoal Burner stayed near the army's camp until nightfall, moving
from one sheltered place to another, observing everything, hearing the
snatches of voices, singing, and laughter in the hush of the wind, sending
his scouts all around the camp or back to Prophet's Town to report on the
army's doings. Finally he himself went back to hear what the chief warriors
would be saying in their council about this army whose bonfires glowed
within sight of the holy town.

He found them in the council lodge, in a semicircle in front of Open
Door, urging him to do something to protect the women and children.
They were making all kinds of suggestions. Some were in favor of moving
the whole population away up the Tippecanoe under cover of darkness;
others recommended that Harrison be seized and stabbed during the parley
the next day.

Open Door sat with his cloak drawn over his shoulders, his face set hard
and stern to conceal the doubts and fears that billowed inside him. As if to
forestall a need to decide, he asked Charcoal Burner to tell everything he
had seen of the American camp.

It was apparent that the Long Knife general was very alert, Charcoal
Burner told them, and he described the thoroughness with which the
defense had been put up even though tomorrow was to be a peace parley
day. White Loon, a Wea warrior chief, seized on that and expressed his fear
that the white men had built no barricades because they had come here to
attack in the night, not to defend themselves. "They will come out of their
camp in the night and fall upon our town!" he cried. "Why else would they
not build barricades when they are so close to us? Would white men dare
to sleep without a fence around them? No! They mean to come and kill us
in our sleep!"

"We must strike them in the night, or they will strike us," insisted the
Kaskaskia war chief, Stone Eater. The Winnebagoes in one excited voice
agreed. They were infuriated by the threat these Americans were posing
to their families, who had traveled so far to be safe in this holy town under
Weshemoneto's cloak. "Though the Great Good Spirit has let the Long
Knives come this far, he will not let them destroy us," said Wood, another
war chief. "Father, you said we will always be safe here, that no one can
hurt the town. You told us that anyone who tries to hurt your people will
die or go crazy."

"Yes," Open Door said in a strange voice. He seemed to be seeing
something far away. He was not slumping as much as he had been, and there

was a keen edge on his eye now. "Yes, that is what I said, and what I say is true." He was thinking now about that vision he had had, of the soldiers lying dead or crazy in their blankets, of Harrison being stabbed in his bed. He turned his eye upon Charcoal Burner and said, "In that army camp, you saw Harrison's tent so that you are sure of it?"

"Yes."

"How does it look?"

"A white tent, larger than the others, held up by a pole in the middle."

"And is it among trees?"

"There are large oaks nearby."

"Are there soldiers near it?"

"As I saw, from far away, there were horse soldiers camping on two sides of it and walking soldiers everywhere else. It is in the middle of hundreds of soldiers."

"And," Open Door asked, "the tent is in firelight?"

"Their entire camp is full of great bonfires to keep them warm." Charcoal Burner wondered what was the reason for these questions. He had already said these things. But he could see that the look in Open Door's face was changing from fearful to sharp. He was quiet, thinking.

And now into the stillness, White Loon spoke. "Since our father tells us they cannot hurt this town, then their coming here means that We-shemoneto has delivered the white men soldiers into our hands. They have come to our town but cannot hurt us, and so it must be that he means for us to kill them here!"

"They are forbidden by their own treaties to be here," said another deep voice, "and so they must be punished for coming. I, Stone Eater, say we must strike them tonight while they sleep, for I fear they mean to do that to us."

"No!" Charcoal Burner cried. "Do you forget what your leader Tecumseh told you? We are not to fight Harrison!"

"Tecumseh is not here, and Harrison is," retorted Stone Eater. "If Tecumseh were here and saw Harrison's fires so close, he would say, 'Kill them!' "

"No! He would not!" exclaimed Charcoal Burner. "He would have had us move out of their way before they got so close!"

"I"—Open Door's voice suddenly overrode this argument—"I, Tenskwatawa, am the leader of the People. It is unfortunate that my brother Tecumseh is far away. But I am the leader in this place! And the Great Good Spirit has told me what must be done. It is true that he has delivered the Americans into our hands. Look at their camp! They are in the open, with no fort to hide in. They have not even built barricades. They are surrounded by darkness, and are lying blind in the heart of my country. We know this land, and they are strangers in it. Not even St. Clair so long ago was in such a sorry circumstance as Harrison has put himself in this night. My children, listen well to me, for I tell you now what the Great Good Spirit has shown me we must do! Listen:

"Some one of our warriors will kill Harrison in his bed, this night!"

Suddenly they were all still, listening, astonished, their eyes ablaze.

"He is to die with a knife in his heart," Open Door said. As he talked, his speech growing rapid now, he was pulling his string of beans through his palm, and his eye was closed. "I have been shown this, in a clear light. Who among you has a knife with a handle of horn?"

Most had British steel knives with red wooden handles. But several warriors raised their knives to show the handles of horn, and both Stone Eater and White Loon were among them. A peculiar light was beginning to show in their eyes now. Perhaps one of them would be the one who was to kill Harrison the land stealer, Harrison the invader. What fame there would be for the warrior who did that! But now Charcoal Burner interrupted again:

"Harrison sleeps among a thousand soldiers, if he sleeps at all! No one could get to his tent! I have seen their camp!"

"Brother," growled Wood, "you have seen only what your eyes showed you. Our father the Prophet has seen what the Master of Life showed him."

"I am a holy man, not a warrior," Open Door said now in that extraordinary voice he used in his sermons and his great pronouncements. "I cannot plan a battle. I can only give warriors the guidance of my vision, and the blessing and protection of the Great Good Spirit. I am not a warrior, but I am aware that no single warrior can penetrate a thousand soldiers to stab their commander. *But!* However many warriors it would take to force their way to Harrison's tent, it would take only one knife to go into his heart!"

"Listen," the warriors began hissing to each other. "Hear him! He says it can be done!"

"No!" Charcoal Burner cried again. His eyes burned on Open Door's profile, but the Prophet would not turn to look in his eyes. White Loon said to Charcoal Burner:

"Brother, do not be afraid of the white men who can shoot squirrels from horseback. They will be in their blankets, not on their horses." Some of the warriors snickered cruelly at Charcoal Burner. White Loon went on: "They are calico peddlers! Their hands are soft! They are afraid! Maybe their commander is brave, but he will be dead!"

"Yes," Open Door cried. "And the soldiers will not be able to defend him. You will find them dead, or crazy! I have seen it, I tell you! Make your plan! Let me hear how you would go into the army camp and kill him. . . . Wait!'' He turned to Charcoal Burner now and said, "Shabbona, are you with me, or against me?''

"Father, you know I counsel against this. But what is decided, if I cannot stop it, I will help you. But I wish you would listen to the words your brother told you before he went away.''

"Charcoal Burner is with us, and I rejoice,'' Open Door told them, "for he is one of the best among us. Now, my warriors. We have a sacred duty given us by the Master of Life. Let us hear how it is to be done.''


Corporal Stephen Mars was awakened by a hand on his shoulder. He was groggy; his limbs were numb; it had taken him two hours to fall asleep despite his fatigue from the march and camp building. The cold, the dampness of his clothes and blanket, the tiny attacks of fleas and lice in the few warm parts of his body, and the necessity of sleeping in full uniform on the hard ground with his hard, knobby rifle for a bedmate had combined with the awful anxiety of being camped in the open one mile from a town of hostile savages and one hundred fifty miles from home to keep him wretchedly, nervously awake until he finally had dropped into a fitful sleep. Now, feeling weak, exhausted, and above all vulnerable, he was being awakened to go outside the firelight into the black, drippy woods and stand there on guard against Indians.

Even while riding in broad daylight, well fed and well rested, on a strong war-horse with a thousand troops around him, Corporal Mars had not been as fearless as he felt he should be. But these next four hours would be, he was sure, the worst test of his private courage he had ever faced or ever would, he was sure it would be, and his dread was so deep and dark that had he not been in the middle of Indian country he might have considered deserting rather than go on guard duty. But there was this to do and no way out.

A few minutes later he was outside the glow of the firelit camp, standing in pitch blackness with his back to a tree trunk, rifle under his cloak to keep the drizzle from wetting his powder, listening with all his might for rustlings or breathings he prayed he would not have to hear. He was outside the northwest corner of the encampment. In front of him, although he could not see it, was the forest. Off to his left he could hear the monotonous trickling of the creek that ran under the bluff. In a way he was glad of the creek's noise; he probably would have been even more scared in a total silence. But on the other hand, sometimes it would override some tiny, stealthy noise he would think he was almost hearing, and then its trickle would be infuriating and frustrating as he tried to penetrate it for the frightful little sound. A possum could sound like a band of sneaking savages, and vice versa. It was better to hear nothing at all. But on the other hand, if there were a noise, he had sure as hell better hear it.

Mars was a member of Captain Geiger's Kentuckians, from Jefferson County near Louisville. He knew that this angle he guarded so blindly was considered a part of the rear line, the front line being the part that faced the redskins' town, and he was a little grateful for that. But would the redskins consider it that way? Had the governor told them *that* was the side they should sneak up on? No. But it would be almost better to be over on that side, he thought. At least I'd be looking over grass and could maybe *see* a dang Injun if one come a-creepin' along. But how am I supposed to see anything here, where everything's all uneven and everything's a little blacker than everything else? Had that comet thing for a bit of light when we started. But these dad-blame rain clouds . . .

Now and then he turned around to look back toward the dim fireglow of the encampment as if to reassure himself that it was still there, that he was not alone in an unlit, dripping universe. He could see, or thought he could, the white peak of General Harrison's tent away back there beyond the branches. Wisht it was him, he thought, havin' to stand out here all stark alone. It's him brought us here.

Then he quit looking back because his eyes would have to adjust to the pitch blackness again. Besides, whenever he moved, his clothes made brushing sounds that spooked him.

A drop of rainwater, falling from a twig onto dead leaf, made him start, his heart slamming, and for a while his fright made him keep watching a place of extra-black blackness that had seemed to shift. But since he couldn't really even see it, how could he see if it had shifted? He shivered. His feet were wet.

And then a hushing sound grew louder, blotting up the trickle of the distant creek, and cold rain began going down his collar.

Ungodly damnation! he thought.

And then he thought that a profanity like that, at a time when he needed all the Almighty's help he could get, might tempt disaster.

Lord, forgive me for cussin'. Lord, help me get through till daylight, and I swear I'll never say another cuss word. Lord, please make sure all them Injuns are sound asleep over in their town. See to it they got enough sense not to be a-sneakin' around in cold rain. Lord, keep all redskins at least a mile off from me till daytime, and I promise I'll be your pious and dutiful sarvant all the rest of my natural days.

But Lordy, Lordy, he thought after a while, wouldn't it pride me to fetch home the scalp o' one o' them goddamn heathens!

Draped in a long fur robe, head covered by the crow-feather cap with its outstretched wings, Open Door dismounted, handed the reins of his horse to one of his bodyguards, and walked carefully down the prairie path through the rainy darkness toward the cliff's edge. Weshemoneto was guiding his steps, but he went very slowly. When he felt the bare rock instead of grass under his feet, he knew he was near the edge of the cliff and stopped. He could not see the drop-off below but could feel the space of it, could hear the rain in the treetops below.

Two hundred feet down and two hundred yards to the southeast, he could see the glow and twinkle of the many bonfires in Harrison's camp. They were still burning high, despite the hours of rain and drizzle; the sentries must have been fueling them throughout the night. Good. It was as he had prophesied. There would be light in the enemy camp for his warriors to see by, as he had told them there would be. The sky in the east had not yet begun to lighten; on a rainy morning like this in this season there would be nearly two more hours of darkness, and the watch soldiers would not be able to see the warriors who were now stealing in on all sides.

Open Door tried to discern Harrison's tent in the glowing camp below, but it was hidden by the screen of bare branches.

There was not a sound above the hiss of the rainfall, the whiff of the cold wind, and the gurgling of water down the rivulets of the bluff and the creek below, not a sound to hint at the movement of nine hundred warriors through the valley. Open Door thought of them, his hardy and courageous young men slithering like snakes through the marshes and meadows and wet woods everywhere down there, closer and closer to the soldier camp, and his heart ached with concern for them. He gripped his medicine fire stick in one hand and his sacred beans in the other and put his head back to pray silently for them, to draw down from above the clouds the protection of Weshemoneto; he could feel the clean cold rain on his face, and his soul, like an opening bellows, drawing downward the power of heaven. His years of doubt were over. At last, as the planning of this holy war had begun in the council lodge a few hours ago, Open Door had felt the power returning to him, and he had begun to see everything that would happen. The entire attack had been planned upon his visions. Through the night the chief warriors of his united tribes had talked over the details of the attack, their confidence of victory growing, and then all the warriors had gathered, painted and armed, some with guns but many with the Indians' own silent and blessed weapon, the bow, and with their tomahawks and clubs, spears and knives; they had gathered in a dimly lit clearing invisible to the Americans, and he had blessed them and told them the Master of Life would protect them. Most of the soldiers would be still in their blankets, dead or crazy and unable to resist. They would be blinded by the darkness in which the Indians moved, but the bonfires in the camp would be like a sun to show the warriors their helpless enemy. The white men's guns would be useless because Open Door would send rain and hail to dampen their powder, but with Weshemoneto's help and their own prudence, those warriors using guns would have dry powder. And of course those using bows would not even have to think of keeping powder dry. He had told them that the Master of Life had given them medicine this night to gain a great victory over the Americans. The medicine would spread confusion in the Long Knives' camp, and even those who could get up from their blankets would fall in a stupor.

But the most sacred duty to be performed in the attack, that which would assure the victory, had been delegated to a hundred warriors under Stone Eater and White Loon. This hundred would steal up from the woods at the creek's edge, the most lightly guarded side, to the northwest edge of the camp, as close as they could get to Harrison's tent, even past the sentries if they could, and at the sound of a deer-hoof rattle they would rush through the sleeping Americans, killing them as they went, straight to the door of Harrison's tent, and they would kill him. All these hundred were warriors with horn-handled knives. If they were discovered before they penetrated the lines, they would give the war cry, and all the other hundreds encircling the camp would take up the cry and attack all around the army camp. In the chaos this would create, the chosen hundred would be able to pour into the heart of the camp and kill Harrison. "In case Harrison might already be awake and moving about in his camp," Charcoal Burner had said, "he rides a light gray horse. My scouts could have shot him from his saddle twenty times, except that we were not supposed to provoke."

"When Harrison dies," Open Door had promised them, "any soldiers that are still alive will run and hide in the grass like little quails, and then they will be caught and made servants to the women of our town!"

So now Open Door, the greatest prophet and shaman the red men had ever known, stood on this stone cliff over the valley, feeling the invisible net tightening around Harrison's army below him, knowing this holy mission could not fail, and he felt his soul to be as vast as the sky that looked down, as he did, upon the approaching victory. The power was all his now. Tecumseh had always warned that the Americans could not be defeated until all the alliance was complete, until his sign of the shaking earth came. But Tecumseh had assumed too much power. He had acted as if he were still the older brother, as if his leadership in games of war were more important than Open Door's magic. And though it was true that Tecumseh had done wondrous things, it was also true that Open Door's own visions and spiritual powers had drawn the Peoples together in the first place and had kept them full of hope and faith. And Tecumseh would come home from the south to find that *Open Door* had defended the town and killed their strongest enemy!

Yes, it was true that Tecumseh was a great leader. But, Open Door thought as he waited on the stone cliff for the great holy battle to begin, was it not I, Tenskwatawa, who commanded the sun to go dark? It was I!

William Henry Harrison had not slept well.

Physically he was comfortable enough. His field cot in the tent was nearly as pleasant as his own big bed at Grouseland, and the rain on the canvas of the tent had been soothing. But conscience and worry had been attacking him, and from several angles. He had thought of his soldiers out there trying to sleep fully clothed on the ground—mud now, surely—in that soaking rain. If only it hadn't rained, he had been thinking. He hoped they wouldn't all come down sick. And the poor lads will require so much cleaning up to make a good show at the parley, he thought.

Then he had started thinking about the parley. Once in the night he had awakened to the nagging hunch that the Shawnee prophet might try to murder him. He had made a mental note to talk with Colonel Owen and Colonel Boyd in the morning about precautions at the council. Only, say, six Indians inside our lines for the parley, perhaps. They wouldn't dare anything then. Then he had thought: I'm glad it's to be the Prophet instead of Tecumseh. I don't think Tecumseh would be afraid to, even under those odds. He remembered, with a shudder, that time more than a year ago when Tecumseh had stood facing him with that gleaming tomahawk raised.

It was hard not to think of Tecumseh, even though he was surely still far away in the south somewhere. But what if he's back? Harrison had thought. A thought like that could grow large in the still of the night, and it had.

Again, surprisingly, Harrison's conscience had nagged him. Tecumseh had asked him not to do anything like this until he could return and talk to the president. And although Harrison certainly had not promised anything, he knew that he was deceiving a man he admired.

But he's my enemy. You deceive your enemy if you can.

And now those thoughts made him doubly glad Tecumseh was away, far away. If Tecumseh were here, he thought, he'd be mad enough, and bold enough, to attack us tonight.

The Prophet wouldn't, he thought. He's intimidated. Our threatening maneuvers near his town really humbled him.

Strange, he thought, that those two are brothers. Such opposites! The best and the worst!

Harrison stretched. The cot creaked. The stretching told him how tired he really was, and he shut his eyes, hoping he might sleep a few minutes more. Surely it isn't four yet, he thought. He always roused the troops at four in the morning when in Indian country, because dawn was the savages' favorite hour for attack. Orthodox military wisdom was that Indians are afraid to fight in the dark, for fear their souls would get lost if they were killed or some such aboriginal superstition.

Harrison listened to the sound of the camp beyond the patter of the rain on the canvas: just the crackling of the fires, now and then a cough, the stamp and snort of the horses tethered beside the officers' tents, and in the distance now and then a restless lowing from down in the beef herd. He let his mind go fuzzy and tried to think of absolutely nothing. For a little while he worried about not having erected breastworks, but then he made himself stop thinking about that. That sham shaman is too meek now to come near this camp, he assured himself, and soon that worry dissolved to naught.

With his eyes shut, General Harrison did not see the man's shadow that moved across the firelit canvas to the door flap of his tent. The shadow paused for a moment. Then the tent flap was raised, and a figure slipped into the tent and stood by the cot. Hesitantly one hand reached toward the cot. Harrison, not quite back to sleep yet, had felt the dank, fresh air come into the tent and could smell wet clothing a few inches away.

"Yes?" he said.

For a moment there was no response. Then:

"Bugler, sir. Shall I sound reveille? It's onto four o'clock."

Harrison chuckled. "No bugle this morning. Those Indians over in town might think it's a bad spirit and stampede. But do go about and start shaking the staff officers. Wake Colonel Owen first, and tell him I need to talk with him right away."

"Yes, sir."

"Thank you, son. Then get the cooks up, if they aren't yet. Like to have the men awake, fed, and watchful by dawn."

"Yes, sir," the bugler replied, and ducked out.

Harrison sighed, threw back his blankets, and sat up on the edge of the creaking cot in his flannel undergarments, his breath condensing, and muttered:

"Dreadful day for a parley. Just dreadful."

Corporal Mars desperately needed to urinate, but he was afraid to move. He still couldn't see much of anything; even though the fires in camp apparently were being built up, he was too far out in the woods to get much benefit from their light. He couldn't really see anything, but he kept thinking he was seeing something. When he would look directly at a place in the dark, he could make out nothing. But sometimes in the corner of his eye he would see—or think he saw—something moving slowly, close to the ground. Then he would stare at it and decide it was a thing—a fallen log, a bush—that had always been there. And he could not quite get up the initiative to move away from his tree and probe whatever it was to make sure. He surely didn't want to probe a log and have it jump up with a tomahawk in its hand.

This had been the longest four hours of his life. He had stuck to the side of that tree like part of its own bark, hardly even turning his head, for about four years, it seemed to him. He ached everywhere, and his bladder was full up to about his ears. Now he was sure his watch was about over. If they were building up the fires, it must be close to four.

He shivered again, thinking, There's scarce any misery known to mortal man worse than being cold and needing to piss, both at once. But he sure wasn't going to unbutton and do it now. Making water would be noisy, for one thing, and by damn, if those *were* Injuns he was seeing in the corners of his eyes, he didn't want to get his throat cut whilst holding his pizzle in his hand. So he would just hold out till the guard sergeant let him off post. I'll wait, he thought, till I'm relieved afore I relieve myself, and he smiled. It was the first time he had smiled in a long time.

Just then he heard something, very close. A soft rustling. A little off to his left. His heart leaped up and pounded like a hammer till he couldn't hear anything but his pulse. And on a low shape he had thought was a fallen log, he saw a glint of reflected firelight.

He drew his rifle out from under his cloak and eased back the hammer, scared that its click would be heard fifty yards in every direction. The click *was* loud.

The glint on the fallen log was gone now, and he began wondering if it had been just a drop of rainwater picking up the firelight. Just to be a bit safer, he pointed the rifle toward it. Then he heard something nearby on his right, a tiny knocking sound, and at the same time he inhaled a sniff of something different from the tangy, loamy smell of the rain-wet woods: something half like tobacco and half like the muskrat smell he had got to know so well as a sometime trapper down home.

God help me, he thought. Now he had the strong notion that there was one Indian on either side of him. And if there were two, how many others might there be? Which one should he shoot? He couldn't see anyone to hit if he did shoot. He would only have time to shoot once, not reload. Frantic plans tumbled in his mind. He would shoot quick, then run back into the lines as fast as he could. So what if he woke up the whole camp? It was time they were up anyway. Especially if these were Indians, not figments of his fright. He'd stood alone long enough, by God. If he shot and there weren't any Indians around after all, that would be as embarrassing as all get-out. But it would be better to be embarrassed than dead.

Then, as he was bringing his gun barrel slowly around to the right, he had a confusing thought:

What if it's just the next sentry?

Lordy, it might be. Everybody in this dang army does smell of tobacco.

He wondered if he dared whisper the challenge. He decided he'd better. The words formed in his mouth as he shivered and strained to hold his bladder, the words *Who goes there?*

But just as he was about to say it, he saw in the edges of his vision that there were movements everywhere around him. Left and right, in front, even something between him and the camp, silhouetted by fireglow.

Oh, almighty God, make me a place in Paradise, he thought. I done waited too long.

He turned away from the tree and aimed at the only one he could really see, the form silhouetted by the fireglow. He squeezed the trigger.

The flash from the flintlock and the muzzle were blinding after all the darkness, and the shot sounded like the end of the world. In its echo came a short scream of pain.

And then, as Corporal Mars started to run toward the camp on his stiffened legs, he could hear movement all around him. He had gone three steps when something hit him in the back with such force that it numbed him clear through his chest, and he fell on his face in the wet leaves. When he put his hand under his chest to raise himself, he felt an arrowhead protruding from his front. Under his palm were cold wet leaves. On the back of his hand was his hot blood. And now he thought he was hearing all the wailing wolves in the world.

He had forgotten about his bladder. He lay there on the cold wet leaves and everything leaked out of him. Hope, strength, everything.


Governor Harrison was sitting on the edge of his cot pulling on his other boot when he heard a shot, then a scream, not far away, surely no more than one or two hundred yards, up in the northwest sector somewhere. The Kentucky flank, he thought.

And then at once there came from that direction that most hair-raising of all the sounds he had ever heard: countless Indians all giving their pulsating shrieks.

An uproar immediately swept through the whole camp. Men were shouting, horses whinnying, things bumping, feet thudding. A staccato racket of gunfire erupted in that same quarter just as Harrison emerged from his tent door, pulling on his saber belt. He stepped out into a garish, firelit chaos. Horses had pulled loose their tethers and were rearing and galloping about, wild-eyed. Men were struggling out of their sodden blankets everywhere, trying to avoid the horses, or were already up, some kneeling, some standing, in every attitude of confusion, some with their muskets and rifles in their hands, their faces looking stricken as men's faces can look only when they are hurled from sleep into panic. Rain was spitting down into the light of the smoky bonfires. The shrill howling was unnerving and frightfully close by. Lead balls were whacking into wagons, tents, horseflesh, men. Some of the soldiers who had just stood up now reeled and fell, arrows sticking in them. A nearby soldier's head twitched, and bits of something spattered the side of Harrison's face. Absently wiping it off, he saw that it was bloody bits of someone's flesh.

"Colonel Owen!" he shouted. "Where are you? Boyd!" Some kind of tremendous mayhem was under way up by the Kentuckians and in that part of the rear line where Major Baen's detachment of the Fourth Infantry had camped: a terrifying uproar of shooting, war whoops, commands, running, clattering, and screaming. And it was coming, spreading toward the center of the camp. Now Harrison thought he was hearing a similar commotion beginning to build up over on the front line, on the east side of the camp. "Up! Up! You officers! Form up your troops! Get them on line!" Harrison bellowed at the top of his mighty voice, trotting around the edge of his tent to get his gray mare. She was not there. He saw her rear end disappear around the tent. There was a bay still tethered there, though, yanking at its tether. Quickly he ran his hand down its face to calm it, undid the reins, and mounted. The animal, terrified by the roar of gunfire and especially by the screaming of Indians, whirled twice before he could get it settled down and put his spurs in to head toward the heaviest fighting. He kept shouting for his aide as he went.

Colonel Abraham Owen, the general's aide, saw his commander's gray mare trotting, riderless, among the tents and darted out to catch her. His first thought was that Harrison must have been shot off her back, but he heard him shouting in the distance, again heard him calling. As he tugged the reins he saw all the officers' tents twitching as bullets slapped through them. Soldiers were gasping and screaming and falling down. An arrow flicked past his nose and broke against a tree. Again now he heard Governor Harrison's voice calling his name in the din and heard him bellow, "Get those fires put out!" Colonel Owen chased the mare through a couple of pirouettes and finally got a foot in the stirrup, swung up, and spurred her in the direction of Harrison's voice. Suddenly he was astonished to see painted warriors running right through the firelit heart of the camp, screaming their curdled screams, shooting at the milling soldiers with guns and bows. At last the troops were awake enough to do something, those who weren't simply petrified, and Blue-Coats were rushing pell-mell against the savages, shooting them down, bayoneting them, or clubbing them with their gunstocks. Two hideous-looking painted warriors with shaved heads were sprinting toward the marquee tent. Colonel Owen cocked his pistol and aimed at one, but the mare wheeled and started running, and he lost his target. He reined her around and spurred her toward General Harrison's voice. He could now see the general riding on a bay horse near the thickest of the fighting, saber upraised, shouting orders. Owen rode toward him, shouting, "I'm here, Gen'l!"

A Winnebago, crouching between a dead soldier and a campfire to reload his rifle, saw the big, splendid-looking officer riding by, shouting, on the gray horse they had spoken of, and he knew it must be Harrison. There was no time to finish loading his own gun. He dropped it, snatched up the weapon of the soldier he had just killed, and shot Colonel Abraham Owen through the body. He screeched with exultation as the officer fell sideways off the horse into the mud and dashed toward the body, drawing his knife to take the most prized scalp. But a bullet slammed into his temple, and he tumbled dead beside the colonel's body.


On the cliff beyond the creek, the Prophet stood in the cold drizzle watching and listening. His heart was pounding fast.

All that was happening down there was his doing! It was he who had made the sun go dark, and now it was he who had made this equally great thing happen! He imagined that every gunshot that rose to his ears was the death of a white soldier. He felt that surely Harrison was dead in his tent by now. His heart drank up the continuous music of the war cries. What a glorious ferocity in his people as they defended their holy town from the white governor's criminal intents!

And all the predictions he had made seemed to be proving true. The rain surely was ruining the Americans' powder. The campfires had grown brighter just before the start of the conflict and must be giving his warriors all the illumination he had promised them. Surely this would all be done soon, a total victory for the allied warriors, every soldier dead or a captive. A strong shudder of exultation shook him, and he raised his face to the unseen rain and spread his arms. The power and spirit of his warriors he had brought down from heaven and directed into their bodies as they had encircled the enemy camp; now they were fighting the enemy with all that power and spirit, and the Master of Life must be thanked.

So, in his piercing, throaty voice he chanted, so loudly it could be heard even in the roar of the battle below, a prayer of thanks and a plea for still more courage and protection for the fighters below.

O Great and Good Master
You have answered my call!
You have sent strength pouring down.
I have caught it in the cup of my heart
And my warriors, your children,
Have drunk from it
And it nourishes their blood!
It warms them as they steal through the cold,
It fills their arms with strength,
And they strike! They strike!
And they are killing the Evil Thing,
Washing away the Spawn of the Serpent!
Hear them O Good Master!
Hear them exult from their throats
As they destroy the Evil Thing!
O Great and Good Master
Father of all our race
Who now stand together unbreakable
A bundle of living sticks!
Give still your courage to us
And put your hand in the way
Of the soldiers' bullets
A little while more
Until the Evil Thing is crushed!

He sang, and his voice was throughout the valley of his home, his voice flew down like a swooping bird and into every pause in the roar of the battle and into the ears of the warriors around the battlefield, and they sped forward through the cold wet grass of the marsh, they slipped forward from tree to tree in the woods, they stood swinging and shooting into the faces of the Blue-Coats and the beaver-hats and the hunting-shirts who kept coming out to the edge of the camp and forming into ranks and lines. Never had warriors stood fighting so furiously in the face of such volleys of gunfire, never had they burst from cover like this to throw themselves at lines of bayonets.

On the cliff, Open Door finished his prayer and looked down now at the blur of yellowish smoke, that glowing, roaring, howling turmoil in this pocket of a black, cold, rainy universe, and even in his exalted state he could see that the combat was not diminishing yet. In fact, it seemed to grow louder and more furious. And something about it was troubling. Instead of being all along the wedge of land, the combat seemed to be concentrated mostly at the north end only.

And if White Loon and Stone Eater and their chosen hundred had penetrated to Harrison's tent and killed him, why was the battle going on so long? By now Open Door had expected to hear nothing but the screams of dying or fleeing soldiers and the joyous yipping of warriors in triumph and pursuit. Instead it was a continuous crackle and thunder of gunshots, going on and on, mostly at the upper end of the camp, and he could hear the big, deep shouts of officer soldiers.

And, strangest of all, it was growing darker down there. He could see muzzle blasts flickering like sparks down among the leafless oaks, but the glow of the bonfires was less and less. Open Door looked down at this change and wondered if something might be going wrong.

He took a necklace of deer hooves from his neck and held it up, and shook it, and rattled the hooves toward the dark sky, and resumed his prayer for help and protection.


Soldiers who were not yet on their lines around the perimeter had got the order to douse the bonfires and were snatching up rain-damp blankets from the ground and throwing them over the flames or beating the flames madly with them; some were kicking the fires apart with their boots and scattering the firebrands over the wet ground; cooks and staff soldiers were fetching pails and kettles of water and emptying them on the flames. In the last dull, reddening light of the dying fires, the army camp was like a half-extinguished inferno of tortured figures all dimmed by a choking pall of smoke and steam, stinking of wet ashes, smoldering wool, and gunpowder. The fires had been giving the savages too much of an advantage, silhouetting their targets and showing them where everything was. Now as the flames were extinguished it became more of an equal contest, but a more terrifying one. Men stood trembling in ranks, firing outward into the blackness where muzzle blasts flashed. They groped in their cartouche bags, tore the paper ends off powder cartridges with their teeth, poured powder down their hot gun barrels in total darkness, rammed home patch and ball, primed their flashpans blindly, and fired into the howling darkness again. And every few moments a comrade would grunt or screech and fall thrashing against their legs, or somebody else's gun muzzle would blast out right at their ear, or men would accidentally strike each other with their guns as they loaded and manipulated them in the dark.

Some of the men stood shooting in the darkness with arrows sticking in their flesh, tears in their eyes, and urine or feces oozing down their leggings. There had been that heart-stopping awakening and then this howling death storm ever since, without a moment for anyone to do the morning labors at the latrines.

In some places along the perimeter, the units had been unable to form or had formed and been scattered, and those places were the most terrifying. Soldiers and warriors were all intermixed, striking and choking, grunting and dying, all around. Here a man would find or collide with another man, and the two would have to grope over each other to know whether this was friend or foe. Shako or feathers? Deerhide or wool? Blades and clubs and rifle butts slashed and thudded unseen, only felt. Only the flash of gunfire nearby would, like intermittent lightning, reveal for an instant the identity of friend or enemy, the shape of the skirmish. Many a man in these tangles of invisible chaos was left wondering if his own last act on earth might have been the maiming or killing of one of his comrades.

Captain Spier Spencer's Yellow Jackets, down at the far southern heel of the encampment, had leaped out of their slumbers at the first shots and shouts, had stumbled in the darkness into ranks facing the marsh, and then had waited there in uncertainty and growing terror for a long time, hearing the din of battle swell to the north of them, hearing the war cries and shooting erupt along the Fourth Infantry sector behind their left flank, hearing now and then through the uproar an ungodly, eerie singsong of a voice from away up on the prairie to their right, and waited for they knew not what or how long, while Captain Spencer's gravelly voice talked their courage up. Then finally from the cold darkness outside their lines came the bellowing and thunderous hoofbeats of the stampeding beef herd, followed at once by a chilling chorus of war whoops and a blazing hail of gunshots. Dozens of militiamen fell at once. Captain Spencer stood bleeding from the head, yelling at his men to stand their ground and fight on. Bullets smashed through both his thighs, and he kept commanding from where he lay in his own blood on the ground. Only when a ball passed through his body did his voice fall still. His lieutenant frantically sent a runner up through the camp to tell the general they needed reinforcements. Then the lieutenant fell dead. And as the Indians came battling their way into the nest of Yellow Jackets, the young Ensign John Tipton was the only officer left to command them. He would not let them fall back, and they held their corner, but the Indians kept coming.

The Prophet was still chanting on the cliff when Charcoal Burner rode up the steep, dark path from the creek valley. The battle raged unabated, as it had for nearly two hours, a deafening storm. It was still dark, but the pitch blackness was just beginning to fade enough that he could negotiate the familiar path up through the woods to the rock bluff at the edge of the prairie. So much blind shooting was being done that even as he rode up this bluff, Charcoal Burner heard stray musketballs snapping among the trees around him.

He reached the top of the bluff and dismounted. He walked close to the dark, strange figure in the fur robe and winged headdress and stood there waiting, not willing to interrupt a prayer between the great Prophet and the Master of Life, but waiting for an opportunity to say a few things that had become important. A few warriors of the Prophet's bodyguard hovered in the windy, rainy gloom nearby. At last becoming aware of Charcoal Burner's presence, Open Door finished his prayer and turned to him.

Charcoal Burner had to shout to make his words heard over the roar of the battle.

"Father, we have failed to destroy them!"

Open Door's expression could not be seen in the darkness. He was a silhouette against the dark gray sky. He replied:

"But soon we will! It is not done yet!"

"Father, they say they still hear the governor's voice everywhere in the army camp. It is believed he escaped the knife. White Loon and his hundred were driven out, many killed."

"Then Harrison will die in battle instead of in bed. But he will die! I have seen it! Are our people not fighting with bravery?"

"Like never before, it is true. They kill many soldiers. But they complain that the soldiers were neither dead nor crazy, as you said they would be. They have rallied, and they fight like devils. Their powder was not wet, as you said it would be."

If Charcoal Burner could have seen the expression on Open Door's face, he would have seen his mouth distorted, a corner of his upper lip between his teeth. Charcoal Burner went on: "Our surprise was lost when a sentry shot one of our warriors. That warrior did not die in silence, and the whitefaces knew we were around them. Had that warrior been still, the others might have got into Harrison's tent."

Open Door waved his hand impatiently. "It is no matter! He will die in battle instead! They will not escape. Their bones will lie forever on that place. Small matters change and shift. But our great victory is determined!"

"When the sentry fired, the warriors on the east and south were still in the marsh and had not reached their places. The attack was ragged, and we lost many. The little-shot from the soldiers' guns is like hail in the woods."

"My son! We are still killing them! A blade or bullet will find Harrison yet, and then they will crumple down! I have felt the power of Weshemoneto go through me to our People. Daylight will reveal Harrison very soon so he can be killed! Daylight will find the Blue-Coats all dead!"

"Daylight," replied Charcoal Burner, "will show the soldiers where we are, and they will turn us with bayonets. Father, I tried to prevent this. The war chiefs say your medicine did not work. They are angry. They say that only courage and skill have killed soldiers, not your medicine. You should know, Father, that they are saying these things."

The Prophet swelled up and hissed, but the contempt was only to conceal his fear. "Go back down," he said in a hoarse voice, "and tell them to kill the rest of the soldiers. Say I have praised their bravery, and that Weshemoneto will help them strike the governor down!"

When Charcoal Burner had started back down the path, Open Door stood grimacing toward the ominous sky. He was quaking inside. He could hear the white officer-soldiers' commands bellowing in the roar of the gunfire. The rain clouds crawled overhead. It was light enough to see the clouds moving now, and features of the land were separating into different shades of gray: the woods, dark but full of the sparks of gunfire and overhung by a pale cloud of smoke, the marshy grasslands beyond, a shade lighter than the woods.

The Prophet's bodyguards could see his robed figure now, the tall bulk of him. They saw him turn from the cliff and come toward them. He took the bridle of his horse from one of them and swung onto the animal without a word. He kicked in his heels and began to trot, then gallop, across the prairie toward his town. Bewildered, they looked at each other, then mounted and rode after him.

Why their prophet would stop invoking the Great Good Spirit's protection while the warriors were still fighting, the bodyguards did not understand. But it was their duty to follow and protect him. So they followed him as he rode in a wide arc across the prairie, around the thunder of the battle, and down the slopes into Prophet's Town.

As the dawn grayed, General Harrison rode from one end of the long campground to the other, riding up behind each unit, conferring with its officers, giving them words of encouragement, then riding on. He was in plain sight now in the half-light, and scores of Indians saw him, saw the huge bicorn hat of an officer among the oaks and the smoke, and shot at him with gun or bow, but the missiles only barked trees around him or flipped through his cloak. It was as if he, not the Indians, had the protection of the Great Spirit around him—or that he had the stronger god. Major Floyd rode up to him and pleaded with him to take cover, but Harrison waved away the suggestion and rode on to the next unit, cheering the troops as he went.

The camp was a shambles of tattered tents and flags, overturned wagons, dead soldiers and Indians and horses, burnt woolen blankets, smoldering ashes, dense smoke, bloodstained mud and puddles, arrows sticking in everything. Every tree in the woods had been completely barked by bullets from waist height to head height. Wounded soldiers by the score lay crowded into half-sheltered coverts, wrapped in muddy blankets and bloody rags, the surgeon moving among them and squatting beside them. There were already at least fifty soldiers dead, Harrison estimated, and of the two hundred or so wounded, there were many who looked almost gone. One man's whole jaw had been shot off, and his ghastly half face with its haggard, stunned eyes was more than Harrison could bear to look at as he went through comforting the wounded and praising them. Some of them were busy in awkward postures trying to clean the waste out of their pants. The surgeon had told Harrison that many of the flesh wounds and abdominal wounds were particularly ugly because many of the savages had chewed their musketballs before going into battle—the surgeon showed him one he had just extracted—apparently to make them flatten or fragment on impact or perhaps to increase the chance of infection. There also were many arrows that had been dipped in excrement. As Harrison had looked at these things, an awful remorse had plummeted in his breast. He was thinking what an intense, profound hatred would have to grow in a people to make them create such things. And in this harsh, soggy, smoking, gray reality of a dismal morning, here within a mile of the Indians' holy town—a place where he really had had no right to come, he could admit to himself now, himself only—he finally understood that the hatred manifested in those chewed musketballs and besmirched arrowheads had been created by his own race.

He clenched his teeth and shook his head to get this forlorn admission out of it and spurred his horse on toward the northern flank, where the shooting was growing heavier again. He was met by Colonel Daveiss of the Kentucky Dragoons, whose face and hands, like those of everybody else, were black from gunpowder and gunsmoke, and Daveiss repeated the same request he had made twice before: permission to charge a wooded rise from which a nest of Indians had been pouring gunfire into the compound. Daveiss's red-rimmed eyes blazed in his sooty face. His white blanket coat, a mark of his flamboyance, was now filthy with mud and chaff and soot. This Joe Daveiss, a noted Kentucky lawyer, had once told Harrison that the two of them were the only two men west of the Alleghenies with any strategic sense. Now he said the best strategy would be to get control of that high place. Finally Harrison said, "Use your discretion, Colonel. If you think it's light enough to see what you're doing." Then he rode off toward the front line, where the Fourth Infantry was having a terrific, noisy gunfight on a bigger scale.

Daveiss grinned and ran to his dragoons. It would not be a mounted charge. Most of their horses were dead or leaking from bullet holes. Daveiss gathered twenty young men and told them to follow him and, saber waving, sprinted in his dirty white coat out of the lines toward the muzzle flashes on the rise. Quite a few of his dragoons thought it was a foolhardy thing to do and didn't follow.

The next time Harrison rode to the dragoons' sector, they were still firing at the same elevation Daveiss had tried to charge. Colonel Daveiss, his dirty blanket coat now soaked with blood, lay at the roots of a sycamore tree where his soldiers had carried him back and laid him down to die.

Now it was nearly daylight, or as light as it was going to get on this drizzly day. Harrison had formed the units at the north end into massed ranks for a bayonet charge into the woods where the battle had started and where the strongest concentration of Indians seemed to be.

The warriors had fought with inspired bravery and unusual prowess for more than two hours, defending something that had somehow become more important to them than even self or tribe. Even as their brothers had fallen before the guns that were not supposed to work, fired by soldiers who were supposed to be dead or crazy, even as they had seen their assured victory thwarted time after time by the brave and stubborn Americans, still the warriors had fought on, even rushing against the dreaded buckshot and bayonets; even after they had lost faith in the Prophet's promises and charms, they had fought on, charging again and again, for something extraordinary that had grown in their hearts.

But finally, seeing the Blue-Coats massing and trooping forward with their indestructible general riding among them with his saber raised, and noticing that the prayers of the Prophet were no longer coming down from the far bluff, the warriors fired a few parting volleys of bullets and arrows into the many-legged army that came crunching and howling toward them, then turned and melted into the forest, taking all their wounded with them.

The white soldiers had not won the battle, nor had the allied warriors. But in the end the red men had lost something more important than a battle: they had lost the faith that for a few years had been the most cherished force in their lives.

The war chiefs withdrew into Prophet's Town with stormy eyes. They placed their warriors to defend the women and children and old men in case the army should come on and try to attack the town. Then they went seeking the Prophet. They found him hunched near a small fire in the gloom of his medicine lodge, running his sacred beans and deer hooves through the smoke, and he called out that he did not want to come out because he was praying for more power to finish destroying Harrison and his army. Before this day, they would never have entered the medicine lodge without his invitation. But by now they had deduced that his medicine was nothing to be timid about, and they pushed in, all sooty and muddy, some smeared with blood, and stood over him. One of them actually shoved the sacred reed effigy aside to make room to stand. They held their blood-dark clubs and tomahawks and looked as if they would be pleased to use them on him. He pretended to be astonished by their menacing manner, but inside his clothes he was pouring the sweat of terror.

"Why are you here?" he asked. "Have you finished the army?"

Charcoal Burner loomed over him and bent to stare fire in his face. "You are a false prophet. You told us Harrison would die at once and his soldiers would be helpless. Harrison still lives and rides, and he made his soldiers fight like demons. Many of our young men died, many are hurt so they will die today. Only their courage hurt the Long Knives. All your medicine was but useless noise!"

Open Door cringed before this devastating indictment, then he replied in a voice that was almost a whine:

"No! I have at last determined what is wrong! It was my wife's fault that the medicine did not work yet." They recoiled in muttering indignation at this outlandish excuse, but he explained: "When she helped me with my prayers before the vision, she handled the sacred articles and had not told me she was in her flowing moon. . . . That as you know is forbidden, and it corrupted the medicine." He emitted a terrible, false laugh, then made his face most earnest and seemed to swell with power for a moment. "I have been cleansing the articles and am ready to enchant the white soldiers so they will be helpless, and you can finish yet this day what you have so bravely begun."

"No!" shouted one of the Kickapoo chieftains, actually shaking his hatchet before Open Door's face. "We are through with all this, with starving in your town while you get us in trouble with the Long Knives! We put our families in your hands, and now the Blue-Coat army is this close to them! Listen! You can hear the women and children crying with fear! I, for one, am going to take my people to the safety of our towns, at once. Will I pause long enough to kill you for what you have done? My brothers' bodies are being mutilated in the army camp now! I should kill you for killing them! But rather will I let you live, cast out of your importance, to slink around the edges of the towns like a beggar dog, crying over your guilt for the rest of your years!"

"Loud Noise," snarled a Shawnee man who had long known him, contemptuously using his old name, "if you want to finish the Americans, perhaps you should go over to their camp by yourself and thunder them with your Thunder-Sucker! Perhaps you should blow them away with the gas of your bowels!"

The worst had happened, and Open Door sat looking down, a sheen of sweat on his ugly face, his heart breaking.

He had fallen to what he had been before.


And so it was that, within sight of each other, the two mightiest forces in the Middle Ground licked their wounds under a drizzling sky and tried to direct themselves toward their futures.

In his muddy, trampled, bullet-riddled, blood-soaked oak grove, Governor Harrison put his exhausted troops to the most dismal sort of hard labor, digging mass graves for sixty dead soldiers, a large proportion of whom had been officers. They laid them in rows, covered them with earth and then with piles of deadwood, then set the wood on fire to hide the signs of grave digging. Other soldiers were put to work with axes and shovels to build the breastworks they should have built the evening before. Harrison was afraid that the Indians, who had fought with such unexpected recklessness and perseverance, were not through and would return under cover of darkness, either this evening or, more likely, on the dawn of the morrow. One mortally wounded warrior was dragged into the camp and questioned about what the Indians intended to do, but he said nothing; he knew nothing.

Harrison tried to learn from him whether Tecumseh had led the Indians' attack. The wounded Indian shook his head and answered that Tecumseh was not back yet from the south and warned Harrison that he had better watch out when he returned.

In their moments of leisure between grave digging and defense building, the troops diverted themselves by sniping at the warriors who had been posted to watch the camp and by scalping and flaying the corpses of the forty warriors they found lying on the ground or in hastily scooped graves around the perimeter. As forty scalps would not go far among several hundred soldiers, most of the scalps were divided among comrades. One scalp, cut into quarters, decorated four rifle barrels the rest of that dismal day. Fingers, moccasins, bracelets, ears, foreskins and scrotums, and strips of skin went farther, however, and hardly a man of that army had to go home without a souvenir. When finally discarded, the Indian corpses were mostly bloody, flayed lumps of carrion. As for noncarnal trophies, there were thousands of arrows, which lay and bristled everywhere.

Across the brown fields toward the Tippecanoe, Star Watcher witnessed the dissolution of the holy town. Warriors, tribal units, families, many orphans and widows, trailed out from the sprawling town all day, walking, riding, pulling their goods and their wounded brothers on travois drags, dispersing along the muddy trails up the Tippecanoe and across the prairie, swinging far out to skirt the army camp, going home in profound sorrow and anger. A few men were burying six warriors who had died since the retreat to town. Many of the bands of embittered warriors, burning with frustration and vengeance, went out vowing to kill every white man and burn every white man's house they saw on the way. By his invasion, Governor Harrison had kicked open a dormant hornets' nest, and the settlers were in more danger than they had been in since the Greenville Treaty of seventeen years ago. Tethered to a stake in front of the council lodge, Open Door sat awaiting a decision about his fate. He understood that had he not been the brother of Tecumseh, he would have been burned at this very stake by now.

Charcoal Burner and Black Partridge, a Winnebago, had tried desperately to persuade the warriors to remain nearby, perhaps to make a new camp across the Wabash-se-pe and await Tecumseh's return from the south. Only a few had decided to stay, some forty young warriors who were still fervently devoted to Tecumseh, who still vaguely yearned toward his beautiful dream of red brotherhood and victory.

And even as the others rode out, taking with them their shares of the harvest that had been cached in the woods, Charcoal Burner would stop them, and take them by the hand, and say:

"Go, then, as every man must follow his own heart. You have been a good and brave friend of the People. But remember as you ride away from here, brother, it is not Tecumseh who has betrayed you. Watch for his sign, for it will be soon, and when it comes, start for Canada, as you were told, and we will all be together again, to finish with the Long Knives at last!"

A few of them on hearing this tightened their hands on his, and their eyes brightened. But many shook their heads or became angry, or simply looked at him as if he were a pitiable fool, dropped his hand, and urged their horses out of this nearly deserted, once sacred town where hundreds of voices once had prayed and rejoiced in unison. Star Watcher was once again fleeing into winter, from still another doomed town.


On the morning of November 8, the dragoons moved out of the army camp and rode cautiously toward the distant gray huts of Prophet's Town. Scouts had reported that the town looked vacant.

The dragoons did not feel much like going there. They had spent a miserable and virtually sleepless night in their fortified camp, exhausted from the battle and all the burying and barricade building. Following the orders of the general, who had in their opinion become cautious rather late in the game, the army had bedded down in darkness, without campfires, and hungry, as the cattle had run off in the battle and there was only a little flour left. Then they had been kept awake by the cold and rain and by jumpy sentries who shot at sneaking forms in the woods. Daylight had revealed that the sneaking forms were only abandoned dogs from Prophet's Town, come to feed on corpses.

When the dragoons entered Prophet's Town, the only living creature they found, other than curs, was an ancient woman too feeble and sick to travel. The great Shawnee holy town was hers now. Their enthusiasm now revived, the soldiers ransacked the town for souvenirs. From one *wigewa* they confiscated a few new British-made muskets, still wrapped in oiled strouding, as evidence to support the governor's eternal suspicions. They found five thousand bushels of corn and beans hidden in the woods nearby and burned all except enough to supply them on their march back down the Wabash. They dug up six fresh graves in the town and scalped and stripped the corpses. Then they set fire to hundreds of the huts, whose seasoned bark and poles made a spectacular conflagration. The dying warrior who had been questioned by Harrison was brought to what was left of the town and placed in the care of the dying old woman.

The next day, with its groaning wounded stacked in twenty-two groaning wagons, General Harrison's army began its trek back down the bank of the

Wabash. The governor himself, never comfortable with the coarse frontier camaraderie, found himself an awfully lonely and disconsolate victor as he rode along at the head of his weary army.

He did not look forward to what his political opponents would be saying about his many casualties—particularly all those officers, most of whom were from influential families.

And then there would be the reaction, which Harrison could fairly predict, of President Madison, who never for a moment would have condoned this invasion.

Harrison knew he was going to have to do much explaining.

Tecumseh stood in the ashes of his lodge, his whole body trembling.

All around him were the ashes and blackened poles and broken pots and tools of what had been the sacred town. Old snow was melting, and its patchy whiteness made the blackened ruins look even more stark and dismal. A piece of deerhide with burned edges swung slowly from a scorched door frame in the dank wind. His warriors, who had traveled thousands of miles through the pines and live oaks and deltas and swamps of the south with him, dancing full of fire, who had gone into Florida and then up into the mountains with him to the Cherokees, then west again to the Missi-se-pe and into the council houses of the Osages and Missourias, often dreaming along the way of home and rest at Prophet's Town, now stood in a cluster at a distance from him, watching him, their faces dark and grim. His mission to the south had failed, thwarted by the old chiefs there who were just like the government chiefs here. He had aroused thousands of young warriors, but only thirty Creeks had come back with him. And finally, returning across Illinois in the icy winds of winter, hungry, he had hoped to find solace at last among his united People here in this town; he had dreamed of succotash cooking in his sister's kettle and of the comfort of the sacred flames in the fire-ring of his own lodge, here, this very spot.

Now instead he stood here in the cold ruins, trembling. But it was not the cold that made him tremble.

All around in the ruins he could hear the silent voices of the warriors who had died trying to protect their home once again from the guns and torches of white invaders. For the sixth time in his life his town had been burned, the sacred harvest burned, the People scattered, hungry and without shelter as the winter came down from the north. He heard the groans of the dead coming up to him from the acrid wet ashes of the holy town, and as he sniffed and listened, his hatred hardened in him; any last fragment of sympathy or pity he might have felt for any American became like a flake of frost. Any notion he had kept of going to the president blew away in the cold wind. He held his hand on his *pa-waw-ka* stone for warmth, for the power to rebuild all this that had been destroyed by that deceitful white man, whom he now knew he should have killed in his own yard at Vincennes in that long-ago fit of fury.

From now on it would be nothing but war, a war of vengeance. He turned his face up toward the low gray clouds and swore it to the Master of Life.

*Harrison,* the still, chill voices of the dead shrieked from the ashes in the snow. *Harrison did this to us!*

Charcoal Burner had been watching for his return. He rode up and dismounted to stand before him. The wind blew the hawk feather that was attached to his fur hat and made it swivel. The two chiefs stood amid the snow and desolation and looked at each other with love and sorrow.

"Come, Father," said Charcoal Burner. "We have made a camp on Wildcat Creek." He pointed southward across the river.

He told Tecumseh what had happened, as they rode out of the ruins and down the valley. He told how he had tried to stop it but with downcast eyes admitted that perhaps he had not tried hard enough. Tecumseh did not hold him to blame for it. He said, "So you did not kill Open Door for this?"

"No. Only because he is your brother."

"You should have. He has undone the work of Weshemoneto himself. What was built over many years and tens of hundreds of miles, with the help of the greatest medicine, he ruined in one night."

"I could not kill your brother, Tecumseh."

"Rather you had. Now I will have to see his face."

Star Watcher and Cat Pouncing came and embraced him. Then Stands Firm held her a long time. Tecumseh told her of their mother's death. She nodded, shut her eyes, and trembled. Tecumseh asked his son if his Spirit Helper had come; the boy shook his head.

The warriors who had not deserted came out to greet Tecumseh. There was joy in seeing him, but pity, too. He smiled at them all with an affection they could feel, but he did not stop yet to talk with them. He walked grimly to a hovel that Charcoal Burner had pointed out to him. Inside in the smoky gloom Open Door sat. His hands were bound behind him, and his neck was tethered to a post. His face brightened for a moment when he saw his brother, but when he saw the storm of anger and contempt in his face, he cringed.

"Stand up," Tecumseh commanded, and as Open Door struggled to his feet, Tecumseh pulled his knife out of the little sheath that hung at his chest.

"Tecumseh," Open Door breathed, looking at the knife. "I am your own brother."

"No. No longer." Tecumseh flicked the knife forward, and Open Door gasped and flinched.

But he was still alive. Tecumseh had only severed the tether. Now he stepped behind his brother and cut the thongs at his wrists, and Open Door's eye began to fill with tears of hope and gratitude. He brought his trembling hands around in front of him and began rubbing his wrists, looking at Tecumseh, his face expectant and his slumping body like a question. At last he said in a half-choked voice: "What have they told you?"

"The truth," Tecumseh said, sheathing his knife.

"The truth is that the war chiefs wanted to attack, and they forced me to help."

"How could they force the man who holds the powers of We-shemoneto?" Tecumseh said with sarcasm. "No. The truth of how your selfishness for glory ruined the faith of a People hungry for faith. Of how you snatched a victory out of their hands and put it in the hands of the white governor. Of how you betrayed me and all your red children."

Then, his teeth bared in rage but his eyes full of the tears he never permitted himself to shed, Tecumseh reached up slowly with both hands as if to cup Open Door's face tenderly in them.

But instead, both hands grasped the hair above the wretch's ears. And with such force that he groaned with the exertion, he jerked Open Door's head back and forth, from side to side, shook him as if he would tear his head from his body, shook him with all the strength of his powerful arms and shoulders, until Open Door's teeth clashed together and chipped, shook him until his feathered turban and his scalplock tube flew off and his earbobs jangled against his gorget, shook him until his brain felt loose in his skull, shook him until blood from his nose and mouth were spattering them both, and finally until the hair came out of his head into Tecumseh's hands.

And as Open Door crumpled to the floor, Tecumseh turned his back on him and went out, panting from the exertion. He stood outside in the snow for a minute, all his warriors looking at him silently, the sixty followers remaining out of thousands.

Open Door's wife came waddling from somewhere, head down, eyes averted, she herself a dweller in disgrace, and ducked into the hovel to see what her husband would need.

After a while Tecumseh's fists at last unclenched, and the handfuls of black hair fell on the white snow.

Inside, Open Door's wife could be heard clucking and cooing over him.

The long-tailed star had passed from the sky. The Year of Signs, which had begun with floods and squirrel migrations, was soon to close. Winter lay upon the land. The tribal chiefs who had accepted bundles of red sticks from Tecumseh now threw away the last stick. Even those whose faith in the Shawnee prophet had been blown away by the tragedy at Tippecanoe, even those in the south who had spurned Tecumseh's pleas, even those west of the Missi-se-pe who had felt too remote from the problem of white invasion to rise to his call, still found themselves unsettled and anxious, watchful for the great sign of which Tecumseh had spoken so ominously, so certainly. Smoke rose from snow-dusted *wigewas* and *tepees* into the night sky. And in virtually every Indian dwelling from Canada to Florida, from New York to the Dakotas, the men were tense, frightened, worried. Some former followers of the Shawnee brothers were eager for the sign, because they did not like living without hope after having lived with it for a few years. And even those who scoffed at talk of the great sign were always thinking of it. Far to the south and southeast, Pushmataha the Choctaw, Big Warrior of the Creeks, Junalaska of the Cherokee, who had all resisted his war talk, lived in a quiet dread. For if the great sign came as Tecumseh had predicted, how much influence over their young warriors they might then lose!

One man who had never heard of the great sign was lying awake and restless, full of anxiety. All night he had heard the clock strike the hours; the last tolling had been two o'clock.

Governor Harrison had been in a turmoil since his invasion of the Indian country. The people of Vincennes and the new settlers in the edges of the treaty lands had at first given him a hero's welcome. But then the critics had set upon him. He was expecting to be called to Washington at any time to defend his actions before President Madison. Here in the Ohio watershed were many influential men who kept protesting about his folly. Even many who had been in favor of the invasion criticized his conduct of it. Why hadn't he attacked at once? Why hadn't he built breastworks around his camp? Among the most outraged was the prominent Kentucky lawyer Humphrey Marshall, whose brother-in-law, Colonel Daveiss, had not come back from Tippecanoe. Marshall was as prodigious a writer as Harrison himself, and he seemed determined to kill the governor with his pen and in his epitaph label him an unlawful aggressor against a small, peaceful nation. In recent weeks Harrison had been parrying with his quill as vigorously as he ever had done with a sword. Harrison had complained on paper:

> My personal enemies now unite with the British agents in representing that the expedition was entirely useless and the Prophet as one of the best and most pacific mortals—a perfect Quaker in principles. . . .

Now, lying restless in his bed and thinking of all their calumny and of the letters and letters of explanation and rebuttal he still had to write, he flopped over from his side onto his back, angrily rearranging quilts and blankets, making the bed shake under his lurching movements.

But when at last he fell still and stopped shaking the bed, the bed began shaking him.

Tecumseh stood on the stony promontory upon which Open Door had stood praying over the battle so many weeks ago and looked over the wedge of land below, where a hundred men had died in a battle that should not have been fought. The battleground was easy to see this night; its trees stood out dark against the starlit snow on the marshes and grasslands around it. Near Tecumseh stood Charcoal Burner, Seekabo, Stands Firm, Black Partridge, and the bodyguard, Thick Water. In the evening Tecumseh had told them: "It is the night for the great sign. Come with me."

A wordless song in his soul had led him to ride down Wildcat Creek, across the ice of the frozen Wabash, and up the valley to this place. The song, like that of a flute inside his head but unheard by the others, had grown louder and louder as he rode. Now it was more than two hours past the middle of the night. The song had become one single high note. Tecumseh waited, looking down on the Wabash-se-pe, this benign and ancient river that began in the old lost Shawnee land of O-hi-o and curved westward past the ruins of Prophet's Town and then southward past Vincennes, its waters eventually flowing into the O-hi-o-se-pe and thence into the Missi-se-pe. . . .

Tecumseh's gaze went toward the horizon in the southwest, beyond which lay that confluence and the place where he had felt the Center of Time. And as he looked, he heard the distant wingbeats of the white dove, growing louder and louder.

The horses nearby began to nicker and move restlessly. The rock under Tecumseh's feet began to tremble, and he heard dislodged fragments of stone begin to fall clattering down the cliff below him.

Now a terrible, deep rumbling rolled up the valley and grew to a roar. Dead trees cracked and fell in the woods below, with crackling of branches and loud thuds. Crows cawed in alarm, and owls fluttered out of the swaying branches and could be seen wheeling over the snow fields. Tecumseh's chieftains cried out in amazement and reached toward him, to pull him back from the cliff's edge, but at that moment, as if the whole earth were a rolling wave of water, the ground swelled and surged under them, knocking them off their feet. The horses fell down, whinnying, rolling about, kicking their legs wildly as they tried to get back up. Slabs of stone as big as houses cracked off the cliff and went thundering end over end down the steep slope below, crushing and flattening trees as they went.

The roaring grew louder, and the earth jolted more violently. But Tecumseh alone did not lose his balance. At times all his life he had felt this shaking earth when no one else had, and now it could not buck him off his feet. His chieftains were on the ground, trying to rise, their voices faint and their cries unintelligible in the deafening roar, which sounded like a war, the cracking and breaking of trees like volleys of musket fire, the great rumbles like the thunder of a hundred cannons.

Tecumseh stood with his right hand raised toward heaven and felt the hand gripped in a field of power; it was as if the hand would hold him up even if the entire cliff should drop out from under his feet. Now in the uproar of grating, grinding, and rumbling he heard the high note again, but now it was the shriek of a multitude of ghostly voices, as if the shaking and splitting of the world were opening the graves of all the red men, those buried since the battle, those buried after the great plagues of the white men's diseases, those buried after the terrible wars with the Iroquois, those buried hundreds of years ago in the big mounds along the riversides; yes, all red men who had drowned when Kokomthena's grandson Rounded-Side had stabbed the water giant's belly and flooded the earth; yes, every red man who had ever died since the Beginning was calling up through the cracking earth.

In his hut on Wildcat Creek, Open Door was having his nightmare again, in which Tecumseh had his hair in his hands and was shaking his brains loose. He always woke from the nightmare whimpering or whining, and his wife would sit up and smack him lightly on the cheek until he would calm down and realize he had been dreaming.

But this time when he awoke and cried out, his wife was screaming beside him, and the fire in the center of the hut was sending up showers of sparks as if it were being poked by a stick, and the ground under their bedding was jolting so hard that his head was being snapped back and forth upon his neck, his neck that was still so sore from the punishment Tecumseh had given him. Pieces of bark fell from the roof onto the bed. Open Door looked up through the gaps in the collapsing roof and saw the stars jerking and trembling in the sky. Pottery was breaking in the house. Trees were falling down in the woods nearby. More bark fell from the roof. Some of it had fallen over the fire and now was starting to blaze up.

Open Door yelled at her to follow him out. They tried to get up but were thrown to the ground. At last they crawled out into the snow. The camp was falling apart. Several huts were, like their own, on fire. The people were yelling and crying and could not stand up in the snow. The whole country-side seemed to be lurching, as if the world were coming to an end.

Star Watcher and Cat Pouncing, unable to stand, were kneeling on the snow together, holding hands to keep from losing each other. Star Watcher was frightened, and there were tears in her eyes, but she was smiling with gratitude and joy. Her brother the Shooting Star had indeed known the great truth.

This was at last the sign he had looked for all his life!


For two days the earth shook, paused, shook again. The air darkened with dust, and the sun grew dull. Houses were wrenched apart; creeks went dry, and streams began flowing where none had before. The water in the Great Lakes swelled and sloshed like water in a jiggling cup. The Missi-se-pe changed its channel in many places, flooding lowlands, raising its bed to the air in great surges. Its muddy waters roiled and bubbled with ooze and in some places even stopped and flowed upstream. In the lowlands near the mouth of the O-hi-o, vast areas of terrain crumpled and changed shape. The land in river bends sank down, and the brown water rushed in, tossing big trees and house timbers and barges about like flotsam. Across the Missi-se-pe from the old Spanish town of New Madrid, the land upon which Tecum-seh had camped on his journey to the south suddenly dropped, and the river water roared into the enormous depression, forming a lake five to ten miles across, filled with seething brown water, with gigantic clouds of mist rising off of it. The frontier was in a turmoil; people and animals were in panic. On the plains west of the Great River, herds of bison were thrown off their feet, scrambled up and stampeded for miles until they were thrown by another jolt. Deer and small animals darted everywhere or stood cowering, their eyes full of fear; some ran until they died.

In the south, the dusty sky was always full of flights of millions of disturbed waterfowl. In the town of Tuckabatchee, Big Warrior ran outside his house and turned to watch it collapse. Everywhere around him, houses were falling down and people were screaming, trapped under rubble and thatch. In Pushmataha's Choctaw town, walls shook and pots fell over, and he knew at once that all his warriors would be remembering Tecumseh.

The great quaking resumed four times in the next two moons and was felt every place Tecumseh had ever trod in his years of traveling. Forests lay in tangles. Hundreds of square miles of lowland lay covered with mud and dead fish and debris. Raw earth gaped where once there had been wooded or grassy slopes. And dust blew and settled over the desolation, making the snow dirty and the sun red.

The Year of the Signs was past. Open Door the Shawnee prophet had lost his power and hung about like a pariah dog. But the damage he had done to the cause of the alliance was already healing itself.

And in his heart Tecumseh felt a greater strength and resolve than he had ever felt. A lifetime of soul questions had been answered for him. His face set like granite, he told Star Watcher:

"The Seventeen Fires and Canada are on the verge of war. When it begins, the British will help us regain our homelands. My followers will come back to me to fight the Long Knives. Warriors everywhere have seen the great sign, and they are remembering my words, and they will be coming to join me in Canada. Your husband will be among them, he has promised me. You come, too."

"Have I not always been with you? Am I not the Watcher of the Shooting Star?"

# PART THREE

PART THREE

# CHAPTER 35

## *Bois Blanc Island, Ontario, Canada*
## *Summer 1812*

Star Watcher had followed Tecumseh to Canada with the thought that the Long Knife intruders would be left far behind, that for a long time she would not have to hear the dreadful thunder of guns.

But already her days were troubled by the nearby noise of battle and the worry that her brother and her husband, in the midst of it, might not come home.

What Tecumseh had predicted had come to be. The Americans had declared war on the English king and immediately tried to invade Canada. Their hunger for the lands of other peoples was insatiable.

Now, in the Blackberry Moon, Star Watcher and the women who had come here from the Wabash-se-pe were trying to prepare for the Green Corn ceremony. They had built a Great House and cleared a Stomp Ground here on the Island of the White Trees in the Detroit River. Now they were grinding meal and preparing packets of seeds for the sacred hoop. They had saved some of their own strains of bean, corn, and squash seeds during the flight from Tippecanoe, and every place they moved, they tried to grow at least enough of these sacred plants to harvest seeds for the next year. This had been one of the hardest things for the women to do in the time of the Long Knives, for seed cannot be hurried, but it was one of their sacred duties.

The women worked and worried. Somehow there would have to be a Green Corn ceremony, war or no war. Our Grandmother expected the tribute; she had never said it would be easy every time, but plainly the People owe everything to their Creator. Besides that, the People enjoyed giving the tribute probably as much as Kokomthena enjoyed receiving it.

Tecumseh had assured these worrying women, "We will have our gath-

ering for Our Grandmother. Even General Hull and his American army
will not prevent it. I will stop him before time for Green Corn."

Everybody, especially the British, had thought that would be impossible.
Hull, the American general who occupied Detroit on the American side of
the river, had summoned an army of twenty-five hundred and brought them
up from O-hi-o even before the war was declared. Then early in this moon
he had crossed the river onto Canadian soil at Sandwich and started down
the fourteen-mile road toward Amherstburg and the undermanned British
post called Fort Malden, intending to capture that fort and the shipbuilding
yard below it. It had seemed that there would be no way to stop him. The
two hundred Redcoats in Fort Malden had thought they were doomed. It
had been expected that the American flag would be on the pole above the
fort by now.

But Star Watcher, from where she sat on the island, could see the British
fort on the east bank of the river, and it still had the pretty English flag over
it. The British were still there because of what her brother had done, and
she was so proud of him that her heart sang as she worked. For with less
than two hundred warriors and a small company of Amherstburg militiamen, Tecumseh had done like the wolves around the herd. He had set up
a series of ambushes and worried the American army to a halt, holding it
there at a safe distance from the fort until a British warship could come in
from Lake Erie and command the road with its cannons.

Then, with that uncanny sense of strategy that had gained him the
immediate admiration of the Redcoat officers, Tecumseh had crossed
quickly to the American side of the river and laid another series of ambushes that had blocked the Americans' messages and supplies between
O-hi-o and Detroit. He had captured important American dispatches and
turned them over to the British at Fort Malden. Thus cut off, the American
general finally had withdrawn his army from the Canadian shore, and they
were now all sitting at Detroit on their own side of the river, surrounded
by Indians and cut off from their supplies. What the Long Knives had started
as a bold offensive had suddenly become a trap, because of Tecumseh's
actions.

Now as Star Watcher worked, she heard gunfire beginning to pop and
rattle, very faint and far up on the other side of the wide river, the noise
barely audible in the still, hot air. It was much shooting, and it went on for
a long time. Star Watcher prayed for her brother and her husband and all
the others as she worked. At one time during the afternoon her heartbeat
began racing, for no reason she knew of, and not long afterward the
shooting noises faded as a breeze from the west arose.

When Tecumseh and his warriors returned to the island in canoes that evening, his legging was soaked with blood from a buckshot wound in his left thigh. Once again, as she had done so often in his life, Star Watcher repaired his torn flesh. He could hardly move the stiffening limb, but he was very cheerful. With the help of a few Redcoats, he and his warriors had ambushed six hundred American horsemen who tried to break out of the encirclement of Detroit and reopen their supply route. "We did well this day, my sister," he said. "They are still caught in their own fort, and they are getting hungry. Ha! They should have stayed in their own country!"

"Tell her the other good thing," said Stands Firm, who was as happy as Tecumseh.

"Yes! We learned that some Redcoats and warriors have captured the American fort at Michilimackinac. Oh, yes! These Long Knives may soon be very sorry they wanted war. When more British come from the east, we will turn the Americans on their heads!"

She smiled as she tied the poultice against his thigh. "While you were gone," she said, "a hundred more of your warriors came across the river. They came from the Illinois and said they have been seeking you since the earth shook."

"Good! All is growing again as in the dream. Have you nearly finished mending that leg, my sister? I want to go and welcome them!"

Only Thick Water was solemn. Star Watcher knew why. She told him, "Brother, do not be angry with yourself. If you stopped every ball that is shot at Tecumseh, your beautiful wife would be a widowed woman now."

Tecumseh turned to his bodyguard, smiling broadly. "Yes! You would be so full of holes your hide would not hold hickory nuts!"

Thick Water finally smiled.


When General Isaac Brock stood up in the barracks headquarters to greet Tecumseh, his short, shining blond hair almost brushed the ceiling, and for a moment Tecumseh remembered that day nearly four decades ago when he had been awed by his first sight of a Redcoat. The Shawnee's eyes widened at the imposing, bold look of this new ally. Brock was a hand's width taller than Tecumseh, brawny and big-boned and erect, and his clean scarlet coat and white breeches fit him like skin. It was his face, though, that most heartened Tecumseh: the direct, friendly blue eyes, massive brow, and resolute mouth.

Brock, who was the lieutenant governor and military commander of Upper Canada, got an equally good first impression of Tecumseh. Even though the Shawnee limped slightly from the wound in his thigh, he was as graceful and poised as any lord. And in his face Brock recognized

something that others saw in Brock himself: the open amiability of one who
has no weaknesses to hide.

The Indian agent Matthew Elliott, who had ushered Tecumseh in, now
said, "Here, sir, is Tecumseh, chief of all our Indian allies. He wished to
be presented to you right away."

Brock stepped forward, beaming, and gripped Tecumseh's hand
strongly, saying, "The fellow who saved this fort from the Yankees! Yes!
Welcome indeed!"

Brock had arrived only two hours ago, in darkness, leading a flotilla
of bateaux and rowboats that had come nearly the whole length of Lake
Erie to bring three hundred Redcoats of the Forty-first Regiment to this
threatened part of Canada. The boats had been rowed nearly a week
along the storm-beaten north shore of the lake, a grueling voyage that had
sickened and weakened all the troops. But within one hour of landing,
Brock had shaved, dressed in a fresh uniform, called a meeting of the officers of Fort Malden, and gone over the whole crisis with them. Here he
had learned the details of Tecumseh's astonishing upset of the American
invasion.

Now he praised Tecumseh lavishly and was introduced to Charcoal
Burner and Black Partridge. Having been told already of the abstinence of
Tecumseh and his people, Brock did not offer them liquor, though his own
officers were by now warm and aromatic with brandy in celebration of
Brock's miraculous arrival. Already flushed to the jowls was Colonel Henry
Procter, the portly officer in charge of Fort Malden. Procter was one of
those haughty officers whose manner revealed a contempt for savages. He
had barely condescended to thank Tecumseh for saving his fort. Tecumseh
did not like Procter, either, and was relieved to see a man of Brock's caliber
here at last.

Brock pointed to the large silver medallion, stamped with the profile of
King George III, that Tecumseh wore hanging by a wampum string on the
breast of his plain deerskin tunic and praised him for his dedication to the
Crown.

But Tecumseh had not come for praise, nor to make a social call. He had
come to propose something he considered necessary and to see whether the
British commandant was the sort of man who would be up to doing it. His
first appraisal of Brock's strength and character was encouraging, so he went
directly to the point:

"Father, it would be a very good thing to capture Detroit, and it should
be done now."

Brock's blond eyebrows went up, but his face at once was suffused with
delight.

"My thoughts exactly!" It was, indeed, something Brock had pondered that evening after hearing the summary of conditions. The dispatches and letters Tecumseh had captured gave evidence that General Hull was indecisive and terribly afraid of Indians—particularly the hordes of Lakes warriors he expected to sweep down since the fall of Michilimackinac—and that his officers had little faith in him. Brock was in command of a very small force, with a thinly populated province to protect against the enormous manpower and resources of the aggressive Americans, and therefore he had vowed to the Canadian government at the outbreak of the war that he would "speak loud and look big." Such a bold move as the capture of Detroit had thus presented itself to his mind, but he had not yet formulated a plan for doing it, nor had he even mentioned it to his officers. But now here was this intense, audacious Shawnee chief who had perhaps a thousand warriors under his command and who had already proven himself an uncommon strategist. "Will you sit down with me, Chief, and let us talk about how we might take Detroit away from the Americans?"

Tecumseh had come to Brock not just with a vague desire to attack Detroit, but with a full-fledged battle plan in mind. He had even had Charcoal Burner bring a roll of bark, upon whose inner side Tecumseh had drawn a detailed map of the terrain and approaches around Detroit, with particular attention to defilades and cover.

The two leaders worked with growing excitement over their strategy, feeling their kinship grow stronger with every hour. Brock, unlike many British officers, did not speak condescendingly to Indians. He and Tecumseh found they could dispute each other's ideas without getting angry with each other and accept each other's amendments without pique. Brock also asked for the opinions of his junior officers, as an Indian chief always did in council, and this further enhanced his stature in Tecumseh's eyes. Only Colonel Procter was opposed to the idea of attacking Detroit, and when it became apparent that his objections were based only upon lack of boldness or imagination, his arguments were disregarded.

The success of a British and Indian attack upon Detroit would depend largely on making their forces seem bigger than they really were. "It is like the mockingbird," Tecumseh said, remembering a lesson of Chiksika. "He sings many songs so that other birds will think there are many birds in his territory. When the American Clark took Vincennes from your Hamilton in the last war, he played mockingbird in a way that we could do." He told how he would have his Indians pass and repass a point visible from the fort, giving the impression that he had thousands of warriors. He would also deliberately let the Americans intercept a messenger who would be carrying a bogus dispatch referring to some five thousand warriors from upper

Michigan—thus playing upon the dread that General Hull had revealed in his dispatches. Brock clapped and rubbed his hands together eagerly at this ruse.

Brock likewise would play mockingbird, by dressing hundreds of Canadian militiamen and farmers in regular army red coats that the quartermaster had in abundance. Added to the real regulars, these would make a formidable-looking display for the eyes of the nervous old American general. The two leaders chuckled like schoolboys plotting mischief and looked into each other's merry eyes with growing appreciation.

Tecumseh's warriors would cross the river first and occupy the ground north and west of Detroit and put on their show of numbers. Brock would bombard the fort with artillery from Sandwich across the river and at dawn of the following day would transport his troops to the American shore by boat and complete the encirclement of Detroit and the fort. Both Brock and Tecumseh felt that Hull had no fighting spirit and would likely talk surrender at that point. His supply train was still stalled far down the road, and the Americans at Detroit were hungry and demoralized.

When this war-planning council ended at four in the morning, the Redcoat officers were sagging with weariness and rank with brandy, but Tecumseh and Brock were wide awake and exuberant, and Tecumseh was feeling something he had not felt for years or even believed he could ever feel again: a full, true, trusting, brotherly friendship with a white man. Here was a blue-eyed man he liked and admired as he had liked and admired Big Fish and Ga-lo-weh. And he said as he left:

"Brock, listen. After the Long Knife Wayne ran over us at the Fallen Timbers on the Maumee-se-pe, the British officer at Fort Miami would not let the red men take refuge in his fort. For many years that memory has been bitter in my breast when I thought of British. But I feel that if that had been *your* fort, you would have had enough heart to shelter my people."

"I would have," Brock said, and he gripped Tecumseh's hand firmly. "Moreover, my troops would have been beside your warriors in the fallen trees."

They held an open council in a grassy field near Amherstburg at noon, to tell the plan to Tecumseh's thousand followers. In the background towered the masts and spars and massive hulls of the British vessels in the shipyard. They were always an awesome sight to the Indians who gathered here. Just the look of them seemed an assurance of the wealth and strength of England. Brock had rested a few hours and looked splendid in the August sunlight. He had added to his uniform a shimmering, varicolored silk sash and a bicorn hat trimmed with gold braid and a cockade. His voice, words, and looks made a powerful impression on the warriors, and Tecumseh was proud and happy as he stood beside his new friend. Brock told the Indians that the Americans were now trying to take the lands of both the red men and the British, and that he was not going to sit here and wait to defend Canada but was going to cross the river and drive them out of the Indians' land. They responded with an excited murmur of approval. Then Tecumseh spoke to Brock.

"We are happy that the father beyond the Great Salt Water has finally awakened from his long sleep and permitted his soldiers to come to the aid of his red children, who have remained steady in their friendship.

"The Americans are our enemies. They came to us hungry long ago, then they cut off the hands of the red man who gave them corn. We gave them rivers of fish, and they poisoned them. We gave them forests and mountains and valleys full of game, and in return, what did they give to our warriors and our women? They gave them rum, and trinkets, and a grave.

"The ghosts of our brothers killed at Tippecanoe can find no rest in the hunting grounds of the dead until the American enemy is destroyed! We must stay united with each other and with our allies the British until this is done!

"Brothers! The Redcoat officers here have been tight-handed until now, and have not given us enough guns. Many of us have fought the Americans with bows and clubs. But now General Brock has come here with a bold heart, and he has ordered them to give us all good guns for our attack across the river, and he and his many soldiers will fight beside us, as they have not done since our fathers were our chiefs." Now he turned and looked at Brock.

"Brothers!" he said, his voice carrying over the field. "This is a *man*!"


Tecumseh's warriors crossed the Detroit River that evening in canoes and moved into the woods above the town and the fort, cutting off the roads. His scouts on the south road came and told him that about 350 mounted militiamen had just ridden out of Detroit, probably to try once again to bring up the supply convoy.

In a way this was good, Tecumseh thought. Hull would feel weaker with those men gone outside.

But on the other hand, a unit outside like that could create problems if it came back and struck at the warriors from behind. So Tecumseh sent word about it to Brock and settled his warriors for the night, to watch the town and guard the roads, particularly that south road. He told them to keep the Americans awake and nervous all night with strange animal calls and other alarms.

The next morning, while Tecumseh's thousand warriors were making themselves look and sound like five thousand, Brock had his troops cut down a clump of oaks across the river at Sandwich, revealing a battery of cannons he had moved into position during the night. When the Americans had had time to look at the cannons for a while and count several thousand Indians crossing a road, Brock sent a messenger to General Hull demanding his surrender. When it was refused, Brock's cannons started bombarding the fort. Tecumseh's warriors were awed and cheered by such smoke, thunder, and fire. Most of them were too young ever to have heard cannon before. Brock had not just been talking big; for the first time in the memory of most of the warriors, the British were actually shooting cannons at the American enemy, and it did not seem possible that the Long Knife soldiers could live long in such a storm of destruction.

Then the cannons of the fort began firing back. The ear-hurting booms and clouds of thick smoke rolled through the river valley, and the shingle roofs of a few buildings in the fort began to fly apart. A building caught on fire. General Hull had all his troops in the fort where the shells were falling, except for one unit of Michigan militia that crouched near the edge of the town, facing the Indian forces. As dusk began to darken the countryside, these militiamen began deserting.

The cannonade continued into the night, a spectacle of red-and-yellow explosions and firelit smoke that kept the warriors enchanted, even though the unaccustomed noise was giving them headaches. They were in high spirits; they were confident that the Americans would give up the next day or maybe even this night.


In the first smoky light of dawn, distant cries of alarm could be heard coming from the fort and the town. The Americans could see many rowboats on the river downstream. Brock's Redcoats were crossing to the American shore. They landed, using the lowest ground to stay covered from the line of artillery fire from the fort. By the time the rising sun was beginning to lighten the hazy, smoky lowlands, the green fields were impressively covered with units of men in red-and-white uniforms, maneuvering into positions for an assault upon the walls of the fort. And while the Americans in the fort were watching this ominous sight, Tecumseh's warriors began trotting in files through a glade visible from the fort, howling their war cries. Once concealed by the trees, they circled back to the end of the line and trotted through the glade again. By the time that ruse had been completed, Hull's observers had counted five or six thousand Indians on two consecutive days, which seemed to confirm the captured message about the horde of warriors coming down from the north.

Now Tecumseh mounted a gray stallion and galloped down past the fort, just a little out of musket range, to the fields where Brock's army was forming. Brock was already prominent on the field, on a high-spirited gray war-horse, and the two leaders galloped to greet each other, within the sight of the fort. They then rode side by side inspecting the fort from a distance, looking confident and nonchalant. But they were aware that this was the point of their greatest risk.

"Now, my friend Tecumseh," Brock said, "let us see whether we've got General Hull appraised right. I'll start the assault. If he resists, we've got a deadly job ahead of us. That's an awful fort to storm, and he's got more fellows in there than you and I have together. You can wager that those cannon pointing down on us are loaded with grapeshot. Oh, how I hate grapeshot! We may not be able to take that fort without a long siege, my friend. Even that's a very long chance. . . ."

"Brock! See that!"

Brock followed Tecumseh's pointing finger. Then he began humming an impromptu little song in his throat and smiling. "Oh, my good fellow," he chortled. "This is just utterly preposterous! It worked!"

A white flag was being raised over the American fort.


Tecumseh gathered his war chiefs and laid down his law.

"I have made a promise to our friend Brock, and it is *our* promise:

"When we go into the town and the fort, we will harm no one. The Americans are our prisoners, and the women and children in Detroit are innocent. I have told you many times that prisoners must not be hurt. If you wish to remain allied with me and win more great victories like this one, you must not let your warriors harm any of the people, nor steal or destroy anything. Remember what I have told you: in my eyes it is the act of a coward to hurt the helpless. The American general has surrendered to Brock in order to save himself and his people from the knife and tomahawk. For the honor of Brock's word and my own, see that your warriors are merciful."


Many of the American soldiers in the fort were weeping with frustration as they watched the American flag come down the flagpole and the British flag go up. Hull had consulted not one officer before making his decision to surrender. They had all been ready and eager to fight and were so astonished when Hull sent his aides out to raise the truce flag that they had hurriedly tried to relieve the old general of command and go on with the battle. But that had failed, and now they were all prisoners—all 2,500 of them, the entire United States Army of the Northwest. Even those 350 who had ridden down the road two days before were included in the surrender terms, though they did not yet know it. Some of the American officers had had tantrums, broken their swords in disgust, or thrown themselves on the ground and wept. Others swore that if they ever got back to their country, they would see to it that Hull was tried as a traitor and a coward.

The misery and depression of the Americans were matched by the jubilation of the British and Indians. As the king's flag went up the flagpole, General Brock was so moved that he untied the beautiful silk sash from around his waist and gave it to Tecumseh. "You deserve the honor for this day of triumph, my friend," he said. Then, as if this token were insufficient for the good feelings overflowing in him, he unbuckled his silver-trimmed pistols and gave them to Tecumseh also, and all the British soldiers and Canadian militiamen who were close enough to see it gave a cheer.

Then, to his total surprise and delight, Brock received a present in return. Tecumseh turned to Billy Caldwell, and the half-breed rode forward and gave a bundle to Tecumseh, who extended it to Brock, saying:

"This was made by the women of Prophet's Town, and I am pleased to put it in the hand of a brave ally. The American governor always tried to tell me that British officers have no courage to help the red men. But you have shown how a great English warrior stands and moves."

Tears welled up in Brock's eyes when he saw the priceless thing Tecumseh was giving him. It was a six-foot wampum belt depicting an oak-leaf design in green-and-white beads.

"For one strong like the oak," Tecumseh said.

"My brother and gracious friend!" Brock said, his voice husky with emotion. "I'll keep this near me till the day I die."

"May that day be far from now," said Tecumseh, who felt that this was perhaps the happiest day of his life, that this was only the first of many victories with Brock's help, which would lead to the salvation of his people. Brock was so important to the outcome of the great task that Tecumseh wondered why he had never seen him in any of the dreams or visions.

For a few days after the capture of Detroit, Tecumseh and Brock shared a deepening friendship and high hopes for more such successes. Brock set up his headquarters in a comfortable house in Detroit, and Tecumseh lived in two rooms of it. Here he was visited by several of the captured American officers who had met him in Vincennes and O-hi-o in past years. They came to thank him for the merciful restraint of his warriors. One of these officers introduced himself as a friend of James Galloway's family. That family, the major reported, was as usual prospering. The major then astonished Tecumseh by referring to Rebekah as "the girl you courted." Tecumseh said nothing about that but listened until he was able to deduce the story: that Rebekah had told people he had proposed marriage to her. It had become the family story.

"Ah," Tecumseh said, looking thoughtfully down at the floor beside the officer's feet. "Such a thing could not be." He remembered her, wistfully, for a moment, remembered the readings, the grammar lessons, the writing, her strange loneliness—their pitiful misunderstanding about the gift she had called dowry. . . . "Is that girl well, then? Perhaps she is a man's wife by now, and the mother of children?"

"Not yet but soon, I hear. They say she's fixing to wed a cousin of hers—'Pennsylvania George,' he's called."

Tecumseh was quiet for a while, half smiling. "That is a good thing to hear," he said. "One should not marry another kind."

Coming now, at this time of his swelling friendship with Brock, the news of Rebekah caused a strange wave of poignancy to move through Tecumseh. Once again, for the first time in many rushing, eventful years, he wondered at this deep affinity he had for a few members of the race that was ruining his world.

Later that day Tecumseh sat in his room, wearing a white man's cloak and no headdress, while a picture maker painted his portrait, which Brock had insisted upon commissioning.

In these heady and pleasant few days, Tecumseh's leg wound finished its healing. The limp went away, and his hopes for the success of his mission grew. With the bold energy of Brock, he felt, the tribes might yet defeat the Long Knives so soundly and so often that they might actually recover their lands in Indiana and O-hi-o and hold those lands forever. Had that region not been considered by the British to be a part of Canada before the Revolution? Might it not be again, if the British won this war? And might not the English king give it back to Tecumseh's people as a reward for their help in the wars? Tecumseh thought of discussing these possibilities someday with Brock. He sniffed the strange paint smell, pondering the notion. He kept it within himself, and would until he might have time to talk deeply with Brock. But first there was this war to win, and it had started out well indeed. By such victories as this, the disaster at Tippecanoe might be fully compensated. He had summoned all the tribes that had followed him before

Tippecanoe, telling them of the conquest of Detroit and inviting them to join him in the rebuilding of the alliance and more great victories. Even as he was sending out these calls, still there came warriors who had been roused by the shaking of the earth.

When the painter was finished, Tecumseh saw the brooding image and laughed at it. "But it does not show how happy Tecumseh is!"

Word soon came of another victory over the Americans, but it was a victory that saddened and angered Tecumseh. His Potawatomi, Sauk, Fox, and Winnebago allies had captured the entire garrison of Fort Dearborn and the people of the village of Chicago near the end of Lake Mis-e-ken. Among the captives had been the Indian agent William Wells. But the warriors had been too tempted by the helplessness of their captives and, forgetting Tecumseh's repeated preachings for mercy, had massacred most of the captives. One of the Potawatomi chiefs in his frenzy had cut Wells's heart out and eaten it. The death of Wells was not bad news to Tecumseh, but this repeated reversion to blood lust twisted his heart. How could the red men expect to become a nation recognized among nations if they never would learn mercy and restraint?

"Yes, I have incited them to fight the Americans as long as they have strength to raise an arm," Tecumseh confided to Brock. "But they forget my pleas to spare the helpless, and are untrained children, who know not what is good or bad, and each time they do that they step farther back from the building of a respectable nation. Every act of cruelty will be repaid a hundred times by the Long Knives, who welcome any excuse to make us be no more. Brock, what am I to do with my poor People?" Tecumseh had never trusted any other white man enough, even Galloway, to say such a thing to him, and to be able to say it to such a friend was an exquisite release of his anguish. He could see in Brock's eyes that he understood.

But the time was coming when there would have to be a distance between them. Activities of the American forces at the other end of Lake Erie compelled Brock to return there. In shipyards at the far end of the lake, the Americans were trying to build a navy fleet. There were raids and battles going on there that threatened the British supply route to Upper Canada. Here at Amherstburg, a young and dignified British navy commander named Barclay was building and arming a huge ship of war to keep control of the lake even if the Americans did succeed in building their fleet. Barclay had lost one arm in a great naval battle somewhere else in the world, and Brock esteemed him highly.

Now Brock put his senior subordinate, Procter, in charge of the western theater and prepared to sail east to Niagara for a while. "But I will always answer to your needs, my friend," he told Tecumseh. "Only send me a message." He gave Tecumseh a gold compass engraved with both their names.

Before boarding a warship for Niagara, Brock penned his report to the Crown on the capture of Detroit. Determined that his country should appreciate the value of its ally, he wrote of Tecumseh:

> A more sagacious man or a more gallant warrior does not, I believe, exist. He has the admiration of everyone. . . . Tecumseh's followers responded to the dictates of honour and humanity; the instant the enemy submitted, his life became sacred.

"Remember, my friend," Brock said, "I cherish this green belt as much as anything I possess. As I told you when you gave it to me, I shall keep it till the day I die."

# CHAPTER 36

## *Fallen Timbers, on the Maumee*
## *April 25, 1813*

Tecumseh and the Redcoat general rode out on the grassy slope of the bluff above the rapids of the Maumee-se-pe.

This place was full of bad memory, even after almost twenty summers. Here Tecumseh had lost a brother and the Shawnees had lost everything that was important. Tecumseh would have spoken of these memories if the British general riding beside him had been Brock. But it was not. It was Procter, with whom Tecumseh would never have tried to share a sentiment. Procter did not seem to believe Indians could have sentiments.

It was Procter riding beside him, an ally only because of the circumstances of war. Tecumseh knew Americans, his enemies, whom he liked better than Procter, his ally, but this fat-jowled Procter was his ally because it was he who had the cannons and supplies and boats and Redcoats Tecumseh needed to wage war on American forts. Thus it was Procter who rode now beside him onto the bluff of the Maumee overlooking the old battleground and the huge new American fort that had been built across the river from it.

It was not Brock, the white man to whom Tecumseh had felt the strongest bond of friendship, because Brock was no more. Where the high spirits and hopefulness of Brock had glowed briefly in Tecumseh's heart, there was now only caution and a kind of despair that would sometimes pull him down and make him doubt that the things that needed to be done could be done after all. Tecumseh had always been confident that the Great Good Spirit would help him do the task, and the inspiration from Brock had made him even more sure, for those two brief moons, but since the news of Brock's death, Tecumseh sometimes had doubted.

Now it seemed that his own spirit was the sole fountain from which his growing army of warriors could drink of hope and confidence. Once Open Door had provided much of their spiritual nourishment, but he had failed and now just hung around Tecumseh's Indians like a bad memory. Once Brock had provided some of it, but a bullet had gone through his massive chest as he led his Redcoats on a charge against the Americans in a battle near Niagara.

It was a sad thing about Brock. For his capture of Detroit he had been made a knight—an honor whose nature Tecumseh could only imagine—but had been killed before he had even known he was a knight.

Tecumseh now was riding a black stallion, one of three that he had obtained at Detroit, and these were the finest horses he had ever ridden. Procter rode a fine, dappled British war-horse that to Tecumseh somehow always seemed far too grand for him. Procter was so portly and mean-looking that Tecumseh thought he would look better riding on a hog. Sometimes by imagining him that way Tecumseh could make himself smile a little.

The grass down the slope and in the Maumee bottomland was tender, fresh spring green. Tecumseh could remember watching the troops of General Wayne maneuver over these same green slopes and bottomlands so long ago; he could remember seeing the Kentucky horse soldiers riding toward the blown-down forest to decoy the warriors out into the open. The fallen trees were hardly visible now. They were rotting into the ground and covered by a new growth of woods, a growth surely nourished by all the Indian blood that had been spilled there by the bayonets and bullets and buckshot of Wayne's army.

Now Tecumseh gazed toward the place where Anthony Wayne's tent had been. He was able to pick out the exact place, though the land had been forever changing in the time since. And when he looked at that place, he remembered seeing Wayne through the spyglass—and also the young Blue-Coat officer who had stood beside him: that young man to whom Tecumseh's eyes had been drawn and who had had the aura of an omen around him: *Harrison!*

Again today that same Harrison was less than a mile away. He was in that enormous new American fort across the river.

It was Harrison who had built the fort.

The strangeness of it was full of meaning for Tecumseh.

A new United States Army of the Northwest had been built to replace the one Hull had surrendered to Tecumseh and Brock at Detroit last summer. And Hull's successor as commander of this new army was Harrison. And now here were Tecumseh and Harrison back at this place, facing each other again, further proof of the truth of Tecumseh's premonitions.

*Harrison! How our fates are woven together!*

As it had seemed to Tecumseh for so many years now, this conflict was like a simple fight to death between two men, behind whom there happened to be gathered the armies of their respective races. Though Tecumseh could not now see Harrison over there in that sprawling, palisaded fort across the river, he felt as close to him as he had in Vincennes that day when they had stood with their eyes locked together, their breath intermingling, one holding a raised tomahawk, the other a bared sword.

Harrison had made himself the grandest fort ever. Its dimensions were stupendous.

As usual, he had had plenty of critics, who did not believe he should have stopped here to build a fort at all but should have gone right on to attack Canada. But he believed the huge stronghold was necessary.

Some of those same critics who said he should not have built the fort were the ones who had roasted him for not building defenses at Tippecanoe, he would recall with a wry smirk.

How many hundreds of thousands of words of explaining he had written to regain favor after Tippecanoe!

Harrison had named the huge post Fort Meigs, in honor of Ohio's new governor. Its palisades enclosed ten acres, and there were eight blockhouses around its perimeter. Cannon stood on platforms facing over the Maumee and also covering the two roads that led to the fort, one from the west along the river, the other from the south. And, despite huge troubles and overcharges by contractors—which gave his critics more fodder—it had turned out to be a well-made fort, with an excellent situation, standing on a high wedge of land where a creek converged with the Maumee just below its rapids.

Harrison meant this to be the primary post to defend Ohio against the British and Indians from Canada and also to serve as a main supply base for the offensives he would make soon enough against Canada. Among the long rows of tents inside the palisade stood a headquarters building and a massive log structure filled to the rafters with supplies.

General Harrison always had replies for his critics. For those who derided his fort, he replied that he was not going to rush headlong into disaster as old Winchester had done last winter.

Recklessly seeking to reverse the capture of Detroit, General James Winchester, a Tennessee planter and Revolutionary War veteran, had sped up the western shore of Lake Erie with eight hundred fifty soldiers, getting as far as Frenchtown on the River Raisin. There, huddling in shelter against zero-degree weather, Winchester's whole army had been killed or captured by a thousand warriors and Redcoats. Roundhead the Wyandot and the British General Procter had simply marched across the frozen mouth of the Detroit River from Fort Malden and attacked in the frigid dawn light by complete surprise. In Tecumseh's absence, the warriors had massacred a hundred sick and wounded Americans. It had been another of those disasters wrought by rashness and poor planning. And Harrison, schooled in campaign warfare by the Roman caesars and by Mad Anthony Wayne, was determined not to make any rash mistakes. His byword was caution now, and this huge fort was a manifestation of that word.

Now Harrison was summoned by an excited aide to come to one of the batteries facing over the Maumee.

"Damned if it ain't Tecumseh and that murderin' Procter themselves," exclaimed an officer of the battery, handing Harrison his spyglass and pointing to two riders high on the opposite bluff, an Indian on a black horse, a Redcoat on a gray. Harrison turned the powerful telescope on them, and his heartbeat quickened. There was no mistaking the slender red man with his long black hair and turban. Harrison had not seen Tecumseh for more than two years, but the Shawnee had been uppermost in his mind ever since, and there was no mistaking him. Harrison had never seen Procter before, but there were men in the battery who had been at the fall of Detroit, and they knew him by sight.

Harrison watched them moving on the distant grassy height, and he knew that their presence must mean only one thing: they were reconnoitering for an assault on Fort Meigs.

"I wonder," Harrison said to the artillery officer, "whether those two gentlemen on that slope over there are in cannon range. Maybe you could satisfy my curiosity, Captain." He did not really expect anything so outrageously lucky as a direct hit on the tiny figures a half mile away, but they were totally exposed, and such fortunes sometimes were granted, and how many problems could be solved if Tecumseh could be killed right now! Harrison listened to the artillery officer's loading commands, watched Tecumseh and Procter through the telescope, and prayed for a bit of outrageous good fortune.

Procter was saying to Tecumseh:

"The man's made himself a nice fort there, but he's done a rather stupid job of placing it." He pointed eastward along the bluff upon which they were standing. "That spot over there is a bit higher than the fort, and a damned good place for my twenty-four-pounders. They could probably throw a thousand cannonballs a day across the river and inside the walls of that fort, and not miss a shot." Then he swung his arm slightly to the southeast and pointed across the river to a mile-wide, stump-dotted clearing beyond the fort, where the logs had been cut to build the blockhouses and palisades. "They've been kind enough to clear us a shooting range over there. Howitzers and mortars set near the edge of that clearing could lob bombshells into that part of the fort the twenty-four-pounders can't reach. And ammunition could be hauled in through those woods and the creek ravine all day with no danger to us whatsoever. I believe your enemy is rather stupid, Chief."

That remark, surprisingly, annoyed Tecumseh. Of course he hoped Harrison would prove himself stupid, and Procter's plan for the artillery positions did seem to make sense. But Procter seemed to think everyone was stupid except himself. Tecumseh had seen some evidence that Harrison was not stupid and considerable evidence that Procter was. But he did not comment on that. He said:

"I think the two-bang balls could make that fort a bad place to live in." That was his term for the explosive shells, which banged when the cannon fired them and banged again when they reached their target. He found these to be most amazing and really did not give Harrison's men, crowded in that fort, much chance against them. He would not want to live inside a palisade like that with nowhere to hide from two-bang balls. And it was so easy to bring all the artillery to this place. British ships controlled Lake Erie and could sail right out from Fort Malden and across the west end of the lake and into the wide mouth of the Maumee, bringing the big guns to within a few miles of this place. Barges could then carry the guns the rest of the way up the river, and that stretch of the lower Maumee was protected by British guns set in the partially rebuilt ruins of old Fort Miami. Procter and Tecumseh had two thousand Redcoats and warriors waiting near the old British fort, to be deployed around Fort Meigs. Tecumseh's hopes were up now. He was carrying the war from Canada back to O-hi-o, back to his old homeland. The recovery of the stolen lands looked more possible all the time, and if this had been Brock beside him instead of Procter, Tecumseh would have had no doubt at all about the outcome.

Now, just as he took another look over at Harrison's fort, he saw puffs of blue-white smoke billow out from the palisade. Instantly he kicked his horse in the flanks and cried, just as the boom of the cannons rolled up: "Go, Procter!"

The horses had hardly moved when clods of grassy earth leaped up from the ground around the place where they had been standing. As they galloped along the slope toward cover, Tecumseh was laughing. Two more booms came, and more dirt flew, but far behind them. Procter was not laughing. His flesh and jowls jiggled as he rode for his life, and against the scarlet of his coat his face was blanched.

When Harrison saw the British building big gun emplacements on that high bluff across the river, he realized at once that his whole big fort would be nothing more than a slaughter pen unless he could come up with something very clever. To keep his whole army from being blown to shreds, he might even have to abandon the fort. But he was determined not to do that. Meanwhile, his troops were growing very nervous about something equally ominous: in the dense woods east of the fort, across the little creek and no more than three hundred feet away, there were Indians. So many of them were infesting the woods there that the spring foliage seemed to be vibrating with movement. Those woods over there should have been cleared back another one or two hundred yards, it was apparent now. To make that matter worse, the cannon in the blockhouse at that end could not be lowered or maneuvered far enough to command those woods. It was painfully clear that Harrison had overlooked a few important details in building his grand fort and that the enemy was already taking advantage of his oversights. Quickly Harrison conferred with his engineers and artillery officers, and they came up with some modifications in the fort's design to meet those emergencies. The blockhouse at the extreme east end of the compound, so recently built that its timbers were still fresh and green, was dismantled and replaced by a low-walled gun battery, in which two or three cannons could be maneuvered easily to fire north, east, or south. To discourage any assault on this salient, the soldiers ringed it with an abatis of slash, pointed poles and tree trunks until the steep ground in front of the emplacement looked as inviting as a porcupine.

The bigger modification of the fort could not be observed from outside, not even from the British batteries high on the other side of the river. Working like slaves in the heat, hundreds of American soldiers and militiamen with picks and shovels dug two trenches, deeper than a man's height, running parallel to each other from one end of the fort to the other, within the palisade. These trenches were seven hundred and nine hundred feet long. The earth thrown out of each trench was piled into a traverse about ten feet high and twenty feet thick. Then, underground rooms were dug off to the sides of the trenches and braced from inside by timbers. A deep powder magazine was excavated, braced up, and covered with several feet of logs and earth. The militiamen, very much an undisciplined collection of individualists, complained loud and long against this exhausting, dirty kind of labor, grumbling that it was "fitten work for niggers." But the sight of the big cannon batteries being built on the far bluff inspired them to labor on.

After twenty-four hours of such work, the troops fell into an exhausted sleep. Harrison, with officers carrying lanterns, toured the ditches. The smell of fresh earth and sweaty bodies was dense, and sometimes he would get a whiff of fresh-cut sassafras roots. Harrison nodded as he went along this subterranean world of clods and roots.

"There's never been anything quite like this, I'll wager," murmured an officer.

"I feel like a proper mole, don't you?" said another.

Harrison smiled. He didn't mind being thought of as an innovator. And no critic would ever be able to fault him again for underfortifying.

Now he was ready for siege. The British guns did worry him. His observers were of the opinion that they were twenty-four-pounders. Neither he nor any of his men had ever been in battle with or against such huge guns, except for a few old officers from the Revolution. He would look at the mass of earth covering a shelter and think, Nothing can get through that.

But then he would think of the force with which a twenty-four-pound iron ball must come down after arcing through the air for half a mile, and he would feel very queasy. He also worried about the Indian-size gaps a missile like that could make in a log palisade. He thought of the twelve hundred men crowded into this ten acres of grass and raw earth and sometimes wondered if any of them would get out alive.

But if any place ever was ready for a siege, he thought, this is. If we can hold it long enough under the pounding that's likely in store for us . . .

Two things were happening that could terminate the siege, but they were so far away that he could hardly guess when or whether they would succeed.

Far east on Lake Erie, in a hastily fabricated shipyard near the New York town of Buffalo, a feverish effort was being made to build an American fleet to put on Lake Erie and break the British navy's control of that body of water. Though the United States had a respectable sea navy, it could not be brought up to Lake Erie because of Niagara Falls, so it had become necessary to build a little navy here. Last fall in a daring night raid, some American officers had boarded and captured a moored British warship, the *Caledonia,* which would be the nucleus of the new fleet. When the new vessels were ready, they were to be put under the command of a cocky young naval officer named Oliver Hazard Perry, whose job it would be to challenge British supremacy on the lake. It was a desperate and audacious plan. But Harrison had met young Perry and had seen in him a man very similar to what he himself had been at the age of twenty-seven. So he expected something to come of that. If the Royal Navy could be blockaded or sunk, it would be much harder for the British to besiege Fort Meigs. But the timing of any help from that quarter could only be guessed at. It could be weeks, or months, or with bad luck, never.

The other assistance was much more imminent, and it would be coming from the other direction. It was a brigade of frontier militiamen under the command of General Green Clay. It would be marching up through western Ohio and boating down the Maumee any day now to reinforce Harrison at Fort Meigs. Harrison had meant to stand fast in his fort until Clay's arrival before setting out to attack Detroit and Canada.

But he had not expected his wait to be under the muzzles of so many big British guns. So now as he prowled in underground rooms with the smell of raw earth in his nostrils, he wished with all his might for the arrival of those reinforcements. When they come down, he vowed to himself, the first job they'll get will be to put those damned big guns out of order.

And to keep his mind off worrying about the Damocles' sword hanging over him, he began planning a way to attack the British batteries across the river. Surely there must be an awful number of Tecumseh's Indians between here and those batteries.

I wish Clay were here now, he thought. Wouldn't it be a splendid thing to spike those guns before they can even fire a shot at us!

Before dawn, Tecumseh mounted his black horse and rode out of the woods where his warriors had slept on their laying poles. They were all awake now. They were crowding toward the edge of the woods nearest the fort, ready to watch the spectacle and to rush the fort whenever they got the word to do so.

In the gray half-light Tecumseh waded his horse through the Maumee at a shallows where a flaky rock island shaped like a bison's head divided the stream. Then he rode across a grassy lowland and up the bluff to the site of the big British guns. The British sentries saluted him. The sky in the east was now streaked with the color of pumpkin, and the red coats of the artillery men looked purple as they moved and carried things around the cannons. The regimental flag hung on its pole above the battery, silhouetted against the sky. There were five huge, earth-and-log gun emplacements, and the black muzzles poked out over them, aimed at Fort Meigs.

Procter now came up the artillery road from old Fort Miami, riding with a bodyguard of dragoons. He dismounted, handed his horse's reins to a dragoon, and said to Tecumseh, "My 'goons here will take your horse back down a way if you like. It's going to be rather noisy up here for a beastie that's not used to it."

"Good, Procter," Tecumseh said. He dismounted and gave a trooper the reins. Procter's face was scarcely visible in the dim light, but his voice was peevish now as he voiced an ongoing grievance:

"I do wish, Chief, that you would address me as *'General* Procter,' just as a token of respect." He had been promoted to general when he was put in charge of operations in this theater, and it meant a lot to him. Tecumseh replied simply:

"I respected Brock. He did not complain that I called him 'Brock.' It was his name. Is not yours Procter?"

Procter hissed a sigh and turned away to talk to the artillery officers. Procter was well aware that Tecumseh had no respect for him, but he always had to humor this haughty chief. If it weren't for Tecumseh's Indians, he knew, the Americans could overrun Upper Canada in a week. Procter had a wife and an ailing daughter and a great many valuable possessions in his house in Amherstburg, and he was desperately worried all the time about some kind of a quick rout that would leave them undefended in the face of the Americans. That was why he had agreed to come out with Tecumseh on this offensive into Ohio and committed so many troops and guns to it. If they could pound Harrison's army into the ground here, Procter's family and treasures would be that much more secure in Amherstburg—and his reputation in London.

It was a little lighter when Procter came back to Tecumseh. He said, "The artillery officers have offered you and me the honor of shooting the first rounds from the big guns. Would you care to?"

Tecumseh liked most of the British officers except Procter and observed as much of their protocol as he could. But the sight of the great black metal monstrosities repelled him. They seemed to give off bad medicine, and he did not want to touch them. They were just not *for* the use of a red man, he felt, and he did not know how to express this to Procter. So he said, "Tell them Tecumseh thanks them for this honor, but the ears of a red man cannot stand so great a noise. Tell them Tecumseh must have both hands over his ears when he stands this close to a shooting big cannon."

Smirking, Procter turned and went back to the guns and spoke to the artillery commander. "The chief's afraid to," he said.

"Afraid to! Ha! I doubt he said *that!*" Procter gave the officer a hard look, and the officer added, "Sir."

"Well, then, Major, if you think it's quite light enough to make out your targets, you may begin firing."

"Yes, sir. You'll do the honor of touching the first match, sir?"

Procter backed off. He himself had always been scared of cannon. He always imagined they would explode at the breech. "Ahmmm . . . I wouldn't want to slight the chief," he said. He walked back a way and put his fat hands over his ears.

"I thought the general and the chief were going to touch off the first rounds," said a lieutenant.

"I guess they're scared to," the major replied.

"Well, 'tis our job," said the lieutenant. "Would *you* care to do the honors, sir?" The lieutenant gave the major the match and then covered his own ears, as did the cannoneers standing about. Tecumseh saw them do it and pressed his palms over his ears.

The burning match in the major's hand was the only spark of warm light in the gray-green dawn, except for the breakfast cookfires now twinkling down in the distant fort. A few birds were starting to twitter in the dark woods behind the battery. Standing beside the massive breech with his feet together as if at attention, the major put the match to the touchhole.

The huge cannon lurched, spurted a tongue of yellow fire and sparks and thick smoke thirty feet long, and cracked open the stillness of the spring morning. Tecumseh felt the ground buck and felt as if he had been struck on the head. The roar rolled over the valley and echoed back, leaving his ears ringing. An instant later the other twenty-four-pounder blasted. Both guns stood smoking under the dust their impact had raised, and then geysers of dirt and debris leaped up inside the distant fort. Even before the sound of their impact could come back, the rest of the British artillery was thundering, flashing smoke and fire and stirring up dust, and the cannoneers were moving to swab and reload the big guns. Now through the ringing in his head and between the thunderclaps of the other cannons, Tecumseh could hear his warriors howling with amazement and delight on the far side of the river.

His head felt as if it were being pounded with a club, and he felt like screaming himself to shut out the overpowering noise.

Now he could hear, too, filtering up through the distance, the shouts of the white soldiers in the fort where the great iron balls were hitting. He thought they must be dying over there by the dozens already, and he felt a little pity for them in the helplessness. But he clenched his jaw and thought:

You should have stayed out of our land.

And by the time the sun was coming up on the horizon and sparkling on the Maumee, and Tecumseh was riding back down to rejoin his warriors,

cannon smoke was puffing out of the palisade of the fort as the Americans
fired back. Tecumseh looked backward and saw the top fall out of a poplar
tree a few hundred feet short of the British batteries. As he rode into the
river, the thundering went on, and he could hear the bleating of a bugle
from inside the fort, a sound like a child crying in a thunderstorm. This
cannonade was a noise that crushed the soul, and he hoped it would not
have to go on very long. Surely most of the Americans would be dead by
the middle of the day, and Harrison would have to surrender.

But though the thunder and the smoke went on all day, no flag of surrender rose in the fort. From their coverts in the woods around the fort, the
Indians could watch bits of earth and splinters fly up and watch the two-
bang balls crack open with an orange flash and hear the shrapnel raining
in the trees and sometimes see a piece of blockhouse roof fly into pieces.
But the Americans in the fort were not all dead yet, even in the late
afternoon; they still came out onto their cannon platforms and fired a few
rounds toward the British batteries across the river, or aimed a load of
grapeshot into the woods where the Indians were, and even appeared on
the palisades with their long rifles once in a while and tried to shoot
Indians. When they showed themselves like that, the Indians would
shower them with musket fire, and they killed a few. Many of the warriors
were Sioux and Chippewa, who had come a long way after the earthquake
to fight for Tecumseh. But he knew they would tire of this kind of fighting before long. After a while the spectacle of the shelling would get
tiresome, and their heads were already starting to hurt from the noise.
Few warriors were willing to lie inactive within range of enemy fire and
wait for something to happen. If they saw no opportunity for a quick
triumph, they grew restless. He knew he would have to spend time with
them now and then and assure them of victory, keep them eager for a
chance to do something glorious. Procter had recommended that the artillery should pound the fort for a long time and kill most of the Americans
and break down some walls and blow up some American cannons before
the warriors and troops should rush the walls.

   Late in the afternoon a new kind of sound erupted amid the cannon
thunder. It was a sort of popping sound, coming from beyond the clearing
south of the fort. Smoke would rise from there, then there would be the
pop, and after a moment there would be a whistling sound and an explosion
in the fort. Tecumseh knew what it was. The mortar batteries had been
finished over there and were lobbing bombshells into the fort from that
angle. Tecumseh explained it to his warriors, tossing a rock high to show

how it would fall on something hidden on the other side of a log, and it kept them entertained for the rest of the day.

When the mortar shells started falling right into the trenches, Harrison ascertained where they were coming from, and that evening his soldiers began digging again. This time they dug ditches and piled up traverses that ran from north to south, at right angles to the long trenches, and dug more rooms.

Never, Harrison thought, had any body of men endured such a bombardment so well. All day the fort had been churned and shaken; all day the air had been full of cannonballs and geysers of dirt and flying splinters and shrapnel; all day the troops had hidden in the underground rooms or crouched in the trenches with dirt raining on their hats and dust sifting down on their shoulders. Now and then a man would crumple with a piece of shrapnel in him or an eye blown out or a face full of oak splinters; sometimes two or three men would be buried alive under a ton of collapsing dirt. But instead of the hundreds of dead that could have been expected after such a day, there were only a couple of dozen dead and wounded. While the shovels chunked in the ditches to repair fortifications, there was also the digging of graves in another part of the compound.

The troops were not as disheartened as might have been expected. Many of them were half-drunk. Borrowing from his studies of past bombardments, Harrison had employed a sporting method used during sieges of the Revolution: he had authorized the issue of a shot of whiskey to each man who turned a reusable British cannonball in to the magazine. A soldier would come in, grinning, covered with dirt, carrying a cannonball he had picked up or dug from the ground, trade it for a shot of whiskey, and go back to the trenches, and soon the ball would be loaded into an American cannon of the same caliber and sent on its way back toward the British guns. One man had staggered in so often that he was joshed by the magazine keeper about catching them in midair.

"Naw, I would catch 'em if I could see 'em," he drawled. "But I *have* ran down a couple afore they stopped rollin'."

The barrage started again at dawn of the second day, and the British officers kept watching for the truce flag that never went up. The Indians surrounding the fort on the east, south, and west grew still more restless in their coverts, and only Tecumseh's persuasion could keep some of the small bands from leaving to go back to Canada or to their homes. They were beginning to doubt the power of cannon; though the noise was as impressive as ever, they were beginning to suspect that most of the damage the cannon could do was to ears.

Some of Tecumseh's scouts were bold enough, or bored enough, to risk the occasional sprays of grapeshot and climb high into the big sycamores beside the creek and look and snipe at the soldiers inside the fort. When they came down they described the ditches and dirt walls and told Tecumseh that they had seen hardly any soldiers—just shells exploding and dirt flying and rows of tents all in shreds. Tecumseh took that news to Procter. It explained why the soldiers in the fort had not surrendered yet. The news seemed both to annoy and frighten Procter. Tecumseh could almost read his thoughts. Procter had been here for days on American soil, and he was sure that more Americans would be coming from somewhere soon—he had often expressed a worry about reinforcements—and the reduction of the fort was apparently going to take much longer than he had expected.

"My stupid American enemy is smarter than you said," Tecumseh remarked.

Procter raised his head and sniffed.


When still another day of bombardment failed to make the Americans hoist a white flag, Procter decided to send down a demand for surrender. He stopped the cannonade and raised a truce flag, and in the ringing silence after the din, he briefed a trim young Redcoat major on what to say to Harrison.

"I too have a message for Harrison," Tecumseh said. "Give me one of your writing soldiers to write it on paper." And he dictated:

> I have with me 800 braves. You have many in your hiding place. Come out with them and give me battle. You talked like a brave when we met at Vincennes, and I respected you, but now you hide behind logs and in the earth, like a groundhog. Give me your answer.
>
> Tecumseh


When the major came back he reported that Harrison had refused to surrender and had implied a readiness to fight to the end. Procter clenched his jaw and ordered the batteries to resume their fire. He went back to his headquarters at Fort Miami, after cautioning Tecumseh to keep scouts far out to watch for the approach of American reinforcements.

Tecumseh himself took a large band of scouts out around the countryside the next day, convinced that the monstrous shelling would have no results against the burrowing Americans. His party rode far in a circuit to check the Sandusky road to the south, then swung up toward the Maumee to watch the river and the western road. As they passed through the cleared fields and farms, the roar of the barrage grew fainter behind them, finally sounding like distant thunder. The countryside was peaceful and fresh with spring foliage. New corn was scarcely knee-high in the fields. To ride through these sunny fields with his bands of scouts reminded him of his journeys to the site of old Chillicothe in the years before the war. He thought of the Galloways, who farmed like this in the old Shawnee lands. He thought of their goodness, then of the evils Harrison had wrought, and he wondered at the ways of the white race. Even Harrison seemed to believe that what he was doing was right. Surely Harrison believed himself to be a righteous man.

The warriors had been fasting in battle, and they were very hungry now, but of course there was no game in all this settled land. Then Thick Water rode up beside Tecumseh and pointed toward a plowed field. Near its far edge was a white boy of ten or twelve years, standing as if petrified, holding the handles of a plow hooked to a pair of oxen. He was looking at the Indians. "Beef," said Thick Water, pulling his tomahawk from his waistband. The other warriors were grinning, looking at the oxen.

Tecumseh held up his hand. He looked at the boy and thought of Gal-lo-weh's sons, who had been about that age when he had first seen them, working in their fields. "No harm to the boy," he said, and led his scouts into the field.

The boy was too terrified to move. He stood, face pale, looking at the painted warriors all around him. In the distance the guns were still thundering under a cloud of gray smoke. Nearby a bluebird was singing. Tecumseh dismounted and smiled at the boy.

"I must have those ox," he said in English. "My young men are most hungry. I must have the beef for them."

It was a while before the boy could speak. Then he whimpered that if they took the oxen, his family would be ruined. He said his father was very sick, and that without the oxen to plow with, his family would die.

"I could take them, as we are at war with your country," Tecumseh said. "But I do not make war on a family. I will pay you a hundred dollar for these ox. They are not worth so much. You can buy more ox for your sick father."

He had Billy Caldwell write an order for one hundred dollars for the beasts, signed it, and told the boy he could take it to Colonel Elliott, the British Indian agent at Fort Miami, who would give him the dollars. "Show the Redcoats my name on the paper, and they will let you in the fort." Having no inclination to protest, the boy took the paper and ran.

The warriors butchered the oxen. Tecumseh hung the harness on the plow and left the yoke nearby for the boy to find. The warriors went into a woods to cook and eat the meat. Billy Caldwell joked to Tecumseh, "You should have told that boy, Go back to Europe and buy new oxen."

They resumed their reconnaissance in good spirits. It had been good to be away from the white armies' terrible cannons, riding together in a peaceful countryside. They found no sign of American reinforcements and so turned and rode back with the late afternoon sun at their backs toward the thundering of the British guns.

It was the fifth day of the bombardment. Tecumseh had gone down to Fort Miami to draw more ammunition and supplies for his warriors and to prod General Procter into doing something decisive. Tecumseh asked for Redcoats to help him storm the fort. Procter chose rather to keep up the shelling. He saw no reason to do anything drastic. There had been no sign of American reinforcements yet.

When Tecumseh rode out of the fort, his face full of anger, someone ran out into the road in front of him. His horse shied and reared, but Tecumseh brought him down. A white boy was standing barefoot in the road. It was the one from whom he had bought the oxen. His dirty face was tear-streaked.

"What, boy?" Tecumseh said.

"Sir, that Colonel Elliott wouldn't pay!" The boy's face crumpled as if he were ready to cry again. "My pa don't have anything now!"

"Come with me." Tecumseh turned his horse and rode back into the fort. The Redcoat sentries looked with amusement at the dirty-faced raggedy boy following the warrior chief's horse.

Tecumseh dismounted at Elliott's building and strode in, pulling the boy by the hand. Elliott was at a paper-strewn counter and looked up. His face was careworn and tired-looking, and he did not seem happy to see the boy here again. He looked up at Tecumseh warily.

"I bought ox from this boy to feed my scouts. He gave you my paper for a hundred dollars. Give him money."

Elliott shifted in his chair and licked his lower lip. "Ah, brother, that's not the way we do things. We don't buy food from Americans."

"I made him one hundred dollar promise, Elliott. My promise is good. Pay this boy."

Elliott shut his lips firmly and shook his head. Suddenly Tecumseh was leaning very close over him. He said in a low voice:

"Before I came with my warriors to fight the battles of king of England, we had enough to eat from our hunting grounds. We had to ask and thank only the Master of Life and the Masters of the Game. We can return to our hunting grounds." Some soldiers and Redcoat officers were standing near the counter, watching with amusement this exchange.

Elliott slumped a bit. "Well, if I *must* pay, I suppose . . ." He pulled a heavy box from the recesses behind the counter. It was chained to the counter and had a hasp and lock. As he unlocked it, he protested, "I do wish you would keep in mind the way we do things, though. . . ." He raised the lid and lifted out some printed currency. But Tecumseh put his hand firmly on his arm and said:

"Give him hard money, not rag money."

Elliott put the bills back with a sigh and counted out the equivalent of a hundred dollars in gold and silver coin and gave it to Tecumseh, who put it in the boy's hand, then turned to Elliott and held out his palm.

"One dollar more," he said.

Elliott closed the box as firmly as his lips, but Tecumseh's rigid fingers nudged his chest.

"One dollar more, Elliott."

Elliott reopened the box with a sigh and gave him another dollar in coin. Tecumseh put it in the boy's hand. "That one is to pay you for trouble you had getting your money. Now come, boy. I have young men who will ride you home safe."


The scouts on the road from the west told Tecumseh that they had discovered some American messengers trying to get to the fort and had chased them.

Quickly he sent a larger scouting party up the Maumee. It was the next morning before they returned, and their news was urgent: Up the river, camped on the shore near many boats, was another American army. Hundreds of militia soldiers. Maybe ten hundreds or more.

Now, Tecumseh thought as he rode toward Fort Miami to report this news to Procter, how will it go now? Will Harrison come out and fight so we can win? Or will he just fill up his hole so full of groundhogs that it will take the cannons a year to kill them? He thought quickly of all the ways it could happen. It would be tomorrow, whatever it was. The scouts had said the army was but two hours up the Maumee.

Harrison surely does not know yet that they are there, Tecumseh thought. Could I attack them where they are with no walls around them? He thought of getting up the river with warriors, Redcoats, and cannon, and ambushing their boats before they reached the American fort.

He knew that would be the best thing to do, but he knew it could not be done because Procter would refuse or take too long to move even if he did agree.

But the initiative was taken out of Tecumseh's hands. A messenger from the reinforcements slipped through and got into the fort to tell Harrison.

Harrison had already decided how to use the arriving militia. He needed to stop that bombardment. There were nearly a hundred graves in the fort by now and almost that many wounded in the hospital. Conferring quickly with his officers, he outlined a daring two-pronged sortie against the British batteries.

The order was for General Clay to float down through to the foot of the rapids and to divide his force just above the fort. The larger part, eight hundred commanded by Colonel William Dudley, was to land on the north shore of the river, storm the British batteries on the bluff, and spike the big cannons to render them useless, then return to their boats and cross to the safety of the fort. The remaining four hundred Kentuckians would land on the south shore near the fort, where a large contingent of Harrison's troops would rush out and join them for a quick assault on the mortar and howitzer emplacements southeast of the fort, and then those troops too would retreat into the fort before they could be fully engaged by Tecumseh's Indians. In his orders, Harrison then warned General Clay against the kinds of mistakes that could result from too much of that reckless Kentucky courage, which, he wrote, "if persisted in is as fatal in its results as cowardice."

The boats came down through the rapids early the next morning, after the daily bombardment had already begun. Tecumseh's warriors were shooting at them from the banks even before they landed, and he could see by the way the boats were being maneuvered that they were going to land on both sides of the river.

Tecumseh kept the main body of his warriors in the woods near the east end of the fort and watched to see what the Americans were going to do. Off in the distance to the north he could hear heavy gunfire as his warriors and a few British soldiers attacked the Americans landing on that shore. Gunsmoke and dust caught the rising sun, and it was hard to see anything.

He could see the hundreds of American troops coming around the road on the south side of the fort now and could see that they were not heading for the south gate, but toward the mortar batteries, running and cheering themselves on. At that moment he saw the south gate of the fort open and heard another throaty yell as about three hundred soldiers from the fort hurried out to join the others in a hard charge through the clearing toward the mortar batteries. And now that it was clear to Tecumseh that these Americans were going for the batteries on this side, he knew that was what those on the other side would be doing, too. They would be trying to storm the big guns. Harrison was smart and bold.

The Americans on this side were too numerous and moving too fast to be stopped. There was not much to be done about them. Their objective was close to the fort, and there was little chance of trapping them. Tecumseh sent Walk-in-Water of the Wyandots off to the left with word for the warriors in those woods simply to shoot as many Americans as possible before they could return to the fort.

His own attention was drawn to the conflict on the far bank. He knew that if the Americans got up the bluff to the big guns, they would be a long way from the fort, on the wrong side of the river, and tired from the uphill assault. Maybe those could be caught.

Quickly he rallied a large number of warriors and sped through the woods to his usual crossing place at the island. There was heavy firing up on the bluff, and he saw in a rift in the smoke that the British flag over the batteries was already being pulled down. The big guns had stopped shooting. Those Americans had done their task quickly; they had already driven out the artillerymen and overrun those batteries. Tecumseh led his warriors pell-mell across the river—some fording, some swimming, some in the canoes that were always left there. A messenger met him on the north bank, saying that the Kentuckians had successfully spiked the cannons and then, apparently carried on by their success, were pursuing the British and Indians on into the woods atop the bluff.

Tecumseh's eyes sparkled at this news. He could not have hoped for the Americans to do anything more foolish. They were doing just what they had done thirty years ago at Blue Licks.

Tecumseh sent the messenger back up with the word that the Indians should keep up a fighting withdrawal and lure the Kentuckians farther away from the river, get them into a trap, then turn on them, that he would come up behind them and close off their escape.

Then he led his own large party quietly and quickly up over the same ground the Kentuckians had taken, following them. They passed through the batteries, surprising and killing the few Kentucky soldiers who had stayed there, and followed the rest on through the woods above the bluff. The river valley around the fort now was quiet, except for some shouting and a few stray gunshots. But in the woods above the batteries, gunfire roared and crackled, and the yodeling and whooping of several hundred exultant Kentucky militiamen filtered through the foliage. Here and there lay a dead, mutilated soldier or Indian amid the trampled undergrowth. Tecumseh sprinted on at the head of his hundreds of silent warriors, waving them onward, Thick Water right beside him. By now the Kentuckians had fought their way more than a mile from the river.

The pursued were doing just what they should. They were leading the Kentuckians up a ravine that would provide a perfect trap.

Tecumseh paused now, detecting a change in the uproar ahead. There was a sudden din of very concentrated gunfire ahead, and the Indians up there were howling their attack cry. There came a bugle call from up in the woods, and Billy Caldwell said it was the call to retreat. Tecumseh motioned to his warriors now to spread up the sides of the ravine and conceal themselves, and in a few moments the hundreds were almost invisible, waiting.

Soon there was a great rush of movement and noise a little way up the ravine. Tecumseh cocked his rifle and waited for the figures to appear through the foliage. He knew that the fleeing warriors had turned on their pursuers and were chasing them back down. The voices of the approaching soldiers were full of alarm now.

Four or five whitefaces in hunting shirts suddenly broke into sight. Tecumseh shot one in the chest. His warriors' guns cracked to the left and right, and in a moment the woods were aswarm with panicky militiamen, some falling, some stopping and raising their guns, others running onto those from behind. Tecumseh's warriors now raised their bloody war cry and loaded and fired as fast as they could. Many were using bows instead of guns. At this short range the bow was a perfect weapon, and it could be shot five times as fast as a gun. A tall militiaman burst into view just in front of Tecumseh, his long legs carrying him at an incredible pace down the slope, but his legs collapsed, and he crashed at Tecumseh's feet with two arrows sticking out of his flank and one out of his ear. Tecumseh, having had no time to reload his rifle, shot two Kentuckians down with the brace of pistols Brock had given him, then stuck the guns back in his belt and began darting to and fro with war club and knife, striking at every militia soldier he could reach. His arms and legs were full of power. He felt as quick and keen as he ever had felt as a young warrior. He was fighting again on the O-hi-o soil of his fathers' lands, fighting face to face with the guilty invaders, and his club and knife grew crimson with their blood. His howls and bellowing cries encouraged his warriors and himself as well. The fleeing Kentuckians were running full tilt down the draw, trying to get back to the river; they came blundering and sprinting through the woods, sometimes stumbling over bodies or colliding with each other, like a roaring river of white men, like a panicky herd. There were so many that the warriors could not shoot and strike fast enough to kill them all. Some plunged by so fast that they got through unscathed. Others staggered through or crashed through, bleeding from wounds. Thick Water was panting from his effort to stay near his leader. Tecumseh was pouring sweat. The air in the woods was thick now with choking, blinding smoke. A few of the Kentuckians had stopped, realizing they were surrounded, and were loading and firing into the woods around them. But they were so crowded in the ravine, and so jostled by their fleeing comrades, that this resistance was ineffective. Some officers were among them, men in beaver hats and frock coats with elegant epaulets and sashes, yelling, waving swords and pistols, and trying to rally the stampeding troops, but these officers were special targets and were shot down as soon as they were seen. The noise was deafening—musket fire, pistol shots, shouts, thuds, crackling and rustling, the clatter and clank of weapons parrying weapons, the groans and screams of the hurt. Tecumseh struck and dodged as fast as he could move, his cries searing his smoke-stung throat, his mouth dry, eyes red and watering. He put himself in the way of every white man he could reach, but none of them could strike or shoot him before he killed them. He had no idea how many he himself had killed or hurt. Somewhere his knife had been knocked from his hand. He ducked down and reloaded the pretty pistols Brock had given him, then stood up, shot a white man in the forehead with one, and with the other shot into the waist of a big, bearish man who was trying to club Thick Water with a rifle butt.

Few Indians were falling. They were fighting with confidence and daring, knowing they were winning something important. The whitefaces were so swept by panic that they seemed to have no strength, no aim. Their bodies were piling up two or three deep; sometimes Tecumseh was stepping on dead men instead of ground as he darted about. His arms were red to the elbows with fresh blood, his palms sticky with it.

Now the circle of warriors was tightening upon the struggling mass of Kentuckians, killing from the edges in toward the center, and some of the white men had thrown down their guns and stood with their hands up screaming for mercy and trying to surrender before they were killed. Others were fighting just as desperately to save themselves from the fate of

Indian captivity. On a far slope of the ravine Tecumseh could see the scarlet of a number of British uniforms; apparently some of the British infantry had come from Fort Miami to help.


When the remaining white men had been rounded up as prisoners, they were a wretched, smoke-blackened, blood-spattered, wild-eyed lot. There were only about a hundred and fifty prisoners. Perhaps that many more had escaped to the river and were trying to make their way back to the fort. But here in the ravine where Tecumseh's warriors had caught them, nearly five hundred lay dead. In this quick action, Tecumseh's warriors had wiped out almost as many Long Knives as Little Turtle's three thousand confederated warriors had done in St. Clair's defeat twenty years before. Now began the harvest of scalps and the gathering of booty.

Tecumseh told the officer of the British troops to march the prisoners safely to Fort Miami, where they could be confined and the wounded could be treated by Procter's army surgeons. As they were led away eastward, Tecumseh looked one more time at the awesome heap of bodies on the slaughter ground, where the warriors were working vigorously with their scalping knives and gathering up weapons. He remembered those days in his youth when Kentuckians like these had ridden up year after year into the Shawnee homelands to kill warriors and burn towns and destroy crops. His chest was heaving and his blood was still hot, and he looked without pity at the carnage, and the words of his mother came into his head again, and he uttered them softly, as if scolding the dead:

"You should have stayed out of our land."

He summoned Charcoal Burner and Stands Firm and Billy Caldwell. "This is done, and done well," he said. "Now we must go back across the river. Harrison might come out of his groundhog burrow. It would finish the day well if we could catch him, too."

When they reached the batteries, they found Major Adam Muir there. His Redcoats had recaptured the big guns and raised the British flag over them again and were pulling out the spikes the Americans had hastily driven into the touchholes, and the artillerymen were preparing to resume the siege of Fort Meigs.


The day was not old yet, but General Harrison had already lost at least three-fourths of the reinforcements for whom he had been so long waiting. He stood on the grand battery in his fort with General Green Clay, stood there red with fury, fists and jaw clenched, watching the remnants of Colonel Dudley's brigade straggle and flounder down the far riverbank to get into the boats and come to safety.

Clay stood nearby on a crutch, face white with pain and despair. He had sprained an ankle in his successful assault on the mortars southeast of the fort, but his dismay over Dudley's disaster on the other side of the river was so great that he could hardly feel anything else.

"I warned you not to let them be rash!" Harrison muttered to Clay.

"I told them that, sir!" Clay protested, as if afraid the blame would fall on him. "I told them, and not just once!"

When that fool Dudley gets back here, I'll court-martial him, Harrison thought.

But the returning survivors made it clear there would be no court-martial needed to do justice to Dudley. "Him bein' a bit hefty, as he was, y'know," sobbed an eyewitness, "he couldn't run fast enough. . . . He was 'mongst the first they got."

Then I can only hope, Harrison thought, that he lived long enough to comprehend the enormity of what he did. "Damn, *damn,*" he groaned. "Why will men never follow my orders?"

Just then, smoke billowed from the British cannon batteries across the river, and fountains of dirt and splinters began spurting up again in the fort, and the officers and troops hurried for the cover of their diggings. Soon the mortars on the other side of the fort began popping, and shrapnel was humming in the air, whacking against everything, as it had been for days. Nothing had changed, except that some five or six or seven hundred Kentuckians who had been alive that morning were now dead. And Harrison's long-held notion that the Shawnee chief Tecumseh might be the most dangerous enemy in the land had once again been confirmed.

Tecumseh was about to leave the batteries when a young Shawnee runner arrived, sent from Fort Miami by a British officer.

The Indians around the fort had got out of control, he said. They were running the American prisoners through a gauntlet and killing them.

With a bellow of dismay and outrage, Tecumseh seized the reins of a British officer's horse, mounted, and lashed it into a gallop down the artillery road. He began passing naked white bodies, battered, cut, and scalped. The war-horse, shying at the smell of blood and the corpses, reared and whirled and pawed the air, trying to bolt, but Tecumseh got him under control, kicked him, and thundered on toward the British fort. The road was littered with torn clothing and bloody shoes, pieces of canteens, hats, broken powder horns, and every kind of discarded paraphernalia, along with the sliced-up corpses, and some warriors making their way along the road were stooping to pick up things and keep them or throw them down. Tecumseh scattered these scavengers as he rode, his heart torn by shame and disgust and pounding with urgency. The gauntlet evidently had been a wanton, murderous affair—he had seen about twenty or thirty corpses on the road already—and he dreaded what he might find when he got into the fort. Or maybe Procter and his officers had put a stop to it this time.

Today had been one of the greatest days of Indian resistance, a day for pride, when his warriors, many of them untried in battle before, had fought swiftly and courageously and intelligently against the invaders and had all but wiped out a whole brigade of American reinforcements. But now they were reverting to their old cowardice, crazed by bloodletting, lusting to make more pain and terror, despite his orders, despite his repeated exhortations. Even if he defeated every army Harrison or any American general could raise, and drove the Americans back over the O-hi-o and the mountains, and achieved the total victory that had been his great dream, the government of the Americans would never council with his red alliance, would never honor its demands, if it regarded it as nothing but a murdering, cruel throng.

*Why?* his mind screamed. *Why will my People never rise to the will of their Creator?*

Now he galloped toward that same gate of Fort Miami that he had limped to in defeat with his slain brother in his arms two decades ago, that same gate the British had shut against his people, and although the gate was open to him now and he was the victor instead of the vanquished, the fury and agony in his heart were no less than they had been then. His own people, like those of Moses in the Bible story of the whites' religion, were his worst enemy.

Already he could hear the screaming and shouting inside. He rode full tilt through the gate, and Redcoats and warriors scattered out of his path as he thundered into the inner compound.

The scene before his eyes was as bad as he could have expected. His angry shout stopped everything for a moment and even froze the Redcoats who were looking down on it from the parapets.

American soldiers, naked or in dirty underwear, lay smeared with blood, while warriors knelt over them, caught in the act of cutting off their scalps. Two soldiers lay on the ground directly in front of him, their skulls battered open, brains on the dirt. One big Potawatomi held in one hand a butcher knife, and another clutched a bound prisoner by the hair. Another warrior had his tomahawk raised over the head of a kneeling prisoner. The Redcoats on the parapets included officers, who apparently were afraid to try to stop the slaughter.

All the bloodthirsty howling had stopped at the eruption of Tecumseh's well-known voice, but the prisoners were still sobbing and wailing. Tecumseh leaped from the horse even before it stopped. With a blaze in his eyes and his war club in his hand, he reached the Potawatomi in two strides and batted him down with a quick blow. With another stride he grabbed the throat of the other warrior and flung him to earth, then shoved back a third. The Indians stood, stunned out of their blood frenzy by the sight of their leader striking down his own warriors. Then they saw the rage and torment in his eyes, and it was more than they could bear to see. They backed off, turning their eyes down, releasing their grip on the prisoners. And if any had failed to understand what was happening, his cry then made it clear to them; its tone was part contempt, part anguish:

"Are there no *men* here?"

As the warriors fell back from his terrible visage, he spoke now in a voice almost strangled. "My poor People! What will become of my poor foolish People?"

And now as he turned, sweeping his gaze over the ghastly scene, trying to mask the emotions he had shown so nakedly, he saw amid a small group of British officers the jowly, pink face of General Procter. At this sight, Tecumseh's outrage boiled over again. Throwing his arm out to point at Procter, he bellowed:

"You! Why did you let this happen in your fort?!"

Procter drew his upper chin into his lower ones. His eyes bulged for an instant, then narrowed. He started to speak, but his throat was tight after what he had just witnessed. He cleared it and replied, just as he had after the massacre at the River Raisin:

"Your . . . your Indians cannot be controlled."

Of course it was a feeble excuse, born out of his own shame; he had just seen Tecumseh alone bring them under control. Tecumseh stared at him with contempt for a long time, his finger still pointed at him. In the near silence then, broken only by the booming of the cannonade up the valley, with all of Procter's soldiers and officers in the fort listening, Tecumseh's voice commanded, in plain English, the officer who was supposed to be the commander-in-chief of all the king's forces and allies in the West:

"Begone, Procter! You are not fit to command! Go and put on petticoats!"

The two stared at each other for another full minute of silence, though Procter still could not look directly at Tecumseh's eyes. Finally, his face livid as his red coat and shining with sweat, Procter turned away, elbowed his way through the knot of officers, and stalked back to his headquarters. He desperately needed a drink.


Tecumseh brooded that night in his camp. A great victory had been made small and ugly by the cruelty of his warriors. Harrison still sat in his groundhog hole, with about as many troops as he had had before it all started. Because his reinforcements had been destroyed, he probably would not try to march on to Detroit or Canada for a while, until more soldiers came. But he was still here, and he was still strong, and eventually there would be new armies of Americans coming up. The Americans would never run out of men. The only way to defeat them would be to destroy one American fort after another, ambush one army after another, to move deeper into O-hi-o and Indiana with thousands of warriors and with Redcoats and cannons. Not long ago, when Brock had lived, Tecumseh had felt certain he could do that. But how could he do it with this slow and cautious and mean-spirited Procter?

Today Tecumseh with swiftness and bold intelligence had won a victory that should have made his heart as big and bright as the sun. And it was just one of many victories he and his warriors and their British allies had won in the eleven months since the start of the war.

He asked Weshemoneto why he had let Brock get killed.

Then he looked up toward the dark, massive shape of the American fort and thought of Harrison in there.

He had a terrible foreboding about Harrison. Harrison was much smarter than General Procter. Only a very smart officer would have built a groundhog hole like that and kept his soldiers alive all these days under so many cannonballs. Only a very smart officer would have devised an attack like that today, knocking out the British cannons on both hills.

It was not Harrison's fault that he had failed today and lost his reinforcements. It was only the stupidity of the Kentucky officer who had allowed himself to be drawn after a decoy and get trapped.

My enemy is better than my ally, Tecumseh thought.

That did not make him feel very good.


Procter kept his cannons shooting at the fort, but it was plain that he had no heart to do anything more bold.

The warriors, who had won a victory but now could see no result, were losing interest. There had been much booty in the boats they had captured from the Kentuckians, so they had kettles and blankets and guns and salt, as well as scalps, and they were not likely to get any more scalps or booty for a long time. It seemed to them that if they stayed here longer, all they would get would be aching heads and deafness from the big guns and maybe unglorious wounds from the riflemen in the American fort. Despite Tecumseh's entreaties, they began leaving in small bands. They thanked and praised Tecumseh for the great victory over the Kentuckians, but nevertheless they were leaving, until some better time.

Meanwhile, Procter's Canadian militiamen also were wanting to leave and get back to their farms, which further wore down the general's resolve. One of the militia officers, a mill owner named Benjamin Arnold, was a strong, calm, big-minded man who reminded Tecumseh of Ga-lo-weh. He could talk about anything of his culture or the red man's. He talked to Tecumseh sometimes at night about the farm and mill he had built on the Thames River above Lake St. Clair and how he loved the land of Canada. He had the same feeling as an Indian about the steady and ominous approach of the Americans toward his land. He was afraid Canada would be taken and overrun by the Americans unless Tecumseh could prevail. He too was a mourner of the loss of Brock and was equally gloomy because the war here was in the hands of a lump like Procter. "Mark my words, Chief," Arnold said sadly, "don't depend on 'im, for he's no field man like you and me."

Arnold proved right. Procter, worn down by the impasse and longing for the comforts of his home in Amherstburg, and still sulking from Tecumseh's rebuke, decided soon that there was no point in going on with it. And so, on the ninth of May, he ordered the siege lifted and began packing up his army for the return to Fort Malden. Tecumseh would have to step back off his homeland of O-hi-o now, if he were to keep his promise of supporting the Redcoats. And he was a man who kept his promises.

It seemed now to Tecumseh, as he sat on his black stallion at the big, trampled gun pits where the siege guns had been, amid all the trash and detritus of war, looking down on the battered palisade and raw, churned earth of Fort Meigs across the river, seeing the countless buzzards circling over the deserted battleground, it seemed now that unless great new signs came, some immense flowing-in of spirit, there would be no way to go forward anymore. It was as if he and Harrison were standing on opposite banks of a river with their blades hanging at their sides, unable to fight and determine the fate of the land.

Until Weshemoneto showed him the way to get to Harrison and fight him face to face, and kill him, there was no hope for a victory.

# CHAPTER 37

*Fort Malden, Ontario*
*September 9, 1813*

T he ships were taller than the trees, so when at last they began to glide down the Detroit River toward the great lake, all the Indians could see them from wherever they were.

Star Watcher was softening an elkhide to make heavy winter moccasins for her family when she heard the people exclaiming about the ships. She held the heavy hide in both hands and tugged it this way and that over the rounded end of a post, working into it the slimy brain ooze, limbering the skin. Elkhide was stiff and heavy, and only a strong woman, or a strong man, could keep working one like this until it was pliable and soft. A deerhide anyone could do, though even that was not easy; an elkhide was almost as tough a job as a bison hide, and rare was the woman who would wrestle one without another woman to help her. But in Star Watcher's mind the moccasins already existed: a pair for Stands Firm, a pair for Cat Pouncing, and a pair for Tecumseh. They would be decorated with oak-leaf designs of beading; they would be impregnated with oil to keep out the cold water and wet snow.

Looking up, sweating, Star Watcher saw the colorful banners at the tops of the masts moving slowly past the leaves in the tops of the trees. Warriors and women and children hurried along the shore to watch them go out. The ships were like black-and-orange forts with white wings and were so big that men were climbing among their wings, yet they moved upon the water as smoothly as little things like canoes or ducks! It was as if the ships were standing still and the island floating by them. Even though Star Watcher was looking at these immense things with her very own eyes and watching them go, it was hard for her to believe they were not visions.

There were thousands of Indians watching them go. All of Tecumseh's warriors were here close to the British fort, and many of them had brought their families, because the British had promised to feed and care for their women and children and elders if the warriors fought for the king. So there were many Shawnee and Wyandot, Potawatomi, Kickapoo, and Winnebago children who hugged close to their mothers' skirts as the great things moved by. Some of the children thought they were seeing moving hills with trees on them, with birds in the branches, but the birds were men.

Even to Tecumseh himself, who had learned what the different kinds of ships were called—brigs, schooners, and sloops—and how many cannons they carried, and where they were now going and why, and who knew the commander of the fleet personally, even to Tecumseh there was a great dreaminess about these ships. They were full of powerful medicine. Shamans of the very old times had dreamed of these things generations before any real ones had come to the eastern shore. Tecumseh remembered the one whose white sail he had seen against the gray-blue distance over Lake Mis-e-ken when he had walked on the sand shore with Chiksika half a lifetime ago. Perhaps it had been one of these very ships.

Now as Tecumseh watched the British warships go out toward the vast flatness of the lake, their canvas wings opening with a noise like fluttering thunder, it was like a sign of hope. Of course it was not a sign, it was just a real thing happening, but it was the first hopeful thing that had happened since the battle at Fort Meigs.

After Procter had given up once on that siege, Tecumseh had persuaded him to go back and help him attack the fort once again, two moons ago, but that had failed because the Americans had again stayed in their groundhog hole and refused to be drawn out to fight. From there the British and Indians had gone to attack a smaller American fort on the Sandusky River, but that attack had failed, too.

Following those failures had been more and more bad news. Harrison had kept building up his army for the invasion of Canada. The old Kentucky governor Shelby had brought still another big army of Kentuckians up through O-hi-o to Fort Meigs. Harrison had persuaded some of the government Indians at the Crane's town to join the Americans against Tecumseh's followers. Worse, even some of old Black Hoof's Shawnee warriors were now scouts for Harrison's army, and that had twisted like a knife in Tecumseh's heart: Shawnees serving the American army! Furthermore, Chief Walk-in-Water, whose Wyandot village was just across the river from Fort Malden, had swayed back and forth between the Americans and the British like a blade of grass blowing in changing winds.

But the worst news had come just in the last moon.

The Americans had finished building their fleet of ships and had launched them. Now for the first time there were enemy warships upon

Lake Erie. Procter had never had the courage or initiative to march east and attack the American shipyards on the American side of the lake, though almost a year ago Brock had said it was an important thing to do, and now it was too late. The new American fleet had come into view two weeks ago and insolently stood in sight outside the mouth of the Detroit River as if to challenge the British ships, then had sailed off over the southern horizon. The British officers said the American fleet was no cause for worry, that the British navy would never be defeated by any other navy, particularly a little fleet of inferior American ships. The commander of the British fleet on the lake was Barclay, a great warrior chief of the British navy and a famous hero, though still quite young. Barclay had lost an arm eight years ago while serving with the navy chief Nelson at Trafalgar, which, the officers explained to Tecumseh, had been the greatest of all sea battles. The newly outfitted ship that Barclay was now sailing out to the lake was the largest warship ever launched on Lake Erie. It was a brig of 490 tons called the *Detroit*. Barclay and Procter had no doubts that the *Detroit* and the five other ships could sweep the American vessels off the lake at once. Tecumseh liked to hear such confident talk, so the going out of the British fleet was like a good sign.

Tecumseh, Thick Water, and Stands Firm stood for a long time watching the ships grow smaller. Then they walked back to Stands Firm's lean-to, where Star Watcher had resumed her strenuous work on the elkhide.


Bois Blanc Island divided the mouth of the Detroit River into two channels. From the southern end of the island one could see far over the western end of the lake. Most of Tecumseh's warriors were camped on this island now, and many of them had hurried down to that end of the island to gaze at the British ships for as long as they could see them. Even after they had become too small to see, many of the warriors had stayed down there, watching the evening settle over the open water. Then they had at last gone back up to their campfires. They had not talked much about the ships during the night, because they knew little about them, but in many a dream that night there were the huge white wings of the ships.

Tecumseh sat late that night by the fire in Stands Firm's lean-to, and around him were all the living members of his own family: Star Watcher, Open Door, and Cat Pouncing. Star Watcher fed everyone from a large kettle of succotash seasoned with herbs and a small stew made of English beef. Tecumseh sat watching her thoughtfully, as if from across the Circle of Time, remembering her great beauty as it had been long ago. She was a gray-haired woman now, her hands rough and veined and big-knuckled from the work of raising crops and two generations of children. Her skin was loose. She no longer had a waist. Her body was straight up and down, all its curves long since gone, and it was lean and hard, and her breasts were wrinkled and pendulous. Only her face and soul were still beautiful, but they were very beautiful. The wrinkles around her eyes and mouth were the lines of smiling. When she looked at Tecumseh it was with the same care and tenderness as when she had tended to him as a child. She was as much like his mother as his sister.

Open Door sat on the other side of the fire. He had eaten prodigiously. After his great disgrace at Tippecanoe and his fall from power, he had begun eating like the hog he had been in his youth, and much of his thought now was of food. But there was some good that could be said of him. He had never gone back to liquor, even after Tippecanoe. He still believed in all the tenets of the religion he had founded and even had a few followers, though his circle of influence had become very small. He was always very careful not to say anything that might annoy Tecumseh; although Tecumseh relied upon him as the shaman of their Shawnee band, he was aware of being barely tolerated by most of the leading men and knew that if he were not Tecumseh's brother, he would be an outcast—or, just as likely, a dead man. Open Door was a sad and gloomy man now, but when he was around Tecumseh he tried to be cheerful and funny.

Cat Pouncing, Tecumseh's son, was handsome and well mannered, a bit shy around his father. He seemed soft. He still had not found a Spirit Helper. It was strange to Tecumseh that this son of himself and the willful She-Is-Favored was so placid. The sight of him was a reproach to Tecumseh, who knew he had never been a good father. He had spent so much time away at war and council throughout his son's lifetime that he had been almost a stranger to him. He had been closer to a white girl, Rebekah Galloway, than to his own son, and to think of that shamed him. He had hardly ever taken time to teach him anything. Raised by his aunt, Cat Pouncing had been more like Stands Firm's son than his own. Tecumseh remembered how much his own father, Hard Striker, had taught him, directly or by way of Chiksika, and he knew he should have made more time to teach his own son the same knowledge. Now he felt that the smooth-faced, shy-eyed young man by the fire was more like a nephew than a son, and it humbled him. He was supposed to be the greatest of all Shawnee men, yet he had failed in something that the most ordinary men did well.

When the war is over, he told himself now, I will come and get my son and hunt with him and take him to the places I have seen, and teach him to be a man. It is not too late to make him into a strong and good man. He is already good; my sister has made him good. He only needs to be strengthened. Stands Firm might have taught him manliness, but Stands Firm himself had been away for so much of his own life as a member of Tecumseh's retinue that he had not had much life in his family, either.

Yes, my son will be a strong and good man someday, Tecumseh thought. It will take time and very much attention, which I have long owed him. Now it is the red people and their homelands that need me.

And if the Shawnee people are not saved, he thought, it will not even matter what kind of man I make my son. He will be but a dog in the white man's yard.

"This tastes better than the horsemeat," Open Door was saying with stew grease shining on his mouth. "Tell them, brother, how you made Procter stop giving our people horsemeat." Open Door, as he had done when he was a boy, tried often these days to make Tecumseh look good in the eyes of others.

Tecumseh came out of his grave ponderings and smiled around at them all. "I went to Procter. I said to him, 'Procter, I have learned that you give beef to your soldiers and horsemeat to my warriors. I know you use my warriors as a hunter uses his dogs, to go out in front and get the game. But my warriors are not your dogs. They do more of your fighting than your soldiers do, and you will give them the same kind of meat.' That is what I told Procter."

"I was there when that was said," remarked Stands Firm. "That fat general's face became as red as his coat."

Open Door laughed, an exaggerated laugh, and slapped his thigh. He laughed louder and longer than the others. Tecumseh looked at him reflectively, with pity and regret, thinking of all the things his brother had been in his lifetime, how he had been great in his smallness and small in his greatness. Tecumseh glanced over at Star Watcher, who was moving cookpots away from the fire, shaking her head at the hysterical sound of Open Door's cackling, a patient, fond smile on her lips.

"Brother," Stands Firm said now to Tecumseh, "what will happen if the American ships defeat the British ships? What will come of things if Procter and One-Arm are wrong about who can win on the battlefield of water?" There had been little talk of such a thing happening, but a few had been thinking of it. Tecumseh replied:

"Procter will be so surprised, he will make soil where he sits."

"Like this!" cackled Open Door. He tilted to raise a buttock off the ground and made a moist wind, which, for once, everyone thought was funny.

Tecumseh did not want to talk seriously about this now; his head had been heavy with serious matters for too long. It seemed he was always in council with his war chiefs or with Elliott or the British officers, and it was good now to be talking about little things with his family and joking about matters. But Stands Firm had asked the question seriously and deserved a serious answer, so Tecumseh said:

"Most of the food and ammunition comes to this place by ships. And when Procter needs to take the big guns and the soldiers anywhere to fight, the best way is to put them on ships, as he did to go to Fort Meigs. If the American ships defeated the British ships, Procter is afraid that no food and ammunition could come here, except by the bad road from the east. And that the Americans then could bring Blue-Coat soldiers in their ships to land on this side of the lake between here and Niagara, and then Procter would be cut off from his king's government, and could not get his chocolate and brandy. Or food and ammunition. This I think he fears more than anything. That is why he would make a mess where he sits if such a thing happened."

They were quiet for a while, looking into the fire, thinking of it in this way for the first time. Before, while watching the British ships go down to the lake, they had not really understood the consequences or how important it was. After a while Stands Firm said, "They took some big guns from the fort to put on the big new ship. How can a ship float with something so heavy?" He smoked for a while, then said, "I saw the big guns shoot at Harrison's fort. When the ships fight other ships, do they shoot at them with those guns? Would it not turn the ship over, as it would seem to me?"

"Think of it this way," Tecumseh said. "You have shot your musket from a canoe?"

"Yes."

"A cannon to a big ship is about like a musket to a canoe. So a cannon does not turn the big ship over when it is shot from it."

"That is your answer?" said Stands Firm. "When I shot my musket from a canoe, the canoe turned over!" Everybody laughed, and Stands Firm smiled around, but then he went on. "Brothers, I will tell you this: I would not want to be on a ship when it is shooting cannons. Nor would I want to be on one ship when another ship is shooting cannons at it. No. I would not. One should stay out of ships and forts. They draw more cannonballs than one would want." He pursed his lips and raised his eyebrows, then nodded to show that he had had his say.

"The one-arm, Barclay, has done that many times," said Tecumseh. "It is why he has one arm only. Yet he goes out again today, knowing it could happen. I admire the one-arm captain. I think he is much more brave than Procter."

"We should pray for the Master of Life to help this one-arm," Open Door said, "even though he is a white man."

The next morning was clear and still. Many of the Indians went down to the end of the island at daybreak, drawn by the memory of their night's dreams to go and look at the lake. There were no ships anywhere in sight, only canoes and fishing boats and army boats near the river's mouth and beyond them the miles of water sparkling with sunlight and the straight silver line of the horizon. There was very little breeze, and the lake water only slurped at the shore of the island. The sun rose over the lake and climbed. The smells of woodsmoke and cooking hung in the air, and in this beautiful place by the water it seemed like a time of peace.

When the sun was at its highest, Tecumseh was talking with Roundhead about the problem of Walk-in-Water. Word had come, by way of a relative of Thick Water's Wyandot wife, that Walk-in-Water was in a secret agreement with the Americans, that if Harrison brought his big army up the western shore of the lake, Walk-in-Water would advise his men to leave Tecumseh and help Harrison. This was not a new problem with Walk-in-Water. When Hull had first invaded Canada, Walk-in-Water had deserted the British, then had rejoined them after Brock and Tecumseh captured Detroit. Walk-in-Water's village was right in the way of the war road, and that was why he always wanted to be on the winning side. At the present time, the Americans showed more promise of winning. Roundhead had been an unshakable follower of Tecumseh since the beginning, and he was ashamed of Walk-in-Water and scorned him. "He is like a weather sign," Roundhead growled. "To know who is winning the war, we only need to sit and watch Walk-in-Water."

At that moment, though the sky was blue and sunny and there was no scent of rain, Tecumseh heard thunder. Roundhead had heard it, too. His anger about Walk-in-Water vanished from his face, and he looked up and around at the sky. Other people in the camp had paused in what they were doing.

It was like thunder, but not quite like thunder.

"The ships are fighting," Tecumseh said.

The people began hurrying down to the lake end of the island. Tecumseh and Roundhead strode along with the crowd.

The lake looked just as it had before: glittering water, the line of the horizon. But the thundering went on and on. It was so constant that Tecumseh knew there were many more cannons shooting than there had been at Fort Meigs during the great sieges there. It was amazing that this rumbling could be so loud even though the big ships were so far away that they could not be seen.

After a while Tecumseh raised his arm and pointed toward the horizon just a little east of south.

There was a smudge of smoke against the pearly-bright sky.

Little Fort Seneca was more than thirty-five miles south of Lake Erie, on the Sandusky River, but General Harrison could hear the naval guns thundering. He stood on a parapet in the sunlight and listened for a while. An officer said, "Listen at 'em, sir! Sounds like young Oliver's giving 'em proper hell, doesn't it?"

Harrison nodded, but he thought: Or vice versa.

He was worried. Captain Perry had set sail with an appalling shortage of trained naval officers. Even his crews were so undermanned that he had had to ask for volunteers from among the Kentucky riflemen, who were anything but sailors.

Harrison went down to his headquarters. He had moved his command post to this little fort from Fort Meigs because it was more central to all the Lake Erie posts, and from here he could respond more quickly to attacks anywhere.

Even here in his room he could hear the thumping grumble of the naval guns and could not concentrate on anything. Just getting a fleet built and launched on Lake Erie had been a miracle. What if it were being sunk now by the British navy?

After an hour or so he went back up on the parapet. And while he was there, listening and thinking, the distant thundering died out. He stood for a long time listening, but there was no more cannon fire.

Now there would be the waiting. How long would it be before the outcome was known?

It was only a few hours. A horseman came galloping up the river road that evening, and he had a message written to Harrison on the back of an envelope:

Dear General: We have met the enemy and they are ours—two ships, two brigs, one schooner and a sloop.
Yours, with great respect and esteem,
Oliver Hazard Perry

For two days after the long thunder of the ship battle, the Indians watched for the British vessels to return from the lake. Tecumseh continued to meet with his warriors and administer to the needs of the people, but he could not keep from wondering where the ships were or why Procter had not sent any word about their victory.

On the second of those two days, some warriors who had been at Fort Malden came to the island and told Tecumseh that they had seen Procter from a distance, and that he had looked like a very troubled man. They had noticed also that some of Procter's aides were making crates and carrying trunks and barrels at Procter's headquarters.

A few days later, the British soldiers were seen taking apart kitchens and armories and offices of the fort and loading wagons. Tecumseh sent a messenger to Procter asking to know what had happened to the ships and for an explanation of the activities in the fort. Procter sent back no reply, but the messenger had noticed that he was still packing. Now it was plain that he was getting ready to flee.

The British had promised to help the red men regain their homelands, but now they were apparently getting ready to retreat farther and farther from the Indians' lands. Tecumseh was growing hot and tight inside. He sent for Matthew Elliott and told him to go to Procter. "Tell the general," Tecumseh said, "that if he does not give me the truth of what is happening, I will cut my end of the wampum belt, and the results will be bad!"

It was a full week after the cannon thunder on the lake before old Elliott finally prevailed upon General Procter to meet with Tecumseh and his chiefs. They were to assemble at the big council hall at Amherstburg.

By this time Tecumseh was almost in a fury at Procter's evasiveness. He had warned Procter in the past that if he ever lied to him, he would take his red men and abandon the British. Tecumseh had had enough experience with such evasiveness in his own brother to deduce that Procter was afraid to lie to him but also afraid to tell the truth.

In the vast hall with its vaulted ceiling, the hundreds of warriors and chieftains filled every foot of floor space, a colorful, agitated, murmuring mass of men. Officers of the militia and the Redcoat Forty-first Regiment stood along the walls.

Procter came in looking sullen, pale, and nervous. Many of the officers with him looked sullen, too. Their noses were in the air, and they would not look at Procter, so it seemed that even they were displeased with him.

Before the panorama of brilliant costumes and garish ornaments and intense, dark faces in the smoky room, Procter announced curtly that plans were being made for a withdrawal to someplace eastward, closer to the other wings of the British forces. He said nothing about the naval battle and made no further explanation. As his words were translated, the voices of the Indians began to rise, droning with consternation and anger in the great hall. Tecumseh rose and spoke loudly:

"Father, listen! Our fleet has gone out; we know they have fought. We have heard the great guns. But we know nothing of what has happened to our father with one arm. Our ships have gone one way, and we are very much astonished to see our father tying up everything and preparing to run away the other, without letting his red children know what his intentions are for them!"

He paused and stared at Procter while this was being translated into English and into the various tribal tongues. He saw that Procter's face was sweaty and red. And he also saw some of the young British officers, who had been his comrades in some of the battles, nod their heads and look accusingly at Procter.

The Indians too were all watching Procter with clouded faces; many of them had already deduced to their own satisfaction that he was deceiving them and going his own way with no concern for their opinions or their welfare.

While Procter sat glowering at Tecumseh with his head back and his lips set thin, Tecumseh went on:

"You always told us to remain here and take care of our lands; it made our hearts glad to hear that was your wish. You always told us that you would never draw your foot off British ground, but now we see you are drawing back, and we are sorry to see our father running without even seeing the enemy!"

He paused again. The warriors were muttering their agreement, their indignation. Procter's eyes were looking glazed; his lip quivered with the hint of a sneer. His face infuriated Tecumseh; this was like the expression that had been on his face while he had stood by and watched the slaughter of prisoners at Fort Miami, afraid to try to stop it. Procter was contemptuous of Indians but afraid of them at the same time, an attitude that insulted Tecumseh and every other red man who perceived it.

So now Tecumseh allowed himself to speak directly of Procter's cowardice; he cared not at all how angry he made him.

"We must compare our father's conduct to that of a fat animal, that carries its bushy tail high upon its back, but when frightened, he drops it between his legs and runs off."

Laughter swept through the whole room when this was translated, and it was not just the Indians laughing but also the British officers around the walls. Several of the officers right beside Procter were biting their lips and flushing, trying to keep from guffawing. Procter's face had darkened almost to livid, and he was shaking visibly, either from mortification or with his effort to contain himself. Suddenly Tecumseh overrode the tittering and laughter with his voice.

"Listen, Father! The Americans have not yet defeated us by land; neither are we sure that they have done so by water. We therefore wish to remain here, and fight our enemy if they should appear. If they defeat us, *then* we will retreat with our father!"

The warriors were very intent upon his words now; here their leader was contrasting their bravery with Procter's cowardice, and they were stirred and proud.

Now Tecumseh reminded them of an English perfidy that a few of them were old enough to remember personally and the rest of them had heard of many times. "At the Battle of the Rapids in the Fallen Trees last war, the Americans defeated us, and when we retreated to our father's fort at that place, the gates were shut against us. We were afraid that the same might be done here, but instead of that, we now see our British father preparing to *march out* of his garrison!

"Father! You have got the arms and ammunition which the great father sent for his red children. If you have an idea of going away, give them to us, and you may go, and welcome. As for us, our lives are in the hands of the Great Spirit. He gave to our ancestors the lands which we possess. We are determined to defend them, and if it be his will, our bones shall whiten on them, but we will never give them up!"

The warriors' response to this was so surprising and menacing that Procter's purpled face drained of color. Many of the warriors leaped to their feet, shaking their tomahawks at the British, their angry voices roaring to the high ceiling.

Procter waited for the din to subside, then rose, saying only that he would answer in another council, and hastened out a nearby door with Tecumseh's anger drilling into his back, palpable as an arrow. Procter's own officers were confused and awkward, torn between their desire to jeer him and their fear that the hundreds of aroused warriors might simply rush at them; some of the officers were standing there applauding Tecumseh while others were sidestepping out of the council hall with tears in their blinking eyes and their chins jutting. It was left to old Elliott to try to restore order in the echoing hall.

So Procter still had not answered, but now there was no doubt in Tecumseh's mind. The British ships had surely been sunk.

Now how could there ever be a hope of carrying the war back into the homelands in O-hi-o?

# CHAPTER 38

*Fort Malden, Ontario*
*September 23, 1813*

The night sky was full of red smoke.

Star Watcher and Open Door stood together, their faces lit by the glow of the burning shipyard and the fort. They stood at the roadside and looked back at the fires while heavy-laden wagons trundled and groaned past, going north on the river road. It was the same road where Tecumseh had ambushed the American army at the beginning of this war, to save Fort Malden from the Redcoats; now, fourteen moons later, the Redcoats themselves had set it on fire and were fleeing from it without an enemy in sight. Nearby stood old Colonel Elliott, his eyes glinting with tears in their wrinkled sockets. Elliott had labored in his old age to build an estate here, and now it would be lost, a ruin. He had helped the Shawnees for as long as they could remember, but now there was nothing they could do to help him, and this made a deep ache in Star Watcher's heart.

The shipyard had been burning like a forest fire all day. The unfinished ship hulls burned with roaring flames that leaped and spiraled a hundred feet high. As their sheathing burned through and fell off to reveal the curving rib timbers, showers and swirls of sparks rose into the lurid smoke and brightened it to yellow. The stacks of oak logs and hewn timbers and planks looked as if they would burn forever. They would burn, then shift and settle and rumble, and the flames would lick higher. Masts and wooden derricks and gin poles flamed like standing torches; when their stays burned through they fell, *whoosh*ing and banging, sending up still more eddies of sparks and setting roofs and shacks and lumber on fire.

After he had ordered the shipyard set afire, General Procter had finished packing everything from Fort Malden, and then the fort too had been set

607

ablaze. The old, dry, wood-shingled roofs flared up so fast, they were almost like explosions.

A company of the Forty-first Regiment Redcoats now tramped by, part of the rear guard for the wagon convoy, and their coats were garish in the firelight. Many of their uniforms had black holes in them where sparks blown by the lake wind had fallen on the soldiers. The soldiers' eyes glinted with fireglow as they glanced at Star Watcher and Open Door.

Now Open Door cried out in his piercing voice, and the Indian families began filling the road behind the Redcoats, hundreds of women and children and elders, carrying bags and kettles and babies, leading horses that carried packs or pulled pole drags. Bent-backed old women limped by, leaning on staffs.

Once again the Indian families were fleeing in the fire-reddened night, refugees from invading Long Knife soldiers, and Star Watcher remembered the many times before. But this time they were not in their homeland in the O-hi-o country, but in Canada, far from old Chillicothe and Piqua and Maykujay Town, far from Tippecanoe and going still farther into an unfamiliar land, following the British, who had promised to protect them and help them regain their homelands but who instead were being protected by the red men—and fleeing from an enemy that was not yet even in sight.

Open Door, his chest aching with sadness and his mouth tasting bitterness, nevertheless smiled and spoke reassurances to his People as they went past, those who did not make war but who were always its sorriest victims. "Be strong," he said. "The Great Good Spirit favors our People; all will be well. Follow the Redcoat soldiers. You will go to a safer place. All will be well. Colonel Elliott will feed you, as he always has done. All will be well, Grandmother. . . ." With a pang in his heart, he remembered how it had been to comfort the People. He glanced at his sister, who was saying the same reassurances. Tecumseh had put them in charge of caring for the refugees and keeping them from straggling too far behind the retreating Redcoats. It would be a heavy and sad burden for them, but the kind of burden they had been carrying for years—the care of the People.

Another wooden roof in the fort caved in, sending up another tower of fire to show them their road.

Thick Water could feel in the wind that much rain was coming. He frowned and pulled his blanket closer around his neck, shifted his tired body in the saddle, and sighed. Another wet autumn was coming, and once again the People were homeless.

To warm his heart then he turned his thoughts to his beautiful wife and children. They at least would be sheltered, though probably hungry, in the Wyandot town on the other side of the great lake. How good it would be to have a time of peace and live with them close to the cookfire, to sleep with the embers warming him on one side and her body warming him on the other.

But Thick Water's duty, by his own choice, was here. Tecumseh sat on his horse a few paces away, between Elliott and Withered Hand, on the road above the smoking ruins of Fort Malden, watching Harrison's huge army come ashore from their ships. The American fleet was large now; it included the ships that Perry had captured from One-Arm Barclay. To guard Tecumseh was Thick Water's self-appointed duty, it had been for many years, and from that duty there came another kind of inner fire. But protecting Tecumseh had always been a difficult duty, full of hardships and dangers, and it was especially so now. Reluctant to retreat, Tecumseh seemed inclined to prowl the very edge of peril. The Redcoats and the warriors and the refugees had long since gone, up the river road to Sandwich Town, then east toward the river Thames, destroying bridges behind them. But Tecumseh lingered miles behind the retreat, choosing to watch the approaching Long Knives from barely a gunshot away, always looking for a sight of Harrison.

General Procter had persuaded Tecumseh not to desert the Redcoats, demonstrating on maps why they needed to retreat to more defensible ground, showing him how the American fleet could go around to Lake St. Clair and cut the Redcoats off from their supply route. Procter had promised Tecumseh that a full-fledged battle against the Americans would be made at the town of Chatham on the Forks of the Thames, where the Thames was too narrow and shallow for the American gunboats to navigate. Once convinced, Tecumseh in turn had persuaded most of his chiefs to stay by the Redcoats, though he would have preferred to fight here and keep Harrison's army from putting one foot onto the Canadian shore at all.

Now Thick Water saw Tecumseh point toward the multitude of Blue-Coats and heard him say:

"Look at them. Now they are out of their groundhog hole, and I can defeat them. But I will have to defeat them at a place called Chatham, whose ground I do not know, instead of here, on a place I know so well. And Detroit, that Brock and I took from them on that good day last year! It will fall back into their hands. Oh, I do not like this!"

Colonel Elliott looked aside at Tecumseh, face full of disbelief. He said in Shawnee, "But look how many! There are forty hundred, at least!"

"Forty hundred is only counting," Tecumseh replied. "Fighting is not counting, old Father. It is strong hearts and being right. In times past you know I have defeated five times as many as my own."

Thick Water's heart swelled at these words. It was true. He knew it because he had been with his chief at many such times past.

Withered Hand, the terrible Potawatomi, was looking at the horde of Americans moving ashore in the near distance and saying nothing. Thick Water thought that Withered Hand did not look very brave now. Much of his celebrated ferocity seemed to have been dampened by the huge scale of things in this white man's war. It was not like raiding Osage villages or isolated cabins of white settlers in Illinois, as in the old days. Thick Water had seen that look in the faces of other chiefs in recent days, chiefs who had grown doubtful about their British allies and had decided to take their people and go home, and Thick Water wondered how much longer Withered Hand would stay faithful to Tecumseh's cause. He sniffed the ashy, tangy smell of smoldering oak as the dank lake wind blew up from the ruins of the shipyard and fort. He felt the hint of the coming autumn rains in the air and heard the deep, steady hush and drone of noises from the invading army, and his heart grew heavy again. He heard hooves on the cobbles at the other end of the little town and saw American horse soldiers come riding slowly around the corner of a stone house. Elliott and Withered Hand looked very impatient, ready to flee up the road.

Finally, then, Tecumseh took one last, long look at the oncoming Blue-Coats, sighed, turned his horse, and rode slowly up the beaten road of retreat. To Thick Water he said as he rode past, "Come, brother. We will destroy that army another day."

The heavy rains began as the retreating Redcoats moved eastward from Sandwich along the shore of Lake St. Clair and continued day after day.

General Procter stayed far ahead of the retreat, traveling in a carriage with his wife and daughter. Far behind him came his army and its enormous baggage convoy and its herd of beef cattle, beating and churning the road into a porridge of mud; behind them came the fatigued and hungry Indian families; behind them came Tecumseh's warriors, a thousand of them. And behind them always came Tecumseh, always a step ahead of Harrison's advancing army, deploying his chieftains to obstruct and harass them at every opportunity, to snipe at scouts, to ambush columns at the bridges and fords, slowing the Long Knives to let the refugees stay ahead at a safe distance. He patrolled the fringes of the invading army like a wolf and nipped it whenever he saw a chance.

But the circumstances grew more and more bleak as the refugees and the

Redcoats plodded eastward toward the mouth of the Thames. Confusing orders came back from General Procter; soon, units of the Forty-first Regiment were out of touch with each other, the commissary was failing to get food to the bivouacs, and riverboats full of arms and supplies fell far behind. The Indian Department could not obtain food for the refugees, and they, weakening, sick, straggled farther and farther behind on the miry roads. Star Watcher and Open Door demanded and begged for their people, but the agents could only shrug and blame the commissary, which in turn blamed the general. Withered Hand groused and sneered about how the British had destroyed his faith in them, then finally broke off and took away large numbers of his Potawatomies, as well as some Ottawas, Ojibways, and Sauks who were under his influence, saying he was tired of running and would rejoin Tecumseh and the Redcoats only if they stopped and defeated Harrison.

Then came a runner to Tecumseh, saying that one of Harrison's brigades, backed up by Perry's American warships in the Detroit River, had driven the few remaining Indian defenders out of Detroit, lowered the British flag that Tecumseh and Brock had raised over the fort a year ago, and raised the American flag. Everything, it seemed, was falling like the dead leaves.

As the retreating column left Lake St. Clair and moved eastward on the road along the Thames under the gray sky, some of the smaller American gunships passed on through the Detroit River channel into Lake St. Clair and entered the mouth of the Thames in pursuit. Tecumseh watched them coming on the rainy west wind, their sails white through the autumn foliage, and saw an opportunity to play wolf again. The river was narrow, so he put warriors along its banks and in trees to shoot down into the American gunships. At last, unable to proceed under such fire, the ships dropped back down the river.

Stopping the gunships was a momentary victory for Tecumseh, but he had no chance to rejoice over it. Another runner came. Roundhead, that staunch friend since the beginning, had been killed while harassing the edges of Harrison's army. Tecumseh's heart grew harder and colder. The bitter worm of vengeance was eating in his soul, and he was impatient to reach Chatham at the Forks. There at Chatham, Procter had said, showing him a map, stood a blockhouse, several strong log houses, and two bridges nearly a mile apart that the Americans would have to try to cross. It did sound like a good place to ambush Harrison and stop his army. Surely Procter was there already with his Redcoats and cannons, building breastworks, as he had promised he would do. The refugees would go across the bridges to safety, then the warriors would cross and tear up the bridges

behind them and turn around to fight Harrison at the Forks, to kill him for
his great crime of trespass. Tecumseh's blood was seething for battle now.
His dead father and brothers, his great friends Brock and Roundhead, his
teacher Black Fish, all who had been killed by the white men's bullets and
diseases, all sang in his soul their wish for revenge, and he was eager to die
if the Master of Life meant to sacrifice him for it.

But when Tecumseh and his rear guard crossed the bridge over the fork
and arrived at Chatham, they found no fortifications. On the other bank of
the river a few Redcoats were casually encamped, doing nothing but trying
to keep themselves dry. Three cannons lay dismantled on the south riverbank, and a hut had been filled with muskets, but there were no British
here, except old Elliott, who stood pale and shaken amid a horde of yelling,
infuriated chieftains and warriors who were demanding to know why there
was no fort here as Procter had promised there would be. Walk-in-Water
was waving a club, howling that he would kill Procter if he saw him, that
he would kill Elliott now. Charcoal Burner seemed to be shielding the old
agent, but only halfheartedly; he, too, turned to him and bellowed, "Father,
your Redcoats are cowards! They are liars!"

Some of the chiefs even met Tecumseh himself with lightning in their
eyes and thunder in their mouths. "Did you not promise us the fat general
would have a fort here, and supplies for us?" cried South Wind, a tall
Ojibway chief, with tears of frustration in his narrowed eyes. As if this
question had suddenly thrown the weight of their suspicion upon Tecumseh, many began crowding toward him, yelling, thrusting up their arms.
Thick Water, suddenly tense, drew his tomahawk and rode his horse between them and his chief, forcing some of them back, and others of the
bodyguard began to form a circle around him.

But Tecumseh himself was soon able to shout down the uproar. He
shamed the crowd for accusing him and convinced them that he was as
bewildered as they were. Elliott got close to Tecumseh and hung near his
stirrup as if to save himself. Tecumseh reached down and grasped the
shoulder of his coat.

"Old Father! What is this fat general doing? Does he not tell even you?"

Elliott was shaking his head, his mouth slack and drooling, his whole
frame trembling. He moved his lips with no voice, then finally croaked out:
"I'm confused. . . . He told us . . . yesterday? . . . told us we would fight
back at the Dolsen farm . . . yes, Dolsen's, it was, that it was a better place
than this . . . more buildings there, but . . . then changed his mind again,
I suppose. I'm sorry! I'm confused. Procter's made such a botch of it all.
. . . My friend, *tell* them it's not *my* fault. My God!" he cried in English then.

"I've given my whole life to your people! My whole bloody life; you know that's true!"

A voice called from downstream that Redcoats were coming up the river road, up the other side. Tecumseh released Elliott's shoulder and stood in his stirrups. He heard troops coming, saw scarlet uniforms through the distant foliage. "Let this be Procter," he said. "I will have an answer from him. Clear a way for me!" he shouted, urging his horse toward the bridge that crossed the river.

When he careened onto the road at the other end of the bridge and galloped to meet the British column, he recognized at its head not Procter but his first subordinate, Colonel Warburton of the Forty-first Regiment. Following the colonel were some three or four hundred foot soldiers, a few dragoons tall on their horses, and a cluster of refugee Indians, mostly women. Tecumseh reined in alongside the officer, crying, "Warburton! Where is Procter?"

Colonel Warburton, looking awfully angry himself, pointed up the river road. "Gone on ahead, I suppose. Who really knows?"

Tecumseh clenched his jaw. "Why has he gone ahead? Why has he made no fort here? Is this not Chatham? He said he would stand here with me and meet the Long Knives! Why is he up that road? *I want to know!*"

Warburton tilted his head and replied with sarcasm: "As you may or not know, Chief, I'm not one of that select group of officers whom the general deigns to favor with information. I'm merely his second-in-command. But from what I can gather of it all, he's changed his mind, and wants to fortify at the missionary town instead."

Tecumseh's eyes for a moment looked like a madman's. "Warburton! Procter gave me his *promise* we would have a fort here and fight the Americans at last! Has he lied to me? You heard me tell him that if he ever lied to me, I would cut off your end of the wampum belt!" Tecumseh was all but grinding his teeth and was ready to ride back across the bridge and lead his warriors away and throw Procter and his army to the Long Knives. Pounding his fist on his knee in frustration, he swept his gaze around in the dusk. It would have been a strong place for a defense, if it had been made ready, and there had been days and days of time to make it ready. But now there was no time. The Long Knives were less than half a day's march behind. Tecumseh groaned. "Warburton! I wish I had never listened to Procter! Everything he promises blows away like smoke!"

Now many of Tecumseh's chieftains and bodyguards had come across the bridge to join him in this confrontation and were gathering around. Among them came Colonel Elliott, hitching along on foot, his face red with exertion and anger. Panting, he looked up at Warburton in the rain and tried to say something, but then broke into abject weeping before he could sob out: "Colonel, do something about this disgraceful rout! I will not by God sacrifice myself!"

Warburton could do hardly anything. Dusk was deepening. He sent a company of grenadiers a mile down the river toward the enemy, to form a picket line on the north bank. Tecumseh had managed at last to contain his own fury and was calming his chieftains, trying to persuade them not to desert their allies just because of Procter's confusion. He counciled with them quickly, and they agreed to stay at the Forks until the next day and make an ambush at the bridges, to slow the American advance and allow the refugees a few more hours of safe flight.

"Your soldiers should be on that side of the river with my warriors," he told Warburton. "Harrison comes on that side."

Warburton replied with more firmness than he felt, "I'll not move them over, Chief. I must stay on this road, if I'm going to the missionary town."

"Then *go!*" Tecumseh snarled. "Go on up and leave *brave* men here to fight your enemy for you! Let your soldiers sleep safe on this side of the river! My red men will stand with me tomorrow and meet Harrison, *without* your cannons or your soldiers! Get out of my way!" He rode a few paces away, then wheeled and came back, an indistinct shape in the early darkness. "Colonel Warburton, I know *you* are a brave soldier. I wish you, not Procter, led your army. I know you must be ashamed of how he always runs backward, like a crayfish." Then he pressed his horse's flanks with his heels and galloped away across the resounding planks of the bridge.


That night for the first time in his life Tecumseh felt age in his bones as he lay on the damp ground and tried to sleep. His wakeful mind prowled every quadrant of the world around him like a night cat: Harrison's relentless army to the west; to the east Procter lying probably in a warm bed with his wife while his misdirected army slept cold, hungry, and disorganized in many places along the river Thames; to the north, winter coming down from the severe lands of the Eskimo people; to the south, the long-lost homelands of the Shawnee now full of square farms and noisy cities. Tecumseh's prayer thoughts then visited the warriors sleeping around him in the wet woods, the refugees a short way up the road, his brother and sister and son among them, and the scouts who had stolen down the riverbank in darkness to prowl the edges of the Long Knives' army camp. His People. His homeless red People. And his heart ached, and his bones ached. It was not until he held the little bag with his *pa-waw-ka* stone in his hand that Weshemoneto told him to sleep.

———

The woods were dripping when Tecumseh awoke in his damp blanket before daylight. Voices were talking low all around, and footsteps stirred the sodden leaves. He heard someone breathing very close by and sat up quickly with his knife drawn, casting off the blanket, scattering the leaves that had fallen on it. A man's figure crouched in the near dark just an arm's length from him. His mind at once filled up with the plight of the day; he had allowed no fires in the camp overnight, lest Long Knife scouts might creep upon them, but now here was somebody. . . .

The crouching man cleared his throat, and then he knew it was Thick Water, just Thick Water watching over him. Now with his quick heartbeat subsiding, Tecumseh was annoyed with himself for not being the first awake. He had slept like an old man with nothing to do, and hundreds of his warriors were already up, moving about in the foggy drizzle, gnawing their last cold shreds and crumbs of food, waiting, praying, readying their weapons for the big ambush. As Tecumseh stood up, stretching his stiff muscles, Thick Water stood up beside him, and his familiar voice, with its cheerful tone, said, as always, "How shall we begin the day, Father?"

It was such a strange thing about this man Thick Water. All day long he was a somber, serious, intense man; the only time his voice and face were cheery was the waking hour, when everyone else was drugged with sleep. Once Tecumseh had asked him about that peculiarity, and Thick Water had replied with a shrug: "Am I like that? Then it must be that I am pleased to see you wake up, Father." And so for a moment on this dire morning, Tecumseh was stirred deeply with care for this brave, selfless man who had made himself Tecumseh's very shadow. There would be surely a severe battle this morning, a battle that would accomplish little besides slowing the enemy. Thick Water was always too quick to put his life at risk, and Tecumseh wished he could somehow spare this beloved man from harm, somehow make him return to his woman and children beyond the great lake. Any life lost today would be wasted.

Thick Water asked again, "How shall we begin this day?"

Brushing and adjusting his clothes, Tecumseh replied, "Bring me Charcoal Burner, O Shawawa-no, Winipegon, and Black Hawk, and we will lay out our ambush. Then I will go up and hurry the women and children on their way."

He assigned most of the warriors to the wedge of land formed by the junction of McGregor's Creek and the Thames and told the chieftains to burn the two bridges. Then he selected scouts to send down the Thames to relieve the ones who had watched Harrison's camp overnight.

"Father," said a boyish voice beside him. It was Cat Pouncing. Until now he had been with Star Watcher and the families. "Let me go with them," the boy said. "With the scouts."

Tecumseh was astonished and alarmed. He wanted to tell his son that it was too dangerous. But for the first time ever, there was resolve in the boy's pretty face, fire in his eyes. Tecumseh in a flash of memory saw a day some thirty summers ago when he, at that same age, had bolted from battle to dump his waste in the woods.

He put his hand on his son's shoulder and, trying to hide the terrible poignancy he felt, replied: "Yes. Go, then. Be brave, my son, but not rash. A dead scout cannot tell what he saw." Then he added the same special instructions he always gave his scouts. "Shoot only to protect your life. . . . But if you can sight on Harrison, kill him, for that would save the People." Then, praying silently for their safety, he watched them trot down the trail toward the bridge, until they were out of sight in the foliage. "Come now," he said to Thick Water, a bittersweet ache in his breast, "we need to rouse the families and make them move on."

Even as they rode up the trampled trail in the gray light of dawn, they found stragglers who had simply dropped from the column the previous evening and sheltered in thickets. They had to bestir these and herd them along. Tecumseh's heart was beginning to race now with anxiety, with the desperate need to get these feeble stragglers to safety, to protect his People and yet to return to the Forks before Harrison's Long Knives got there. *The Long Knives!* How often they had scattered the women and children and elders like autumn leaves! He wanted to hurry back to the Forks. There, he kept imagining, there the Master of Life might place Harrison in front of his rifle. He envisioned the figure on horseback that always came at him in his dream, the figure in a tall hat. . . . I want to kill Harrison! he thought wildly as he urged the stragglers along toward the pall of smoke that marked the refugees' campground.

Hundreds of gaunt wretches lay scattered about a weedy, brushy field, sheltered under any hides or rags or blankets they had been able to hang up. Many still lay exhausted in their bedding or squatted around fires trying to make a morning meal out of anything. Some were boiling roots with scraps of rawhide in kettles. Others were cracking nuts or leaching acorn meal. Some had obtained the half-spoiled head and entrails of a cow slaughtered by the British and were roasting shreds of this pungent offal over the flames. They came calling and crowding toward him as he rode up.

Star Watcher came forth from under a crude shelter made from skins thrown over bowed saplings. Her clothes were mud-stained, but she was as always erect and elegant, with bright beads around her neck, with the red thumbprints on her brown cheekbones, with the straight white teeth in her smiling mouth. Open Door too came hurrying through the smoke, his sleep-puffy face full of anxiety. Everything about him looked wretched and scruffy, as in the old days before his greatness.

"My sister, my brother," Tecumseh told them, "you must make these people leave here at once and go on toward the Christian town. Do not allow them to lose each other or fall behind anymore, as did these! I know they are tired and sick, but you must move them as fast as they can go. If one cannot walk, put bundles off a horse and put him on. The Long Knives are close behind! I am going down to the Forks to sting them hard and delay them. But I cannot hold them back very long, for the Redcoats have fled with their rolling guns. Get these people as far from danger as you can."

Star Watcher's brow furrowed with an expression of despair, but only for a moment. "They are so weak and slow," she said. Tecumseh reached down and took her hand and said:

"If you push them hard, you can reach the missionaries' town tomorrow. Brother," he said intensely, turning to Open Door, "I will tell Elliott to find the food officer named Bent and make him give you food for them. I will tell Ironside the same. Maybe you will see Bent before they do. If you do, *make* him give food! Listen to no lies or excuses! Make him give them enough!"

"Yes," Open Door replied, drawing himself up tall. "I shall make him listen!"

"Some families are with Colonel Warburton on the other side of the river. Maybe they are safer. But the Long Knives come on this side. So make the people walk!" A wistful smile softened his features for a moment as he looked around the wretched camp and back to her. "You have always had so many children to care for, my sister; even I was one of them, do you remember? But never so many as now." With a sweep of his hand he indicated the hundreds of refugees. "*Tanakia,* my good sister, my good brother. Farewell!" Then he turned the horse and lashed it into a gallop back toward the fork of the river.


The warriors had not been able to burn the bridge over McGregor's Creek; everything was too wet from the days of rain. So they had used poles to pry up all the planks and had thrown them into the creek, leaving only the spanning timbers. The other bridge, the one across the Thames, had caught fire, by some better luck, and was burning slowly, with much smoke. Other columns of dark smoke still climbed into the gray sky downriver, where the retreating Redcoats had set fire to abandoned supplies the day before. Tons of valuable tools and munitions had been lost because of General Procter's confusion and his inept assignment of boats and wagons. Now the last of Warburton's Redcoats had marched away up the road on the north bank toward the Christian town, and even the rumble and rustle of their going was fading away, and only Tecumseh's warriors were here to defend the Forks at Chatham.

Tecumseh posted himself in the brush near the huge trunk of a fallen beech tree, facing the creek at the road. As the noise of the Redcoat army grew fainter and fainter upstream, that of the Blue-Coats grew louder and louder below. The spanners of the bridge reached across from the road on that side of the creek to the road on this side. Wisps of smoke still rose from the ends of the timbers, where the warriors had tried to burn them.

The last few Shawnee scouts emerged from the foliage on the other side, one by one, running crouched. Several scurried down into the creek and waded across, but Cat Pouncing came straight up the road and ran across the creek on one of the beams with the sure balance of a panther on a limb, his smile showing white in his dark face, a boy showing his prowess even at this critical moment, and the sight of him stirred Tecumseh's love for his Shawnee people as nothing had for a long time. He called his son to him and squeezed his arm.

"Their horse soldiers come first, Father. The walking soldiers are being put in an angle where the streams flow together."

"Good, my son. How do you like the look of our enemy?"

"They are beyond counting. And they make such a noise moving!"

"Such a noise! Now go back out of harm's way. You are young."

"I want to fight them, Father."

Tecumseh thought. Here on the point by the broken bridge would surely be the heaviest fire. "Go, then, to South Wind, down there," he said. That would put his son closer to the road of retreat. "I am proud of you, my son. And I rejoiced when I saw you returning safe up that road." When the boy left, his eyes were bright.

"I think I saw General Harrison among those horse soldiers," reported another scout, one who had fought at Tippecanoe and knew Harrison by sight. "But he was too far to shoot."

"Ah!" Tecumseh's eyes flashed. "What color horse?"

"White, Father, with black legs."

"Then go tell our shooters. Who kills Harrison will have a great name forever."

Tecumseh grew impatient as he listened to the approaching rattle and

rustle of the cavalry and tried to penetrate with his eyes the woods on the
other side, anxious to see the horsemen on the road. But the Americans,
who had been ambushed too many times along this road, did not come
galloping recklessly up to the bridge. Instead, a few mounted scouts and
skirmishers were seen passing through the undergrowth on that side, reconnoitering. Then there was a long stillness before the movements could be
seen again, and suddenly the whole woods over there seemed to be moving.
When a large number of the horse soldiers had emerged into the open near
the bridge, Tecumseh cocked his rifle and searched intently among them
for the face of Harrison, for the white horse with black legs, but he did not
see them. The American officers wore tall, cockaded beaver hats and long
frock coats, and Tecumseh knew that these were the Kentucky mounted
militia. How many of these he had killed in years past! The worst of the
Long Knives! The town burners, the woman slayers!

Soon there were many Long Knives in plain sight, and musket fire
erupted all along the Indian line, accompanied by their fierce yodeling and
a shower of arcing arrows. At once the Americans returned a lively fire,
then turned, rode back into cover, and dismounted to set up firing lines.

Tecumseh still had not seen Harrison. So, saving his rifle load in case his
yearned-for target should appear, Tecumseh darted along his lines of warriors with Thick Water on his heels, directing them, inspiring them with his
voice, which issued clear as a trumpet call from his deep chest. They needed
great spirit to stay here on the line, because the enemy's musket balls and
buckshot were spattering through the brush like a hailstorm. Many of the
warriors were already bleeding from the wounds of small shot and splinters.
Some lay twitching and writhing, until their comrades came and carried or
dragged them back to safety. A few lay crumpled in their coverts, dead.

Then, within minutes after the shooting started, the Americans rolled
two cannons up into place beyond their end of the bridge. Warriors who
feared nothing else feared the rolling guns. When the cannons fired with
their yellow flashes and smoke clouds and their head-slamming noise, everything in their way lurched and flew apart in splinters and clods, dust, shreds,
and bark chips, and any warrior who was not hit by some of these flying
bits or by the grapeshot itself knew that Weshemoneto was protecting him.

As always, Tecumseh's clarion voice and boldly visible figure attracted
more than his share of the enemy's fire. But his motions were so quick and
darting that riflemen could not sight on him. And as for the random shot
flying all about, he seemed always to have the guidance of the Master of
Life in keeping out of the way. He had passed unscathed through so many
bullet storms that Thick Water sometimes believed he was unkillable. To
be his bodyguard during a battle was of course to be in the way of every-

thing that was shot at him, so Thick Water himself was thought to be charmed as well.

Suddenly Tecumseh's eye caught a glimpse of gold braid on a horseman on the far side. An elegant officer in top hat and gold-faced frock coat was looming in the smoke, sword raised high, boldly maneuvering along behind the firing rank on a capering white war-horse with black legs. Tecumseh's heartbeat quickened, and he brought his rifle to bear on the officer, who surely was Harrison. In the smoke with his tall hat, this was the figure that had rushed upon Tecumseh time after time through the mists of his dreams!

But when his sights were on him and his rifle cocked, Tecumseh heard the officer's voice and saw his face and even at this distance and through the smoke saw that it was not Harrison at all, but a younger, prettier officer. In this moment's hesitation, Tecumseh's target disappeared into the distant thickets.

So now Tecumseh despaired of getting a shot at Harrison, who probably was somewhere in the rear, safe among his Blue-Coat soldiers. Without killing Harrison, the warriors could not hope to have a victory here at the Forks of the Thames.

If only Procter had stayed here with his cannons!

This thought rose again and again in Tecumseh's boiling mind, distracting him, souring his soul, making him hate his ally Procter as much as he hated his enemy.

Suddenly such a fusillade of fire came from across the creek that the warriors had to hug the ground to avoid the lead storm. And then under its cover, fifteen or twenty soldiers emerged from the cloud of gunsmoke and plunged down the far creek bank and waded into the water. Within the time of a few breaths they had rooted themselves under the near bank, almost under the muzzles of the Indian defenders—a precarious perch, but one that made them a worrisome presence. Some of Charcoal Burner's warriors tried to go to the edge of the bank and dislodge them but were driven back by another fusillade.

Tecumseh felt a tug on the sleeve of his hunting shirt. He turned. There as always was the long face of Thick Water, who shouted over the gunfire:

"Naiwash sent this man to tell you something!"

It was one of the Ottawas, who were fighting on the left end of the line, near the other bridge. Tecumseh and the messenger knelt behind a thick-trunked oak to get out of the rain of lead. The Ottawa, using hand language and a few Shawnee words, told him that the Wyandot chief Walk-in-Water had deserted his sector of the battle line with sixty of his warriors and was going over to the Americans' side to offer Harrison their hand. "Ahhhh," Tecumseh growled in his smoke-tortured throat.

It was not a surprise; Walk-in-Water had swayed for months back and forth always with the stronger wind. But happening now, it was still another sign that the great cause was falling apart.

Thick Water was kneeling in the brush beyond the shelter of the great oak, head swiveling, watching for any approaching danger, hardly bothering to fold his long frame down into real cover.

"Thick Water!" Tecumseh suddenly called to him. The bodyguard turned and scooted down closer in the wet leaves. One of the American cannons discharged again, shaking the ground and splintering another swath of underbrush. Tecumseh leaned toward Thick Water to make himself heard and told him:

"Brother, do this for me. I want you to go away. . . ." With his left arm he indicated a sweep around to the north and west and saw the pathetic look of disbelief in Thick Water's face. "Go," Tecumseh said, sweeping his arm wide again, shouting over the battle din, "and follow Walk-in-Water. . . ."

A gunshot cracked very close by, and Tecumseh lurched backward, grunting as he fell into the leaves. His left arm was suddenly numb, but his shoulder felt as if it had been pulled out of its socket. Thick Water hovered over him, face full of anguish, and with the help of the Ottawa raised him and leaned his back against the roots of the oak. Blood was seeping all over Tecumseh's upper sleeve. Grimacing, Thick Water pulled his knife and slit open the sleeve, and they examined the wound. Tecumseh could see the oozing, puckered hole where the ball had slammed into his bicep muscle.

"Here it came out," Thick Water said, looking at the tattered flesh on the rear of the arm. Tecumseh raised and moved the benumbed arm and was satisfied that the ball had missed bone. Several warriors nearby had seen their chief fall and were gathering, crouched around him.

"See!" he told them, waving the limb and grinning ferociously. "It is only little! Go back and shoot the Long Knives! This bullet came from down there, those soldiers under the bank! We must drive them out! Quick, now!"

And then, while the battle roared on and Thick Water packed the wound with moss and humus and bound a white strouding cloth around it to stanch the bleeding, Tecumseh continued his instructions: "Follow Walk-in-Water," he said. "Go where he goes, if he does not stay in the American camp. If you can find him and talk to him, tell him to come back and rejoin us, and we will not think or say evil of him." Rifle balls were still whickering through the foliage, bringing down a rain of bark and twigs and yellow bits of leaves, and the dank air was full of concussions, rank with powder smoke. Tecumseh studied the grief on Thick Water's face and went on: "Tell him we will win when we fight with the British cannons tomorrow at the Jesus town. Tell him we want him to be with us instead of the Long Knives when we defeat them. You know his tongue. Go tell him that, Thick Water.''

"I do not want to go."

"Yes. Go, brother. You can do us good this way!"

"But if I leave the battle now, our brothers will say I was a coward!"

"Our brothers know you are no coward. And I will tell them what I sent you for. I ask you to go, my brother. Do this!" In Tecumseh's arm there was no bad pain, just a great ache underlying the numbness. He did not feel faint or weakened at all and rose and picked up his rifle with his right hand, looking around, seeing his warriors still shooting, still howling, still bleeding. More soldiers were trying to get down under the near creekbank. "Soon we will have to get out of this," he said. "We will all draw back, to fight better tomorrow, with the cannons and Redcoats beside us. You will miss nothing by going now to do what I asked you." And he reached over with his left arm, as if it were not even hurt, and clasped his hand on the side of Thick Water's neck, then grinned and pushed him away.

When the bodyguard was gone into the undergrowth, Tecumseh pulled the Ottawa messenger close and told him: "Go and say this to your chief Naiwash: tell him to burn down the building where the Redcoats left the things they couldn't carry. Do this so the Long Knives cannot use those things when they come over. Say that when it is on fire, we will begin to leave this place. We have done all we can do here. We have given our families some time. Tomorrow we will have the fight we have wanted with the Long Knives, and there we will stop them, or there we will leave our bones."


Thick Water stalked through the rainy woods, away from the noise of the battle. He clenched his teeth to keep from crying out with the desolation in his heart.

It was true, what he had protested to Tecumseh; he did not want the others to think he had left the battlefield in fear. But even more true was the other thing.

He was afraid that if he went far from Tecumseh, his great friend would be killed, and he would never get back to his side. Weshemoneto had put him here and made him invulnerable so that he could always protect the greatest chief of the People. They had gone all over this land together and had escaped death more times than he could remember.

Now Tecumseh was without his protection, and Thick Water was so full of fear for him that he could hardly breathe, could hardly see, as he thrashed through the wet, yellowing woods.


Inside his white tent that night, William Henry Harrison dismissed his secretary and aide-de-camp and stood up beside his field desk, the fingertips of his left hand resting lightly on the green deal cloth that covered it. The young men clicked their heels and ducked out of the tent. A whale-oil lamp and an inkstand sat on the green cloth, and a stack of papers and maps lay beside them. Governor Harrison kept meticulous papers, even in the field, even on days like this when he had battled Indians. Being such a dedicated student of military history, he was always aware that he was making more history, and he always liked to get his version down on paper as quickly as possible, before anyone else's interpretation of his actions could circulate.

From all around came the late evening sounds of a large army camp: axes and shovels chunking as breastworks were finished up around the perimeter; the drone of hundreds of voices talking, boasting, laughing; here and there a Jew's harp twanging and a fragment of song, now and then a yelp or scream from the surgeon's tent where bullets and arrows were being extracted from flesh. . . .

It had been a hot skirmish, but surely it had not been the retreating enemy's last stand. There had been only Indians at the Forks, no British artillery, infantry, or cavalry. Just Tecumseh's Indians.

Or maybe only Tecumseh himself alone, Harrison thought with a smirk of amusement; just about every soldier who had taken part in the engagement claimed to have shot at Tecumseh or been shot at by him, even though in this whole army there were only a handful who knew the chief by sight. Tecumseh was their bugbear; they hardly thought about the Redcoats. Harrison was aware that the British army was in disarray; it was shedding equipment and boats and vehicles all along the road. Nevertheless, the Redcoats were up ahead there someplace and could not be dismissed. The fact that it had not been engaged in any of the rearguard skirmishes indicated to Harrison that it was going to be used in a big way someplace ahead. Yes, there had been a fight today. But somewhere ahead, there would be a battle. Harrison thus knew that his best hope lay in pursuing the British so closely that they would not have time to set up a real defense anywhere. It was true that for now Tecumseh was *the* enemy, and sometimes Harrison fancied that he was in a personal conflict with that Shawnee, which would not be concluded until one of them lay dead.

Harrison had become chilled in the unheated tent while dictating his reports and dispatches and got up stiffly from the camp chair intending to go out and warm himself among his officers at the bonfire. He paused beside the desk, slowly twisting in the top button of his cloak, musing on a thought that had just visited him.

He had just thought of Julius Caesar: Caesar standing like this in a tent by lamplight, a tent somewhere in Gaul, perhaps, or beside the Rhine, or in ancient Britain . . . Caesar in a tent on foreign soil, at any rate, surrounded by the men of his legions and their campfires, and those in turn surrounded by night and barbarians. Harrison thought of Caesar with a surge of empathy.

He had had that feeling often. More and more lately he had reviewed the Roman conquerors, and to him, Caesar and Tacitus and Aurelian were very sympathetic souls. He could see their faces in his thoughts sometimes, and he had a habit, in his voluminous correspondences and the gigantic tracts on honor and discipline that he penned for the Vincennes newspaper, of making analogies between his purposes and theirs. As he paused now in the cold tent, his fingertips trailing on the table, he felt his soul leap back nineteen centuries, and he *was* Caesar, Caesar crossing borders into wild and hostile lands, the vanguard of a great empire, call it Rome or call it America, and out there someplace in the wild darkness was Tecumseh the Shawnee, his own Vercingetorix, the barbarian leader he must conquer in the building of empire. "Hm," he said in his throat, cocking his head. He ran his hand from his crown down over his forehead, smoothing his short Caesar-styled hair forward onto his brow. Then he put on his bicorn hat, ducked out of the tent door, and strolled to the bonfire.

Several officers and scouts, sipping from cups, sat on camp stools and on large logs flanking the bonfire. Their talk and laughter fell off, and some of them started to rise as Harrison came into the firelight, but he told them in a soft voice, "As you were, gentlemen," and they eased back, holding their cups and basking in the comfort of the crackling fire. They had smelled gunsmoke today—their army had killed perhaps a dozen savages, at a loss of only three dead soldiers—and were mellow with whiskey, enjoying that satisfying sense of camaraderie and manly purpose that old campaigners feel when there has been a not-too-costly victory.

Those who sat in this privileged circle were all heroes—either very recent heroes like Captain Perry or long-ago heroes like Shelby and Kenton. Their uniforms, except for the blue-and-braid of the regular army, were an anarchy of comic-opera soldier suits, many designed by the militia commanders themselves or perhaps by their wives or mistresses: top hats with rosettes and plumes, frock coats of many colors and cuts, hunting shirts, silk sashes, thigh-high boots or leather leggings. These heroes, Harrison knew and often regretted, were not the sort of obedient, anonymous drones that would make up an ideal legion. They were frontier adventurers, undisciplined individualists, glory seekers, politicians, scoundrels, aging revolutionaries, each bent upon making himself a legend, it seemed. They were a commandant's nightmare. Though at times they were as brave as centurions, their discipline was as motley as their fancy costumes. As they had shown at Fort Meigs six months ago, they were as quick to flee in panic as to charge with reckless bravery.

Especially so were the Kentucky Mounted Riflemen, whose commanding officer just now had risen and was coming toward Harrison, carrying in each hand a pewter cup that gleamed in the firelight. This officer, of patrician features and grand bearing, was Colonel Richard Mentor Johnson. He was also Congressman Johnson. He was one of the congressmen known as the war hawks, and he had left Washington to come out and gain laurels in this war he had helped to start. Colonel Johnson's dress reflected his two roles: the beaver top hat and elegant, fur-collared frock coat of the statesman were veneered with the plume and gold braid of the soldier.

Harrison accepted the proffered cup with a nod and a wry little smile, put his left hand behind his back, and touched the rim of his cup to the congressman's.

*"Fortes fortuna juvat,"* toasted Colonel Johnson, who had learned enough Latin to become a lawyer and to awe voters.

*"Deo adjuvante, non timendum,"* replied Harrison.

The Latin toasts delighted him, his head just now having been so full of Caesar. Another officer, looking almost a twin to Johnson, appeared beside him and raised his own cup to theirs. This was Colonel James Johnson, the congressman's brother and second-in-command of his brigade. "Death to the slippery red bugger," proposed this lesser Colonel Johnson, who was known at home as Reverend Johnson.

"Which red bugger d'ye mean, Jimmy?" the congressman smirked. "Redcoat or redskin? Ha, ha!"

"I mean that Tecumseh. I do aim to take home a patch of his hide, God willing."

"And just so does every man here," came the raspy voice of old Colonel Whitley, an aging Indian fighter sitting near the fire, all clad in deerskins and wampum belts. "That there Shawnee better have a lot o' skin, I'll say!"

"Well, sir," said the congressman, "if he's as big as all the talk has it, he should have enough hide to go round." That brought more hard laughter from around the bonfire.

Now Harrison spoke, his tone a bit condescending. "Contrary to his legend, gentlemen, he's not all that big; no more than your height, I'd say,

Congressman. But on my word, when he jumps up before you with his tomahawk, he does *seem* gigantic, take it from one who knows."

Those around the fire murmured appreciation. They knew that story: Harrison facing off against an angry Tecumseh with drawn sword, all in a large crowd of witnesses and with a newspaper journalist present. Harrison tended to mention it often, to remind people of it. He would still get shivers when he remembered that cocked, taut, copper-skinned arm, those hazel eyes blazing into his own. And yet, sometimes, Harrison would remember those eyes instead shining with charming mischief as the Shawnee crowded him toward the end of their log bench. It was a shame Tecumseh was such an intractable enemy, for Harrison would have loved to have him as a friend. The governor believed that aside from his color, Tecumseh was superior to any of these heroes around this bonfire, except himself. He glanced around at their firelit faces. He pointed with his cup toward a huge, graying man in a woolen cloak, with a mane and face like an old lion's. "General Kenton, you know Tecumseh. He's not such a giant, is he?"

Somebody called out, "Hellfire, Gov'nor, to Simon Kenton *anybody'd* look little!"

In the laughter, Kenton wagged his big, shaggy head, then replied in his cavernous voice, "Gov'nor, I'll just say this, ye tangle with that'n, size don't count. It's like havin' a bobcat caught by his privates. Th' harder ye squeeze, the longer his claws git." He paused and shook his head again, gazing into the blaze, remembering across his eventful years. He started to say more but instead just nodded and sat back. Kenton did not wish to get into particulars; it embarrassed him to remember the times Tecumseh had turned the tables on him.

Harrison, thoughtfully swirling the liquor in his cup, said, "But then, as the maxim goes, gentlemen, 'The greater the enemy, the greater the victory.' "

"Hear, hear," cried the congressman. *"Aut vincere aut mori!"* It was a phrase he had liked to use while stirring up congressional enthusiasm for this war.

"To conquer, or to die," echoed Harrison, raising his cup high.

"Aye!"

"Hey, hey!"

"Remember the River Raisin!"

"Remember the River Raisin! Death to all the red buggers!"

"A patch o' Tecumseh's hide for every man jack of us!"

"Here's to our hero of Tippecanoe! Tecumseh's scalp for Gov'nor Harrison, hey, boys?"

Harrison acknowledged their hearty sentiments with stately nods befitting a Caesar, though they grated on his soul. No one wanted more than he to see the British smashed in Canada and Tecumseh's stubborn Indian confederation scattered. Harrison himself—he and young Oliver Perry— stood fair to become the saviors of the Northwest in this war. Harrison knew that well, and it chimed with his ambitions. Like Caesar the campaigner who had gone home from the wars to rule Rome, William Henry Harrison aimed to go home someday and be president. The support of these rowdy westerners would help him get there. But he had always felt, secretly, that he was of a finer grade than they. And though he had done more than any of them to destroy the world of the red man, he did not relish the vision of their bloody hands scalping and flaying a noble leader—even though he was only an aborigine of the woods.

A red maple leaf fell loose from its twig in the darkness of a treetop and tumbled down through the air toward the glow of a small fire. It danced and turned among the branches, falling toward one campfire among a hundred campfires. Six red men sat around this campfire, sharing a pipe.

Tecumseh saw the red leaf coming down from the high darkness into the smoky fireglow. It looked as if it would fall into the flames. But when it reached the heated air above the fire-ring it hesitated, rose slightly, veered outward, caught the eye of Stands Firm, and then came to rest on the edge of Tecumseh's scarlet British army cloak. Tecumseh looked at it and thought about the short life season of that leaf and the uncountable other leaves covering the ground, falling on the blankets of hundreds of sleeping warriors, falling on the new graves of fourteen warriors who had died today at the Forks of the Thames, ten miles back.

Now scores of wounded warriors were lying in the barn and sheds, the mill and even the house, of Captain Arnold's farm, while the unhurt ones camped under these trees. Arnold and his wife and sons had doctored the wounded and cooked kettles of porridge for the rest. And Arnold himself, Tecumseh's acquaintance from the siege of Fort Meigs, had helped dig the graves for the fourteen. He had invited his friend to stay the night in the farmhouse, but Tecumseh had asked him to keep the badly wounded in the warm house instead; he needed to stay outside and council with his chieftains.

Now it was the middle of the night, and Tecumseh and these five chieftains sat in a circle of friendship that was so old and deep that he could not hide his doubts from them. He had talked to them tonight and tried to raise their hopes for a great victory tomorrow, speaking eagerly of the long-awaited confrontation, but inside himself he could feel the cause grow-

ing hopeless, falling like an autumn leaf whose season is over, and they
could see this in his face. These five knew him so well that his face was like
another language to them. They had gone to the Four Winds with him and
helped him carry his great message. They had danced with him to bestir the
nations. They had been with him when he had made his prophecies and
when they had come true. They had seen him fight with the swift force of
the panther, but they had also seen the uncommon mercy of his heart and
the long vision of peace in his head. They had flown on the wings of his
words and had crawled in mud and blood with him. They had helped him
triumph over whole brigades and armies of the Long Knives, but they had
also seen him howl amid the ashes of his home. Following Tecumseh had
consumed their lives and for many seasons had kept them from the em-
braces of their families, and yet they felt that they were the most privileged
of all men, to have been with him along this hard road.

Now they sat together late, after a long, long day of retreat and battle,
more retreat, burying, and council. They smoked together from Tecumseh's tomahawk pipe, the same one they had seen him raise over Harrison's
head, the one they had seen him smoke with Harrison in council, the one
he had smoked with the old chiefs in the red nations all over this land. They
breathed the fragrant smoke of the kinnick-kinnick, their bodies weary and
bruised, their heads buzzing with fatigue and turbid with last thoughts.
Tecumseh's wounded arm had been re-dressed with a poultice of healing
herbs, and it throbbed with a dull ache as his heart beat. The campfire in
their midst had almost burned down to shimmering coals, but they made
no move to put on more wood, as they would have to sleep soon.

Stands Firm looked up to Tecumseh's firelit profile. Just then Tecumseh's
somber gaze turned to meet his. Tecumseh handed the pipe off to Charcoal
Burner at his right and said to Stands Firm:

"I have been thinking, brother, you should go up the road at the earliest
light tomorrow, and help Star Watcher with the families, help her move
them along faster. Help Open Door get food for them. The children and
old ones are suffering very much."

Stands Firm drew back and regarded him for a moment, then replied,
"I, I do not think I should do that." They stared at each other for a while
as if they might argue. Then Stands Firm said politely, "As you know, my
brother, I am always pleased to do what you ask me. But until now you have
never asked me to leave you before the start of a battle and go join the old
men and women. And so I say, I do not think I shall do that."

After another time of silence, Tecumseh said, "I would like you to do
it." And Stands Firm replied:

"My brother, today in the fight at the Forks, you sent Thick Water away with that message to Walk-in-Water. It was a message that Walk-in-Water will not listen to, as I know and you know. And so it seemed to me that you were really just sending Thick Water out of the way of danger, because of your love for him. Is that perhaps true?"

For a moment Tecumseh looked very annoyed. But then he compressed his lips to keep from smiling and finally could not keep from it, and he breathed a small laugh out from his nose.

It was true. Tecumseh today had sent the bodyguard after the Wyandots expecting that when his mission failed, Thick Water would be closer to his wife's village and would simply go there, to that beautiful wife, to those beautiful children who were always on the verge of becoming fatherless because of Thick Water's rash bravery.

"I know you care for me as for Thick Water," said Stands Firm, "and that you do not want your sister to be a widow. And that you care for the rest of us here as well. . . ." He swept his hand around to indicate the other chieftains at the fireside. "But if you send your best chieftains to a safe place, how will it go in battle tomorrow? I, for one, mean to be at your side when we face Harrison."

And the others, at once, grunted their agreement. So Tecumseh, with a sigh, let his gaze drop to the burning oak branches in the fire-ring, a look of acceptance and resignation. It was plain that none of these intended to choose safety. These were not like Withered Hand and Walk-in-Water. These were the true ones.

Billy Caldwell said, "Do you *believe*, Father, that Procter will stand with us and fight tomorrow, instead of running again?"

"Yes. At last he has no choice. By doing everything so badly, Procter has made himself unable to run any longer. Now he must turn and fight. He knows that if he does not help us fight tomorrow, we will all go and leave him to face the Long Knife army by himself. That he fears more than anything. Yes. Tomorrow we will be in the smoke of their guns again, and the Redcoats will be at our side. On the field there we will beat Harrison, or there we will leave our bones. Harrison is very far out of his own country now, far from his supplies. He can be stopped, and cut off, as we cut off Hull in Detroit. All this we can do, I believe, if the British fight bravely beside us as they have promised to do."

The Winnebago, Chief Wood, passed the pipe to his fellow chief, Four Legs, murmuring in approval of Tecumseh's words. Four Legs drew from the pipe and let the fragrant smoke flow up from his lips into his nostrils, gazing into the dying fire. A last tongue of flame trembled on the end of a charred chunk of oak, playing its light on the gray ashes and the six faces, then winked out, and the faces at once faded back into the night's gloom;

now the six were dark shapes silhouetted against the diffused glow of the many other campfires around them in Arnold's Woods. Still the six faced inward over the shimmering orange embers of their own fire. They were all exhausted, but reluctant to leave each other.

Tecumseh could feel their presence around him like a warm cloak. He felt the dank autumn fog on his face and hands, smelled the sharp smell of smoke from maple and birch and oak, heard the soft voices of the warriors all around who had not yet bedded down beside their own fires; he could feel their presence around him, too. He felt that his soul extended to the outer circle of his camp, that these hundreds of souls were parts of his own soul. He had felt this often: he *was* his People. Tecumseh picked from his cloak the red leaf that had fallen on him from the treetop and leaned forward to drop it on the embers. The leaf curled, smoked, blackened, then flared up and went out, brief as a shooting star.

This night, here among his chieftains, Tecumseh had been feeling a coldness growing in his center. His heartbeat throbbed in his wounded arm.

The fire inside him had never cooled before. Ever since Chiksika had taught him how to keep the inner fire, it had always been in him, and though his feet and hands and face might have been numbed by winter winds, he had never quaked with chill or been dominated by cold. But now, even though the autumn night was not severely cold, and though he was warmly dressed and warmed by the presence of his comrades near a bed of embers, his inner fire was lessening and a coldness was spreading in him.

And now as he sat here, the murmur of voices in the camp became in his head the murmur of all the voices of his People, those present and those absent, those alive and those departed, and the faces came with the voices; they came along as if passing him in a long file on a trail in the dark of the night, each face in turn lighted dimly for a moment as it passed near and murmured to him in its own voice and then faded into the darkness ahead: Turtle Mother, happy in youth, bitter in age. Pucsinwah, the Hard Striker, his father, the Shawnee nation's main war chief but a man who had laughed and had been tender. Chiksika, great warrior and teacher, the brother he had buried in the south. Cat Follower, killed robbing a honey tree. Stands-Between, his brother whom he had buried by the Maumee-se-pe. Open Door, who had nurtured the red man's hope and then nearly ruined it. Star Watcher, who was like the other half of himself. Change-of-Feathers, the shaman . . . Eagle Speaker, the first to see the great events . . . Black Fish, his foster father . . . Black Snake, Blue Jacket, Cornstalk, the chief Tall Soldier Woman, Black Hoof, She-Is-Favored . . . all passed. . . .

Then Tecumseh saw his father and mother sitting outside their lodge in old Kispoko Town, a town that was no more, saw himself as a boy standing before them, saw his father's mouth moving as he said something that he could not hear because of the murmur of all the other voices. . . .

The coals of the fire for a moment reappeared before Tecumseh's eyes, filling the place where the scene of his childhood had been, and the murmur of the camp was there for a moment where the passing voices had been.

But then a thundering began, a thundering not in his ears but inside his head. And shouts sounded amid the thunder. The din of it increased, like a coming storm, roaring, pounding, the voices howling, and a pressure built behind his eyes, a powerful, swelling, reddening pressure.

And suddenly, as if the pressure had cracked open his head, light flooded in, yellow as the sun is on one's closed eyelids, and shapes were coming in the brilliance, shapes vague, blurred by the yellow but growing more distinct as they came running toward him. He could feel the presence of Stands Firm beside him in this storm of noise and yellowness, and now he could see that the shapes coming toward him were large-headed men on horseback, white men on horses, white men with huge hats. He had seen them coming like this in other dreams. They rushed upon him, and one of them loomed to fill up all the brightness, and then the noise crashed and all was darkness at once. He felt Stands Firm tapping him with something, then the light came again, and then all the vision faded, the men and horses dissolving in yellow mist, the noise falling to a rumble, a whisper, then a silence, and he was looking into the coals, hearing only the tired voices of the warriors in his camp.

Stands Firm had been tapping him with the pipe stem, offering the pipe back to him in the darkness, when the five chieftains had heard something pass among them like a bullet, and had heard Tecumseh gasp, and seen his body stiffen in the dim light, as if he had been shot. They started, leaning toward him in alarm. For a while no other sound came from him.

Then his voice came from his silhouette, his voice deep and resonant like a voice in a cave, saying the words they would always remember. And although they had learned long ago that he spoke only truth to them, they could not believe what he now said.

"Listen, my brothers. I have just seen tomorrow. In the battle, I will fall."

It was as if they had all stopped breathing. None spoke. Their hearts seemed to them louder than drums of a Stomp Ground.

Tecumseh rose and stood over the glow of the embers, a dark, cloaked shape.

"I saw," he told them. "My body will lie on the field. Listen, for I must tell you what to do when you see me fall."

He began opening the collar button of his British cloak with his right hand. He looked from one to another of the shapes around the fire as he turned the button out and pondered on the meanings of what he had seen and felt. He could see that Charcoal Burner was beginning to move his large head from side to side. Billy Caldwell and the Winnebagoes were holding their hands out toward him from beyond the fire, as if entreating him to unsay the words. Tecumseh shrugged off the cloak and let it slide to the ground behind him. Softly, so that his words would not be heard beyond this circle, he said:

"Tomorrow when the Long Knives attack us, we will not run, not as long as I live. Brothers, we will not be long in their smoke before I fall." Now he put a hand on Stands Firm's shoulder and said to him, "Brother, since you will not go to a safe place, I ask you to stay near me if you can. When I fall you must come to me at once, and strike me four times with your ramrod. If you can do this, I shall be able to rise, and we will defeat the Americans. But if you cannot touch me, I am dead, and we have lost, and it will be the end of what we have tried to do. Then our warriors should leave the field and not waste their lives for the British. Perhaps if we fight very well from the beginning, we can rout them before I fall. I did not see how the day is to end."

Stands Firm reached up and put his hand on Tecumseh's wrist and said, "No, brother. . . ."

"Yes, brother. I know you do not wish to believe. But you know that I am always to be believed. Listen . . ."

They were shaken. They had never felt such a fear, such a grief. He went on now in a harsh whisper:

"Have you not learned that what I say is always so? Did I not tell you that the earth would shake and houses fall, and the rivers change their courses? And did this not happen as I foretold?"

They remembered all that, that wondrous and terrible thing that had happened the winter before last, just as he and only he had somehow known it would. He went on:

"You know that on the night before the battle at the Kanawha-se-pe, my father saw that he would die in the battle, and he told my brother Chiksika that he would, and it was true.

"You know that my brother Chiksika told me he was going to be killed in the battle at Buchanan's Fort, and he died in my arms there, just as he had said. This is true sight among the warriors of my family, and is not to be denied."

They remembered all this, and now they could not deny that he had seen tomorrow. And knowing that it would come true was crushing their hearts in their breasts.

He held his hand still on the shoulder of Stands Firm, Star Watcher's husband, and said in a voice now almost cheerful, "Don't you see that you must believe me and do as I ask you, my good brother? Do you not remember that the Panther Star crossed the sky when I was born from the womb?

"So you must believe me, and we must all have our hearts ready for tomorrow. Let us sleep now. It is so late."

# CHAPTER 39

*Moraviantown, Ontario*
*October 5, 1813*

He was ready to die now, so he had painted the black of death on the left side of his face. But if he died, he would die fighting his enemy, so he had painted the red of war on the right side of his face.

His father Hard Striker had fought long and well knowing he was going over the edge of death. His brother Chiksika had done the same. Now Tecumseh could feel how they had been able to do so.

The great question of what to do no longer wrestled in him. Weshemoneto had taken back into his own hands all the choices. Tecumseh's hands were free to do the one thing: to slay his enemy. He felt as ready and strong and vibrant as a drawn bow. Though he would fall, he might kill Harrison first, and he no longer needed to guard his own life while doing it. Perhaps he might last long enough in the battle to take victory in his hand and give it to his warriors to finish.

That would be the best thing!

He was ready to die now. He had ridden up that morning and said farewell to his sister and brother. He had not told them he was going to die, but Star Watcher surely knew. Anything that was ever in his heart was also in hers.

He thought, as he rode with his chieftains toward the battleground, about how things go on after a man dies. For the man it ends there, and there is no more breathing for him on this side of the Circle of Time, and he has to lay down what he has been carrying on the earth. But what has been happening keeps on happening because those who still live carry it on with them. When his father Hard Striker had died and when Black Fish had died and when Chiksika had died, and when his white brother Brock had died, it had gone on, because he had picked up what they had been carrying and brought it forward to this day, when he himself would have to lay it down. He did not know who would pick it up when he died today. It might be his son, who had run across a broken bridge with a smile on his face yesterday. It might be Charcoal Burner, or it might be Black Hawk, or it might be Stands Firm or Seekabo or Wood, or it might be Thick Water or some Choctaw or Muskogee he had aroused in the south, or it might be all of them or some of them carrying it together. It might be Thick Water or one of Thick Water's sons or grandsons; yes, it might be someone who was not even born yet. Always things had kept going on around the circle even after the people who had started them had died and laid them down.

And whoever picked up what Tecumseh was going to lay down today would not have to carry it the same way he had carried it. Every right man was his own chief and would carry the thing in his own way. The messengers from the Great Good Spirit would come down and remind him to keep carrying it and give him signs and hints, but how he carried it would depend upon what kind of a man he was.

Or woman, he thought. Maybe it will be a woman who picks it up and carries it. It is woman who connects the man of yesterday with the man of tomorrow, who closes the gaps in the Circle of Time; it is woman who carries most of the burden of the People; she carries the carrier, in her heart, in her womb, in the cradleboard on her back, in the slain body of her son across her lap. It is woman who carries most of it. He thought of his mother, whom he had last seen four and twenty summers ago, and of Star Watcher, whom he had last seen no more than four and twenty minutes ago. Star Watcher was already carrying it as she bore the lives of the families on toward safety. He thought of Kokomthena, Our Grandmother the Creator, who had carried it since the Beginning. Yes, the women really carried it and now and then gave some of it to the warriors or the chiefs and shamans to carry. Yes, the shamans. His brother Open Door had carried it until he forgot what he was doing.

Then Tecumseh found the place where he would die today. He drew back on the reins. His chieftains reined in beside him. He knew it was the place. In a hundred dreams he had seen a place that felt like this.

It was not the Moraviantown high ground where General Procter had said he would stand his army; the general had apparently changed his mind again. The town of the Jesus Indians was a league farther up the road. In a part of the woods near the river and the road, hundreds of British soldiers were standing or moving about, a mass of red coats, black hats, white shoulder belts. A team of steam-snorting horses was turning in the road, pulling a cannon into place. Nearby stood another team of horses, hitched to Procter's muddy carriage. A driver in a red coat sat on the front seat, hugging himself, his hands under his arms. The general was not in the carriage, but Tecumseh saw him standing with some of his officers down near the cannon.

At first sight this did not look like as good a battlefield as Chatham on the Forks had looked. It had no creek, no bridges, no buildings.

Here the road passed between a bend in the river and a wood of big maples and oaks and beeches. The trunks of great fallen trees lay on the forest floor covered with moss and drifted deep with dead leaves.

Now with his chieftains Tecumseh rode to Procter. The general's jowly face was sallow and puffy, his eyes were squinting, his nose and cheeks etched with scarlet capillaries; his hands were shaky. But for once he was able to look at Tecumseh's eyes instead of around them, because he had stopped running from the enemy.

"You choose to fight here, not at the Moraviantown. Why is this, Father?" Tecumseh asked.

"The Americans are too close behind, I believe. We wouldn't have time to march there and fortify the place. So we will turn and face them here."

Tecumseh felt a wave of scorn and old anger and wanted to flail Procter for not fortifying the Forks instead—but this was the day he was to die, so yesterday did not matter, and it was too late to cure a man's stupidity. So he said instead, "Perhaps that is better." He thought of the refugee families that would be filling the town by afternoon. It would be better to keep the battle far from them. "But," he said, "are your cannons not already at the town? I see only one here."

At this, Procter's face grew flushed, and his hands flopped at his sides. Tecumseh could see in this gesture alone that Procter had indeed lost control of everything and knew it, and that he was making his stand only because he had no more choices. He said, "Have you not sent for them to be brought here, Procter?"

"I . . . well . . . not yet. . . ."

"You have five cannons in a place where you have decided not to fight, and one cannon here where you mean to fight," Tecumseh said. "Would it not be better the other way?"

Procter, pawing at his chin, turned and looked about till he saw a major, whose name he seemed not even to remember, and he stammered, "Uh, you . . . send, uh, somebody, and tell Troughton to bring the artillery back. . . . Oh, no, I'm sure there's not time. . . ."

Tecumseh glanced toward Colonel Warburton, who stood nearby, his expression fallen into a set of resignation and disgust. Other officers were grouped around as if waiting to be told what to do.

"Come," Tecumseh said to his chieftains, "let us look at this place where we will fight."

It was not a good way for a general to choose his battlefield. But of course Procter could not help that, really, because this was the place the Great Good Spirit had long ago appointed for Tecumseh to die.

His hopes rose as he looked over the place. It was better than he had thought. The huge fallen trees made natural breastworks. The western edge of the old woods opened onto thickets of second growth, which would hinder any charge of horse troops and give dense cover for his warriors. He rode weaving slowly through this, having to duck and fend off branches. He emerged on the edge of a reedy swamp where dead tree trunks stood gray and barkless in the muck. Two hundred paces to his left was the road, clearly visible. On the right of the swamp was a brushy meadow and beyond it a larger swamp, extending far to the west, parallel to the road.

To his eye it looked like a fine place for either an ambush or a stubborn defense. The steep-banked Thames would protect the defenders' left flank. The road led straight between that barrier and the woods and the small swamp. Any attacker who tried to outflank the defenders by swinging away from the riverside would be caught in a wide meadow between two swamps, facing a dense thicket. With those swamps and woods and thickets filled with warriors and Redcoats, and with cannons set up behind barricades and aimed down the road, it would be perfectly set up to trap an army.

Tecumseh rode out across the meadow now, galloped out westward toward the road, then turned and rode toward the thicket in order to sense the terrain from the Americans' viewpoint. As he rode back in, he could see that the Long Knives, in order to get close enough to attack, would have to funnel themselves into either one or both of two traps: between the two swamps or between the little swamp and the river.

"The Master of Life has shown us a good place to meet the Long Knives," he said. "Let us bring our warriors up and place them."

Procter's orders to his officers were vague and contradictory. The Redcoats responded by milling about, getting in the way of each other and grumbling because they had been marching hungry and there was no breakfast in view. Procter failed to tell them to build breastworks, so they didn't. The artillerymen set up the six-pounder cannon in the roadway and aimed it down the road but built no barricade in front of it. Colonel Warburton was put in command of the first line, which was deployed athwart the roadway, from the river to the small swamp, and a second line was stationed in reserve two hundred yards to their rear. The Redcoats did not stand in ranks in the open, as was their custom, but took cover behind the big trees of the woods and in clumps of brush.

As the hour of battle drew near, Tecumseh grew very animated and keen. He moved along the lines quickly, a fresh white bandage on his left arm, stationing his warriors in the margins of thicket and swamp and encouraging them. He seemed to shine with light, though he had discarded all ornaments and wore only his plain, close-fitting buckskins. Stands Firm could hardly keep up with him; he followed him with the ramrod clutched in his hand, thinking that Tecumseh did not act like a man who expected to die.

Tecumseh gave command of his right wing to the Ojibway chief South Wind, who had influence over both his own tribe and the Sioux, and told him and Naiwash to infest the edge of the large swamp on the right. Then Tecumseh himself, with Winipegon, Black Hawk, Black Partridge, and Charcoal Burner under him, took charge of the tribes who would defend the thicket between the two swamps and the forest behind it. This put his Shawnees next to the right flank of the Redcoats. He felt that Procter would need watching, and he wanted to be close enough to coordinate the actions of the Redcoats and the tribes. Billy Caldwell with his good command of the English tongue and his ability to write messages would be the liaison between them.

Every warrior had been given a finger-size stick as he approached the battlefront. When these sticks were collected along the battle line at noon, they numbered five hundred. The British force, soldiers of the Forty-first Regiment, with Canadian dragoons and the Royal Newfoundland Regiment, were no more than that, as so many had been scattered out on details at Moraviantown and along the road. So it would be a thousand against the three or four thousand of Harrison's Long Knives. But Tecumseh could not feel discouraged. Five hundred Redcoats were a magnificent sight, and Tecumseh felt that any one of his warriors was worth five Americans in a contest of this sort. They had wanted this fight for a long time. And they knew they were the only barrier between their families and the Long Knife soldiers.

After midday Open Door came down from Moraviantown, where he had left the refugees, and now he rode out along the battle line in a flowing cape, sitting tall and looking almost as grand as he had in his days of prominence, and he even handled his horse tolerably, as he went along assuring the warriors that he was praying for power from the Great Good Spirit and was caring for their families. He held Tecumseh's hand for a moment, saying nothing about Tecumseh's premonition, which Star Watcher had confided to him. His eye glimmered with tears, and Tecumseh could feel coming from him some of that unselfish love that Open Door had possessed for a few years while giving his best service to the People. Tecumseh looked at his brother's dead eyesocket and remembered that long-ago accident with the arrow, and his heart swelled with pity and affection for this strange brother of his. Then Open Door squeezed Tecumseh's hand very hard and rode back to take a place near Procter's carriage and sat there holding his medicine fire stick tightly in both hands, praying as he had used to pray when he was Weshemoneto's vessel.

Soon the scouts came up to report that the Americans had already forded to this side of the river. They had crossed very quickly, each horse soldier carrying an infantry soldier across behind his saddle, and now they were but a mile down the road, though still out of sight in the woods beyond a bend in the road. There the army had stopped, and their Leathershirts and their Shawnee scouts from the band of old Black Hoof were coming ahead to reconnoiter.

So now Tecumseh set out to make a final tour of his battle line, riding with his head high and his painted face agleam with eagerness. He carried his rifle slung on his back, his sheath knife hanging from his neck, his tomahawk and Brock's silvered pistols in his belt.

He rode first to Procter, who was standing nervous and pale and blinking behind the center of his reserve line. Seeing the general's abject wretchedness, he decided to encourage him if he could. He dismounted, went to him, and extended his hand. Procter's palm was clammy.

"Father," said Tecumseh, smiling at him, "have a big heart. Tell your soldiers to be firm, and all will be well!"

Procter, who knew nothing of Tecumseh's premonition, stood puzzled by this effusion of goodwill. "I hope," Tecumseh said, "the other cannons arrive before Harrison attacks."

Then he swung onto his horse and trotted down to the Redcoats' first line. He gripped the hand of Colonel Warburton and suggested that he should have his cannoneers place some kind of protection in front of the cannon. Then he shook hands with Colonel Evans and Major Richardson, sometime comrades in the defense of Fort Malden, wished them strong hearts, and rode northward to his sector and dismounted. On foot then he moved swiftly along his line of warriors. "*Weshecat-too-web,* be strong! Stand your ground! Shoot well! They are out of their groundhog hole at last! Have a big heart! *Weshe-kesheke,* a fine day!"

They felt the warmth pour from him into their own hearts. They knew what they were to do if he fell and could not rise again. But they saw his brother-in-law right beside him with that magical ramrod, and they believed that even if he fell, he would be touched by it and given back his life, to fight on, as he had said. They had no doubt that this could happen on such a day. This was their father who had made the earth shake and who had defeated American armies almost every time he had fought them. They drank up the warmth and love and strength that came from him, and they did not believe he could die, they did not believe he could lose, and so they were in good heart for the battle. Along the right wing he found his son, whom South Wind had asked to fight alongside him again today. He wanted to embrace his son, but now this was a warrior, not a boy, not someone to be embarrassed or weakened by a show of affection. So Tecumseh only reached over, shook him by the shoulder, and said, "*Weshecat-too-weh!* Make our People proud of you, as I am now. *Tanakia,* farewell!"

"*Tanakia,* Father."


"Why does this Blue-Coat general wait so long?" Stands Firm asked in the middle of the afternoon. He was clutching the ramrod as if in a death grip, and he had stayed within two paces of Tecumseh all day, ready to tap him four times with it the moment anything happened. Far down the road, through gaps in the golden foliage, the American army could be seen moving, and the blended noise of all their movements and voices was like the rush of water. It was not raining today, but the ground was soft and the sky was overcast. Tecumseh said:

"Remember, brother, this is General Groundhog. He is cautious outside his burrow." But the waiting was almost too hard to joke about, and Tecumseh was so eager for the final things to happen that he felt ready to leap out of his skin.

Then at last the brassy blare of the bugles sounded through the chilly air, the munching and rustling of thousands of boots through the brush, and the long formations of the walking soldiers could be seen coming into the open, seeming to come very slowly. Behind the walking soldiers, visible over their heads, were the mounted troops. There looked to be at least ten hundreds of men on horses.

Tecumseh, standing on a log, saw what he had been looking for. He pointed. "*Harrison!*" he shouted.

There he was, a half mile away, riding his light gray mare slowly up the road, at a little distance off to the side of one of the masses of walking soldiers. Tecumseh tried to think hard enough that Harrison would feel the thoughts. Come close, Harrison! Let us sit on this log together, and this time you will fall off! Here I am, and we are our peoples, you and I! Come close enough!

Tecumseh wondered if the cannon Redcoats were aiming down the road at Harrison, with grapeshot in the barrel. The road was straight. Surely they could see him. Tecumseh wanted above all to kill Harrison himself, but if he got no opportunity to do that, it would be almost equally satisfying to hear the cannon blast and see Harrison blown out of his saddle way over there.

But the cannon did not shoot, and Harrison came no closer but just held up his saber and made his horse prance around out there beyond gunshot range, and the walking soldiers came on.

Harrison, O enemy, will you never come as close as you did once, there by your own house, when you pointed your little sword at me?

When the walking soldiers were a little closer and their crunch and rustle came louder in the breeze, their officers shouted, and their formations began changing shape; their front seemed to widen and veer northward. And two long lines of them were now flanking toward the big swamp where the Ojibways, his son among them, lay in wait. Harrison's scouts had done their work well; Harrison knew just where all his enemies lay concealed, and there would be no surprise.

But yes, Tecumseh thought, the surprise will be how firm we stand before his numbers.

Another line of the walking soldiers was coming straight toward the thicket where Tecumseh stood. In the distance another neat formation of the Blue-Coat regulars tramped alongside the road toward the British, their bayonets thick as the quills of a porcupine.

It was awesome how a white commander could make so many hundreds of soldiers move as if they were not men with souls and minds but fingers of his hands. Tecumseh remembered what it had been like to train two dozen dancers to do a ceremonial dance in unison. This that the white soldiers did was something like an enormous dance. As he waited with rifle ready, he remembered the first time he had seen that phenomenon, when as a boy he had watched the Long Knife Clark attack Piqua Town. . . .

*The walking soldiers!* Suddenly Tecumseh felt strange stirrings, both of hope and doubt. For in his dreams the forms coming at him out of the noise and yellow light had not been walking soldiers, they had been horse soldiers. Could it mean that the dream had been only that, a dream, that the *walking* soldiers would be leading this attack as they were doing, and that he was *not* going to be killed today by horse soldiers? If he had dreamed something different from what was happening now, could it mean that he was *not* to fall in battle? Or that horse soldiers would kill him some other day, not this day?

Then Harrison down on the road pointed his saber, and bugles bleated again, and hundreds of voices rose up whooping and yipping in the distance, and the rumble of hoofbeats overrode the tread of the walking soldiers. The mounted troops came streaming around the walking army, galloping headlong up the road. Half a thousand horse soldiers were thundering straight up the road toward the Redcoats, vanishing beyond the screen of woods at Tecumseh's left. As many more horsemen suddenly turned out and angled across the meadows between the marching army and the swamp. They were riding more slowly because of the brush and boggy ground but nevertheless moving straight up the meadow into the trap, right up toward the Shawnee sector of the battle line. The warriors in the thicket cocked their guns and nocked their arrows and waited with prayers and pounding hearts for them to come close enough. Tecumseh stood on the thick log, and through the thicket he could see the heads and shoulders of hundreds of Kentuckians and their horses, all becoming more distinct as they rode closer. He glanced down at the gray head of his brother-in-law, who was now where Thick Water had always been, and put his hand on his right shoulder. Stands Firm pressed his cheek against that hard, cold hand for a moment. He gripped the ramrod that had become the most potent and important artifact in all the world, more sacred now than any of the Prophet's carved cedar sticks.

A volley of musket fire erupted on the left where the British were, and a great uproar of yelling and neighing and sporadic gunfire, and the continuing rumble of thousands of hooves, then another thunderous volley. But the sound that Tecumseh yearned to hear—the crash of the cannon spewing case shot into the Blue-Coats—never came.

Now in front of the Shawnees the Kentuckians had skirted the narrow swamp and were spurring their war-horses, charging up through the brushy meadow and howling for revenge, the brush crackling and shuddering under them.

And now it was as it had been in the dream after all: the earth quaking under hoofbeats, voices howling, Stands Firm at his side, the tall horsemen becoming distinct among the yellow leaves. . . .

Now they were too close to miss. The war cry pulsated from Tecumseh's throat. Hundreds of muskets and rifles went off at once, and flights of arrows arced through the powder smoke. Riderless horses reared and whinnied and collided and tumbled, and many soldiers fell to the ground. Tecumseh bellowed, "*Tschi,* kill them!" and the ground nearby was stirring with crawling, writhing, fallen horse soldiers. "*Pe-eh-wah,* this way,"

Tecumseh's voice trumpeted. "Chase them!" He sprang forward off the log and darted through the undergrowth toward the milling, hesitating Kentuckians and straight into their midst, Stands Firm right behind him, and a hundred warriors rose to follow. Tecumseh leaped at a soldier and dragged him backward off his rearing horse, bashed his head in with his rifle butt, then sprang for another. A soldier who had fallen from his saddle in the first volley stood up and leveled his rifle at Tecumseh. A Shawnee hurled a tomahawk from ten paces away, and it penetrated the soldier's temple. The Shawnee leaped on the soldier the moment he fell and scalped him.

Tecumseh felt in his sinews all the strength of the panther. He felt as if he could leap over horses. Boughs and branches slashed at him as he sped after the retreating riders.

An officer in a top hat was spurring a big horse and waving a sword, trying to rally the milling riders. Tecumseh pulled from his belt one of the little pistols Brock had given him. The moment he fired it, the horse reared; the ball hit the officer's thigh, and he lurched in his saddle but did not fall. Then a horse with no rider ran between them before Tecumseh could shoot the officer with the other pistol.

His warriors had followed him into the very midst of the Kentuckians now, yipping and sprinting, leaping and slashing, dragging them from their saddles, driving them back onto the meadow and into the edge of the swamp. Horses shrieked and stumbled, bloodied by arrows and lances. Their riders, trying to shoot from their maddened horses, blundered into each other's way but were easy prey for the agile warriors. Triumph and gratitude sang keening in Tecumseh's soul; the power of the Master of Life, the righteous power, was pouring into his warriors, and Harrison's arrogant Long Knives were falling back, confused, afraid. Tecumseh howled and laughed and struck with a tireless arm. The handle of his tomahawk was sticky with blood. Thrilled by the sound of his joyous voice and the sight of his brutal charges, his warriors found more courage and strength in themselves than ever before and charged with him, hearts ablaze.

But when the horse soldiers were at last driven back upon their own advancing ranks, they could be pushed no farther. They became a wall of pistols and swords and rifles and flailing hooves, and the shouts of their officers rallied them. Now the warriors began edging back toward their thickets, sidestepping, covering each other, picking up their wounded as they yielded the ground, pausing to scalp soldiers.

When they were back in their coverts they turned, reloaded, and resumed the deadly fire that had first broken the charge. Tecumseh was everywhere, praising them and exhorting them to be strong and shoot well, to save their People. A messenger came down from the right, saying that the Ojibways had struck the lines of walking soldiers so hard that they were fleeing in a panic and the warriors were chasing them. *"Weh-sah!"* Tecumseh cried. "We will have this day yet!"

But here at Tecumseh's front the horse soldiers kept coming. They seemed to be without number, and they were not frightened now, but brave and crazed. They kept spurring their big horses, crowding closer to the thicket, not trying to ride into it but firing in with their rifles and pistols, howling their vengeance cry, milling and trampling in the haze of gunsmoke, the agitated mass of them crushing closer and closer on the edge of the thicket. Tecumseh saw Charcoal Burner and Black Hawk off to the right, fighting like demons. Stands Firm was still at his side.

Tecumseh remembered that he had heard no cannon fire, and now stray bullets were spitting through the woods from his left, where the Redcoats were. In a moment a Shawnee messenger ran over from the British sector, sent by Billy Caldwell. He said the British lines had given way at once before the charge of the mounted Kentuckians, that some Redcoats had fled in the woods and the rest were throwing down their muskets and walking out with their hands up. The cannon soldiers had fled without firing the six-pounder even once, and the Americans now had the gun.

"And Procter?"

The messenger pointed up the road toward Moraviantown. "Gone away. He scolded his soldiers one time for running, then he outran them."

Tecumseh shouted, a wordless bellow of outrage.

So now he had horse soldiers around on his left flank, too. That was the result of it: where five hundred Redcoats were to have held, the Indians were left to fight alone, as usual.

Quickly Tecumseh turned again to his warriors, who were howling and fighting with unabated vigor, still shooting horsemen out of their saddles. But now some of the Americans were dismounting and fighting afoot, taking cover in the weeds and pouring bullets into the thicket. There were so many hundreds of them, and they came faster than they could be shot down. Some had penetrated into the thicket and were fighting with pistols and swords, grappling with warriors, clubbing them with rifles. Others, still mounted, were spurring their horses right in through the undergrowth, their mighty horses crashing through the branches, wild-eyed and snorting, their mouths foaming and bleeding from the bits, into the gaps where warriors had fallen.

Tecumseh raised a pistol and shot one of those soldiers in the face, then ran along the line calling for some of the warriors in reserve to go and form a line on the left where the British had been; Blue-Coats were already starting to appear in the woods over there. Stands Firm was still with him, but stumbling and panting.

Then, through the roiling, choking gunsmoke, Tecumseh saw a huge, blood-smeared white horse with an officer on it, that familiar, tall-hatted figure from the dream, his face and his clothing drenched with blood, crashing closer through the brush, coming around the root bole of a fallen tree, filling the daylight with his silhouette. Suddenly sure that Harrison was just before him in the thick smoke, Tecumseh raised his rifle and cocked it. He pulled the trigger.

For a moment he could not see through the smoke of his own rifle. Then he saw that the bleeding horse had half collapsed, pinning its rider's leg against the tree. With a joyous shout Tecumseh dropped his rifle, snatched his tomahawk from his belt, and sprang toward him.

He saw two things as he leaped through the air. The bloody face was not Harrison's face.

And this officer who was not Harrison had a pistol in his right hand. Smoke blossomed from the pistol. Everything disappeared in a red flash. Then there was half darkness, as on a day of *Mukutaaweethe Keelswah,* the Black Sun.

Stands Firm howled with agony when he saw Tecumseh tumble in front of the bloody officer. He tried to run to him. He must touch him with the ramrod four times, the sacred number. In life there were four seasons, four winds, four ages of a man. The four touches would make him live. He had said so. Stands Firm knocked two soldiers aside as he struggled toward his fallen leader. But then something exploded by his ear and he stumbled, seeing nothing but redness, and the last thing he felt was something long and sharp passing through his body from back to front.


Tecumseh opened his eyes and saw fallen leaves. He tried to shout for his warriors to be strong. Blood spewed out of his mouth and reddened the leaves on the ground. He called for Stands Firm, but the name only gurgled in his throat.

He tried to rise from the ground but was too heavy, and the effort made more warm blood gush from his mouth and nostrils, bathing his hands red. When he took a breath his throat was filled with blood, as if he were drowning in it, and it made him choke and cough, and he was bubbling deep inside his chest. He was dizzy and seemed to be hearing a blizzard with women's voices lamenting in it. He turned his head to look for Stands Firm but could not see him in the swirl of smoke and shadow, which now was starting to fade from yellow to blizzard white.

He wanted to see Stands Firm, but the fading shadows were tilting and whirling now and disappearing in the blizzard of whiteness; all the lamenting voices in the blizzard wind were blending into one high, keen note. He felt out of control of himself, that awful feeling he had had the one time he had drunk rum. He was growing cold in the center. He rolled onto his side and groped into his tunic for the *pa-waw-ka.* Its bag was sticky with blood in his palm, but it gave warmth. The whiteness receded a little, and he could see shadows and moving shapes. At last he saw Stands Firm. He was lying a little distance away. A soldier had one foot on his back and was trying to pull out the bayonet he had stuck through him. Stands Firm was dead with the ramrod still in his hand.

It did not matter about the ramrod anyway. Even if Stands Firm could have reached him and tapped him with it, it could not have made him get up and go on. If he was dying, he would die. That about the ramrod had been the only untruth he had ever told his warrior chieftains. If he had not told them he could rise from death and fight on, how would they have had the will to fight today?

The ramrod was nothing. But no longer would Star Watcher have this good husband, and Tecumseh was sorry for her.

My poor People, he thought. What will become of my poor People?

Then all the noises and all the violent motions faded into the blizzard, and the weight of the burden lifted off of him. The blizzard white was the white dove flying upward before his eyes, leading him. At each side of him was a handsome warrior dressed in only a dark blue breechcloth and moccasins glittering with stars. They rose, one holding him by each arm, following the white dove, into a perfect silence.

The two sky warriors carried him between them to the fork in the Road of Stars.

Then he was walking by himself in a beautiful and misty land of green meadows and corn fields and gigantic elm trees and blue streams where herds of bison and elk stood in dewy grass as high as their shoulders, and multitudes of rainbow-shimmering birds veered through the sky. Chiksika was hunting in a meadow and smiled and waved at Tecumseh. At the end of the road was a large town of gray bark *wigewas* in a wide river valley, between bluffs gushing with springs. His father and mother were waiting for him, and he could see them in the clear, bright light, sitting before their lodge. They were young, and Tecumseh was a boy. He was sitting before them, and his father was saying to him:

"You were born under a great sign, the sign of the Panther leaping across the sky. To be born under a great sign means that you will have a great thing to do, and your life will not be easy."

"We may never know," General Harrison said the next morning, speaking to the officers and scouts who stood with him looking down at the mutilated corpse of an Indian. It was all the general could manage to say at this moment because he was on the verge of having to vomit. Young Captain Perry stood with them, and though he was miles from his fleet, he looked seasick. Acres of woodland and thicket and swamp were trampled and blood-spattered, littered with smashed hats, broken weapons, and torn paper powder cartridges.

Scores of soldiers were claiming that they had either killed Tecumseh or witnessed his death, though hardly any of them would have known the chief if they had seen him. There were only thirty-three Indian corpses on the battleground, and not enough was left of them to tell which one, if any, had been the chief. The soldiers had come out on the battlefield early this morning and had taken everything from the corpses, even some of their skin.

Yesterday evening John Conner had said he was pretty sure this body now lying at their feet was Tecumseh's, and Anthony Shane had said the same, as had some captured British officers. But now neither they nor Harrison nor Simon Kenton could tell enough from the blood-encrusted lump of flayed meat to verify it.

Harrison had walked all over the battleground and had looked down at each corpse and had thought that surely he would feel something, some intuition if nothing else, that would tell him when he stood over the right body. How could the entire identity of such a splendid enemy, a man whose face had been visible in his memory's eye for two years, just vanish?

Some of Congressman Johnson's troops were swearing that they had seen him kill Tecumseh with a pistol beside the fallen tree, but Johnson was lying in the hospital tent with five bullet wounds and unable to make such a claim or come and point out a particular carcass. Johnson had never been acquainted with Tecumseh before, so how could he know, anyway? Or how could his men? Some other witnesses had said they saw Colonel Bill Whitley and a magnificent-looking savage kill each other simultaneously with pistols. Others said they had seen a soldier pin the chief to the ground with his bayonet. Tecumseh seemed to have been killed two dozen times on this field yesterday. But now in broad daylight no one could say surely, "There he is."

Though Harrison had won a major battle and captured half the British force in Upper Canada, he felt troubled and hollow. These damned frontier brutes who made up his army had fought well with their usual swashbuckling bravery, but as usual they had lost control of themselves after tasting blood; some of them had torn on up the road and sacked and burned the missionary town and hurt innocent Indians there.

But in mutilating these corpses here on the battlefield, they had done their worst mischief, in Harrison's mind. Now he could not say for certain

whether Tecumseh was dead or not. Harrison knew his old anxiety would
be with him until he was sure Tecumseh was dead. And now he could not
be sure. So for now in his reports to the government he would not make
such a claim, only to have it refuted someday when Tecumseh showed up
alive on still another battlefield. Harrison had learned the hard way, after
Tippecanoe, not to exaggerate his claims of what he had done against these
Shawnees.

The only things that made him feel reasonably sure Tecumseh had fallen
were the sudden cessation of the chief's great voice and the curious way the
battle had ended. One minute the Indians had been fighting with stubborn
ferocity. But after that voice had fallen still, the resistance had simply melted
away.


In another part of the battlefield, Canadian farmers were digging graves for
Indian corpses. They had been called together for the task by Benjamin
Arnold the mill owner. Arnold was grim and silent. The sight of the
American militiaman and soldiers prowling the field like buzzards picking
away at the dead warriors disgusted him more than anything he had ever
seen in his life. He believed the Indians' statements that his friend Tecumseh was dead. But he had not seen his body on this field, and he was thankful
for that.

One of his grave diggers threw a shovelful of dirt, wiped his forehead
with his sleeve, then paused to watch some Kentuckians cutting and then
strenuously pulling skin off the thigh of a dead warrior. The grave digger
spat in their direction and said, "Workin' hard, aren't you, boys?"

"Damn right, Canajun! This here Tecumsey's tough as an ol' tom turkey!"

"I hate to dash y' down after all your hard labor, lads, but you aren't
skinning who you think you are."

A soldier snickered.

"I reckon when we get back to Kaintuck, won't nobody know no difference!"

# EPILOGUE

*On This Side of the Circle of Time*
*A Village Near Lake St. Clair*
*October 6, 1813*

O n the morning when the Americans were peeling carcasses at the Thames River battleground, four Shawnee warriors many miles away were peeling slabs of bark off a large elm. The tree was very hard to peel. The bark squealed and groaned as if the living tree were in pain.

Two hundred paces away, warriors and chieftains were digging a grave, using none of the iron tools of white men. They dug with elk-bone hoes in the rich ground beside a creek, under a tree they had aligned with other landmarks. They had made a pledge among themselves. They would never forget where the grave was, and no white man would ever be told of it.

In a *wigewa* off from the edge of a village, Star Watcher knelt on a reed mat on the floor beside the naked body of her brother. Her gray hair was unbraided and hung about her head and shoulders, hiding her face. She washed off his red and black war paint and the dried blood from his mouth and chin. She squeezed the cloth in a kettle of warm water, and then she began washing and rubbing off the encrusted blood that covered the deep chest. In the thick muscle near his left nipple were a puckered, black-edged bullet hole and three small buckshot holes. She washed the wounds gently, as if they might hurt. Upon her heart was a weight so heavy she could hardly draw breath. She remembered how, when he was newborn, she had helped wipe the slime of birth off his tiny body. She remembered how, when he was a boy, she had washed the cuts and gashes and splinter gouges that he got in his rough play, and that he had never cried or even whimpered. She could still see some of those little scars on his hairless bronze skin and could remember how he had gotten each one, and the sight of each little scar gave her a sweet pain.

And there were the bigger scars.

649

She cleaned the dark-scabbed wound in his left arm from the battle two days ago at the Forks and the hard-ridged shot scar in his leg from the battle at Monguagon a year ago. And she washed his sinewy legs, the straight one, then the crooked one broken in a bison hunt on the prairie near the Mother of Rivers half a lifetime ago.

Weshemoneto may help a man escape death many times, she thought. But he does not let a man live forever in one body.

And as she washed his skin she was remembering too the many wounds she had washed and healed on the beloved flesh of her husband, Stands Firm, in the years of his life. The sweet and bitter burden grew still heavier on her heart. Her husband's body still lay wherever it had fallen on the battlefield far away.

At nightfall yesterday after the battle, Charcoal Burner had stolen in among the American sentries on the battlefield with two warriors, and they had gone to the place by the big fallen tree where they had seen the bloody officer kill their chief. In the black night they had found Tecumseh's body by touch. Through the greatest stealth and effort, they had carried his body off the battlefield from among the sentries, outside the glow of Harrison's hundreds of campfires, hearing in the distant camp the thousands of Long Knives laughing and singing in celebration of their victory. Charcoal Burner and his warriors had carried the body of Tecumseh a long way through swamps and dark woods to their horses. They had tied his body across the saddle of his own white horse and had ridden the rest of the night to this town, the town of a tribe that the Americans supposed was neutral in the white men's war.

They had not been able to find the body of Stands Firm. If they had, Star Watcher could not have prepared it anyway because Stands Firm had been a Chalagawtha Shawnee, and she, his wife, was a Kispoko. So now she touched her husband's body only in her memory while she washed her brother's body with her hands.

And as she washed her brother's wounds, she was also washing the many wounds of all the Shawandasse, the South Wind People, because Tecumseh had been the People.

When she had finished bathing the body of her brother and had combed his hair, she dressed him in a clean and unadorned suit of deerskins and put upon his feet a new pair of elkhide moccasins decorated with beads, the pair she had made for him before the flight from Fort Malden. When she had made them she had thought he would wear them to walk upon this earth. She pulled down on his crooked leg and pushed up the other so that the feet were side by side, so that he would not have to limp anymore where he went. Tears were running down both sides of her nose, leaving cold wetness on her mouth.

Now he was ready. She sat back on her heels and parted her hair from her face and looked at him. In the smoky beam of daylight from the smokehole in the roof, his face looked serene and young and beautiful, shimmering with silver light through the wetness of her eyes. He appeared to be a man who had never been troubled, a peaceable man who was having a pleasant dream. As she looked at him she remembered the other side of the Circle of Time, before the Long Knives had come, and she saw a misty land of green meadows and corn fields and a large town of gray *wigewas* in a valley between bluffs gushing with springs, and her father and mother sitting in front of their lodge, and Tecumseh as a boy sitting before them and listening to what his father told him.

Now that she had done the preparations and had no more to do, she could no longer bear the weight on her heart, and she began the lament.

When they heard the vibrating wail from inside the *wigewa*, Open Door, Thick Water, Charcoal Burner, and Cat Pouncing rose from where they had been sitting in prayer. They walked single file down to the creek and waded into the cold water. They drank from their hands until they could hold no more water, then made themselves vomit until their insides were empty and clean. Then they went back up to the *wigewa* and went in. Each took one end of a pole at a corner of the blanket litter upon which the body now lay, and with Star Watcher following and wailing they carried him down to the grave. They lowered him down and placed him within the bark slabs, in such a way that if anyone ever dug up a body and said it was the body of Tecumseh, as many would surely do over the next hundred years, the Shawnees would know whether it was true.

Open Door pinched sacred tobacco out of a bag and went to each of the four sides of the grave and sprinkled it in, chanting barely above a whisper. Then he stood and held his fire stick against his chest. Star Watcher stopped wailing. The wind off the wide lake flapped Open Door's cape and shook the feathers and ornaments of the grave diggers and bearers and blew Star Watcher's thick gray hair away from her face. Her face was smeared with ashes and was as gray as her hair. Her fists were clenched at her abdomen as if she were trying to keep from falling open.

Then her brother the Prophet moved the fire stick over the grave. And Thick Water, who had not wanted to leave his beloved leader before the great battle, groaned and shivered as the last slab of elm bark was put in place, hiding forever this body of Tecumseh. Cat Pouncing shut his eyes and bit inside his mouth until he tasted blood, and kept from crying out.

Now they would all have to do the hardest thing they had ever done since the Eye of the Panther had crossed the sky. They would have to go on, with Tecumseh behind their hopes instead of in front of them. They would have to go on that way until he found a way to come around to them again.

# Author's Note

For the red man of that day, the warpath was the path to a quick death; peace was the path to a lingering death. For the white man, the warpath was often the path toward the White House or Governor's Mansion.

William Henry Harrison campaigned successfully for the presidency in 1840 with a slogan evoking his "victory" at Tippecanoe. Never a man to use one word when a thousand would do, he gave a two-hour inaugural address in a cold wind, took ill, and died after only thirty-one days in office.

Richard Mentor Johnson rode to the vice presidency in 1836 on the jingle "Rumpsey dumpsey, rumpsey dumpsey, Richard Johnson killed Tecumseh"—though in the chaos of that battle it was never determined who really shot the great warrior down. Other veterans of the Battle of the Thames garnered votes for decades afterward for their part in defeating Tecumseh's warriors.

Tenskwatawa, the Shawnee prophet, lingered on with a dwindling following of believers until 1836, when he died in Kansas. He was not, as some popular writers have stated, disowned or banished from the tribe by his brother.

Black Hoof, who had led the Shawnees in decades of resistance and then had tried to accommodate the conquerors, lived to see the last corner of Ohio partitioned out from under his people. He died at the age of 105 in 1831, and that year his followers left Ohio for Kansas.

The Shawnees who had remained loyal to Tecumseh until his death fought on against the Americans through the War of 1812 but were not effective without his leadership. Years after the war they began filtering back from Canada into Ohio and Indiana. Now a few hundred of their descendants make up the Shawnee Nation United Remnant Band, whose principal chief is Tukemas/Hawk Pope, a descendant of Thick Water. With patience and effort, they have managed to buy a secluded eight-acre plot in their ancestral lands for a ceremonial ground. For the first time in more than a century and a half, Tecumseh's people have a piece of their homeland, and it is sacred to them.

In the 175 years since Tecumseh was killed, scholars and historians have quibbled over details of his life, career, and death—thus perpetuating and compounding some myths and, here and there, probably preserving a truth.

Was Tecumseh born near Piqua, as he reportedly told some white men, or near Chillicothe, as one of his descendants reportedly told other white men? Was he married once or twice? Was he a sexual profligate who left half-breed descendants all over the country? Did he really propose marriage to Rebekah Galloway, or was that just the Galloway family's romanticized version of a more earthy incident? Did Tecumseh make one recruiting journey among the southern tribes or two? Was Tecumseh the whole intelligence behind his brother's religious movement, or was the Shawnee prophet an inspired leader in his own right? Did Simon Kenton recognize and refuse to identify Tecumseh's corpse on the battlefield the morning after the Battle of the Thames, or had the body been removed during the night?

My own extensive research for this book was not for the purpose of resolving those and other perennial disputes, many of which I know cannot be answered unequivocally. Not only do white scholars still argue over them, the various surviving factions of the Shawnee nation have their conflicting traditions. Even eyewitnesses, both red and white, changed their accounts as they grew old and started depending more upon what they had heard than on what they had seen.

No, my research was aimed at something beyond those old contentions. Though I pored over the usual documents, diaries, treaties, memoirs, history books, and battle accounts, paced over old battlegrounds in the United States and Canada, and interviewed experts red and white to be as historically right as possible throughout this book, I was looking especially for insights into the culture, morality, ceremony, and psychic condition of the Shawnee people in the time of their greatest crisis. Neither Tecumseh nor Tenskwatawa nor other great chiefs of the woodland tribes can be understood outside the context of their tribal ways or the disasters visited upon them by the Anglo-American invasion.

Often in this book I have written the red people's version of some particular incident. Sometimes their version can be reconciled with that of white historians, but not always. Often I have chosen the red man's version because that is the way my principal characters would have perceived it and sometimes just because I found it more credible.

Although I have carefully sought the ascertainable truth, sometimes I have had to choose one unprovable version over another in order to proceed with the story; I hope that readers will not cite my work as an authority on one side or the other of any of the perennial quibbles. Too many readers have been led astray already by authors who claimed to have found the last word. I have not broken much new ground; this field has already been plowed over too often. I have instead tried to understand and interpret, to make my reader walk in the Shawnees' moccasins, to help him appreciate what they once had and comprehend the devastation they were suffering.

One element of my story that might raise still another dispute is the relationship between Tecumseh and Rebekah Galloway. The idyllic account given by the Galloway family historian, verified nowhere else and repeated uncritically by scores of book, magazine, and newspaper writers ever since, I have long found suspect. I could not believe that this exemplary red leader would mock and jeopardize the holy cause of his life by proposing to marry a white teenage girl.

My research showed me that the attitude of the red man toward his homeland was never obvious to Anglo-Americans, even when explained by Tecumseh and many other eloquent chiefs.

It still isn't, as I learned one evening beside a campfire. Two talkers, a compassionate, liberal-minded white man and a Shawnee veteran of Viet Nam, had been conversing earnestly for hours about matters close to their hearts. Now my fellow white man shook his head and blurted something I had almost known he would say:

"But, my God! How can you go and fight a war for a country that's treated your people the way it has?"

The Shawnee smiled and wagged his head slowly. He put his fist against the man's knee, chuckled, and said, "You palefaces still can't understand that this is our country, can you?"

# About the Author

James Alexander Thom lives in the Indiana hill country near Blooming-ton, in an old log cabin he moved onto his own wooded land. He has been a U.S. Marine, a newspaper and magazine editor, a free-lance writer, and a member of the Indiana University Journalism School faculty. He now devotes all his time to writing, researching his American historical novels meticulously, traveling, tracking down primary sources, and even walking in the footsteps of his characters. Jim Thom is the author of *Long Knife,* *Follow the River,* and *From Sea to Shining Sea,* which *Publishers Weekly* said "is distinguished by its careful research, clear style, and the author's obvious love of his subject."

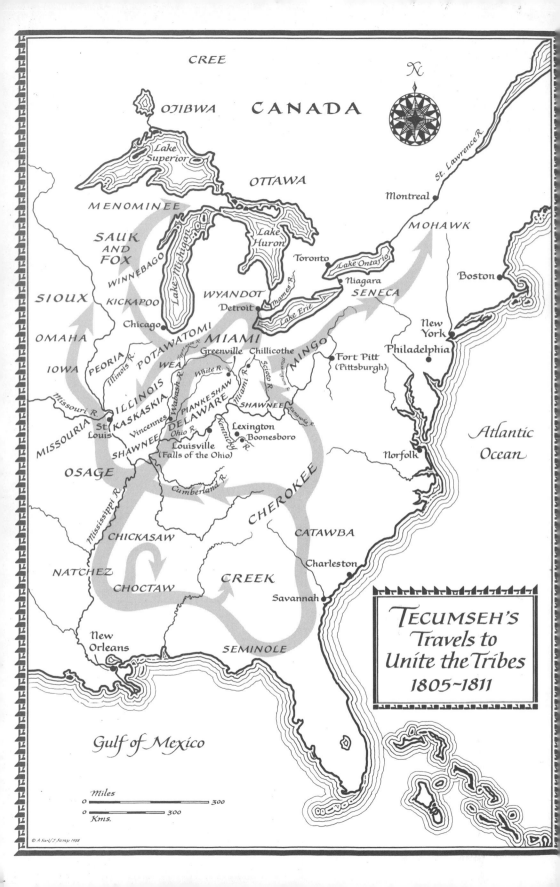

CREE

OJIBWA          CANADA          N

Lake
Superior          OTTAWA          St. Lawrence R.

MENOMINEE                         Montreal

SAUK          Lake          MOHAWK
AND          Huron
FOX          WINNEBAGO          Toronto          Lake Ontario          Boston

SIOUX          KICKAPOO          WYANDOT          Niagara          SENECA

OMAHA                    Chicago          Detroit          Lake Erie          New York

IOWA          PEORIA          POTAWATOMI          MIAMI          Philadelphia

MISSOURIA          ILLINOIS          WEA          Greenville          Chillicothe          MINGO          Fort Pitt
St.          KASKASKIA          Vincennes          White R.          (Pittsburgh)
Louis          SHAWNEE          PIANKESHAW          DELAWARE          SHAWNEE
          Louisville          Ohio R.          Lexington          Norfolk
          (Falls of the Ohio)          Boonesboro

OSAGE                    Cumberland R.          CHEROKEE          Atlantic
                                                                   Ocean

CHICKASAW          CATAWBA

NATCHEZ          CREEK          Charleston

CHOCTAW          Savannah

New
Orleans          SEMINOLE

Gulf of Mexico

Miles
0          300
Kms.
0          300

© A. Karl/J. Kemp 1988

TECUMSEH'S
Travels to
Unite the Tribes
1805~1811